DEVIL'S NIGHT DAWNING

Book One of the Broken Stone Series

DAMIEN BLACK

ABOUT THE AUTHOR

Damien Black...

... grew up in north-west London, and is of mixed French and Scottish ancestry...

... is a professional writer, editor and musician with more than fifteen years' experience...

... has lived and worked in the UK, France, Thailand, Spain and Australia...

... played lead guitar in an originals rock band for six years on the London 'toilet circuit'...

... can be contacted at **www.damienblackwords.com**

To Cris, for his intelligent beta reading

CONTENTS

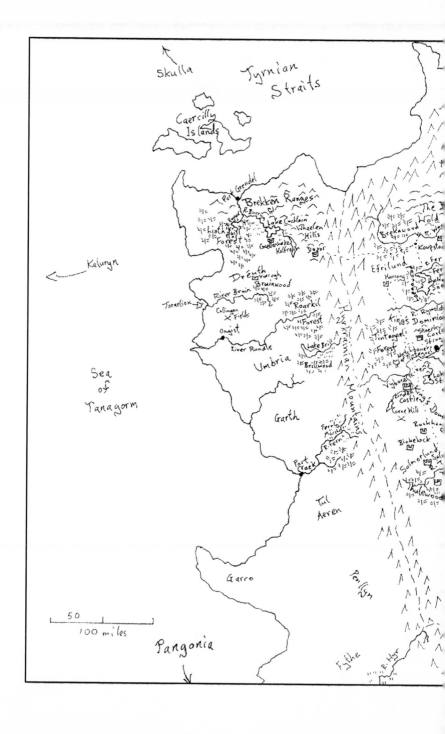

Realms
of
Northalde,
Thraxia
and
Vorstlund

(being part of the northerly Free Kingdoms)

cers

Faror Islands

Sea of Valhalla

Marvik

Port Cravern

Cravern Estuary

vern Bay

iem

Wyvern Sea

The Empire

Port Ursing

Saltecaste

Argael Forest

Fire City of Meerborg

Dulsinor

Lothon Monastery

Graukolos Castle

Glimmerholt

Merkstaed

PART ONE

← CHAPTER I →

A Duel With A Devil

The hut's interior was exactly as they had left it: the same stench defiled the air, and again Adelko found himself gagging on the foul atmosphere. The walls were daubed with dried faeces and blood; the young monk shuddered at the memory of the girl gouging strips of flesh off her body in a frenzy.

That had been three nights ago, when her condition was at its worst. He could not recall how many of the Redeemer's psalms it had taken to compel her back into bed on that occasion.

In the faint morning light peering through the single covered window Adelko could see her lying in bed, only her head discernible above the soiled blanket. In the half gloom it looked as though she were sleeping, though the novice knew that Gizel had not done that for a tenday now.

Only when his mentor lit the first tallow candle on the makeshift table near the entrance did the thing inside her show any sign of life. Hissing resentfully it forced the girl's head to look up at the two monks without moving the rest of her body.

The eyelids flicked open. Soulless orbs scrutinised the pair balefully. Her pupils were horribly dilated, the bloodshot whites flecked with an unnatural yellowish tinge. The suppurating skin on the girl's face began to twitch spasmodically, as though a thousand nervous tics suddenly consumed her morbid flesh.

Unperturbed, Adelko's mentor lit the second candle on the other side of the entrance. Turning to face the possessed girl, the adept brandished his circifix. It was a simple silver rood, depicting the Redeemer being broken on the Wheel – but there was power in such a thing, if wielded by a true initiate.

As it had done on previous occasions, the thing that was and was not Gizel flinched back, pulling up the dirty blanket to abjure the hated symbol.

With a deft movement of his other hand Adelko's mentor reached into the folds of his grey habit and produced a silver phial, flicking several drops at her green-tinged hand. A piteous cry escaped the girl as the drops burned her fingers, causing her to let go of the blanket. To Adelko's ears it sounded like an infant in pain, but he knew better than to fall for the deception.

Moving in swiftly, he presented his own circifix and before long the two monks had Gizel backed up against the wall, crouching feebly on the far end of the bed.

In a sonorous voice the adept began to recite the Psalm of Banishing: 'O Reus Almighty, in thy heavenly kingdom, we implore thee: grant thy humble servants the power to cast out this denizen of the Other Side! Palomedes, sacred Prophet and Redeemer, broken on the Wheel in mortal form for our salvation, grant us now the strength of mind to resist this chimera of wickedness! In thy name, and by the grace of the Unseen, let the servants of the Fallen One be driven from the mortal vale!'

The thing that was and was not Gizel squealed louder, writhing around on the filthy cot and trying in vain to block out the hated words. Flicking more drops at her, Adelko's mentor began to address the spirit directly.

'No more shall you torment this innocent creature of the earth! Release that which is not yours to own! The works of Abaddon shall melt before the burning zeal of the righteous, as tallow melts beneath the flame! The deceits of Sha'amiel shall be blown asunder as mist before a keen wind! Look on the Wheel, the unbroken circle of our faith, devil-spawn, and despair!'

Recognising his cue, Adelko stammered the appropriate response from his copy of The Holy Book Of Psalms And Scriptures.

'It is the power of the Redeemer that compels thee! His body was broken but through his death the Creed was born! The aegis of our faith shall turn aside the sword of Azazel!'

His young voice sounded reedy in his ears. Adelko hoped he had mustered the necessary conviction, as he had done yesterday. For the first three days he had struggled to channel the Redeemer's words properly; exorcisms were a lot harder to conduct than he'd previously reckoned.

His mentor picked up the counter-response, again reciting scripture flawlessly from memory: 'It is the power of the Redeemer that commands thee! The fleshless horsemen of Abaddon shall turn and flee before the bright wings of the Archangels! The honest man shall not fear, though the stings of Ma'alfeccnu'ur assail him!

Tell us your name, foul spirit, that we may encircle it with words of holy prayer, and send thee back to Gehenna!'

⁂

Over and over they repeated the litany, and the fifth morning of their clash with demonkind grew old. As the candles burned down, Adelko felt his strength waning too. Despite the brisk weather the hut grew steadily warmer until it was stiflingly hot; the sweat poured from his body, soaking through his brown novice's habit.

Throughout the ordeal the thing that was and was not Gizel continued to toss and turn frantically while screaming piteously in a thin high voice that was not her own. It sounded to Adelko like the noise a burning child would make.

He felt an unseen presence fighting him with unearthly weapons; a thousand doubts and worries that had never entered his mind before the exorcism gnawed at his soul. Were it not for the Redeemer's words he knew he might well have succumbed to the spirit's power and been driven mad.

But today he noticed a difference: that power was growing weaker, the unclean voices in his head fainter.

⁂

It was shortly before noon when they finally broke the spirit's will. Brandishing his circifix, the older monk bellowed for the umpteenth time: 'By the Seven Seraphim and the blood of the Redeemer, through his agency as the Lord Almighty's right hand, I command thee, demon, TELL US YOUR NAME!!!'

Suddenly sitting bolt upright, the thing that was and was not Gizel stared at them again, face and limbs contorting horribly, her skin undulating across her flesh with a sick life of its own. From deep inside her young throat an awful and ancient voice spat out a handful of words: 'My... name... is... BELAACH!'

The older monk's eyes widened in horror. For one brief but crucial second he was robbed of his composure. His grip on the circifix loosened slightly, his psychic hold on the fiend inside the headman's daughter doing likewise.

Seizing its opportunity, the demon called Belaach propelled Gizel's body forwards. Even at the best of times, she was only a slight thing, but the strength of ten bears was in her now. With a malignant hiss, she struck the rood from the older monk's hand, breaking its chain and sending it skittering against the wall.

With her other hand she grasped the adept's that clutched the phial, whilst raking at his face with a savage strength. The two fell to the ground grappling, the monk desperately repeating the Psalm he had so calamitously broken off from uttering. The holy words instantly weakened the demon's grip on the girl, but even so it had recovered a temporary advantage not easily dispelled.

Letting go of his own circifix, which hung by its chain around his neck, Adelko fumbled for his holy water.

He had to risk not being able to keep the thing at bay with his own rood, because he couldn't abandon the scripture book – he still didn't know every word by heart. Though they had recited little else for the past four days, the Psalms of Banishing and Abjuration were lengthy and complex passages – they had caught many a journeyman out before, his mentor had said. Never mind a mere novice like him.

He had to hope the thing would keep attacking his mentor long enough to give him a chance to help him...

Producing the phial while continuing to read aloud, Adelko rained drops down on Gizel's back. The thing inside her howled, causing her to shrink away as her body responded to its tormentor's diabolical instincts. Seizing his chance, the older monk broke her weakened grip and scrambled frantically across the rubbish-strewn floor towards his circifix.

With an ugly hiss the possessed girl turned to face Adelko. Instinctively, he dropped his scripture book and reached for his circifix, giving the possessed girl another splash of holy water as he did.

Faced with the hallowed drops and the holy rood, the thing that was not Gizel screeched and flinched back again towards the cot. Even so, the loss of one recital might have allowed Belaach to regain enough strength for another lunge.

But to his elation, Adelko had not dropped a syllable. The words he'd once feared he might never learn now came to him flawlessly – correctly pronounced and spoken with perfect conviction. He did know them after all!

By now the older monk had recovered his own circifix – and his composure – and working fluently together again they forced the possessed girl back on to the cot.

Now for the endgame.

Adelko's mentor uttered the final verse of the Psalm of Banishing, inserting the demon's name in the appropriate places: 'Belaach, denizen of the Third Tier of the City of Burning Brass, by the power of the Seven Seraphim, the Redeemer and the spirit-father Reus Almighty, I compel thee to return to thy tower!

'Belaach, let the hellfires there engulf thee, let darkness enshroud thee! Return now to languish in the prison to which thy black betrayal condemned thee aeons ago!

'Belaach, pollute this mortal vale no more! The Third Tier awaits thee! Go now and seek thy infernal master, crawl to his feet like the serpent thou art, and trouble mortalkind no longer! It is the heavenly powers that compel thee!'

'It is the heavenly powers that compel thee!' chimed Adelko. At least this part of the exorcism wasn't hard to remember.

The demon gave vent to a horrid shriek as it reluctantly exited Gizel's body, which convulsed frightfully before collapsing in a still heap on the bed.

As the spirit left her the shriek did not diminish, but seemed to hang in the air, disembodied.

And then Adelko heard it speak one last time, pronouncing voiceless words that echoed in his mind: *So ye have cast me out of this wretch's body, and won a skirmish! Well done, wise monks, well done! Ye have earned yourselves a prophecy, so mark this:*

Hell's Prophet shall reawaken/the Five and Seven and One shall lead the hosts of Gehenna to victory

Silver shall be tarnished black as night/the fires will rise and consume all in their path/the righteous shall moan beneath the scourge

Those who oppose us shall scream for eternity/the flesh shall be broiled from their bones/their souls shall be bound in burning brass

For the war of worlds is coming...

Which side will you be on, my clever friars? I bid thee a fond farewell, until we meet again...!

A gust of rank air suddenly swept through the room; the low-burning candles went out and the hut was plunged into gloom. Gradually, light from outside began to penetrate again. All was silent now but for the sound of Adelko's master intoning a blessing over Gizel, the customary closing ritual for a successful exorcism.

At his bidding Adelko went over to the window and pulled back the curtain. More light spilled into the room; weak and grey though it was, he felt glad of it. Looking back he saw his mentor drawing the blanket over Gizel, who appeared to be in a deep exhausted sleep.

Her face was deathly pale and bore the marks of her self-mutilation, ugly red grooves caked over with encrusted blood. But it had at least lost its ghastly hue and looked like mortal flesh again, albeit torn flesh.

Adelko's mentor walked over to the entrance and pulled the hide flap aside. Two timorous peasants were standing outside guarding the hut – village folk had been known to take matters into their own hands where the possessed were concerned. Ignoring their startled expressions, the adept addressed them in a flat weary voice.

'Summon the elders. Our work is done.'

✥ ✥ ✥

An anxious crowd of village folk was soon gathered around the hut to hear Adelko's mentor break the good news. It being Rest-day, no one had gone to graze their flocks in the highland valleys below, and most of the four score inhabitants of Rykken had chosen to stay indoors and add their prayers to the friars' pious exhortations.

Foremost among them was their headman Lubo, beside himself with relief and desperate to look upon his daughter, now free of the dreadful spirit that had possessed her so cruelly. Adelko's master gently but firmly insisted that rest was best for Gizel, to which Lubo reluctantly assented before inviting the pair back to his hut to break their fast.

At the mention of food Adelko's ears pricked up. It had been a long and challenging morning, and he was rightly famished – even the prospect of poor peasant fare sounded like a feast fit for the great banqueting halls of the Free Kingdoms.

✥ ✥ ✥

Presently the two friars were taking their much-needed meal in Lubo's hut as Adelko's mentor gave him a full account of Gizel's condition. The headman's watery grey eyes held a mixture of relief and gratitude at his daughter's salvation, mingled with sorrow for her suffering. He was a short rustic fellow in late middle age with skin like the gnarled bark of an old tree.

His rotund, flaxen-haired wife Lara had managed to stop weeping tears of joy long enough to busy herself with putting a fire on and feeding her child's saviours. The adept had had to stop her throwing herself on the ground and kissing the hem of his grey habit as though he were the Prophet himself.

Adelko was too busy with his second bowl of gruel to pay much heed to his mentor's post-exorcism counsel. It wasn't aimed at him, although strictly speaking he was obliged to listen as the adept might test him at any time on his knowledge of the Argolian Order and its ways. Thus far he had proved an able student, or at least he hoped he had. But few novices at Ulfang Monastery were lucky enough to be seconded to its most celebrated adept, and true to his reputation Horskram of Vilno could be a stern taskmaster.

'Master Horskram, may the Redeemer be praised!' exclaimed Lubo. 'A poor mountain peasant like me can never hope to repay you, except with humble prayers that the Almighty grants you a long and blessed life! But tell me truly, will my poor Gizel ever be... right again?'

The adept met the peasants' anxious stares with a reassuring smile.

'She will live, though her body will take time to heal and her mind will not recover immediately from such an affliction,' he replied. 'Keep her fed and warm, and above all be vigilant at night – make sure she doesn't fall asleep with the candle on again! Devilspawn are drawn to such signals – for an unguarded flame reminds them of the hellfire they use to torment their victims on the Other Side. Before we leave I will daub the sign of the Redeemer on her – that should help her if there are any further attempts to claim her body and corrupt her soul.'

'You think there will be... others?' The faces of the peasants grew anxious again.

But Horskram shook his head. 'It's just a precaution, never fear. The denizens of the Other Side sometimes return to inhabit the recently possessed while they are still weak, but it's rare. It's more likely that, having been cast out of one person, they seek another where the prayers of our Order are not so fresh. Reus willing, no further harm shall befall your daughter.'

'The Redeemer be praised!' Lubo exclaimed again. 'And thanks be to the Almighty for the friars of St Argo!'

'I thought I'd lost her forever, master monk,' said Lara, breaking into tears again. 'I can never thank you enough! Oh, glory be, what a day is this!'

Horskram smiled graciously and stretched briefly on his stool, before taking another sip of goats milk. Despite the recent ordeal he showed little sign of physical fatigue – during their past six months on the road Adelko had noticed that his mentor rarely seemed to tire. Although he must have seen sixty winters, his robust frame remained gifted with the vigour of youth.

Adelko could not help but reflect somewhat ruefully at how much this contrasted with his own chubby body. But then he had seen only fourteen summers, and he supposed he had time left to grow yet. He certainly hoped so – a little more height and a little less puppy fat would suit him well.

'No need to thank us,' Horskram was saying. 'Our reward is the work we do – every soul saved is a stroke against the Fallen One, as the Prophet sayeth. Now, I will put the sign on your daughter while she is sleeping, and then we shall be on our way. There is just one more thing I would ask you – are you quite sure, as you said before, that Gizel had not fallen into any... trouble before she was taken?'

They had been through this four nights ago, when the pair of them arrived at Rykken in the pouring rain after word of Gizel's plight reached them at the nearby priory where they were staying. Lubo had answered this question as candidly as he could – or so Adelko thought – along with all the others the adept had asked him as part of his preliminary enquiries.

Hearing the matter brought up again now, in a more relaxed atmosphere, gave the adept's words a more pointed slant. For a moment no one said anything, and the fire crackled loudly in Adelko's ears.

Then with a bemused shrug Lubo replied: 'Master monk, what more assurances can I give? As Reus sees all, to the best of my knowledge my daughter was – *is* – a good and virtuous girl. She prays on Rest-day as a good Palomedian should, and on all the others you'll find her helping her ma, as a good daughter ought. Until now, that is.'

The village headman gazed at the dirt floor of his hut, sadness creeping over him again.

'A more dutiful child you could not hope for, Master Horskram,' said Lara in a voice that now betrayed a mother's pride. 'Why, since she was a little lass I've barely had a day's trouble with her! And as for the menfolk – if that's what you're gettin' at – well she's had no want of offers, but she's turned them down, every one! Said her duty was to her family, and she'd have no business marrying a man and takin' up with his kin. I ask you, sir, what more could honest folk expect from a good daughter?'

Horskram nodded, giving the kindly couple another reassuring smile. 'I quite understand. Please don't be offended by my asking again. I am sure Gizel is indeed as pure of heart as you say she is. It's my job to make sure of these things, that's all... and now, I'll look in on her once more before we depart. Adelko, put aside that bowl and come along!'

Taking one last mouthful before reluctantly leaving Lara's watery gruel, Adelko did as he was told. Their leave-taking of the grateful peasants was cordial enough, but as they rejoined the trail outside Adelko noticed that his master's face had darkened again.

✠ ✠ ✠

While Horskram was daubing the sign of the Wheel on Gizel, Adelko went back to the hut where they had slept to pack up their things and ready their horses. He had just finished loading on the saddlebags when his master returned. The village was quiet; the peasants had returned indoors to spend the rest of the day giving prayers of thanks for Gizel's deliverance.

Slinging their iron-shod quarterstaves across their backs, the two Argolians took to the saddle and followed the trail out of Rykken at a brisk canter. A thick mist had begun to fill the valley, nestling against the knuckled crags of the highland ranges as afternoon slid inexorably towards dusk.

Resigning himself to a night of snatched sleep under open skies, Adelko consoled himself with the thought that he would soon look upon the home he had not seen for nearly five years – Narvik was a day's ride away and Horskram had said they could stop there on the way to their next assignment. The thought of his long-missed family and friends was a welcome antidote to the cheerless road they now took.

Once or twice before they stopped to make camp he glanced sidelong at his mentor, but the older monk had fallen into one of his brooding silences. The dark expression had not left his face.

⊹ CHAPTER II ⊹

Of Humble Beginnings

Memories of home stayed with him on the trail out of Rykken. As dusk deepened into night, they found a tree-lined dell in which to make camp and bed down.

Sat on a rock idly poking at the fire he had built, Adelko glanced at his mentor sitting on another rock next to him. He was staring into the flames, lost in his own thoughts. The old monk had barely said a word since they left the village, but for once the silence suited Adelko. Poking the burning branches again, he let his mind drift back into his childhood.

⊹ ⊹ ⊹

Narvik was a day's ride from Rykken. Several times larger, its people were no less tightly knit, and few strangers ever passed between its crooked wattle huts.

That suited most of its inhabitants well enough, including Arun the blacksmith, Adelko's father; but from an early age his youngest son had nurtured a deep yearning to expand his limited horizons.

On summer afternoons he would climb the slopes overlooking his village and listen to the far-off cries of the last Gigants, as they mourned the passing of their gargantuan race from the loftiest peaks of the Hyrkrainians.

His mother Lettie – before the ague took her – would admonish her reckless youngest son. If he strayed too far, she warned, the spirits of the North Wind would carry him off to their airy palaces on the Other Side, never to return.

To no avail. Adelko was steadfastly in a world of his own most of the time, and before long the other villagers began to nickname him 'the dreaming wanderer' in gentle mockery of his fanciful excursions through the valleys around Narvik. His father Arun was exasperated – after all, his two elder sons, Arik and Malrok, were sturdy, dependable lads more than happy to learn the family trade. But his youngest could not have been more different.

When the Archangel Morphonus refused to bestow the gift of sleep on him Adelko would lie awake at night, dreaming of what he would become. A swordsman perhaps, or an archer. Or maybe an outrider, scouting for armies – he wasn't all that nimble if the truth be told but he certainly liked to roam.

Well, he was the dreaming wanderer after all.

He went about his chores at the smithy with a sullen reluctance, and neither scolding nor belt across the backside could put a spring in his step. Reus knew, his parents tried both more than once, but somehow the message never sank in.

Simply put, horseshoes just weren't for him.

In his ninth year Adelko's mother passed away. A bad harvest and harsh winter robbed her of her strength, and several other villagers shared her fate that year.

As they had done for generations, the inhabitants of Narvik pulled together in times of strife. Food was rationed and shared, and the young and strong lent a hand to help the weak and ailing. Arun's sister Madrice came to stay with them and help keep house now that Lettie was gone.

Little by little, the villagers' tolerance of hardship paid off, and as the long winter thawed into spring they began once more to graze their goats and sow crops.

'Well, it could be worse – at least we don't have it so bad with the highland chieftains,' Arun would say over his stoop of ale in the evenings. 'Not compared to some o' the lowlanders anyway.'

Most of the blacksmith's friends agreed. Down south, the Highlands gradually gave way to the Brenning Wold, a rugged expanse of rolling hills that ended with the River Warryn and the Brekawood to the south-west. There the lowland Wolding barons held sway, unchecked by royal law, squeezing their common folk with harsh taxes and unfair tithes. Arun and the other grown-ups in Narvik would shake their heads disapprovingly whenever they spoke of them.

'Reus Almighty, we may be poor Highlanders, but at least we aren't Wolding peasants!' the blacksmith was fond of saying, to a general chorus of 'ayes' and 'amens'.

Things were different in the mountains, where for centuries the semi-autonomous clans had ruled their peoples with more leniency and less pride. A royal edict issued by King Freidheim II of Northalde early on in his long reign had preserved a state of quasi-independence in the Highlands, although Adelko's father often said that what really kept the Wolding barons from making trouble up north was the simple fact that there was little worth taking: not easily assailed and still less easily borne, the harsh landscape they called home afforded a meagre existence to clansman and commoner alike.

As Arun played host to his drinking cronies, Adelko would lie awake in the next room, refusing sleep and eagerly devouring the grown-ups' talk of the outside world. Sometimes their words would carry his greedy imagination further afield, out across the Wold and over the Warryn onto the fertile plains of Efrilund and the King's Dominions beyond. He had often heard the grown-ups muttering that down south the yeomanry were better treated than the sorry Wolding lot, for they were ruled by barons loyal to the King, or directly by Freidheim himself.

'He's alright as kings go,' Arun would pronounce over his stoop. 'At least Freidheim saw fit to leave us Highlanders alone – he's got enough sense to see there's no call to be botherin' us mountain folk.'

'Not unless there's a war on,' his best friend Yurik would always remind him. A condition of Highland independence was that the clans had to contribute warriors in times of strife. That wasn't too likely to affect ordinary villagers, as clansmen seldom used conscripts, but men like Arun with useful skills might be called up. Not that Arun was ever concerned about that.

'Aye, but when was the last time we had one of those?' he would reply. 'He thrashed the Thraxians at Corne Hill before any of us were born, then he put paid to the pretender Kanga – and that were fifteen years ago! Wins the wars and keeps the peace, that's Freidheim for you – we won't see another war in his reign, mark my words.'

And then they would fall to talking more generally of the kingdom. Their beery conversation evoked splendid visions in Adelko's mind: of lush green meadows and tilled hedgerows, grand castles and manor houses, and decorated knights tilting at one another in lavish tournaments beneath sunny skies. To hear the grown-ups tell it, such things were commonplace in the Dominions.

As they went on talking of the wider world, or what little they knew of it, and Aunt Madrice poured them more ale and Adelko's brothers snored beside him, he would shut his eyes and dream of a life of far-flung journeys and high adventure.

✧ ✧ ✧

A year after his mother's death, his nightly prayers to the avatar Ionus, patron saint of travellers, were unexpectedly answered by a calamity.

Old Balor, one of Narvik's three headmen, was suddenly possessed. The local perfect, a timid priest who preferred a life of simple prayer and gentle extortion from his parish in the form of Temple donations, could do nothing. Word was sent to Whaelfric, their local clansman, and a rider was despatched to Ulfang Monastery to summon an Argolian to perform an exorcism.

A tenday passed before he arrived. During that time Balor worsened. An unearthly strength seemed to possess the old man, and he howled like a banshee through the night as he strained at the chains Arun had been forced to put on him. After performing this unenviable task, Adelko's father had drunk twice the usual amount that night, and staring grimly at the fire had said nothing to anyone until the following day. Once only had he glanced over at his three sons and sister, eyeing them blankly as if they were strangers.

Adelko never forgot that haunted look in his father's eyes. It excited his curiosity. What could strike such fear into the hearts of the adults he had looked up to all his life? Something in him longed to know.

He never forgot his first impression of Horskram either. His future mentor had cut an imposing figure when he arrived at the village. Dismounting from his chestnut rouncy he formally greeted Malgar and Radna, the husband and wife who formed the other two thirds of Narvik's not-so-mighty triumvirate of headmen. His dark grey habit, worn by all journeymen and adepts of the Order, matched the colour of his hair and trimmed beard.

But it was his eyes that really stood out, hard and blue like a pair of sapphires. Set in a chiselled, aristocratic face they sparkled with a keen intensity the boy had never seen before. Malgar, who had seen fifty winters, seemed like a green youth next to him.

Intoning a prayer the monk made the sign of the Wheel, touching his forehead reverentially before placing the palm of his hand flat across his chest, fingers splayed to represent the spokes on which the Redeemer's limbs had been broken a thousand years before. Producing his circifix, he entered the hut and did not emerge again until the following morning.

The spirit had fortunately proved to be a lesser entity of the Other Side, one of the many anti-angels of Gehenna. After a night-long struggle Horskram had cast it out, sending it back to cluster about the Fallen One's throne of obsidian in his City of Burning Brass, the words of the Redeemer ringing in its ears.

Drained as he was by his psychic travails the monk was persuaded to rest a while at Malgar's dwelling. By the time he awoke it was mid-afternoon, and the villagers had arranged a celebration feast to give thanks to the Almighty, with Horskram as guest of honour.

✤ ✤ ✤

Poking idly at the fire again Adelko smiled as he recalled that momentous evening. Being summer, it had been warm enough by highland standards. The villagers had set up a small pavilion and a ring of rough stools and tables on a sward of grass overlooking the valley just outside Narvik. The last harvest had been kinder than the one before, and most were happy enough to bring provender to the feast.

As the sun lowered in the skies Ludo Sharpears the goatherd and his two brothers began to strike up a merry ditty on lute, flute and fiddle as the womenfolk began bringing salted meats, cheese, turnips and gourds of ale to the table.

The villagers knew they would have to tighten their belts for the next few weeks to make up for the night's extravagance, but given the occasion most agreed it was worth it. The notable exception was old Valgrit Sourtongue, who muttered disconsolately that no good would come of such wantonness – but then such miserable remarks were typical of him and nobody listened.

As the sun gradually slipped out of sight beyond the Hyrkrainians and more villagers gathered, Adelko helped his aunt with putting lanterns on the tables and lighting them.

His duties brought him to the table of honour where Horskram sat talking with Malgar and Radna. Lighting another lantern, Adelko looked up to find his eyes meeting the monk's. He flinched. It felt as though the old adept was looking directly into his innermost thoughts and feelings, as if his soul were under scrutiny.

'This is young Adelko, Arun the blacksmith's youngest.'

Malgar's voice broke the spell, and Adelko found himself blinking and looking at the three of them, feeling slightly foolish – though he wasn't sure exactly why.

'He's an adventurous lad – we call him the Wanderer on account o' his roaming! Always roaming around the place and getting into trouble, eh lad?'

Without waiting for a response Malgar went on: 'Like the time he went on one o' his wanderings, and got lost in the Rhotang Passes half a day from here and slipped down a ravine – his poor mother thought 'e was a gonner, Reus rest her soul!' The headman gave an avuncular beam.

'Ah but we found him in the end, didn't we Adelko? Still e's a good lad, bright as a button too! Make a fine smith one day he will – if only he can settle down and stop his wandering!'

Adelko felt his cheeks flush crimson in the flickering yellow lantern light. He was well used to Malgar's chiding – as village headman it was his duty to cajole him into wiser ways – but right now this was the last thing he needed.

Here was an outsider, an interesting stranger – a learned man, with *powers* to boot. What must he think of Adelko now?

But the monk simply smiled at him, before turning to address Malgar: 'The Almighty forgives an impetuous spirit, when it is wedded to a good heart. I am sure young Adelko will make his father proud yet. And a keen mind, they say, is a great gift from the Unseen.'

Turning back to Adelko he fixed him again with his penetrating blue eyes and asked him: 'How many summers have you seen, lad?'

'Ten, including this one,' the boy stammered back.

The monk smiled again. 'I'm sure the next ten will reveal much about you, young Adelko. And the blacksmith's trade is an honourable one to follow.'

Adelko's heart sank. Things had been going so well, but now it looked as though all the mysterious friar was telling him to do was accept his fate and be glad about it.

His unhappiness was completed by Radna, who told him: 'Adelko, I think your aunt is waiting for you at the next table. There's lanterns that need lighting, now run along.'

Turning he saw Madrice standing at the next table, frowning at him. Bidding the monk farewell he went back to his chores reluctantly. But glancing over his shoulder he saw Horskram was still staring at him.

✧ ✧ ✧

Before long all the tables were set and most of the villagers were present. Ludo and his brothers in full flow now, striking up a merry ditty about a goatherd who'd lost his flock and had to go through all sorts of misadventures to get it back. It was an old favourite in those parts and some of the more enthusiastic villagers had already started to dance.

Things were brought to a halt, as usual, by Albhra Widehips the busybody, who came marching over to interrupt the music and started berating Ludo for putting pleasure before devotion.

Ludo, an exceptionally short, rotund fellow with a comical look accentuated by the ridiculous straw hat he always wore, looked up from his fiddle playing and effortlessly foiled all her attempts to make him feel contrite. She completed the tirade by storming off in a huff. At that he turned and nodded to his brothers. They put aside their instruments to hear prayers – as had been the rascally trio's intention all along. It was always more fun to wind up Albhra before you did what she wanted you to.

From where he was standing beside his aunt, Adelko heard Erith Handyman chuckle over his first flagon and mutter to his best friend Derek sat next to him: 'Albhra and Ludo, at it again! Those two should've married years ago.' Derek chuckled softly into his ale and Adelko grinned – this was a grown-up joke he felt he could appreciate. Sort of.

Then Malgar got to his feet to call silence. The headman said a few words of thanks on behalf of everyone, and most of all old Balor, who was recovering in his hut with a bowl of his favourite pottage.

At the end of his short speech there was a general 'hear hear' around the tables, and many raised their flagons to the friar, who humbly acknowledged their praise. After Malgar had sat down, his wife Radna rose and said: 'And now Horskram will lead us in prayer.'

The Argolian rose, and in a melodious voice he intoned the Psalm of Thankfulness, suffixing this with an extra verse from scripture celebrating the vanquishing of evil.

The observance completed, the villagers sat down to eat and drink, Ludo and his brothers taking it in turns to supply the music so all three could satisfy their hunger and thirst before beginning the night's revels in earnest.

Adelko was sharing a table with his family and Silma Green-eyes, whom his eldest brother Arik was courting. They were expected to wed before long – Arik was already sixteen summers and Silma was only a year younger – but Adelko's father had been insistent that his eldest spend more time at the forge learning his trade before getting into a marriage, and all the distractions that would bring with it.

With blonde hair and a buxom figure, Silma typified the Northlending ideal of feminine attractiveness, and though her face was not classically beautiful her vivacious spirit more than made up for it.

Not that Adelko really took much notice of any of this. As far as he was concerned girls were all well and good, but there were far more interesting things to hold one's attention.

And right now there was only one person at the feast who was doing that.

From his perch at the end of the table he strained to get a better look at the monk several tables up from him, but there was too much hustle and bustle, especially now that more villagers were getting up to dance. Once or twice his Aunt Madrice pointedly heaped another spoonful of vegetables onto his wooden platter, or poured him some of the milder ale reserved for the children.

When she did this she would give him a look, as if to say: *Don't let your imagination keep running away with you.* She knew him only too well.

The evening drew on and turned into night. One by one the stars came out to join the gibbous moon. It wasn't a full one, so there should be no need to worry about any more evil spirits – at least not for tonight.

As the older womenfolk cleared away empty platters and brought more gourds of ale to the tables, a mood of euphoria began to sweep the villagers. Ludo and his brothers were back in full swing, and not even a hundred Albhras bolstered by all the hordes of Gehenna would stop him now. Most of the younger men and women, and quite a few of the older ones too, were frolicking around the circle of green formed by the trestle tables in groups of six or eight, swapping dance partners with a skill and grace borne of seasons of practice.

A few young lovers, including Arik and Silma, had slunk off to embrace one another beneath some trees near the edge of the sward. Adelko caught his elder brother Malrok gazing at the two with a yearning look in his eyes – he was thirteen summers and seemed to be more interested in girls every day. Adelko still didn't see what all the fuss was about.

Horskram had not left his spot at the table of honour, and seemed content to spend the night talking to Malgar, Radna and the other village notables.

As some of the menfolk began to prepare a fire and Madrice instructed him to help out, Adelko began racking his brains for an excuse to go over and talk to the monk again. As he was thinking this it also occurred to him that his idea was rather silly – after all, even if he did invent an excuse, what would he say to him?

The villagers had prepared firewood earlier in the day and they soon had a healthy pile set up in the middle of the green. Adelko's father didn't take long to get a blaze going: as a blacksmith, he was no stranger to fire and prayed to the avatar Nurë every night. As the flames added their light to the lanterns Ludo and his brothers took the music up another notch, and soon more than half the village was spinning madly to the energetic swirl of sound.

The fire spread a cheering warmth across the sward, and soon even those not dancing were joining in, thumping out a rhythm on the tables with their tankards and laughing merrily. Adelko had wandered back to his table with his father, who affectionately ruffled his youngest

son's hair before pouring him another mild as a reward for his labours
and sidling over to talk to Yurik. Aunt Madrice had gone over to
share a stoop with the womenfolk, so Adelko was left temporarily
unsupervised. He looked over at the table of honour.

Again he saw the monk, but this time – and Adelko could swear
it was no coincidence – the Argolian glanced over without breaking
off his conversation and met his gaze again.

As the music lifted through the night air and villagers cavorted
about him, Adelko felt the heady scene retreat sharply into the
background: all he could focus on were those azure eyes, sparkling
as they caught the flames.

Taking a deep breath, he steeled himself and did something that
would change his life forever.

Putting down his small pewter pot, he walked the length of the
tables until he was standing before the old monk again. The others
turned to look at him with a mixture of amusement and inquisitiveness
– what was Arun's strange and unpredictable son up to now?

In a small voice that trembled Adelko began to stammer words,
but found himself struggling to be heard above the night-time revel.
Raising his voice, he began again: 'P-please, Master Horskram,
begging your pardon but – '

The music rose to a crescendo, eliciting whoops and yells from
the dancing villagers.

' – but I don't want to be a blacksmith – '

With a final refrain Ludo and his brothers brought the music to an
abrupt halt, and Adelko's last sentence sounded loud and clear through
the silence: 'I want to come with you and learn about the world.'

A fresh ripple of sound washed across the clearing as exhilarated
villagers applauded Ludo and his brothers. Most of them had been
too busy enjoying the music to register his words, but those sitting
at the table with Horskram certainly had, and exchanged frowning
glances. The monk stared at him inscrutably, although a faint smile
now played across his lips.

Flushing again, Adelko surprised himself by repeating his words
above the clapping: 'I want to come with you and see the world – I'm
bored of Narvik.'

The monk's smile dropped to a frown of his own – not lightly
did men scorn their homes in the highland provinces.

But his voice was level as he replied: 'You are indeed an adventurous
young lad. But those who wish to learn more of the world must first show
a mind open to the *discipline* of learning. Perhaps we shall talk of this

further in the morning, young Adelko – however, now is not the time. My advice to you is to join your friends and enjoy the rest of the celebration – I rather suspect you have done more than enough thinking for one night. We shall see each other on the morrow.'

Turning to Malgar, who was looking at Adelko with a shocked expression, the monk said in a quieter voice: 'Malgar, if I might have a brief word with you in person, I would be most grateful.'

Looking from the boy to the friar the headman blinked, shrugged, and nodded.

Both men got up and left the clearing. Radna fixed Adelko with a pointed stare that was not entirely unkind and said: 'Well young man, you heard the master monk – why don't you go and play with your friends now? I think you've spent quite enough time bothering the grown-ups.'

For once Adelko did as he was told. Shuffling off in a daze as the music started up again he soon found his best friend Ulam, busy leading the other boys in an ingenious new game that involved throwing pebbles at the couples under the trees and running off laughing. Adelko joined in enthusiastically. He didn't really know what the next day would bring but he felt he'd put something into play. Something big.

✥ ✥ ✥

The rest had been history, as the loremasters said. The next day Horskram had met Adelko in Malgar and Radna's home, and asked him if he wished to join the Most Learned Order of St Argo. When Adelko replied that he did the adept had given him a strange item called a *book*.

He'd heard about such things – wise men like Horskram put secrets in them.

His first book. He still remembered it. It had felt strangely welcoming to his touch; a faint musty smell that he found appealing rose from it as he slowly opened the cover. On the yellowy white surface of the first page was a strange spiky symbol he had never seen before and a drawing of an apple, which of course he had seen – and eaten – on feast days several times a year.

Horskram had told him that the book was designed to teach one how to read other books. He had spent the rest of the day showing him how to use it while the nonplussed grown-ups left them to it and went about their chores.

Upon Horskram's return to Narvik a month later Adelko had astonished his family by showing a near mastery of the Thalamian Alphabet used throughout the Free Kingdoms. Even the stoical friar had been visibly impressed when he'd turned to the last page and begun reading the text inscribed on it. It was a simplified extract from the Thraxian troubadour Maegellin's *Lays of the Heroes of the Golden Age* that described one of the many adventures undertaken by the legendary mariner Antaeus. Adelko had read it haltingly, but already he showed a grasp of literacy previously unknown in his village.

Horskram had pronounced the boy a prodigy on the spot and, with Radna and Malgar acting as witnesses, obtained Arun's formal consent to indenture him into the Order of the Friars of St Argo as a novice.

The next morning he had left Narvik riding pillion behind the friar. It had been a clear summer's day. The peaks and valleys around him had seemed even brighter than usual, full of possibilities.

⁜ ⁜ ⁜

He spent the next four years at Ulfang Monastery. The monastic life was not an easy one, and sometimes he wished he was back at home being bossed around by his Aunt Madrice.

Dawn prayers were followed by morning lessons under the stern tutelage of the adepts before the noon meal. This provided a brief respite before the novices went to help in the fields, for like all Argolian sanctuaries Ulfang was entirely self-sufficient, and the monks were as much farmers as they were scholars and witch-hunters. Mid-afternoon prayers and more lessons brought them wearily to supper at sunset, followed by another round of devotion and study. After that they would be released for sleep, having said their final prayers ahead of the Wytching Hour.

But the long hours had paid off. Adelko perfected his knowledge of the Thalamian Alphabet and learned Decorlangue, the native tongue of Ancient Thalamy. Although a dead language, it was still used as a common speech among loremasters and perfects throughout Urovia, so it was very useful to know. He also studied the Old Norric tongue spoken by the First Reavers who had journeyed across the Wyvern Sea from the Frozen Principalities and settled the fertile coastlands of Northalde more than seven centuries ago, and learned to read the runes used by their pagan priests.

Reading opened up a new world to him. Gazing at maps in the monastery's venerable library he realised it was vast, far beyond his prior reckoning: its seas, plains and mountain ranges stretched for leagues without number; the cities of men were scattered across the earth, as numerous as the stars in the night skies.

There was Strongholm, the grey-walled cityport built by the First Reavers, royal seat of the present-day King of Northalde;

splendid stuccoed Rima, capital of Pangonia, most powerful of the Free Kingdoms; crumbling, colonnaded Tyrannos, where the Redeemer had been broken on the Wheel for defying the Thalamian Empire. A shadow of its former glory, Ancient Thalamy's foremost city had long since fallen into a semi-ruinous state, just as Palom had foretold it would.

The Redeemer had been born in Ushalayim, a vast city across the Sundering Sea in the desert lands of Sassania, said to be so beautiful it resembled a thing of jewels and cloth-of-gold more than brick and stone. Pangonian crusaders had conquered that holy place from the infidel worshippers of the False Prophet Sha'abat during the First Pilgrim War several generations ago, but Adelko could find little evidence of the Redeemer's work in the histories of that bloody slaughter.

The world was older than he'd thought too: some five millennia had passed since the Elder Wizards of Varya had provoked the wrath of the Unseen and ushered in the First Age of Darkness. Legend had it the priest-kings of that fabled civilisation had been seduced by the Fallen One and punished for it by the Almighty, just as Abaddon himself had been after daring to challenge Reus for mastery of the universe.

'The Redeemer tells us the servants of Abaddon were turned into demons as divine punishment for siding with him in the battle for heaven and earth at the Dawn of Time,' Brother Rothrik, the adept who taught them Counter-Demonology, had explained in his first class. 'Banished to the island of Gehenna, they fashioned the City of Burning Brass at its epicentre. In his visions Palom saw five levels in that accursed metropolis: the Seven Princes of Perfidy and other archdemons dwell on the First Tier, at Abaddon's right hand. And there, the scriptures tell us, the Fallen One shall sit on his throne of obsidian till the end of time, as just punishment for his divine betrayal.'

The spirit that had possessed Balor belonged to the lowliest Fifth Tier – no match for a skilled adept like Horskram, but even a lesser demon could wreak havoc among mortals unversed in Argolian lore. More powerful manifestations could potentially be calamitous.

'The mortal vale and the Other Side are forever divided by Reus' will – but there are weaknesses, rents if you will, that spirits use to cross over into the mortal vale,' Brother Rothrik continued. 'The more powerful the spirit, the bigger the rent it needs to pass into our world. That is why sorcery is such a foul and dangerous thing. Aside from its blasphemous meddling in the natural order of things ordained by Reus, its use causes rents in the sacred barrier separating our world from the spirit-lands. The more mortals use such powers, the more opportunity there is for greater demons to cross into our world.'

Greater manifestations were rare – but they did occur. It was even noised among the echoing cloisters of Ulfang that the Pilgrim Wars had been started by two archdemons posing as influential mortals on either side. But of this theory Adelko learned little beyond the whispered rumours – it was controversial to say the least, as the mainstream Temple wholeheartedly sanctioned the crusade against the Sassanians. The Order of St Argo had remained steadfastly neutral on the issue, refusing to endorse it but stopping short of condemning it outright.

As his stay at the monastery lengthened, Adelko noticed that the older monks would become tight-lipped on any subjects that touched on the True Temple. His developing sixth sense, which all monks honed through years of devotion and prayer, registered a tension among the adepts and journeymen whenever it was mentioned – even though technically the Order belonged within its fold and its Grand Master answered to the Supreme Perfect in Rima.

Young as he was, he began to get an inkling that relations within the wider Temple were not entirely harmonious.

✣ ✣ ✣

Last autumn Horskram had returned to Ulfang after an absence of more than four years.

Adelko was gathering in the harvest with the other novices and journeymen when a lone rider appeared on the crest of the high hill overlooking the monastery. Soon the cry was going up around the fields and in the courtyard where the wheat and vegetables were being piled. Ulfang's most cherished son had been brought back safely, by Reus' will.

By then Adelko knew of his benefactor's status within the Order. Horskram possessed an unusual gift for the psychic arts and was sought throughout Northalde and beyond for his ability to lift curses and banish spirits. He was said to have travelled throughout the Free Kingdoms and beyond, so it wasn't uncommon for him to be gone for years at a time. A peculiar zeal to confront the servants of darkness burned within him; rumour had it the Redeemer had appeared to him in a vision many winters ago, charging him with his lifelong mission.

Harvest duties were forgotten as the monks crowded round to greet him. The abbot, Sacristen, was especially pleased to see his old friend, for Horskram had been his protégé. Adelko had once overheard a journeyman muttering that Sacristen was always pleased to see Horskram because his fame reflected well on him and enhanced his own prestige. That smacked of vanity – a sin and certainly not a trait becoming an abbot of the Order. But then even the pious Argolians were only mortal.

At a feast held to celebrate the twin blessings of a decent harvest and the return of Horskram, Adelko had been reintroduced to the adept. He had questioned him closely on his studies before dismissing him with a curt nod.

Adelko remembered thinking that he looked considerably older than before. It was more spiritual than physical – the intervening years had given him a few more grey hairs and wrinkles, but beyond this Adelko thought he sensed a peculiar ageing of his soul. There was something in his demeanour that had not been there before: he had the look of a man who had confronted some great evil, or perhaps seen too much of it throughout his long life.

On the day of Horskram's departure Adelko had been summoned to the Abbot's room after dawn prayers. Entering he saw Horskram standing by the window, gazing out across the wheat fields into the deep green valley beyond.

Adelko had found himself in that chamber more than once, for the Abbot used it to prescribe punishments for misdemeanours and offer praise for outstanding performance among novices. Adelko qualified on both counts – fine student though he was, he was also just as fond of high jinks as his mischievous circle of friends.

On this occasion he had a sinking feeling that he knew exactly why he had been summoned, and was just about to offer some feeble excuse to allay punishment and perhaps avoid humiliation in front of Horskram, when the Abbot cut him off.

'Adelko, you have been tested by Brother Horskram here, and after some confabulation on the matter we have decided that further instruction would be beneficial to you.'

The corpulent abbot's voice was impassively neutral, his jowly face the same.

The novice felt himself flushing. He thought he had answered the adept's searching questions the other night fully enough. Had he overestimated himself? Horskram had not turned from the window.

The abbot was staring at him. Clearly a response was expected.

'I... I had not realised my knowledge was so wanting, Prior Sacristen,' he stammered, bowing his head deferentially. This already felt worse than being upbraided for pinching ale from the scullery storehouse – being criticised for his lack of prowess at the lectern hurt his pride far more. Not that good Palomedians were supposed to feel pride.

To his bafflement, a broad smile suddenly split the abbot's pudgy face.

'Wanting?' he beamed. 'Oh no, my dear novice, on the contrary – your knowledge to date has been found to be exemplary. After just four years at Ulfang you already know more than most novices your age – and quite a few who are older than you for that matter. What remains to be seen is how your spiritual fortitude will measure up in the coming months.'

Sacristen was still staring at him. Only now his eyes were twinkling. The smile had not left his face.

'Spiritual fortitude...' Adelko repeated dumbly. He still couldn't fathom where this was going.

'Why yes,' replied the abbot, a note of seriousness entering his voice. 'For that is precisely what will be tested most rigorously over the next year. Brother Horskram has asked my leave to take you on as his second, and after due consideration I have given my consent. I trust this decision pleases you, Adelko.'

Adelko blinked. Had he walked into a dream weaved for him by the Archangel Oneira, celestial wife of Morphonus? He barely noticed as Sacristen told him to ready his things and make haste to the stables where a saddled rouncy awaited him.

The adept still had not turned from his contemplation of the wheat fields, but at last it sank in.

He was Brother Horskram's second – an honour far beyond his expectations.

It was hardly unheard of for novices to be seconded to a journeyman or adept. Only in the test of spiritual combat – confronted with the madness of possession or the terror of a real-life haunting – could an Argolian's mettle be truly determined. The Order's history abounded with tales of those who had excelled at the lectern only to turn to lunacy before the Fallen One's servants.

What was so surprising was how soon he had been singled out – he had only just come of age, and he had joined the Order later than many.

He could still barely believe his senses when he rode out of the monastery's main gate with Horskram an hour later, the envious looks of his best friends etched on his mind and their words of farewell ringing in his ears.

⁜ ⁜ ⁜

That had been nearly half a year ago. During the first couple of months Adelko and his new mentor had travelled continually – though not as widely as he could have wished, and not in the direction he yearned for.

For rather than heading south to the Lowlands, of which the snatched tales of his childhood had painted such bright pictures, Horskram took them deeper into the Highlands. At least its remote dells and isolated dwellings abounded with minor hauntings and lesser manifestations – Adelko soon had a few juicy tales stored up to tell his friends back at Ulfang.

By the time the onset of winter had forced them to hole up at a mountain priory for the Year's End Festival, he had criss-crossed the rugged peaks of his homeland several times. The austere beauty of its stark landscape pleased his highland spirit, but even so he hankered after something different. Dialects aside, one mountain village was much like another, the people and customs little different to his own.

Throughout this time Adelko found himself thinking of the library at Ulfang, with its centuries-old maps and treatises on strange and foreign lands. The desire to broaden his travels burned more strongly than ever within him. He wasn't done with praying to St Ionus just yet.

✢ ✢ ✢

The fire was burning low in the dell as Adelko's thoughts returned to his village. He couldn't deny the thought of it made him feel a little nervous. So much time had passed – what would his family make of him now?

He didn't even know if they were still all alive. His father had occasionally sent his best wishes via the odd traveller or friar that happened to pass through Narvik on the way to Ulfang – but that hadn't happened for at least a couple of years now. He supposed Arik had married Silma, they must surely have children as well by now, Reus willing. Maybe Malrok would be courting somebody too.

At this thought Adelko felt a pang of longing strafe his youthful body – that was one thing he would never know, for the monks of the Order could love the Almighty and no other. A sigh escaped his lips, frosting up the brittle night air before him. Yes he was different, he supposed – but still he'd be glad to see them all.

Narvik lay between Rykken and their next destination, another village where Horskram wanted to check on a malicious Terrus, an earth spirit he had banished the previous summer. Terri were one of the four Elementi, the other three – Aethi, Saraphi and Lymphi – corresponding to air, fire and water respectively.

Terri could return to spots they had previously visited and had a tendency to wreak havoc, digging pits that swallowed huts and villagers whole and ruining crop fields with their mischievous antics. They weren't really evil, not like the devils that served the Fallen One, but they certainly weren't good either. After they were done with the earth spirit Adelko hoped they would continue south into the Lowlands he longed to explore.

Suddenly his mentor looked over at him and broke his long silence: 'Well, Adelko, it's getting late and the fire is nearly spent. We should both get some rest, for it's been a long day and we still have quite a journey ahead of us.'

Adelko looked at the adept. In the dying firelight his face looked haggard and mysterious. 'Well, I suppose so – but my village isn't far from here. We should reach it by dusk tomorrow, I think.'

Horskram glanced back over at the embers. 'Yes well, I'm afraid we aren't going to Narvik anymore. We're going back to Ulfang.'

Adelko was tired, and it took him a few seconds to register Horskram's words.

'What!? But... I thought you said...'

Horskram huffed irritably and brought his fingers up to the bridge of his nose, squeezing tightly.

'Adelko, if you've learned anything these past four and a half years you will know that most exorcisms are performed within a day or two by experienced adepts such as myself – especially if they are accompanied by an assistant,' he said. 'This one took nearly five, and no wonder – Belaach is no archdemon, but he's certainly no lesser spirit either. Such manifestations are rare – that's why I was so shocked to learn his name. High-ranking demons do not tend to visit the mortal vale unless summoned by a powerful black magician. That's also why I had to be sure of Gizel's character.'

Adelko frowned. 'You don't mean you suspected the girl – '

'Of being a black magician?' his mentor finished for him. 'Heavens no. But curious peasants have been known to fall in with the wrong kind of people before, especially if they are young or foolish. That said, if there really was an accomplished warlock practising in these parts, I'm sure I would have heard about it before... which leaves only one other possibility.'

His mentor broke off, rubbing his hand over his beard absent-mindedly.

'But, we won...' said Adelko. 'I mean, we beat it – didn't we?'

His mentor sighed heavily again. 'Yes, we did, but that isn't the point, Adelko. The bigger the rent, the more powerful the spirits that can pass through it – you know all this perfectly well.'

'Yes, of course Master Horskram – but, I still don't under – '

'Oh for goodness' sake, Adelko, use your reason!' Horskram snapped. 'I didn't pick you out of that mountain lair of goatherds and crop-shearers so you could plague me with stupid questions! What causes a bigger rent? Witchcraft – that's what! We've just fought with every ounce of our strength to banish a demon of the Third Tier, which means that someone somewhere is practising some damnably powerful Left-Handed magic! They may not have summoned Belaach directly – but they've been using magic for other purposes, somewhere in this vicinity. We have to go straight back to Ulfang because I need to tell the Abbot about this right away – he will probably sanction a divination to try and determine the sorcerer's location.'

Adelko looked sheepishly at the ground, feeling foolish for having provoked his mentor.

'I'm sorry,' he muttered. 'I didn't realise. I just wanted to see my family, that's all.'

Horskram looked at his apprentice with kindlier eyes – always quick to anger, his temper subsided just as rapidly. 'I know, lad. If I could change things I would – but this is a serious matter. You know the rules of the Order. Now, in Reus' name, let's get some rest!'

They unrolled their pallets and lay down to sleep, wrapping themselves tightly in their cloaks and blankets. As he drifted off, Adelko could not help but wonder if the change in plan wasn't a reminder from the Almighty – he'd chosen his path, and the Order was his family now. His childhood suddenly seemed very distant.

⇥ CHAPTER III ⇤

The Quixotic Knight

'Again! One more time!'

Bringing his steed around, Vaskrian levelled his spear again and waited for the two attendants to reposition the target. It was a cold morning, and most of the castle nobility would only just be stirring in the keep. The leaden skies matched the colour of the grimy bailey walls, but the squire had eyes only for the quintain before him.

This was a tall stout pole with a smaller horizontal beam attached to a swivel mechanism mounted on top of it; a battered torso-shaped board of wood dangled from it by a chain on one side, on the other hung a sack filled with dirt.

Spurring his courser into a gallop, he hit the target dead centre, sending the beam swinging around and bringing the sack hurtling towards his back. He ducked in the saddle just in time and it glanced his shoulder as it flew past.

The blow wasn't strong enough to hurt him through his brigandine, but it did force him to clutch the reins more tightly and bring his steed up early. Vaskrian glowered at the quintain, still lazily turning from the aftershock of his charge.

That was the third time in a row he'd hit the target perfectly but failed to avoid the counterpunch. At least it hadn't unhorsed him on any of his tilts – he was improving daily.

He was about to tell the attendants to reposition the target when he heard a familiar throaty voice yelling at him across the courtyard: 'Vaskrian! In Reus' name what are you playing at? I told you to pick up my sword from the smithy more than an hour ago! We were supposed to leave at daybreak!'

Sir Branas, a stout hoary knight of about fifty winters, came trudging through the mud, his tatty hauberk jingling. The attendants, fearing the well-known shortness of his temper, tugged their forelocks and made themselves scarce.

The ageing knight drew level with his squire and glared up at him.

'Your saddle bags aren't even on! And I daresay that means mine aren't either! Too busy tilting when you should be squiring, as usual!'

'But you said I could use the castle facilities to practise,' protested Vaskrian. 'And I *have* packed the other horses – they're all ready, the sumpter's doing most of the carrying and I just wanted to keep mine unburdened so I could –'

'Enough!' roared the old knight. 'I said you could use the castle facilities to practise *whenever it didn't conflict with your duties!* Now in Reus' name go and collect my blade! We're late enough as it is!'

Suppressing a sigh, Vaskrian nudged his courser towards the gatehouse where the laden sumpter and his master's charger were being looked after by a bored-looking page boy. Dismounting, he made his way over to the armourer's forge on foot.

By now the castle courtyard was stirring into life as its resident craftsmen began their daily labours, along with the husbandmen who looked after the animals that provided for the Jarl of Hroghar's broad tables. The familiar reek of stale sweat, refuse and burning cinder greeted him as he pushed his way through the dirty gaggle of commoners and beasts. It didn't bother him all that much, he was used to it.

A smile played across his lips as he remembered his mother Aletha's words: 'A castle looks a fine thing when you see it from a distance, but inside it stinks worse than a town square on market day!'

She'd died of food poisoning six winters ago – castle life meant you ate better than most, but sometimes eating your fill could kill you as sure as starvation. A simple washerwoman, she'd been as honest a soul as any. That meant he'd see her again in the Heavenly Halls, when his own mortal span was done.

Likewise the dull ache that permeated his limbs from constant practice during the winter didn't trouble him over much: a knight was supposed to endure hardship with fortitude after all. The shoulder injury he'd sustained in his last sword bout had healed up nicely too, though the fracture had been painful enough at the time.

Not nearly as painful as the broken jaw he'd left his opponent nursing, mind. Practice bouts weren't supposed to be lethal – but even a blunted sword was a heavy piece of metal, and armour didn't always protect. He'd come at Dorik fast on the counter attack, knocking him senseless. The other squire had had a prolonged spell in the castle infirmary after that, and Vaskrian hadn't seen much of him since.

The forge lay in the shadow of one of the castle bailey's five towers, in a sturdy lean-to made of brick that jutted out of the wall. Ereth the armourer was there as usual, working up a sweat.

Vaskrian's heart surged briefly as he stepped into the forge's fiery precinct. Its steely smell tanged pleasantly in his nostrils after the grimy courtyard. All about him hauberks, helms and weapons in various states of manufacture and disrepair hung from hooks in the walls or lay piled up in corners.

Ereth looked up from the mail shirt he was working on and smiled broadly at Vaskrian. A stocky, muscular man covered head to toe in soot, his blackened hairless head resembled the anvil he worked on.

'Well, if it in't young Vaskrian,' he grinned. 'I thought you'd never show up! Been tilting in the yard again, I'll warrant.'

Vaskrian flushed, trying not to think of the royal bollocking he'd just earned himself. 'Always!' he said brightly, shrugging off his chagrin. 'Do you have the guvnor's sword then? He'll probably use it on me if I keep him waiting much longer!'

Ereth chuckled good-naturedly, wiping the sweat off his brow and laying down the shirt.

'Of course! Had it ready first thing this morning! Here we are...' Reaching behind him he took it down off the wall and handed it to Vaskrian: his master's sword, sheathed in a leather scabbard bound with iron. Drawing it, he paused to inspect its keen edge in the light of Ereth's forge.

'Should be good as new,' said Ereth, returning to work on the mail shirt. 'I've taken all the notches out of it and sharpened the edges. Some of the binding on the hilt had come loose as well – I wound a new one on.'

Vaskrian nodded, only half listening, his eyes fixed on the glinting blade. He owned a sword too: it had belonged to his father, but it wasn't as well made – it was less long and broad, and the balance wasn't quite as good.

Stepping back outside the smithy, he took a couple of swings with it for good measure. He loved the feel of the weapon – if only he had one like it, he'd be an even better swordsman than he already was. He'd show all the bluebloods in Hroghar what he could do with a blade then.

'Still dreaming the impossible dream are we, Vaskrian?''

Vaskrian whirled to face the speaker, his heart sinking as he recognised the voice immediately. Sat on coursers just before the smithy were Sir Rutgar, his nemesis, and two of his cronies, Sir Marten and Sir Bors. He hadn't heard them approaching above the din of the castle. They were kitted out for a day's hunting in the woodlands overlooking the nearby River Warryn. Behind them rode their own squires with bows, spears and other equipment. He felt painfully aware of his own worn apparel – as a squire to a landed vassal he was reasonably well outfitted, but Branas refused to have his clothing replaced more than once a year.

'Look, he thinks he's a knight!' brayed Rutgar, his companions exchanging unpleasant grins. 'What invisible monsters are you slaying this time, churl? You're supposed to polish your master's weapons, not play with them.'

Several of the artisans working nearby began laughing. Ereth frowned and shook his head. 'Take no notice of him, Vaskrian,' he breathed. 'He's just trying to bait you.'

'Laugh all you want, but at least I know how to use a blade, Rutgar,' snarled Vaskrian, ignoring the smith.

Rutgar stopped laughing. 'I think this common squire is getting ideas above his station, boys,' he said to the other two. 'Perhaps it's time we taught him a lesson in manners.'

'I'd like to see you try it, Rutgar,' sneered Vaskrian. 'I haven't forgotten our last practice bout, even if you have. Tell me, how's that broken clavicle of yours? It looked painful enough at the time, when you were howling in the dirt!'

'Now that's done it,' muttered Ereth. 'You shouldn'ta said that, Vaskrian – he's a knight now.'

'I don't care,' said the squire, loudly enough so everyone could hear. 'Spurs or no, he can't fight worth a damn – he wouldn't even be a knight if his father hadn't died of food poisoning last autumn. But then I suppose it's a knight has to inherit lands, hey Rutgar? Even if it's a useless one who wields his sword like a plough!'

Rutgar glared furiously at Vaskrian. Then he snarled: 'By Reus, you'll regret saying that before you breathe your last.'

Vaskrian could have sworn he heard Rutgar's voice quaver.

But then that was no surprise. Rutgar was a blue-blooded braggart who took his spurs for granted. Vaskrian trained hard every day – he wasn't as heavily built as some of the fighters in the castle, but with his wiry frame he was quick and able. And he had a fierce track record as a swordsman – the lance came less naturally to him, but he was better with a blade than most his age.

Rutgar had learned that the hard way when they'd been paired off for combat practice last summer. It had been a moment to savour – Vaskrian's naked ambition hadn't made him popular with Hroghar's haughtier inhabitants, and Rutgar and his ilk poured scorn on him for it.

He'd stopped doing that for a while after Vaskrian sent him crying to the infirmary for a month. But then he'd been knighted and resumed his daily mockery with impunity. This time there could be no redress – lowly squires were forbidden from challenging knights to combat. Rutgar knew it, they both did.

Rutgar gave a curt nod and the three knights beckoned for swords from their squires.

'I'm fetching Sir Branas,' said Ereth, rushing off towards the yard.

'No don't!' barked Vaskrian, but it was too late. Turning to face Rutgar again he saw the three knights dismounting, swords in hand.

'Drop the blade, churl,' snarled Rutgar. 'It's death by hanging if you strike a knight – you can't win this fight. Just come quietly and we'll make this as painless as possible.'

Sir Marten and Sir Bors grinned mercilessly. Vaskrian felt his blood boil. He was damned if he'd submit meekly. Sir Rutgar was right – he would hang for this – but at least he'd take the blue-blooded bastard with him.

Rutgar and his cronies advanced, blades in hand. Vaskrian dug his heels into the mud. Adjusting his fighting stance, he tilted the keen edge of Branas's sword towards Sir Rutgar as he advanced hesitantly. At eighteen summers, he was a year older than Vaskrian, but less strong and quick. Vaskrian could positively smell the fear coming off him. Three against one and he was still afraid.

Sir Marten and Sir Bors fanned out to his left and right as Rutgar came at him head on. Vaskrian knew there was no way he could win; the other two were a couple of years older than Rutgar and better swordsmen. If he could take down Rutgar before they finished him at least he'd die happy.

Darting forwards he lunged at Rutgar's face. Taken aback by the alacrity of the squire's attack, he barely managed to parry, blanching as he retreated a couple of paces.

Sir Marten stepped in and slashed at his exposed midriff. Reacting quickly, Vaskrian stepped back out of range – straight into Sir Bors' line of attack. His head exploded with pain as the knight caught him a painful blow with the flat of his blade.

The force of it knocked him to his knees. Laughing cruelly Sir Marten kicked him in the jaw, sending him sprawling in the mud. He hadn't let go of his master's sword though.

'What are you doing?' he heard Rutgar scream. 'Stop playing around! He just tried to strike a dubbed knight – kill him!'

'What, and spoil our fun?' Marten shot back. 'Where's the sport in killing him straight away? Come on, Vaskrian, get up and show us what you're made of!'

With a roar Vaskrian complied. His jaw ached and his head was ringing painfully, but pure blind rage was a good salve.

He rushed at Sir Marten angrily, but the attack was wild and ill-timed, and the knight blocked it easily before riposting.

Vaskrian ducked the blow, but then Sir Bors stepped in again, cracking his knee sharply with the flat side of his sword. Wincing, he tottered back on one leg. Sir Marten aimed a brutal kick at his stomach. Gasping as he felt the air pushed out of him, the squire doubled up and collapsed into the mud again, letting go of Branas's sword.

Only then did Rutgar step in. Placing his foot on Vaskrian's neck he sneered as he raised his blade, holding it point downwards above the squire's face.

'Glad... to see... you've finally... found your courage,' he managed to gasp.

'He still hasn't learned his lesson,' sneered Rutgar, slowly bringing his sword down towards Vaskrian's face. 'I think I'll put his eyes out before I cut his throat.'

'That's ENOUGH!'

Sir Branas's voice tore across the ward. The nearby craftsmen who had stopped working to watch the fight suddenly became interested in their tools again. Ereth was standing timorously behind the grizzled old knight. He shot a sympathetic look at Vaskrian.

'Sir Rutgar, put up your sword and get your damn foot off my squire's neck,' snarled the veteran, approaching the young knight with a measured tread. Rutgar blanched again and backed off immediately. Grimacing, Vaskrian pulled himself into a half-sitting position. He was covered in mud and ached from the beating.

'And as for you two,' roared the old knight, rounding on Sir Marten and Sir Bors. 'I fought with both your fathers in the last war – what d'you think they'd say if they could see you now, hazing a young squire three to one?! You should both be ashamed of yourselves – sheathe your blades, you're not fit to carry them!'

Sir Marten flushed at that. He looked poised to retort but Sir Bors shot him a warning glance and shook his head. Reluctantly both knights beckoned for their squires to divest them of their weapons.

'Your squire forgot his place,' spluttered Rutgar. 'When we reminded him of it, he attacked us. By the laws of Hroghar that means he should hang!'

'That isn't true!' yelled Vaskrian, getting his breath back.

'Silence!' roared Branas. 'I'm dealing with this!'

Squaring up to the young knight the veteran fixed him with beady eyes. Rutgar flinched. 'Oh, I don't know the man, but I know the type,' he said in a low dangerous voice. 'Always talks a good fight. I knew your father too, and I didn't like him over much either. Tell me, did you even land a blow on my squire until he was lying prone in the dirt?'

The old knight was breathing heavily now. Rutgar lowered his eyes, unable to hold his stare.

'That's what I thought,' sneered Branas. 'So how about this? You say yon squire should hang – I say he's innocent of the charges laid against him, and that you picked a fight with a common man contrary to the rules of knighthood. Deny this, and you are calling me a liar – for which I will have satisfaction. Vaskrian, sword!'

Staggering to his feet, Vaskrian picked up the blade and handed it to his master. Though Branas was saving his skin, he felt sick and humiliated. Being rescued by his master was the last thing he wanted.

'Well?' growled the old knight, grasping the weapon without taking his eyes off Rutgar. 'Which is it to be?'

Flushing with shame Rutgar backed off, mumbling a half-hearted apology before barking at his squire to take his sword.

'Good, that's settled,' said the old knight. 'You three get about your business, before I change my mind and report you all to the Jarl. Vaskrian, put my sword back in its scabbard where it belongs – I didn't have Ereth reforge it anew so you could run amok with it! It's time we left – you'll have to clean yourself up later.'

Turning on his heel Branas marched away, nodding a curt farewell to Ereth. As Vaskrian sloped off after him Rutgar yelled out a last parting shot: 'You'll never be a knight, Vaskrian. They don't let *commoners* wear spurs – your father never even sat a horse!'

The words cut deeper than any sword could. Rutgar was right – a low-born son of a man-at-arms was an unlikely candidate for knighthood. There were instances when commoners had been dubbed for exemplary service in the field, but they were very rare.

He wasn't about to let a slight aimed at his father go unchecked though.

'My father may have been a footsoldier, but that didn't stop him saving the Jarl's life – or had you forgotten that?' he yelled back over his shoulder.

Even saving Lord Fenrig from a Wolding ambush hadn't been enough to get the old man knighted, but it had got his only son squired to Sir Branas, a rare honour for one of common stock.

'Vaskrian!' bellowed Branas. Giving it up as lost the squire turned and followed his master back to the gatehouse, Rutgar calling curses after him.

He mounted his courser and took hold of the sumpter's reins in sullen silence. Rutgar's last insults still bothered him far more than the beating he had just taken.

His father Ethelric had died a happy man. His deathbed words four years ago came floating back to Vaskrian: 'You'll learn to be a man and fight and serve others, just like I did. But you'll also have opportunities I never had – you'll ride a horse, and get out of the castle a lot more than I did! Ah my own son, a squire of the realm! Your mother would've been proud.'

Thinking on that had him going all misty-eyed. He also felt guilty. If the old man's shade could see him from the Heavenly Halls, he'd probably disapprove of his behaviour – Ethelric had been nothing if not humble.

But nothing could change the way he felt. A squire of the realm wasn't enough. He wanted to be a proper knight. Preferably a landed one like Rutgar.

Pushing his despondent thoughts away with some difficulty, he did his best to lighten his spirits by thinking of the road ahead.

There would be plenty of knights and squires both where he and Branas were going. For all his irritableness the old knight wasn't such a bad guvnor – he loved tourneying as much as Vaskrian, so they had that much in common at least. Spring was in the air, and after wintering at Hroghar his master was ready to hit the tournament circuit again.

The first major event of the season in those parts was at Harrang, several days' ride to the south-west. Already its Jarl would be supervising the building of the wooden stockades for the jousting lists, and the bleachers where the high-born lords and ladies and their entourages would sit and watch the contest.

The main attraction was the melee – and Lord Vymar's ample demesnes provided no shortage of venues on which to stage the mock battle. Vaskrian relished the event because it gave squires a chance to get involved in the fighting alongside the knights. Technically it wasn't meant to be lethal combat, but deaths and injuries occurred frequently. That only made it more exciting, of course.

Last year there had been more than a hundred fighters on either side at Harrang. He'd unhorsed three squires – he wasn't allowed to attack knights because it wasn't a real battle – and received a handful of silver marks for each of them as per the rules of the contest.

One of his defeated opponents wouldn't walk again. He'd felt bad about that – after all he'd had no grudge against him, it was only a game. But what could you do? You took your chances at a tourney, if you couldn't fight well or sit a horse properly you were asking to get hurt. And Vaskrian hadn't escaped unscathed himself. His second opponent had hit him hard enough to gash open his forehead, even with a blunted blade.

Not that he minded – on the contrary, another scar to add to his growing collection.

For knights the stakes were much higher – any dubbed fighter disabled or captured by the enemy had to pay a ransom, and depending on how prestigious the combatant was this could run into hundreds of marks. Such rewards were beyond his grasp for now, but at least the melee gave him a chance to do something he loved to do more than anything else. Fight.

Fighting was everything. It was even better than sex. And for all its dangers, at least you wouldn't catch the crotch-rot from a good scrap. He'd seen a few folks die from that foul wasting disease, it didn't look like a pleasant way to go. And how would you ever live that down, getting killed by a wench? Give him a sword death any day.

⁂

Riding out through the castle gates they began descending the road, which snaked downwards from the summit of the hill from where Hroghar sternly overlooked the rugged landscape with patrician gravity. To the north Vaskrian could make out the silver trickle of the Warryn; the lands tilled by Lord Fenrig's peasantry stretched up to meet it, by its banks nestled the woodlands where Rutgar and his cronies were going hunting.

With some difficulty he suppressed his angry thoughts. His injuries hurt less now, though Rutgar's last words carried a lingering sting. He'd prove him wrong – when he became a knight he'd seek out all three of them and avenge himself, in single combat. See who got the beating then.

After meandering between the odd roadside hovel and a lone priory the road took them on to level ground before joining the highway skirting the river. They took this in a westerly direction towards Kaupstad. It was an old crossroads market town about a couple of days' ride away. From there they would take the south road to Harrang.

The pair ambled on at a leisurely pace. For all his complaints about their tardiness Sir Branas wasn't really in a hurry. Like anyone of noble blood he disdained rushing unless it was an emergency. The tourney wasn't due to start for a week but there was an entry quota, and it was best to arrive early to be sure of getting a place. Besides, it was always good to soak up the atmosphere, listen to the latest troubadours and size up the competition.

Vaskrian whistled an old marching tune as he led the sumpter carrying his master's weapons, supplies and pennant, which flapped gently in the breeze. It was emblazoned with Branas's heraldic coat of arms, a coiled green wyvern on a blue background. Vaskrian gazed enviously at it, mulling over a handful of ideas he'd had for his own.

⁂

In the afternoon they spotted another pennant on the road ahead: an orange leopard couchant on a vivid green background.

Vaskrian tensed. The coat of arms belonged to Sir Anrod of Dalton. He had nothing against the knight, who was on friendly terms with his master. It was his squire Derrick who was the problem – he was a crony of Rutgar's. He wasn't much better than him in a fight, but he had a tongue like a flail.

Vaskrian eyed Derrick sullenly as they caught up with them, the two knights bidding each other well met and falling immediately to chatting about the tourney they rode to. Derrick returned his sour stare with a lop-sided grin.

It didn't take long before he started dishing it out.

'So you must be excited about Harrang,' he said with mock levity, nudging his courser a bit closer to Vaskrian's so the knights wouldn't hear what he said next. 'So many horses for you to rut. But then that's what common folk do when they can't get any better, isn't it?'

Vaskrian clutched the reins with white-knuckled fingers. This wasn't going to end well. Every season he promised himself it would be different, that he'd stay out of trouble. Every season it came calling, and he obliged.

'The only time I'll pay attention to horses that don't belong to Sir Branas is when I'm knocking squires off them,' he replied, trying to keep his voice calm. 'One day you might get to know what that feels like, when you learn to sit one properly.'

Derrick turned and spat into the pock-marked road. He was Rutgar's age, of a height and build with Vaskrian. His hair was an unruly blond mop and did little for his long ugly face.

'I suppose we can't all be as adept at riding them as you,' Derrick sneered. 'Seeing as you like to mount them night and day. But then one beast cleaves to another I suppose – that's only natural with churls like you.'

It went on like that, for the rest of the day. At dusk they made camp off the road in a copse of birches. Branas had originally planned to call on the local vassal Sir Alban, but Sir Anrod wouldn't hear of it. Some gambling dispute or other. Sir Branas evidently enjoyed his old friend's company enough to forego a night under a roof.

Vaskrian cursed inwardly at that. By now he was thoroughly riled. He did not enjoy verbal sparring with Derrick. The young noble was just too sharp. Every jibe was followed up by another, more cutting than the last. If he'd been half the swordsman he would have been a knight in the making indeed.

They had a blaze going in the little clearing in the middle of the copse. Branas had ordered broth for his supper. A simple roast would have been much easier but the old knight was picky about his food. He was sitting on a log next to Anrod, the pair of them getting stuck into a wineskin and reminiscing about tournaments past.

Vaskrian set to preparing supper. In accordance with his guvnor's wishes he seasoned the chicken and bacon with a healthy dose of bear's fat. That made for a thick greasy soup all right, but that's how Branas liked it. Not that he was complaining – the nights were still cold, the heartier the meal the better. A good sprinkling of salt and marjoram for extra flavour and a loaf of crusty bread to go with it, and they'd have themselves a feast.

Sir Anrod was content with cured meats and hard cheeses. He was a tallish spare man and evidently did not share his friend's appetite. That gave Derrick the easier job – but at least it meant the two squires didn't have to jockey for who got to use the fire first for cooking.

Sir Anrod got up to relieve himself in the trees. Vaskrian stirred the broth with a stick to stop the sizzling fat from congealing too much. He'd forgotten to pack the ladle, but hoped Branas wouldn't notice. The old knight seemed content with staring off into the trees, a dreamy smile on his face as he hummed a war-tune and drank his wine.

'A stick?' asked Derrick suddenly, with mock incredulity. 'Why, Vaskrian, I would have thought even a glorified peasant like you should know better! Haven't your years about your betters taught you anything?'

He was sitting by the fire, a platter of food next to him. Custom dictated that a squire couldn't start eating until his master had taken the first bite of his own meal, and Anrod was still busy wetting the trees.

Branas raised an eyebrow. 'Too busy tilting when he should have been preparing for the road!' he growled. 'Always the same – I'll thank you not to get any bark in my broth, Vaskrian!'

The squire flushed hotly. It had little to do with the fire – now Derrick was showing him up in front of his master. 'I shaved the bark off it, sire,' was all he could mumble.

That seemed to placate Branas, who turned back to his wine with a harrumph. Derrick was another matter. He let a braying laugh off the leash. 'Well, there's no end to your ingenuity... oh, I'm sorry, you won't know what that word means, will you? How shall I put it then? Low animal cunning – that's you all over isn't it? Well, more of the first two anyway.'

Taking the stick from the spitting broth Vaskrian did his best to shut Derrick's words out as he prepared to serve it up. No ladle meant he'd have to pour it in. Wrapping his hands in the thick folds of his cloak, he lifted the iron pot from the fire and bent low over the first bowl. Sir Anrod was making his way back over to the centre of the clearing. Sir Branas was still humming away, his eyes now fixed expectantly on the steaming soup as Vaskrian filled his bowl. He'd made sure there was plenty enough for two servings each.

He could feel Derrick still staring at him. He hadn't said anything for at least five seconds. Perhaps he'd finally shut up now his own master was drawing back within earshot.

He stooped over the second bowl, his own. Technically he shouldn't serve himself until he'd served his master, but lifting the heavy pot on and off the fire was a pain, and the day's unwelcome events had left him feeling drained.

'What's this! Serving yourself before you've brought your knightly master his food? Didn't your churl mother teach you any manners, Vaskrian?'

He did it without thinking. The next thing he knew Derrick was rolling around on the ground screaming, hands clawing at his face. Vaskrian was holding an empty pot, steam rising from its bottom into the uncaring night.

Branas lurched to his feet, a horrified cry escaping his bearded lips. Anrod was nearly on Vaskrian, the whisper of cold steel mingling with a yell of hot anger as he drew his blade.

He would have run him through there and then if Branas had not stepped up to bar his way.

'Now then, Sir Anrod, peace!' he growled, laying a broad mailed hand on his friend's shoulder to restrain him.

'What... is the meaning of this?!' Anrod managed to splutter. Derrick's screams continued to tear the silence.

'Derrick provoked my squire,' said Sir Branas, making a point of catching his friend's eyes. 'Dishonoured his mother. Common or no, that's a hard slight for a man of arms to bear.' His voice was dangerously even. You could say one thing for the old veteran, he was a fair man. Hard, but fair.

But Anrod was having none of it. 'Why hell and blazes, man, he's *blinded* my squire! What use is he to me in this state? I'll have to ride back to Hroghar and get him seen to! Even if I manage to find a replacement, I'll miss the entry signing for the tournament! And all because you can't keep your whoreson villein in check! In Reus' name, Sir Branas, you should know better than to take commoners into knightly service – this is what comes of it!'

Branas's eyes narrowed at that, his eyes like flints in the firelight. 'I don't recall you saying anything of the kind before,' he growled. 'And mayhaps you should have had your squire keep his tongue in check – he's been sniping at my Vaskrian all day. What did you think would come of it!?'

Sir Anrod took a step back at that, breaking contact between them. He was still clutching his sword. The blade carried an orange flicker in the fire's glow. Derrick's screams had subsided into low moaning sobs as he writhed in the grass. Vaskrian stood stock still, clutching the pot stupidly. He knew he must look like a village idiot. He felt like one too. What had he just done?

But the two knights had eyes only for each other.

'I demand a reckoning for this,' yelled Anrod. 'I'll be wanting compensation – and so will the lad's family. Why, he's my wife's nephew! There'll be hell to pay for this – and I'll not be footing the bill, Sir Branas!'

Branas let his hand drop to the hilt of his own sword. 'I'll be damned if I pay a penny for your fool squire's big mouth, Sir Anrod,' he snarled.

That was Branas all over – hard, fair, and tight-fisted as the day was long.

'Reus damn you, Branas, I'll have satisfaction over this, damn you but I will!' exploded Anrod, really losing his temper now.

'Oh aye?' replied the old knight, the edge in his voice sharpening. 'Well, Sir Anrod of Dalton may have satisfaction any time he wishes!'

His meaning was unmistakeable. The spat had become a duel of honour, and there was no backing out now.

'Draw that blade of yours, Reus damn you,' seethed Sir Anrod, dropping into a fighting stance. 'I'll not attack a defenceless man, like yon coward squire of yours.'

The pot slipped from Vaskrian's fingers at that. The words stung him. He was no coward. He'd wanted to fight Derrick properly – not maim him with a pot of boiling broth. But it was too late for regrets now.

Branas's blade left its scabbard with a steely whisper as he dropped into a fighting stance of his own. The two of them circled each other warily in the light of the fire. The drink had slowed them a little, but not enough to seriously impede their fighting abilities.

Vaskrian fixed his eyes on them, all thoughts of Derrick banished by the prospect of a good fight. Sir Anrod was at least fifteen years younger than Branas, and half a head taller too. That meant his reach was slightly longer – but Branas was a seasoned campaigner. He'd fought in the War of the Southern Secession against the pretender Kanga – Anrod had just missed out on the front line of that conflict, serving out his squirehood instead.

Vaskrian hoped experience would trump old age – he didn't fancy his chances fighting an enraged armoured knight if Branas lost.

Their blades rang as they passed and feinted at one another, each trying to outfoot his opponent. Sir Anrod was a good swordsman, and did everything by the book. But Sir Branas fought with a stubborn tenacity that had seen him live through years of warfare, skirmishes and tourneying. He wasn't an exceptional knight – but he was a survivor who knew his trade.

It was knowledge that paid off in the end. Sir Anrod came at him high; the grizzled old knight caught the blade and turned it forcefully.

He was stronger than his antagonist despite his superior years. Anrod stumbled to one side and before he could recover Sir Branas caught him in the side with a swift riposte. His hauberk took the worst of it, but even so the impact was probably enough to crack a couple of ribs. Sir Anrod grunted and staggered back on legs that tottered.

Sir Branas could have pressed his advantage and finished him, but he didn't.

'All right, Anrod,' he said, breathing heavily. 'You've had your satisfaction, now let's put this matter behind us and - '

With a roar Anrod came at him again. Branas's eyes widened momentarily in surprise, but he quickly recovered the initiative. The attack was that of a wounded animal – clumsy and angry. The old knight sidestepped the swipe and took Anrod full in the face as he did. Neither of them were wearing helms; in the heat of the argument Anrod had not even thought to pull up his coif.

He didn't cry out. He just brought up short, turning a half circle on feet that were suddenly slow. It brought him face to face with Vaskrian as his sword slipped from nerveless fingers. Blood welled from a diagonal slit that straddled his nose bone, reaching from lower cheek to forehead. It cascaded over his mouth and chin in a torrent made black by the half-light of the fire. Without a word he toppled to the ground in a jingle of mail links.

Branas stood, leaning heavily on his sword and panting. Vaskrian dashed over to inspect the fallen knight. Branas's blade had bit deep, its renewed edge shearing through the front half of his skull. Ereth had done his work well.

'He... he's dead,' said the squire in a hushed voice. Derrick's low moaning continued to keep the silence at bay. Even now Vaskrian couldn't help but feel excited. They hadn't even reached Harrang yet, and he'd already watched his master win a duel.

'He came at you with everything he had!' he said feverishly as Branas straightened himself and let go of his sword. 'He had to be at least fifteen winters younger than you, and you got him anyway - '

Striding over, Branas pulled him up by his brigandine and slapped him hard across the face. His gauntleted hand drew blood, tearing his lower lip. Vaskrian didn't even have time to register pain as the stocky knight held him over the fire and exploded in his face.

'What in Palom's name do you think you were playing at!?' he screamed, spittle spraying in Vaskrian's face. Never mind a split lip, he could feel the heat of the fire on his backside. It was uncomfortably close. 'I just had to kill a good knight I've known for ten years because of you and your temper! I've a good mind to do the same to you!'

Branas had the neckline of his brigandine in both hands. There was a ferocious strength in them.

'I... I'm sorry,' Vaskrian stammered. A painful heat was coursing through his rear now.

'You're sorry?' repeated the knight, his voice an unpleasant mixture of rage and incredulity. 'Yes, I daresay you are – though not half as sorry as poor Anrod and yon squire, I should think!'

'Please, sire, the fire...'

Branas's eyes were burning with a fire of their own. Vaskrian knew which one he feared most.

With a disgusted noise the veteran turned him from the blaze and flung him to the hard ground.

'Well, you caused this mess and you're going to damn well clean it up,' he thundered. The cool earth felt good beneath Vaskrian, but it didn't look as though he would be enjoying it for long. 'I'm certainly not missing the tourney at Harrang escorting that blinded idiot back to Hroghar!' Suddenly lowering his voice ominously, he added: 'So you'd better finish what you started.'

His eyes had turned from fire to ice. Derrick had started wailing again – evidently his pain wasn't getting any better over time.

'Wh-what?' Vaskrian managed to stammer. He didn't like where this was going.

His master loomed over him, an implacable silhouette against the firelight.

'What's the matter, Vaskrian, esquire of Hroghar? Surely you of all people aren't one to quail at a bit more bloodshed? It's not as if you've never killed a man before – now get to it!'

Vaskrian turned to glance at Derrick. His agonised throes had taken him to the edge of the circle of light. The darkened wilderness stretched behind him.

What his guvnor said was true enough. This wouldn't be the first time he'd killed. That had been two years ago, when he and Sir Branas had fought against Baron Olvar, a rapacious Wolding who had crossed the Warryn to raid Lord Fenrig's lands. He'd felt proud of himself that day – an enemy squire and a footsoldier had both met their ends on his blade. At fifteen summers, he'd been well on his way to becoming a knight of renown. Or so he'd reckoned at the time.

But this was different. He certainly had no love for Derrick – yet even so, he was incapacitated. Chivalrous knights weren't supposed to do this sort of thing.

Sir Branas must have read his mind. 'No, not very knightly is it, to kill a defenceless opponent?' he snarled. 'That's why I certainly won't be doing it!'

'But... can't we just leave him here?' Vaskrian tried desperately.
'He's completely helpless. I can't just kill him in cold blood!'

'You should have thought about that before you threw a pot of boiling
fat and water in his face! Reus' wounds, look at him! Blinded and disfigured
– what place do you think he'll have at the Jarl's table now? You've as good
as killed him already – now finish the job, for mercy's sake!'

Looking over at Derrick again he saw it was true. He'd taken to
clawing at the long grass, revealing a face that was hideously burned
and scalded. The eyes were gone – he couldn't distinguish them from
the lumps of sizzling bear fat clustered about them.

Picking himself up with leaden limbs Vaskrian drew his dirk
and walked over to Derrick.

He'd heard veteran knights at the castle say there was no
strength like that of a dying man. And so it proved with Derrick,
who wrestled like a Wadwo, his cries swiftly turning fearful as death
embraced him. Perhaps there was a lesson in that – no matter how
bad pain could get, fear of worse always trumped it.

In the end Vaskrian had to sit astride him, pinning both his arms to
the ground with his knees. Derrick's legs thrashed up manically, kicking
helplessly at his back before he sank the dirk into his throat. As his screams
subsided into gurgles Vaskrian kept his eyes tightly shut, trying not to think
of Derrick's pitiful pleading before the sharp blade silenced him forever.

He wrenched the dagger free with hands darkened to the wrists
with blood. Lurching up he staggered over to the nearest tree and
threw up bile. All was silent now but for the crackling of the fire
and the lone hooting of an owl.

Without looking at Derrick's corpse he made his way back over to the
fire and slumped down next to it. Sir Branas was still standing, staring at Sir
Anrod's crumpled form, shaking his head sadly and muttering to himself.

'We'll leave them here,' he said presently, his voice flat and
emotionless. 'I'll tell the peasants at the next village to send word
so his family can collect his remains – his horses and chattels too,
I'll not profit from an old friend's death. It was a duel of honour so
at least there'll be no blood-price to pay.'

Turning to look at Vaskrian he added coldly: 'Go and clean yourself
up at the river. After that you can do the same for my blade and see about
cooking up another supper – fighting is hungry work and I'm rightly
famished. See it doesn't stray between pot and bowl this time.'

Vaskrian nodded blankly and did as he was told. It wasn't until
he was stirring a second pot of broth that the old knight spoke again.
He was finishing off the wine, staring grimly into the night.

'Be thankful Derrick was only the second son of a minor vassal,' he said. 'If his family were more powerful we could both have been in a lot of trouble, duel of honour or no. All the same you've a nobleman's blood on your hands, Vaskrian, and you'll have to tread carefully from now on.'

'I'm sorry,' replied Vaskrian sullenly. 'I didn't mean for things to get so out of hand, but everyone at Hroghar's been taking pot shots at me today - '

Branas silenced him with a curt wave of the hand.

'Derrick is - *was* - a big-mouthed fool, no better than his cronies. If they could couch a lance half as well as they can hurl insults then Lord Fenrig would have a fearsome garrison in the making. As it is he has a spoiled bunch of rakehells who talk better than they fight.'

'But I can fight!' protested Vaskrian. 'Why can't *I* be a knight? I'd serve Lord Fenrig as well as anyone if only they'd give me a chance!'

He'd spoken well out of turn. He was half expecting Branas to rise and chastise him again, but the grizzled knight only laughed and took another pull on the wineskin. He was well in his cups now.

'Nay, Vaskrian of Hroghar,' he said, shaking his head. 'You've no idea what it means to be a knight. It takes more than a strong right arm to serve with honour. You commoners want it too badly, that's your problem. That's why only men of noble blood are fit to wear the spurs - not even that fool Derrick would have done what you just did.'

His eyes narrowed to mean slits as he gestured at the squire's corpse with the wineskin. 'Didn't I teach you your lesson just now? You start a fight ugly, it's going to finish ugly. Killing a defenceless man in peacetime doesn't feel as good as taking a life on the battlefield does it?'

'But he provoked me! You said so yourself!'

'Aye! And what did you do?' roared Branas. 'Sniped back at him - all blasted day! You could have held your tongue - do you think I won't have to do the same when some high-born lordling's son gainsays me during battle planning for the melee at Harrang? When some idiot half my age presumes to know better than me because he's bluer-blooded than I am? Oh, I may be of noble lineage, Vaskrian, but I have to stand in line too! Even lords have to bend the knee before their royal liege - why should you of all people be any different?'

Vaskrian stared sullenly down at the bubbling soup. He felt exhausted. It had not been a good day.

'If Lord Fenrig didn't owe your father his life I'd have dismissed you from my service months ago - you're nothing but a liability!' snarled the old knight. 'As it is, I've no choice but to put up with you - because I too have to do what I'm told, whether I like it or not!'

Guzzling down the last of the wine he tossed the skin angrily to one side. 'I can only pray that Reus grants me the power to knock some sense into that hot head of yours,' he slurred. 'You'll never make a knight, Vaskrian, but one day you might just make a half-decent squire. Now serve up my blasted supper – I've more than earned it.'

They ate in cheerless silence before turning in. Derrick's body caught Vaskrian's eye just as he was climbing into their tent. His limbs were bent in the unnatural pose of death.

He felt no remorse. The truth was, he'd sicked that up with the bile. His hands were washed clean in the waters of the Warryn, the bloodstains barely visible against the mud-caked red of his tunic sleeves. Derrick was just another corpse he'd made.

Still, he'd learned his lesson, whatever Branas might think. He wouldn't kill like that again.

Because when he became a knight, he would never have to listen to anyone taunt him all day long. He could demand satisfaction at the first insult, just like Branas and Anrod had. Kill a man in a duel of honour and you were beyond reproach.

He realised then that it wasn't how many you killed, or even who you killed that mattered – it was *how* you killed them.

Sir Branas was definitely wrong about one thing. Vaskrian understood perfectly well what it meant to be a knight.

⊷ CHAPTER IV ⊷

A Reunion With Old Friends

Adelko felt his heart quicken as he gazed across the valley at Ulfang Monastery. Three days' ride from Rykken had brought them back, and travel-thirsty as he was he had to admit he'd missed his adoptive home.

Its outer stone wall, sturdy and buttressed like a castle's, traced a circle around the crown of the hill it rested on. Adelko could make out the familiar storehouses, granaries and stables dotting the outer enclosure of the circular courtyard, and the stone buildings clustered about its centre that housed the refectory, kitchen, lectern halls, prayer room, sleeping quarters and common library. These were arranged in a smaller circle that enclosed the pillared cloisters where the adepts and journeymen spent the day in contemplation and study, when not teaching the novices. The cloisters encircled the monastery's inner sanctum, forbidden to all but the Abbot and senior members of the Order.

The only part of the monastery to have more than one floor, the sanctum was a small fortress in its own right, housing the Abbot's private rooms and study. Its round turret loomed above the grit-strewn courtyard, a flag perched atop it flapping in the brisk wind. This was emblazoned with the Order's motif, a silver lectern inside a circle of the same colour on a grey background. Beneath it, written in Decorlangue, were the words *Knowledge of Evil Brings the Strength to do Good*.

That had been the Order's motto since it was founded by St Argo more than five hundred years ago, when the learned savant had called on the people of the fledgling Free Kingdoms to favour reason and faith over sword and spear in the age-old struggle against wickedness and injustice. The Redeemer had said just the same thing of course, but by St Argo's time the world was languishing in the Second Age of Darkness and the lesson had been forgotten somewhat. But then the Almighty could always be counted on to send His servants to help the faithful, if they were wise enough to listen.

Adelko glanced at his master. His face was stern and unyielding and betrayed no emotion at their return. He supposed Horskram had made this journey too many times to be really moved by the spectacle. The two monks pressed on down into the valley before ascending the gentle slopes to draw level with the crop fields surrounding the monastery. These were carved from the hills in a series of platforms: a veritable giant's stairway of wheat, barley, corn and other good things.

Adelko felt his stomach rumble as he thought of Ulfang's capacious storehouses. One thing the Order did not lack was provender, and he had sorely missed hearty mealtimes in the refectory during his travels.

As they had done last autumn, the journeymen of the Order crowded around Horskram as they approached the monastery, bidding him well met. Brother Silas, the adept in charge of farming for the season, strode over and joined his leathery voice to the greetings.

'Brother Horskram, returned so soon!' he exclaimed. 'We had not expected to see you back here for at least another half year! Pray what brings you back?'

Horskram's face remained stoical as he replied: 'We have had unforeseen encounters upon the road, and I must speak with the Abbot. The forces of darkness are abroad in the land, and I have words for his ears only.'

Silas' drawn face lengthened even further, and he and several other monks nearby made the sign of the Wheel.

'That is ill news, Brother, and I am sorry to hear it. You will find Sacristen in his receiving chamber, for he is giving audience to a party of merchants from Port Cravern. They will be breaking their journey with us this night.'

An expression of distaste crossed Horskram's face. Adelko had heard him voice his disdain for the merchant class on more than one occasion, and knew his mistrust of the city-born commoners who placed a tidy profit above all else was shared by many in the Order. But their hefty contributions to Temple coffers, given to purchase prayers for their crooked souls, were valued. The Abbot, though a pious monk, knew only too well that the Order could not afford to pass up on its share of donations. Sacristen was clever like that.

Giving Silas a curt nod Horskram nudged his steed up the trail towards the monastery gates, Adelko following. In times of war the great oak portals would be bolted shut, but today was a clear spring day in time of peace, and they were spread invitingly. Riding beneath the gateway's buttressed arch the two monks ambled over to the stables.

Yudi, a ruddy-faced novice about Adelko's age, rushed over to take care of their horses.

'Adelko! You're back!' he said excitedly. 'We didn't expect to see you so soon – though it seems an age since you left! And humble greetings to you too, Master Horskram,' he added, suddenly remembering his manners and giving the distinguished adept a flustered half bow.

Horskram allowed a slight smile to break his features as he replied: 'Never mind all that, young novice! See to our horses – there'll be plenty of time for gossip later!'

Yudi gave another awkward bow as Horskram and Adelko dismounted, and hurriedly did as he was told.

Looking across the courtyard Adelko saw a dozen other novices returning quarterstaves to the barracks. He frowned at the memory. They'd just had combat practice – by far his least favourite discipline. But the Order applied a stern and thorough regimen, and Argolians were expected to be physical exemplars too; when not busy helping to farm the monastery lands novices were trained to ride and fight.

Both skills were taught in anticipation of the day when they would serve as friars and roam the wilderness in service of the Almighty. Just as knights sometimes forsook their liege lords to travel hither and yon as errants, fighting enemies of the King's Law wherever they could, Argolians would leave their monasteries to confront the servants of the Fallen One wherever they could find them.

Their weapons were the Words of the Redeemer, but all too often man was his own worst enemy – so the Argolians practised martial arts as well. Even with Freidheim on the throne ruling benevolently many of the roads and ways lying outside the King's Dominions were not safe, and robbers and highwaymen roamed at will through lands unguarded by the Knights of the White Valravyn.

Udo was still barking orders at the hapless novices in his hoarse, cracking voice – though the lesson was plainly over. The hardy old monk had served as a knight for many years under a Wolding baron before his conscience moved him to take holy orders.

His conscience hadn't quenched his fighting spirit, though, and it was whispered in the cloisters that he still loved the lance more than the lectern. The Abbot had apparently worked this out some time ago and decided that Udo's yearnings would be best served by putting him in charge of martial training, simultaneously harnessing his talents for the good of the Order. Sacristen was clever like that.

Adelko felt a shiver run down his spine as he watched Udo. He might have been an excellent scholar, but he was a near hopeless fighter.

A harsh and unforgiving taskmaster, Udo knew it too. In his first year at Ulfang he had singled him out mercilessly, often sweeping his legs out from under him to 'improve his stance' or deliberately pairing him with one of the bigger, stronger novices to 'encourage him to up his game'. Then there were the humiliating admonishments, which typically went something like: '*Adelko!* Follow through on your swing, for Reus' sake! My horse could wield a staff better than that!'

Adelko wasn't sure which he had hated most – the bruising blows or the barbed jibes.

At least some good had come of it, Adelko thought ruefully. He'd improved somewhat over the years, and by the time he had left with Horskram his quarterstaff technique was nearly passable. Passable enough to last maybe a couple of minutes in a fight with a brigand.

Three of the novices had spotted him. Adelko recognised his best friends with a smile as they approached excitedly.

Fat Yalba was first to rush up and greet him. About a year older than Adelko, he moved with a speed that belied his girth, and anyone unfortunate enough to be paired with him in quarterstaff practice was likely to wind up flat on his back nursing bruises.

Adelko knew it only too well, and unfortunately for him so did Udo. Yalba was as sharp-tongued as he was strong, and a natural leader, but his prowess at the lectern left something to be desired, and often he would trade a fighting tip or two for a page of Adelko's flawless Decorlangue translations.

'Adelko! I can't believe it's you!' he exclaimed loudly. 'It feels like you've been gone forever! My, but you've grown!'

'You too, Yalba!' Adelko faltered nervously. Though they were best friends, Yalba could get sensitive about his weight. He added quickly: 'It's good to see you! It's good to see you all!'

'Tell us, where have you been?' asked Hargus. 'You must have seen so many places – we want to know everything!'

Hargus's big round face bobbed comically up and down as he looked up at Adelko and beamed. He was very short – even for his fourteen summers – but his cheerfulness made him popular, along with his impressions of the adepts, with his turn on old Udo being widely considered his best.

'Oh don't worry – you will!' said Adelko dramatically. He'd been fantasising for weeks about impressing his friends with stories of travelling, exorcisms and witch-hunting, and he wasn't about to pass up on his opportunity. 'You won't believe some of the things I've seen this last fortnight!'

'Adelko!' Horskram snapped. 'Nothing beckons the anti-angels like the loose wagging of idle tongues – remember your scripture and don't be so boastful!'

'Yes, Master Horskram,' Adelko said, quickly curbing his ebullience. The others did likewise. The adept's reputation at Ulfang meant that no novice dared cross him.

'As I have said already,' Horskram continued sternly, 'there will be plenty of time for gossip, if you really must indulge in such tittle-tattle. For now it behoves us to make our report to the Abbot, so look lively Adelko – and I trust that your account of your adventures, when you doubtless give it, will be a fittingly *sober* affair.'

'Of course, Master Horskram,' replied Adelko in a hushed voice.

'Very good, now come along – Sacristen will doubtless have heard of our arrival and be waiting for us.'

Horskram turned on his heel. Adelko was just about to follow when the third novice, Arik, caught his sleeve.

Fixing Adelko with a conspiratorial look he said in a low voice: 'Adelko, good to see you. If you still care to regale us with your stories after evening lessons, come to my pallet – this afternoon I managed to purloin some... refreshments from the scullery.'

Arik, who shared the same name as Adelko's brother, grinned and winked before turning to leave with the other two.

Adelko liked Arik a lot. He was very clever – along with Adelko, he was probably the brightest novice in their cohort, and they often studied together and compared notes. It was a rare friendship. A lanky and somewhat ungainly youth, Arik wasn't the most popular novice in the monastery – with his intelligence came an arrogance that didn't endear him to many. Adelko often suspected that if it wasn't for Yalba vouching for him Arik might not have fared half so well at Ulfang.

✣ ✣ ✣

Four men were just leaving the Abbot's chamber as they approached. Horskram pointedly ignored them, but even without this clue Adelko could tell from their corpulent frames, sumptuous clothing and forked beards that they were the merchants. Taking in their smug, self-satisfied demeanour, he could well understand why his master despised their kind. But then he supposed somebody had to provide all the good things that the rich lowland nobles wanted.

If the merchants had come from Port Cravern then most likely they would be accompanied by mercenaries and pack horses laden with goods, purchased from the trading ships at harbour. These would have been brought across the Wyvern Sea from the mighty Empire to the east – a vast and powerful realm separated from the Free Kingdoms by the Great White Mountains that minded its own affairs but still deigned to trade with its lesser neighbours.

Following his master into the chamber Adelko found Sacristen much as he had left him. As portly as the merchants they had just passed, his kind jowly face was offset by keen grey eyes that betrayed a sharp intelligence. He was about the same age as Horskram, but the years had been much less kind to him – his love of food and drink was well known.

Getting to his feet and moving around his thick oak table with some effort, Sacristen embraced Horskram, exclaiming: 'Brother, well met! I trust St Ionus guarded you well on your travels! Pray what brings you back so soon? We had not expected to see you for another season at least.'

'The Redeemer be praised for returning us safely and in good health,' replied Horskram, keeping to monastic formality. 'And may the Prophet's peace be on Ulfang, and all who shelter within its walls! We are indeed returned right soon, for though Reus granted that our labours were successful, we encountered trouble that necessitated our coming back without delay.'

Sacristen's face darkened. 'Ah, old friend, that is bitter news indeed. In that case I can only presume you have an account to give. What is it? A haunting, or some other manifestation?'

'It pertains to an exorcism we conducted less than a week ago at Rykken. We managed to cast out the spirit, but there are... other ramifications.'

Sacristen looked at Horskram and Adelko nervously. He was naturally of a jittery temperament, but the novice thought that today he looked especially agitated, even allowing for the gravity of Horskram's statement. He wondered what the merchants had been saying.

Moving back behind his table the Abbot picked up a small iron bell and rang it.

'Sit you down both, and wait while I call for some refreshments – then you can tell me everything. You yourselves must be hungry after your long journey, and you know how I hate to receive bad news on an empty stomach.'

The three monks waited for a novice to bring some bread, cheese and cured fish and a flagon of watered wine. Sacristen helped himself liberally to these. Adelko followed suit gladly but Horskram ate and drank sparingly as was his wont.

While they ate the avuncular Abbot commented breezily on how Adelko had grown, quizzing him perfunctorily on his experiences. Too breezy, too perfunctory. Something was bothering him, Adelko's keen sixth sense told him that much.

Horskram reported their less gruelling encounters with the forces of darkness, the same tales Adelko was looking forward to regaling his friends with later. But all the while he sensed a lingering tension in the room. It was almost enough to spoil his appetite.

Presently Horskram began to tell Sacristen of their struggle with the evil spirit at Rykken. The Abbot's face grew even graver, and when Horskram finished by telling him that Gizel had been possessed by Belaach, he ran his pudgy fingers across his bald pate and let out a troubled sigh.

'Belaach is too powerful an entity to get across to our world without some kind of potent witchcraft being involved,' Horskram reminded him. 'Whether it's a case of his being directly summoned or being able to exploit a temporary widening of the rent - '

'Yes, yes!' snapped Sacristen in a voice Adelko thought far more irritable than it should have been. 'I'm not a novice, Horskram, and I understand these matters as well as you do – even if it is more than two decades since I served as a friar.'

Then he sighed again, and in less harsher tones he asked: 'If it is a demonologist at work, do you have any idea who it might be? What about ... ?' His voice trailed off as he glanced over at Adelko.

'I don't know,' said Horskram, picking up the slack. 'It could be. But without a divination there's no way we can be certain, as you well know.'

Sacristen nodded, staring distractedly into his half-empty wine cup. 'Yes, yes of course... Well, tonight we must entertain our prosperous guests. But tomorrow morning they shall be gone. Then we can gather the adepts together and... see what can be determined.'

Horskram was now staring intently at the Abbot. 'What is it? What else is troubling you?' he asked.

Sacristen licked his lips nervously and continued to stare at his cup. With his other hand he absently stroked the silver circifix around his neck. Then he raised his eyes to meet Horskram's.

'We had better speak in my private chambers. Tonight, after sunset prayers. I have things to tell you that are not fit for a novice's ears.'

✤ ✤ ✤

The rest of the afternoon was a giddy blur to Adelko. Naturally all the other novices were desperately keen to hear of his adventures, and they had just managed to squeeze a couple of stories out of him before the great iron bell in the courtyard rang for the evening meal.

Filing into the refectory, Adelko felt renewed pangs of hunger knot his stomach as he laid eyes on its trestle tables for the first time in months.

The vaulted chamber had been built well over three hundred years ago, along with the cloisters, inner sanctum and other older parts of the monastery. Two-thirds of it was given over to the main common area where the novices and journeymen ate together, with the remaining part raised above floor level and reached by a broad stairway. This was where the Abbot and the adepts ate and discussed important matters concerning the Order, save of course on Silence Days.

The high stone walls were punctuated by arched windows and draped with tapestries depicting scriptural scenes from the life of the Redeemer. Life-size statues of the saints looked down gravely at the diners from alcoves, an eternal reminder of the sacrifice and labours that had preceded their abundant repast.

From its lofty perch in one corner the statue of St Ionus caught Adelko's eye. It was his favourite. Of all the statues in the refectory it was the only one that betrayed a hint of a smile on its stone lips. Adelko liked to think it meant the savant had learned things on his travels that brought him a joy none of the others could know.

Yalba, who was just behind him in the orderly line of novices filing towards the tables, nudged him and whispered excitedly: 'Adelko! Did Arik tell you? We've been raiding the scullery again! We've managed to get a flagon of cider! Old Sholto never even knew! We'll be over at Arik's pallet after sunset prayers – come and drink with us then and tell us the *real* story of your travels!'

Adelko glanced back at Yalba and managed a half-smile before the four friends sat down together at the far end of a table. Sholto was nearly blind with cataracts: it hardly came as a surprise that he never picked up on their regular excursions to the storehouses – in fact why he was still in charge of them was anybody's guess. Arik had suggested that the Abbot simply didn't have the heart to dismiss the fiercely proud and irascible old monk from his duties, and that in any case he would probably die soon anyway. Hargus's more jocular theory was that Sacristen was only too glad to have someone virtually blind in charge of Ulfang's food stores, so he could help himself whenever he liked.

Adelko suddenly felt a little anxious. As much as he liked the idea of getting tipsy on Sholto's potent scrumpy while playing the returning wanderer, he hadn't forgotten his mentor's stern admonishments.

He suppressed a shudder as the memory of Gizel's suppurating skin and the hellish voice of her tormentor flashed through his mind. *The Five and the Seven and the One...* he'd never heard of devils giving prophecy, unless disguised as false prophets to deceive mortalkind. Perhaps Horskram was right – was that really the sort of thing to make light of over a gourd of cider?

And what had the Abbot been hiding? *Not fit for a novice's ears.* That remark had been rolling around in his head all afternoon. Something was clearly afoot.

‡ ‡ ‡

When the novices and journeymen were seated in the lower hall the adepts filed in, according to monastic custom. The thirty-odd senior monks walked solemnly up the middle of the refectory and ascended the stairs to the upper part of the hall. Horskram, the Abbot, and Udo were among them.

So were the merchants – as honoured guests they would eat at the high table. That was normally a privilege given only to visitors of noble birth, Temple perfects, or friars visiting from other chapters of the Order. Adelko guessed that the traders had been generous with their donations.

Looking around the refectory he caught sight of their bodyguards for the first time: sitting at a separate table near the entrance were about a dozen burly men. Heavily scarred and dressed for the road, they had a rough, ill-favoured look about them, and he was glad they were sat apart from everyone else.

All the adepts took their seats at the high table save one. This was Brother Calistrum, a hoary old scholar who had seen well over eighty winters and was in charge of the library. He also presided over the recitation before supper.

This was unfortunate, because for all his scholastic talents, Calistrum wasn't an inspired speaker.

Yalba glanced over at Adelko and rolled his eyes, as if to say *bet you haven't missed this much*. But no pious monk dared break with monastic observance, and so as Calistrum began droning his way through a chapter from the *Life of St Argo* on the lectern by the high table, Adelko and the four hundred novices, journeymen and adepts of Ulfang clasped their hands and bowed their heads.

The sun was low on the horizon by the time Calistrum finished. The prayers over, novices and journeymen on refectory duty busied themselves lighting torches ensconced in brackets about the hall, while others brought trenchers and carving knives to the tables.

Their feasting fell short of the groaning boards of the gluttonous Wolding barons, but the monks ate well. Adelko's mouth watered as pewter platters holding wild boar, goat's meat, salted fish and an abundance of vegetables were set along the tables. Of course today the food was especially fine because the Order wished to celebrate Horskram's safe return – and impress its wealthy visitors.

During the hearty meal, washed down with watered wine, Adelko's friends and other novices nearby pressed him for further accounts of his travels, but his mouth was too full most of the time to tell any tales.

'Adelko must have been possessed himself!' joked Hargus. 'He's eating for ten!'

Though the wine was too weak to have a strong effect, spirits ran high, and Adelko's friends laughed and chatted boisterously throughout dinner until the nearest journeyman told them sternly to pipe down.

Afterwards, with the platters cleared away and the tables wiped clean, the Order prepared for evening prayers.

The prayer hall was next to the refectory on the circuit of buildings that perambulated the cloisters and inner sanctum. The monks filed across in customary silence, broken only by their sandals crunching noisily across the gravel.

A nondescript domed edifice, the hall's interior consisted of a round auditorium supported by high columns of stone. No decorations graced its cold precinct save for a vast stone rood depicting the Redeemer being broken on the Wheel – unlike Temple perfects, Argolians believed that places of worship should be austere.

The rood was set directly behind a dais at the centre of the chamber, from which the Abbot addressed his congregation. Wooden pallets were set at regular intervals on the stone floor so the rest of the Order could kneel in prayer. Behind the dais and rood was a separate walled enclosure housing the sacristy. The Order's most treasured relics were kept there, including a set of prayer beads strung together with hairs from St Argo's head, along with the monastery's supply of holy water. Adelko had never set foot in there – like the cloisters and inner sanctum it was out of bounds to novices.

The Abbot led the prayers and gave additional thanks to the Almighty for returning Horskram and Adelko to the Order safely – and moving the hearts of the merchants to grace it with a handsome donation. Adelko's head was bowed in prayer, so he couldn't see the expression on Horskram's face as Sacristen spoke, but he could imagine what he was thinking and guessed it wasn't all that charitable.

The merchants themselves were present, doubtless only too glad to join the pious Order in prayer and reap the spiritual rewards of their material generosity, but of the freeswords that protected them Adelko had seen nothing since supper. He wondered if such men were so godless that even the prayers of the Order could not save them.

Their devotions over, the monks filed out of the chapel. Outside it was dusk. A chill wind was blowing through the valleys that lay about the monastery. The adepts and journeymen retired to their quarters or the cloisters, to study for another hour or two before sleep.

Adelko and his friends made their way back to their dormitory. There were about a hundred and twenty novices at Ulfang, crammed into four long low buildings situated in the same circular compound that housed the prayer hall and refectory. The four dorms were situated at the main points of the compass, lending each a ready nickname.

Adelko and his friends belonged to North House. At fifteen summers, Yalba and Arik were among the eldest there – upon reaching their eighteenth year novices who passed their exams became journeymen and moved out of the dormitories. Many of the strictest older boys were seconded to friars and would not be present. The remainder would be busy studying in the cloisters for their final exams. As for the younger novices, none of them would dare cross Yalba.

✢ ✢ ✢

The four of them gathered around Hargus's pallet an hour after sunset. Lights were not permitted after curfew, but the clouds had parted to reveal a waxing moon. Hargus pinned back the curtain covering the window nearest his bed to allow enough light to seep in. One of the novices their age lying nearby began to complain until Yalba told him to shut up.

Each novice had a small trunk at the head of his pallet in which to store his meagre possessions. Hargus rummaged through his and produced his prize, a round stoppered gourd fashioned of hide. His yellowy teeth flashed in the moonlight as he beamed at it.

'Well don't just sit there staring at it!' said Yalba in a loud whisper. 'It's a gourd, not a parchment scroll! Open it up and pass it round!'

With a last furtive glance around the darkened dorm to make sure no one bigger than them was watching, Hargus removed the stopper, took a swig, and handed the gourd to Yalba.

Adelko took a good long pull on it when it came to him. Sholto's scrumpy tasted delicious: say what you like about his skills as a quartermaster, the old coot certainly made good cider. The predictable taste of the monastery orchard's apples was offset with something else – Adelko had once overheard a journeyman say that Sholto used something called *lemons* for extra flavour, strange exotic fruit from the Southlands that he bought from the odd passing merchant.

As Adelko's senses exploded with warmth he reflected that perhaps those fork-bearded devils were good for something after all. His reverie was interrupted by Arik poking him impatiently.

'Adelko! Be a good chap and pass it on! One sip and you're already grinning like a village idiot!'

The other two burst out laughing at this, quickly stifling their mirth into none-too-quiet sniggers so as not to draw too much attention. Sheepishly Adelko did as he was told, trying not to laugh too loudly himself.

They passed the gourd around a few more times. Sholto's scrumpy was as strong as it was tasty, and before long Adelko's head was feeling pleasantly light. After filling him in on a few of the more interesting things that had happened at Ulfang, his friends pressed him eagerly for more stories of his travels.

Made merry by the potent combination of the Archangel Kaia's gifts of nature and human ingenuity, Adelko was more than happy to oblige. Besides the demon at Rykken, he reckoned the witch at Lönkopang and the banshee spirit at Urebro were probably his best stories.

The banshee had been the unclean spirit of a village girl who had taken her own life after murdering her husband. Her essence had coalesced in a dark cave overlooking the village three days after her burial in an unmarked grave nearby. Every night for seven weeks she had driven its inhabitants to distraction with her continual screeching, to such an extent that several of the frailer villagers had died of exhaustion or sheer fright by the time they arrived.

'She was a fearful sight alright,' said Adelko, drinking in the rapt gaze of his friends as eagerly as Sholto's scrumpy. 'A shimmering likeness of a village girl, but you could see the rain falling right through her – her face was all twisted, covered in ghostly blood it was! Her hands too... I was scared, but Horskram just marched right up to her and started reciting the Psalm of Banishing. I joined in with him, she didn't last long. But that wailing *screech* – if we hadn't been chanting the Psalm of Fortitude all the way up the hill towards her cave I reckon we'd have died of fright too!'

'What did you do afterwards?' asked Arik, his black eyes glinting keenly in the moonlight.

It was a shrewd question. Any good exorcist knew that a banishing should nearly always be followed by a blessing.

'We marched straight back to her grave,' said Adelko, taking another sip of the cider. His head was humming pleasantly by now. 'Horskram put a blessing on the grave and sprinkled it with holy water. That's one banshee you won't be hearing from again – she'll be in Gehenna now where she belongs.'

The others exchanged glances and nodded approvingly as Adelko launched into his next story. A few weeks after the banshee they had arrived at the hamlet of Lönkopang, to find its distraught folk at a loss as to why their harvest crop was in a state of decay, and the milk and cheese intended to sustain them through winter curdled instantly every time it was exposed to the air.

After a few days spent divining in the local area they had apprehended the witch responsible. Shackling her with cold iron to stop her using pagan sorcery on them, Horskram had brought her back to the villagers and convened a council. It soon transpired that the witch, Uselda, had lived in Urebro until she was forced to leave after being caught using Enchantment, one of the Seven Schools of Magick, to charm the local tradesmen into giving her discounts.

At the council she claimed she had been exiled without her belongings, which the greedy villagers had taken and kept for themselves. This, she claimed, had provoked her into using Transformation, another of the Seven Schools, to ruin their precious food crop.

'Hah, typical!' snorted Yalba, upon hearing this. 'Witches always lie!'

'Hush!' said Arik, gesturing irritably with the cider gourd. 'I want to hear what happened next!'

Yalba glowered at Arik and snatched the gourd from him as Adelko continued his story. It had taken Horskram a full day to extract the truth, but eventually the villagers had confessed that Uselda wasn't lying.

'Hah!' said Hargus. 'There you go, Yalba – what happened to "witches always lie"? You should become a Temple inquisitor – you've got the right amount of zeal and the right amount of brains!'

Arik snorted with barely suppressed mirth. Yalba stared menacingly at the pair of them. Arik and Hargus stopped laughing abruptly. You didn't want to get on the wrong side of Yalba if you were in his quarterstaff class.

'So what happened?' asked the burly novice, turning back to Adelko. 'Did you have to burn her?'

Arik rolled his eyes. Hargus turned away so the bigger novice wouldn't see him laughing again. It was a well known fact that in the Kingdom of Northalde such cruel punishments were reserved for those who practised the diabolical Left-Hand Path of magick. Uselda, a hedge witch at best, hardly qualified. Even her powers of Transformation were relatively weak, and could only effect a minor change upon things. A legendary practitioner like Proteana, the Golden Age sorceress who infamously turned the mariner Antaeus's crew into slugs, would have laughed at Uselda's fumbling attempts at revenge.

'Of course not!' said Adelko, humouring Yalba with a straight answer. 'He even ordered the villagers who stole from Uselda to pay compensation to the others who had suffered from her curses – said it was their fault for provoking her!'

The others let out a few gasps and whistles at this. It wasn't so uncommon though – Argolian friars often found themselves acting as much as justices of the peace as exorcists and witch hunters in remote areas cut off from the authorities.

'What about the witch?' asked Arik. 'He didn't let her off surely?'

'No,' Adelko shook his head. 'Horskram took his own shackles back and ordered the local blacksmith to put iron bands about her wrists, to stop her using sorcery again, then he had her branded as a witch so everyone would know what she was in future.'

'Quite right too,' said Yalba, his voice slurring. 'She got what she deserved – filthy pagan witch!'

Adelko bit his lip. He wasn't so sure about that. Uselda had been spiteful and malicious, but she'd also had some reason to be angry, and it wasn't as if she'd killed anyone. He had even protested at the apparent vindictiveness and cruelty of the punishment at the time. But Horskram had countered that it was necessary, because convicted witches had been known to submit to iron bracelets before travelling to another village and seducing another blacksmith into freeing them. If everyone knew a witch immediately when they saw one, such seductions would be more difficult to accomplish. Or so the reasoning went. Adelko wasn't entirely convinced. His training was testing him in ways he'd never expected.

They passed the gourd around some more, their conversation stoked up by Adelko's storytelling. He revelled in the moment, and was especially pleased with himself when he was able to counter Arik, who challenged him a couple of times on some of the Psalms he said they'd used (much to the consternation of Hargus and Yalba, who told Arik to stop being such a rivalrous swot for one evening at least).

Even so, he couldn't quite bring himself to tell his friends about his most recent and harrowing encounter. Despite the cider's effects, something in the back of his mind told him this was no tale fit to tell in an open space, where anyone might overhear. In fact he wasn't sure it was a tale fit to tell at all.

Presently they drifted off on to more general subjects, the conversation taking a random turn as it always does when drink is involved. Hargus started in with his latest mockery of Udo, which had them all in stitches. Arik, relentless scholar that he was, turned the subject back to Adelko's use of scripture. The other two looked at each other, rolled their eyes and went back to lampooning their grizzled combat trainer, while Adelko did his best to answer Arik's searching questions. By now he was getting the distinct impression that Arik was jealous of him for having been chosen above him by Horskram, and was trying to find some flaw in his account of their travels to show him up.

Arik was absently holding on to the gourd. Hargus, who was next in line for a swig, tugged at his brown habit impatiently. Without breaking off or turning around Arik stretched out his arm and let go of the gourd, dropping it on to Hargus's pallet and spilling its contents.

'You fool!' exploded Yalba. 'What are you doing?!'

Arik turned and gaped as Hargus leapt forwards to recover the gourd before it could roll away out of sight.

'I... I thought Hargus had it,' he stammered stupidly.

'You weren't even looking at him!' hissed Yalba. 'You were too busy trying to catch Adelko out at scripture, as usual! Now look what you've done!'

'I wasn't! I – I'm just a bit drunk, that's all... Hargus, I'm sorry, is it all right?'

Hargus was staring in distress at the near-empty gourd and his sopping pallet. 'No, Arik, it is most definitely not all right. Apart from losing us the last of the cider you've soaked my pallet through.'

'Arik, you bloody idiot!' snarled Yalba. 'You're as clumsy as a Wadwo! The Redeemer knows how someone so clever can be so stupid!'

'I'm sorry – look, you can have my pallet, I'll turn yours over and sleep on it, it'll be fine.' Arik looked as though he'd just been scolded by Udo.

Hargus shook his head grimly. 'No, don't you see? That stuff *stinks* – when the journeymen on prefect duty inspect us tomorrow they'll be able to smell it from a mile off. We're going to get into trouble – and it's all your fault!'

Arik was looking more and more downcast. 'I'll take the blame,' he said sullenly.

'No one's taking any blame.'

Adelko spoke in an unusually firm tone of voice. His three friends looked at him in surprise – but after everything he'd been through in the past six months he wasn't going to let something like this fluster him.

'Look, it'll be fine,' he said. 'You three stay here and keep a look-out – I'll go to the well and fetch some water. I can bring it back in the pail and we can get this cleaned up before anyone notices. Then I'll take the pail back and we're done. The others will be studying for at least another hour – we've plenty of time, so don't panic.'

Getting woozily to his feet Adelko found himself savouring for a second time that night his superior experience. Arik could try and catch him out on his theory all he liked, but right now empirical knowledge of how to deal with adversity was his alone.

'Are you sure you don't want me to come with you?' asked Yalba, looking unusually hesitant. Adelko smiled breezily at him. The cider had inflated his confidence magnificently.

'No, I'll be fine. Besides, there still may be journeymen out and about – the fewer of us running around at this time of night the better. Just keep your eyes peeled and give the signal if you see one!'

✢ ✢ ✢

Adelko lurched off, his heart pounding and his head swimming. The well was on the south-east side of the circuit of buildings, next to the scullery and storehouse. To reach it he would have to tiptoe past the journeymen's quarters and East House. Thanks to Udo's constant endeavours he was by now fairly nimble, so he was confident of sneaking past without attracting any attention. He would have to hope none of the other monks were taking in the night air, but given the chilly weather that was unlikely.

Still, he felt painfully exposed beneath the glaring light of moon and stars, and found himself wishing for a cloud or two. He couldn't risk moving into the shadows as this would mean passing right next to the journeymen's quarters.

Doing his best to make as little noise as possible he made his way past, keeping them to his right. He could see flickering candlelight from the windows of some of the buildings. The journeymen were generally quartered a dozen to a building; there were some two hundred and fifty of them altogether, housed in twenty buildings dotted around the compound. A few were situated along the monastery's outer wall along with the stables, smithy and outhouses, which meant keeping an eye to his left as well.

He reached the well without incident. Peering over its stone lip he felt a shiver go down his spine. The silvery moonlight contrasted starkly with its lightless depths. Glancing furtively about him he reached for the rusty iron chain and began slowly pulling up the pail from the depths below. A couple of times it grated noisily against the side. Adelko winced but kept his cool, and soon he was clutching a full bucket of water.

Setting it down gingerly he spent an agonising minute detaching the rusted chain from the pail before setting off back to his dorm.

It was harder to walk quietly clutching the bucket and Adelko could not help the water slopping about, but he had just skirted East House without incident when he heard it: the sound of a raven.

Hargus's adroit imitation was unmistakeable – the signal.

Hurriedly he retreated into the shadows, crouching low by one of the journeymen's quarters that had no lights on. Clutching the pail tightly Adelko hardly dared breathe as he saw two monks round the next building from the direction of North House.

Closing his eyes he prayed silently to Ushira, archangel of good fortune. The two monks drew nearer. They were talking quietly to one another. Adelko heard them pass by, their footfalls crunching in the gravel. Their voices receded.

Opening his eyes and glancing back to make sure they were gone, he got to his feet and continued on his way, still clutching the pail tightly.

The rest of the way back to North House felt like an age, and it was with some relief that he made his way back into the dorm and over to where his friends were waiting for him.

'Adelko!' exclaimed Yalba in a loud hiss. 'You made it! There were two journeymen! We saw them go by and Hargus gave the signal! Did you manage to avoid them?'

'I wouldn't be here alone if I hadn't,' replied Adelko dryly. 'Let's hurry and clean this up so I can get the bucket back!'

The four of them got to it. Hargus had produced some old rags from his chest, the others had done the same. Soaking these in the water they set about mopping up the spilt cider. Several of the other novices lying nearby complained, and one even threatened to call a journeyman until Yalba grabbed him by the habit and told him he'd give him bloody teeth if he dared.

Adelko often found himself hoping his friend would grow out of his bully-boy ways, which were ill befitting a monk of the Order – but he had to admit that right now they were proving useful.

They soon had the mess cleaned up. Hargus's pallet might well stain, but if he turned it over no one would notice. Yalba had already succeeded in cowing the nearby novices into swearing silence.

'All right,' whispered Adelko when they were finished. 'We're done. Now all I have to do is take back the pail and we're in the clear.'

Yalba looked at him, biting his lip and looking a little uncertain in the half light of the moon. 'Adelko, are you sure? You've already taken a risk – and the older boys will be coming back from their studies soon...'

Adelko smiled at his friends – they looked so funny, all nervous and unsure of themselves.

'There's still time if I go now,' he replied. 'Besides, if we don't take it back they'll soon know something's up. Don't worry – compared to hunting witches and banishing evil spirits, this is nothing!'

Snatching up the pail he bounded out of the dorm before the others could say anything. He was still riding the crest of an exuberant mood – the thrill of a minor adventure had amplified his intoxication.

He made his way back to the well without being spotted. Fixing the bucket back onto the chain he lowered it gently down into the water.

He had no sooner done this when he heard the sound of voices. Looking up he saw the silhouettes of cowled figures emerging from the arched entrance to the cloisters between the scullery and South House. He cursed inwardly. The older novices, returning from their studies.

He nipped around the well so they would not see him, and crouching down he peered over it furtively. After wishing each other a perfunctory good night, the novices split into two groups. Some were heading clockwise towards South House and West House, the rest were heading the way he had come back to the other two dorms.

He waited for them to file away before considering his next move. The cold had intensified. Adelko shivered as he drew his own hood over his head.

It was then that it caught his eye.

The circular edifice housing the cloisters was low: above it he could see the central tower of the inner sanctum, and on its first floor he could see the steady yellow light of a lantern burning at a window. Silhouetted against this was an imposing figure. He guessed its identity immediately.

His mentor. No sooner had he realised than the words of the Abbot came flooding back into his mind: *I have things to tell you that are not fit for a novice's ears.* For one tense moment Adelko thought Horskram had spotted him, but then he turned away from the window and walked out of sight.

Adelko glanced about him once more. The older novices would take some time to bed down for the night – he would have to stay here a while and endure the cold before sneaking back to his dorm. Returning his gaze to the window he felt something stir in him. It was the same feeling that had prompted him to approach Horskram at the celebration feast in Narvik five years ago.

Taking a deep breath, Adelko slipped out from behind the well and, for a second time, made a decision that would radically alter the course of his life.

⇥ CHAPTER V ⇤

An Unwelcome Revelation

It was not far from the well to the entrance to the cloisters, and Adelko reached it without drawing attention to himself. On either side of the arched gateway statues of the avatars Argo and Weirhilde, patron saint of Ulfang, stared down at him blankly. Their pitted stone likenesses looked eerie in the moonlight, and Adelko shivered all the more in the highland cold.

There was no gate: adepts and journeymen could come and go freely to this part of the monastery, although novices were discouraged from doing so when their elders were using them.

Designed for study and quiet contemplation, the cloisters were also where the adepts would meet to conduct divinations. Stepping through the entrance Adelko looked about him. To either side the cloisters curved off, forming a circle around the inner sanctum. Set off it at regular intervals were small alcoves with stone pews and lecterns where monks could take their books and scrolls. Others would tread the flagstoned path in a circle, reciting prayers they had memorised from the *Holy Book of Psalms and Scriptures*.

The study alcoves were carved from the outer wall of the cloister, which was as thick as it was high; the inner side of the ring facing the sanctum was open and colonnaded at regular intervals. From where he was Adelko could clearly see the Abbot's private quarters, the tower housing them surrounded by a small circular garden.

The Abbot's forbidden inner sanctum. Where no novice was permitted to set foot, on pain of expulsion from the Order. Adelko took a deep breath. Then he took another step forwards.

Following the cloister in a clockwise direction according to custom, he stopped at the short path crossing the Abbot's private gardens from the edge of the cloisters. At its far end the single door guarding the inner sanctum stood, silently beckoning him onwards. The path was flagstoned like the cloister floor, but the bushes and plants to either side threw it into a shadowy gloom.

Glancing up at the night sky Adelko saw the moon staring down at him accusingly. In ancient times before the coming of the True Prophet the peoples of Urovia had worshipped her as a goddess: Kaia, mistress of tides and sister of the sun, avatar of nature and still venerated in some lands as one of the archangels.

Was she looking at him now? Casting aside such thoughts and steeling himself, Adelko set one foot on the path before him.

He knew that in doing so he had broken one of the core rules that bound the monastery. Although no one had yet discovered him, he felt there could be no going back now.

A few swift footfalls brought him to the threshold of the door. He had half expected something to happen, but nothing did. Faith and obedience guarded the forbidden parts of Ulfang; he would encounter no sorcerous traps here.

The ancient oak door was bound in bronze and presented a sturdy obstacle. A great knocker made of the same metal stared Adelko in the face: its tarnished hoop was clutched in the maw of a lion's head. Something in the way it had been wrought gave it an unearthly, devilish look. This came as little surprise to the novice, for the imperial grandees of Ancient Thalamy had fed the early followers of the Prophet to the lions in their blood-soaked amphitheatres for sport, and those fabled creatures were often portrayed as ghastly beasts in the tomes and parchments he had looked at in the library. Adelko felt his sense of foreboding increase. Ignoring his sixth sense was not easy, but he blocked it out nonetheless.

The door would ordinarily be bolted from the inside at all times: even adepts such as Horskram could not enter the sanctum without the Abbot's invitation.

Was it merely instinct that guided his hand that moonlit night, or some higher power that told him he would not find it barred on this occasion? It was a question he would ask himself many times thereafter. Whatever the truth of it, pushing at the door he was strangely unsurprised to feel it yield to his touch, grinding softly across the sanctum's precinct.

The vestibule was windowless; wan candlelight greeted Adelko as he gingerly pushed back the door. As if in a dream, he stepped inside and gently closed the door behind him.

The chamber was cold and dank. Aside from two rusted iron candelabra affixed to the curving walls on either side of him there was nothing in it apart from a wooden circifix on the far side and a carpet of horsehair that covered most of the floor. A spiral staircase began to his left, curling upwards and terminating directly above the rood at an aperture in the ceiling, from which stronger light spilled. His quick hearing also picked out the faint sound of voices somewhere upstairs.

Taking another deep breath, he tiptoed over to the staircase and began slowly to ascend it. His body cast a long shadow on the circular wall. He found himself thinking of the banshee they had fought at Urebro, how her form had flickered and undulated beneath the light of the stars, at times seeming horribly distended and contorted. Not for the first time that night, he shivered.

Making his way up the stairs he emerged onto the first floor. The room he was in was semi-circular and half the size of the vestibule below. It was much better appointed: torches were ensconced in bronze brackets at regular intervals, the walls adorned with embroidered hangings that depicted scenes from the life of the Prophet, and the stone floor was carpeted with a fur trimming that came from some animal too exotic for Adelko to recognise. Arched windows not unlike the one he had seen his master at were dotted at several intervals about the room, covered with translucent panes of bone.

The stairs emerged next to the wall that curved. Set into the straight wall opposite was another bronze-bound oak door, smaller than the main entrance and less sturdy. To either side of it stood two tall burning braziers of iron in each corner. The smoke from the burning embers wafted into small apertures above each brazier: Adelko guessed that these led to flue shafts designed to filter out unwanted fumes, for the engineers that built Ulfang had been canny craftsmen, well versed in the ancient lore of the Golden Age.

The voices were louder now, coming from behind the door. Next to it was a small mahogany table, on which were an unlit candelabrum and a tinderbox, presumably to light the Abbot's way downstairs should he need to receive visitors after dark. Thinking this, Adelko felt his heart contract guiltily at the enormity of what he was doing.

Creeping across the antechamber he pressed his ear to the door. He heard his mentor's strong voice, low but distinct. He sounded deeply perturbed and displeased.

'... but what in St Argo's name were you doing keeping it here? It should have been kept in the sacristy, with all the relics, for Reus' sake!'

'In the sacristy?! Where we keep our holiest treasures? Horskram, think of what you are saying! To – to keep a thing of such evil there, of all places, where we pray to the Almighty, where we ask Him to reward our unworthy spirits with His beneficence! Not for all the blessings of the angels would I have done such a thing!'

It was the Abbot's voice, higher pitched than Horskram's, and a good deal louder and more agitated too. Horskram replied – he must have turned away from the door or lowered his voice, because Adelko had difficulty making out what he was saying.

'... too exposed. Only the essence of the Redeemer or the saints can ward... You say it was taken two nights ago? Who else in the monastery knows about this?'

'No one. In truth, I had not yet decided what to do about it, until the Redeemer brought you back to us. Oh Horskram, if the Temple authorities learn of this there shall be hell to pay! You know how those godless curs have despised our Order ever since the Purge! There are many among the high perfecthood at Rima who would do anything to bring us down! This will provide them with the perfect excuse!'

'For Reus' sake, calm down!' His master had raised his voice now, and Adelko could hear the anger and tension in it. 'And stop wailing like a banshee – there may still be novices up revising for their exams. Not all the Temple priests mean us harm – and if anyone should know whether they do, I do ... years ago ... but I haven't forgotten... First I need to inspect... the fragment was taken from...'

'... in the summit.'

'... show me...'

Adelko heard the sound of a chair scraping heavily against the floor. It took him just a couple of seconds to remember that the stairs did not continue on his side of the door, and that therefore the top of the tower could not be reached via the room he was in.

But by then it was too late. In his startled haste he had involuntarily started back, his elbow catching the candelabrum on the table next to him. Adelko felt his heart shoot into the roof of his mouth as it landed, as ill luck would have it, just beyond the edge of the carpet. It hit the stone floor with a resounding clang.

Adelko turned to run back across the ante-chamber and was just at the top of the stairs when the door was flung open. His master stood imperiously in the doorway, eyes fixed on his unruly charge.

'Adelko!' he bellowed, 'Just where do you think you're going? Come back here at once!'

Horskram's tone brooked no argument. He was already found out anyway: his future in the Order hung by a thread. Adelko shuffled fearfully back over to where his mentor stood, the Abbot gazing incredulously over his shoulder.

No sooner had he done so than Horskram grabbed him, yanked him inside the Abbot's private study, and pinned him up against the wall.

'How long have you been listening?' His voice was lower now, but twice as menacing. Adelko could barely summon up the wherewithal to respond.

'N-not long. Maybe a couple of minutes... I didn't hear much – nothing at all really!'

'How much! What did you hear? Tell me every word, now!'
Horskram demanded, raising his voice. His tanned face was pressed up
close to the novice's, and his eyes burned with a strange light that Adelko
found frightening.

'N-nothing! Just some things about... some fragment of evil that
should've been kept in the sacristy being pinched from the Abbot's
private chambers upstairs, and something called the Purge, and the
Temple perfects not liking us much – that's all!'

Horskram relaxed his grip on Adelko, his careworn features
slipping from anger into despondency. Shaking his head he sighed and
said wearily: 'So in other words, you've heard far too much already.'

'No – really, I haven't! And I can explain everything about why I'm here...'

Adelko's voice trailed off, because the truth was that he couldn't
explain at all. Out of nothing more than sheer curiosity he had gotten
himself into huge trouble.

But Horskram paid him no heed in any case. 'How did you get
in here?' he demanded, the sternness returning to his voice.

'The door was unlocked. I was over by the well returning the pail
after fetching water when I saw you at the window. I decided to come – '

'Yes, yes, spare me the foolish reasons behind your intrusion for now.'
Letting go of Adelko the grizzled adept rounded on the Abbot. 'Sacristen,
you blasted fool! How could you have been so careless? Leaving your
front door unbolted, tonight of all nights! It's no wonder... *it* has been
stolen from us!'

The Abbot was gazing dumbfounded at the pair of them, his round
eyes wide open, his jowls quivering with consternation. In different
circumstances Adelko would have been tempted to burst out laughing.

'But... I'm *sure* I locked it,' he stuttered. 'Ordinarily I never... oh
Redeemer's wounds, what a week is this!' Sacristen made the sign
and raised his eyes to the heavens.

'The Redeemer only helps those who help themselves –
preferably by not being as simple-minded as a village idiot,' said
Horskram roughly. 'Adelko, I take it you didn't bother to lock the
door behind you when you decided to pay us your surprise visit?'

The novice shook his head sorrowfully and looked at the ground.
Horskram turned back to the Abbot and looked at him disdainfully.

'Well, go and bolt the damned thing, Sacristen – before half of
Ulfang decides to join us!'

The hapless Abbot blinked and shuffled off to do as Horskram bade
him. Adelko's master turned to look at him again. 'So tell me the rest,' he
said in a flat voice. 'What were you doing up after curfew in the first place?'

✢ ✢ ✢

Reluctantly Adelko told his mentor the whole story. By the time he had finished the Abbot had returned – holding the now-lit candelabrum that had betrayed him. Shutting the door behind him he locked it with a key that he kept with several others like it on a chain about his waist.

Adelko had read about locks: clever, new-fangled devices that originated in the Empire but were rarely used in the Free Kingdoms, save perhaps in the cities where the merchants guarded their wealth jealously. He had never seen one up close until now, apart from the one on the door to the common library. The keyhole had escaped Adelko's attention before because he had simply not thought to look for it – otherwise he might have been able to peer through it, he reflected.

The study was another well-kept room. Like the antechamber it had several windows, the largest of which was directly opposite the door. That was the one Adelko had seen his master standing at. Unlike the other windows it was not covered with bone, but two wooden shutters stood flung open to either side of it – the chamber felt unusually hot and Adelko guessed that his hardy master must have hankered for the cold night air. Two more braziers burned brightly – clearly Sacristen did not share his master's opinion of the benefits of chilly weather.

The room was well lit: several lanterns hung from iron hooks set into the walls. Two chairs and a long low table of oak were set in the middle of the chamber, whose walls were lined with creaking shelves holding more than a hundred books and scrolls and assorted bits and pieces of paraphernalia used for study and prayer.

The overall effect was one of homely disorderliness: however tightly he ran the monastery's finances, the Abbot certainly wasn't personally tidy. The right-hand side of the chamber's semi-circular wall was given over to another spiral staircase leading up to the next floor.

Adelko absorbed all these details peripherally: most of his attention was taken up with fielding his master's scrutiny and wondering what would now become of him. He found little solace in Horskram's flat-voiced declaration when he had given a full account of his misdemeanours.

'Adelko, you have twice broken the rules of our Order this night,' the old monk said. 'The first infraction of being abroad unsupervised after curfew is a forgivable offence, albeit not without punishment. But the second is far more serious: no one, novice, journeyman or adept, is permitted to enter the inner sanctum without the Abbot's express permission. You have presumed to do so, for what precise reason I have yet to fathom. Our Order is founded on discipline and a respect for authority, which you have broken with. As such I cannot intercede on your behalf, and it falls to Prior Sacristen, whose precinct you have unlawfully entered, to determine your fate.'

Horskram turned to look at the Abbot with a deferential gesture. Only a moment ago he had been the one in control, but in the blinking of an eye he had reversed the situation, and authority was in the portly prior's hands again.

Adelko held his breath as he looked at the avuncular Abbot, who stared back at him and did his best to look stern and authoritative as he barked: 'Adelko, of all the foolish games you might have played this is surely the worst you could have chosen!'

Adelko's head slumped – he must surely be finished now.

The Abbot continued: 'Such behaviour would ordinarily warrant instant expulsion from the Order. But tonight is no ordinary night, as you have doubtless begun to fathom.'

Adelko raised his head to look at the Abbot, whose eyes were sparkling in the lantern light. He felt hope return to him as Sacristen continued: 'You are devilishly bright, young novice, and far too curious for your own good – but I believe that the Redeemer has sent you here for a purpose, though I cannot divine as yet what that may be.'

Adelko saw the Abbot glance sidelong at Horskram, who nodded imperceptibly to indicate his assent. The novice felt his pulse quicken.

'And so, by the power vested in me, I shall waive the usual punishment and withhold your expulsion from the Order – provided you swear on the Holy Rood that you shall not breathe a word of what you have heard here tonight to anyone!'

Both monks were looking keenly at Adelko. The novice felt the sweat trickling down his back as he realised he must have stumbled onto something big.

'Of course, Master Sacristen! I won't tell anyone, I promise!'

Adelko hoped he sounded sincere. At that moment in time, he certainly was – but whether they would believe him was another matter.

Sacristen turned to look at Horskram, who turned to look at Adelko. Producing his silver circifix from the folds of his habit, Adelko's master bade him kneel. And there, in the name of the Almighty and His Prophet and the Seven Seraphim, Adelko swore to keep secret everything he had seen and would see that night, on pain of immediate expulsion from the Order if he broke his troth.

'Your time in Purgatory where Azrael weighs the souls of all the dead shall be lengthened by days beyond count if you break with your oath,

Adelko,' warned Sacristen, 'for the Unseen do not take kindly to those who break promises made to them on consecrated ground. Remember that! For it is not just your future in the Order of St Argo that is at stake now!'

Hearing this Adelko had to fight back tears. The night had proved more emotional than he had expected, and he felt his nerves stretched to breaking point. Why oh why did he have to go and be such an intrepid fool?

His face must have betrayed his anguish, because Horskram placed a calloused brown hand on his shoulder and said in gentler tones: 'Now then lad, don't despair. The Almighty knows you've done a foolish and disobedient thing tonight, but as Prior Sacristen says there may well be some divine purpose in it. Now get up and pull yourself together. If you keep to your word no evil will befall you.'

Snuffling back his incipient tears Adelko did as he was told. He wondered what his friends would be thinking now, and hoped he hadn't gotten them into too much trouble. He felt bad about having dropped them in it – but what else could he have done?

He had no time to mull this over, because just then Horskram turned to Sacristen and said: 'Well, Master Abbot, I think it is time you showed us the scene of the crime, so to speak.'

Taking up the candelabrum once again Sacristen motioned for them to follow him up the stairs. Adelko felt his pulse quicken again, his old thirst for adventure and natural curiosity quickly subsuming his guilty feelings.

The next floor was the Abbot's bedchamber. Again Adelko was surprised to see a certain amount of opulence, with hangings, furs and carpets decked about the room. As men given up to spiritual service of the Almighty, the monks were supposed to lead austere lives, and Adelko knew that the buildings housing the journeymen and adepts were divided into cells that afforded few creature comforts. At least Sacristen's pallet was a simple affair, and half the room was given over to a personal shrine, with a great rood of painted hardwood dominating it.

Looking at the Redeemer's gaping wounds in the eerie candlelight, Adelko felt himself less reassured than usual by the image of his spiritual saviour. There was so much evil in the world, even one of the Unseen descended to earth in mortal form had fallen foul of it.

The Abbot led them up another flight of stairs. This emerged into another circular chamber, with a lower ceiling than the others; the two older monks almost had to stoop. This room was windowless, and a foul musty odour of dankness permeated the cloying air. The wavering light from Sacristen's candelabrum fell on dozens of books stacked up around the walls, some of them piled in rotting wooden boxes, others standing free.

Seeing this Horskram turned to look at the prior. He was frowning, and his aquiline features looked ghostly in the candlelight.

'Sacristen, some of these books are very... you know what some of them contain. They should not be kept so freely!'

'What would you have me do?' snapped the other monk, his eyes suddenly flashing. 'Waylay every passing merchant for his strongbox? Is their presence in the inner sanctum not enough?'

Sacristen's voice trailed off as his eyes fell on Adelko. 'None of them contain the kind of... knowledge you are doubtless referring to in any case,' he said sullenly. 'They would have been burnt long ago if so.'

'If they contain the other kind of "knowledge" as you put it, they should have been destroyed regardless,' replied Horskram testily. 'In my opinion there's no such thing as good – ' He cut himself off abruptly as the novice caught his eye too. 'Never mind. Is this where you were keeping *it* too?'

The Abbot shook his head emphatically. 'Redeemer's wounds, no! A fine night's sleep I would get with such a thing directly above my pallet! The sanctum has one final chamber. It's this way.'

Adelko listened to this exchange in silence, but his mind was racing. What secrets did the inner sanctum hold? He was already beginning to fathom what some of them might be, but dared not believe he could be right.

While the elder monks bickered he tried to make out the tomes they were arguing over in more detail, but the light from Sacristen's candelabrum was quite weak and all he could see was that many of them looked very old indeed.

But where his eyes failed him, his other senses were picking things up.

Beyond the dank smell to be expected from an airless stone chamber was something else: a more profound foulness permeated the air and put him instantly in mind of the room where poor Gizel had lain possessed. His sixth sense had ratcheted up another notch, and he felt an insidious dread creeping through his entrails, growing stronger with every passing moment. Looking at the taut expressions on the older monks' faces, he could well believe they felt it too.

Sacristen led them through the piles of books to another flight of stairs leading up in a diagonal line from the centre of the chamber and terminating in a trapdoor. Sacristen held up the candelabrum to give a clearer view of the latter: like the other doors in the sanctum it was made of oak, but this one was bound in iron and had the Wheel carved into its surface. The Abbot glanced sidelong at Horskram.

'Everything you need to see lies beyond yonder trapdoor. If you don't mind, I would prefer not to go up there again.'

In the wan candlelight Adelko could see beads of nervous sweat on the Abbot's pudgy face. Even Horskram looked visibly perturbed. Adelko's feeling of creeping horror had increased, as had the foulness of the stench. Both were undeniably coming from beyond the trapdoor.

Reaching into his habit Horskram produced his circifix and began intoning a prayer to the Redeemer. It was the same one they had recited before beginning their assault on the evil spirit at Rykken, and without thinking twice Adelko found himself doing the same. Then, taking the candelabrum from the Abbot, Horskram began slowly to ascend the stairs to the trapdoor. Again without thinking, Adelko followed. That Sacristen preferred to stay alone in the dark surrounded by all the strange books barely crossed his mind.

The trapdoor was as heavy as it looked and with some effort Horskram pushed it open one-handed. As he did so a gust of foetid air rushed down into the chamber. Both monks recoiled at the reek; for an instant Adelko feared one or both of them would lose their footing and tumble down the stairs. The air was hot, far too hot for the season or circumstances, and Adelko felt himself break out into a cold sweat that confused his senses horribly. As the hellish draft passed through the room it rustled the dry leaves of the old books, which seemed to whisper eerily in the half darkness.

Then all was silent again, although the increased stench lingered. Horskram pushed back the trapdoor with a dull thud and entered the uppermost chamber. Adelko mouthed another quick prayer and followed before his courage failed him. He could hear Sacristen below him in the dark, reciting psalms in a soft voice that quavered.

✢ ✢ ✢

Looking about him Adelko was almost disappointed. The room he was in was no bigger than the last one, and almost empty. There was no obvious manifestation of evil, but its lingering presence was undeniable. Down in the chamber below the smell had been unpleasant; up here it was enough to make him gag. Even the monastery's latrine could not smell so awful: indeed there was something profoundly *unnatural* about the putrid odour that now set his gullet heaving and forced him to put the sleeve of his habit across his mouth.

Horskram was casting about in an agitated state, the candelabrum clutched in one hand and his circifix in the other. The ceiling of the uppermost chamber was no more than a man's height above their heads. A rusty iron ladder affixed to the far wall led up to an aperture that presumably led onto the turreted roof where the flag of the Order perched. The ruins of another trapdoor hung loosely from its one remaining hinge; Adelko gawped as he realised the thing had been made of stone. In the flickering candlelight he now noticed shards and splinters scattered about the foot of the ladder. The night skies peered down at them as they stared up at the mangled stone block dangling precariously above them.

'Very clever,' breathed Horskram in a low voice. 'Right at the summit of the tower. No one from the outside would notice – you'd have to be a thaumaturgist to see this!'

'A thaumaturgist? What do you mean?' Adelko breathed. He had unconsciously lowered his voice to a half whisper. The air was still oppressively hot.

'Only someone capable of flying would be able to notice that there had been a break-in,' Horskram clarified. 'None of the other brothers at Ulfang would ever spot it from the ground. You wouldn't even see it from the hills around the monastery.'

That made sense, Adelko supposed. Thaumaturgy was the school of magic that gave a warlock power over the elements in defiance of the natural laws of the world decreed by the Almighty. Skilled thaumaturgists could bind Elementi to their will, including air spirits or Aethi, enabling them to fly.

Horskram's gaze involuntarily flicked downwards as he answered Adelko's question. The novice wasn't sure whether he was thinking of the Abbot, the strange books, or both.

Slowly they perambulated the chamber. Horskram handed the candelabrum to Adelko and produced his phial of holy water, sprinkling it about the dusty floor and intoning the Psalm of Reconsecration as he went, just in case Sacristen had neglected to do so in his fear.

The flickering candlelight fell on the only item in the room: a large strongbox, at least half the size of a man, wrought of solid iron. Adelko glanced over at his master, who had just finished the blessing, but he seemed unsurprised.

Putting his holy water away the older monk took the candelabrum back and stepped over to examine the chest, still clutching his circifix.

As the light fell on it directly Adelko nearly gasped out loud. Given his childhood days spent at his father's forge there could be no mistaking his eyes.

Something had *melted* more than half the side of the chest.

The top and other sides were covered in engraved quotations from scripture: Adelko's studies had not rendered him familiar with these passages, but he could make out that they invoked the Redeemer's protection against some great evil. That didn't surprise him. As he stood beside his master nervously fingering his own circifix the residual presence of that evil seemed to heighten, battening keenly on his psyche.

The casket was empty, although as his master passed the light to and fro above it the novice could see that the engravings continued on the inside.

After inspecting the casket Horskram drew himself up and intoned a final blessing. As he sprinkled holy water on the iron casket it smoked slightly, giving off a resentful hissing noise. Both monks made the sign before Horskram turned to Adelko.

'We have seen everything that there is to see – our work here is done. Let us make haste and return below, before the Abbot faints in the dark.'

Horskram's grim humour did little to dispel the novice's feeling of trepidation, although precisely what he feared would happen he could not say. The two monks returned below, to where the Abbot was still muttering psalms. Horskram was last to descend, closing the trapdoor behind them.

'Well, it's as bad as you said it was,' said Horskram laconically as he drew level with Sacristen. 'We had better go back to your study and talk this over.'

Taking the candelabrum that had so changed the course of Adelko's night from Horskram, the Abbot led them back over to the stairwell. As he did so the novice caught sight of one of the old books, momentarily illuminated by a flaring candle. It was made of a strange-looking hide, and on its cover were inscribed bizarre symbols, the like of which he had never seen before. Something about the alienness of them made Adelko feel even more uncomfortable.

✣ ✣ ✣

'And you are quite certain it is but two nights since it was stolen?' Horskram's face looked graver than ever. They were back in the Abbot's study. The older monks were sat on chairs with the novice squatting beside them on a thin rug that did little to keep out the cold from the stone floor.

'Quite sure,' the Abbot said. 'And, unless some of our brothers have unnaturally keen eyesight, no one else at Ulfang knows about it... although some of the adepts may have begun to sense all is not as it should be.'

Horskram nodded absently. He was deep in thought.

Presently he spoke again: 'Something's afoot, that's clear enough. A greater spirit manifests itself in an innocent host displaying no vice or wickedness, while at the same time some other infernal entity makes off with one of the most dangerous artefacts to survive the Breaking of the World. It can't be a coincidence.'

'Horskram, you cannot be sure of that!' Sacristen's voice sounded tremulous. Adelko had an inkling he was trying to convince himself that all would be well.

'Why else would somebody try to take the fragment?' said Horskram. 'Its potency is well known to all who take an interest in such things... and only a warlock of considerable repute could harness such powers of the Other Side as we have seen here displayed.

'The spirit that possessed the girl Gizel could easily have got through the rent between worlds while our unknown antagonist was conjuring up whatever fiend it was that stole the fragment. And then there were Belaach's own words... the Five and Seven and One would return, he suggested. That would correspond to the Five Tiers of Gehenna, led by the Seven Princes of Perfidy and the Fallen One himself! And our hellish "prophet" who will supposedly bring this about would be our Left-Handed warlock, presumably.'

Sacristen made the sign. 'Horskram, we cannot trust the words of devilspawn! They are designed to mislead!'

'Perhaps... or maybe our devilish antagonist couldn't resist crowing at us to assuage his defeat at our hands. Fallen angels are by their very essence fallible. Look, I can't be sure of anything right now, Sacristen, but the scenario I've just described seems plausible enough to me!'

'Well who do you think could be behind it? Do you think it's...'

'Andragorix? That's the question I've been asking myself. This deed bears all his hallmarks, that's for sure. If only I had slain him when I had the chance!'

Adelko was shocked by the vehemence with which his mentor said this. He had no idea who Andragorix was, but this was the first time he had ever heard the adept talking about wanting to kill someone.

'Do not chastise yourself for holding to your vows, Horskram,' replied the Abbot in soothing tones. 'Those who keep their troth shall never be counted sinful in the eyes of the Almighty, as the Redeemer sayeth.'

'Aye, Sacristen, and he also said that sometimes a lesser evil must be done to avert the greater. Would that I had done such three years ago.'

But the Abbot shook his head. 'There is little use now in crying over spilt milk – or unspilt blood, in this case. Reus fashioned us from the celestial clay and gave us free will, to choose our paths in life as we see fit. We must do that now, for it falls to us to decide what to do next, not rake over the past and might-have-beens.'

'You're right of course,' said Horskram with a deep sigh, though the blank look had not left his eyes. 'The first thing we must do is take counsel with the rest of the adepts, then hold a divination to see – '

'No, Horskram! That would be folly!' exclaimed the Abbot. 'The fewer people know of this, the better! If the adepts learn of it, sooner or later the rest of the chapter will know and then... who knows who else? We must guard this secret closely – many in the Order do not even know the Headstone fragment was being kept here!'

The light had come back into Horskram's eyes, and he was staring keenly at the Abbot now. 'So what do you propose we do? Sit on this and do nothing!? Sacristen! You should know better!'

The old Abbot shook his head. He looked tired and confused. It was certainly late. Adelko guessed it must be approaching the Wytching Hour.

'No... no. I'm not suggesting that,' replied the Abbot in subdued tones. 'But... Horskram, you of all people should appreciate what could happen to us if the Temple learns of this, after everything we went through with them before! In Reus' name, you were one of the – '

The Abbot cut himself off abruptly, glancing at Adelko again. The novice noticed a pained look cross his master's face, which he immediately suppressed.

'Be that as it may,' said the latter evenly. 'But we can't deal with this alone – and the mainstream perfects will find out eventually. But perhaps you're right. It might make sense to keep this to ourselves for a while – at least until we have a better idea of who's behind it and what they're up to.'

He paused then, and the three monks sat silently, all of them deep in thought. Presently Horskram spoke again.

'We must tell Hannequin. If we can keep it secret for a while from the rest of the Order and the Temple at large, there's no keeping it from him. It was stolen from a chapter belonging to the Order, so technically it's his responsibility.'

The Abbot nodded, albeit reluctantly. Adelko could fathom why: Hannequin was Grand Master of the entire Order, every Argolian chapter across the Free Kingdoms ultimately answered to him. Though he was only just beginning to get his head around what was going on, the novice guessed that Hannequin would not be pleased by what had transpired at Ulfang.

'I suppose you have the right of it,' replied Sacristen. 'Though Reus knows what he'll say when he learns of this!'

'Yes, well, you leave me to worry about that.'

The Abbot blinked and looked at Horskram in surprise. 'You're going? To Rima?'

'Well who else is going to make the journey there to tell him?' replied Horskram testily. 'We've both just agreed to keep this a secret, and I can't see you travelling hundreds of miles to do it. When was the last time you even sat on horseback?'

Sacristen's eyes fell to the ground, a look of shame crossing his corpulent face. 'Horskram, though I am prior of Ulfang, you truly humble me. What would the Order do without you?'

'It would muddle along, I suppose,' replied Horskram, his voice not completely devoid of humour. 'No, it falls to me in any case – if Andragorix *is* behind this then I am as responsible as anyone for what has happened. And travelling to Rima makes sense – to get there we must pass by Graukolos Castle in Vorstlund, and we'd do well to look in and check that the fragment kept there is still safe. As for the others... well, Rima wasn't built in a day, so to speak.'

The Abbot nodded again. 'When will you leave?' he asked.

'At daybreak,' replied Horskram. 'And that being established, it's time we got some rest. Adelko! Come along – tomorrow we begin a very long journey, I hope you're in the mood for riding. Oh, and I think you can spend what's left of this night in my cell... oath or no oath, I don't think returning to the dormitory to be surrounded by your garrulous friends is a good idea. Come now, lad, look lively! You wanted to see more of the world – well, by Reus, you shall!'

Sacristen ushered the pair of them out of the sanctum, pausing only at the threshold of the cloister to embrace Horskram and bestow his blessing on both of them for the long road ahead.

The thought of it made Adelko's head spin. The Pangonian capital lay many leagues to the south; to get there would be a journey of weeks, taking them across lands he had read about but never seen.

Adelko felt a feeling of euphoria welling up inside him at the thought of it, and he struggled to get to sleep in Horskram's cell despite all the rigours of the long day. He thought of his favourite icon in the refectory smiling down on him with its delicate stone lips and smiled gladly himself – at last, his prayers to St Ionus had been answered!

Overjoyed at the prospect of his new adventure, Adelko could have no inkling of the danger into which he had unwittingly propelled himself.

⇒ CHAPTER VI ⇒

The Dreaming Damsel

From her chamber on the highest floor of the inner ward's south-west tower Adhelina could see many things.

If she chose to look south-east, across the battlements of the castle she had been born in, she could see the silvery waters of the Graufluss, and the barges bringing trade to Merkstaed from the Free City of Meerborg. If she chose another window she could look upon Merkstaed itself, a prosperous town for many generations, simultaneously blessed with the river trade and the protection afforded by Graukolos. Look to the south-west, and she could just about make out the green line of the Glimmerholt, where her father loved to hunt – or had done until he became too fat to sit a courser. Spread out in a verdant canvas between all of these lay the green fields of Dulsinor, the realm her ancestors had ruled for nearly three hundred years.

On a sunny day – which this was not – it was a vista that would take the breath away if seen by fresh eyes.

But the eyes of Lady Adhelina of Graukolos, sole living child of Wilhelm Stonefist, Ninth Eorl of Dulsinor, were anything but fresh. The splendid view only reminded her of how confined her world really was. Privileged as she was, Adhelina often felt she would trade places with any of the low-born bargemen and passing merchants on the river below.

'Milady, come quickly! You'll want to see this!'

Sunk in her jaded reverie, Adhelina barely registered the words spoken by Hettie, her lady in waiting and best friend.

'Will I?' she asked languidly, turning from the window and absent-mindedly laying a hand on the book she had been reading. It was a compendium of the *Lays of King Vasirius and Queen Mallisande* by the Pangonian poet Gracius. She'd read them a dozen times, but unlike the view outside the walls of Graukolos, they never seemed to tire her. The world evoked by Gracius seemed so much more just and elegant than the one she occupied.

Had Pangonia really been like that once? She often wondered. She had only ever heard her father's vassals talk about the people of that realm disparagingly, although it was still undeniably the most powerful of the Free Kingdoms.

But then that was probably half the reason her Vorstlending kinsmen despised their southern neighbours. Vanity and envy seemed to be the principal virtues of most of the knights she knew.

'No really, Adhelina, you'll want to see this!'

Hettie's insistent tone roused Adhelina from her gloomy thoughts – her lady in waiting only used her given name when she really wanted to get her attention.

Looking up from the book she saw Hettie peering out of the north-west window of the chamber. That overlooked the main courtyard, located in the middle ward along with the feasting hall, armoury, barracks and other essential buildings. Beyond that lay the outer ward, where the horses were stabled and the resident craftsmen and artisans pitched their stalls during the day.

That could only be of interest for one reason – unexpected visitors.

Leaving her book Adhelina lifted her white samite skirts as she walked across the room, inwardly cursing the impracticality of the garment. Usually she rebelled, defying her father and choosing to wear a shorter gown that allowed more mobility. Mostly she succeeded in defying him, for she was every bit as headstrong as he was, but on special occasions and feast-days – when she would be on show as his heir – he would put a broad foot down and insist in a thundery voice. Even Adhelina knew better than to oppose him in such a mood.

'So, Hettie, tell me,' said the damsel with a wan smile as she moved slowly over to join her by the window. 'Who comes to dine with us at the feast tonight, and regale us with his tales of hunting, warfare and tourneying? Surely not someone I might actually find interesting for more than five minutes?'

'No, it's Lord Hengist!' replied Hettie, stepping aside to let her mistress have a clearer look.

The middle and outer wards were divided by a crenelated wall and gatehouse, but unlike the outer fortifications of the castle these were less than ten men tall. From her lofty chamber window, the heiress of Dulsinor could easily make out the new arrivals in the outer courtyard.

Adhelina recognised Hengist's banner instantly – a coiled silver serpent on a deep purple background.

She even hated his coat of arms – just who did those Lanraks think they were, taking a royal colour for their emblem? And as for the snake – well it positively echoed the heathen adherents of the Faith, and weren't good Palomedians supposed to be fighting a crusade against that lot?

The Herzog was accompanied by ten armed knights, each one attended by two squires.

Such extravagance! Wasn't one apiece enough? Together with the other servants he had brought there must have been a good forty of them assembled in the courtyard, making a great fuss and clamour. She supposed her father was meant to feed and shelter all of them – as if he didn't have other important guests coming tonight.

Now she could see Berthal, the seneschal, striding over to meet the dismounting lord and his pack of toadying sycophants.

Adhelina's heart went out to the old steward. He had always spoken kindly and respectfully to her, treating her like the intelligent person she hoped she was, and she was genuinely fond of him. Hengist would have the unfortunate septuagenarian running around after him for the next hour at least.

She hadn't seen the loathsome Herzog since the last feast, when he had behaved abominably, groping every passing serving wench and becoming hideously drunk – even by Vorstlending standards. Things had finally come to a head when he had tried the same thing with Hettie at the dance – Adhelina had had a thing or two to say about that, and if her father had not intervened things might have turned ugly.

'What in Reus' name is he doing here?' exclaimed Adhelina in a disgusted voice. 'After last time... my father should know better than to invite such a boor to our table!'

'I can't disagree with you there, milady, but then I suppose Hengist is our neighbour, and a very powerful baron at that...'

'Oh Hettie!' exclaimed the damsel again, stroking her friend's brown tresses affectionately. 'Don't worry – I'll make sure he doesn't come within a country mile of you this time!'

Hettie smiled, her eyes sparkling mischievously. 'With all due respect, milady, I doubt you'll need to bother – I don't think he'll even remember meeting me, state he was in, and I'll certainly know better than to come within a country mile of *him*!'

Adhelina smiled back, flicking a stray tress of strawberry blonde hair over her shoulder. 'How right you are,' she replied in a knowing voice. 'Well, let's see to it that he doesn't come within a country mile of either of us! If I never have to speak with him again I'll consider it a blessing from the Almighty Himself!'

�֍ �֍ ✶

The day drew on and gradually more guests began to arrive in the outer courtyard, vassals and their ladies from the demesnes of

Dulsinor come to pay fealty and feast with their liege lord. In that time Adhelina had forsaken Gracius to tend the abundance of herbs and plants she cultivated in her chamber.

One could scarcely move for all the hanging baskets, as Hettie pointed out continually. All in vain, because Adhelina loved growing things.

Since her youth she had plunged herself into the study of herb lore, visiting the Marionite monks at Lothag Monastery nearby to learn all she could from those masters of the healing arts. At twenty summers she had already attained a knowledge approaching the learned disciples of St Marius, amassing an abundant supply of all the necessaries used in chirurgery: King's Wort for infected wounds, St Marius' Weed to expedite the healing of injuries, Linfrick's Node for the easing of abrasions and armour rash.

At the library and gardens of Lothag she had learned to prepare other kinds of simples too: St Alfias' Herb for the melancholy sickness, Morphonus' Root for inducing sleep, Luviah's Teet, a powerful aphrodisiac... these and many more herbs and roots were clustered about her chamber, hanging up to dry or in various stages of growth or preparation.

Her father had not discouraged her from taking up the healing arts – the presence of a gifted healer in the castle carried obvious benefits – but had he known about all the other things she was growing he might have felt inclined to put his broad foot down again. Not that there was ever any danger of that – Lord Wilhelm knew about as much of herb lore as he did of scripture.

In any case, it wasn't that Adhelina planned ever to use her more illicit plants – it was just fun growing and preparing them.

And there were few other pursuits permitted a lady, besides reading, riding and the occasional spot of hawking, that really appealed to her. She'd tried taking up the harp when she was younger but had made little progress, much to the consternation of her music tutor. It hadn't bothered her all that much – like most of the knights and ladies in the castle she could dance well enough, and so long as the household troubadour Baalric was around who needed another noble-born amateur behind the strings?

Adhelina was busy chopping up a fresh crop of Wose's Bane when there came a knock at the door.

Putting aside her embroidery Hettie picked her way adroitly between the hanging baskets and opened it. Berthal was standing there, dressed in his dark brocade robes of office and looking harried and weary.

'My ladies,' he said, smiling at Adhelina and nodding deferentially as he stepped inside. 'I trust you are both well today! Still busy turning your quarters into the Hanging Gardens of Shamaria, I see.'

'Hardly,' replied the damsel, putting aside her work with a smile. 'And in any case I should hope not to invoke the misfortunes of that fabled city – it was sacked by the Thalamian warlord Tycius if my memory serves me well.'

The old seneschal beamed. Like Adhelina he was one of the few occupants of Graukolos who had bothered to master the Thalamian Alphabet, and he shared her passion for reading the poetry of that ancient realm.

'Ah indeed – though he reaped the just deserts of his cruel conquests when his concubine slew him... you have been reading my copy of Aedelric's translation of *Hessian's Fables* then?'

'Several times over,' laughed Adhelina. 'You can have it back if you wish – I can probably recite half of it from memory by now!'

Berthal shook his head emphatically, his wispy white beard waving. 'Oh no, please keep it – I'm afraid an old man hardly has the energy to read after a long day's work.'

Adhelina's smile became a frown. 'My dear Berthal – are they working you so very hard?'

'I'm afraid so,' replied the seneschal, his slender wrinkled face darkening. 'That young rapscallion, the Herzog of Stornelund, has arrived – and I don't need to tell you what a fuss he's capable of stirring up! Already he and his men are demanding wine and victuals and complaining about the size of their quarters. Such indecorous behaviour! Really! Not half the man his father was!'

'Yes well, you don't need to tell us what an unwelcome guest he is,' said Adhelina coolly, exchanging meaningful glances with Hettie. 'But pray what brings you here? You're obviously far too busy to be making social calls...'

'Hmm, yes indeed. As a matter of fact I was just discussing some final arrangements for tonight's banquet with your father, and he requested that I call in on you on my way back to the grind, so to speak. He says he wants to see you in his quarters.'

'What, right now?' asked Adhelina, suppressing a sigh.

'Oh yes, I'm afraid so – the Hanging Gardens will have to wait a little while!' said Berthal with an avuncular smile. 'Now if you'll excuse me, dear ladies...'

'Of course, Berthal, please don't let us keep you from your work a moment longer,' replied Adhelina as Hettie showed the seneschal out.

'Would that you could milady!' said Berthal, looking over his bony shoulder with a rueful smile. 'Oh well, goodbye for now – Miss Hettie, a pleasure as always, goodbye.'

Hettie shut the door behind him. Adhelina walked back over to the table and picked up the knife again.

'Aren't you going to go and see your father?' asked Hettie, fixing her mistress with a pointed stare.

'Yes... yes I am,' replied the damsel, as she started chopping up the pungent bristly leaves again. 'Just as soon as I've finished doing this.'

✣ ✣ ✣

When she was done, Adhelina rinsed her hands in the fingerbowl and went to call on her father. His private chambers were just one floor down, the roof of the central keep being lower than its turrets.

Spread across the top floor of the castle's inner ward, which would have dwarfed many a fortress in its own right, Wilhelm's quarters afforded him the space a rich merchant would envy. When Adhelina was a small child and her mother was still alive, she had lived there with them, and her younger brother Adhos, before smallpox took him in his third year. By the time she was ten summers old Adhelina was clamouring for her own quarters. Her father, only too glad to have his troublesome daughter out from under his nose, had readily agreed.

All the same, Wilhelm hadn't been about to let his only child disappear completely from his oversight – so he'd installed her in one of the inner ward's four turrets, where just a short flight of stairs and a small landing separated her door from his.

He would never admit it, but most of Graukolos' inhabitants could see that their liege loved his only surviving child with a fiercely protective passion. Those who had known the elder Lady Dulsinor said Adhelina was the spitting image of her mother. Wilhelm had loved his wife dearly, and grieved for her night and day after she was killed in a riding accident.

Some even said his spousal passion was altogether unnaturally strong: as if to say that a man born to rule other men should never conceive such powerful love for a mere woman.

Adhelina resented such remarks, which were typical of men. Whatever the truth of them, Wilhelm had never remarried. He hadn't even taken a concubine after Adhelina was moved to her own chamber.

Adhelina knew the castle gossips talked about all these things. She also knew that some even dared suggest that Lord Dulsinor's obsession with her dead mother had something to do with his letting her reject every marriage proposal she'd had since turning fourteen.

Drawing level with the riveted oak door Adhelina rapped loudly on the iron knocker.

'Enter!' Muffled though it was by thick wood, her father's stentorian voice was instantly recognisable. Pushing the door open Adhelina stepped into his solar.

This was an expansive chamber that ran nearly two-thirds the length of the keep's western wall. It was perfectly positioned – from windows to either side of the room overlooking the castle's inner and middle wards the Eorl of Dulsinor could survey his holding at leisure.

Bearskins lined the walls, along with the preserved heads of deer, aurochs and other beasts of the chase: the room was more a collection of her father's beloved hunting trophies than anything else. A few tapestries mostly continued the theme, depicting scenes of the chase, the largest being a noticeable exception.

Running almost the entire length of the eastern wall, this portrayed the Eorl's victory over the neighbouring barons of Ostveld and Upper Thulia ten years ago before the gargantuan walls of Graukolos. Stylised knights and men-at-arms being driven back in an embroidered flurry of severed limbs and broken helms dotted its rich fabric.

Adhelina could understand why her father liked it – it was an idealised representation of the violent world they occupied. Just like her courtly romances, it captured the noblest aspects of their way of life – whilst conveniently glossing over its grisly reality. She had treated injured soldiers in the last war, and knew all too well that a few scarlet stitches could not hope to convey the horror of a butchered knight or the screams of the mortally wounded as they bled their lives away.

And yet, a stubborn romantic streak in her refused to subside – surely all the courtly lays and elegiac poems she'd read held some glimmer of truth too...

The only bookshelf in her father's room held a tatty pile of scrolls and tomes detailing the ancient laws and customs of the Griffenwyrd. The coat of dust filming them testified to their lack of use. But then, Lord Dulsinor was fond of asking, why should he have to memorise the finer points of the law when Lotho, his scrivener and amanuensis, was there to do it for him?

Lotho was there now, sharing a stoop of wine with his liege, and to Adhelina's dismay her father had a third visitor.

Rising to his feet along with the scrivener, Lord Hengist bowed curtly as she entered the room. He was stocky, as typical Vorstlendings were, but even shorter than average. Worse still, his hairless head was too big for the rest of his body, giving him an absurd look. This was only accentuated by his finery – the latest Pangonian court clothes adorned his uncomely frame, and his carefully trimmed beard was oiled after the fashion of the southern nobles.

Doubtless Hengist meant to be stylish. Adhelina thought he looked like a buffoon.

'Hengist, Herzog of Stornelund, Sixteenth Scion of the House of Lanrak,' boomed Wilhelm, rattling off the formalities with a casual wave of his huge hand.

'You have of course met my daughter previously – Adhelina, First Lady of the House of Markward, heiress to the holdings of Dulsinor and very, very late – as usual! In Reus' name where have you been!?'

'I was tending to my herb garden, my lord,' replied the damsel, curtseying coldly at the Herzog and doing a bad job of masking her contempt. 'I did not realise the matter was so urgent.'

'Did not realise...?' echoed the Eorl peevishly, fixing her with angry grey eyes. He was a mountain of a man, more than a head taller than average, with huge powerful shoulders. His bushy greying beard was cut in a square shape that had looked fierce in his youth but was now somewhat at odds with his rotundity.

'Fie! You and that blasted herb garden! Your horticultural obsession is taking over your life, young lady! That and the blasted books! You should see it, Hengist – she's only gone and covered one of my turrets with creeping ivy! Not content with turning her chamber into a pleasure garden, she has to do likewise with the outside of it too! Make me a laughing stock all over the Griffenwyrd! Next thing she'll be turning the whole bloody castle into a forest!'

'It looks becoming,' replied Adhelina softly. She knew when it was best to raise her voice to her father – and when it was more amusing not to.

'Dammit, a castle isn't supposed to look becoming!' yelled Wilhelm, taking the bait and slamming down his wine cup with such force that Lotho almost dropped his own. 'It's supposed to inspire awe and terror! For miles around! Not look pretty – Reus' sake! And next time I send you a message to *come see me in my quarters directly*, it means *now*, do you understand? You may be of age but you're still living under my roof while I'm alive – and don't you forget it!'

'Yes, my lord,' replied Adhelina coolly, doing her best to suppress a smile. Her father's capacity for washing the dirty linen in public was as legendary as his prowess at hunting, feasting and fighting. Childish though it was, she still found it rather funny.

But then, didn't the philosopher Tachymus say that the essence of humour was the perceived difference between the ways things ought to be and the way they actually were? Her father certainly had a habit of behaving in a very un-lordlike manner at times... one of many reasons why, in spite of all their differences, she still loved him dearly.

The Eorl's desk was located towards the south wall for optimal light, but Wilhelm had characteristically forsaken quill, parchment and seal to sit at a low broad table near the huge fireplace.

To either side of this reared a pair of sculpted hippogriffs, each bigger than a man. The arched lintel was surmounted by another sculpture of similar stature, its great stone wings centring on a frescoed bust of the Archangel Ezekiel, avatar of defensive war. The House of Markward had invoked Ezekiel's essence for three centuries, since King Danton had given Wilhelm's ancestor Ranveldt the castle as his seat, back when Vorstlund had been a united realm.

Since that time the kingdom had crumbled, fragmenting back into its constituent baronies, but the Markwards had held onto their ancestral holding. Directly above the fireplace, surmounting Ezekiel's stoical features, was a great cloth of woven silk depicting the Markward coat of arms: a black gauntleted fist on a silvery-grey background.

The Eorl had remained seated while the other two got up to greet Adhelina. At the former's insistence Lotho sat down again, but Hengist remained standing.

'My lady, the months have been too long – it seems an age since I last saw you,' said the Herzog obsequiously.

His voice had a horrible rasping tone, like broken ceramic being drawn across gravel.

'Really?' Adhelina replied with a frosty smile. 'To me it seems an age since you returned.'

'Adhelina!' roared her father, leaning forward menacingly in his creaking walnut chair. 'Be civil! How dare you insult an honoured guest!'

'Forgive me father,' replied the damsel without losing her composure. 'But how can I be expected to be civil to someone who used my lady-in-waiting so churlishly the last time we met?'

Turning to regard the flustered Herzog with frosty eyes she addressed him coldly: 'I hope you will find the time to apologise to Hettie now you are settled in. If you do, I promise to show you every courtesy while you are here, as befits your station.'

The Herzog smiled thinly. She could sense his displeasure and knew her hatred of him was mutual. What was her father playing at, holding a private audience in his chambers? Adhelina supposed the Great Hall was given over to preparations for the feast, but still...

'It is hardly becoming for a peer of the realm to give apologies to a lowly maidservant,' said Hengist flatly.

'That "lowly maidservant" happens to be the daughter of a knight of the realm!' flared Adhelina. 'Landed or not, that makes her of noble birth!'

'Now, Adhelina!' interjected Wilhelm in a warning voice. The damsel struggled to suppress her anger, biting her lip. Why was it always like this? Men ganging up on women and changing the rules of courtesy to suit them? A nobleman could behave like a boor and get away with it, but if a lady so much as spoke out of turn...

'Of course,' Hengist replied in his cold, cracking voice, stroking the over-elaborate mustachios he wore to compensate for his bald pate. He was a young man but an early receding hairline had piqued his vanity, obliging him to shave off the rest of his ailing locks.

'I understand that I have given some offence to the honourable lady since I was last here,' he continued without emotion. 'The Herzog of Stornelund does not forget his debts. As such, it would please me greatly if my lady would be so kind as to accept this humble gift, by way of recompense for my... misbehaviour last time I was here.'

Clicking his fingers, he beckoned to a liveried squire who had been standing to attention by one of the south-facing windows behind Adhelina. The squire approached, bearing something in his arms.

He drew level and proffered the gift: a purple ermine cloak trimmed with gold lace set with precious gemstones.

She paused for a second or two then, with all eyes on her, she took the cloak before turning to face the Herzog again and curtseying perfunctorily.

'The Lady Adhelina thanks the Lord Storne for his kind and generous gift,' said the damsel, deliberately mocking his bombastic speech. 'But it was not I who was offended – rather it was my lady in waiting, Hettie Freihertz, who was the aggrieved party. And so I will accept your gift and pass it on to her along with your sincerest apologies – since it does not befit you to condescend to the daughter of a household knight who served your host faithfully for thirty years.'

'Adhelina!' The loudness was gone from her father's voice now; he merely breathed her name in shocked disbelief as he lurched to his feet. Even by her rebellious standards this was overstepping the mark. Adhelina knew it, but she didn't care.

'Father, will that be all?' she asked peremptorily, ignoring Hengist, his flushed face now rendered even more ugly by an angry scowl.

'As a matter of fact, no it won't,' rumbled Wilhelm in an ominous tone. He placed a broad hand on the Herzog's shoulder. 'Lord Storne,' he said, 'best if you leave us a while – as you can see my only daughter is wilful and headstrong. When her passions subside you will find her to be of a sweet and forgiving nature.'

'I can only hope so,' snarled the Herzog. 'As you wish. I go now to join my retinue – I trust your kitchen scullions are more welcoming than your noble heir!'

Spitting out the last two words he gave a curt bow to each of them before clicking his fingers at his squire to follow and swaggering out of the room.

✛ ✛ ✛

'Detestable man,' said Adhelina when they had gone. 'Why do you let him talk so? I wonder that you even invite him to our table!'

'All right, young madam,' replied her father, his voice sinking to a low growl. 'We'll have this conversation in the appropriate place, for this is formal business – Lotho, drink-time is over! Assume your post!'

Lotho, a skinny, nervous fellow in early middle age, dutifully complied with the Eorl's command, taking his seat at his own table, positioned at a right angle to Wilhelm's desk. The lord of Graukolos strode over to sit behind it, taking a full cup of wine with him.

'Take a seat!' he growled, indicating the finely carved walnut chair opposite his own. Like all the others in the room it had been imported at considerable expense from Mercadia, the most southerly of the Free Kingdoms. As if in recognition of its provenance the sun was finally making its presence known, streaking in through the windows. Its cold rays did little to cheer Adhelina's spirits. Something was up, she knew it.

Walking slowly over to her father's table she sat down in the chair as she was told. In the clear sunlight she could see tiny motes of dust floating languidly through the air. For one absurd instant she felt she could almost identify with the aimless specks, moved by a power beyond their control.

Her father took another slug of wine, looked at her with deep grey eyes. Then he spoke.

'Lotho, don't record what I am about to say. Adhelina, you are my daughter, blood of my blood, and in spite of what you may think, I love you dearly. And you are no fool. I should hope not, being my kin! Being no fool, you are absolutely right about Hengist. The man is a boor and a popinjay – I've more respect for our buffoon, Jaelis, who at least knows when he is playing the idiot. But more importantly than all of these things, Lord Storne owns all the lands from the east side of the Graufluss to the Great White Mountains. And he is our neighbour. That makes him either a powerful ally, or a formidable enemy.'

The Eorl paused to quaff from his wine cup again, allowing his daughter to absorb the words. His faith in her was not misplaced, for though headstrong the heiress of Dulsinor was indeed no fool. Slowly and reluctantly she nodded.

'I understand,' she said sullenly.

'Not entirely, not yet you don't,' her father replied, shaking his head solemnly. 'In time I will sicken and die, or perhaps even meet my end in combat as befits a true knight. The perfects will come and shrive me, and say prayers for my immortal soul. My body shall be laid to rest in the Werecrypt below, where the bones of our ancestors have found their repose for centuries. Then, it will be left for my shade to wander the unseen islands of the Other Side until, Almighty willing, it finds admittance to the Heavenly Halls by His grace.'

Adhelina stared at her father in stunned silence. He never talked like this – next thing he'd be quoting scripture, he practically already was.

The Eorl continued: 'One thing that will ease my troubled spirit on its celestial journey – wherever it be my doom to end it – will be knowing that I did the right thing by my House, and left Dulsinor in good and able hands.'

Adhelina felt her heart rise into her mouth as her father paused again to take another drink. She knew exactly where this was going. But before she could utter a word the Lord of Graukolos went on.

'Lotho, you may start recording. For generations, the Vorstlending barons have fought one another. Alliances have been forged and broken, wars prosecuted and peace made thereafter, for a time. The House of Markward has been no stranger to such conflicts. Thrice in my reign have we been to war with the Kaarls and the Ürls. Like many before them, they have tried and failed to take this castle. Doubtless they will try again – they, or another House. As far as I am concerned they shall never succeed, for is it not rightly said that the eight turrets of Graukolos have never fallen? But sadly, that's not an end to the story...

'This castle is a jewel, coveted by every man who commands swords in the northern reaches of our realm. Many say it is a seat fit for a king, and should never have passed to a mere eorl – but I say fie on them! For three hundred years there has been a Markward at the helm of Graukolos, and so there shall continue to be – though sadly, not entirely in name.'

'But I shall bear the family name!' protested Adhelina, trying to stave off the inevitable. 'Under the laws of our land I can inherit! Who says I have to marry and take another man's name?'

Her father shook his head again, this time in sorrow. 'When I said this castle was a jewel, I did not mean it as a good thing. For decades this holding has provoked one invasion after another – oh, they've all come to grief against the walls of this place, but that hasn't stopped them ravaging their way through Dulsinor to get to it. I'm tired of picking up the pieces of lives broken by other men's vanity...'

'I don't understand.'

'Yes, you do. Think on it. If the castle alone is enough to provoke one invasion every ten years, what do you think the spectacle of Graukolos ruled over by a virgin Eorla will do? They'll redouble their efforts! Every lord within a hundred miles of Dulsinor will want to be remembered as the one who took the castle – and its unspoilt mistress too! But that won't happen if you're married off first.' His voice suddenly became steely as he uttered the last sentence.

Adhelina rose abruptly to her feet. 'No father, don't even say it!' she cried. 'I won't! You know I won't do it!'

'Heavens, Adhelina!' thundered the Eorl, rising to face her. 'How long did you think you could put off marriage? I've indulged you far too much over the years, all for the sake of your mother – Reus rest her soul! It's time to grow up! Your position is a privileged one – did you really imagine it would come without responsibilities?'

'No, I won't! I won't marry him!' Adhelina was close to tears as she stared into her father's flint grey eyes, her body trembling with barely suppressed rage and frustration.

'Aye, you will marry him!' barked Wilhelm angrily. 'The Lanraks are the only neighbouring House that haven't been to war with the Markwards in the past hundred years! They are our only ally, in a viper's nest!'

'But why!?' exclaimed the damsel. 'Who's idea was this? Surely not...' she couldn't bear to utter the loathsome Herzog's name.

'Hengist's?' laughed the Eorl. 'Reus' teeth, no! It was his steward's. The truth is they covet the castle as much as the others do, but they're smart enough to know there's an easier way to get into it – now that you're my only heir and I'm on the way out.'

'Don't talk so! You'll live another twenty years!'

'Oh aye, and what then? What happens when your time comes? No children of your own – then who inherits? My siblings are all dead, except my sister – and she's holed up in a priory somewhere in the mountains, childless... they'll have to dig up one of my cousins, drinking himself to oblivion in a fleshpot in Meerborg. Fie on that! I'll not have it! The family name deserves better!'

'But if you marry me to... him, the family name will die out anyway!'

A crafty look came into the Eorl's eyes. 'Not altogether it won't, not according to our little arrangement.'

'What arrangement? How long have you been planning my future?' demanded Adhelina, her voice cold with rage.

'Long enough to know what's good for it! Under the terms of our proposal, Lord Hengist would come and reside here – the Herewyrd of Stornelund and the Griffenwyrd of Dulsinor would be joined and become the Grand Herewyrd of Stornelund-Dulsinor, with Graukolos as its official seat. Our houses would be forever joined together into one – the House of Lanrak-Markward! Think on it, Adhelina, we'd become the most powerful family in Vorstlund! And you'd be instrumental in bringing it about!'

'You mean my enslavement would be instrumental,' snarled Adhelina, her lip curling in disgust.

Wilhelm's face darkened. 'Now girl, don't try me. Reus knows, I've been patient with you for too long, but it's not an inexhaustible well. And don't think of crossing me – this has been a long time in the making.'

'Then it can be swift in the breaking! I'll not have him, not if all the lands of the Free Kingdoms came with him!'

'Oh yes you will,' snarled Wilhelm. 'I'm announcing your nuptials at the feast tonight – Hengist's mother and his other important family members should be here shortly. Don't disappoint me, daughter – your future, all our futures, depend on your reining in that infamous impetuous streak of yours. You and Hengist will be wedded a moon from today.'

Adhelina felt the blood drain out of her. The feast... of course. That had been her father's purpose all along – hidden beneath the smokescreen of his well-known love of a good feed.

Her heart went numb as the realisation sank in. Then, in an icy voice, she asked: 'May I be dismissed now, father?'

'Yes, you certainly may,' he replied, walking back across the room to pour himself another cup of wine. 'Get back to your chamber and prepare for the feast. I suggest in the interim that you think long and hard about what it means to be a nobleman's daughter.' He gestured expansively at the study's rudely opulent interior. 'In case you hadn't realised, all of this wasn't built on romances and herb lore – it's founded on blood, tears and sacrifice.'

✣ ✣ ✣

Hettie combed her mistress's long tresses in silence. Adhelina stared wordlessly at the polished silver mirror on the dressing table in front of her, but her sullen angry eyes told a story all of their own. She had raged for well over an hour after she returned to her bedchamber with the news, and it had taken all of Hettie's level-headed forbearance to calm her down.

Even so, her mistress was inconsolable. Hettie had to sympathise – the Almighty knew, Hengist was a loathsome prospect of a bedfellow. And yet her natural common sense told her an awful truth – Adhelina's father was right, the match *did* make good sense politically. She had not dared to venture this opinion, however.

When she was done combing her friend's hair she took up a circlet of white gold and set it on her brows. It had been a gift from the Eorl when Adhelina had come of age, and though since then he had showered her with many other baubles it was the only piece of jewellery she could ever be persuaded to wear. The design was simple and elegant; it was set with a single ruby that caught the flickering candlelight with a fierce lustre.

Stepping back Hettie surveyed her handiwork with quiet satisfaction. Her mistress was beautiful. She was tall, with a full-bodied figure, her heart-shaped face pleasing to look upon – or would be if she would only smile more often. Her pale skin was offset by her full red lips and sparkling blue-green eyes; her red-gold hair fell abundantly to her lower back. Yes, any man with eyes in his head and red blood in his veins could not fail to find her attractive.

'You look stunning, my lady,' Hettie breathed softly in the shifting light of the room.

Adhelina managed a wan smile. 'If only such things pleased me, Hettie,' she replied in a subdued voice. 'But tonight of all nights, I'd give all my tresses and fineries to look as ugly as a Wadwo.'

An involuntary shiver ran up Hettie's spine as she said this. She didn't like hearing the beast-folk mentioned so lightly – she could still remember her uncle Tomas's fireside tales, of how he had narrowly escaped being ripped to shreds by one of them in the Argael Forest during a period of errantry. Her mistress seemed to think they only existed as a byword for ugliness – but Hettie knew better.

'I should have hoped for a little more appreciation for all my hard work than that,' was what she contented herself with saying.

'Oh Hettie!' Adhelina turned in her chair, looking up at her best friend with eyes that were sad and apologetic. 'I don't mean to take any of this out on you! But can't you see what a horrible fix I'm in?'

'I feel for you milady, really I do...' Hettie faltered. 'As I've said already, I of all people know how... unappealing the Lord Storne is. But...' – she screwed up her courage and spoke frankly – 'your father speaks *sense*. You are the heiress of Dulsinor – that means you must marry. Indeed most in your position would have been long since – you've been of age for six years now. You've been lucky enough to preserve your freedom this long – and don't you want a husband to warm your bed at night and give you children to bear your name?'

'Oh I *do* eventually – but why him?! He is... vile, in every way!'

✢ ✢ ✢

Adhelina lapsed back into moody silence. She didn't know what else to say – she had dreamed of being married one day, that was true enough. But in her dreams it had always been a perfect knight who won her hand – fighting for her love in one of her father's tourneys, courting her assiduously for months...

She wanted to know the man she would marry before she married him, was that so unreasonable? That's how it happened in the courtly romances – surely Gracius and his ilk weren't complete fantasists?

And yet, as she had grown older and mingled more freely with the castle knights and her father's landed vassals she had grown swiftly disillusioned.

It wasn't that they weren't brave, or loyal, or skilled in combat – they were all of those things. But the warriors who served her father were mostly boors. The knights she read of in the *Lays of King Vasirius* could all fight too, but they were modest and merciful as well – and when they wooed a lady, they did so with sweet words as well as bold deeds. Sir Aremis of the White Rose had earned his epithet after climbing the peaks of Valacia in full armour to pick the rare bloom for his lady-love, Gorlivere. Sir Malagaunce of Triste had composed twelve verses of love poetry for his amour, each one detailing a trait of hers that he worshipped.

Such a far cry from the knights of Graukolos. She knew that this evening she would have to listen to Sir Balthor boasting of his latest triumphs. He was her father's greatest knight and had won countless victories on the field of war, his tournament trophies clogged up an entire room in his manor house, maidens had swooned for him in his youth... as he liked to tell everyone within earshot, again and again and again.

Most of her father's other vassals were every bit as haughty as Balthor, if less accomplished. When they weren't fighting or boasting they spent the rest of their time feasting, wenching and hunting. But what appalled her most was their cruelty and lack of mercy – during the last war her father's men had despatched fallen foes on the left hand and the right, driving bloodied sword between chink of armour without compunction. In the days of King Vasirius only the wicked knights opposed to his reign had done that kind of thing.

When she'd protested this to her father he'd laughed and told her that Gracius might be a fine poet, but had little idea how to fight a war. She had been fifteen then, and his cynicism had stung her – but even so she'd refused to accept his argument. Where did it say that a war could only be won by butchering surrendered captives or an injured foe?

As it was, her father's knights would only spare a man if they thought his ransom money made him worth more alive than dead. In her eyes that made them little better than mercenaries with knighthoods.

⁂

Presently Sir Urist Stronghand, Wilhelm's marshal, arrived with three other knights to escort Adhelina to the feast.

Urist was middle aged but well preserved – his dark brown hair was barely streaked with grey as it hung about his shoulders in unkempt strands. He was ruggedly handsome and slightly taller than average – with his keen grey eyes and stoical demeanour he well looked the part of the man in charge of the household knights and the castle's defences.

He was dressed simply, in a deep blue doublet and breeches, some simple silver filigree on the hemline of the sleeves his only concession to finery.

'Good e'en, milady,' he said with a stiff bow. 'I trust you are ready for the feast. And may I take the trouble to say you look ravishing this evening. Your father will be pleased.'

'Thank you, Sir Urist,' replied Adhelina, curtseying perfunctorily.

At least Urist didn't share the boastful arrogance of most other knights at the castle. He had been widely regarded as the Eorl's fiercest fighter, until Balthor bested him in the lists some ten years ago and followed this up by downing him in the melee, breaking his thighbone. Urist had taken this all with characteristic stoicism, contenting himself with remarking that he might only be the second best knight in the Griffenwyrd now but he was still in charge of Graukolos – a duty that came before everything else.

But he was so *stiff* – Adhelina couldn't imagine him composing a line of verse, let alone a dozen stanzas, and as for climbing a mountain to pick some flowers... she wasn't even sure Urist had enough humour to laugh at the idea, such a request would probably have simply baffled him. Besides that he was married – and far too old.

'We are nearly ready, my lord,' replied Hettie, stepping around a hanging basket of sweet-smelling herbs to fetch the cloak Hengist had bought her mistress.

Adhelina knew she was obliged to wear it – that and the damned long skirt. She held her tongue as Hettie fastened it around her neck, using a platinum brooch fashioned in the shape of a rose. *Give me white roses over platinum ones any day*, she thought disconsolately.

When she was done Hettie gently turned her mistress to look again in the polished silver mirror.

'Never mind a duchess, you look like a queen,' she dared to breathe in her ear.

Gazing at her reflection, Adhelina had to admit her friend was right – dressed in elegant white samite, cloaked with royal purple and crowned with bright gold, she did look regal. But if she was so regal then why was she so powerless?

Her fate sealed by men of real power, she had been perched on a throne that was hollow to the core.

⊶ CHAPTER VII ⊷

For King And Country

Sir Aronn crumpled in the dirt, his sword skittering out of his hand, his broken shield hanging uselessly off his left arm as his opponent loomed over him.

'Touch!' cried Sir Baltimere, raising a gauntleted hand to indicate a successful strike.

'I think you had best yield Aronn,' said Sir Torgun with a grin, placing the tip of his blunted blade close to his throat. 'I have the advantage.'

'As usual,' replied Aronn with a scowl, as Torgun reversed his sword and offered a hand to help him up.

'It was well fought,' said Torgun, clapping the burly knight on the shoulder and doing his best to placate him. 'You nearly had me a couple of times and no bout against you is ever easy.'

'Nor ever lost, in your case,' muttered Aronn, his ruddy face flushing a deeper red as both knights shook hands. 'One day I'll have you, Torgun, don't know when, but one day by Reus I shall!'

Torgun grinned again. Though Aronn was a little too proud, he had a valiant heart and was as honest a man as any Torgun had ever met. It was an honour to serve alongside him in the Order of the White Valravyn.

'I look forward to that day,' he said humbly. 'One can learn as much in defeat as in victory.'

Aronn raised an eyebrow at this. 'Well that's half your education missing!' His scarred face cracked into a grin, and both men laughed gladly. Torgun felt his heart soar, as it so often did – he was in his prime, serving in the most prestigious order of the land. He had devoted his life to the Code of Chivalry and service of the King – a good King at that. Did it get any better than that?

Sir Baltimere, in charge of combat training for the day, was already motioning for the next pair of knights to step into the yard and square off for battle. The white walls of Staerkvit loomed high and proud above them. Flags atop its four turrets boasted a white raven taking flight above two crossed spears on a sable background, the Order's coat of arms.

Some twenty mailed knights were gathered about the practice yard, all keen to hone their skills. There hadn't been a real war for a good long while, so it was all about training and tourneying. Of course there would be the odd skirmish here and there, but generally the Knights of the White Valravyn did their job so well that the King's Dominions were free of marauders.

Not that the Order was inexperienced – to be admitted in the first place you had to have proven yourself in battle. That meant seeking out trouble wherever you could find it – more often than not in the lawless hinterlands and restive southern provinces.

Torgun had done plenty of that since being knighted in his seventeenth summer. He'd completed his squirehood in half the time it normally took a good knight to do so. People said he was gifted – Torgun just put it down to hard work and application. If something was worth doing, it was worth doing well.

He'd spent the next three years as an errant, travelling the lands beyond the Dominions where he'd been born and raised. Fewer and fewer knights did that nowadays – a damn shame too, errantry was a fine tradition and it toughened you up no end.

Good years those, he recalled them fondly. He'd distinguished himself in tournaments, rescued the odd damsel, slain robber knights (mostly Woldings – a bad lot that, no respect for the King's Law), and even vanquished a hedge wizard or two. Not that he ever boasted – that would be bad form of course. Heralds, troubadours and town criers were quick to pick up on his deeds in any case, so there was no need to.

Three years ago the King, hearing of his exploits, had made him an offer he couldn't refuse. Joining the Order was a rare honour for one so young – most of the knights here had seen at least twenty-five summers before they were admitted.

True, sometimes he missed the wandering days of his wild youth. But he had been happiest here, in Order's century-old headquarters. He loved the strict regimen, the camaraderie of fellow knights, the emphasis on duty. Knights were meant to serve their lords but they should also protect the poor and weak – that's what it said in the Code of Chivalry, so it must be true.

Torgun knew that too many knights were proud and arrogant. Too many neglected their duties to the less fortunate, robbing the defenceless at will and defying royal law. Such men were little better than common freeswords as far as he was concerned – they didn't understand what knighthood was really all about. And their souls were poorer for it.

Torgun belonged to one of the oldest noble houses in Northalde, and his sister was married to Prince Wolfram, heir to the throne. But more than that Freidheim was a just liege, a true successor to his great-grandfather Thorsvald. His famous victories against the Thraxians and the southron traitor Kanga in the War of the Southern Secession had cemented his reputation, but it was his devotion to chivalry and justice that Torgun admired most.

King Freidheim II and old Northalde forever!

Striding over to the weapon rack, Torgun and Aronn replaced their blunted blades. Aronn's shield would have to go straight back to the armoury after the battering it had received. This Torgun did himself – the rules of the Order stated that knights must be self-sufficient and take no squires, in keeping with the custom of the errants of old.

All the same, he wasn't looking forward to the poor armourer's rueful looks when he brought him the shield – it was the fifth one he'd broken this month. And he hadn't even been using his full strength, seeing as it was non-lethal combat.

He was about to head over to the armoury when he caught a familiar figure strutting his way across the courtyard towards the practice yard. He felt his high spirits dampen slightly – it was Sir Wolmar. Following his gaze Sir Aronn muttered a curse.

'Well look who it is,' the ruddy-faced knight said darkly. 'The High Commander's son comes to grace us with his presence – an hour late as usual. I wonder that they admitted him to the Order, I really do.'

Torgun's face was even as he replied softly: 'To be fair, Sir Wolmar couches a decent lance, and his swordsmanship is excellent. He is a valuable addition to our ranks.'

Though the first part was true enough, his last remark lacked conviction, and Aronn knew it.

'He's here because he's a Prince's son, Torgun – let's not deceive ourselves, even if we have to lie out loud to the rest of the Order about his qualities. It takes more than being a good warrior to be a White Raven, Torgun – you of all people know that.'

The flaxen-haired knight's deep blue eyes were on the ground as he replied: 'Wolmar could be a little more... virtuous, it is true.'

Aronn snorted. 'He could learn to understand the concepts of mercy and justice, is what he could do! I still haven't forgotten what he did to those poachers he caught at Marring. Would that I had been there to stop him! It's a travesty, I tell you – the man is a living stain on our Order!'

Torgun felt a surge of guilt as the unpleasant memory came back to him – even though he'd had nothing to do with it. Like the rest of their company he had ridden up to the village on the border of the Staerk Ranges and been horrified to find that Sir Wolmar had meted out summary justice to the peasants he'd caught thieving from yeoman farmers in the area.

'The law says you're only supposed to mete out capital punishment if it's a third offence,' said Aronn, shaking his head. 'And even then it's only supposed to be a single hand – by the time he was done with the three of them they were in pieces! And how old do you think the youngest of them was? Sixteen summers?'

Torgun grimaced. 'If that – we should never have agreed to let him scout ahead while we were refreshing our horses. What was Tarlquist – I mean... forgive me, Aronn, I am speaking out of turn. Sir Tarlquist is a fine commander. He could not have foreseen what would happen.'

Aronn scowled. 'Tarlquist has his hands full enough as it is, without keeping a spoilt princeling with a lust for blood in check – Reus knows Prince Freidhoff is as fine a leader as the Order could wish for, but where his son is concerned he's as blind as Yareth the Predictor!'

'We should not speak ill of the High Commander,' Torgun admonished the older knight gently. 'A father cannot be blamed for loving his son.'

'No, but his son can be blamed for loving himself,' replied Aronn bitterly. 'Look at him – he's breaking up the bout so he can step in and fight straight away. How I wish I hadn't already gone – I'd love another chance to knock him in the dirt!'

Torgun was far too polite to say it, but he silently wondered what the chances of that were. The two knights had sparred three times, and Wolmar had won every bout. Though Aronn was the stronger of the two, Wolmar was deadly quick on his feet, and faster than a striking snake. He had even bested Torgun at swordplay on one occasion – no one in their company besides Tarlquist had ever managed that. After his victory Wolmar had boasted non-stop for a week – never mind that Torgun had bested him five times before and never mentioned it once. But then the likes of Wolmar could hardly be expected to show the modesty befitting a true knight.

One of the chequered twins, Doric, had accepted Wolmar's challenge and was getting ready to square off against the haughty princeling, who flicked back his red-gold tresses with an air of casual arrogance before donning a light helm to complement his hauberk, sword and shield. Doric's brother Cirod called out encouragement as the two began circling each other.

'Come, let's go and give Doric some moral support,' said Aronn.

'In a minute,' replied Torgun. 'I'll just drop your shield off at the armoury first.'

Aronn nodded curtly before striding back over toward the practice yard, cheering loudly for Doric every step of the way.

✥ ✥ ✥

By the time Torgun returned from the armoury it was all over. Doric was being taken by his brother to the castle chirurgeon to be treated for mild concussion. There was more to it, though. A crowd of angry knights was circling around Wolmar. Aronn had to be restrained by two more, his face beetroot red as he snarled one insulting challenge after another at the princeling.

'What happened?' asked Torgun of the nearest knight.

'Wolmar beat Doric fair and square,' replied the raven. 'He outfooted him and knocked him to the ground. Seems that wasn't enough for him - he had to step in and hit him again, even after Doric called yield. Lucky his helm took the brunt of it - he'd have a cloven skull otherwise.'

Sir Torgun struggled to control his mounting anger. Of all the churlish things to do - striking a fallen foe who had surrendered! Was there no end to Wolmar's shocking disregard for the Code?

Sir Baltimere and several more knights had interposed themselves between Wolmar and his antagonists. Just as well, because Wolmar was still clutching his sword and shield and looked happy to fight some more.

'Aye come then, Aronn!' he snarled venomously, his cruelly handsome face contorted in a sneer. 'Let's see if you can match that colourful language with some equally colourful swordplay! Or shall I make you look an oaf again - as I did the last three times we met?'

Aronn roared, struggling to free himself. 'Let go of me dammit! I want to fight again! I'll show you who's the oaf, you vicious scoundrel!'

Wolmar brayed with laughter. Torgun hated that laugh, full of spite and arrogance it was. 'Is that the best insult you can come up with?' sneered the princeling. 'Why, your words are as weak as your swordsmanship!'

That was quite enough. Stepping up to Wolmar, Torgun met his gaze before saying calmly: 'Perhaps you would care to take a bout with me, Sir Wolmar? I have already sparred once today, but if the others permit it, I would be happy to oblige you - seeing as you have such a thirst for combat.'

He held his gaze. Wolmar blinked first. Torgun could see a look of uncertainty in the princeling's face. Then it was replaced by one of pure hatred.

'Well, if it isn't our resident perfect knight,' he said, his green eyes narrowing to slits. 'If I recall, the last time we met I bested you too!

Come then! A foe far more worthy of my prowess than yon armoured bullock! Let's to it!'

You could say one thing for Wolmar: he was no coward. Merciless, proud, vain and cruel, yes – but he wasn't one to back off from a fight. Torgun favoured him with a curt nod before turning back to the weapon rack to rearm himself.

They squared off and prepared to fight. Most of the company was cheering for Torgun, but he banished their voices from his mind as he focused on his opponent. Wolmar was a confident fighter – too confident. He would come out swinging, which meant a defensive posture could allow an effective counter-strike.

But defensive fighting wasn't in Torgun's nature.

When Sir Baltimere gave the order to begin Torgun launched himself at his rival. Wolmar was taken aback by the sheer ferocity of his attack, and at first it took all his agility and guile just to keep Torgun at bay. But as he adjusted to the onslaught he began to get in several good ripostes of his own, and the contest started to look more even.

Again and again their blades rang as they lunged and hacked at one another, punctuated by the dull thunk of steel on oak as they parried with their shields. The cries of their comrades intensified as they circled one another, sweat running down their faces. These were swelled by the arrival of the next company due for sword practice, and soon a crowd of more than forty knights ringed the two warriors.

With a snarl Wolmar feinted at Torgun's head, before nimbly sidestepping and thrusting towards his midriff on his right side where he couldn't interpose his shield. It was a cunning move, but Torgun had fought Wolmar enough times to see it coming, and turning the blade aside dismissively he brought his sword up towards his chest with a deft flick of the wrist. From a lesser knight such a blow would have lacked power, but Torgun was as strong as an ox. It took all of Wolmar's agility to step back out of reach, and as he did so he nearly fell over backwards.

'At him Torgun!' yelled Aronn from amidst the press of knights. 'You've got him now!'

Torgun needed no encouragement. Stepping forwards he aimed another strike at Wolmar's head, forcing him to bring his shield up to block. The force of the blow was enough to knock him off balance, but even so Torgun had to twist sideways to avoid a counter-attack to his midriff as Wolmar went down.

Even now the princeling would not yield. Torgun raised his sword to strike again, the yells of the knights resounding in his ears... But at the last minute Wolmar rolled away, and Torgun's blade bit dirt.

He recovered himself quickly and wheeled around to face the princeling, who had pulled himself up into a crouching position, his blade extended and a feral snarl on his lips.

He's going to come at me low, thought Torgun. He was just preparing himself for the attack when a clarion call rang across the courtyard.

It was a summons to the Great Hall.

'Bout suspended due to garrison duties!' cried Baltimere above the clamour of the crowd. 'All right, Sir Torgun, Sir Wolmar, put your blades up and return them to the rack. The High Commander must have something important to say if he's interrupting martial training.'

Torgun and Wolmar both turned to look at Baltimere with a frown. He was right. Their mock duel would just have to wait.

Removing his helmet Wolmar shook out his fiery tresses and smiled icily at Torgun. 'To be continued, Sir Torgun,' he said, underscoring every word with contempt. 'I'm not done with you, not by a long chalk.'

Torgun glared back at him. He was normally courteous to all his opponents, but Wolmar was impossible. 'Nor I with you, Sir Wolmar,' he replied in a dangerously calm voice.

✦ ✦ ✦

Presently every knight not on patrol duty was gathered in the Great Hall. A vast square chamber, its buttressed walls were the height of many men. Scenes from the life of St Ulred, the poor knight whose legendary retribution had inspired the Hero King Thorsvald to found the Order, were painted the length and breadth of it. Two hangings on the far wall behind the dais supporting the Chair of Judgment depicted the symbol of the White Valravyn and the royal coat of arms of the Ruling House of Ingwin, two rearing white unicorns facing each other on a purple background.

The High Commander Prince Freidhoff, brother to the King, was sat on the Chair of Judgment, a plain affair of white marble. Sir Toric of Runstadt, his deputy, sat at his right hand. The seven other commanders had taken their seats – Sir Tarlquist, Sir Yorrick, Sir Redrun and the others.

Sir Danrik, the Herald, stamped his great iron staff thrice on the floor of the dais for silence. Within a few seconds the excited hubbub had died to a deathly hush.

Prince Freidhoff rose and approached a stone lectern in front of his siege. His tall frame seemed to fill the hall – though well past fifty he was still hale, and the years had not diminished his presence.

'Knights of the Order!' he began, the echoing hall amplifying his gravelly voice. 'As you may have gathered from the abruptness of the summons, I have important news – news that is both grave and good.'

The High Commander paused momentarily to clear his throat. Sir Aronn glanced sidelong at Sir Torgun, who responded with a slight shrug of his broad shoulders.

The High Commander went on: 'I am not one for wasting words as you know, so I will come straight to it – war is imminent. That is the good news for those of you eager to test your mettle in the field!'

The assembled knights fell to chattering again excitedly. Prince Freidhoff was right of course – tourneys were all well and good, and by no means non-lethal affairs, but real war was meat and drink to any true knight. Torgun glanced at Aronn and could not help but return his grin.

'Silence!' bellowed Freidhoff, getting it instantly. 'I also said it was grave news – and so it is. For we shall be fighting our own countrymen again – Krulheim, Jarl of Thule, has declared himself a Prince in his own right, over all lands south of the River Thule. He has united the Southron barons behind him and means to supplant our rightful King, just as his father sought to a generation ago!'

Freidhoff fell silent again. Once again the hall was plunged into babble, only now the angry voices of the knights sounded like a hive of bees.

'Krulheim!' exclaimed Sir Aronn, his face twisting with anger. 'But... the King spared him years ago – when he could have legally had him executed for his father's treasonous crimes!'

'His Majesty was ever a merciful liege,' replied Torgun, only raising his voice loud enough to be heard above the din. 'It is a sad truism that the wicked will often take advantage of mercy to do an ill deed.'

Prince Freidhoff bellowed again for silence. This time the Herald had to bang his staff repeatedly to get it.

'The last we heard the King had sent messengers beseeching the Jarl of Thule to desist in this madness,' the High Commander continued. 'But if, as seems likely, he refuses we shall once again be in a state of civil war. Naturally it shall fall to us, as the doughtiest warriors in the realm, to lead in the coming conflict. As such, every knight is to double combat practice from this day on – we're going to *war*, men of the White Valravyn, and I mean to see that we don't dishonour our standard!'

A roar of approval met his words. Sir Torgun and Sir Aronn joined in with gusto, punching the air with mailed fists. Even Sir Wolmar seemed swept up in the fever – no doubt relishing the chance to shed blood legitimately to his heart's content.

But as excited as he was, Torgun also felt a tinge of sadness – his first full-blown war would be fought against his countrymen, albeit treasonous ones. Freidheim had worked hard to consolidate his kingdom, yet still there were truculent provincial barons who refused to heed his message of strength through unity.

Thule and the rest of the southern baronies had lain quiescent since Freidheim crushed them at Aumric Fields fifteen years ago. In an act of characteristic generosity he had even allowed the traitors' sons to inherit, so long as they had been too young to take an active part in the rebellion. Krulheim had been among them. He had kept a very low profile since coming into his title several years ago – who could have guessed he was up to such treachery?

Sir Torgun supposed he wanted to avenge his father. Then again, perhaps he was just being naive thinking that – Hjala had always said he was naive.

Thinking on the lissom princess he had once called lover brought mingled feelings of desire and guilt. He pushed the thought of her away as they filed out of the Great Hall.

✢ ✢ ✢

The days went by and the castle courtyard became a daily bustle of activity. Everyone was drilling in earnest now – not just the knights but the regular men-at-arms and bowmen who also served the Order. Castle servants scurried to and fro, and Staerkvit's blacksmiths, armourers, bladesmiths and ostlers had work aplenty.

Sir Tarlquist, commander of the company that Torgun, Aronn and Wolmar served in, supervised their redoubled training with vigour. His bearded face was set grim – a scarred veteran who had seen more than forty winters, he'd followed King Freidheim to war against the Old Pretender, as they were already calling Krulheim's father Kanga.

The men respected him, and none more so than Torgun. He was married to his aunt Karlya of Vandheim, but that had little to do with why he liked the older knight – Sir Tarlquist was a staunch fighter who had spent his life in loyal service. That made him a man Torgun would have been proud to call uncle, if pride weren't an unknightly virtue.

His sister's marriage to the King's son meant his house was also tied to the royal family – and that meant he was connected to Sir Wolmar too, albeit distantly. That he didn't feel good about.

But there'd be no further reckonings where the princeling was concerned – not for a while anyway. With the impending war all personal grievances had been set aside. Tarlquist had told Aronn none too subtly to save his anger for the battlefield, and rumour had it even the High Commander had found time to have a few choice words in his unruly son's ear.

News had slowly filtered back to Staerkvit: Krulheim had rejected the King's last attempt to make peace and war had been declared.

Krulheim had been officially attainted and stripped of his title – not that he cared one jot for being called Jarl anymore. Only force would stop him now.

That had been a week after the first news of his treason reached the castle. Since then there had been worse. Krulheim had led his forces in a lightning strike across the Thule, laying siege to the Jarl of Salmor's castle. That had come as something of a surprise. No one had expected Thule to act so quickly. Besides that, he had two other armies on the move – even now these were harrying the southern reaches of the King's Dominions while Salmor Castle was pinned down under siege.

'The Pretender's been planning this for a while, that much is obvious,' Sir Aronn had muttered at board the day the news reached them. The sturdy trestle tables had been abundant as ever with roast meats, thick loaves and hard cheeses: the White Valravyn didn't believe in marching on an empty stomach. All the same, the usual cheer had been largely absent from the assembled knights.

'The King is mustering an army of his own and he has the White Valravyn on his side,' Sir Torgun had replied, taking a mouthful of watered wine. 'We'll soon put a stop to Thule's madness.' His pewter trencher had a rather more modest helping of food on it than Aronn's – the Code specified that good knights shouldn't eat or drink to excess, though it was a stipulation many struggled to obey.

'Not as soon as you'd like,' Aronn had growled in between mouthfuls of braised pheasant. 'It'll take weeks before the muster is complete, and Krulheim won't dawdle in the meantime. The Young Pretender's well and truly stolen a march on us!'

Optimistic as he was by nature, Torgun hadn't had it in him to gainsay the older knight. Though Aronn's prowess fell short of his own, he'd lived through the War of the Southern Secession. He knew what he was talking about – a modest knight should know when to bow to superior experience. The serious faces of some of the other veterans sat near them told the younger knight that they were thinking much the same thing as Aronn.

That only made Torgun more determined to give the coming war his utmost. Thule was a traitor who had to be stopped at all costs – even if that meant all loyal knights dying to a man.

But other, stranger, rumours had begun to filter northwards since then. It was told that the self-styled Prince of Thule rode with a mysterious foreigner in tow, an imposing figure who dressed in robes the colour of the sea and carried a trident of similar hues. Some of the rumours claimed he was a sorcerer, a pagan priest from the

Frozen Wastes who had taken up with the Southron rebels – for what purpose, Reus only knew.

There was a palpable aura of tension in the garrison when Sir Tarlquist marched into the barracks one morning and addressed his company as they were donning their armour for another day's training.

'All right, sir knights, look lively!' said Sir Tarlquist, his normally stern face cracking a broad grin as he addressed his company. 'We've a mission! You will all have heard that Lord Kelmor is sorely pressed at Salmor. It will take the King some weeks before he can raise an army of his own, especially if the Wolding barons drag their feet as usual!'

A few curses were uttered at this. The Woldings were universally resented by all and sundry, and with good reason. Torgun was too courteous to voice his thoughts out loud, but he thoroughly agreed with the blunter knights in his company. He'd fought and killed enough of them to know what they were like.

Tarlquist went on: 'But the White Valravyn is always ready for a fight! That's why our company has been chosen to join a sortie – we're heading south, gentlemen, to rescue Salmor if we can. The High Commander wants a hundred ravens down there on the double – we'll be sore outnumbered but we should have the advantage of surprise on our side. If we can take them unawares and harry them enough we should hopefully inspire Kelmor's lot to sally forth and join us. Then, Reus willing, we can lift the siege. It's a mad plan, it's a bold plan, it's a *raven's* plan – what say you, sir knights!?'

'AYE!!!' More than twenty throats roared their approval as one.

Torgun felt excitement welling up in him again. This was perfect. If the preliminary reports they had heard were true, they'd be outnumbered at least ten to one. But then not all of the enemy would be knights. And none of them were ravens. This was the kind of heroic undertaking he'd dreamed of when he first joined the Order.

'I'll see you all in full panoply of war in the courtyard in one hour – King Freidheim II and old Northalde forever!' bellowed Sir Tarlquist, before turning on his heel and marching out of the barracks.

As he finished buckling on his armour, Sir Torgun barely noticed that he was grinning like a village idiot.

⇥ CHAPTER VIII ⇤

An Ancient Curse

The sun rose weakly on a pale grey day. Horskram and Adelko did not join the rest of the Order in dawn prayers, but busied themselves requisitioning supplies from the scullery for their long journey. Sholto was there on duty, regular as clockwork, already barking orders at his hapless assistants.

Sholto was well over seventy and almost entirely bald. His skin was white like alabaster and peeled off him in flakes: an ailment that even the apothecary Lordqvist had been unable to cure. But his most striking feature was his cloudy eyes, their colour long obscured by cataracts.

As his master bade him good morning Adelko felt a surge of guilt at the thought of the previous night's antics, followed by shock at the realisation of where they had led him.

Of all this Sholto could have no inkling as he responded to Horskram's greeting in his rasping, irritable voice: 'So, Brother Horskram comes to pay me a visit on this fine morning, doubtless to make my life even more difficult with some tardy last-minute request for victualling – as ever!'

Horskram offered a placatory smile. 'Sholto, for years you have nourished the Order's capacity to do good,' he replied, 'for as the Redeemer sayeth not even an army blessed by Reus can march on an empty stomach!'

'Pah! Flattery is the honey-coated poison of the Fallen One's agents!' retorted the irascible old monk. 'Don't bandy Scripture with me, Horskram – I was in the Order studying it when you were still clad in mail fighting the so-called holy war! Now, be quick about it and tell me what you want – for I've four hundred monks and four fat merchants to feed this morning!'

Adelko glanced sidelong at his mentor, whose face betrayed a flicker of anger. He'd known Horskram was once a knight, long ago – after all, he was of noble birth – but he'd had no idea he'd been a crusader too. That shouldn't sit well with most Argolians, given their stance on the Pilgrim Wars. And yet his mentor was highly regarded within the Order.

He thought back to the previous night, when Horskram had talked about wanting to kill the mysterious Andragorix... Adelko was fast beginning to appreciate that grown-ups had a history just as complex the countries he had read about.

'We need as much as you can spare,' Horskram replied, keeping his composure. 'We've a very long journey ahead of us... so we need plenty of food that will keep. Biscuit and hard cheeses will do, and any dried fruits you can spare. Some water from the well would be useful, too.'

Sholto did his best to fix Horskram with a scrutinising glare. 'Oh, a "long journey" eh? Brother Horskram, off wandering again! And just where is he wandering to this time, eh? Doesn't care to disclose, I'll be bound... Well, let's see what we can fix up for you, I'm sure as you imply it's the Redeemer's *good work* you're going about... Urk! Where are you, you scoundrel?'

Urk, a slight lad of about eleven summers, rushed over from where he was helping to cook a great iron pot of soup. He looked flustered enough already but Sholto showed him no respite as he bellowed: 'Well don't just stand there gawking – go to the storerooms and fetch biscuit, cheese and dried fruits for the two friars! They've a *long journey* ahead of them too, so make sure you give them stuff that keeps, you barnacle! And when you've done that you can go to the well and fetch them some water – then you can get back to helping with the soup! Get to it boy, on the double!'

The hapless Urk bounded off like a hunting dog set off the leash. Sholto turned back to face Horskram, continuing to ignore Adelko.

'Well, Brother Horskram, that concludes that. Bring your horses over here and you can pack your victuals yourself if you don't mind – in case you hadn't fathomed yet, I'm rather *busy* right now.'

'Of course, Brother Sholto, and thank you again for all your help. Adelko, come along.'

The two friars trudged over to the stables, Horskram muttering under his breath so only Adelko could hear: 'That irascible old fool would test the patience of the Redeemer. Twenty years in charge of the scullery and he thinks he's a saint!'

Yudi had taken good care of their steeds, which were fed and watered and had a fresh supply of oats. Taking their horses the two monks returned to the scullery, where they loaded the food Urk brought them into their saddlebags while he scampered off to fetch them a pail of water.

Adelko couldn't help but look at the iron bucket with some bemusement as Urk brought it back and used it fill their gourds to the brim.

If he hadn't needed to use it, he wouldn't have spotted Horskram at the Abbot's window, and then... the Almighty used curious instruments to shape the destinies of His children.

Slinging their quarterstaves across their backs and mounting their steeds they rode towards the main gate. A thin drizzle had started to fall. *Not a very auspicious start,* Adelko thought as he pulled his cowl over his head.

There was no one to see them off. The Order would be finishing prayers before heading over to the refectory for breakfast. As his stomach rumbled painfully Adelko realised he hadn't seen his friends since dashing off from the dormitory to return the pail.

There had been no time for goodbyes, and yet he did not know when he would see them again.

✦ ✦ ✦

Despite the rain they made fair progress, following the mountain trail and striking south towards the Brenning Wold. As the day drew on the high crags about them gradually began to decline into hill-lands, their swardy tops dotted with trees. The drizzle came and went, hardening into a downpour during the early afternoon and prompting them to stop for food and shelter under an old yew tree.

Though he was famished, Adelko thought it a miserable meal, and already he was missing the broad tables of Ulfang and his friends' urbane chatter, both so briefly rediscovered. He knew he would get little of the latter for the time being, for his master was in one of his taciturn moods, and stared grimly across the rugged landscape with eyes that betrayed nothing of his thoughts.

As they were preparing to set off again a hoarse cry alerted the novice to a raven, which had been perched silently above them throughout their meagre lunch. Watching it take flight on ebony wings through the driving rain, Adelko felt uneasy: long regarded as a harbinger of doom in the lands of the North, the raven had sounded the death knell for many a hero down through the centuries.

The most well-known of these was the Northlander, Søren, who had heard the cursed creature's call no sooner than he had slain the warlock Ashokainan on his sixth and penultimate Deed. That got him thinking of the Thraxian troubadour Maegellin's *Lays of the Seven Deeds of Søren*, which he had read countless times in the library at Ulfang. They told how, standing triumphant over the wizard's corpse atop the fractured summit of the Watchtower of Mount Brazen high in the Great White Mountains, Søren had felt his blood run cold and seen his victory turn to ashes at the sound –

for no one who heard the raven's call in their moment of triumph could expect good fortune to last long. The great Northlandic warrior had proved to be no exception.

Thinking of that tale and its sad conclusion made Adelko feel even more uneasy, although he couldn't fathom why.

Presently the rain stopped, although the skies stayed stubbornly overcast. By the time the sun was setting behind its blanket of cloud the two monks had almost left the Highlands behind, for the trail Horskram had taken them on had steadily meandered downwards. Rounding a bend the pair came upon a cave. Horskram gave a curt nod – this was where they would spend the night.

Dismounting, Adelko paused to gaze across the gently rolling hills of the Brenning Wold in the fading light. They looked little less bleak than the Highlands, but even so he felt a sense of excitement at the prospect of expanding his horizons at long last. To his right he could see the western ranges of the Hyrkrainian Mountains, their silhouetted peaks just visible against the darkening skyline.

They tethered their horses to a nearby ash, which also provided them with plentiful firewood. They soon had a crackling blaze going as they tucked into their second and last meal of the day. As luck would have it, young Urk had provided them with some cured rashers of bacon, probably owing more to flustered incompetence than any designs of generosity. Nevertheless Adelko was more than grateful as he tucked into a couple of strips along with another slab of hardened cheese and some tough bread. He was also glad of the shelter the shallow cave afforded them, for a keen northerly wind had begun to blow, bringing with it an unseasonable wintry chill.

The cave's depth was little more than a man's length, so the two friars did their best to huddle back out of the wind on their thick woollen pallets, the fire between them.

Presently Adelko's master spoke: 'Well, we've made good progress despite the weather, though I daresay it may worsen tomorrow.'

Adelko nodded, saying nothing. He felt curiously subdued.

Horskram continued: 'If we make sufficient haste, we should be able to sleep under a roof a few nights from now. There's an old crofter who lives on the Wold called Landebert whom I'm on friendly terms with. He'll shelter us.'

Adelko was a little surprised and disappointed – when his master had mentioned sleeping under a roof he had immediately hoped for something more salubrious than a peasant farmer's dwelling.

'But what about the Wolding barons?' he queried. 'Or one of their knights? Aren't you on friendly terms with them too?'

'Not as many of them as you might like to think, young Adelko – for as you probably well know, the Wolding nobles are on the whole an ungodly lot. I do know one or two good apples among them as it were, but it won't do. A landed knight or a lord would ask too many questions, especially of wayfarers travelling through their fiefdom. Landebert is a shrewd but simple soul – he won't pry where it's none of his business to pry. Would that others had such virtue.'

Horskram was staring pointedly at Adelko now, and the novice felt himself wilting under his piercing gaze. His cheeks, already warmed by the fire, flushed a deeper red. By the rigorous standards of the Order, his conduct the previous night had indeed been shameful.

'I'm sorry for what I did, Master Horskram,' he said quietly as he stared at the flames. 'I suppose if it wasn't for the Abbot's forgiveness I would have been expelled.'

'Prior Sacristen did exactly what I wanted him to,' replied Horskram testily. 'Of course the decision was his to make – that's why I deferred to him in the matter – but the outcome was never in doubt.'

Adelko blinked and looked up. 'What do you mean?' he asked.

Horskram rolled his eyes. 'Oh for Heaven's sake use your wits, Adelko – you've been privy to a secret that could gravely jeopardise the Order! Do you think Sacristen was going to expel you summarily so you could go straight back to Narvik and tell everybody what you'd heard? No, far better to swear you to secrecy and keep you closer than ever, to make sure your tongue doesn't wag.'

He frowned and poked at the fire with a stick. 'Consider yourself very fortunate indeed, young man,' he continued. 'Many other organisations, and many more ruthless men of power than the Abbot, would have taken far more drastic steps to ensure your silence.'

Horskram broke off and looked outside the cave into the evening gloom, leaving a shiver to run down Adelko's spine as he grasped the full meaning of his words.

Presently the adept turned back to stare into the fire and spoke again: 'And speaking of last night's revelations, I think it is time I explained to you a little more about their significance – doubtless you will already have begun to glean their important nature, and if you're to accompany me in this thing you'll need to understand just how important, and why secrecy is therefore essential.'

Adelko nodded. 'Of course, Master Horskram.'

He tried to moderate the enthusiasm in his voice, but once again his thirst for knowledge, so rarely quenched, was welling up inside him. His mentor was about to tell him more secrets, this time without his even having to ask any annoying questions. Disobedient as he had been of late, it was hard to avoid the conclusion that his audacious behaviour was paying off.

Horskram took a deep breath and let out a weary sigh as he poked the fire again. The flames flared momentarily and threw the adept's shadow up on to the cave wall behind him – Adelko fancied for an instant he beheld a wraith-like mimic of his mentor, come to haunt them like the banshee at Urebro. He shrugged off the unpleasant thought as Horskram began his instruction.

'Doubtless you will have read of the elder days, when the world was newly fashioned at the Almighty's command from the celestial clay by the Unseen – that we today call the archangels and our pagan forefathers called gods,' said the monk. 'The wisest loremasters tell of the Varyans, an ancient race ruled by wizards, who were taught the music of the spheres by the Unseen – for in those halcyon days the angels walked openly among mankind, and spoke freely with those who had ears for their wisdom.

'Now in time the Varyans waxed great and powerful, for the Unseen taught them many things. They built a mighty city on the shores of the island where they lived, called Varya, from where they take their name. The Thalamians called it Seneca, which as you will know means "city of light" in their tongue. But today most simply call it the Forbidden Isle, and its ruins lie in the midst of the Great Inland Sea.'

Adelko nodded perfunctorily. The sea his master referred to was a vast land-locked ocean hundreds of leagues away, surrounded by strange kingdoms inhabited by stranger peoples. He knew something of the legend of the Elder Wizards of Seneca – everyone did, and even remote peasant communities such as his had some inkling of an ancient and terrible power that had ruled most of the Known World thousands of years ago. Occasionally the odd wayfarer would mention having seen some vast haunted ruin of strange design, a fragment of the age-old empire made by Them, and anyone listening would shudder and make the sign.

His master continued: 'Now the Vedict Texts tell us that the Priest-Kings of Varya began to look beyond their shores, for though they lived on an island paradise they were curious about the rest of the world, and it is said that the Unseen encouraged them to explore beyond the Sceptred Isle, as it was then also called. And so the Varyans built a mighty navy, and sent high-prowed ships sailing in all directions. Before long they reached land, for the Inland Sea was less vast before the Breaking of the World. The Vedict Texts tell us that during the following centuries they conquered all the lands about its shores – from the baking deserts of Sendhé in the Far South to the very shores of this land.

As well as teaching them surpassing skill in all earthly crafts, the Unseen taught the Priest-Kings great and powerful sorceries, allowing them to bend nature to their will so that none might withstand them.'

Adelko's ears pricked up. This he hadn't known. 'The archangels teaching magic to mortals? But... that's blasphemy!' he exclaimed. He had promised himself he would listen quietly, but he could not help butting in.

Horskram did not seem irritated or surprised by his interruption, but merely nodded and continued: 'Indeed, it is rightly held so now, for we have the benefit of hindsight to aid us in our reckoning. But the world was a far younger place then, and the folly of giving mortals such power had not yet been made apparent. The Unseen taught the Elder Wizards the secret language of magic, words of power that would allow them to summon spirits from the Other Side to do their bidding. Using this power, and that of their mighty armies and fleets of ships, the Varyans raised an empire that lasted a thousand years.

'For much of that time all was well, or so the Vedict Texts would have us believe – for though terrible when crossed the Priest-Kings were munificent in victory, and soon all the lands under their thrall shared in their glory. Indeed, some loremasters even believe that people in those days enjoyed blessed lives, living far beyond the years of mortal men nowadays, free of disease, famine, war and strife. Such scholars refer to this period as the Platinum Age, and we have not seen its like since, nor probably ever shall.'

Horskram paused to warm his hands at the fire, first casting a couple more branches on to it. Adelko barely noticed the cold or the wind outside, by now howling fit to raise the dead.

'So what happened?' Adelko knew that some of most powerful Elder Wizards had angered the archangels, and that the Almighty had ordered them to destroy their mighty city as a punishment for their transgression, but he was a bit light on the details.

'I was coming to that,' replied Horskram. 'In time, the Vedict Texts tell us, there arose among the Grand Synod of Priest-Kings one who surpassed all the others in knowledge and understanding.'

'Wait, I do know this!' interjected Adelko again excitedly. 'His name was Mammon! He was the most powerful of the Elder Wizards, but his vanity and pride got the better of him... he was seduced by the Fallen One and became corrupted... then he corrupted the others...' Adelko's voice trailed off – he was fast reaching the limits of his knowledge.

'Yes, that is correct,' said Horskram. 'Although the name you give him is but an Urovian corruption of "Ma'amun", which means "Bringer Of Night" in the Pavana tongue of Sendhé, whose latter-day priest-caste are said to be direct descendants of the Varyans. It is the name given to him in the Vedict Texts that I have referred to, which are an account of the days of the Priest-Kings written by their descendants more than a thousand years after the Breaking of the World.'

Adelko had read a little about that mysterious realm. The Hierocracy of Sendhé was a vast land on the southern fringes of the Great Inland Sea, beyond the Pilgrim Kingdoms and Sassanian Sultanates, home to a strange and esoteric people who practised human sacrifice and worshipped devils openly. He could well believe they were descended from the blasphemous Elder Wizards.

'During his communion with the Unseen, Ma'amun did indeed become corrupted by Abaddon,' continued the adept. 'He ventured too far on his astral wanderings, and strayed where he should not have strayed. For in those days, the rent between worlds was greatly widened, and it was easier to travel to and from the Other Side. In fact it's commonly believed among loremasters and sorcerers alike that most visitations we experience to this day are a direct result of that era, when the Elder Wizards practised sorcery at will. Our world has been changed forever and made less natural as a result of their diabolical meddling.'

Horskram paused to make the sign. Adelko almost forgot to do the same, he was so enthralled by his mentor's story.

The adept continued: 'And so in time Ma'amun found himself at the gates of Gehenna, where the Fallen One had been imprisoned for aeons with his servants. These were the anti-angels and lesser spirits who had joined him in the Battle for Heaven and Earth at the Dawn of Time, when at the Almighty's behest the First Clarion signalled its emergence from the Void.'

Adelko knew this part, any good disciple of scripture did. Abaddon had been the greatest of the archangels, until he became corrupted by his own pride and vanity. He had helped Reus to make the world but soon desired to rule over it exclusively. So he had gathered a formidable host of archangels, angels and lesser spirits and gone to war against the Almighty and those of the Unseen that remained loyal to him. Through the long ages of celestial war that followed Abaddon and his followers became horribly corrupted, still able to take beautiful forms for a time but always reverting to hideous shapes in the end. After an unimaginable length of time, Reus and the loyal angels had succeeded in overpowering Abaddon and his followers, banishing them to Gehenna in the remotest corner of the Other Side.

Horskram continued: 'Standing at the gates of smouldering brass that had kept Abaddon and his infernal brood at bay for so long, Ma'amun entered into discourse with him, and there the Fallen One taught him things that he should never have learned. He showed him how to twist the words of power he had learned of the other archangels, to use magic for great harm to increase his own stature.

'And all the while, as the Vedict Texts and the Scriptures both tell us, the Fallen Archangel poured words of honeyed poison into Ma'amun's willing ears, so that he gained greater power only to become a pawn of the Author of All Evil. Ensnared by his greed for knowledge and spurred on by his waxing hubris, Ma'amun returned night after night to converse with his new master.

'His power and influence grew steadily, so that before a hundred years had passed he had subjected most of the Grand Synod to his will. From that time the happy days of the Varyan Empire began to wane, and its diverse peoples felt the yoke of oppression, as the Elder Wizards sacrificed the weak and ailing, burning them alive on vast pyres or rending them in two on marble altars stained red with blood from morning till night. Watching this the true archangels of the Unseen were horrified, and bewailed what had become of their grand creation through mortal folly.'

Adelko could not resist interrupting again. 'But why didn't they do something? Surely they could have stopped it from happening?'

Horskram shook his head sadly. 'The Almighty had gifted mortalkind with free will from the outset – the angels could counsel them but they could not compel them. But in his contumely, the Fallen One reckoned not well, and he overplayed his hand. For in teaching Ma'amun the secrets of black magic, he had made him powerful beyond all measure, what the pagan ancients of the Golden Age that came thereafter would have called a demi-god. Gathering his followers about him, he bade them prepare for the appointed hour when he would unleash the forces of the Other Side. Co-rulership of the Known World, extended long life, and wisdom and power beyond mortal ken were not enough for him, for he desired like his diabolical tutor to become sole possessor of all that he saw. And in dark vaults deep below the City of Light, Ma'amun wrought his masterpiece, an artefact of dread power that would help him summon the hosts of Gehenna to do his bidding and sweep aside all that remained to oppose him. The Vedict Texts describe it as a great tablet, on which he set down the most potent words ever written in the sorcerer's script. And legends refer to it as the Headstone of Ma'amun, for its power is said to be enough to put the world in its grave should it ever be unleashed.'

Adelko frowned. The Headstone... yes, it was familiar, vaguely. He was sure he'd read about it somewhere, but he seemed to recall it being regarded as little more than a myth. Once more he felt an inexplicable sense of unease. He wasn't sure he liked where this story was going.

Horskram continued: 'Now when the conjunction of the planets hailed by Ma'amun came to pass, he took himself to a place he had long prepared at the summit of his white-walled tower at the heart of the City of Light. Upon it he set the Headstone, and he chanted mighty incantations through the night. Whether Ma'amun's intention was to try and wrest power from Abaddon and assume control of his hellish host using the Headstone, the Vedict Texts do not say, nor any other source that I have come across. But what we do know is that neither Abaddon nor Ma'amun had reckoned on the wrath of the Almighty.'

'The Breaking of the World...' said Adelko softly. Most scholars agreed that devastating cataclysm had taken place around five thousand years ago.

Horskram nodded grimly, his eyes burning as he became swept up in his own story. 'His fury waxed terribly, and He resolved that if His creations could not be compelled, yet they must be reckoned with. And so He chose to visit ruin upon the world they had so marred. But He was right to do so, as He is in all things, Adelko! Even such a cataclysm was preferable to a world ruled entirely by evil in its purest form!'

Adelko had to look away from his master's zealous stare. When the old monk was at his most intense holding his gaze was like trying to hold a hot iron.

Horskram continued regardless: 'And so at His behest the Unseen pulverised the Sceptred Isle, and they caused the seas about it to be greatly expanded, drowning the surrounding lands for many leagues so that none would come near it again. Some accounts even say He caused the Great World Serpent, his first sentient creation, to stir momentarily from her perpetual slumber at the centre of the earth. And such was the ruin wreaked on the world that the civilisations of mankind were blown asunder, the towers and palaces that the Priest-Kings built shelved, their cities levelled and their highways smashed into tiny fragments. Some loremasters even say the world's very shape was altered.'

That rang a bell. In the library Adelko had looked at a fragment of an ancient tablet said to pre-date the Breaking. It was supposed to cover the southern portion of the Free Kingdoms, but it looked very different to every other map of that region he'd looked at.

'Ma'amun and his followers were banished to the outer limits of the Void, to join his infernal seducer in the burning halls of Gehenna. But the ruin they had brought about could never be fully undone. And so began the First Age of Darkness, which lasted another thousand years before new civilisations flourished, first in Sendhé and afterwards in Ancient Thalamy and other places – which as you know heralded the Golden Age that preceded our own.'

Their own era was commonly referred to as the Silver Age. Adelko knew enough about precious metals to grasp the metaphor – the world wasn't getting any better for old age.

His master had paused to put a few more branches on the fire. Clearly he wasn't done with telling stories for the night, not by some way. Adelko pulled his cloak more tightly about him as the wind outside the cave intensified, keening hungrily like an evil spirit.

When the fire was renewed Horskram went on with his tale. He told how the Headstone had lain forgotten among the ruins of Varya, for it had been erected with the help of the Unseen and not even in their utmost wrath could they destroy utterly what they had helped to make. Accounts of those few adventurers foolhardy enough to seek its fabled treasures who had somehow returned with their minds and bodies intact told of an island shrouded in thick mists that coalesced into ghostly phantasms: incarnations of devils once bound to the Elder Wizards, or the cursed shades of Varya's former citizens. But no freebooters had ever managed to penetrate its ancient heart, from where Ma'amun had brought the wrath of the archangels down upon him.

No one that is, until the Northlandic hero Søren braved its shores seven hundred years ago.

Adelko's ears pricked up another notch when he heard his master mention the legendary warrior's name. He recalled the raven that afternoon, and his uneasy feeling at being reminded of the doomed mariner.

'You will doubtless be familiar with many of Søren's adventures,' said Horskram, 'how he led the First Fleet that brought our ancestors from the Frozen Wastes of the North, and helped their kings carve out new realms for themselves on these shores. But the Northern Chronicle tells that Søren grew weary of war and conquest, for he did not desire to settle the lands he had helped to subdue, but yearned for new adventures.

'And so in time the Chronicle tells us he took to the waters once again on his mighty longship, Jürmengaard, which legend has it was gifted to him by the Archangel Sjórkunan, Lord of Oceans, whom the Northlanders still worship as a god. Legend also has it that Sjórkunan was Søren's father – even today they hold him a demi-god. And Søren sailed west across the Tyrnian Straits, until he came to the shores of the Island Realms.'

More strange lands. The Island Realms were home to a reclusive and ancient group of tight-knit clans, ruled over by the Marcher Lords and their druidic priests, who venerated the Archangel Kaia as a nature goddess.

'And neither are the Tyrnian Straits for the faint-hearted,' said the adept, 'for many a traveller's tale tells of water spirits and ghosts of drowned mariners glimpsed upon the loam that moan and whisper as one draws near the Islands.'

As if on cue, a sound came suddenly to them out of the wilderness. Barely audible through the driving rain, it sounded like the howling of some distant beast, although it was too faint to identify.

'Probably wolves,' said Horskram, noting Adelko's discomfort. 'The Wold is full of them.'

The novice shivered in the folds of his cloak as his master poked the fire some more and resumed his story.

'The Northern Chronicle tells how, standing on the prow of his self-guiding longship, Søren looked across the haunted waves and espied a great tower looming over the shoreline of Skulla, the largest island of the Realms. Drawing closer he realised it was much further inland than he had at first thought, for it was vast indeed, the height of many castles. This was the Watchtower of the Valley of the Barrow Kings, which the Priest-Kings of old erected to guard over that part of their world empire. Like the City of Light, these could not be completely unmade by the wrath of the Unseen, and many like it still exist – you will no doubt have heard of the Watchtowers of Mount Brazen, where Søren slew Ashokainan, and Tintagael, which lies directly south of here.

'When Søren stumbled on it, the Watchtower was the residence of the enchantress Morwena. She was originally a member of the druidic synod that ruled the Island Realms with the Marcher Lords, and it is told in both the Northern Chronicle and histories kept by the Islanders how she became passing knowledgeable in the workings of magic. This was not uncommon in the Realms, nor is it today, for legend tells how Kaia visited the Island folk towards the end of the First Age of Darkness and broke with the covenant set by the Unseen, teaching them Right-Handed magic.'

'Why did she do that?' Regarded as an un-angel, neither good nor bad, Kaia had a reputation for disobedience and fickle behaviour. Even Adelko had no inkling why she would have transgressed against so serious an injunction. Truly the Unseen moved in mysterious ways.

'Who can reason at the motives of the Unseen?' replied Horskram, reading his thought. 'But the Island's druidic codices claim Kaia acted out of compassion, for the Islanders' lives were relentlessly harsh and bleak – the Realms in those distant days were rocky and barren, affording little sustenance. Under her divine tutelage they learned to coax plants from the soil, and fruits ripened on the bough, and for many centuries the island clans lived in peace and prosperity.

'The druids who practise the arts she taught them adhere to strict rules, and anyone found practising the black magic of the Left-Hand Path is put to death immediately. But where one viper is rooted out and crushed another will always pass unnoticed and flourish, as the Redeemer sayeth – and so it was with Morwena, who began to study the forbidden Left-Hand Path in secret. And this is why I always say there is no such thing as white magic, Adelko! Even the most well-intentioned souls can stray and become corrupted in their thirst for knowledge and seeming desire to do good – just as Ma'amun himself was. Fools will ever light their own way to darkness and damnation, to quote Maegellin, and no doubt it is from his renowned works that you will have heard some of this story.

'Beaching his longship and striking inland, Søren entered the Valley of the Barrow Kings, and there he met Morwena. Inviting him into her damned precinct she ensorcelled him, and before he knew where he was that mighty warrior was enthralled by her and seduced to her will.

'And thus began the Seven Deeds of Søren, and every one of those mighty adventures he undertook was purposed but to extend her power, and thus the tales of his exploits are underpinned with tragedy from start to finish. I shall not dwell on these, for doubtless you will have read Maegellin's account of them, how he wrestled great Wyrms and slew Gigants in the Frozen Wastes of the uttermost North, and cast down Ashokainan, crushing his demonic servants and destroying his tower in the Great White Mountains. Søren's seventh and most perilous deed took him to the heart of the Forbidden City, where he endured and fought nameless horrors beyond imagining, for it was infested with devilish guardians long conjured up from the Void that still haunted its cyclopean walls. But through great terror and hardship he won the Headstone, casting down Hydrae the Many Headed, Queen of Wyrms, enduring countless grievous burns from her venomous spittle.

'But I will tell you what Maegellin does not treat of in his *Lays* – namely, what happened to Søren afterwards. Taking the Headstone on his back, he returned after a journey of many weeks to the Islands, where his witch-mistress awaited him. And upon his triumphant return he exulted, for he truly believed that with his final task complete his reward was at hand, and that he would hold his paramour in his arms forever.

'But taking the stone from him she waxed terribly proud, for all her designs were come to fruition if only she might learn the using of the Headstone and unlock its ghastly powers. And, his usefulness at an end, she spurned Søren cruelly. And with such words, harder than the hardest steel, Søren's heart was broken – but so too was Morwena's spell over him. From the depths of his mighty spirit a fierce pride kindled, waxing into a terrible fire of wroth. And he pulled out his sword, *Orm-Killerin*.'

Adelko's eyes lit up at the mention of that legendary blade. Its name meant the 'serpent killer' in the Norric tongue – it was probably called that because Søren had used it to kill Hydrae. The *Lays* told how Søren had worn the silver blade at his side after Morwena fashioned it for him from a sliver taken from the great axe wielded by the Gigant, Arthrax, whom he had slain on his third deed.

'Morwena turned from contemplating her newest prize and spoke a word of power that condensed the air between them, making it hard as iron,' continued Horskram. 'But the strength of a dozen Wadwos was in Søren's right arm, made all the mightier by the rage of a spurned lover, and the blade of *Orm-Killerin*, forged by his erstwhile mistress's potent sorceries, was harder than any earthly metal. His blow pierced past Morwena's magic shield, passing through her fair breast and cleaving her cankered heart in twain.

'As she fell dying to the floor of the great balcony overlooking the steep valley, Morwena reached one last time in vain towards the Headstone of Ma'amun. And as Søren gazed upon the dying form of the woman he had loved above all else, he saw her eyes fixed in the lifeless stare of death upon the ancient stone he had suffered so much to obtain on her behalf. And in a rage borne of bitterness he took the Headstone his faithless mistress had so coveted, and lifting it high above his head, he cast it down into the rocky valley below with a great cry of furious anger and terrible despair, where it sundered into four pieces.'

Horskram paused as if for dramatic effect, his keen blue eyes gleaming intensely in the firelight. Looking into them Adelko could almost believe his master had actually been present when Søren's mighty adventures reached their dramatic conclusion. Outside the cramped cave, their horses whinnied nervously, although the wind and rain had subsided somewhat. Again he heard the piercing cry; this time it seemed closer than before. It didn't sound like wolves to Adelko. His master was too busy with his story to notice.

'What fate Søren met after that no tale tells,' he said. 'All that is known is that the grief-stricken hero left the Island Realms on his ship Jürmengaard, and sailed out across the Great Western Ocean, never again to be seen again by mortal eyes.

'What became of the fragmented pieces of the Headstone is somewhat better documented. Morwena's tower burned to the ground shortly after her death, and who knows what diabolical powers finished the work of destruction left incomplete by the Unseen centuries before?

With it perished most of her treasures, including those brought back by Søren on his Deeds, and her demonic servants vanished back to their hellish domain on the Other Side, the spells binding them to the mortal realm broken.

'But the fragments of the Headstone remained, lying in the valley where the Watchtower had once stood. As time went by many said it was not just the remnants of its ghastly sorceries that cast an evil pall over that once-fair region. The island druids whispered amongst themselves fearfully, of a far more ancient and dreadful power than any its witch-mistress had dared conjure up.

'Eventually the druids and clan chieftains came together and agreed that something had to be done – a thing of such obvious evil could not be left in the open unguarded forever. After much lengthy debate, it was decided to take the pieces and scatter them to the four corners of the Known World, so that none might reunite them.

'One of the pieces was entrusted to the clan chieftain Orbegon and the high priestess Jedda, who resolved to take it to the Principalities of the Frozen Wastes – for it was rightly deemed that those people should bear some responsibility for the burden, seeing as it was a Northlander who had brought the Headstone out into the world. And so they sought an audience at Landarök with Prince Olav Iron-Hand, so called because of his prowess at war – and also his unwillingness to lend money to anyone, friend or foe.'

Adelko shared a half-smile with his master at this. Prince Olav's unpleasant traits were well documented.

'And to this unlikely source of help Orbegon and Jedda made many a grim entreaty,' Horskram went on. 'For Olav was on his mother's side a descendent of Gunnehilde that had borne Søren, and on his father's was connected to Orbegon's clan by a truce marriage that had helped to broker a peace treaty between the Islanders and Northlanders, who had been at war for many years. Eventually, the barbarian prince was prevailed upon to accept the shard – it probably pleased his vanity to possess a keepsake of his legendary forebear's mighty travails, for by that time tale of Søren's deeds had spread far and wide. But woe betide an alliance through pride, as the Redeemer sayeth! For Prince Olav strayed from his promise, which was to keep the shard locked in the dungeons beneath his great stone fort at Landarök, and before long he went off to war against the mainland, as Søren had done before him.'

Adelko almost felt relieved to get back on familiar ground. Olav had been among the First Reavers, bloodthirsty colonists who settled the lands that would eventually become Northalde. He had founded the Old Kingdom of Nylund and built Strongholm on its southern border.

'And in his pride and contumely Olav took with him the shard of Ma'amun's headstone, thinking to build his new throne upon it,' said Horskram. 'But not lightly should petty kings of latter days use the heirlooms of the greatest race of wizards the world has ever seen! The Northern Chronicle tells of the curse that fell on Olav and all his line, for daring to use that eldritch stone as a foundation for his royal seat. He was the first to wither away, a tortured victim of the Rotting Death, which none but his wife and children contracted from him, and they all met a similar fate.

'All that is, but one. His son Ulfric escaped the disease and succeeded him, only to be driven slowly mad by spectral voices that whispered to him from his throne at night. One red morning he could bear it no more, and cast himself into the sea from the high stone walls of the city his father had built, where his body was dashed to pieces on the rocks below. And of Ulfric's three sons the first, Wulfric, drowned at sea when he was eighteen. The second was slain by a poisoned arrow during a border war with the neighbouring Kingdom of Wessia, which comprised the lands directly south of Strongholm. The third disappeared into the haunted forest of Tintagael on a mad quest to find a bridge to Gods-home, never to return.'

'Gods-home? What's that?' asked Adelko.

'That is the name our ancestors gave to the Other Side,' replied his master, frowning at his unusual lack of elementary knowledge. 'Hence when Ulfric died none of his lineage was left to succeed him. His eventual successor was Manfred the Ready, another barbarian ruler from the Principalities. Upon taking the crown of Nylund, he had the throne that had brought so much trouble broken up, and the accursed fragment taken to a shrine in the Highlands for safe-keeping with the priests there. These were pagan times, but before another century had passed the Creed had spread its light across Urovia, and the Northland settlers had embraced the Redeemer. And as the old rites gave way to the new, the shrine was reconsecrated as a monastery – the very monastery that you have called home these five years past.'

Adelko's eyes widened as the significance of that statement dawned on him. Though he knew it held many secrets, he would never in all of time have guessed that Ulfang held such a powerful artefact. Not that it did any more, come to think of it. The magnitude of the theft he had unwittingly learned of suddenly loomed large in his consciousness.

'But why... why keep it there?' he asked. 'Ulfang is a holy place – surely such things are not fit to be housed there?'

'The monastery had already been built by the time the pagan shrine's darker secrets were discovered,' replied Horskram. 'It was decided that the Headstone fragment – and other things you may have seen in the Abbot's inner sanctum – should remain precisely because it was judged safer to keep such things on holy sanctuary than elsewhere, where the unwise might try to use them. And for five long centuries it would seem the wisdom of such thinking has been borne out – until now.'

The adept gave a deep sigh and fell into silent contemplation of the flames. Adelko was left speechless, and for a long while he joined his mentor in silence as he did his best to digest everything he had heard.

At length he spoke up. 'So... is somebody trying to reunite the Headstone then?'

'It would certainly appear so,' replied Horskram flatly, continuing to stare into the fire. 'Though we cannot be certain until we visit Graukolos.'

'Is that where the other fragments are being kept?'

'One of them, yes. But I will not speak of the other shards tonight. You have learned enough for one evening.'

'Very well, Master Horskram... just one more question, I promise – those strange books in the Abbot's attic, the ones with the peculiar markings on them, were they magic books? You said the monastery kept other dangerous things, apart from the fragment...'

Horskram raised his eyes from the fire to look into the novice's. As on so many other occasions, he felt as though his mentor were reading his very thoughts.

'Yes. They are not tomes instructing use of the Left-Hand Path, which is why the Abbot permits them to survive intact and not be burned. Had it been my say in the matter, I would have had them destroyed regardless, for as you know I do not believe there is such a thing as "good" magic.'

'And how did they get to be in the monastery in the first place?' Adelko knew he was pushing his luck asking another question, but thought it worth a try all the same.

'The pagan priests of old sometimes practised Right-Handed magic. But, as my fireside stories tonight should amply illustrate, to meddle with such powers is to put one's very soul at risk.'

Adelko fell silent again as he pondered this for a while, before yet another question occurred to him.

'And what about Andragorix? Is he a Left – '

'Heavens Adelko!' thundered Horskram, his face darkening. 'Do you not know when to cease your questioning and fall silent? A castle torturer would envy your persistence!'

Adelko reluctantly held his tongue. He was just about to offer an awkward apology when it cut through the drizzling rain like a knife. It was the same howling sound as before, only now it was loud enough for him to be certain of one thing.

It most definitely was not a wolf, or anything else belonging to the animal kingdom.

Outside the cave their horses, visibly agitated, neighed and stirred. Getting to his feet hurriedly and motioning for Adelko to stay put, Horskram stared fruitlessly out into the darkness for a few moments before turning and stamping the fire out.

His face was grim as he said: 'Well, young Adelko, you may yet even have your last question answered – more swiftly than you might hope. No more lights tonight! Whatever made that awful noise means us no good, I'll warrant! Now lie down and be still! Make no sound!'

His heart pounding, Adelko did as he was told. As he lay next to the dying embers of the fire, he heard the sound again: something in its unearthly timbre set his teeth on edge and reminded him of the top chamber of the Abbot's inner sanctum. Once more he heard it, and then it was gone, leaving him wide awake in the darkness with nothing but the keening wind to trouble the silence.

⭐ CHAPTER IX ⭐

A Run Of Bad Luck

S ir Branas howled in agony on the bed, his rotund form writhing around like a beached whale.

'The apothecary says to drink it down while it's hot,' said Vaskrian, trying not to laugh. 'The herbs are at their most potent when the water they're mixed with is boiling.'

Gritting his teeth the old knight propped himself up and took the proffered cup from his squire. He grimaced again as he sipped at the foul brew – if it tasted anything like it smelled Vaskrian did not envy him.

Fortunately there wasn't much to swallow. Having taken his bitter medicine Sir Branas let himself sink back into bed with a groan.

'Of all the things to lay me low,' he growled, gritting his teeth again. 'Gout! I've a good mind to demand a refund from that churl Vagan – it's his stew that's caused this, I'll be bound!'

Or the fact that you guzzled three bowls of it on our first night here, Vaskrian thought. He felt some sympathy for his guvnor, but all the same it *was* funny – to see a hardened veteran howling like a smacked child over a touch of gout was, frankly, hilarious.

At any rate, they were stuck in Kaupstad for a few days at least, which meant they would probably miss the entry-signing to the tournament at Harrang. That wasn't funny at all. But it couldn't be helped – Branas could barely rise right now, never mind sit a horse or fight. They might still get a place in the melee at least – it was less exclusive than the jousting event.

The apothecary up the road had said the infusion would do its work in a couple of days. That probably meant three or four. At least it wasn't food poisoning – more than one good knight had met his end at the groaning board due to over-indulgence.

'All right, leave me be,' said the knight, waving a thick-fingered hand at his squire. 'See that the horses are being well kept. After you've done that you can spend the rest of the afternoon as you wish.

But don't get too drunk – and above all, don't get into any fights! I'm in no state to contest another duel on behalf of your reckless temper!'

Vaskrian breezed out of the room they were sharing on the middle floor of the *Crossroads Inn*. They always used it on the way to Harrang and other tourneys – Branas insisted it did the finest ale this side of the Rymold. Not that he was praising it now.

A couple of days had simmered things down between the two of them. Well, somewhat anyway. He still felt bad about the way he'd killed Derrick – he'd rather have done him over in a fair fight. But then again Derrick should have kept his mouth shut.

He would have thought the pasting he gave Rutgar last summer was enough to warn the others – you didn't want to mess with Vaskrian of Hroghar, commoner or no. But then Rutgar had got his spurs and started up again. That had obviously encouraged his cronies.

Thing is, they weren't knights yet. That meant they couldn't hide behind a title. Derrick had learned that the hard way.

He'd been worried at first – Branas had warned him he'd have to tread carefully after killing a noble. But then he'd got to thinking about it after they notified the peasantry at the next village. The killing had technically happened during a duel of honour. It wasn't unknown for squires to second their masters during such affairs and square off against each other. In that case any fatality was legitimate. Low-born or not he was still a squire of the realm – that meant he hadn't broken any law. There was no way a stickler for form like Branas would have ordered him to finish Derrick off otherwise.

Of course that didn't mean Derrick's family might not take matters into their own hands and seek revenge – the same went for Anrod's too. But if that was the case then so be it – let them try their luck. Nothing like a good old-fashioned blood feud to spice up your life.

Descending the rickety wooden steps two at a time Vaskrian emerged into the taproom. The shutters were flung open despite its being a miserable drizzly day outside; patrons were already clogging up the common room, getting stuck into Vagan's famous ale. Rudi, his harassed assistant, was struggling to take their orders in the innkeeper's absence. Two serving wenches were also on duty. Vaskrian had an eye for one of them. He was fairly sure she had an eye for him too, but he hadn't found the time to make something of it.

He felt a pang of longing as he took in her buxom curves and dark wavy tresses. It had been a while... but then he was so busy training hard every day he hadn't had much time to think about girls at all. And there was precious little opportunity for him at Hroghar, now that Rutgar had personally seen to it that he was the laughing stock of the castle.

There were a couple of more distinguished arrivals at the inn – two more knights serving the Jarl of Hroghar. Sir Rudd and Sir Ulfius, if his memory served him – both landed vassals. Both the kind of person he wanted to be one day.

Pushing open the side door leading into the stabling yard he stepped deftly over the slick cobblestones and went to check on their horses.

They seemed contented enough. Rudi had made sure they were well fed, and the straw was fresh and clean. That was to be expected – Vagan ran one of the tightest ships for miles around. Vaskrian knew that his guvnor was just finding excuses to keep him busy. To keep him out of trouble. Honestly, what kind of trouble could he possibly –

'Hey, look who it is – Hroghar's greatest imaginary knight!'

Vaskrian stiffened as he registered the half-recognised voice. Turning he saw Edric – Sir Ulfius' new squire. Edric was a commoner like himself – he hailed from the Brenning Wold, and had come south seeking service after his old master passed away. Or that was the story he told. More likely he had been let go for unruly behaviour – he'd already been in plenty of brawls since arriving at Hroghar last year. He'd won all of them too.

Why Sir Ulfius had taken him on was uncertain – the other knights had muttered something about the old fellow trying to be charitable and give an opportunity to the less fortunate. Or perhaps he just wanted a squire who knew how to fight and didn't care much for the rest. At any rate, Edric was certainly obsequious enough around his master: like all bullies, he knew just when to knuckle under.

Edric had quickly learned of Vaskrian's ambitions upon joining the castle retinue, and taken an instant dislike to him on that account. One of many enemies he had Rutgar to thank for, he supposed.

'Well met, Edric,' said Vaskrian cautiously, remembering his guvnor's admonition. Edric was accompanied by Cedric, Sir Rudd's son and heir. Unlike Edric he was of noble birth, but there his superiority over his fellow squire ended. Edric was tall and thick-limbed, with a bull neck and a face to match. No charmer, but not one to pick a fight with lightly. Cedric on the other hand was pale, sickly looking and weak. What's more he knew it.

Edric brayed with laughter. 'Well met? Hah, he even tries to talk like a proper knight! You're no knight, Vaskrian – you're a commoner, just like me. What's your problem, eh? Always got to put on airs and graces – just who do you think you are, eh?'

Edric edged forward through the drizzle towards Vaskrian as he spoke. There was an unmistakeable menace in his tone. Cedric hung back, looking confused and worried.

Vaskrian sized him up. Edric was dressed in a leather jerkin crisscrossed with iron studs. He wore a long poignard at his belt.

'All right, Edric,' said Vaskrian, stepping from the shelter of the stables and into the rain to show he wasn't afraid. 'My guvnor told me not to fight – not until we get to Harrang at least, so why don't you – '

'Why don't you shut your hole?' Edric snarled. 'I'm not taking orders from the likes of you – you might think you're better than other folks, but I know damn well you're just a common squire like me!'

Vaskrian felt the familiar anger stoke his breast. He clenched his fists at his sides as struggled to keep his composure.

'Look, Edric, I don't know what your beef is, but I'm damned if I'll dance to your tune! Now why don't you be a good lad and get out of my way – before I see to it that you lose your first fight in Efrilund.'

He hadn't intended to say that. But as usual, his impetuous nature had got the better of him. Well, he was who he was. If it came to a fight, so be it. At least this time he'd make sure it was a fair one.

Edric's face cracked into an ugly grin. 'Aw no, d'you hear what he just said to me, Cedric? Think I'm gonna have to show him a thing or two, think I'm just gonna have to...'

Cedric had turned paler. 'Um, Edric, is that really such a good idea...?' his voice trailed off. Vaskrian thought him utterly contemptible. Rutgar and Derrick were second-rate – but this one was positively frail. Was this the kind of person they guaranteed knighthoods to? The thought of it made him sick. At least Edric looked like he had some fight in him.

'Don't worry yourself none, Cedric,' said Edric without taking his eyes off Vaskrian. 'This'll be over quite soon.'

Without warning he launched forwards, coming at Vaskrian with ham-like fists. He'd seen Edric beat his last opponent, the blacksmith's assistant, leaving him with two missing teeth and a broken nose. He knew that if one of those hams landed on him he stood to meet a similar fate.

Vaskrian darted to one side as Edric closed on him. His fists hit rain and thin air. Stepping in quickly he caught him in the ear with a swift hammer punch.

Edric howled in pain and rage as he whirled around and aimed a blow at his face. Vaskrian ducked it, then dodged a second punch, before stepping in again and delivering a vicious uppercut to Edric's chin.

It should have felled a normal man but Edric was tougher and stronger than most. He staggered back spitting blood, but quickly regained his composure.

Vaskrian was content to let Edric come at him again. He always fought well from the defensive, counter-punching came naturally to him. He nimbly dodged another flurry of blows before stepping in again and delivering a solid punch to Edric's right eye. He grunted with the force of the impact. That would bruise nicely come morning.

Vaskrian could have gone for another attack but again he pulled back, circling his foe, goading him to try another onslaught. This time Edric seemed wary, but he soon lost his patience. With a roar he came at him again, fists flailing...

Whack! Again Vaskrian sidestepped and caught him another bruising blow, right on the nose. This time he followed it up instantly with another one in the same place. Edric staggered back, blood streaming down his face.

Vaskrian pressed forward, ready to deliver the knock-out punch...

In his eagerness to finish the fight he forgot his footing. Slipping on a wet cobblestone he suddenly found himself flat on his back.

He struggled to regain his feet in time but it was too late: Edric was down on him, crushing him back to the ground with his weight. Desperately Vaskrian reached up and closed his hands around Edric's wrists, but it was a straight contest of brute strength now and one he could not hope to win. With an evil smile the bloodied squire wrenched his right hand free and curled it into a huge fist...

'All right, that's enough!'

Both squires froze then turned to look at the speaker. It was Sir Ulfius, standing at the doorway, the innkeeper Vagan just behind him frowning disapprovingly. Cedric had backed off, a fearful expression stamped across his weakling face.

'I said, that's enough!' repeated Ulfius with a growl. He was a well-made knight in middle age, and had a stern patrician manner. You didn't disobey a man like that, especially not if he was your benefactor.

'Forgive me, Sir Ulfius,' said Edric, lurching to his feet and grovelling in the rain. 'But the churl Vaskrian cheeked your house – I had no choice but to teach him a lesson!'

'That's a damned lie!' yelled Vaskrian, also getting up. You weren't meant to curse around your superiors, but the false accusation and adrenalin from the fight had robbed him of his self-possession. Not that he had much at the best of times.

Luckily Sir Ulfius was having none of it. 'All right, that's enough from both of you! A pair of hot-heads, and no mistake! Why can't you learn to conduct yourselves like the gentlemen you're supposed to be – like Cedric here?

I should've known that common blood runs thicker than water! You belong in the stables with the horses, both of you!'

Vaskrian had to bite his lip to stop himself from saying something foolish. Glancing sidelong at Edric he could see the big man trying to suppress similar emotions, panting heavily as blood streamed from his nose.

'Edric – I sent you out here to check on my horses, not roll around in the dirt like the peasant you are! So get to it – and then clean yourself up, for Reus' sake! You disgrace my name, and the name of my house!'

'Yes sire,' replied Edric, glowering, before turning to do as he was told.

The knight fixed Vaskrian with a steely glare. 'And you, master Vaskrian – never far from trouble! At least Edric has the excuse of being a Wolding churl – but your father served Hroghar's garrison with dignity and honour his whole life! A poor successor to him you are – I'll be having words with your master, mark that! Sir Branas has evidently been far too lenient with you.'

With a sneer Sir Ulfius turned on his heel and disappeared back into the common room.

Vaskrian was left standing in the rain, trembling with rage. Vagan eyed him not without sympathy from the doorway. Cedric looked about him with a face like a hooked fish, before stumbling back indoors past the innkeeper.

'Aye, c'mon lad,' said Vagan in a kindly voice. 'Get thee indoors – the rain's hardening and you'll catch your death. I'm sorry I called the knight out now – but I can't have brawling on the premises, you understand. This is a respectable establishment.'

'I don't see much in the way of respect,' retorted Vaskrian bitterly.

The innkeeper rolled his eyes. 'Heavens, lad, you're making mountains out of molehills now! This'll all blow over, don't you worry – I've known Sir Ulfius and Sir Branas both for many a year now, their bark's worse'n their bite. Come inside – I'll shout you a stoop of ale, on the house. It's Old Whitsom's Finest – a good drop for a fevered head, do wonders for your choler it will.'

Sighing, Vaskrian decided to take the innkeeper's advice – and his offer of a free ale. Vagan was gruff enough but a kindly soul too, he had no quarrel with him.

Back inside the taproom he saw no sign of Sir Ulfius. Probably off upstairs to speak with his guvnor. That would land him right in it and no mistake – the last thing Sir Branas wanted to hear in his state was that his squire had succeeded in doing exactly the opposite of what he'd been told. Vaskrian tried not to think about it as he took another pull on his ale. It was frothy and sweet – by far, the best thing yet about his day.

Just then he caught sight of the serving wench with the dark hair. She was bringing a tray of empty tankards back to the counter, where Vagan had resumed bartending, much to the evident relief of the hapless Rudi.

Taking her in, Vaskrian reflected that maybe his day was about to get better. Gulping back another swig of strong beer he screwed up his courage and caught the girl's sleeve as she was passing by.

'Hey... what's your name?' he asked bluntly. Well, subtlety had never been his strong point.

'Kyra,' she replied, a quizzical look on her winsome face. He felt her dark eyes on him. Oh, she was interested alright.

'Kyra... I'm Vaskrian. I know you're working right now, but how about you join me for a drink later on?'

She smiled prettily, her eyes flashing. 'Vaskrian? Esquire of Hroghar?' she asked.

'That's me,' he replied, elated that she knew who he was.

She laughed. A merry dismissive laugh. 'Oh no! I know all about you – you've just been fighting in the yard, haven't you? I can see the mud on your brigandine. Sorry, Vaskrian, but I'm a nice girl and I don't go in for brawlers. Shame really – you're quite handsome as it goes.'

Without another word she breezed off. Slumping over his beer the squire shook his head disconsolately. When oh when would his luck change?

⇥ CHAPTER X ⇤

The Hunter In The Dark

The two friars took their leave of the cave after a snatched breakfast of biscuit and raisins. Hungry as he usually was, Adelko could barely force down even this meagre fare; he had spent a sleepless night, his half-waking dreams troubled by frightful visions.

The strange and horrible cry lingered in his mind long after they had set off along the muddy trail taking them down into the Brenning Wold. Only when they stopped for another bite at noon did his jangling nerves begin to ease.

The terrain they were now travelling through afforded little comfort; its rude low-lying hills lacked even the harsh beauty of the Highlands, with just the odd distant hamlet or forlorn copse to break the monotony. The weather too was unsparing, and a mean drizzle blown by a steady wind gradually permeated his habit and undergarments, spitting derisively in his face with a maddening persistence.

Their first day's journey across the lowland wilderness ended in a wretched night spent under an old chestnut tree that ill afforded them shelter. Worse still, the infernal howling returned to plague them, although thankfully it was less loud than on the previous night. All the same, it set Adelko's teeth on edge, and his body tensed and shivered with renewed vigour under his rain-soaked blanket. The following day they rode hard, for Horskram was clearly troubled and in no mood to tarry. The rain mercifully abated, although the clouds remained densely packed, rubbing their shoulders together menacingly like brooding giants.

As they journeyed further south, the novice began to notice more signs of habitation, espying on a couple of occasions a stout wooden hall that signified a knight's residence. But the sight brought him little cheer, for with it came thoughts of food and shelter, of which there was little to be had – Horskram was determined that they should speak to no strangers, refusing even to stop at the few villages they passed through.

Feeling the resentful eyes of their unfortunate inhabitants as they trotted briskly past, Adelko was glad of that much at least. Their stunted malnourished forms were shockingly less sturdy than those of his highland brethren: clearly his father's old stories of their mistreatment by the Wolding barons had been no lie.

Around late afternoon they reached a crossroads, where a grisly sight greeted them. From a makeshift gibbet overlooking the intersecting trails two corpses slowly turned in the breeze. Their bodies had been coated in tar to delay decomposition, but even so a cluster of enterprising flies could be seen circulating about the remains of the two unfortunates. Looking up at their ghastly faces, contorted in the awful rictus of strangulation, Adelko blenched.

'Wolding justice,' said his master in a scornful voice that also betrayed a hint of sadness. 'The barons take all they can from their miserable peasantry, and then hang them when they dare to resist or take to thievery to feed their families. Let us not tarry here Adelko, there are fairer places in the world in which to linger – but perhaps now you begin to understand why I am so chary of seeking the Wolding nobility's hospitality.'

Taking the south-west road, the pair made good progress before finding a burnt-out priory in which to spend the night. Semi-ruined as it was, Adelko was more than grateful of its scant shelter as the wind and rain started up again. As the pair hunkered down in a corner of the priory's single room beneath the sole surviving section of roof, Adelko found himself wondering what had befallen it. Asking his mentor, he was by now not surprised by his answer.

'It was robbed and burned, years ago,' said Horskram grimly.

'Who did it? Highwaymen?'

'No. Local robber knights.'

'But... why would knights rob a place of holy sanctuary?' he asked, shocked.

'For the alms money,' replied his master. 'I used to know the perfect who administered here. He was a good and pious soul, who devoted his life to helping the poor and disaffected in these parts. As word spread of his good works, travellers would stop by and donate money, perhaps hoping to receive a blessing in return from a true priest. Then, one day, the local baron got wind of what was happening. He sent some of his men to make him an offer: half of his takings, in return for... protection.'

The adept fell silent, staring out of a nearby window at the deepening gloom.

'So... what happened?' pressed Adelko.

Horskram sighed. 'The perfect refused. Said it was an insult to the Almighty to spend money given freely in His name on filling the coffers of a corrupt and loathsome overlord. So the baron's men killed the priest, and all his lay followers, before robbing this place and burning it down – as a warning to the rest of the perfecthood in the area not to get ideas above their station.'

Adelko was aghast. 'But surely that couldn't happen... what about the King? He would never permit such a thing on his lands – that's what my father always said!'

'Yes,' sighed Horskram again. 'Freidheim is in many ways a good and just liege – far better than most. But his royal seat is a long way from here. Not even the most powerful of monarchs can effectively rule their entire realm. And that means that here the Wolding barons *are* the law.'

Adelko fell into a gloomy silence. He thought of his master's story two nights ago, of how Mammon had been tempted into evil by the Fallen Archangel, then corrupted everyone else around him. In his mind's eye he saw a never-ending chain of human iniquity, stretching down through the ages, each link a vicious cycle of selfishness and suffering. Surely this couldn't be what the Almighty had intended for His most precious creation? But then, if He hadn't intended it, why had He made mankind so fallible, so flawed?

The thought depressed him, and for a long while he stared blankly around the shattered priory as the rain outside pressed down relentlessly. He could sense there were no real ghosts here, but it still felt haunted. He almost wished they were back underneath the chestnut tree again.

Presently they settled down to sleep. The rain had not abated, but the charred walls of the priory shielded them from the worst of it. Deprived of proper rest for three nights, Adelko soon drifted off into slumber, only to be disturbed by frightful dreams again.

✣ ✣ ✣

With a start he woke up, to find his master also sitting bolt upright on his pallet. Then he heard it. He felt his insides churn as he recognised the awful sound immediately.

It was much louder than it had been the previous two nights – he could now discern it had an avian quality to it, but there was something else too: its timbre was tinged with a peculiar buzzing that reminded him of angry hornets. He felt himself break out into a cold sweat. Horskram glanced over at him sharply, indicating that he should make no movement while putting a finger to his lips for silence.

For what seemed like an interminable length of time they sat stock still, while the buzzing screech continued at unnaturally regular intervals.

It could almost have been music, albeit of the most ghastly kind – perhaps this was what they listened to in Gehenna, the novice thought with a shudder. At one point it grew louder, and Adelko would have put his hands over his ears had he not been petrified.

Then abruptly it began to recede until they could hear it no more. Horskram bade them wait a while longer, before going outside to check on their horses, which were tethered to a tree. Now the noise had stopped they could be heard whinnying and stamping frenziedly. Presently his master returned, and gradually the clamour of their terrified steeds subsided.

'Try and get some more rest if you can,' he said. 'If we ride hard enough tomorrow we should reach Landebert's farm by nightfall. I'm beginning to think that nights spent in the open wilderness are no longer conducive to our safety.'

The old monk's voice was even, but Adelko could hear the tension in it. For once he did as he was told without asking any more questions – the way he saw it, the less he knew about what was making that awful noise the better.

✤ ✤ ✤

The next day it rained harder than it had done since they left Ulfang. Horskram pushed them on relentlessly, and Adelko soon lost track of the number of twists and turns they took as he guided them expertly across the harsh hill-lands. They passed through several more villages, although the inclement weather meant that this time not a soul was to be seen.

Around noon they passed a castle to the east, belonging to a Wolding baron. It was a squat ugly thing built of dark grey stone, and looked nothing like the elegant structures Adelko had read about. With its rudely crenelated turrets and glaring embrasures the young monk thought it looked more like a prison. Which it probably was, for more than one unfortunate inhabitant.

His mentor offered no words of introduction, but spurred his steed onwards through the torrential rain.

A little later, glancing over to his right, Adelko thought he could see another corpse swinging from a tree crowning a hill in the middle distance. Beyond that the Hyrkrainian Mountains were etched on the horizon; a looming presence, their giddy blue-grey tops were wreathed in mist.

Adelko supposed the Gigants would be up there gnashing their teeth at the weather's hostility, stirring up the North Wind to greater fury with their mighty provocations. Sometimes in their anger the ancient brutes were known to take up boulders and hurl them, causing ruinous avalanches and destroying the mountain communities huddled fearfully against the lower flanks of the ranges. Luckily the adjoining Highlands where he'd grown up weren't part of the mountain ranges proper; his people had been spared the depredations of those gargantuan monsters, who preferred to dwell in the loftiest peaks.

He'd read in Celestian's *Compendium of Creatures Ancient and Strange* how the Almighty had fashioned them from the flesh of Aurgelmir, Father of Gigants, a first attempt at creating a race in His image. The experiment had gone awry, for though somewhat more intelligent than their near-mindless forebear the Gigants were brutish, slow creatures, incapable of self-improvement. Other tomes told how Reus had created the world when he squeezed the Great World Serpent and the Father of Gigants together, wrapping the latter around the former to stop them destroying the firmament in their mindless rage. And so the Gigants were like living rock and earth, being made of the same substance as the bones of the world. Being unwilling to extinguish any species He had made, Reus had permitted them to live, sending them to the remotest corners of the world that had spawned them. But the Gigants had quickly grown jealous of their successors, and coming down from the mountain fastnesses they had preyed on mankind, smashing his fledgling communities in the Dawn of Time. That was until the coming of the Elder Wizards, who had slain most of their race and enslaved the rest.

Since those days the few remaining Gigants had fled back into the mountains – although some loremasters including Celestian claimed that a handful had chosen to dive into the deep oceans and take refuge beneath the waves, where the Seakindred and Tritons were too busy warring against one another to bother with them.

✤ ✤ ✤

It was well past nightfall when they reached Landebert's homestead, for the downpour had churned up the muddy hill roads, making swift progress difficult.

As they drew nearer Adelko could see it was a low but sturdy dwelling made of large stones pack tightly together. Unusually for a crofter's hut, the roof was also tiled in stone. Probably a former outpost or barracks for that region's warlike soldiery, he supposed. Its present occupant had converted it into the epicentre of a small farm. In the light of Horskram's lantern Adelko could discern a wooden enclosure surrounding it, although it was too dark to see any crops.

A rude gate barred the way in. Lifting the latch Horskram rode inside the enclosure with Adelko close behind. Since dusk a foreboding sense of unease had begun to grow steadily within him again;

humble as it was, the crofter's stout dwelling looked like an appealing place of refuge.

The hut had a single low door made of oak. The two monks were just dismounting when it was flung open to reveal a wizened figure silhouetted against the bright light that now spilled from the hut.

'Who goes there?!' came a rasping voice. 'Don't be thinking to trouble me on this evil night – I enjoy the lord's protection and my dues are all paid up till summer!'

Adelko squinted against the glare at the crofter standing in the doorway. He was very short, even for men of those parts, and bow-legged. Dressed in rude peasant clothes, he also wore a loose cloth cap several sizes too big for him. This, together with his gimlet eyes and snaggle-toothed mouth, gave him a comical appearance. His back was hunched and crooked, not uncommon among those who tilled the land for a living. In one hand he held a lantern, in the other he clutched a pitchfork. He hardly looked fearsome, but all the same Adelko decided to conceal his mirth.

'Landebert, have no fear,' cried Horskram above the pelting rain. 'It is no brigand who comes to trouble you this inclement night, but an old friend seeking shelter!'

The crofter craned his head forwards, looking even funnier as his puzzled face turned to one of recognition.

'Why Horskram!' he exclaimed with a gap-toothed grin. 'I haven't seen you in a twelvemonth at least! A cursed night is this for a reunion of old friends, but I shall be glad to have you under my roof all the same! Come, let's get your horses tethered, and then we'll get us inside and have some nice warm pottage!'

Horskram nodded and gestured at Adelko. 'This is Adelko of Narvik, a novice of Ulfang seconded to me. I hope you have enough for three.'

'Why of course, anything for my friends from the chapter!' beamed the crofter. 'A pleasure to meet ye, young sir. Now come, let's see to your horses and be getting inside!'

They tethered their rouncies to an ash tree before hurrying indoors. The stench of sweaty animals greeted Adelko as they entered the hut's cramped precinct. Landebert had brought all his livestock inside to shelter them from the weather and provide extra warmth, and more than half the hut was given over to a riotous gaggle of pigs, chickens, hens and geese. In one corner a lone goat sulked quietly.

To one side of the room a fire was burning low in the stove. Next to it was a pile of firewood, from which the crofter pulled a couple of hefty pieces to throw on the blaze. The hut's single window was directly opposite the hearth, battened down with thick wooden shutters. Though rude and smelly, the hut was also warm and dry, and for the first time in a while Adelko began to feel safe again.

'Now then sirs, sit yourselves down by the fire,' said Landebert in a cheerful voice as he busied himself with preparing a vegetable broth in an iron pot hanging above the hearth. 'I've no ale to offer ye, but y'can 'ave some goats' milk while ye wait. Here...'

Reaching for a gourd he filled two earthenware cups and handed them to the monks. Adelko sipped his gratefully as he sat on a stool proffered by the kindly crofter. Outside he could hear the rain splashing thickly against the hut, but as the increasing blaze began to warm his bones and dry his sodden clothes he felt something akin to cheer return to him.

Landebert and Horskram busied themselves with small talk. The crofter was soon complaining liberally about the rapacity of the local lord, who had raised his seasonal dues twice in the past six months. From their conversation Adelko learned that Landebert was lucky enough to own his farmstead, which his grandfather had purchased cheaply after the Red Plague decimated the local population, rendering able-bodied labourers in ready demand. But far from being exempt from tithes thanks to their nominally free status, Landebert and his ilk were obliged to pay protection money to their local overlords. Thinking on his master's tale of the perfect who had dared to defy his, Adelko felt no need to ask what would happen to those who didn't pay.

Horskram could offer little more than sympathy. 'The Wolding barons are a weed in the King's fair garden,' he said sadly. 'As a man of the cloth it is not for me to advocate bloodshed, but I often wonder if it would not have been better if Freidheim had gone to war with them as well as the rebellious Southrons.'

'You're forgettin' that it's the Woldin' barons wot helped him win the war against the Southrons,' replied the shrewd crofter from where he stood hunched over the pot.

Horskram snorted. 'So they like to say – they almost turned up too late to be of any use, if I remember rightly. But then that is typical of them – always quick to help themselves and slow to help others! But no, after two gruelling wars Freidheim wanted peace at any cost.'

'Aye, and it's a cost borne by us, the poorer folk of Brenning!' said the crofter, shaking his head. Horskram did not disagree.

Observing his host over his cup of goats milk, Adelko sensed a peculiar unease about him. Something else besides the Wolding barons was troubling him.

His mentor clearly felt the same. 'And what other news of these parts, Landebert?' he asked pointedly.

'Aye, well,' rejoined the crofter uneasily. 'This is your line of work, Master Horskram, so perhaps you can tell me more of what I've been hearing lately. People round 'ere say there's been... unnatural goings on. Old Yurgen, wot owns the next plot of free land, about a mile from 'ere, was in bed just t'other night when suddenly he wakes up in a cold sweat. Hears a terrible sound, like nothing he's ever 'eard before. His wife, Kresta, she's sittin' bolt upright in bed next to 'im, an' she's shaking like a leaf. Reus be praised, Master Horskram, ain't nothin' in the world ever scared that woman in 'er life, not that I've ever seen anyways!'

Horskram frowned as the crofter went on with his story.

'He calms 'er down and they both goes back to sleep. Next mornin' when he goes out to tend his flock o' sheep, Almighty strike me down but if they 'aven't all gone *blind* overnight! Now I ask you master monk, what's that all about? Smells like witchcraft to me, and no mistake!'

Horskram stared keenly into the crofter's anxious face.

'When did this occur?' he asked sharply.

'Well, I 'eard it from Yurgen's son, Yurik, who came by yesterday afternoon, so that would make it two nights ago. Somethin' on your mind, Master Horskram?' he added, eyeing the old monk keenly. His weather-beaten face looked strange in the shadows cast by the fire.

Horskram paused and shook his head. 'No... no. Give me directions to Yurgen's farmstead before we leave tomorrow. If it's only a mile away it will do no harm to look in on his holding and put a blessing on it. I am sorry to learn of his plight.'

The old monk fell silent, staring distractedly into the fire. Landebert eyed him for a second or two before replying, 'Well, thank you master monk, in truth that's what I was hopin' you'd say.'

Landebert turned back to his cooking, humming an awkward tune to himself.

✢ ✢ ✢

When the pottage was served the crofter pulled up a third stool and sat down to join his guests. Though it was plain fare, the old farmer had packed each of their bowls with a generous helping of turnips and swedes, and Adelko gulped the meal down greedily.

As they ate Landebert scrutinised them over slurping spoonfuls.

'So, where are you travelling to this time, sirs, if ye don't mind my askin' that is?' he asked abruptly.

Without looking up from his bowl Horskram replied: 'We are travelling south, to the King's Dominions. I have not ventured there for a while, but I recently heard a rumour that one of his castellans has a daughter who has begun to dabble in black magic.'

The wizened crofter gaped upon hearing this, and promptly made the sign. 'Bless me, but that is an evil piece of news! In the heart of the kingdom, of all places! Whose daughter would that be then – and I thought the nobles round 'ere were bad enough!'

'If you don't mind,' replied Horskram, taking another spoonful of pottage and measuring his words, 'I would prefer not to disclose that. She is innocent until proven guilty, and it may well be nothing more than a pernicious rumour started by one of her father's rivals at court.'

'Well,' replied the crofter, 'I'm sure you know best, Master Horskram, and will get to the bottom of it one way or t'other. I still 'aven't forgotten the day when you delivered my humble home from those fiendish air spirits all those years ago... I've never been able to repay you since.'

'On the contrary,' said Horskram with a kindly smile as he finished his pottage. 'You repay me every time you give me food and shelter. And in any case an Argolian neither demands nor expects payment for sending the Aethi or any other spirit back to the Other Side where it belongs. Now, if you'll – '

With an awful clarity it came tearing across the wilderness – an infernal cry of reckless malice, half buzzing, half birdcall. Adelko felt his blood run cold. His master stood up immediately, his body tensing visibly. A look of dread twisted the crofter's face. Again they heard it, and then again. It was growing steadily louder. Landebert's sequestered animals began to panic, their fearful screams mingling with the horrid sound.

Shrugging off his paralysis of fear, Horskram looked over sharply at his novice.

'Adelko!' he cried. 'Bring out your scripture book, quickly! We must put a Psalm of Protection on this house now!'

Fumbling in the folds of his damp habit with trembling hands Adelko did as he was told. Horskram had already begun pacing around the cramped hut, feverishly reciting scripture from memory and splashing the interior at regular intervals with holy water.

Shakily locating the correct page, Adelko reached for his own phial and followed suit. His end of the room was the enclosure where the terrified animals were now running amok. He had to fight to keep his footing among them but he was grateful for the cacophony, which at least did something to drown out the far less natural sound closing on them. Landebert, unsteeled by years of spiritual devotion, fell to the floor moaning, his hands clamped firmly to his ears as his body convulsed spasmodically.

No sooner had the monks finished sanctifying the hut when the screeching noise suddenly stopped. The animals crowded in Landebert's makeshift pen continued their frightful clamour – all except the goat, which remained strangely serene and seemed completely untroubled.

Both monks stood still, trying to discern any new sound over the din. Adelko felt his chest heaving with ragged gasps. The air suddenly seemed leaden. Panic welled up in him, which he controlled with an effort.

Now he could make it out – a low buzzing hum, similar yet different to the terrible cry and steadily growing louder. It rose to a whining pitch where it was clearly audible above everything else, then ceased – just as the roof above them shook with a low *thunk*. Stone dust descended through the wooden rafters and fell about them in scattered showers.

Both monks turned to look up at the ceiling as the thing now perched on the roof gave vent to a sound Adelko felt sure he would remember for the rest of his days.

At this proximity it was almost unbearable. Adelko dropped his circifix and phial as he clasped his hands to his ears and fell to his knees. He was trembling feverishly. Landebert was now writhing around, gripped by some awful agony of the mind, while his fowl pecked each other's eyes out in a mad frenzy.

Horskram, sweat pouring from his brow, steeled himself and held his circifix aloft. Gazing resolutely up at the ceiling, he began yelling scripture at the top of his lungs.

'Desist, dark-winged phantasm of the Other Side! Unlawfully have you exited the Isle of Gehenna to desecrate the Almighty's Kingdom on Earth, whence you and all your ilk were banished aeons ago! Therefore I say begone! Go back to your lightless realm! The mark of the Redeemer is upon this house! The unbroken circle of our faith protects us – you shall not enter this dwelling!'

As if in response, a strange gurgling sound came from the roof. Though it was scarcely human, Adelko could sense the unbridled malice in it.

Barely pausing for breath, Horskram continued yelling scripture: 'Let the iniquitous followers of Abaddon cower before the bright gaze of the Archangels! Virtus! Ezekiel! Stygnos! Morphonus! From the four corners of Heaven hear my plea – your humble servant implores you, lend him the strength to drive this creature back into the pit! It is their power and the power of the Redeemer that compels thee!'

The thing on the roof responded, another blood-curdling screech that now carried a note of pure hatred as it registered the detested words. A scraping sound could be heard as well – more dust began to fall from the ceiling in thick streams, causing both monks to cough and splutter. Adelko could hear the heavy stone tiles of the roof rattling and falling outside as the thing began clawing them away.

Undaunted, Horskram repeated his intonation over and over, raising his voice still louder until it seemed as if he was a demon himself, shrieking the words that the Redeemer had first uttered ten centuries ago, when the Arch Deceiver's wickedest servants chastised him on the Plains of Abram.

But gradually the old monk's voice began to weaken and lose conviction. His face grew drawn and his throat became hoarse from trying to shout above the thing's horrid screeching.

Still kneeling on the dirt floor, Adelko bent over double, breathing rapidly, his hands raking the dirt floor as he struggled to ward off the awful madness engulfing him. He felt himself retreating into the innermost recesses of his mind. His life flashed before him. He was back in the clearing overlooking the valley next to his village, his eyes meeting Horskram's for the first time...

And somewhere deep within him, he felt a strange strength muster its power, galvanising his limbs and steadying his mind.

Suddenly he raised his head and opened his eyes. The words that the Redeemer had spoken on the Plains of Abram came to him with a perfect clarity, resounding in his head like the tolling of heavenly bells.

Reaching calmly for his circifix, he stood up slowly as if in a dream and raised his eyes to the ceiling, which was raining dust as the creature of nightmare above them wrenched at the packed stone tiles. Even now Horskram was still reciting the Psalm of Abjuration, but his voice had grown faint and he sounded like a dying man praying for his own soul.

Holding the rood aloft Adelko joined his voice to Horskram's, matching him word for word. The beleaguered adept spared a stupefied glance at him before chanting the Psalm with renewed vigour.

Again and again they recited the words, their voices steadily growing stronger in unison. The unseen devil above them began thrashing around wildly, its awful voice now registering pain as the Psalm penetrated its profane consciousness. Adelko felt cold sweat pouring from his body as a yawning gulf threatened to swallow his mind...

Again he recited the words, in a voice he never knew he had. He had never felt such conviction as he did then, save perhaps when he had first told Horskram he wanted to leave Narvik and see the world.

Again he recited the words...

And then he felt something give. A profound shift, like a ledge of rock giving way above a precipice, breaking into small pieces and tumbling into darkness...

With a final cry of frustrated malice, the thing lurched off the roof. Adelko felt his spirit surge with relief and exultation. They had done it! They had broken the demon's will! It was fleeing their pious might!

Then his heart clenched again as he heard the screaming of horses and a wet tearing sound. A mad notion seized him, his natural compassion getting the better of him.

'Our horses! It's killing our horses!' he yelled as he made a dash for the door. He was saved by Horskram, who grabbed him in a vice-like grip and restrained him.

'There's nothing we can do for them now, Adelko!' shouted the adept. 'Stand fast, and trust in the Almighty! Only He can deliver us now!'

The tortured screams of their hapless steeds soon subsided into deathly silence, punctuated only by another low buzzing sound that swiftly receded into the distance. A final hideous shriek and it was gone, careering off into a night made pregnant with fear.

Exhausted by their ordeal, the monks collapsed to the ground, clutching one another like fearful children. Beside them Landebert convulsed on the ground, his spasmodic shivers gradually subsiding into the stillness of profound shock. His surviving animals grew calmer, although they remained extremely agitated.

With one exception. Over in its corner, the goat stared impassively at its animal brethren and the three men on the floor, and calmly chewed some oats.

⊹ CHAPTER XI ⊹

A Refuge In The Wild

It was well past sunrise when the three of them screwed up the courage to venture outdoors. Landebert had recovered enough to regain his senses, although by his drawn white face and blank eyes it was apparent he was still in shock.

Amazingly, the damage to his hut was not extensive. The thing had succeeded in dislodging some of the smaller stones, which lay scattered about the enclosure like the broken teeth of a giant. Their poor horses made for a far more upsetting spectacle. Staring at their torn and bloody carcasses, Adelko shuddered at the thought of the terrible strength that had killed them. He offered up a heartfelt prayer of thanks that the hut which had sheltered them was made of stone and not wood.

Luckily, the demon in its mindless rage had not thought to despoil their saddlebags, leaving all their carefully packed provisions untouched along with their iron-shod quarterstaves. Looking on the latter the young friar wondered what use mortal weapons would be against such a thing.

At Horskram's bidding they built a fire on which to burn the dead animals, and Adelko noticed that his master took care to intone a Psalm of Blessing over the smouldering corpses.

After they had brought their supplies into the hut the three men sat down to decide what to do next. Poor Landebert was clearly still out of his wits with terror, and Horskram took considerable pains to convince him that he would be safe once they were gone.

'Whatever it was that troubled us last night is clearly pursuing us,' the adept said, doing his best to sound reassuring. 'Soon we will be on our way, and no further harm will come to you – so have no more fear, good Landebert!'

The traumatised crofter nodded his head abstractedly, clearly doubting this but too exhausted and frightened to argue.

'We'll strike south-west towards the Brekawood,' continued Horskram, addressing Adelko. 'Our ghastly malefactor appears to have the power of flight – the trees should shelter us and provide us with some cover until we reach the River Warryn. It should take us three days on foot – if we're swift, so we'll have to pack lightly. We can break cover of the woods and rejoin the highway just before it crosses the bridge – from there it's a short distance to Kaupstad. It's an old market town, we'll be able to buy new horses there and find shelter at an inn.'

'What do we do then?' Adelko could not help but ask.

Horskram eyed him testily, before replying: 'I suggest you think about packing for our journey, and leave me to worry about that. Time is of the essence, and we've delayed long enough as it is. Come now, let's sort through our saddlebags!'

Delving inside these the monks produced two small knapsacks, which they crammed with enough provisions to last them five days plus their blankets and sleeping pallets. To these Horskram added his lantern and tinderbox, a fat purse stuffed with silver marks, and a few other essential items.

Turning to Landebert, he pressed five coins on the reluctant crofter in compensation for his damaged roof and livestock before tucking the pouch deep into the folds of his habit. They also availed themselves of a spare phial of holy water, which they used to refill their depleted vessels. Then they filled two gourds with drinking water from the well outside, to which the kindly crofter added another full of fresh goats milk.

Taking up their quarterstaves the two monks bade him a hurried farewell before setting off into the cold grey morning.

✣ ✣ ✣

The way was hard, and before long Adelko, deprived yet again of a good night's sleep, felt himself tiring. Horskram, buoyed by his iron constitution and possessed with a feverish intent, harried them on, permitting only one break shortly after noon to snatch a meal. They walked for hours, slogging through rain-soaked hill trails that were often knee-deep in mud. At one point Adelko felt he could go no further; without breaking his stride Horskram seized him by the upper arm and continued to march, pulling the exhausted novice along with him.

Dusk came, obscuring the hills in a deepening gloom, and still there was no sign of the Brekawood. Horskram cursed under his breath before stopping to light his lantern, allowing Adelko to collapse gratefully against a rugged hillock. But in five minutes they were up again, striding into the gathering night with an endurance borne of desperation. Even Adelko, broken as he felt by their ten-hour march, found new vigour returning to his aching limbs as the encroaching darkness brought thoughts of their horrid pursuer flooding back into his mind.

They struggled on for another couple of hours. Dusk deepened into stygian night, and nothing could be seen beyond the yellow circle of light which shrouded them. In any case Adelko by now would have been capable of registering little, for he felt that his body was detached from his mind; it seemed to him that he looked down as if from a great distance at his lumbering feet.

On and on they went. Adelko felt like a sleepwalker, barely conscious. And then suddenly he heard his master speak.

'We've reached the Brekawood. Lie down and get some rest. We'll continue at daybreak.'

Looking up for the first time in hours the novice saw the gnarled boughs of oak and laurel trees looming around him, their green leaves glowing softly in the lantern-light. Just off the trail they had relentlessly followed was a patch of grass. Removing his knapsack to use as a pillow, he threw himself on the sward, not even bothering to take out his pallet. In less than a minute he was fast asleep.

✣ ✣ ✣

Adelko woke to find his mentor tugging at his shoulder. Rolling over he winced; every part of his body was stiff and sore. Sitting up with some difficulty he blinked away sleep and gazed at the lofty trees in the morning light. All about him he could hear the sound of birds making their love songs to the spirits of the sky. Inhaling deeply he registered with faint pleasure the fragrance of wild mushrooms and damp foliage. After the rough hill-lands they had endured his present surroundings almost seemed like a paradise.

Horskram was obviously in no mood for such pastoral reflections. Handing him a cup of goats milk, some biscuit, cheese and raisins, he said curtly: 'Eat these quickly and get your strength up. We've no time to lose.'

Falling ravenously on his first meal in nearly a day, Adelko replied between mouthfuls: 'But what about you, Master Horskram?'

'I've already eaten. You overslept. Now hurry up and finish – we've only reached the outskirts of the Brekawood and we need to get deeper in, for our own safety. That otherworldly fiend cannot harm us by day – only at night-time can such diabolical monsters venture onto the mortal plane in physical form. That gives us one slender advantage. By my reckoning we should be able to make the journey to the river under cover of the trees in two days – if we break cover on the morning of the third that gives us plenty of time to rejoin the highway, cross the river and get to Kaupstad by nightfall. But it's a while since I wandered the paths of the Brekawood, and I'm concerned about getting lost.'

Adelko was somewhat surprised by this candid admission. As far as he could recall, his mentor never seemed to get anything wrong.

They made good progress, and as the morning drew on the sun – so long a stranger to their journey – slipped out from behind the sundering clouds, casting its rays in golden cascades through the tops of the trees and painting their arboreal surroundings in a sylvan light. Tired as he was, Adelko felt his troubled spirits rise, and found renewed energy to traverse the wooded hills through which Horskram now led them.

⁂

When they stopped by a babbling stream in the early afternoon to fill their water bottles and take another meal something caught Adelko's eye. Glancing over to his right he saw it again: a little way up the side of the hill, where the stream came tumbling over a jumble of mossy rocks, he could make out an ephemeral humanoid shape in the water.

No, not in the water – it was *part of* it. As he stared open-mouthed, the tiny figure – surely no bigger than his forearm – seemed to turn and look at him, its slender, curving form undulating and sparkling translucently in the glinting sunlight.

The body resembled a naked female – or what Adelko in some of his more guilty dreams imagined such to look like – but the head was entirely androgynous, appearing smooth-crowned and hairless.

Adelko continued to stare. It stared back at him and, he could have sworn, *winked* at him before suddenly shooting upwards against the flow and disappearing over the top of the hill.

'Adelko!' barked his mentor. 'What are you staring at?'

'I... I think I just saw a water spirit – a Lymphus,' replied the novice, quickly remembering the correct definition in Decorlangue. Even now he didn't want to be caught short on his knowledge of the Elementi.

Horskram humphed testily before saying: 'Yes, well, that's hardly the worst inhabitant of the Other Side you've been dealing with lately, Adelko – my advice is to finish your lunch and not concern yourself with such things.'

'No... I wasn't scared. It looked at me and... it was beautiful.'

Horskram put a firm hand on his shoulder and turned him around to face him.

'Be careful of thinking such things, Adelko,' he said, staring keenly at the novice with his piercing eyes. 'Lymphi are generally harmless if left well alone, but they have occasionally charmed unwary travellers into drowning themselves. This forest is mostly safe, but you would do well to keep a level head in it all the same.'

'Is it haunted, then?' asked Adelko.

Horskram shook his head. 'Not really, no. I'm just being cautious, that's all. The Brekawood is an old forest but its inhabitants – earthly and unearthly – are for the most part benign. It was never really polluted by the Elder Wizards' magic, unlike Tintagael to the south.'

Adelko had heard many tales of haunted Tintagael. It was said to be inhabited by the Fay Folk, immortal nature spirits who delighted in crossing over from the Other Side to trick mortals into bringing about their own ruin. Sometimes the creatures would appear as a distant pinprick of light at night, goading hapless wayfarers into becoming hopelessly lost in treacherous marshes. But those that chose to sojourn in Tintagael were said to be especially vicious, and few travellers mad enough to venture beneath its forbidding eaves ever emerged. The novice had heard his Aunt Madrice whisper in fireside tales how the spirits of those who perished there were cursed never to leave, but stayed trapped in the forest till the end of time, becoming ghostly eidolons whose only joy was in tormenting their unfortunate successors before they joined them forever.

The most well-known tale of such damned souls was that of the Thirteen Knights of Thorsvald the Hero King. They had been the greatest of the Northlending chivalry a hundred years ago. Their fame had spread far and wide, and tales of their quests and deeds in battle were legion. But they were tricked by an enchantress into declaring war against the Fays, and riding without a backward glance into gloomy Tintagael on a sunlit morning they were never seen again.

The number thirteen had been deemed to betide ill fortune ever since by superstitious Northlendings.

It was rumoured that more ghastly and wicked things than fays and eidolons also called Tintagael home, but Adelko knew little of those.

'Is that why Tintagael is such an evil place – because of the Elder Wizards' magic?' he asked.

'For the most part, yes,' replied Horskram. 'It lies next to the Watchtower of Tintagael – one of the ancient fortresses built by them across the Known World that I mentioned in the cave. The Vedict Texts claim that in their heyday these would have been a great benefice to the people, for their wizardly masters took pains to provide every comfort and luxury for the tribes they had conquered.'

But the more they practised their arcane arts, the adept explained, the wider grew the rent between worlds, allowing spirits from the Other Side to spill across in ever greater numbers and pervert the natural laws decreed by the Almighty at the Dawn of Time. And as the poison of Ma'amun spread far and wide and the practices of the Elder

Wizards became increasingly corrupted, the great forest that was once green and good became polluted by its proximity to the steadfast evil emanating from the Watchtower that had once guarded it.

'That devilish edifice was levelled at the Breaking of the World,' concluded Horskram. 'But like others of its ilk it was not completely destroyed, and even now it is a ghastly place and none will live for miles around it. In fact only the most foolhardy adventurers, lured by legends of the Priest-Kings' ancient wealth, would dream of approaching it, and of those that do few if any return.'

Gazing at the dappled sunlight filtering gently through the trees of the Brekawood, Adelko found it hard to picture the horrors of Tintagael. But he did not look at the stream again.

✤ ✤ ✤

The rest of the day passed uneventfully, Horskram only once retracing their steps to take a better choice of turning. Most of the trails were easy enough to follow, for foresters maintained them regularly for the Wolding nobility to use on their hunting trips.

Towards late afternoon the two monks encountered a deer, which sped away fleet-footedly no sooner had it seen them. Thinking on this as they stopped to rest for the night in the hollow of a dead oak tree, Adelko suddenly recalled the goat at Landebert's hut and how calm it had remained throughout their terrifying ordeal.

As they sat down to their final meal of the day he asked his mentor about this.

'That is hardly surprising,' replied Horskram. 'Goats are one of the few creatures of the animal kingdom that were created by Abaddon. As such they feel no fear in the presence of his diabolical servants, who will never do them any harm.'

Adelko spat out his goats milk in horror. Was he drinking the very blood of the Fallen One?

'What!?' he exclaimed. 'But how can that be? I – I've fed on goats all my life, one way or another!'

'You should make more effort to remember your scripture,' said Horskram with sardonic humour. 'Don't forget the Fallen One was once one of the archangels – the foremost among them in fact. As such, he had a hand in making the world on the Almighty's behalf – and goats are one of the creatures he invented, before his fall. But don't concern yourself! They are quite harmless, for he did not yet intend any malice when he made them – although it is true that in some parts they are held by the overly superstitious to be wicked creatures.'

Adelko thought about this for a moment. Looking around the forest in the evening twilight and listening to the fading birdsong, he began to wonder what else the arch enemy of mortalkind had created.

'Young novices who ask far too many questions,' Horskram answered wryly when he asked. Adelko pressed him further and he conceded another nugget of information.

'Cats – of all kinds, great and small,' said the adept. 'But of those you will probably see little, Adelko, for such creatures are native to the hot lands of the Far South.'

'Cats? Does that include lions? The Thalamians used to feed early Palomedians to the lions, didn't they?' Adelko was thinking of the bronze knocker on the front door of the Abbot's inner sanctum, when he had unwittingly stood on the threshold of his great adventure.

'Yes, that includes lions,' replied his master, his face suddenly growing grim again. 'I am sure the Author Of All Evil appreciated the delicious appropriateness at the time. Now, finish up your devil's juice, and get some rest. Let us hope our unearthly pursuer spares us another night of torment!'

Adelko had been thinking about that as well. 'Why *are* we being pursued? Is it to do with everything that happened at the monastery?'

Horskram's face grew darker still. 'That is something I have been trying to work out myself. Go to sleep! Tonight is not the time to discuss such things.'

⁜ ⁜ ⁜

It was well past the Wytching Hour when Adelko found himself sitting bolt upright again, staring feverishly at the darkly silhouetted trees. He fought to control his rising panic. The awful cry he had learned so well to fear was much further away than it had been on previous nights. That was some relief at least.

'It's not as loud as before! Does that mean it's lost our trail?' He glanced nervously at Horskram, sat beside him on his pallet and looking tense and drawn.

'Possibly,' he replied. 'It can only materialise on our plane at night – that means it has to start over each time. Such entities cannot always choose exactly where to materialise – if sent to pursue someone, a demon will always appear within a certain radius of its intended victim, but rarely in the exact same spot. Two nights ago it got very close – we were lucky to escape alive.'

'But how did it find us? It came on us in the dead of night!'

'Night-time means nothing to the devilspawn of Gehenna – for them the deepest dark is as a sunlit plain to mortals. It probably saw us from several miles as we were approaching Landebert's hut.

Fortunate indeed for us that it cannot fly as fast as it can see far! That's why I sought the cover of the trees – not even the Fallen One's servants can see through material things. Or not this one, at any rate.'

'So... it has limitations then? Weaknesses – after all, we drove it off didn't we?'

Horskram's voice betrayed a hint of admiration as he answered: 'Yes – *we* certainly did. I must say your efforts that night were impressive, and quite possibly saved us from ruin. Your conviction in the words of the Redeemer in the face of so great an evil was commendable. And I had not realised you knew the Psalm of Abjuration by heart.'

Adelko felt himself flushing at this rare compliment from his normally taciturn mentor. 'I... I didn't,' he replied. 'Not until I heard you repeating it that night. You were screaming it so loudly... I suppose it just went in.'

Horskram looked at him with even greater admiration. 'Well, young Adelko, a journeyman of the Order in the making indeed! For all your youthful exuberance, I see my faith in you has been far from misplaced – but listen! It's getting fainter still – the damned thing has lost us this night, Reus willing!'

Another question occurred to Adelko. 'How powerful is it?' he asked. 'I mean... compared to Belaach for instance?'

'Without knowing a demon's name that is difficult to assess,' replied Horskram. 'But generally speaking, the more powerful a demon the more difficult it is for it to take corporeal form in our world – a greater demon in physical shape would be a terrible thing indeed. But only a great power could bring about such a happening...'

'Like the reunited Headstone?' Adelko finished for him. His anxiety was growing at the thought. Sometimes he wished he didn't think so much – he didn't always feel comfortable in the places his thoughts took him to.

Horskram looked away. Clearly he didn't like contemplating the subject either. 'Indeed,' was all he said. Then he added: 'Our pursuer is probably a devil of the Fifth Tier, or perhaps the Fourth at most.'

Adelko felt his anxiety twist up another notch. If the thing that had almost killed them at Landebert's hut was just a minor demon in physical form, it didn't take a savant to work out what the reunited Headstone could mean for the world.

Belaach's words at Rykken came slinking back to him: *The Five and Seven and One... the fires will rise... those who oppose us shall scream for eternity...*

Adelko shivered in the night.

⇌ CHAPTER XII ⇌

A Celebration Soured

The feast was already under way when Adhelina arrived in the Great Hall. The vaulted chamber where the lords of Graukolos had heard petitions, received important guests and feasted their vassals for generations was vast enough to fit three rows of trestle tables, each long enough to sit more than a hundred people. Most of the knights and ladies attending were already there, laughing and chatting freely as they guzzled strong wine and picked at platters of cold meats set before them in anticipation of the banquet proper.

The heiress of Dulsinor was accompanied by Hettie, Sir Urist, and an escort of bachelors. She had a passing fancy for one of them, a newcomer called Agravine who seemed to have mastered the art of paying her the most appropriate compliments – while flirting with her most inappropriately. With his sandy curls and charming smile he was handsome enough, and she liked the attention in spite of herself. In truth the young knight was just as shallow as the rest of them, concerned only with war, women and spoil – but at least he was modest and courteous, like the fabled heroes she'd read about.

If only the same could be said of Sir Balthor – he was well in his cups already, boasting to a flock of hangers-on about his latest hunting trip to the Glimmerholt. To hear him tell it, you would think he had slain the two-headed boar of Alixos, felled by the mariner Antaeus on his sixth voyage, or captured the enchanted silver hart sent by Kaia to test the Northlending hero Sir Damrod, famed for his hunting prowess... Balthor had felled an aurochs, albeit a huge one (according to him).

Her future husband was also present, surrounded by his own fawning retinue. He had changed clothes for the feast, and was dressed even more outrageously than before. He wore a rich woollen doublet and hose of striped orange and purple trimmed with gold silk lace, a blood-red cloak fashioned from dyed feathers and a sky-blue velvet cap topped with three more taken from a peacock.

As custom dictated, the betrothed-to-be were sat next to one another at the table of honour just before the Eorl's high seat, on a dais overlooking the triangular hall from its broadest end. The tension between them was palpable. She felt as if the air between them were congealing.

Her father sat at his usual place next to her, with Berthal the seneschal to his right. The rest of the honour table was occupied by Sir Urist, Sir Balthor, the castle perfect Tobias, and the guests of honour. These were scarcely a welcome sight. Hengist's elder sisters, Festilia and Griselle, rivalled their brother in fashion-sense and ugliness, and their mother Lady Berta was as frigid an old dame as Adhelina had ever seen.

And then there were Hengist's two favourite toadies, Sir Reghar Headstrong and Sir Hangrit Foolhardy, a loutish pair of rakehells who revelled in their reputation. Watching them pour wine into each other's mouths as servants began bringing out the first course, a thick fish broth that was more like a stew, Adhelina hoped they wouldn't cause any trouble.

On the other side of Hengist sat Sir Albercelsus, Seneschal of Castle Storne. A tall spare pale man, he had a granite face that gave nothing away and eyes of cold flint that told an even more meagre story. Everybody knew Albercelsus was the brains behind the Lanrak family – had been even in Lord Henrich's day, and by all accounts he had been a far wiser scion than his popinjay of a son. Adhelina could well believe he had concocted the plan to inter-marry the Houses of Lanrak and Markward.

The feast didn't lack for entertainment. Baalric Swiftfingers, the castle's troubadour in residence, was on top form, dazzling the assembled guests with virtuoso renditions of old favourites. As the banquet progressed he threw in a few bawdy songs, the best loved being an old ditty about a merchant's wife who was cursed by a witch and developed an insatiable lust for the most inappropriate of swains – stable boys, beggars, apprentices and the like.

Vorstlending humour was coarse and simple – and the aspiring merchant class an easy target for a high-born audience – but it was Baalric's renditions of the Pangonian classics telling tales of chivalry and derring-do that moved Adhelina the most.

As the troubadour drew elegant fingers over harp, lute and mandola and trilled one song after the next in his accomplished contralto and the wine and food flowed freely, Adhelina felt herself relax slightly. She was careful not to drink too much, though the Herzog showed no such temperance, knocking back the stuff as if it were grape juice and loudly calling for more when the silver wine-jug at his elbow was empty.

So far neither of them had said a word each other.

During the fifth course Jaelis Wenchbottom, Wilhelm's fool, took to the boards of the central table.

Adhelina smiled fondly as the jester began his routine. Jaelis was a short, pudgy fellow with elaborately tapered black mustachios who wore a ridiculous straw-coloured wig. In keeping with the gravity of the occasion, he'd toned down his usual filthy language – somewhat.

Not that that hampered him in the slightest. He soon had everyone roaring with laughter, and several guests nearly choked on their food. Even pompous Hengist brayed at his antics. Only one man in the hall did not so much as crack a smile, Adhelina noticed: Albercelsus remained as lifeless as a waxwork throughout the performance.

Some fools relied solely on antics, but Jaelis was more developed in his art, interweaving humorous stories between frolics. Sometimes he would even improvise, inventing gags on the spot at the expense of random audience members, taking full advantage of the immunity that his patronage granted.

He was one of the best loved fools throughout the land, and as a child Adhelina had adored him, when he would seemingly pick crab apples and chestnuts out of her ear while singing silly songs that had her in hysterics.

It was even said by some that after Graukolos itself and its lovely heiress, the Stonefist's most widely coveted possession was his jester.

'Well m'lords 'n ladies,' Jaelis declared presently, pausing to let the audience recover from their laughter. 'I must say I'm right glad t'see you all 'ere laughing at your 'umble servant – especially *you* Lord Storne.'

The jester removed his toupée as if it were a hat and bowed low at the Herzog, the tiny pewter bells sewn into his chequered yellow and black motley jingling. A few titters here and there trailed off into silence – no one quite knew what to expect next.

Hengist nodded curtly, not deigning to meet the fool's eyes, and snarled into his goblet. Compared to last time he had stinted on the wine, but he'd still had enough to leave his face flushed and even uglier than usual. He evidently did not appreciate being addressed directly by a commoner – even one permitted to do so by the circumstances of his profession.

Adhelina could have kissed Jaelis for what he said next.

'Aye, I must confess, bein' a simple man as I am, I didn't recognise him at first,' the jester continued, addressing the rest of the hall again. 'Took one look at him and I thought: "Bugger me, I'm out of an effin' *job!*"'

Roars of laughter shook the foundations of the hall. Balthor laughed so hard that wine spurted from his nostrils, and down in the lower hall Hettie giggled mischievously and exchanged knowing glances with the wife of a vassal next to her. No one laughed harder than her father, Adhelina noted with satisfaction.

Wilhelm's canny fool had hit the nail on the head. By and large, Vorstlending nobles were fairly restrained dressers. Even allowing for the importance of the occasion, Lord Storne had overstepped the mark, and few outside his sycophantic entourage could have approved of his ludicrous weeds.

Jaelis bowed again triumphantly. His riskiest joke had paid off and everyone had seen the funny side.

Everyone, of course, except for the butt of the joke.

Hengist turned a deep purple, looking even more enraged than when Adhelina had insulted him in her father's solar. Lurching suddenly to his feet he stormed from the hall, flinging his cup furiously at Jaelis as he did. Drunk as he was, it missed the jester by a country mile, but that was small consolation for the poor serving wench who caught the ill-aimed shot in the face with a piteous scream.

Reghar and Hangrit scrambled to their feet and went after the Herzog as silence descended on the shocked knights and ladies. Out of the corner of her eye Adhelina caught Lady Berta frowning before exchanging meaningful glances with Albercelsus.

'Damn and blast!' boomed Wilhelm, getting to his feet angrily and motioning for Berthal to follow the offended Herzog outside and placate him. 'There always has to be someone who can't take a bloody joke! All right, Jaelis, that'll do for now. The next course, please! Baalric, more music! And more wine, for heaven's sake!'

Her father turned to glower accusingly at Albercelsus, who had tapped him on the arm and seemed about to say something but suddenly thought better of it. Favouring the Eorl with a frosty smile he sipped perfunctorily at his wine instead. Adhelina reached for her goblet too as she and Hettie exchanged meaningful glances of their own across the hall.

✣ ✣ ✣

Halfway through the next course Adhelina could still hear her future husband ranting in the courtyard outside.

Berthal had had little success with the enraged Herzog, returning to the feast and shaking his head and muttering disparagingly. Hengist's mother and his own steward had gone out to try where Berthal had failed, but they didn't seem to be having much luck either.

Not that that bothered Adhelina: the more time she spent away from the Herzog the better.

Presently Albercelcus re-entered the hall and approached Wilhelm.

'Is the boy recovered?' said the Eorl, in between mouthfuls of roasted goat and onions. 'He should be present – after all it's his betrothal feast.' Adhelina noticed that her father didn't seem all that concerned.

'His Grace has been subjected to the most frightful abuse and is chary of returning,' replied the seneschal, proffering another frosty smile. 'But perhaps if your jester were to receive... due punishment for his insolence, it might expedite Lord Storne's recovery.'

Wilhelm put down his goblet and favoured the steward with a fiery stare.

'Retribution against fools is against custom – as well you know. Lord Storne will just have to draw on his fortitude to recover.'

The seneschal's face tightened. 'I can only commend your respect for tradition, Lord Wilhelm,' he replied. 'However, without some chastisement, I fear the Herzog will be in no fit state to rejoin – '

'Dammit, I said no!' roared Wilhelm, slamming a meaty palm down on the table and upending his goblet. 'A joke is a joke, for Reus' sake! I won't hear another word on it! If a man can't take being made a fool of by a fool then he ought not to dress up like one in the first place!'

The table lapsed into nervous silence again. Lady Berta's face, cold at the best of times, hardened to ice, but Albercelcus smiled self-deprecatingly and offered a half-bow.

'Lord Markward, as you see fit,' he replied in a brittle voice. 'You are of course free to govern as you will in your own hall.'

His words were courteous enough, but the flint-eyed stare he fixed her father with before leaving again was anything but friendly.

Adhelina felt her blood boil. *How dare he?* To suggest having a fool flogged – or worse – simply for doing his job... Just what kind of people were they joining themselves to? She tried not to think about her fate as she took another swallow of wine.

When Hengist learned that Jaelis would not even receive a flogging, he took his ranting up to a new pitch. Thankfully at that moment Baalric started up again, this time accompanied by a hired band of wandering minstrels.

Jaelis, who had retired to his own small table in the corner, looked decidedly nervous, and was slugging back the wine as liberally as his master. Adhelina tried to catch his eye, to give him a reassuring look to tell him all would be well.

Her heart went out to him, even as it was filled with rage at the thought of the Lanraks and all their haughty arrogance – people she would soon be bound to for life.

⁘ ⁘ ⁘

It took another flagon of wine to finally persuade the Herzog to rejoin the feast.

Adhelina felt her body tense as he lurched back over to his seat. Slumping into it he called rudely for more drink in a voice already thick with the stuff.

He said nothing by way of apology. Adhelina ignored him pointedly.

The rest of the nobles continued their revels with a gay abandon that papered over a palpable sense of relief. Vorstlendings hated angry scenes during feasts – food and drink time was practically revered in her country, a joyous occasion.

The wine continued to flow freely as serving wenches brought out platters laden with roast boar drenched in apple frumenty, quince pies and jellied eels, braised lamb shanks and boiled haunches of venison garnished with roast vegetables, and grilled trout encrusted with herbs and drizzled with garlic sauce.

Adhelina ate sparingly, washing her food down with a couple more goblets of Mercadian dry white to steady her nerves. Berthal found time to go and whisper a few words in Jaelis's ear, which seemed to improve his nervous state.

If only my fears were as easily assuaged, Adhelina thought sadly.

Her sinking heart reached rock bottom when her father stood during a dessert of honey and almond cakes fashioned to resemble forest fruit to formally announce the occasion.

The rest of the celebration was an ugly blur. When her father's speech declaring the formal unification of houses by marriage was done, Father Tobias stood and wrapped a binding cloth around their joined hands, intoning scripture and pronouncing them betrothed in sight of the Almighty.

Her future husband was barely able to stand throughout the ceremony, his eyes rolling up into the back of his head as he struggled to maintain his composure and retain some awareness of his surroundings. His hand felt clammy beneath hers – Adhelina tried unsuccessfully to repress a shudder at the thought of sharing a bed with this man for the rest of her life.

And then, just like that, the pre-nuptial ceremony was done. Her father sealed it with a toast, announcing that the marriage would be held in the house of the bride, as custom dictated, on the next moon.

One more month of freedom, thought Adhelina with a cold horror. *Not even that.*

Hengist stumbled back into his seat, calling for more wine. Adhelina stood and stared as knights and ladies got up to let the servants clear the hall for dancing, her ears deaf to the change in tempo as Baalric and his troubadours took the music up a notch.

Her eyes briefly caught Hettie's and the smile died on her oldest friend's face as she saw how unhappy she was. Berthal came over and placed a gentle hand on her shoulder, whispering in her ear: 'There now, my lady, the worst part is over with – you won't even have to dance with him now.'

Looking over she saw it was true: her future husband was keeled over the side of his chair, his oversized head lolling to one side. He was snoring loudly enough to be heard over the music. On the table before him the contents of his spilled goblet were dripping steadily into his lap.

The celebration would continue long into the night, but Adhelina excused herself after dancing perfunctorily with her father, Berthal and Urist.

She would gladly have danced with Agravine too – just to spite her unconscious fiancé and send a message to her father that she still loathed the match body and soul – but the dashing young knight was too busy seducing a comely serving wench.

Well, let him have his fun, she thought bitterly. After all, he was a man: even a lowly bachelor could enjoy freedoms she never would.

That night she cried herself to sleep. She who prided herself on rarely shedding a tear. Hettie reached over to console her, but she shrugged her away.

She wanted to be alone with her grief.

✢ ✢ ✢

The pale morning found her staring out of a window blankly at the green fields of Dulsinor. Or should that be Stornelund-Dulsinor? It mattered little – she might have been staring at the fire-scorched plains of Gehenna for all it mattered now.

Turning back to the bed they shared in times of cold weather, Adhelina saw Hettie was still sleeping off the wine.

That was good. What she had to do, she must do alone.

She had to act quickly too, before the castle got too busy. Graukolos normally held some five hundred inhabitants – the knights, squires, men-at-arms, farriers, cooks, servants and other menials privileged enough to call its mighty walls home. What with all the guests and their own squires and servants, nearly a thousand souls had gone to sleep or passed out beneath its watchful aegis last night.

Her father had not reigned for so many years by being careless, and the night's watch would have been stronger than usual to compensate for his lack of sober knights and guarantee protection for so many honoured guests.

But even so, there would be fewer people up and about than usual. Most if not all of the bachelors would still be sleeping off their wine. That just left the men-at-arms – but they were commoners, and commoners could be cowed by authority. Unless Brigmore, the captain of the guards and a notorious stickler for form, was on duty.

Chances are he was – but what other choice did she have? She had to try now, this might be her only opportunity to escape. She would make her way down to the stables, take her favourite horse and ride out of the front gates... It would be a daring escape, just like in the romances.

She barely thought about what she was doing as she hastily donned her riding clothes, swaddling herself in a thick cloak and exiting the room quietly while Hettie snored softly.

Halfway down the tower the absurdity of the idea hit her. She pressed on regardless.

As she stepped into the flagstoned courtyard of the inner ward, absurdity became futility.

She had no supplies, no food, no ready money. No idea where she was going. No idea what she was doing.

Taking in a deep breath and letting it out, she stopped in her tracks and pressed a pale hand to her forehead, shutting her eyes tightly to compose her thoughts.

It was when she opened them that she noticed something was amiss.

On the other side of the courtyard, Brigmore and Tobias were engaged in an animated conversation. The captain looked perturbed and not a little bit angry, shaking his head continually. But the perfect looked like a man who had just seen a ghost. His face was white, and he was extremely agitated.

They were standing just outside the entrance to the private chapel on the north side of the ward, where the Markward family and their most senior retainers heard prayers – the rest of the castle went to temple in the outer ward.

Tobias was pointing towards the chapel entrance and babbling frantically. They were too far away for her to hear what they were talking about.

Adhelina frowned. She was indifferent to Brigmore, a loyal servant to her father, but she disliked Tobias. She had long grown weary of his pompous aphorisms and sententious maxims – most of which centred around his disapproval of her headstrong and unladylike behaviour.

All the same, some instinct told her that this time he had a good reason for being upset. But what could be troubling him? Below the chapel was the Werecrypt, where the bones of her ancestors and their loyal seneschals had been laid to rest for generations. Being located directly below a consecrated chapel it was unlikely to fall victim to a haunting –

Her heart stopped as she remembered.

There were no ghosts in the Werecrypt. There was something much worse.

She was just reminding herself that she was supposed to be escaping and that Brigmore's distraction was a good time to try when he suddenly broke off and began striding towards the gatehouse leading to the middle ward. Catching sight of her he detoured swiftly and drew level with her. He was a short, stocky man, with a bulldog face and thinning grey hair.

'Milady,' he said, bowing stiffly in his immaculate mail armour. 'I must say it is a surprise to see you up so early after your pre-nuptial feast. May I offer my congratulations - '

'Yes, yes – thank you,' said Adhelina, cutting him off with a wave of the hand. 'What was all that about, Brigmore? Father Tobias seemed very anxious just now.'

The perfect had disappeared back into the chapel. Glancing over his shoulder Brigmore licked his lips nervously and refused to meet her eye. 'Begging your pardon, milady, but I'm afraid I can't disclose that until I've spoken with your father.'

This was annoying, but typical of castle protocol. Her mind working quickly, Adhelina said: 'Please don't let me hold you up, Brigmore, I was... just going for a ride, to clear my head after last night's revels. It was indeed a mighty feast.'

She hoped she sounded casual. But Brigmore barely seemed to be listening. He wasn't moving either – and he was blocking her way to the gatehouse.

He licked his lips again. 'Ah, milady, I'm afraid that won't be possible this morning. I've to speak with the Eorl right away and no one is to leave the castle.'

Adhelina felt her anxiety increase. She knew what was below the Werecrypt, better than the uneducated Brigmore did.

She pressed him for details. 'Brigmore, if I can't go out riding when I please there had better be a good reason for it. Tell me.'

'I only know what the perfect told me,' said the captain. 'You know... you know the men won't go into the Werecrypt, not for a while now.'

Adhelina nodded impatiently. 'Yes, I know – some superstitious nonsense about a haunting, of all things!'

Brigmore shuffled his feet nervously as he replied: 'Well now, this has to stay just between you and me, you understand – I'll catch it from His Lordship if he finds out you heard first.'

Adhelina forced a smile and did her best to sound soothing. 'If it's as dramatic as you and Tobias seem to think it is, everyone will find out about it soon enough. I think I can keep a secret for a few hours.' Had it been considered proper to do so, she would have laid a hand on the commoner's shoulder to reassure him.

Brigmore nodded. He already had one eye behind Adhelina, anticipating the long journey up to the Eorl's private chambers in the painful knowledge that he was the bearer of bad news.

'Well, Father Tobias seems to think there's been some kind of break-in,' he murmured, his voice barely more than a whisper. 'Don't see how that could have happened, seeing as the Werecrypt is several men's height underground and surrounded by stone and earth on all sides. But whatever's beneath it that we were supposed to be guarding – it's gone.'

Mumbling an apology, Brigmore stepped around her and hurried into the ward.

Adhelina was too shocked to say anything else. Gone? After all these years? The chilly morning suddenly felt colder.

No wonder Brigmore was nervous – as captain of the guards, keeping watch on the Werecrypt was his responsibility. Not that he hadn't tried to do his job – but that had become next to impossible of late.

Adhelina paused to consider her next move. Brigmore would be a while waking up her father and telling him – she still had time to make her escape. But then with the castle in a state of high alert they'd soon come after her. They might even think she'd had something to do with the theft.

And her idea had been a stupid one anyway. Running away on the spur of the moment like that, without any supplies, any planning – what had she been thinking? Life was not a romance, much as she hated to admit it. It must have been the wine from last night, clouding her head and affecting her judgement.

Heaving a sigh, she turned to retrace her steps. She would have to resign herself to her fate. Perhaps what she had just learned put it into perspective, if only a little.

As she trudged back up to her chambers her keen mind was already turning towards the theft and what it might portend. Opening the door quietly and tiptoeing across the room so as not to wake Hettie, she removed her travelling clothes and scanned her bookshelves until she found the volume she was looking for.

Sitting next to the window she had been gazing out of, Adhelina settled down to a morning of brushing up on her ancient history, and began once again to read of the breaking of the tablet that had so nearly put the world in its grave.

⊱ CHAPTER XIII ⊰

A Turn for the Worse

The friars caught their first glimpse of the Warryn shortly after noon. The portion of the Brekawood they had exited straddled a higher swathe of hills, and as they headed south-east these descended gradually. As they rounded a bend to face due south Adelko saw that the hills declined steadily before dropping sharply and flattening out altogether into rolling plains on which he could make out the river, its bright waters sparkling in the sunlight.

He knew from the maps he had looked at that the Warryn flowed east for leagues before draining into the Bay of Belhavern and thence the Wyvern Sea. That thought stirred him – he had seen rivers before during his highland travels, but his young eyes had never yet looked upon the churning waves.

Horskram took them south-east again, intending to rejoin the main highway where it descended from the plateau that separated the southern reaches of the Wold from the plains below. Approaching its edge they found themselves looking down on the river, now barely more than a mile away. To the left the highway snaked down an incline towards the plains before meeting a stone arched bridge fording the Warryn.

Directly before the bridge on either side of the highway were clustered what looked like ten or fifteen horsemen, it was hard to be sure of the number at that distance.

Adelko glanced at his mentor. The old monk had a suspicious look etched on his weatherworn features.

At his behest they struck out directly east, skirting the lip of the plateau but stopping short of rejoining the highway, instead turning south again to follow an outcropping that stretched towards the river. Clambering up a chalky hill at its very edge they found themselves almost directly overlooking the bridge.

The outcropping they were now perched on was no more than thirty or forty yards from the highway, and the two monks crouched behind a straggly bush to observe the riders unseen.

There were about a dozen in all, dressed in travel-worn clothes and clad in mail shirts. All were armed. Their flaxen hair was long and braided, as were their beards. With their burly frames and threatening demeanour they reminded Adelko of the freeswords he had seen with the merchant party at Ulfang.

Only these men looked even nastier. There was a raw wildness about them he hadn't seen before. As he took in their warlike bearing he felt a conviction growing within him that such men could not mean them well.

His mentor was clearly forming the same judgement, for just then he muttered: 'Well, it seems as though the most direct route to Kaupstad is barred to us, for I do not think we should chance a meeting with these gentlemen.'

'Are they highwaymen?' whispered Adelko, ignoring his master's irony.

'I wouldn't be at all surprised, in this lawless region. All the same, there's something else that doesn't quite add up... but never mind that for now! Our first priority is to get across the river – come! We must retrace our steps, let's tarry here no longer.'

His heart sinking at the probability of another missed meal and yet more hard walking without a proper rest, Adelko struggled along beside his master as they began retracing their steps.

'Where are we going?' he asked breathlessly.

'Back into the Brekawood,' replied Horskram without stopping. 'The river runs through it – if my memory serves there's a natural ford of stepping stones about a mile or two in. If we cross there we can make our way through the lower forest on the other side of the Warryn and approach Kaupstad from the west – I doubt we'll encounter any brigands on that route, it's rarely used nowadays.'

✢ ✢ ✢

The afternoon was drawing on by the time they re-entered the Brekawood, closely hugging the river as it carved a path through its verdant canopy. The going was slow, for Horskram could not risk abandoning the river for a trail and missing the crossing point, but by late afternoon he was pointing triumphantly through the trees.

Peering ahead Adelko could make out a jumble of crude rocks bisecting the river about a hundred yards ahead. To reach this they had to scramble down the rocky plateau, with only a few side-growing trees and the odd bush for hand-holds. Adelko navigated this obstacle with as much confidence as his master – he wasn't naturally as sure footed as other mountain lads but his childhood excursions as the Dreaming Wanderer had paid off. Besides that four years of torturous attention from Udo had improved his footwork somewhat, although he would not be thanking the crusty old monk for that in a hurry.

As they reached the bottom he felt his confidence drain away. Earth was one thing, water quite another. The river was wider at this point than where it crossed the bridge further downstream.

'We'll need both hands free to navigate the stepping stones,' said Horskram. 'The trick is to clamber across – don't walk upright, or as like as not you'll slip and take a tumble!'

As the roaring river all but drowned out the old monk's words, Adelko felt an anxious feeling gnawing at his insides.

'Um, how deep is the river here, Master Horskram?' he asked in a small voice. He couldn't see very far beneath the surface of the water, which churned up into a froth as it coursed over the lumpen rocks stretching before them like the spine of a dragon.

'Deep enough to meet your end if you fall in – so don't!' replied his master.

'It's just that... I can't swim,' blurted Adelko nervously.

'Well of course you can't!' exclaimed Horskram. 'You're a mountain lad, not a fisherman's son! Now, if you're done stating the obvious, follow my lead. Remember, these rocks are slippery, so always have three points of contact with them – you'll be fine, just do as I do!'

Horskram stepped lightly onto the first rock, crouching low and clambering up on to the next one, which was half a man's height above the first. Turning around to look at Adelko he beckoned for him to follow with his free hand.

Taking a deep breath the young monk stepped gingerly on to the first rock. The water flowed and splashed across it with the free abandon of wild nature. Trying not to look at it, he picked his way unsteadily onto the next rock, just as Horskram moved on to another.

They were more than halfway across when Adelko began to feel surer of himself. He had slipped a couple of times, and felt his heart in his mouth when he did, but managed to recover his balance and avoid falling into the river. His mentor was by now several rocks ahead of him, and once again Adelko had to marvel at the able-bodied nimbleness of one so advanced in years. But then Horskram had spent most of his life on the road, his body hardened by decades of grappling with the unforgiving wildernesses of the world.

Adelko could hardly say the same – he had found the last six months as exhausting as they had been exhilarating.

He was nearly across when he slipped again. This time he almost tumbled headlong into the water, and only saved himself by grabbing frantically at a mossy outcropping of rock. Getting to his feet with a stream of curses unbefitting a pious monk he winced; he had grazed his knee, but at least he hadn't fallen in.

Looking up he saw Horskram standing at the edge of the river with his hands on his hips, a wry half-smile on his face as he barked: 'Well, come on! We haven't got all day – we're behind schedule as it is!'

Adelko frowned and bit his tongue, and focused on navigating the rest of the crossing in safety. He was growing weary of his mentor's caustic humour – at times he felt Horskram was deliberately poking fun at him to test his resolve in the face of adversity.

It only occurred to him later that perhaps Horskram's uncharacteristic quips were intended to take both their minds off the mortal peril they were in.

On this side of the river the Brekawood lay on the fertile plains of the lowlands proper, so at least it was less tiring to travel through. Adelko was more than grateful for this, for he now had a sore knee to add to his woes.

They reached the western highway at dusk. Adelko groaned inwardly as he registered its shocking state of disrepair.

'I've seen fewer holes in Yalba's Norric translations,' he said glumly. 'I would have thought the local baron would have kept a road this size in better condition.'

'It used to serve as a main trading route with Thraxia,' explained Horskram without breaking his stride, 'before it fell into disuse during the Border Wars.'

That series of internecine skirmishes between the two kingdoms had lasted more than a century. The Border Wars had finally come to an end with King Freidheim's decisive victory over the Thraxians at the Battle of Corne Hill. It had been half a century since the Boy King had routed the invading army and their mercenary allies from Vorstlund, and that mighty struggle had passed into Northlending folklore. In keeping with his unusually wise and benevolent nature, Freidheim had chosen not to press his advantage against the defeated Thraxians, instead suing for peace. His advisers had protested this decision, putting it down to the optimistic folly of youth, but the Boy King had proved to be shrewd beyond his years.

Not long after peace was made between the two kingdoms, Morwyne, Thraxia's fierce patrician king, had died. His son Cullodyn was a far more level-headed man than his fiery father and had recognised the wisdom in maintaining cordial relations with his Northlending rivals; for within a few short years Freidheim had laboured to make Northalde a sturdy kingdom once again, reviving the Order of the White Valravyn and garrisoning and repairing the castles that his great-grandfather had built.

With lasting peace made with the Thraxians, and the age-old threat from the Northland reavers extinguished by Freidheim's grandfather Aelfric, the young monarch had been free to consolidate his realm. He had proved to be as able a ruler as he was a general and diplomat, and the years that followed Corne Hill were mostly happy and prosperous for those living in the King's Dominions and the surrounding lands ruled by loyal barons.

But not even so wise a liege as Freidheim could please everybody or pacify all. Though the highland clans where Adelko was born used their autonomy wisely enough, their neighbours on the Wold were another matter.

'The barons there can always be relied upon to cease their bickering and present a united front whenever the King tries to bring them to heel,' said Horskram ruefully as they got onto that subject. 'They will never apply his just laws to their oppressed people.'

'Why not?' asked Adelko, feeling suddenly naive.

'Because it would cost them money,' answered Horskram. 'Justice always costs rulers money, one way or another.'

He said no more on the matter. Adelko found himself thinking of his mentor's conversation with Landebert before the demon attacked.

'What about the southern barons?' he asked. 'I haven't read much about them – I know they rebelled against the King after the Thraxians were beaten at Corne Hill, but why did they do it?'

'Their quarrel was an old one,' explained Horskram. 'For in bygone days before the Unity of Crowns, when Northalde was three separate realms, the lands they ruled comprised the Old Kingdom of Thule, from where the present-day jarldom takes its name. The pretender Kanga meant to revive his antiquated royal seat and have himself crowned as head of a breakaway kingdom. So together he and half a dozen of the most powerful southron nobles raised an army to fight for secession. It took seven years of bitter civil war to thwart him, until finally he perished by the King's own sword at the Battle of Aumric Fields, in sight of the very walls of Strongholm.'

Once again Freidheim had shown mercy in victory, and against all advice had refused to execute Kanga's young son Krulheim, as was customary when dealing with traitors. Instead he had made conciliation with the southern provinces, forbidding his victorious armies from despoiling their lands.

That had been fifteen years ago. Since the War of the Southern Secession the King had reigned in peace, and many living in the

Dominions and loyalist territories had even begun to say that Northalde was almost back to its heyday of a century ago, when Thorsvald the Hero King had sat on the throne of a regional power.

But others murmured that the present King's kindness was a weakness, and that no good would come of his excessive clemency; many loyal knights and nobles with holdings on the southern borders of the Dominions eyed their neighbours with suspicion, and kept their swords sharpened.

The two monks trudged along the highway in the deepening dark, with only the steady yellow glow of Horskram's lantern for company as they debated their country's troubled history. The road was deeply rutted and potholed. Despite the peace, trade between the two nations had never fully recovered from the wars.

'In any case the route across the mountains is now too dangerous to travel,' said Horskram when Adelko complained about the road again.

'Why is that?' asked the novice. 'The Border Wars are long over.'

'Northalde is not the only kingdom to suffer the privations of civil war,' replied his mentor. 'Over on the other side of the Hyrkrainians, mountain tribes have been fighting the lowland Thraxian nobles for generations.'

'Why?'

'Much the same reason as we fought the southern barons. History, land, power. When you have seen enough of the world, young Adelko, you will learn that most conflicts boil down to the same handful of ideas in the end. They're seldom very good ideas either, but that doesn't stop them being revisited time and again.'

Horskram fell silent again, grimly staring into the night as the pair of them trudged on towards Kaupstad.

Though Adelko supposed he was too young fully to appreciate what his master was telling him, he felt a twinge of pity for the old monk – he had seen so much of life, yet so little of it seemed to bring him any joy.

Contemplating this, he began to wonder if he had chosen the best path in life. Then he thought of himself back at his father's forge in Narvik, hunched over yet another horseshoe, and his doubts vanished.

✢ ✢ ✢

It was more than two hours after sunset when they finally reached Kaupstad. The town was enclosed on all sides by a roughly rectangular wooden palisade built of logs twice a man's height, hewn into square shapes and fitted closely together. From the lintel of the western gate they approached hung two lanterns, their flickering light meanly reproaching the still darkness. Perched atop this on a platform hidden from view behind the palisade slouched a balding town dweller, dressed in a tatty brigandine and clutching a rusty spear.

He must have been half asleep, as he didn't notice them until they were well within the circle of lantern light. As if to make up for his lackadaisical sentry-keeping, the hapless guard now made a great show of challenging them.

'Who goes there?! What time of night is this to be wayfaring?'

'Far too late for respectable men of the cloth to be bandying words with a dozy guardsman,' replied Horskram sharply. 'We are Argolian friars, from Ulfang chapter in the highland ranges. Our journey has been a long and hard one, and all we crave is food and shelter on a chilly night.'

The sentry eyed them suspiciously. 'Ulfang, you say? I thought that lay to the north – what brings you 'ere by this route, if you don't mind my asking?'

Adelko couldn't stop himself frowning. Of all their luck – had they landed themselves a shrewd watchman?

But Horskram was unruffled. Without a pause he replied: 'A forester's daughter was recently taken grievously ill. A friend of mine on the Wold connected to his family by marriage told me of this when we took shelter with him several nights ago. I considered it my duty to make a detour so I could give the poor girl her Last Rites. There are few perfects to be seen in the lawless lands hereabouts, as you no doubt know.'

The sentry licked his lips nervously. 'Well, I'm awfully sorry to 'ear that, sirrah, and please don't be offended by my askin' such questions – it's just that it's me job, you understand. Hang on a minute and I'll let you in.'

Descending a short flight of wooden steps behind the wall the sentry lifted the bar before opening the gate to admit them.

Adelko had to marvel again at how readily his mentor was prepared to lie when necessary – the first time had been in Landebert's hut, when Horskram invented the story about the castellan's daughter turning to witchcraft.

The secrecy excited and unsettled him. For his mentor to break with good Palomedian behaviour by uttering falsehoods so liberally underscored how vital and dangerous their mission was.

Entering the town they trudged up the highway, which now became one of Kaupstad's main streets. Lights flickered in the windows of mean-looking buildings that hunched over them menacingly like lurching footpads. The stink of human and animal refuse and discarded rubbish assaulted his nostrils as they made their way towards the market square at the town's centre.

During their evening journey Horskram had told him what little he needed to know about Kaupstad. For generations it had thrived on its renowned horse market, gradually drawing artisans and craftsmen from the lands about to hawk their wares and further increase its fortunes. The loss of the Thraxian trading route had hurt these somewhat, such that its prosperity was less than of old; yet still the fifteen hundred citizens who huddled within its crooked walls gleaned a fair enough living from their varied trades. Castle Hroghar lay a day's hard ride to the east. It was the seat of the Jarl Fenrig, a loyalist baron who owned the town and much of the surrounding lands. The proximity of a strong garrison was enough to discourage most outlaws and robber knights from despoiling its wealth.

Adelko breathed an inward sigh of relief when they drew level with the inn. The way things had been going of late he would not have been surprised to find a ramshackle affair with cramped rooms and a leaking roof, but at first glance his master's choice of hostelry appeared to be reassuringly well appointed.

A sizeable wooden building three storeys high overlooked an enclosed courtyard where the horses were stabled; light peeped through cracks in the shutters on the ground floor and a raucous din could be heard from inside. Beside the mews entry to the courtyard was another door leading directly into what must be the taproom, judging by the noise.

A painted wooden sign above the door swung aimlessly in the gathering wind. The simple cross daubed in gold on a red background proclaimed the hostelry's name: *The Crossroads Inn*.

Pushing open the door the monks stepped into the reeking common room. At one end was a counter, behind which were shelves crammed with flagons and barrels piled up on top of one another. The rest of the place was no less crowded; nearly every table was taken, and Adelko found himself blinking in the candlelight after the relative darkness of the ill-lit street outside. The common area formed a U shape around the counter; next to it a flight of stairs led up to the rooms on the next floor. Over to the right another door led out into the courtyard, whilst a fire roared in the hearth against the far left wall.

The taproom's occupants were mostly a motley crew of merchants, freeswords, travelling artisans, and what looked like pilgrims, probably bound for the Blessed Realm in Sassania. There must have been some forty or fifty drinkers there, and Adelko began to despair of finding lodgings, but the innkeeper nodded at Horskram in recognition as they approached him at the counter.

'Well, well, if it ain't Brother Horskram, the master witchfinder himself,' he exclaimed. A stocky, ruddy-faced man of middling stature and middling age, his brown beard was flecked with tinges of grey that matched his keen eyes. 'Haven't seen you round here in a month of rest-days! What brings you up to these parts then? Trouble, I'll wager – there's never any need for an Argolian unless there's trouble brewing!'

'I'm glad to see the inclement weather has done nothing to dampen your dry sense of humour,' replied the adept with a wan smile. Then, lowering his voice: 'Yes, trouble of a kind you might say, although not around here… or not yet at any rate.'

A couple of merchants slouched over the counter next to them were eyeing them blearily. Adelko guessed they'd had a few stoops of ale already.

Registering them with a sidelong glance Horskram raised his voice again: 'The famed quality of your ale is always enough to bring me back, Vagan, trouble or no. This is Adelko of Narvik, a novice of the Order seconded to me for training. However, tonight I think he is in need of refreshment more than anything else – so two stoops if you please!'

Without changing his neutral expression Vagan nodded and reached behind him for two pewter tankards, which he filled to the brim from a nearby barrel with frothy amber-coloured ale. Setting these before them he asked: 'I take it you'll be needing lodgings for the night then?'

'You presume correctly,' replied Horskram, nodding and taking a sip of ale. 'Preferably a room – we've had a long hard journey and we'd rather not sleep on the common room floor if possible.'

Vagan nodded, pursing his lips noncommittally. 'It's a busy night as you can tell, but I'll see what I can do.'

Someone called loudly for more ale. Excusing himself the innkeeper went off to tend to their needs. Taking a slug of his beer, Adelko instantly felt better: it was indeed impeccable, and after all his labours it didn't take much to induce a feeling of light-headed euphoria in him.

Gazing idly around the common room he pulled up short as he recognised the merchants who had stayed at Ulfang.

They were sat in the corner playing eagerly at dice, stroking their forked beards with an air of great concentration while their freeswords clustered noisily around two broad tables close by. They were drinking heavily and yelling coarse jibes at the flustered serving wenches.

The novice turned back to see if his master had noticed, but he appeared sunk in one of his reveries and barely seemed to register his surroundings.

Soon Vagan returned to tell them a room was free on the top floor. He was about to say more when his stable boy came tugging at his sleeve.

'Vagan, sir, the night watch are in the courtyard,' said the grimy-faced boy in a high, reedy voice. 'They say they've 'ad anover complaint about the noise.'

Vagan rolled his eyes and cursed. 'That'll be Vara Busyhands kicking up a fuss again – I've told her a hundred times I've a licence to keep tavern behind closed doors for three hours after curfew, but she won't listen. Her husband runs for town mayor once and she thinks she owns the place!'

Turning to Horskram, he said: 'I'd better go and deal with this. I'll show you to your room afterwards – Rudi, mind the barrels while I'm gone, there's a good lad.' Shaking his head wearily he went off to appease the watch.

Horskram took another slug of ale and smiled. 'He's always getting into trouble with his neighbours – it's his ale, it's too strong for its own good! Makes his clientele overly rowdy.'

Looking around him at the unfolding debauch, Adelko could well believe it. He had never been in a proper inn until now – none of the mountain villages he had passed through were large enough to warrant having one – and to tell the truth he was rather enjoying the experience.

❖ ❖ ❖

The monks drank their ale in silence for a while and Vagan did not return. Presently Rudi rushed off to help the serving wenches, who were having difficulty keeping up with the freeswords' voracious demands for more ale.

Putting his half-empty tankard down with a sigh Horskram said: 'I have to ask Vagan about the horse markets. There should be one tomorrow, but he'll know who's best to approach. You stay here and finish your ale – I'm going to go outside and speak to him now, otherwise I'll never pin him down on a busy night like this. Besides, it looks as if he might need a respectable member of the religious community to vouch for his establishment.'

Left alone with his ale, Adelko finished it off and immediately thought about getting some more. A minor commotion had broken out on the far side of the common room, where a freesword had caused a scene by grabbing one of the more attractive wenches by the haunches. A winsome peasant girl with long dark tresses and a full figure – not that that was any excuse, of course.

An old knight had come over to intervene, and was now squaring off against the loutish bodyguards. He was clearly outnumbered and looked somewhat pale and drawn in the face despite his well-fed girth. Still, he seemed hardy enough, dressed in mail and carrying a stout sword at his belt. He wore a sky-blue tabard over his armour bearing his coat of arms – a stylised coiled green serpent, or perhaps a wyrm.

Someone else was joining the dispute now. A tall, wiry youth with a scar on his forehead and a dangerous light in his eyes stalked over to stand wordlessly beside the knight. He was dressed in travel-soiled clothes and a well-worn brigandine and carried a blade of his own. Probably the old knight's squire.

With both parties exchanging harsh words and staring at each other menacingly things looked set to turn ugly – until one of the merchants stood up to intervene, admonishing the men in his service and apologising humbly to the knight before proffering a silver mark to the offended girl. That seemed to mollify the stern old vassal, who stomped back to where he was sitting out of Adelko's view, accompanied by his sullen young squire.

Returning to the counter with an armful of empty mugs Rudi looked at Adelko and rolled his eyes. He could not have been much more than a few summers younger than the novice, but with his skinny frame and pallid skin he looked far away from manhood.

Realising that the lad would probably serve him, Adelko looked down at his empty tankard and, glancing sidelong at the door to the courtyard, said: 'I think I'll have another if you please.'

Even so, he was half expecting Rudi to laugh and shake his head, but the boy simply nodded and took his tankard, filling it up again from the same barrel.

Feeling triumphant, Adelko took up his master's half-finished stoop too and moved around the U-shaped bar to a stool, which had just become vacated by a drunken craftsman falling off it in a stupor.

From here he still had a good view of the bodyguards, who were now singing an old mercenary marching song. Given their coarse manners they were surprisingly tuneful, and Adelko caught some of the words as they came floating across the hubbub of the inn:

The blood sun rises on the morn
And sees us off to war, hey!
We'll go marching up the hill
To meet the crimson dawn!

A soldier of fortune has no home
But the camp and field of war, hey!
His brothers in arms his family
No other friends he owns!

We fight for a purse of silver marks
Gold bids us go to war, hey!
No king commands us lest he pay
No perfect moves our hearts!

The only fate a freesword craves
Is a glorious end in war, hey!
And when his time comes he'll be found
Lying in an unmarked grave!

So it's off to fight in the cold grey morn
To try the chance of war, hey!
We'll come marching down the hill
Stained with the crimson dawn!

Supping on his ale as he listened to the grim verses Adelko couldn't help but feel a rush of excitement – these men knew full well the dangerous nature of the life they had chosen, yet they embraced it with gusto regardless.

Then he caught himself – what was he thinking? They were hired killers, revelling godlessly in that sinful fact. Staring at his second ale he began to wonder just how strong Vagan's stuff really was.

Just then he heard the sound of many horses pulling to a halt outside the taproom. Several of the patrons sitting by the windows had noticed too, and were turning to peer through the cracks in the shutters.

A minute later the main door was flung open and four burly warriors strode purposefully inside. Adelko felt his hackles rise: with their braided hair and beards they had to be part of the group of riders at the bridge. Highland clansmen braided their hair too, but at this range he could see the style was different. Nor did they wear the distinctive clan colours: these men were definitely foreigners. Nasty-looking ones at that.

Approaching the counter they eyed poor Rudi with a mixture of amusement and contempt before one of them, a muscle-bound, red-haired man with a look of cruelty etched into his rough face, barked at him in a thickly accented voice: 'Gif us strong drink, *now*, boy.'

As Rudi scurried to obey, the four men stared around the common room. A pilgrim sitting nearby made the mistake of catching the eye of the red-haired warrior, who snarled viciously at him and made as if to step over. The terrified pilgrim turned immediately to stare down at his ale, his companions quickly following suit.

The warrior laughed, a harsh grating sound, and turned back to face the counter.

Somewhere across the common room somebody had broken out a lute, and now the raucous singing of the freeswords was accompanied by a wild frenetic strumming that briefly put Adelko in mind of old Lubo and his brothers back in Narvik. It certainly seemed a world away now.

Rudi set the tankards of ale before the four men, who picked them up and quaffed them eagerly. Slamming his down with unnecessary force the red-haired brigand, who appeared to be the leader, leaned over the bar menacingly to address Rudi again.

From where he was sat half in the shadows Adelko strained to hear what he was saying over the music. He couldn't make it out, but then he heard the stable boy reply in a high, nervous voice: 'I – I'm not sure if we've got enough room for that many, sire, and the stables are quite full tonight. I'll 'ave to go and check wiv the guvnor.'

Gratefully rounding the counter, Rudi bounded out into the courtyard.

Just as he did one of the four men glanced over in Adelko's direction. He was a hulking brute with a rough piece of cloth covering one eye; the other burned with a malign light. Instinctively the novice drew his head back so it was in the shadows – the one-eyed brute turned to size up the singing bodyguards, drunkenly oblivious to their new rivals.

Adelko pulled his cowl over his head to better obscure his face. His sixth sense was jangling unpleasantly.

Vagan's ale did a good job of dulling his nerves, but even so he made a point of staring down at his mug as the cowed pilgrims had done. Glancing up surreptitiously a minute later he felt his anxiety increase as he registered the red-haired man peering at him in the gloom over his flagon, trying to make him out.

Just then the brigand was distracted by Rudi returning to tell him that begging his pardon but the guvnor was coming to see to him now.

Seizing his chance, Adelko slipped off his stool and made for the courtyard door, almost bumping into Vagan, who was coming back in wearing a harassed look on his face.

Outside it was chilly. The clouds had drawn in again and a mist had rolled in from across the plains, giving the air a thick dampness. His master was standing in the torchlit courtyard, an impatient look on his face. The watch were nowhere to be seen.

Rushing up to Horskram, he exclaimed: 'In the common room! I've just seen... them! The horsemen we saw at the bridge!'

Adelko lowered his voice, looking around nervously as he remembered the rest of the brigands would be in the street just outside.

Horskram frowned. 'Are you sure? How many?' he asked softly.

'Four of them. But I think there's more outside – they were asking for lodgings, that's why Rudi called Vagan in just now. Two of them were looking at me – one of them was wearing an eye-patch and there was another one with red hair who seemed to be the leader...'

'Did they get a clear look at you?' Horskram's face was intent and serious now.

'I don't think so... I'd moved to a stool away from the lantern-light.'

Horskram stood still, his eyes glinting in the torchlight as he pondered their options.

'Master Horskram, what should we do?' hissed Adelko after a short while had passed. His master waved him to silence. Moments later he nodded to himself, appearing to make his mind up about something.

'Stay here,' he said to Adelko firmly, before re-entering the common room.

✢ ✢ ✢

With a cocksure swagger Vaskrian got up to order more ale at his master's behest. As predicted, it had taken several days for the apothecary's poultice to work its wonders – if indeed it had had anything to do with the prickly old knight's recovery at all. By then Sir Rudd and Sir Ulfius had left for Harrang, taking Edric and Cedric with them.

That was some relief. He'd come close to having his melee privileges revoked – he didn't need Edric in his face goading him into another fight. As it was, he reckoned he'd narrowly avoided the worst thanks to a long-standing antipathy between his guvnor and Sir Ulfius. That hadn't got him off the hook completely, but it had at least made Sir Branas less inclined to take the complaint against his squire seriously. If he hadn't been bedridden there might even have been another duel of honour on the cards.

'Who does that pompous idiot think he is?' he'd growled at Vaskrian, who had been summoned to receive his due bollocking after the haughty knight complained. 'At least I didn't *choose* a common churl for a squire, let alone a Wolding one! I might just make up for missing the jousting by demanding satisfaction when we get to Harrang!'

Then he'd got his bollocking. Turning beady eyes on his squire Branas had covered him in scorn, berating him fiercely and cursing him for a low-born coxcomb and other unsavoury things. No one did bollockings quite like Sir Branas – yet all the same Vaskrian couldn't help but feel loyal to him. The old knight still put up with him – he'd never once voiced a word of complaint to Lord Fenrig, despite everything.

'That's twice you've brought trouble to my door!' he'd yelled, wincing with every word. 'It'll be a wonder if we get to Harrang in one piece – at this rate you'll bring every knight we meet down on us in a blood-feud to end the ages! I swear you get worse with every passing season!'

Vaskrian had bit his lip and stared sullenly at the floorboards, for once knowing better than to protest. Branas had finished by docking his prize money for the next three tournaments. It must be nice to mete out a punishment that filled your own purse, he'd reflected bitterly.

With Branas fully recovered, they were due to leave first thing tomorrow. After spending several days bedridden, his guvnor was in a drinking mood. Vaskrian was pleased – that meant he could enjoy a few flagons too.

It got better. Vagan and his wenches were swept off their feet tonight, and that gave him the perfect excuse to approach the counter and order. That meant he'd have to pass the freeswords they'd just quarrelled with – maybe one of them would shout something at him and provoke him. Though men of arms, they were commoners, so he could legitimately pick a fight if they did.

Even his irascible guvnor would have to allow it to happen, for honour's sake – old Branas had fairly been spoiling for a fight himself just now. That had been a lot of fun, the two of them squaring up to a dozen fighters, just like in Maegellin's *Lays of King Vasirius and His Noble Knights*.

And he was itching for another scrap – anything to assuage his wounded pride from the last one. Edric had been quick to boast of his 'near victory' to anyone who cared to listen, knowing full well there wouldn't be a rematch.

That had riled him and no mistake – he'd had the oaf on his last legs before he slipped over. His luck of late had been miserable – had some hedge witch cursed him, he wondered?

He reached the counter without incident. Caught up in their raucous singing, the freeswords hadn't even noticed him pass by.

Oh well, perhaps Vagan's ale had dulled their senses. Good job for them.

Besides, here was a sight to quickly take his mind off the boorish bodyguards. Stood at the counter were four more warriors – but these had a very different look about them.

Vaskrian eyed them keenly. Dressed in light mail shirts and armed with axes and swords. Probably just another band of mercenaries seeking strong drink and shelter for the night. Definitely not local though – foreigners, they had to be, no self-respecting fighters from these parts wore their hair and beards like that. They looked like barbarians – clansmen from the Highlands perhaps, or possibly even Northlanders from the Frozen Wastes.

All four were scowling as Vagan bravely met their eyes and shook his head.

'I'm sorry, sirrahs, as I say we've no room for a dozen horsemen tonight – and I've seen no one of that description round 'ere. The *Journeyman's Rest* down the road past the square might still 'ave room, beyond that I'm afraid I can't help you.'

'Ja ja, you vaste our time,' snarled one of the men, a beefy looking fellow with flame-red hair. 'But ve take der free ale as payment.'

Turning to the others he laughed nastily and said: 'How you say in your tongue? On der *house*, ja?'

The others laughed too before all four exited the common room as suddenly as they had entered, barging their way past the stoical innkeeper and not bothering to close the door behind them.

Following on their heels Vaskrian had half a mind to yell out a challenge, but thought better of it as he saw there were at least half a dozen other barbarians waiting for their comrades out in the street. All were likewise armed, and mounted to boot.

No – if he challenged this lot to a fight without Sir Branas's approval he'd be in serious trouble. Also they might be from noble clans in their own benighted lands – and Vaskrian wasn't sure if that meant they counted as knights according to the Code of Chivalry.

That he would also lose such an encounter through sheer weight of numbers barely occurred to him.

With a sigh he shut the door and turned to see the innkeeper talking agitatedly with an Argolian friar who had just entered from the courtyard.

'... think it would be best if you showed us to our room,' the friar was saying. He was a sturdy looking fellow, about his guvnor's age or perhaps a little older. Something in his hard blue eyes and taciturn demeanour told Vaskrian that this was a man who could hold his own, monk or no.

That didn't stop him interrupting. The squire was voicing a request for more ale when the innkeeper cut him off.

'Ah, young Vaskrian, please wait a minute – young Rudi is just serving yonder artisans, and will attend to your order right after.'

Vagan motioned for the friar to follow him up the stairs. Just at that moment the door to the courtyard opened again, and another friar – perhaps a couple of years younger than Vaskrian – entered the common room.

'Ah, Adelko,' said the older monk in a voice that was gruff but not unkind. 'I thought I could rely on you to disobey my order, but at least on this occasion it saves me going back out into the cold. Come along, Vagan will show us to our room now.'

Hastily the young monk scurried over, catching Vaskrian's eyes as he did. He seemed a timid fellow, with his round face and goggle eyes. Nothing like his stern master. But then that's what a life spent in the cloister sheltered from the rough and tumble of the world did to you, he supposed.

As the three of them went upstairs, the squire leaned against the bar and glanced over impatiently at Rudi, struggling to hear the craftsmen order above the din.

Vaskrian rolled his eyes to the rafters. A frustrating night, all in all: what did it take to get a drink or a fight in this place?

✤ ✤ ✤

Their room was a cramped, dingy affair on the corner of the uppermost floor with two beds and a small table by the shuttered window.

The innkeeper ushered the monks inside before following them and shutting the door behind him.

'Well now, Master Horskram,' he said. 'I'd better tell you what those... gentlemen had to say just now.' He spoke in a hushed voice even though he had just closed the door. 'So as I was sayin' downstairs, there's four of them and they say they're looking for stabling and floor space for a dozen. I told them I've no such room – which as you'll have gathered is the truth – and they went all sour on me. Mean bunch of fellows, soldiers of fortune like yonder louts downstairs, but foreigners as well to boot. Don't get me wrong, I don't mind foreigners or freeswords, so long as they mind their own business and pay their way – but these look like they don't do neither.

'Anyway, I'm about to steer them towards the *Journeyman* down the road hoping they won't cause any trouble, when one of them – a red-headed, evil-looking fellow if ever I saw one – asks me if there's any priests staying here tonight. I don't rightly follow him at first, then he leans in my face and says: "Priests, *monks*, worship *Argo*! Wise god, ja? Any here tonight?"'

Vagan paused and made the sign. Only a pagan would refer to a saint as a god. 'Forgive me my talk, Horskram, but that's the Almighty's honest truth what he said. I told him I wouldn't be havin' any blaspheming under my roof and he looked at me again all nastily. I weren't about to back down before any pagan blasphemers in my own house, so I just stared back at him and said I'd seen no men of the cloth here for several moons. Hardly the kind of place such men'd frequent in any case, I said.'

Horskram and Adelko exchanged glances in the gloomy light of Vagan's single candle.

'Rest assured Master Horskram,' continued the innkeeper hastily. 'I know a bunch of rotten apples when I see one, and I wasn't about to take a bite. I made my excuses and told him I had customers to attend to. They left after that – didn't pay for their drinks o' course and looked none too pleased, but I reckon I've thrown them off the scent at least.'

Horskram placed a hand on the innkeeper's shoulder. 'Vagan, you've excelled yourself this evening,' he said. 'You have my thanks, and the gratitude of the Order.'

Vagan shook his head. 'Anything to help an Argolian friar. There are few enough good men in the world as it is. But if you don't mind my asking – is there anything I should know?'

The innkeeper was looking at Horskram keenly now.

'Vagan, you've already deduced enough I think, but there are good reasons why I can't tell you everything,' replied the adept. 'We are being pursued – I have a good inkling as to why but I don't know who is behind it yet. I can't tell you any more except that we have to get south –

as far away from here as possible, and right soon. Our steeds were taken from us several nights ago, hence my asking you about the horse markets just now. We'll go and visit the fellow you recommended tomorrow at first light and make a trade, after that we'll be gone from Kaupstad. But Vagan – and this is very important – you must not breathe a word of our coming or going to *anyone*. Not a soul, do you understand?'

Vagan nodded, his face stoically neutral. 'As you wish, master monk, I'll not say a word – though Reus knows what kind of a pickle you've got yourselves into.' Glancing over at Adelko he added: 'This lad seems tender of years to be in such danger.'

Horskram allowed himself a slight smile. 'Don't you worry about young Adelko. Though he be a novice, he's already tried his mettle on more than one occasion. And I do believe that underneath all that youthful foolishness he has a sharp mind in that head of his too.'

'Well, very good then,' replied the innkeeper. 'I should know well enough to trust the Argolians to weather stormy tides, after all. Now if you'll excuse me I'd better get back to work. There's candles on yonder table should you need a light. I'll wake you for breakfast just before dawn – if you need anything else in the meantime I'll be downstairs until drinking-up time.'

Bidding Vagan goodnight, the monks barred the door behind him before fumbling around in the darkness for the candles and tinder. Once they had these lit they took off their knapsacks and quarterstaves and sat down on their beds.

Presently there was a knock at their door. That had them reaching for their quarterstaves, but to their relief – and Adelko's delight – it was only Rudi with a tray bearing bread, two more flagons of ale and bowls of goat stew.

Thanking the boy they sat down to eat, first making sure the door was bolted again. The stew was a little on the gristly side, but tasty all the same, and mopping up the sauce with his chunk of bread Adelko could almost fancy himself back in the refectory at Ulfang, listening to Yalba hold forth in his boisterous voice. When they were done they sat back to enjoy the rest of their ale.

But Horskram clearly had more serious matters on his mind. Presently he said: 'Well, Adelko, I think now is as good a time as any to take stock of events of the past week. I have been doing much thinking on the matter, and I believe I have arrived at several conclusions, although in truth many questions linger that need to be answered.'

Taking another sip of his ale Adelko leaned forward nodding. Though he felt an incipient fear dampening his natural curiosity, he thought it best he know more about the pickle they were in, as Vagan had put it.

'It is by now obvious, I'm sure you will agree, that we are being pursued by agents that intend us harm. By night we are stalked by a demon of the netherworld – and now it would appear that brigands from a foreign land are hunting us by day. The first salient question is *why* – and I think there can be only one feasible answer to that. Whoever was responsible for the theft of the Headstone fragment has learned that we know of it, and is trying to eliminate us before we can warn anyone about it.'

Adelko felt a shiver run down his spine. His master's euphemistic language did nothing to make the prospect of being murdered in the wilderness less frightening. One question did occur to him though.

'But... whoever they are, how would they know that we know?'

'A good question,' replied Horskram. 'But one that can be answered easily enough, I think. You will recall the half-melted casket in the uppermost chamber of the Abbot's inner sanctum. Only a demon of the netherworld could command such flame – and only a powerful Left-Handed sorcerer would know how to summon such an entity and bind it to his will. I propose that whoever did such a thing also has the powers of Scrying, another of the Seven Disciplines of Magick. This would allow our putative culprit to observe things from afar – and therefore to have seen us poking around in the top chamber of the inner sanctum at Ulfang.'

Horskram paused to take another sip of his ale. 'So, to return to my theory, I propose that our unknown adversary sent his blasphemous servant to steal the fragment, knowing that the only person at the monastery who would learn of its theft would be impelled to keep it secret.'

'But why is Sacristen so afraid of others finding out? After all, it's hardly his fault the thing was taken!'

'Adelko, I'm afraid to say that the world is a more complicated place than you yet fathom,' sighed Horskram, looking down at his ale. 'Though venerated throughout the Free Kingdoms and beyond, our Order has not always been... popular with the mainstream Temple.'

'Is this something to do with the purging that... that I overheard you and the Abbot talking about?'

Horskram fixed Adelko again with keen eyes. 'You are indeed shrewd. Not for nothing do I praise your faculties! Yes, it is indeed to do with the Purge. But I will not speak of that now except to say that unfortunately its repercussions are far too widely known, and an enemy of the Almighty might easily use such knowledge to his own benefit.

'But to return to my hypothesis. Our unknown enemy despatches his infernal servant, which makes off with the fragment in the dead of night. He perceives all is well, until something he has not foreseen takes place:

we arrive at the monastery to report on our unusually trying demonic encounter at Rykken. Of course in hindsight it's obvious why poor Gizel was so foully possessed: our Left-Handed practitioner, in summoning up devils to do his work, has widened the rent between worlds – thus allowing a greater entity to cross over and possess a girl pure of heart.

'Ironically, this is the very reason that impels me to go to the Abbot, which prompts him to risk breaking his silence and tell me of the theft. In his headlong dash for power, our cunning mage has failed to predict the consequences of his diabolical actions, and chance has put us in the way of his schemes. Had we not turned up when we did I can well believe Sacristen would have kept the theft secret for far longer.

'Upon learning of his mistake, and our plans to journey south and alert the head of our Order, our adversary immediately conjures up another servant to pursue us. However, knowing full well that a creature that can only emerge on to the material plane at night may not suffice to despatch two resourceful Argolians, he – or she for that matter – commissions a band of mercenaries from abroad to seek us during the day. And so we are pursued relentlessly, from one hour to the next.'

The adept paused to take another draught of ale. Adelko's mind was racing.

'But, just a second...' he began falteringly. 'The stone trapdoor at the top of the Abbot's sanctum was smashed to pieces. I suppose that's how it entered in the first place. If this wizard is powerful enough to send something like that to steal the fragment, why not just send... well, another one just like it to do for us? The thing that tried to attack us in Landebert's hut wasn't strong enough to claw through his stone roof.'

'Excellent!' exclaimed Horskram, his eyes lighting up. 'You do me proud, Adelko! I was myself wondering the same thing for a day or two, and the answer only just occurred to me in the common room this evening. Our knowledge of wizards from testimonies at witch trials leads us to believe that any sorcerer, no matter how powerful, can only control a certain number of entities at any one time. You see, when a devil is conjured up from the Other Side, it instantly longs to be free, so it can wreak havoc on its new surroundings at leisure – it doesn't want to serve the wizard who has summoned it. Therefore, to keep it in his thrall, a black magician must continually strive in a battle of wills.'

The adept paused to make the sign. 'A fiendish contest if ever there was one! As such I can only conjecture that our warlock still needed to retain the services of his first demon – presumably to transport the stolen fragment back to his lair, or some other appointed place. Therefore his will would still be partially diverted to keep it in check, meaning he would be forced to content himself with summoning up a lesser being of the lowest Tier to pursue us. This would also explain his resorting to more earthly means of having us killed. Do you follow?'

Adelko nodded eagerly, by now too caught up in the fascinating puzzle to register that someone he had never met wanted him dead.

'So what about the brigands? Where are they from? They're definitely not Northlendings – they look similar to clansmen but they're not quite the same.'

'No,' Horskram shook his head. 'Most probably they are Northlanders – from the Frozen Principalities across the Sea of Valhalla, whence our ancestors came. Even today they are a barbaric folk, who repudiate the Redeemer and cling to the pagan gods of old. They certainly care nothing for the niceties of chivalry, but they are a fierce and warlike people – many of them take service as freeswords, guarding trade ships laden with goods from the Empire. My guess is that they were commissioned in Port Cravern, less than a week's hard ride north-east of here.'

'So, is that where our bad wizard is then?'

'Possibly, but we can't be certain of that. Some wizards have the power to communicate with each other across space and even time... but that hypothesis assumes that we have more than one enemy, perhaps an apprentice who serves the master. At this point, we cannot be sure of that either.'

'So, what do we do? I don't fancy our chances, Master Horskram, travelling hundreds of miles to get to Pangonia with a band of ruthless swordsmen and a devil on our trail!'

'Neither do I,' replied Horskram, frowning. 'But what choice do we really have? At least we know the demon can be turned by such prayers as we two can muster – and there are places of holy sanctuary that will increase our chances of a night. But what concerns me is what happens when our adversary has dispensed with the services of his first demon – he might then choose to divert all his will into summoning up a more powerful entity to chase us. If such a thing were to find us alone, I doubt even our combined efforts could save us then.'

Adelko took a nervous gulp on his beer. He did not like his mentor's pessimistic tone.

'Now then, lad, be of some cheer,' said the adept. 'I did not say all was lost. At any rate, if we do manage to reach the Grand High Monastery in Pangonia we shall be safe – the prayers of the Order's most powerful chapter should be enough to protect us from whatever our unknown villain throws at us!'

Another question occurred to Adelko. 'Do you have any idea who he is?'

Horskram's face darkened again. 'I have one or two ideas, but again none of them are certain. The most likely guess is Andragorix – whom you heard me speak of when you eavesdropped.'

Despite everything that had happened, Adelko still couldn't help blushing as he remembered his transgression. 'I was going to ask... but you didn't seem to like talking about him.'

'I don't. He is a black magician of no small repute, the worst and most dastardly that these lands have seen for generations. I sought him out several years ago, myself and one other – Sir Belinos of Runcymede, a pious knight from Thraxia. Together we bearded him in his lair in Roarkil, a haunted fortress surrounded by dense woodlands on the eastern edge of that kingdom. Poor Belinos did not survive, but before he perished by Andragorix's potent sorceries he managed to cut off his hand. As he lay writhing in pain on the floor of his cursed tower I had the chance to slay him... ah, but mercy stayed my hand! Foolish notion! It would have been far better to commit an ill stroke then, to preserve the world from his evil! My moment of doubt allowed him to transform himself into a raven and escape. And thus was the turning of my victory to ashes symbolised.'

Horskram paused to take another pull at his ale, staring down into the half-empty tankard with regretful eyes. Adelko wanted to offer him words of comfort, but found none forthcoming.

At length the old monk looked up and continued: 'It was not until last year that I heard rumours he had resurfaced, travelling incognito from village to village, bringing ruin on the unsuspecting peasantry with his poisonous words and stealing their children for his ghastly rituals. In vain I tried to seek him, so I could confront him again and finish what I should have when I had the chance, but he has learned from his mistakes and never stays in one place for too long.

'The last I heard he was somewhere in Vorstlund – so we may even encounter him on our journey. There are several chapters belonging to our Order in that realm, I sent word to the priors there to keep a close watch. I always knew he could not run and hide forever, for his lust for power will always get the better of him – eventually he'll seek another stronghold in which to settle. But – if it really is him behind all this – it seems that his warped ambitions have outstripped even my darkest expectations, and now he has us on the back foot.'

'But how can we know for sure? I mean, this is all just speculation isn't it, Master Horskram?'

'Aye, it is. But there are thankfully few who can wield such powers, which is why Andragorix is the most likely suspect. You are right however – we can only be sure when we get to the Grand High Monastery.

No doubt Hannequin will call for a divination. That should reveal who's really behind this – assuming we don't meet them first! In truth I would sooner have held one straight away at Ulfang, but as you saw the Abbot would not hear of it, and in this I must defer to him. So we must endure prolonged danger thanks to Temple politics.'

The two monks finished the rest of their ale in silence before going to bed. The cots were small but comfortable, the blankets thick and warm. But even so they were denied a good night's rest.

Less than an hour after putting the candles out they were awoken by the sound of their demonic pursuer. Though mercifully far away this time, its awful voice seemed to fill the dark wilderness about them, pronouncing their doom in a language unfit for mortal ears.

⊸ CHAPTER XIV ⊶

An Ambush in the Night

The common room was already a bustle of activity when they descended to take their breakfast. Outside in the courtyard the freeswords could be heard noisily taking their horses from the stables as they prepared to leave the inn. Their fork-bearded employers were in the taproom, finishing a gluttonous breakfast of chopped liver, roast lamb, bacon and bread washed down with watered wine. Scattered around the rest of the room were the same motley crew of pilgrims and artisans, struggling with their hangovers as they tucked into humbler fare.

Most of the inn's patrons had been woken in the night by the frightful noises. Several whispered fearfully among themselves, making the sign and exchanging scared looks. During breakfast Adelko noticed a few people looking over at their table, perhaps hoping to hear some words of reassurance from an Argolian friar. But Horskram said nothing, and did not raise his eyes from the table until Vagan approached them to settle up the bill.

The adept insisted on pressing an extra silver mark into the innkeeper's hand to pay for the drinks consumed by the brigands the night before. Vagan protested that it was far too much, but Horskram shook his head and waved him away kindly.

Bidding Vagan farewell they were just taking their leave of the *Crossroads* when Adelko noticed the old knight and his squire sitting down to a late breakfast at a corner table. The wiry youth caught his eye, as he had done the previous night. He looked proud and sure of himself – perhaps too sure of himself, although his upright bearing and athletic figure suggested a young man well trained to arms.

They stepped out into a cold grey morning. The market square was a short distance from the inn. They found it already crowded with stalls, and Adelko's eyes feasted on an abundance of fruit, vegetables and other victuals, crafted goods of leather and wood, cooking utensils and other household items.

He had never seen a market as large as this one. Not even the monthly
fair at Rykelling, a day's journey from his village, was as big. Competing
for space among the stalls were several wooden stockades where dozens
of horses of various ages and quality whinnied and stamped.

Already there were well over two hundred townsfolk in the square,
haggling with the merchants and artisans. Adelko recognised several from
the inn, and off to one side he saw the freeswords slouching idly by their
horses while the merchants from Ulfang began their morning's work.

'Follow me, and stay close,' instructed Horskram, as though
they were about to navigate another difficult stretch of wilderness.
'These scoundrels would sell you the sky if they thought they could
get away with it. And watch out for pickpockets!'

'But I don't have anything worth stealing,' Adelko pointed out.

'Well, just watch out anyway!'

It took them a while to make their way through the crowds to the
horse stall recommended by Vagan. During that time Adelko found
himself obliged to follow his master's suit and use his quarterstaff to
wave away the vendors, who weren't shy about grabbing his habit and
proclaiming their wares in loud voices from mouths that reeked of rotten
teeth: 'Eggs, my lord? Got the best eggs in the province! Only sixpence a
dozen – giving them away!...' 'How about a nice cooking pot, sirrah? Made
of solid iron too – half a sovereign! Not heavy at all – you can carry it back
to your monastery! You monks love a good feed, doncha?...' 'My good
friars, how are your holinesses this day? Sharpest sickles in Kaupstad, for
tending your gardens – buy two and I'll do you a special price...'

The horse trader recommended by Vagan was a stout fellow
of medium height in early middle age. Drawing level with him
Horskram proffered his hand, asking: 'Are you Radko?'

'Aye, who wants to know?' replied the other, without taking
the monk's hand.

'I'm a friend of Vagan's. My companion and I need good strong
horses – he said you'd be the man to help.'

'Aye, that I am,' said Radko, now taking Horskram's hand and
shaking it. 'Always pleased to help a friend of Vagan's. And where
be you from? Down south judging by your accent.'

'I hail from the King's Dominions originally, but my calling
takes me hither and yon. If you'll forgive the impertinence, we are
in something of a hurry – so let's get down to business.'

'Begging your pardon, sirrah, I meant no offence – just making
conversation is all. Yes, let's see now... what are you looking to
spend? Got two of the finest coursers in Efrilund right over here...'

⁜ ⁜ ⁜

The process of selection and haggling was long and painful, for Horskram's slender stock of money also had to cover saddling and fresh provisions for their journey. Eventually they settled on two mangy-looking rouncies. They were far inferior to their old steeds, but they had to hope they would last the long and arduous journey to Rima. Despite their poor quality and Horskram's fierce bargaining, his purse was virtually emptied by the transaction.

'There now, master monk,' said Radko, seeing the grudging look on his face. 'These horses ain't so bad as they look! Fine Northlending stock they are, they'll last a lot longer than some o' them fancy southern breeds. They just 'aven't been kept as well as they should by their last owner, that's all. Feed 'em up nicely with plenty of oats and they'll make out fine in time.'

'If only time were in abundance,' replied Horskram. 'But that's something we're as short of as money! Speaking of which... Adelko! We need to buy two good saddles, and some bags to go with them, then we need oats for the horses and food for ourselves, so let's look lively!'

By the time they returned to Radko's stall they had everything they needed including food for a week, and an empty money pouch.

'I know people we can stay with on the road, so we shan't need money for an inn,' said Horskram as they hurriedly saddled their new horses. 'And if we really need coin we can always take a detour to visit one of the chapters – I should be able to raise some funds if we get really desperate.'

Adelko nodded wordlessly, only half listening. Right then he was just glad that their days of walking cross country were behind them; his knee still stung and his thighs still ached.

They were just about to mount their new steeds when they heard a commotion at the other side of the square. Looking over they could make out a crowd of angry townsfolk clustered around one of the stalls.

Suddenly the flash of cold steel caught the morning light. The townsfolk stepped back to reveal the red-haired warrior from the inn, clutching a sword and flanked by his one-eyed comrade and the two others Adelko had seen. Half a dozen town watchmen were pushing their way through the throng towards the scene. The red-haired brigand barked something at his companions in Norric before all four leapt onto sturdy-looking chargers nearby. Striking up a gallop, they sent the panicked townsfolk scattering as they made for the south road leading out of town.

'Adelko, get your head down!' hissed Horskram as the four riders tore past them. Adelko rapidly did as he was told, and when they looked up the men had gone, leaving dust clouds in their wake.

'Outlanders, causing trouble again,' said Radko, shaking his head. 'Good thing they brought their own horses at least – I shouldn't like to 'ave 'ad any dealings with such rogues!'

Horskram nodded and muttered his assent before turning to address Adelko. 'Stay here. I'm going over to talk to yonder merchants.'

Adelko stared at him, gobsmacked. 'But, I thought you didn't like – '

But Horskram was already jostling his way through the townsfolk, towards the merchants who were busy were doing business with some local traders. Adelko lost sight of him, but presently he returned, declaring flatly: 'That settles that. The merchants and their freeswords are due to leave in an hour. We're travelling with them – there's safety in numbers, and we can't be too careful with such brigands on the road!'

Radko nodded wisely. 'Aye, master monk, quite right – the lawless lands hereabouts are no place for men of the cloth to travel through unguarded. Though I daresay those louts that you plan on joining would cause just as much mischief if they weren't already hired.'

'Indeed,' replied Horskram. 'But at least we'll have one warrior of some integrity with us – Sir Branas of Veerholt and his squire were staying at our inn and will be travelling in our party. I spoke to them just now and advised them of the danger on the road. He's a vassal of the Jarl of Hroghar – he'll keep an eye on our unruly travelling companions, and he should be handy in a fight if any highwaymen make trouble.'

✢ ✢ ✢

An hour later the travelling party assembled in the square and prepared to leave Kaupstad. Many of the pilgrims and travelling artisans had decided to join for their own safety, along with the troubadour who had accompanied the soldiers at the inn.

'Well, Adelko, it seems as though fortuity is on our side today,' said Horskram in a low voice as they nudged their new steeds into a canter alongside the merchants and freeswords. 'Our reckless pursuers seem unable to avoid drawing attention to themselves, and now we may seek security against them without appearing suspicious. If anyone asks where we are bound, tell them we are headed to the Blessed Realm, like yonder pilgrims.'

Adelko blinked in surprise. 'I thought our Order didn't endorse the Pilgrim Wars?'

'It doesn't. But the Sassanians have a long tradition of fine scholarship, and our adepts and journeymen often visit the Pilgrim Kingdoms to hold learned discourse with their sages. It's one of many reasons why the mainstream Temple disapproves of the Argolians. Most temple perfects believe that exchanging knowledge with the followers of the First Prophet is ungodly, although they don't seem to apply that line of thinking to exchanging goods with them. Just after I spoke to the merchants I overheard someone saying our foreign friends had been turned away from the *Journeyman* too – so they must have had to spend the night out of town. Hopefully that means they didn't get a chance to ask around about us, which means that no one in our party, I hope, will know that they are looking for us. We should therefore be able to travel incognito with added security for at least some of our journey.'

'Yes, but what about... the other thing?' Even whispering in broad daylight, Adelko was reluctant to name the horror pursuing them.

Horskram's face was characteristically grim as he replied: 'We must pray to the Almighty that it doesn't come upon us out in the open – I doubt even a host of armed men will avail us much if it does. But no more talk of such things now! Remember what I've told you!'

✣ ✣ ✣

The south road took them out of town into tilled fields and meadows, through which they travelled for an hour or so before being embraced again by the wilderness. During this time Adelko saw peasants hard at work, but if their labours seemed onerous, at least they appeared less oppressed and malnourished than the Wolding peasantry.

Breathing in the fresh spring air he felt the excitement of new adventures and experiences beckoning, though a lingering awareness of the dangers ahead gnawed insidiously at his youthful high spirits.

The merchants rode on well-fed palfreys as befitted their pretensions to high birth; but this illusion was betrayed by their each leading a sumpter laden with goods. Their bodyguards, clad in shabby brigandines and wearing light helms, rode ahead and behind their paymasters in two groups, belted swords within easy reach and shields slung insouciantly across their broad shoulders. The other wayfarers straggled behind on foot along the muddy potholed road. Occasionally some of the pilgrims would break out into holy song, while the craftsmen contented themselves with the occasional muttered exchange.

As befitted his high status, Sir Branas, whom Adelko recognised immediately as the old knight from the inn, rode in front of the party. His squire rode behind him, leading a sumpter laden with weapons and other supplies. At Horskram's indication, he and Adelko joined themselves to these two, the adept riding beside the knight. The two youths found themselves riding next to each other. It wasn't long before the squire struck up a conversation.

'So you're an Argolian friar then?' The way he asked this suggested he wasn't all that impressed.

Undeterred, Adelko replied: 'Yes, although I'm not a journeyman – I'm only a novice. I've been seconded to my master, the most learned Brother Horskram, so I can learn more of the ways of our Order.'

The other youth, who looked to be at least a couple of summers older than him, pursed his lips and nodded perfunctorily. 'Respectable... well, in a manner of speaking. I hear many good things about the Order of St Argo, and other things too.'

'What other things?' Adelko was instantly alert to the squire's implied meaning, recalling his master's words the previous night.

'You're supposed to travel the land, fighting evil spirits and suchlike, aren't you?' said the squire, not really answering Adelko's question. 'That's all well and good, but I'm only interested in fighting things of flesh and blood.'

Adelko wasn't sure he liked the way the squire said this. 'I suppose you're training to be a knight then?' he asked, persevering.

The squires eyes suddenly lit up. 'That's right – someday I'll be a great knight too! Bards and troubadours will sing songs of my deeds, and I'll have a host of men at my beck and call! Can you say the same?'

'Er, not really...' replied Adelko, somewhat confused. 'It doesn't quite work like that. You see – '

'Anyway, what's your name?' asked the squire, cutting him off. 'Mine's Vaskrian of Hroghar – mind you remember it, it'll be known throughout the land someday.'

'I'm Adelko... Adelko of Narvik.' Even now using his birthplace as an honorific struck the novice as a strange custom. In the Highlands noble clansmen used patronymics, taking their fathers' names; commoners like him simply used the family trade as a surname, if they bothered with surnames at all.

'We're going to Harrang,' Vaskrian continued. 'There's a big tournament there, every year. There's jousting and feasting, and then they have a melee.'

'A melee? What's that – you mean, like a big fight?'

The squire laughed. 'Yes, if you want to put it that way – like a battle. Only, it's not a real battle, I mean people do get hurt but you're not supposed to kill anyone. Although that does happen, of course.'

'That sounds horrible,' said Adelko. Of late the idea of being a fighting man, even a titled one, had begun to appeal to him much less than it had in his childhood dreams.

Vaskrian looked at him with contempt before replying: 'No, it's not – it's wonderful! It gives squires of – squires like me a chance to hone their fighting skills. And if you knock anyone off their horse or best them in combat, you get paid. I won five silver marks for each man I bested last year.'

'Oh... is that a lot?'

Vaskrian frowned. 'Not really – not compared to what you get if you vanquish a knight. But I can't fight them yet – I'm not allowed to until I've been dubbed myself.'

Something in the downcast way the squire said this made Adelko feel a little more kindly disposed towards him – perhaps there was more to his bombastic bearing than met the eye.

'How long does it take to become a knight?' he asked, following the thread. 'Is there a test you have to pass? We have to pass lots of tests to become journeymen of the Order – in fact that's why I'm travelling with Master Horskram. A good Argolian has to confront the entities of the Other Side first hand to be fully initiated – it's not all books and learning if that's what you're thinking, although there's plenty of that too!'

Vaskrian's face grew longer. 'To become a knight takes courage on the field of battle, and skill at arms – and you have to be a good horseman too. I've got all of those things.'

'So... why do you look so sad?' Adelko was genuinely puzzled. The squire's demeanour seemed to have swung from exultant arrogance to sullen bitterness in the blinking of an eye.

'Never you mind,' he replied sulkily. Changing the subject he asked: 'Have you been in Efrilund before?'

Adelko shook his head. 'No, this is the furthest south I've ever been.'

Vaskrian gestured expansively. 'These lands are ruled by Lord Fenrig, Jarl of Hroghar, whom I serve.'

At this Sir Branas turned in the saddle and said testily: 'No, young Vaskrian, *I* serve Lord Fenrig. You serve *me*, and don't you forget it! You should know better than to try and foist your delusions of grandeur on a learned member of the Order.'

The old knight harrumphed loudly and turned back to continue his conversation with Horskram, leaving his chastened squire flushing a deep red.

Taking pity on him, Adelko did his best to keep the conversation going. 'So does Lord Fenrig rule all of Efrilund then?'

'No,' said Vaskrian, shaking his head. 'Just the northern part we're in now. In a couple of days we should reach Lake Sördegil. All the lands west of that as far as the mountains are ruled by Vymar, Jarl of Harrang. All the lands east of the lake as far as the sea are the domains of Lord Aesgir. I don't know much about that part of the country, because to get there from Hroghar you'd have to cross the Ferren Marshes, and no one goes there because they're haunted. Job for you and your guvnor, right there!'

Now it was Adelko's turn to frown. 'It doesn't quite work like that,' he explained. 'We can't rid whole areas of ghosts or evil spirits just like that! If we could we'd have done it long since!'

Vaskrian shrugged. 'Suppose you've got a point. Can't win all the battles in a day, eh?'

✤ ✤ ✤

The way was slow, the road being almost as full of potholes as the one they had taken into Kaupstad, and they did not reach Lake Sördegil until the sun was lowering in the sky on their second day out of town.

The road ascended a bank of ridges affording them spectacular first views of its glassy green surface. From there they could see the Ferren River pouring its waters from the east into the lake's long shallow basin. On the west bank the Laegawood stretched as far as the eye could see, closely hugging the still waters. The road dipped down and curved towards its verdant depths, slowly losing their lustre in the dying rays of sunlight.

The wayfarers had not travelled long beneath its gloomy eaves before they came upon a clearing lying off the road to their left. The grassy sward stretched level for a distance of some twenty yards before dipping down at a shallow gradient to meet the western edge of the lake's northernmost tip. All agreed to camp there for the night as the deepening dusk robbed the lands about them of shape and colour.

Distributing themselves about the clearing the assembled company found their several spots and unfurled sleeping pallets. Vaskrian and Branas pitched their tent next to the monks' pallets, the old knight's pennant flapping listlessly in the gentle evening breeze. A group of craftsmen had already gone off to forage for firewood. Presently they returned and soon had a merry blaze going to augment the light of lanterns lit by Horskram and Vaskrian.

Frowning and shaking his head the adept went over to remonstrate, warning them against drawing too much attention to themselves and exhorting them to make do with lantern light instead, but he was shouted down by one and all, for the night was cold and the overconfident bodyguards scornfully dared any roving brigands to try their luck.

Muttering to himself the old monk stomped back over to his pallet. Glancing over at the merchants awkwardly sitting down on their own pallets to sup, Adelko was surprised to see that they hadn't brought tents like the old knight – until he realised that these would have further burdened their horses, depriving them of the opportunity to carry more wares.

He had to smile at the ironic thought of their innate greed compelling them to endure the very hardships they strived so hard to elevate themselves above.

Gazing across the lake, which had begun dully to reflect the emerging stars, he felt a familiar sense of unease return to him.

The marshes lay on the other side, and though he could not see them he fancied he sensed the troubled shades of that haunted fenland stirring in the dark beyond its deceptively calm waters.

Vaskrian went off to fetch water. Taking up a tin pot they had bought at the market, Adelko accompanied him. The air was chillier down by the edge of the lake. Overhead the full moon glared at them with ominous portent. Adelko muttered a prayer as they gathered up water. Vaskrian hummed a tune with a carefree cheer that he envied.

The pair of them were just about to turn around and head back up the rock-strewn slope when they heard it: the sound of breaking wood, followed by a muffled noise that could have been a low voice or an animal call.

'What was that?!' hissed Adelko in a loud whisper.

'I'm not sure,' replied Vaskrian. The two listened together in silence. What sounded like something retreating back through the woods could be briefly discerned for a few moments. Then it was gone.

Adelko turned to look the squire. 'Did you hear that?'

Vaskrian nodded. 'Could have been anything though – there are plenty of deer in these woods. Let's get back to the camp.'

They found most of the travellers gathered around the fire. The wandering minstrel had brought out his lute again; he and some of the freeswords began to strike up a song while the rest took their evening meal. The four companions, sat together a little apart from the others, set about their own supper, Vaskrian first preparing his master's meal while the two monks sat down beneath their lantern, which Horskram had slung over the pommel of his horse's saddle.

Glancing at the rest of the party disparagingly the adept frowned again, muttering in between mouthfuls: 'Those churls know no restraint. If highwaymen are in the area they should certainly have no trouble finding us! I'm beginning to think this wasn't such a good idea after all.'

Adelko exchanged a meaningful glance with Vaskrian before speaking up. 'Master Horskram – when we were down by the lake getting water... we heard something in the trees to the south! What if it was one of them?'

'It may well have been, so don't go wandering off! We need to stick together – if they are in the area we've a better chance in numbers, even with allies such as these.'

'Aye,' said Sir Branas. 'I like this no more than you, master monk – yon churlish louts are more trouble than they're worth! But have no fear – we'll not be found wanting if those brigands try to surprise us. Vaskrian, keep your blade handy!'

The old knight loosened his sword in its scabbard. Vaskrian leaped energetically to his feet and went over to their horses, bringing back his master's shield and a buckler for himself. Placing them on the ground next to both of them he fingered the hilt of his own sword and said in a breathless voice: 'I'm ready.'

Adelko wondered at his new friend's excitement – the prospect of being attacked hardly seemed like much fun to him.

Finishing their supper the four travellers sat together in tense silence while the other travellers revelled. Once only did Sir Branas approach them to remind them of the danger and admonish them for their carelessness, but nobody listened. As an afterthought Horskram covered his lantern, Vaskrian following suit and plunging them into darkness on the edge of the firelight.

Their foresight proved well founded. Not long after, an artisan who had gone to relieve himself at the edge of the clearing came yelling and running back to the campfire.

'It's them! They're in the – ' He fell to the ground in mid-sentence, a crossbow bolt buried in his back.

Just then a hail of quarrels swept across the clearing from the trees on either side of the entrance. Three mercenaries fell to the ground screaming and did not get up again. A fourth quarrel whistled past the shoulder of another and buried itself in the face of one of the merchants, who had risen to his feet on hearing the artisan yell. With a cry he fell backwards into the fire, his body convulsing horribly. Two other mercenaries went down injured; the rest of the bolts missed their mark.

Panic broke out in the clearing, with pilgrims and artisans running to and fro like headless chickens. Some had enough presence of mind to flee back towards the road; others ran into the woods, where their cries soon told of their grim fate.

The remaining seven bodyguards grabbed shields and drew swords, forming a close circle around the remaining three merchants, who hugged each other and trembled. Vaskrian and Branas were likewise prepared for combat, while Horskram gripped his quarterstaff with firm hands as he tried to discern their foes in the flickering firelight.

'They're over to either side of the entrance of the clearing!' growled the knight. 'They're staying put – they'd sooner shoot us all than square up to us in a fair fight, the craven dogs!'

'Let's charge them!' cried Vaskrian. 'We'll soon flush them out!'

'Don't be a fool!' snarled Branas. 'We've no idea how many they are – they'll cut us down like cornstalks if we do that! Hold your ground!'

No sooner had he spoken than another volley strafed the clearing. This time the bodyguards, crouched down behind their broad shields, were prepared, although their two wounded comrades were mercilessly despatched, along with several pilgrims and artisans who had not managed to flee the clearing.

The four companions must have been visible at the edge of the fire's glow, because two of the quarrels were aimed at them: one whistled past Adelko's head while the other buried itself in Sir Branas's shield.

At this a dark rage suffused the veteran's features, and in a stentorian voice he yelled across the clearing: 'Craven dogs! Are you too afraid to face us in mortal combat, like true men? Is this how the feeble warrior class of the barbarian wastes makes war? I've seen more courage in women!'

His proud words must have struck a nerve, because a few moments later a dozen brigands rushed into the clearing. They had discarded their crossbows for swords, axes and shields, which together with their mail shirts glinted menacingly in the light of fire fuelled by charring flesh.

With a roar Vaskrian and Branas charged. The bodyguards, naturally assuming that their paymasters' booty was the prime target of the assault, broke their defensive formation to meet their foes hand to hand, and soon the night air was ringing with the sound of clashing steel and angry war cries.

Horskram cursed. 'They're outnumbered, I have to help,' he said to Adelko. 'Stay here – don't get involved! If any of them come at you, mount your horse and ride!'

Without another word he sprang forwards to join the fray.

⁜ ⁜ ⁜

Vaskrian squared off against a brigand wielding an axe and a shield. He was hugely strong, and for a while he pressed the squire hard with fierce strokes. But Vaskrian was light on his feet, and wielded his blade with a disciplined precision unknown in the Frozen Wastes. He stayed on the defensive, luring his opponent into making one stroke too many. Then, nimbly sidestepping the last sweep of the brigand's axe, he stepped in, lunging downwards with the point of his blade above the top of his opponent's shield. It was an unorthodox move his father had taught him, and caught his assailant unawares – the life went out of him with a gurgling cry as Vaskrian's sword pierced his throat.

He turned and saw Branas cut down another brigand who fell screaming in a rain of blood, his skull cloven in twain.

'Sir Branas, watch out!' he yelled, as the red-haired leader charged the old knight from behind. Whirling around, Branas parried his deadly stroke just in time, forcing him back as he launched a counter-offensive.

⁜ ⁜ ⁜

Feeling utterly useless, Adelko watched with his heart in his mouth as a Northlander hacked at his master frenziedly. He was a sneering brute who clearly thought a monk easy fodder for his axe. But the doughty adept stood his ground firmly, parrying his crude strokes easily with his iron-shod quarterstaff before ducking under another swing and knocking him senseless with a lightning stroke to the head.

But even so the fortunes of war were not with them, for the remaining brigands had got the better of the freeswords. Two more lay mortally wounded, and the remaining five were hard pressed.

Adelko felt his innards clench as one of the barbarians, the hulking one-eyed brute, spotted him. With an evil leer he bounded across the clearing towards him. Terrified, Adelko clutched his quarterstaff and tried to remember everything Udo had taught him. With a nerve borne of desperation he managed to parry the Northlander's opening salvo of sword-strokes. His arms shuddered painfully with every blow. Stepping back beneath the onslaught he saw his young life flash before his eyes...

Bellowing a war cry, Vaskrian came at the one-eyed brigand from behind. The Northlander turned and parried the blow, hitting back ferociously and breaking the squire's buckler with a single fierce stroke.

The force of the blow brought Vaskrian to his knees but he was quick to react. Lunging upwards he would have disembowelled the brigand were it not for his mail shirt. Gripping his quarterstaff Adelko aimed downwards at the back of the brigand's head but missed, instead catching him a glancing blow on the shoulder. Lashing out with his foot, the one-eyed Northlander kicked Vaskrian in the chest, sending him flying back to sprawl winded on the ground. Turning back to face Adelko with a snarl he was about to renew his onslaught when Horskram engaged him.

And then suddenly there it was. The sound that Adelko now feared would haunt them forever returned, approaching steadily across the lake. For a surreal moment everyone in the clearing ceased fighting, breaking off to stare fearfully into the blackened firmament.

Horskram was the first to recover his wits. With a low swipe of his quarterstaff he struck the one-eyed brigand hard across the knee, bringing him low.

Turning to Adelko he cried: 'Make for the horses, now! We cannot fight what approaches!' Repeating the command to the other two he bounded over to the horses.

The two warriors would probably have paid him no heed, but at that moment one of the merchants screamed and began tearing at his beard.

Following his terrified gaze Adelko saw a ghastly silhouette against the moon, growing steadily larger as it approached on giant membranous wings that seemed to trap the pale light. Its body appeared to be tubular, like a giant eel's, tapering into a wickedly sharp tail that swished menacingly behind it. It was still mercifully too far away to make out in any more detail but everything about the thing screamed defiance of the natural world.

One of the younger freeswords dropped his sword and fell to his knees, retching. The others backed away, fearfully making the sign and imploring the Redeemer to save them. The brigand leader yelled something in his tongue to the others, and quick as a flash they fled back into the woods.

Reaching their horses, Horskram and Adelko mounted. Shrugging off their terror with some difficulty Vaskrian and Branas followed suit.

Spurring his horse into a gallop Horskram yelled: 'Back towards the road! Follow me!'

As he rode the adept uncovered his lantern with his free hand. The other three followed the bobbing light through the darkness as it swung madly from the saddle.

Rejoining the main road they tore along it, plunging deeper into the Laegawood. Of the brigands and their own horses there was no sign. With a hybrid shriek the nightmarish thing careened after them.

Though the overhanging branches of the trees prevented it from descending to attack them, their diabolical pursuer was not quite bereft of ways to hurt them. Something wet and viscous flew past Horskram: landing on the path it sizzled and hissed, emitting an acrid smoke that made Adelko gag as he rode in his master's wake.

The winged devil pursued them above the trees for a while, spitting vile gobbets of unearthly sputum at them through the branches, which burned and sloughed pitifully at its awful touch.

Presently the canopy became more densely clustered, mercifully obscuring them from the terrible creature's view. At Horskram's signal they all pulled up on the darkened road. The thing's hideous shrieks grew fainter as it flew onwards, before growing louder again. Soon it could be heard circling above the trees that now concealed them.

'We need to stay under cover of the foliage,' said Horskram, his voice tinged with urgency. Glancing off to the right of the road, they could see the forested land dipped down at a steep incline. They dismounted, dragging their frightened steeds between the trees and down into the undergrowth. By Horskram's lantern light they found a dell clotted with briars and bushes in which to spend an uncomfortable night. But better uncomfortable than dead. Glancing furtively upwards at the thickly clustered branches, the monk dimmed his lantern. Gradually the demon's awful voice receded into silence again.

'We should be safe here,' he said in a soft voice. 'Yonder thing cannot see through the natural world, though darkness impairs it not. Let's tether our horses and rest awhile.'

'What in Reus' name was that?' Branas's face was cold with horror, while Vaskrian appeared too stunned to speak.

'A demon of the netherworld,' replied Horskram. 'Sent to pursue us by an unknown foe. A fortnight ago my novice and I learned of a calamitous theft, one which could have grave consequences if its perpetrator goes unchecked. I believe that perpetrator is now trying to eliminate us so we cannot warn anyone.'

Branas peered at Horskram in the subdued lantern light. 'Theft? What theft? You speak in riddles, master monk! What thief could conjure up such horrors?'

'I am not at liberty to disclose such details until I've had a chance to speak to the head of my Order in Rima. Until then, suffice to say that we are in grave danger, for I believe that the brigands we fought just now were also sent after us.'

The old knight's eyes widened. 'You mentioned nothing of this when I spoke to you on the road! Are you saying that you are the cause of all this trouble?'

'Not the cause, more like the catalyst.'

Branas stared at him again in bafflement.

'Never mind,' resumed the friar. 'I had hoped that we would not have to deal with both problems at once – that is why I thought it best to travel incognito in a larger party, for safety. If we'd set out from Kaupstad alone we would have been outnumbered by the Northlanders, our fate sealed. But against a creature of Gehenna only the combined powers of my Order can prevail, and unfortunately I cannot alert them until I have spoken to the Grand Master in person.'

'But... Rima's hundreds of miles away!' the old knight protested. 'How do you expect to survive such a journey?'

'Yes, well,' said Horskram, smiling grimly in the half-dark, 'that is a question I have been asking myself for some time now.'

'Well that settles it,' said the veteran. 'We must go back to Hroghar and tell my liege of this – he'll be able to help.'

Horskram shook his head fiercely. 'No! As you love the Redeemer, I implore you, make no mention of this to anyone! Tomorrow Adelko and I will continue our journey – once we go our separate ways you should both be safe. The only reason why you were attacked was because you were with us – it grieves me to have brought such danger on you all, but I'd hoped that our freesword friends would prove less careless and our enemies less cunning.

The noise Adelko and Vaskrian heard earlier must have been a scout, sent to espy our position. I warned those fools not to make a fire!'

'If they were otherwise good in life, the Redeemer will forgive their sins in the heavenly halls,' replied Branas, making the sign. 'But if you insist on continuing your daredevil mission, at least you shall not do so alone. We'll come with you as far as the Vorstlending border – your journey through Northalde shall not be without trusty swords to accompany you!'

Vaskrian suddenly came to his senses. 'But, Sir Branas, what about the tourney at Harrang?' he asked, now looking more downcast than horrified.

The old worthy sighed and shook his head. 'I've lived long enough to know a good cause when I see one. There'll be plenty more tournaments – but this smacks to me of a quest.' A glint came into his eye. 'It's been a long while since I took a period of errantry. Besides, Vaskrian, you seem to be forgetting that we left our pack horse behind in our haste. I doubt much will be there tomorrow morning – if yon brigands don't return to steal it, those churlish mercenaries certainly will! I can't very well turn up at Harrang without spears to joust with, a tent to pitch or a pennant to proclaim my coat of arms, can I? It simply wouldn't do.'

Horskram was shaking his head impatiently. 'Sir knight, your offer is a worthy one and denotes a stout heart – but I cannot put you in such danger. We have imperilled you enough already.'

But Branas would not hear of it, and settled the matter promptly by swearing an oath on the spot to accompany the two monks as far as the Argael Forest on the southern fringes of Northalde.

Horskram sighed. 'Well, if you are resolved in this, I cannot but accept your offer gratefully – while warning you again of the grave dangers to which you expose yourself.' It seemed to Adelko as if his master was secretly glad of the help, however much he had tried to refuse it.

'Hah!' said the old knight with some cheer. 'Grave dangers are meat and drink to a knight errant! Now, I'd suggest we all try and get some rest – and pray that thing doesn't come back tonight!'

✥ ✥ ✥

The four of them settled down as best they could in the overgrown dell. Mulling over the night's extraordinary events, Vaskrian felt his spirits rise again. It was really a shame to miss the tournament at Harrang, but there were compensations... Squire to a knight errant on a dangerous quest – that didn't sound too bad at all. If only Rutgar could see him now!

⇌ CHAPTER XV ⇌

From One Danger To Another

The bloodstained clearing told an even unhappier story than they had expected. All the supplies they had left behind had been taken or despoiled. Branas's sumpter was also gone. His tent had been cut to ribbons and lay in tatters on the bloody grass alongside his torn and broken standard. Seeing this Vaskrian groaned inwardly: that would put his guvnor in a foul mood and no mistake.

Among the scattered corpses of slain pilgrims and craftsmen they found the bloodstained bodies of all ten freeswords and the four merchants heaped in a grisly pile. Some were transfixed by quarrels, others had been butchered at close range by the returning brigands. The bodies of the three Northlanders had vanished.

'Those ungodly curs!' roared Sir Branas. 'Look what they did to my coat of arms! Reus willing, I'll soon have a reckoning with those dogs! At least we slew three of them.'

'Two,' corrected Horskram. 'My blow was not lethal. Doubtless my erstwhile opponent will recover presently, although he may find that his wits are addled and his head aches for some time.'

'Well that only leaves ten of them,' said Vaskrian. Excited by his new adventure, he felt full of confidence. 'With one of them injured at least. We're not that badly outnumbered!'

His guvnor had to smile at this, but the old monk stared at him incredulously before shaking his head wearily. His novice looked frightened.

But then that's why they'd sworn an oath to protect them. Let the monks do the praying – Vaskrian was more than happy to take on enough fighting for two. Or three, come to that.

Resignedly they salvaged what they could in the way of food, an unappetising task amid the flies and crows that had already begun to feast on the bodies of the dead. Branas's lamp lay smashed, his spears broken. The Northland brigands had done their work thoroughly.

'Adelko and I didn't lose any of our food and I still have my lantern,' said Horskram. 'We should have enough supplies to last a while but one thing we do lack is money.'

'Have no fear there,' replied the old knight, patting a small saddle bag on his charger. 'I'd know better than to keep mine anywhere else but handy – provide for us now and I'll see to it that we amply repay the compliment when we reach the next market town.'

'That may be later than you think,' said Horskram. 'We should try to avoid the main road for a while.'

'But what about all these poor people?' interjected Adelko. 'We can't just leave them here unburied!'

The adept placed a hand on Adelko's shoulder and shook his head sadly. 'We have no choice, I'm afraid. Our mission is of paramount importance and we've already taken a risk in returning here. But let us intone a blessing for their souls now – this spot is often used by wayfarers, it won't be long before word is sent to the nearest village, especially if some of those poor fellows managed to escape. Lord Vymar of Harrang will send men to bury them, so have no fear!'

Vaskrian stared distractedly across the lake as Horskram led his novice in a prayer for the souls of the departed. Its glossy sheen underpinned the ridges south of the marshlands with a stark beauty. It certainly made for a contrast with the scene of carnage in the clearing. Against the cloudy skies a flock of birds wheeled and carped across the still waters. He hoped they weren't ravens, he'd heard they were meant to be bad luck.

Thinking on the horror that had come at them from that direction, he suppressed a shudder and turned back to face the corpse-strewn clearing. Corpses he didn't mind – workaday butchery he could understand.

✛ ✛ ✛

Returning to the main road they retraced their steps, passing the dell where they had spent a sleepless night made even more uncomfortable by the returning cries of the demon as it searched for them relentlessly.

They spent the rest of the day following the south road through the forest. Although its verdant depths seemed pleasant enough, Adelko began to wonder if they would be forced to spend the rest of their lives hiding under trees, and a longing for the open country of his highland home grew steadily within him.

Towards dusk they veered off in a south-westerly direction, Horskram's intention being to break cover of the woods the following day and rejoin the highway south of Harrang.

The sun was low in the skies when they heard the sound of coarse singing filtering through the leaves. Horskram and Branas exchanged glances.

'That'll be forest folk,' said the old knight. 'The Jarl of Harrang is a generous liege, and permits them to hunt deer on certain days of the week. No doubt they'll be cooking up a fine feast in yonder clearing – we should go and join them!'

The adept shook his head firmly. 'No, we must stay under cover. I've already brought enough ruin on innocent people, though Reus knows it wasn't my intention! Let's get off the path – I'm sure we can find another overgrown nook in which to enjoy a good night's rest.'

Horskram's irony brought little cheer to the weary travellers, who complied with heavy hearts.

'I don't know about you, but this business of errantry isn't all it's made out to be!' Vaskrian muttered to Adelko as they dismounted and led their steeds deeper into the hoary bosom of the forest. 'I don't remember hearing the troubadours singing about cramped forest floors and wormy biscuit for supper in the *Lays of King Vasirius!*'

'Me neither!' replied the novice in a low voice so their masters couldn't hear. 'Then again, I've read most of them, and they do mention a lot of stuff about "enduring the privations of a harsh wilderness" and so on.'

'I suppose so,' said Vaskrian. 'Enduring hardship is a knightly virtue, it's true – it's just not nearly as much fun as the others, like fighting and feasting!'

'I don't know that I care much for the first one,' said Adelko, 'but I certainly miss the latter! I'd give anything to be sitting down to supper in the refectory at Ulfang!'

'Mmm, Lord Fenrig's feasting hall at Hroghar would be a nice place to be right now too!' grinned the squire.

The two of them spent the evening swapping tales of home and the places they had seen. It lightened their hearts a little. Presently a fire could be discerned in the clearing occupied by the huntsmen, who went on singing till well after dark before retiring. Uncomfortable as they were amid the tangled undergrowth of the forest, the weary companions soon drifted off to sleep.

✢ ✢ ✢

Mercifully, that night it was untroubled. Emerging from the forest at around noon the next day they found themselves gazing upon lush countryside. Striking up a gallop they passed through meadows and fields dotted with well-kept hamlets and manor houses: Lord Vymar was loyal to the King's Law and ruled his prosperous domains with a firm but even hand.

Seeking shelter for the night at a priory known to him, Horskram was forced to lie again about their real reason for travelling. Thankfully the old perfect who presided over that parish was a gentle soul, sympathetic to the Argolian Order and clearly too in awe of the adept's reputation to ask many questions.

They rejoined the highway around mid-morning of the following day. Taking this south they soon encountered other wayfarers travelling in both directions. Vaskrian sighed regretfully every time they passed a haughty knight heading north to the tournament at Harrang, riding at leisure before a liveried squire.

Occasionally Sir Branas would exclaim: 'See that knight there, that we just passed? I bested him in the lists, some years ago – I'd do it again this week if I had the chance!'

'I can't help but notice that he never seems to point out any knights who've beaten *him*,' muttered Adelko to Vaskrian as they slowed their horses to navigate a rough patch of road.

The squire glanced over his shoulder at Adelko with a wry grin. 'Oh no,' he answered. 'That would *never* do! Haven't I taught you anything of the ways of chivalry by now?'

The two youths chuckled as they picked up the pace again. High spirits seemed to be in short supply, and it felt good to share a joke.

✣ ✣ ✣

A few hours later they stopped to eat and rest their horses. The water they had taken from the lake was nearly spent, so they replenished their skins from a nearby stream.

'We should reach the River Rymold in an hour,' said Horskram, gazing across the meadowed plains. 'When we cross over, we'll be in the King's Dominions. That should afford us better protection against the brigands that pursue us, for those lands are guarded closely by the Knights of the White Valravyn.'

Vaskrian felt his heart skip a beat as Horskram mentioned the doughty warriors sworn to uphold the King's Justice. He had only laid eyes on them once before, when his master had gone tourneying across the Rymold last summer. Linden was the greatest tournament he had been to, and more than five hundred brave knights had competed there for the castellan's daughter's hand in marriage and a hundred gold sovereigns.

Needless to say, Sir Branas hadn't won first prize, although he'd secured his fair share of booty in the melee. Vaskrian hadn't done too badly either, unhorsing a couple of squires and claiming his modest share of prize money. Since that time he had dreamed endlessly of one day winning the grand event.

The actual victor, Sir Torgun of Vandheim, had caused some controversy by graciously but firmly refusing the castellan's daughter, explaining that he was beholden to another lady for whose love he had entered the joust. He had donated the prize money to the White Valravyn, according to the rules of the Order.

When Vaskrian related all this breathlessly to Adelko, the novice nodded slowly before asking: 'So... who's Torgun of Vandheim?'

Honestly – these monks, didn't they know anything about the real world?

'Only the greatest knight in the realm!' he spluttered. 'Don't you get any news up north? He's been making a real stir at court – some even say he's the mightiest warrior in the whole of the Free Kingdoms, except maybe Sir Azelin of Valacia – you do know who *he* is, don't you?'

Adelko rolled his eyes. 'Of course – he's the Pangonian knight who slew the last of the Wyrms and went off to the Pilgrim Wars, even I know that! He joined the Knights Bethler and donated all his lands to the Holy Order, didn't he?'

Vaskrian frowned. They were getting off the subject and away from his story. 'Yes, well never mind him,' he said, 'no one in the Free Kingdoms has seen or heard from him since he left for the Blessed Realm years ago. But I tell you, Sir Torgun is a true hero – he'd never forsake his country to fight some foreign crusade! That's why he joined the Order of the White Valravyn – they've all sworn an oath to protect the Kings' Dominions, no brigands will be a match for them, you'll see!'

The novice didn't look entirely convinced. How naïve was he?

'They say Torgun's never been knocked off his horse,' persisted Vaskrian, trying to inspire some courage in his new companion. 'He's jousted against hundreds of knights, and no one's ever beaten him! I watched all his matches when I was at Linden – he was amazing! When he beat Sir Brogun of Dantor in the final I was right up at the front of the crowd, cheering with the rest of them – he looked over, and I swear he caught my eye and smiled! I took that as an omen, right then and there – some day I'd be a true knight and famous, just like him!'

The young monk simply stared at him. Vaskrian rolled his eyes and shook his head as Horskram and Branas called for them to remount and continue their journey. There was no talking to these Argolians about anything interesting – it was all spirits and scripture with them.

✠ ✠ ✠

Presently they reached the Rymold. It was a mighty river, twice as broad as the Warryn. Further east beyond their view barges would be plying their trade to and fro, carrying goods brought across the sea from the Empire and Vorstlund to the bustling riverside towns of the northern reaches of the King's Dominions. The river was forded by a triple-arched bridge of grey stone, built during the reign of King Wulfraed I, founder of the ruling House of Ingwin. On the north side was a small guard tower manned by sentries dressed in mail hauberks and armed with spears and shields. From the roof of the tower the King's standard stood as it had done for nearly two hundred years, proudly displaying the white unicorns of the Ruling House.

Approaching the sentries at a canter the four travellers pulled up before them as Horskram declared their names.

'And what business brings you to the King's land, may I enquire?' asked the serjeant-at-arms, clearly noting their unusually dishevelled appearance.

'Our travelling party was attacked by brigands three nights ago up in the Laegawood,' replied Horskram. 'Many were slain, and we were lucky to escape with our lives. We have sent word to the Jarl of Harrang that his lands are despoiled by depredators, and now hope to seek safety in His Majesty's demesnes.'

'Brigands, you say?' replied the serjeant in an unruffled tone of voice. 'Well that's the upperlands for you – though you may not find the safety you seek down south. Where are you travelling to, if you don't mind my asking, sire?'

'My novice and I are travelling to the Blessed Realm – this worthy knight and his squire have elected to accompany us as far as Linden Castle, where he plans to visit an old friend in the castellan's service.'

Horskram broke off and held his peace. The serjeant turned a squint-eyed glance expectantly in the old knight's direction.

'Ahem, that's right,' said the latter somewhat awkwardly. 'Might well have a word with the castellan about sending a few of his men across the Rymold too, while I'm there – the northern roads are clearly not safe!'

The serjeant smiled crookedly at this. 'I doubt you'll succeed in persuading him, sire – the way things are looking he'll soon be needing all the men he can muster. Have you not heard there's war brewing down south?'

Horskram and Branas exchanged bemused glances before looking at the serjeant and shaking their heads. 'Aye, the southern provinces are at it again,' continued the sentry. 'They say that Kanga's heir has been stirring up fresh talk of secession, and he's got the rest of the southern provinces behind him. You'd think the fools would have learned their lesson last time.'

Horskram's eyes widened in surprise. 'Krulheim?' he exclaimed. 'You mean Krulheim, the new Jarl of Thule? He's leading another separatist revolt? That is ill news indeed.'

'Pah, the King should have slaughtered him when he had the chance!' snarled Sir Branas. 'I always said no good would come of such a merciful deed!'

'Every virtue has its price, as the Redeemer sayeth, and mercy is foremost among the virtues,' replied Horskram sadly. 'We had best be getting along – before more ill tidings catch up with us!'

They crossed the bridge in thoughtful silence. All about them sprawled the tidy farmsteads of the King's Dominions, their abundant fields, well-kept copses and sturdy huts testifying to a land that had enjoyed years of peace and prosperity. Adelko wondered if all that would soon be reversed by the misfortunes of war. On the western horizon the Hyrkrainians sprawled languidly, their indifferent peaks wreathed in ephemeral clouds.

Presently he gave voice to his less gloomy thoughts. 'At least we should be safe from the brigands now? After all, they won't get past those sentries will they?'

'Unfortunately they might,' replied Horskram, unsmiling. 'The Rymold Bridge guardhouse is really just a formality – the King has never had much reason to fear attack from the loyalist provinces directly to the north. There's another bridge ten miles east – it used to be guarded many years ago, but not any more. As we've just established, Freidheim fears an assault from the southlands more than anything, and that's where most of his defences are concentrated. Plus if there's war brewing in that direction the knights of the White Valravyn will be less likely to be patrolling the northern reaches of the Dominions. So even on royal land we are not safe, it seems.'

Everyone lapsed back into silence after that. Clouds began gradually to thicken and condense across the blue skies, heightening their sense of foreboding. The highway snaked on relentlessly, and an encroaching shadow appeared on the horizon to their right, blotting out the distant mountain ranges.

As they drew nearer, Adelko noticed that the tilled and arable land dropped off sharply, the well-tended fields of wheat and barley abruptly giving way to a sparse unkempt wilderness. Presently they could see it more clearly: the dark clusters of thick oaks that now lined the western horizon seemed to suck the light from the failing skies above, intensifying the bleakness of the strangely barren lands they now found themselves in.

Adelko felt his trepidation increase as he realised it was no ordinary woodland they were skirting. The haunted eaves of Tintagael seemed every bit as spooky as his mentor had led him to believe they were.

Glancing over at its lightless depths Sir Branas made the sign and muttered: 'Tintagael Forest! A cursed place if ever I saw one! I wouldn't be surprised if yon fiend pursuing us was spawned in such a place!'

'Do not speak of such things here!' exclaimed Horskram, his voice flaring angrily.

At that moment they heard a sound they had all been half expecting. Wheeling their horses around they saw five horsemen hurtling towards them across the plains from the north-east. Their exultant war whoops seemed to hang heavy in the air.

Sir Branas drew his sword. 'There's only five – we can take them!' he growled. Vaskrian unsheathed his own blade, a look of relish on his face. Horskram sat still in the saddle, clearly undecided whether to flee or fight. Adelko looked from him to the approaching brigands fearfully.

As they drew nearer they unleashed a volley, gripping their steeds with their legs whilst using both hands to fire their crossbows. Though still too far away to aim well, a couple of quarrels nearly found their mark – one bolt passed through the side of Horskram's habit while another glanced off Branas's mailed shoulder.

That seemed to galvanise the adept into action. 'We must charge them now, before they can reload!' he yelled.

'Wait, there's more!' cried Adelko, pointing south. 'They're coming at us from two directions!' Five more riders were tearing up the highway towards them.

'In Reus' name, how did they get so far ahead of us?' exclaimed Sir Branas. 'I thought they had to detour!'

'They must have ridden through the night!' said Horskram. 'Those foreign devils must be as hardy as Wadwos!'

'We can take them anyway!' yelled Vaskrian, although even he now sounded uncertain.

'Don't be a fool!' snarled Horskram. 'We're outnumbered more than two to one – and one of us barely knows how to fight! We must flee into the forest – they won't dare chase us in there!'

'Tintagael?' Branas stared at him with bulging eyes. 'You're mad – no one who goes in there ever comes back! It'll surely be the death of us!'

'It'll be the death of us if we don't!' cried Horskram, turning and spurring his horse towards the dark line of trees. 'They've got us cut off – we've no choice! Fly! Fly for the forest!'

As if to emphasise his words, another volley of quarrels flew past them, this time fired by the second group of brigands. Cursing, Branas kicked his charger into a gallop, the two youths following suit.

As the four of them rode hell for leather towards Tintagael both parties of Northlanders converged in hot pursuit. They had abandoned their crossbows and were now brandishing swords and axes above their heads and yelling fearfully. The berserker rage of their ancestors was in them, all thoughts of reward subsumed by sheer bloodlust.

But of this Adelko registered little, for his perception was all but consumed by the growing horizon of Tintagael, which rather than see he seemed to sense as an expanding presence in his consciousness. From somewhere in the deepest recesses of his mind he fancied he could hear thousands of voices whispering to him, their susurration drowning out the thundering of his panting horse's hooves.

A sense of rising panic gripped him, and just then he imagined he felt the long grass of the plains drop away from him at a breakneck pace. He was looking down at four tiny figures on horseback, riding desperately towards a forest that stretched for leagues without number. It suddenly occurred to him that there was no path by which they could enter.

As if answering this unspoken thought the foremost trees suddenly pulled apart, their boles bending impossibly. With an unearthly flash of green light, the four horsemen were swallowed up by the forest, and the trees closed behind them.

PART TWO

⇥ CHAPTER I ⇤

Of Fathers And Sons

Hardened as he was by war and toil, Sir Braxus almost wept with relief when he and the other survivors crossed the river. It was good to be back on firm dry land again. Even then they did not stop to rest, but spurred their exhausted steeds across the fields for another hour before finally pausing.

Dismounting, the young knight turned to gaze back across the treacherous land that had so nearly doomed their escape. Beyond the marshlands on the other side of the river the Whaelen Hills could still be seen in the late afternoon sun, rolling up to meet the Hyrkrainian Mountains in the east.

Raising a mailed fist he shook it at the indifferent peaks melodramatically. Over the years he had come to despise those ranges with an irrational hatred. But then he knew full well what dangers they harboured.

'A thousand curses on the mountain clans!' he cried, giving full vent to his rage. 'And a thousand more on the tribes of the Brekkens,' he added, turning north to face the adjoining range and shaking his fist again. He was acting like a man gone wood in front of his men, but he didn't care.

One of the three other knights who had survived the ambush walked over and placed a gauntleted hand on his shoulder.

'Peace, Sir Braxus,' he said gently. 'You'll need all the energy you've left for the rest of the journey home.'

Looking into the older knight's careworn face Braxus felt his anger dwindle into despondency. He was not looking forward to returning to Gaellen. Certainly not under these circumstances.

'I had hoped you wouldn't remind me of that,' he said drily. 'Seven good knights lost, and nothing to show for it! My father will disown me for this, you see if he doesn't Sir Vertrix!'

The grey-haired knight shook his head. 'Don't take on so, Braxus – you weren't to blame. Ever since the mountain clans elected a new High Chieftain they've had us on the back foot. Reus knows but this Slánga Mac Bryon must have Azazel sitting on his right shoulder! I've never in all my years seen highlanders fight with such ruthless cunning – never.'

Running his fingers through his auburn locks, Braxus felt some resistance. That would be the blood that had spattered over him when he'd opened a highlander's throat. One more at least that wouldn't cause further trouble.

Turning away from Vertrix he strode over to check on the other two. Sir Curulyn had taken a nasty wound to the shoulder, but it was Sir Cadwy who worried him most. He'd taken a spear in the back and he was coughing up blood. His armour had saved him from being spitted like a wild boar, but hadn't been enough to prevent his lung being punctured.

Felled by a thrown spear. It wasn't a death Braxus would choose. But then the highlanders fought like the savages they were.

Curulyn had Cadwy's head cradled in his lap. He was still breathing, but wouldn't be for much longer. Only by a superhuman effort of will had he managed to make it this far.

Kneeling beside him Braxus took his limp hand in his own and lied as best he could. 'Never fear, noble Cadwy, we're back in Gaellentir - we'll get you patched up as soon as we make the castle.'

Cadwy, a young knight of twenty summers who had only recently been dubbed, coughed up more blood by way of answer. It dribbled down his cheeks and into his hair as he croaked: 'You may be good at lying to your mistresses, Braxus, but you can't fool a true knight!' His bloody face cracked into a deathly parody of a grin as he added: 'I just... wanted to die... on home soil. Sure you understand... I didn't want to be any trouble...'

His voice trailed off. They waited a few moments for Cadwy to speak again. He didn't. His head slumped to one side, his eyes frozen and sightless.

Curulyn wept. Getting to his feet Braxus felt a tear roll down his own cheek. Thraxians were less ashamed to show their emotions than their stoical rivals east of the mountains. Northlendings often mocked them for it, but Braxus knew better. A man could cry and still be brave and strong.

Still, now wasn't the time for grief. Swallowing his, Braxus barked a few curt orders in a hoarse voice.

'Let's get him back on his horse - we'll see that he gets a decent burial at least. More than can be said for the other poor devils. Vertrix, bind up Curulyn's injury first. Then we'd best get going. I wouldn't put it past the highlanders to try crossing the river after dark, way things have been going lately.'

Brushing his tears away Sir Curulyn began to protest. 'I'll be fine until we get back - '

Braxus cut him off harshly. 'I said to bind up your wound! I'll not have another brave knight bleeding to death on my watch - we've lost enough good men today as it is.'

Kicking a stone angrily across the long grass he strode back over to his horse and wearily remounted. All told, a dreadful day. And it was about to get even worse.

✢ ✢ ✢

His father was waiting for him up in his solar. A modest chamber, what it lacked in size it more than made up for in location. Its three north-facing circular windows commanded a spectacular view across the citadel and the silvery waters of Lake Cuchlain. Beyond that, the Brekken Ranges.

Mountains, always the mountains.

Lord Braun of Gaellen, First Man of Clan Fitzrow and ruler of the Ward of Gaellentir, turned to greet his only son with a scowl. He was shorter than Braxus but considerably thicker about the shoulders. In fact the only attribute he shared with his offspring was his auburn hair and beard, surprisingly ungreyed given his fifty-five winters. The two were different in just about every other way, and not just physically.

'Well?' he said curtly as Braxus favoured his father with a grudging half-bow. 'What have you to report?'

Braxus licked his lips nervously. He'd tried as best he could to prepare himself for this moment on the rest of the journey home. But faced with the patrician father he hated as much as he loved, all his carefully prepared words drained out of his head.

'I... I regret to report that we were ambushed, taken unawares, that is to say, father - '

'Aye, I know that already!' exclaimed the burly lord. 'D'you take me for a fool, young man?'

Braxus blinked. 'I... how do you know?'

'What are those?' he barked again, suddenly pointing at the round windows behind him.

Braxus blinked again. 'They're... they're windows, father.' He felt his heart sink another fathom. This was to be yet another exercise in paternal humiliation.

'Yes, that's right! Very good, son of mine!' replied his father, a steely edge entering his voice. 'They're windows. And more to the point, they're windows that overlook the approach to the castle. So imagine my surprise when I see my son and heir returning with just three knights in tow, one of whom looks decidedly worse for wear! Remind me, how many knights did I send out with you?'

Braxus dropped his eyes to the floor. Though the braziers had been lit against the encroaching night and a fire crackled in the hearth, he felt as cold as the flagstones beneath his feet.

'Ten, father,' he answered in a small voice.

'Aye,' roared Lord Braun, advancing towards him heavily. 'Ten! And only three returned! So that's how I know you were ambushed! And that's why I always keep the castle approach well lit – so I can know immediately when my useless, good-for-nothing-but-wenching-and-merry-making heir has failed, yet again, in his duties! Now tell me something I don't know! How did it happen?'

Braxus knew better by now than to try and embellish the truth with his wily sire. So he told him the plain truth instead.

They had been on their way to reconnoitre with another contingent of knights sent by Lord Tarneogh of Daxtir in the Whaelen Hills. Over the past week reports of incursions into the hills by highlanders had increased. They had struck like lightning, razing villages and slaughtering their occupants before vanishing. Such tactics were typical of their kind, but this was different: they had never been so organised before, so coordinated.

'We managed to catch one band, as they were burning Meath about five leagues north-east of the Cuchlain River,' said Braxus, secretly pleased to be able to give his father some good news. 'We came on them and slew them to a man, but we were too late to save the village.'

'You took no prisoners for interrogation?' his father asked, keen-eyed.

Braxus shook his head. 'There was one that survived our attack, but he took his own life before we could stop him.'

'Pagan scum,' muttered Lord Braun, shaking his head in disgust. 'Go on.'

'A couple of days after that we reached the rendezvous point at Fangwyn Hill,' continued Braxus. 'We saw their pennants waving in the breeze. We rode up the hill to meet them and it was only then that we realised... that we realised they weren't Tarneogh's men. They were highlanders dressed up as his knights. By the time we spotted their corpses piled in the middle of the hilltop it was too late. The highlanders were at us.'

'Ye Almighty!' breathed Lord Braun, genuinely shocked. 'These savages grow more cunning by the day! I swear this Mac Bryon is in league with the Arch Deceiver himself!'

'They killed Sir Aedan and Sir Maedoc before we could react. Even so, we started to get the best of them, for highlanders don't move well in heavy armour, and they were little match for us in a straight fight at close quarters. There were about a dozen of them – we killed half and the rest broke and fled down the other side of the hill. So we gave chase.'

His father closed his eyes and shook his head painfully. A seasoned campaigner, he was too long in the tooth not to see what was coming next.

'I know it seems reckless now, but our blood was up and, well – we were out there to kill highland rebels after all,' the young knight faltered.

'You're knights,' said his father with unusual forbearance, his hard manner softening somewhat. 'I'd have done the same in your position. Go on.'

'We chased them down the hill. We didn't see the others coming until we were at the bottom of the next valley. They came swooping down at us from either side. There must have been thirty of them at least. We lost another couple of men to spear-throwers before we could even engage with them. The ones we'd been chasing turned about face and joined their comrades. It was then that we realised they'd been nothing more than the bait all along.'

His father sighed heavily. 'So, out with it. How did you manage to escape?'

'Almighty as my witness, we stood our ground and fought as best we could,' said Braxus, flushing. Now if anything he felt too hot. 'I myself cut down three or four of them, and the rest of the lads acquitted themselves admirably under the circumstances. But even with most of them on foot, we were still outnumbered four to one. When I realised we couldn't overcome them, I ordered a retreat. Four of us including me managed to cut our way out and flee, although Sir Cadwy took a spear in the back as we disengaged.'

'The one I saw slumped over his horse,' said his father grimly. 'How is he?'

For a second time Braxus failed to meet his eyes. 'He died of his injuries. We were bringing his body back so we could bury him.'

Lord Braun's face looked more sad than angry now. 'A great pity. Promising young knight. Don't suppose being named after our wonderful king brought him much luck.' The first statement was sincere; the second tinged with sarcasm.

Walking over to an oak table by the windows his father reached for a jug and poured two horns of mead. Handing one to his son he said: 'Well, you did what you could. Fighting's your trade not dying, after all, and Reus knows the Fitzrow line must stay intact. It's not as if you've any sons of your own to succeed you if you die – apart from the illegitimate ones of course, and they don't count.'

Braxus started over his mead horn. His father's words stung him – even by his standards, that was cold. Was that all he meant to the old man now? An heir to keep the family name going, and nothing more? He felt a bitterness that not even the finest Thraxian mead could assuage.

'This is getting worse by the day,' his father went on, oblivious. 'Ever since Slánga took over the Brekken tribes they've been getting more disciplined. This new alliance with Tíerchán's lot in the Hyrkrainians will be our undoing – united, the mountain clans pose a greater threat than we barons of Dréuth alone can hope to contain.'

Braxus nodded perfunctorily over his horn of mead. All his father was doing was reiterating what the northern lords of Thraxia and their vassals had known with a dread certainty for weeks.

'What about the King?' he asked reluctantly, expecting little joy there either. 'Has he yet replied to your latest summons for help?'

'Oh yes, he has,' replied Lord Braun with mock levity, turning back to the table and reaching for an unfurled vellum scroll. 'Here,' he said, handing it to his son. 'At least you managed to get your letters before you took your own wayward path in life. See for yourself.'

Ignoring the umpteenth rebuke of his personal character, Braxus scanned the letter while his father quaffed his mead darkly. It bore the royal seal of the High Clan Cierny; the handwriting was probably Cadwy's, although one couldn't be sure even of that nowadays.

At any rate, there was not much written to test the young knight's rudimentary literacy: *No troops available. The northern lords are to do their job. Any attempt to make peace with the highland rebels shall be deemed an act of treason – fight on till victory or death.*

Very succinct. Glancing up from the letter he registered his father's face in the ephemeral shadows cast by the light from the braziers. It looked eerie, and something in his dark eyes told the young knight the unpleasant audience was not finished by some way.

'Is that all?' asked Braxus, incredulous. Even allowing for what was now widely suspected throughout Dréuth province, the King's curt reply seemed beyond all the boundaries of common sense. 'You made it clear to His Majesty the terms that Slánga is demanding?'

His father gestured irritably with his horn. 'Well of course I did! He wants all the lands north of the Cuchlain, plus the Whaelen Hills as far as Daxor and including Port Grendel, for his people. The Hyrkrainian tribes are to be allowed to settle the hill-lands, and all of Tarneogh's people are to be relocated to make room for them. In return for which Slánga promises an end to hostilities – a likely promise indeed!'

Shaking his head he drained his horn and turned back to the jug for a refill.

'And what about Tarneogh?' pressed Braxus. 'Has he sent messengers of his own?'

'Oh yes,' replied his father, pouring more mead for himself before handing the jug to Braxus. 'He stands to lose most from the terms – well, imminently at any rate. And Lord Cael of Varrogh has despatched riders of his own. So Cadwy's heard from all three lords of Dréuth by now – small difference that'll make.'

For a while the two drank in silence. Lord Braun paced over to the central window and stood staring at the dark line of mountains, now disappearing beneath the deepening shroud of night. The absence of the hated peaks did little to allay Braxus' discomfort. Despite his father's low opinion of him, he was a seasoned campaigner of nearly ten years, and no stranger to battle. But the threat now facing them was the worst yet. If the King could not be persuaded to help them, all would surely be lost. It would only be a matter of time before the combined might of the mountain clans overwhelmed them, inferior arms or no.

Their new tactics alone were enough to make the blood run cold. As part of a reported shake-up of the Brekken clan order, Slánga had appointed Cormic Mac Brennan as his lieutenant. Cormic Death's Head they called him, and with good reason: apart from the unusual wound that caused him to have a perpetual rictus grin, he was notorious for his bloodthirsty ways.

Braxus had seen with his own eyes what had been done to villagers and knights and other soldiers unfortunate enough to fall into his clutches. The Cormic Cravat was fast becoming a dread thing of folklore: throat slashed open ear to ear, the victim's tongue wrenched down to hang from the gaping wound.

And that wasn't the worst of it. If a knight or soldier fought especially bravely, it was said, the Death's Head spared his life. Instead he put out his eyes, severed his fingers, tongue, nose and ears and punctured his eardrums. Most victims went mad within a few days.

Not all the knights in his company had been felled by lethal blows. Braxus shuddered to think what torments they would be suffering now. He prayed it would at least be quick. No wonder Sir Cadwy had been so keen to die on home soil.

Presently his father turned from the window and stared at his son again. 'She has to go,' he said flatly. 'By any means necessary.'

Taking another draft of mead Braxus nodded slowly. He had been thinking much the same thing. The question was...

'How? She's the King's royal concubine. He keeps her by his side day and night, they share the Royal Cot. She's surrounded by Cadwy's own knights at all times, and some of the rumours I've been hearing from down south say half of them are under her spell, same as the King himself!'

Abrexta the Prescient, they called her. A damsel of reputedly striking beauty, she hailed from the foothills of the Hyrkrainian mountains just south of Roarkil Forest. Some said she had been taught her devilish craft by air spirits high up in the ranges; others whispered she had learned it from the eidolons that haunted those cursed woods. There had already been reports some years ago of another sorcerer who had taken up residence in Roarkil, some Northlending mage who called himself Andragor, or some such. But he had apparently been driven out of his lair some years ago by an Argolian friar from Northalde and Sir Belinos of Runcymede, a knight errant from the province of Umbria famed for his piety. He hadn't been seen or heard of since. Nor the mysterious friar, come to think of it.

At any rate, alarm bells should have been set ringing when Abrexta rode up to the King's palace at Ongist eighteen moons ago. Instead the guards had let her through without a word of complaint, as if she were a member of the Royal Clan. Soon after she had gained an audience with the King himself. He had been taken with her immediately, and taken her into his bed.

It was not long after that that strange things started to happen. Trusted advisers were summarily dismissed, to be replaced with non-entities, men ill qualified for the high office of state. The King began to grow indolent, locking himself away in his private chambers and disporting himself with his mistress and a growing pack of toadies and hangers-on. The royal treasury's coffers, previously so well tended, began to be emptied, lavished on extravagant feasts and tournaments.

Tournaments! That was the worst of it. Tourneys were all well and good when there were no real wars to fight, but now they needed every strong knight more than ever to resist Slánga and his highlanders. The thought of the King's knights jousting on the plains before Ongist while Cadwy and his witch mistress watched from his pleasure barge on the River Rundle made Braxus feel sick.

People had complained. Loyal courtiers, stalwart vassals of the King. Most had come to grief. Those Abrexta thought she could charm had been admitted to a private audience with her, to air their grievances. They had soon emerged with an entirely different disposition. Those that she could not ensorcell had simply disappeared. Whether by her own dark crafts or at the hands of hired blades, no one was quite sure.

What was sure was this – within a year of Abrexta presenting herself before the Seat of High Kings, half the noble subjects of the King's Ward were dancing to her tune. The other half were deadly afraid. As for the commoners, their lot grew more miserable by the day, as one harsh tax after another was levied on the peasantry and townsfolk to pay for the King's suddenly extravagant lifestyle. There had already been several uprisings in Umbria, all of them brutally quashed.

Put bluntly, the royal realm was in a royal mess.

'You're right of course,' Lord Braun replied, acknowledging his son's objections. 'Several brave men have already tried. Sir Axel of Wieran was hanged ten days ago for trying to murder her at a feast held to celebrate the latest tourney. And Solon, Prior of the Argolian Monastery at Kilucan, was impaled along with a dozen other men after being found guilty of conspiring to capture Abrexta and put her in cold irons. Now the Argolian Order faces closure across the Kingdom – for national security of course.'

Lord Braun sneered in disgust. Unlike his only son, he was a pious man, and respected the monks of St Argo. Evidence of his devotion could be seen about his solar: in place of the usual bearskins and crossed weapons its walls were decorated with great vellum hangings bearing quotations from Scripture. It was said the old lord knew all of them by heart.

Braxus knew only too well that rumour was perfectly true – as he had learned to his chagrin when his father had tried to get his heir to follow suit and learn them all as a boy. That hadn't gone well. Braxus could recall the lyrics to hundreds of songs great and small at will, but not a word of holy scripture had ever found its way into his comely head. Yet another bone of contention between them.

'So what do we do?' asked the young knight helplessly. 'I mean to say... the only way we could get to Abrexta is by... well, by staging a coup...'

His father smiled for the first time that night. 'Exactly,' he said, his eyes suddenly glinting in the firelight.

Braxus blinked. He must have misheard.

'I said "a coup", father – I wasn't being entirely serious. You know - '

'Oh you may not have been, son of mine, but I am being deadly serious.' A dangerous tone had entered his father's voice.

'But... we can't overthrow him,' protested Braxus. 'Even with things the state they're in, it would be nothing short of high treason, our lives and lands would be forfeit - '

'They'll be forfeit anyway!' roared his father, suddenly losing his composure. 'What d'you think will happen to us in the next few months, if things go on unchecked the way they have been? Mac Bryon, Tíerchán and all their men will overrun these lands. The lords of Dréuth and their vassals shall fall to a man! Then there'll be nothing to stop them sweeping south to attack Umbria! This kingdom is on the brink of ruin – and I for one will not stand by and do nothing about it!'

His father paused. The crackling fire sounded loud in the sudden silence. Braxus swallowed, thought carefully. He and his father had their differences, but he had to acknowledge it – the old man was right.

Nodding slowly and taking a deep breath, the heir of Gaellentir said: 'All right. Let's say you're right. How do we do it? We've our hands more than full keeping Slánga's lot at bay – Umbria's under the King's, or should I say Abrexta's, thrall. That leaves the southern reaches of the Kingdom. But they'll do little to help – this state of play suits them too

well. They've few mountain clans to worry about down there – all the
ranges south of Roarkil are long settled by lowlanders. A weak king
is good for them – it means they can run their wards to their hearts'
content as they see fit! So even if we wanted to, we can't do it!'

His father smiled again, a crafty smile. Braxus felt sure he did not like it.

'What you say is true. But you seem to be forgetting one thing, son
of mine.'

Braxus blinked again, puzzled. 'Which is what?'

'Our neighbours to the east. For two generations now, we have been
at peace with the Northlendings. They are no longer our implacable foe,
as they once were. Their King is a wise and just ruler. Perhaps he can be
persuaded to help us in our direst need.'

Now it was Braxus's turn to smile, but he didn't. He laughed. 'The
Northlendings?! With all due respect father, but for once I'd say it's
you who's been quaffing too much mead! How on earth do you plan to
persuade the King of the Northlendings to help us? Oh aye, we're at peace
with them, but that hardly makes us bosom friends! Why, we still don't
even trade with them as much as we should.'

'Ah, there you have partly answered your own question, son of
mine,' his father replied craftily. Reaching for another scroll, he unfurled
it and handed it to his son. 'Here is a contract drawn up, of trade terms
and concessions that we would grant to the Northlendings, for sending
a contingent of knights to our aid. Generous terms on all consignments
of Thraxian mead and furs from Dréuth, not to mention iron mining
concessions in the Whaelen Hills – and likewise for extracting ebonite
from the Brekken Ranges, if we can wrest those from Slánga after we
deal with the King.'

Braxus scanned the vellum with bulging eyes. Together with his
father's words, it was a lot to take in. All the terms and conditions
were there, drawn up by his father's scrivener. At the bottom of the
document were three signatures. He recognised his father's own spiky
hand. The other two were written by Tarneogh and Cael.

He looked up from the contract. 'You... you've got the other lords
of Dréuth to agree? How long have you been planning this?'

'For some weeks now. The time is ripe. King Freidheim's realm has
enjoyed peace for many a year now. The Northlendings are a hardy
lot, as I know only too well from experience. Fighting is what they
do best – a peaceful realm is a joyous thing, but it can be frustrating
for an ambitious knight. Give the youngbloods of Northalde a
chance to test their mettle, and I'm sure they'll jump at the chance.
For King Freidheim's part, I'm sure he'd be only too glad to get some of

his more truculent vassals out from under his nose. Why, the Southern Kingdoms use the so-called Pilgrim Wars for just the same purpose.'

His father spat into the hearth. His contempt for the notion of holy war was well known, and shared by most inhabitants of the Northern Kingdoms.

Turning back to the vellum Braxus scanned it again. He nodded to himself as he did. Yes – he had to admit, this plan made sense, in theory at least. But it still troubled him nonetheless.

'All right, say it works. Say Freidheim takes you up on your offer. We're still committing high treason. To kill a king – '

'Heavenly thunder, did I say anything about killing the King?' his father interjected sharply. 'We're not going to kill Cadwy, you fool! No, we're going to kill as many of his ensorcelled knights as it takes to get to that bitch of a witch he calls concubine. Then we're going to try her and burn her at the stake – or hang her at the very least. Kill the witch, break the spell. You don't need to be an Argolian to know how that works.'

Braxus nodded again. Once again, he had to admit his father was making sense – as bold and dangerous as his plan was.

'Once we get rid of her it should, Reus willing, bring the King to his senses,' Lord Braun continued. 'Then we can restore him to his proper throne – right now it's clear from everything we've been hearing out of Umbria that his will is no longer his own. That makes this Abrexta – and everyone who serves her – guilty of high treason, not us. The Argolians have been clandestinely apprised of our intentions, as has the High Perfect at Ongist. They will support our justification once the thing is done.'

Braxus wasn't entirely surprised to hear the Temple was on side. A pagan witch in control of a Palomedian kingdom, even a not particularly devout one like Thraxia, was definitely not in its interests.

'All right, I'm convinced,' he said. 'It's certainly risky, but at least it gives us a chance of survival. And who will you send with this offer to the King of the Northlendings?'

His father favoured him with another wan smile. Braxus knew the answer before he spoke it.

'Why, you of course, son of mine.'

⚔ CHAPTER II ⚔

A War Against Water

S ir Tarlquist and his company were a day out of Staerkvit when they learned of Blakelock's surrender. Thule's vanguard had reached it some days after his main army invested Salmor, the castle they were riding to save. Blakelock was poorly garrisoned, and its old castellan could not have hoped to conduct a successful siege. Better to yield that brave knights might be taken for ransom and live to fight another day.

Or that was the kinder view taken by some of the white ravens in the hundred-strong sortie sent to relieve Salmor. Others muttered darkly that Sir Ulfheim was a coward and a traitor for giving up the castle without a fight.

Foremost among these was Sir Wolmar, but then such an unforgiving view was typical of the arrogant princeling.

'If I had my way, he'd be hanged for dereliction of his duties,' spat the High Commander's son as they warmed themselves at a campfire on the second night of their journey. 'Ulfheim is weak. He has been tested and found wanting.'

Sir Tarlquist rolled his eyes. Best to nip this one in the bud. There was enough dissent over the matter brewing in the ranks without the idiot princeling making it worse.

'And I suppose you feel the same way about your cousin, the King's royal son and heir, Prince Wolfram?' he queried pointedly. 'He and his men had no choice but to flee when faced with overwhelmingly superior numbers. The last we heard he's fallen back towards Linden, to stiffen the garrison there. But I suppose that still makes him a coward in your eyes too?'

An uneasy silence fell about the company. Sir Tarlquist suspected that many of the knights in his charge *did* disapprove of the royal heir's decision to fall back – after all, were they not even now riding to face odds as great as those that had confronted Wolfram?

'How could His Royal Highness have done otherwise, when presented with the castellan's abject cowardice?' spluttered Wolmar, recovering quickly. He glared at his commander, his green eyes menacing slits in the half-light of the campfires.

Tarlquist glared back at him. If it were not for his duties as commander and the princeling's royal blood, he would have taken Wolmar to the lists and given him the sound thrashing he deserved long ago. He was about to reply when Sir Aronn interjected.

'You're a fool to talk so, Sir Wolmar,' said the burly knight, his scarred cheeks flaming scarlet in the fire's heat. 'At a time like this we should be uniting, not causing trouble amongst ourselves. We're outnumbered enough as it is.'

'Aronn has the right of it,' said Tarlquist, quickly picking up the thread. 'This is no time for casting base aspersions on the honour of subjects loyal to our King. We've plenty of disloyal ones to deal with, as the good knight says.'

'Pah!' Wolmar spat into the fire to show what he thought of that, before stalking off to check on his supplies.

'That man is trying my patience by the second,' said Sir Aronn between gritted teeth. 'If he goes on like this much longer, I swear there'll be another civil war – between the King's loyal subjects!'

'And that's why it's so important not to rise to his bait,' replied Sir Tarlquist. 'Try to stay cool, in that hot head of yours, Aronn. When he talks like that it's best just to ignore him. Don't give him the ammunition he craves – a bow without an arrow is a useless weapon. The same goes for the rest of you,' he added gruffly, addressing the fifteen or so knights gathered around the fire.

Aronn was about to reply when the sound of galloping horses alerted them. As one they drew swords and seized torches. All about them the rest of the sortie did likewise: its four campfires were ringed with steel by the time the riders approached from across the darkened plains.

It was only Sir Torgun and his men, returning from their reconnoitre as expected, but in times like these it was best to be prepared for any eventuality.

Dismounting, Torgun stepped up to the main campfire to debrief the four commanders including Tarlquist. The other knights gathered around to listen to his report.

'It is as we feared,' said the towering blond knight. 'Thule has a third army, besides the two investing Salmor and Blakelock, ravaging the countryside as we speak, laying waste and burning. We came on two survivors fleeing north. They say their entire village was burnt, its occupants put to the sword.'

Cries of anger resounded about the camp. Most knights of the White Valravyn had a strong sense of justice, and at least tried to hold to the Code of Chivalry. Others like Wolmar would merely have been outraged at an attack on the King's property.

'Who commands them?' asked Sir Øren. He was a heavy-set knight in early middle age, and in charge of the entire sortie of four companies. His granite face looked even grimmer than usual.

Sir Torgun shook his head. 'The peasants we questioned didn't know for sure. One of the more prominent southron barons, they think. Lord Johan of Orack perhaps, or Lord Aelrød of Saltcaste – we can't be sure.'

'This sounds more like Johan's work,' muttered Sir Larson, another company commander. 'That man's reputation for bloodthirsty violence long precedes this war.'

'It makes little difference who is behind it,' replied Sir Øren. 'This is a war of attrition, and such scorched-earth tactics are only to be expected from men capable of treason. Torgun, do we have any idea of the whereabouts of this third army?'

Torgun shook his head again, a sorrowful look on his ruggedly handsome face. 'Would that we did,' he answered. 'Most likely they are in the vicinity. We may even encounter them on the way to Salmor, though more likely we will miss them, given they appear to be headed north.'

'We must seek them out!' cried one young knight. 'We are knights of the White Valravyn! We cannot let this injustice go unchecked and unpunished!' A chorus of hearty throats voiced their approval.

'Be that as it may, noblemen, orders are orders,' replied Sir Øren, raising a hand for silence. 'Our mission is to relieve Salmor, if we can. That means we must press on regardless, however painful it is to leave the King's subjects unprotected.'

'But we're sworn to protect those subjects!' cried another knight, to a chorus of 'ayes'. Tarlquist felt a tightness in his gut. Many of the younger men had never experienced the horrors of a full-scale war before. Young idealists who were used to dealing with villains and lawbreakers in smaller numbers, where problems presented themselves one at a time. This kind of dissent might not be easy to quell.

'Yes, we are sworn to protect them,' said Øren firmly. 'And that's precisely why we must stick to our mission. Right now Thule's armies have a free run over the southern reaches of the King's Dominions precisely because the greatest castle protecting them is pinned down. Blakelock has surrendered, Rookhammer is next – its garrison is bigger but even so its castellan Sir Aelfric won't be able to hold off Thule's vanguard for long. That's why it's imperative that we relieve Salmor –

if our plan succeeds we can muster with Kelmor's forces and harry the rebels in the rear. Either that or we could march across the Thule and give the Young Pretender a taste of his own medicine.'

That got a mixed reaction. Wolmar and his cronies clearly liked the latter idea very much; but many of the more decent knights clearly found the realities of war distasteful.

'We didn't join the Order to slaughter civilians!' yelled the first knight who had spoken up. 'Even if they are ruled by traitors! And as for your first suggestion, with respect commander, by the time we relieve Salmor and turn north again they'll have ravaged half the countryside hereabouts!'

Øren nodded, grimly acknowledging the truth of those words. 'Aye they will,' he said sadly. 'War is full of painful decisions, and not all of them lead to glory. But if Thule retains Salmor he'll have a permanent foothold in the southern Dominions. That will mean the entire stretch of King's land as far as Linden will be all but lost. And then he'll be able to join his forces and invest that too. And if he takes Linden he'll have all the lands between the Thule and the Vyborg in his grasp. I don't need to spell out what disaster that would mean for the kingdom.'

Øren fell silent, allowing his words to sink in. Angry cries dwindled into disconsolate muttering, but the commander-in-chief's point had been hammered home. Tarlquist felt a sense of relief – the last thing they needed was the younger hotheads breaking ranks. Admittedly that was unlikely among the disciplined knights of the Order, but still he knew only too well that war did strange things to men.

Øren must have been thinking along similar lines, for then he said: 'All right, men of the White Valravyn! We've had our supper, and we've heard our report! Time to post watch and turn in – Salmor is still another couple of days' hard ride away, so we've leagues to cover. Dismissed!'

✣ ✣ ✣

The rest of the journey passed without any engagements. By now spies would have been sent ahead with the necessary disinformation: the King was mustering a full contingent of knights, complete with supplies and footsoldiers, to meet Thule's forces at Rookhammer. The Pretender wouldn't expect a bold sortie of a hundred unaccompanied knights riding hard cross country to attack his forces at Salmor, which by now was virtually behind enemy lines.

The journey was harrowing nonetheless. Tarlquist gritted his teeth as they came upon the third ravaged village that afternoon, on their fourth day out of Staerkvit. The huts had been burned down.

The livestock had been taken to feed the rebel armies. The villagers had been slaughtered without regard to age or gender.

Their corpses hung from makeshift gibbets, their crow-pecked cadavers twisting in the breeze. They had not even been tarred, which made for an even worse spectacle in the grey afternoon light.

Tarlquist clutched his reins tightly as he gazed at pulped eyes and mangled limbs. Loyal yeomen, whose only crime had been to serve the rightful King that Thule sought to supplant.

He took a deep breath to calm himself. They were not far from Salmor now. Soon there would be a reckoning, a reckoning of steel. War could be dreadful, but it had its rewards too.

✤ ✤ ✤

It was dusk when they reached the castle environs. Naturally the rebel army had posted scouts, but the White Valravyn anticipated this and sent some of their own to pick them off. Most were quickly slain. Two survivors were dragged back to camp beyond the foothills overlooking the castle. Sir Øren pronounced them traitors and hanged them both from a lone yew tree.

But not before he questioned them. Men terrified at the prospect of imminent death had little to say that was coherent, but one daunting piece of information they did glean from the scouts before they died: the waiting rebel army was not commanded by any lord of the southlands. The Sea Wizard was in charge, a Northland pagan priest whom they seemed to fear as much as death itself. As the two rebel scouts danced the mad dance of death upon their makeshift gallows, the knights exchanged grim glances. Men of arms they knew how to fight. A warlock was another matter entirely.

The hills ringing Salmor Castle were an advantage long factored into their plans. Another advance party of knights was dispatched on foot to climb them and spy on the rebel army before the light failed altogether.

They soon returned. The news they brought came as little surprise. The Sea Wizard's army outnumbered them more than ten to one. But less than half of them were knights. And they would catch them unawares. Even now they were settling down to their cookfires and whoring – as was usual in times of war, a sizeable number of hangers-on had attached themselves to the marching army.

Sir Øren gathered the men about him for one last briefing.

'All right, you know the plan,' he began. 'We'll lead our horses on foot to the summit of the hills and gather at the marker left by our scouts. Then we mount and ride like the wind down into the valley. Target their knights – it's important we kill or wound as many as we can before they have a

chance to take the saddle. After that it's the serjeants and footsoldiers.
Don't bother about the archers – by the time they know what's happening
we'll be in amongst their ranks and they'll be next to useless.'

He paused and looked around at the grim faces of the armoured
men about him.

'There's a lot of civilians attached to the main army – washerwomen,
whores, peddlers and the like,' he added. 'On no account are they to be
attacked – we've a precious advantage and I don't want it squandered on
unchivalrous and pointless slayings.'

As he said this Tarlquist was sure the barrel-chested commander
fixed a squint-eyed glare at Wolmar.

'So this is it!' said Sir Øren. 'We've done well to get this far, but now
we go to war in earnest! Strike hard, strike fast, and be worthy of the
White Valravyn!'

Muted cheers answered him. They were a league away from the
castle, but it was best not to risk drawing any attention. Their success
depended on the element of surprise.

✣ ✣ ✣

Their battle plan worked like a charm. Reaching the short white flag
planted by their scouts the White Valravyn took to the saddle. With
a roar they swept down the foothills, couching lances as they did.

The enemy knights were easy to spot in their heraldic surcoats. Before
they had time to realise they were being attacked dozens lay dying about their
campfires, spitted like wild boar. Spinning their Farovian destriers around
with well-drilled precision, the ravens drew swords and began to lay about them at
the remainder. They slew on the left hand and the right; knights and serjeants
fell screaming as their comrades began to muster a desperate counter attack.

Several dozen had by now managed to mount their steeds. Sir Tarlquist
closed with one of them amidst the screaming and clamour. Camp followers
were running about pell-mell, trying to avoid being trampled in the
melee. Footsoldiers had availed themselves of spears and were trying to
knock ravens off their horses, but many of their serjeants had been killed
or wounded in the first onslaught, and their efforts were ill disciplined.

Tarlquist parried his adversary's first blow. Bringing his sword
back he slashed fiercely downwards at the young knight's head.
He hadn't had time to put on a helm and was clearly not used to
defending strikes above the shoulder. Tarlquist's blade bit deep
into his skull; the young knight shrieked pitifully, his own sword
slipping from dying fingers. Tarlquist wrenched his weapon free,
and the knight slipped off his horse in a shower of blood and brains.

Glancing to his left at the castle, which was surrounded with siege engines and catapults, Tarlquist hoped Lord Kelmor would realise the plan and muster his own forces to sally forth and join them.

That was the second crucial part of the plan: now the element of surprise was over, it depended on allied reinforcements from the castle. Even with the dreadful casualties they had inflicted on Thule's best men, they still outnumbered them more than five to one. Kelmor was known to be a cautious general, but when he witnessed the desperate and brave effort to relieve him, surely he would come to their aid...

A footsoldier lunged at him with a spear. Reacting quickly, Tarlquist brought his blade down in a powerful sideswipe, knocking the polearm from his hands. Before he had a chance to rearm, the knight spurred his charger straight at him. With a great whinny it reared up, catching the soldier in the face with a lashing hoof. Spraying rotten teeth, the man went down with a cry.

Suddenly a great horn blast shook the hills to either side of the castle approach where they were fighting. It was their herald Sir Albared, sounding the call for help. Tarlquist hoped Kelmor would get the message.

Doric and Cirod, the twin knights, were nearest to him. They fought as one, their swords flashing in the firelight as they staunchly fended off the three knights harrying them. Charging into the fray, Tarlquist evened up the odds. He exchanged several fierce strokes with his new adversary, a battle-scarred veteran of the southlands who had probably squired in the last uprising. He swung his sword at Tarlquist's forehead – but unlike the young knight he'd just killed he was well used to fighting without a helm. Turning the lethal blow aside at the last second he countered with a thrusting riposte, catching the knight through a chink in his armour. He gave a low groan as Tarlquist's blade sank into his bowels. As he finished him off with a cut to the throat the twins simultaneously despatched their foemen.

It was then that he heard it. A strange chanting in a peculiar tongue, one that immediately sent shivers down his spine. Glancing up from the combat he could see its source. Perched atop a high hill overlooking the scene of battle was a tall man dressed in flowing robes the colour of the sea. In his hand was a strange weapon; it looked like a trident and matched the colour of his robes. His arms were aloft and he was bellowing the strange words at the top of his lungs. Somehow they managed to cut across the raging war-song that filled the castle approach.

Once again Tarlquist glanced towards Salmor, stood impassively behind its protective moat. Its grey flanks bore the scars of siege, though it was still far from falling. Again Sir Albared's horn sounded, mingling oddly with the Northland wizard's strange chanting.

Come on Kelmor, for Palom's sake, thought Tarlquist desperately as he wheeled his horse around to face yet another attack. *We're risking our lives to bring you succour – repay us in kind, dammit!*

The battle raged on. By now most of the surviving rebel knights had managed to mount their horses. The remaining serjeants had finally succeeded in ordering their men, and even archers and sappers were being pressed into hand combat. Doughty as they were, even the white ravens were sore pressed by such odds.

Gradually the rebel forces began to surround them and push them back towards the moat. As Albared blew his horn again and again, the pagan priest continued his chanting, his eldritch words assaulting the night skies with the monotonous persistence of a battering ram...

It's now or never, thought Tarlquist as he fended off two knights. *If Kelmor doesn't ride out soon, we're done for. Where in Reus' name is he?*

The press of men and horses and steel was too thick for him to risk a glance backwards in the direction of the castle. One of his foeman swiped at him with an axe; Tarlquist took it on his shield, but was prevented from counter-attacking by his second opponent. He took his blade on his own before riposting, but the knight was quick and dodged the hurried blow. As both knights renewed their offensive Tarlquist pulled his horse back towards the moat.

They're hemming us in, he thought desperately. *They're going to pin us against the moat of the castle we've come to save and crush us like flies.* The bitter irony was not lost on him even in the midst of battle.

All about him his comrades were beginning to feel the effects of superior numbers. Many ravens had been knocked off their horses. Some were able to continue the fight on foot. They made light work of the footsoldiers, but were easy prey for mounted enemy knights.

By the time they had been pushed back to within a stone's throw of the moat Tarlquist estimated that less than half their number remained. The rest had been captured, slain or incapacitated.

At least they won't be able to surround us with the moat at our backs, he thought with grim triumph. *We'll make a brave last stand, worthy of bard's song.*

A great cry suddenly went up amidst the throng of fighters. It wasn't coming from their own men, but from the enemy soldiers facing the castle.

'The Sea Wizard has spoken! The Sea Wizard has spoken and his words are doom!' The words of a rebel footsoldier sounded as much horrified as they did triumphant.

The rebel fighters had fallen back momentarily. Taking advantage of this to risk a glance over his shoulder, Tarlquist gaped.

Now he understood Kelmor's hesitation to act. There would be no succour from Salmor.

Where a short while before he had glimpsed the still waters of the moat, there now raged and roiled a tidal wave, one that circled the castle unnaturally like a cartwheel spinning on its side. Staring at it with eyes he scarcely believed, Tarlquist registered the ethereal forms of galloping knights within its roaring depths, their watery blades held high as they rode round and round Salmor in a devilish elemental parody of a carousel. Each one was the size of small tower; they seemed to undulate and merge with the rest of the ensorcelled waters at will, hooves of surf lashing the ground by the moat with the force of a hundred rainstorms.

At that moment he heard Albared's trumpet again. It wasn't summoning a sally-forth anymore – it was signalling retreat. Turning to gaze in its direction, Sir Tarlquist saw the battle standard go down. Sir Øren and his men usually rode with the standard bearer and herald – Tarlquist couldn't pick him out in the press, but rebel fighters were swarming thick and fast around his company. It didn't look good.

The knights and soldiers harassing Tarlquist's own men had meanwhile recovered from the shock of witnessing the Sea Wizard's sorcery to renew their attack.

Hurriedly he barked orders at the remainder of his company. 'Close ranks and prepare to charge! We're getting out of here if we can!'

Drawing his neighing Farovian up beside him Sir Wolmar looked at him askance. 'But, Salmor Castle, we can't abandon it...'

'Salmor's lost!' snarled Sir Tarlquist through gritted teeth. 'Look behind you if you haven't already! No mortal can get through that – neither them nor us! We've no choice but to flee!'

Some dozen white ravens still ahorse had gathered about him and the princeling, Torgun, the chequered twins and Aaron among them. The enemy was coming thick and fast from several directions now, menacing them with a bristling rash of swords and spears. This would not be easy.

Raising his blade high in the air, Sir Tarlquist bellowed the words he had prayed he would not have to utter.

'Knights of the White Valravyn, charge the enemy and cut yourselves out if you can! The battle is lost – the Sea Wizard has won! Damn his pagan hide, but he's won!'

⚜ CHAPTER III ⚜

In the Footsteps of Vanished Heroes

A delko had no idea how long they had been in the forest. One moment it seemed only seconds since the four of them had plunged into its forbidding depths, the war-cries of the brigands sounding loud in their ears. The next it felt like years... and he struggled to remember the events that had brought them there in the first place.

All around them, the thick boles of strange trees stretched in all directions. From the outside they had looked like oaks, but in here they deceived the eye continually. Their shapes would shift and bend subtly, come tantalisingly close to resembling a recognisable species... before shifting again and becoming something altogether alien. Occasionally he would look back at a cluster of trees he had just passed – each time he could swear they had changed positions.

He repeated this experiment several times, until Horskram told him in a quiet but firm voice to stop – playing such tricks on his own mind would only increase the likelihood of turning to madness.

Whatever power it was that caused the trees to metamorphose had sealed their fate the instant they passed beneath the dark eaves of Tintagael: the boles behind them had snapped back into place, abruptly cutting off the whelps of the brigands. A slab to seal their tomb.

Reining in their panicky horses they had turned to see the trees stretching back behind them seemingly without end, as though there had never been a world beyond them: of the sparse plains of the wilderness not a single blade of grass could be seen.

Horskram had told them all to stay calm, and above all not to raise their voices unless absolutely necessary. He seemed outwardly composed, but Adelko could sense his master was deeply uncertain about the choice of path he had led them on.

But the time for making decisions was over. The trees parted to reveal a trail that snaked maddeningly as they proceeded along it.

Adelko was quite sure it led exactly where the forest – or whatever unseen force controlled it – wanted it to.

Regardless of the form they took the trees always rose high above them, their snaking branches intertwining grotesquely to form a tangled web of foliage, dense and impenetrable, that blocked out the skies entirely. Yet they had no need of Horskram's lamp, for the forest was suffused in a peculiar silvery-green light, an unnatural hue that seemed to mock the colours of a normal wood.

The leaves of the trees were a rotten dead brown colour, and put the novice in mind of autumn; but instead of falling they clung to the menacing branches with a horrible tenacity. After a while he noticed that they were the only part of the trees that never changed.

Their way was not easy, for the undergrowth of Tintagael had a malign intent all of its own, and more than once their horses' hooves became inexplicably caught in its tangled briars, until eventually they had no choice but to dismount and lead their reluctant steeds.

Perhaps worst of all were the noises. Tintagael sounded like no earthly forest Adelko had ever set foot in: no sounds of wildlife could be discerned, just the sussurant rustling of leaves and ominous creaking of the trees as they shimmered and altered about them.

But there was something else too, *behind* those sounds; a faint whispering of countless voices, always just on the edge of human hearing. A thousand tiny pinpricks, poking relentlessly at the blurred threshold between the soul and senses...

'Do you hear them, Master Horskram?' the novice asked furtively as he walked beside the old monk. 'Voices... or at least I think they are, but I'm not sure. I think I heard them just before we entered the forest. What are they?'

Horskram's face was a mask as he replied flatly: 'If you can hear those, it means your sixth sense is as attuned as mine is. The Fay Folk are the masters of Tintagael – most like it is their voices you can hear, though you would not understand their tongue even if you could do so clearly.'

The novice glanced back behind their horses to where Branas and Vaskrian were bringing up the rear, both looking pale and unusually frightened. 'Can... can they hear them too?'

Horskram frowned and looked thoughtful. 'Possibly not. Our trusty swords are much less psychically attuned than we are. Probably just as well for them.'

'What do you mean? Are we... in greater danger if we can hear them?'

'Just remember what I said to you all when we first entered: as much as you possibly can, do not look upon the forest, do not listen for its noises, do not try to comprehend it! The more you allow your senses to interact with its denizens, the more chance you have of becoming ensnared by its evil.'

'Ensnared, yes, but by what kind of evil?'

But Horskram shook his head and refused to answer, instead casting his eyes to the dark soil of the forest trail as it led them blindly onwards.

✢ ✢ ✢

Vaskrian stumbled along the winding trail as if in a dream. It was one he would fain have awoken from, for the ghastly forest that undulated around them was likely to drive him mad if he paid it too much heed.

Resolutely he did his best to remember what the wise monk had told them, and tried to think of castle battlements, courtyards and tourneys – anything familiar that he could cram into his troubled mind. Once or twice he glanced over at Sir Branas for reassurance, but the old knight's ashen face did little to inspire him with courage.

He could hear no sound besides the creaking of the shapeshifting trees accompanied by the eerie susurration of their dead leaves, which seemed to brush against them menacingly as they passed by. Together they made for a sinister medley, occasionally punctuated by a crack of briars as the sedge moved in to hinder their way, their alien flowers puckering grotesquely. It was as if the forest itself were registering its disapproval of intruders.

And yet the squire couldn't shake the feeling that some of the denizens of Tintagael were only too delighted to have them under its eaves...

Like everyone, he knew the legend of the Thirteen Knights of King Thorsvald: he'd seen the castle troubadour Thoros perform it on several occasions. At the time it had just been one more entertainment to enjoy during cold winter nights in the great hall of Hroghar; but now the fate of those brave men evoked by the cogent lyrics made for a sinister recollection – if the best knights of old had met their end here, what chance did the four of them have? At least they had a couple of Argolian friars with them – they knew how to fight the spirits of the Other Side. That was some consolation at least...

The trees shimmered around him, their boles warping obscenely. Vaskrian suppressed a shudder and tried to think about the time he had knocked Rutgar flat on his back – as if to defy him in this consoling thought, a low-hanging branch suddenly dipped in front of his face. Bringing up a tremulous arm he pushed it away, half expecting it whip back at him.

As he struggled past it the branch receded. It was then that he noticed that no matter what shape the trees assumed the leaves were always the same – spiked like morning stars and of a lifeless iron grey hue. Oh well, at least that was a constant of sorts. He wondered, had the others noticed?

✢ ✢ ✢

It was impossible to tell how long they had been walking, but Adelko's feet were sore when the mists began to thicken around them. It was of the same silvery hue as the interminable light, and he was unsure whether it was not simply the latter that was changing, becoming less transparent by the minute. It congealed steadily around them; Adelko fancied then that they were in the belly of a great amorphous creature, slowly being digested and absorbed into its monstrous bowels.

He thought of the old Norric legends his master had mentioned that spoke of the vast World Serpent, which slept at the heart of the earth. The benighted Northland priests had predicted that one day it would stir from its chthonian lair, bringing about a second breaking of the world, far more ruinous even than the first.

He shuddered at the thought, which was the last thing he needed right now; and it was then that he began to hear the whispering sounds grow clearer, reaching out to him across the penumbra of his consciousness.

It was indeed a language he could not hope to understand, but the very sound of the words set his teeth on edge, their soft syllables deftly slicing through his composure like an assassin's oiled knife. An alien tongue sent to murder his sanity... swiftly Adelko began repeating the Psalm of Fortitude, softly to himself at first, but then steadily louder with a growing conviction. When he reached the final set of verses he was almost shouting the words:

Though I walk a crooked path through the darkened vale
My feet shall not falter, nor my soul be corrupted
For the King of Heaven shall not forsake His children!

The wings of Morphonus will be my shield
His celestial consort Oneira will bless my dreams
Stygnos will be my strength; Virtus my resolve!

The Betrayer's words shall stick in his mouth
For the manna of the archangels shall be my balm
Against the poisoned words of his perfidy!

The Almighty hears the prayers of strong and weak
The archangels shall give them the wings to fly
And though the road be broken it shall not hinder them!

Though he was not sure that the ethereal voices tormenting him actually served the Fallen One, the Psalm made him feel better, and gradually the sacred words drowned out everything else.

He had kept walking blindly throughout his recital, trusting to the Almighty, the Redeemer and St Ionus to guide him. And then suddenly he stopped and looked around.

His companions were nowhere to be seen.

Even his horse was gone: its reins must have slipped from his nerveless fingers as he struggled to retain possession of his mind against the baleful whisperings of the Faerie Kindred. At least the mist was starting to disperse somewhat... and now he could hear something altogether new up ahead, its soft gurgling calling him enticingly through diaphanous tendrils that parted invitingly.

Stumbling onwards as if he were walking in his sleep he came suddenly upon a river. It bisected the woods, which had stopped shifting and now resembled the oaks he had first looked upon before adversity chased them into the cursed forest.

Even now the skies remained hidden; the trees here contrived to stretch across the river on either side, their gnarled boughs forming rough stitches in a sylvan veil that steadfastly defied the natural world outside.

Glancing down at the water Adelko shuddered: its stygian black depths offered no comfort, spurning life and light alike. Before him a trail of stepping stones traversed the murky stretch. Their grey surfaces, unnaturally polished and smooth, could be seen glinting beneath the bilious green moss that clung to them.

The novice looked back but found nothing behind him, just an impenetrable wall of oak trees where the trail had been moments ago.

Plucking up his courage he called out: 'Master Horskram?' His voice sounded thin and reedy. The words fell flat no sooner had they exited his mouth – he felt sure that even if his master had been standing right next to him they would not have reached his ears.

Steeling his resolve he stepped on to the first stone. The river stopped, its flow ceasing as abruptly as a horse being reined in, the matt black waters rippling turgidly to and fro before lapsing sullenly into eerie stillness.

Taking a deep breath he took another step. This time he didn't slip, as he had done back in the Brekawood, for the moss was curiously dry.

They want me to get across the river, he thought suddenly, and no sooner had this occurred to him than he found himself on the other side, a fresh pathway opening up for him.

Unlike the trail they had been following this one ran straight as an arrow, and hastening along it Adelko could make out a white light ahead of him. He felt the ground gently rising beneath his weary feet, but some unknown force was now pushing him, nudging him onwards with an invisible hand both firm and gentle. The light up ahead grew steadily brighter. For a while it almost blinded him, but he pressed on regardless, until...

Without warning the brightness receded, and the novice found himself in a tiny clearing shielded from the sky by the intertwining branches. Directly in front of him sat his master on a rock, his quarterstaff nestled in the crook of his arm and his cowled head bowed – in thought, prayer or sleep, Adelko could not tell.

'Master Horskram?' he called softly. When his master did not reply, he repeated himself more loudly. Still the monk did not stir, remaining motionless on the rock. Was he even breathing? Slowly, Adelko stepped towards him...

'Adelko! Stop right now! Don't touch it!'

The novice whirled, his heart leaping into his mouth. Standing behind him was another monk, dressed exactly as his master, the cowl of his habit pulled down over his head. The voice was unmistakeably Horskram's, but it had a strange tinny timbre to it. In his right hand he clutched a quarterstaff. The other was stretched out imploringly towards Adelko.

'Come hither, lad – don't be fooled by your eyes. Yonder apparition is a Gaunt – an eidolon of the forest sent to trick us!'

The voice was definitely his master's, the words reassuringly like his own, and yet... something in that tinniness set Adelko's sixth sense ringing.

'How do I know it's not you who is fooling my eyes...?' asked the novice warily. 'You couldn't have got to the river – the trees closed behind me...'

'What river?' asked the cowled figure testily. 'There was no river – the forest is playing tricks on us, it makes each of us see different things... come away from that apparition, Adelko, it isn't safe to stand so close to it!'

Adelko's sixth sense was screaming. But who – or what – was the cause? Looking uneasily from the cowled figure sitting on the rock to the one standing at the edge of the clearing he shook his head, slowly but resolutely.

'If... if you are who you say you are, then remove your hood. If you are truly my master then show me your face!'

'What in Reus' name are you talking about, boy?' snapped the tinny voice. 'My face is right before you, plain as day! Ah, but Tintagael is playing with your mind – come here!'

The cowled figure took a step towards Adelko. Quick as a flash the novice produced his circifix from the folds of his habit.

'Servitor of Sha'amiel, thy deceit is undone!' he cried. 'Begone! Back to the everlasting wilderness of Gehenna I banish thee! It is the power of the Redeemer that compels you!'

The cowled figure that claimed to be his mentor recoiled, crying out in horror. Triumphantly Adelko stepped forwards, brandishing his circifix and repeating the words.

It was then that he felt a presence at his back. Turning he saw that the monk sitting on the rock had risen and pulled back its cowl.

But it was not his master's face he looked upon.

The skin was chalk-white and taut, pulled back over the skull, forcing the mouth into an awful grimace. Its teeth were unnaturally large, while its glaring eyes were a bloodshot-red with no irises, only pupils of deepest night. The thing towered over him, a head taller than his mentor, reaching for him with impossibly long alabaster fingers that bent and cracked unnaturally.

Adelko felt his mind go numb with horror. Dropping his circifix he fell to his knees as the strength drained out of his body. Behind and above him, as if from a great distance, he heard a tinny voice shouting words that had a vaguely familiar, comforting sound. Then a great shudder passed through him and a yawning void opened at the base of his mind. Without another thought, he plunged into it.

✦ ✦ ✦

Vaskrian had no idea how long he had been wandering blindly through the mist, friendless and horseless, before it slowly gave way to reveal his surroundings. He was standing on a broad outcropping of rock that appeared to overlook a ravine; he could hear the splashing of fast-flowing waters below but a thick shroud of white fog obliterated all sight of the river beneath it. Looking behind him he could see a line of trees following the fractured lip of the ravine in both directions as far as the eye could see. At the far end of the outcropping, a ramshackle-looking rope bridge crossed over to the other side of the chasm, beyond which the forest stretched onwards with an awful certainty.

Gazing upwards he found little to raise his flagging spirits: for even now the obtruding branches somehow contrived to extend across the width of the ravine, interlocking high above his head and abandoning him to the queer light of Tintagael. It was cold; deathly so, and young as he was the squire fancied there was something of the grave about the bitter chill.

As the mist continued to recede the figure of another person became visible. Drawing his sword Vaskrian stepped gingerly towards where it knelt, about halfway across the outcropping between the rope bridge and the trees on his side of the ravine. As he drew closer he could see it was a knight, broad-shouldered and powerfully built. His back was to Vaskrian, and he appeared to be praying: his sword was point down against the cold rough rock, his head bent to the semi-circular crosspiece as he clutched the upturned hilt in gauntleted hands. His white tabard and cloak were slashed and torn in many places; patches of dried blood clung to the rusted links of his armour. He wore an old-fashioned helm that was dented and scratched all over.

The knight did not budge as Vaskrian approached. Stepping around to look at him the squire could see the lineaments of a once proud and noble face, now drawn and lifeless. The deep brown eyes had a soulless look about them, one of a man who has forsaken all hope. His hair hung about his shoulders in greasy black tresses beneath his helm.

'Sir knight?' Vaskrian found himself addressing the warrior, although he had not consciously thought to speak.

'Who disturbs my prayers?' The voice was cold and disembodied. The warrior's ragged lips barely moved as he spoke.

'I... Vaskrian, esquire of Hroghar,' he replied falteringly. It seemed strange to use chivalric protocol in this unhuman place.

'Esquire of Hroghar...' repeated the knight vacantly. His accent had a slightly curious lilt to it, at once foreign and familiar. 'Have they built the place, then? Last I heard the castle foundations had only just been finished... Ah, I've been stuck in this accursed forest for so long...'

'You're one of the Thirteen, aren't you?' Again Vaskrian found himself speaking almost without will, as if his actions preceded his volition.

'One of... is that what they call us now?' replied the knight, still unmoving. 'Yes, I suppose so... my name is Sir Mablung of Teerholt.'

'I know,' replied the squire distantly, as if in a dream. 'They called you The Raven...'

'... because of the colour of my hair and my swiftness in combat,' the ghostly knight finished for him. A touch of wistfulness had crept into his ethereal voice. 'I was the swiftest sword in the land, but the *vylivigs* put an end to that... A raven indeed! Alas, a harbinger of my own doom!'

'The *vylivigs?* Who are they?' The word sounded strange in Vaskrian's ears. It was thoroughly alien; he didn't like it.

'They're the Keepers of Tintagael,' replied the shade of Sir Mablung, his voice dropping to a cracking whisper. 'That's the name the Fay Folk give to themselves... ah, I can still feel their black spears inside me! The pain is never gone from my bones... it's *cold!* It's so very, very cold...'

As he spoke, blood began to run down the shade's gaunt face from beneath his battered helm, splashing silently over his surcoat. It was indeed cold, even more so than before, and Vaskrian found himself shivering uncontrollably. The mist had not receded entirely, but undulated around the pair of them in a mad silvery-green dance of death. From somewhere deep in the ravine a powerful gust of keening wind had started up. It billowed Vaskrian's cloak, which snapped manically about him, but Mablung's ragged threads were limp and lifeless beneath its sere icy touch.

'Tell me where my companions are!' yelled the squire above the rising wind. 'Tell me how to get out of this forest!'

'You'll never get out!' replied the spirit in a despairing voice. 'Forget your friends, they are lost to you now! All is lost! You're in the realm of the *vylivigs* now, and there can be no returning!' The shade's lips had become more animated, spitting particles of ghostly blood that vanished into thin air.

'That can't be!' Vaskrian yelled again, raising his voice yet another pitch. 'There must be some way out of here!' The wind had whipped itself into a roaring frenzy. It howled in his stinging ears.

'There is none!' replied the knight with a sudden fierceness that took the squire aback. As suddenly as it had come, the wind died. The cavorting wreathes of mist twirled abruptly to a halt and sloped to a sullen rest against the rocky ground.

'There is none,' repeated the ghost, this time in another whisper, the sorrow returning to his eerie voice. 'I thought to cross this ravine, many years ago, but this was as far I got. The *vylivigs* came for me here.'

'Well, they haven't come for me yet,' replied Vaskrian, trying to keep his own voice from trembling.

Stepping over to the ravine he glanced down into it again, but the white fog lay thick and heavy and still no water could be seen. Surveying the rope bridge suspiciously he turned back to ask the ghost of Sir Mablung a question... but where the semblance of a living man had been there was now naught but a kneeling skeleton clad in rotting armour. Its sword was rusted and caked with dirt; hollow eye sockets stared back at him beneath a tarnished helm.

✣ ✣ ✣

'... Adelko! Adelko! Can you hear me?'

The novice's eyes flicked open with a start. Had he been dreaming?

Yes... he had. But of what? A forest, a dark pit... he couldn't recall. Horskram was bending over him, looking anxiously into his eyes and holding aloft his circifix. The silver rood glinted dully in the strange light of the forest...

The forest. So that part hadn't been a dream then. Slowly raising himself to a sitting position, Adelko rubbed his eyes and looked about him.

It was the clearing where he had been: the rock was there the same as before, only this time it was empty... a shiver went down his spine as everything came flooding back to him.

'What – what happened, to the...'

'The apparition?' replied Horskram. 'Twas a Gaunt, a wicked eidolon that lingers on the earthly plane to torment and afflict the living.'

Though his face was paler than usual he appeared to have recovered his composure. He placed his circifix back into the folds of his cloak, apparently satisfied that Adelko had not become tainted during his encounter with the ghastly shade.

'But I don't understand... I was so sure it – that *you* were the ghost,' said Adelko. 'Your voice sounded strange and tinny...'

'That was the Gaunt's way of deceiving you. Or the Fay Folk's, for that matter. I told you before, this forest can play with your senses if you let it. Incidentally, I didn't have my cowl pulled up either – another magic mind trick designed to confuse you.'

'But,' protested Adelko, 'when I intoned the Psalm of Abjuration you recoiled...'

His master smiled grimly. 'Yes I did – but not because of your holy ministrations! The real Gaunt had risen behind you, and even one as seasoned as I cannot look upon such deadly apparitions without feeling a chill of horror on my soul. In fact we were very lucky – I almost lost my wits as you did. Oh, here – ' The older monk handed Adelko's own circifix back to him.

Accepting it sheepishly, he asked: 'So you banished it then?'

'Yes, though not without a struggle. The ghosts of Tintagael are unusually strong: their essence is sustained by fay magick, making them all the more difficult to exorcise.'

'What happened to us? One moment we were walking along, the four of us and our horses... the next thing we got swallowed up by mist and then... I started invoking the Psalm of Fortitude and we all got separated.'

Horskram frowned. 'Yes well, that was your first mistake – the Fay Folk don't like to hear the Redeemer's words spoken in their realm. Our being separated was probably their idea of a punishment for your infraction.'

Adelko lowered his eyes to the ground, which was covered in thick emerald grass that sparkled with a deceptive beauty. 'I'm sorry, Master Horskram – it's just... the voices got louder and louder in my head – I had to do something to keep them out.'

Raising his eyes he saw his mentor looking at him strangely. He seemed about to say something and then changed his mind. 'Well, perhaps it makes no difference anyway. We're in the Faerie Kingdom, and only by their sufferance will we survive.'

That begged the question Adelko had been burning to ask. 'So if they're in charge, what can we do to get out of the forest?'

Horskram looked thoughtful as he sat down on the rock, oblivious to the thrill of horror this provoked in his novice.

'I have a feeling we are being tested in some way,' he continued. 'The Fays have ever been capricious and mercurial, serving neither the archangels nor choosing to align themselves with demonkind – although they are most certainly closer to the latter. But if my suspicion is right then we have no choice but to go on, wherever they compel us – and hope that we pass their test.'

'And... what happens if we do? What then?'

'Then we must hope for an audience with the Fays. If we have... amused them sufficiently, we should hopefully be able to persuade them to let us go.'

Adelko was aghast, so much so that he forgot himself. 'That's it?!' he exclaimed. 'That was your plan when you led us into Tintagael?'

Horskram scowled. 'In case you've forgotten, we were somewhat hard pressed – I hardly had time to draw up a treatise on how one survives being outnumbered threefold by bloodthirsty paid killers, Adelko,' he replied acidly. 'But yes, that was, roughly speaking, the adumbration of my intentions. Had we stood our ground we would almost certainly have perished. At least this way we have a chance of survival.'

'But... after all the dark stories you told me of Tintagael! How can you be so sure?'

'I'm sure of nothing,' replied the older monk, unsmiling. 'But not all adventurers have been so brazen, so foolish, as the Thirteen Knights – I know of at least one member of our learned Order who ventured into Tintagael and lived to tell the tale. I know of none who would have survived the odds we faced. You can barely fight, yon youth is bold but inexperienced... and Branas and I are getting too old to single-handedly despatch five berserkers each.

'Nay, lad, I have not spent the past forty years fighting the denizens of the Other Side to quail before a haunted forest, legends be hanged! Trust in the Almighty, keep the Redeemer in your heart, and by his bones we'll find a way out of this accursed place! Now come! We've tarried long enough as it is. We must be on our way, and hope that the Kindred see fit to reunite us with our boon companions – assuming they are still alive and sane.'

Taking up their quarterstaves the two monks looked around the clearing for an exit. Creaking wordlessly, the twisting trees parted obligingly for them, their leaves rustling ominously.

✠ ✠ ✠

Clutching his father's sword in nervous fingers Vaskrian put a tentative first foot on to the rope bridge's gnarled wooden walkway. It let out an elongated sigh as he did. Doing his best to ignore this phenomenon he put another foot forward, trusting his entire body weight to the mercies of the peculiar bridge. This time it let out an agonised groan, and for a split second Vaskrian was tempted to jump back onto the rock behind him.

Plucking up his courage he began to traverse the strange bridge gingerly. His every footfall was registered unpleasantly: sometimes the bridge sounded like a youth having a barbed arrow pulled from his flesh, at others it sounded like an old man dying of the plague. Vaskrian did his best to ignore it, trying to remember what Horskram had told him.

All the while, the white fog rose slowly from the ravine below; by the time he was halfway across it had risen to envelop his legs and lower torso. Resolutely he pressed on, his eyes fixed on the other side where a narrow path had opened up tantalisingly between the trees. The fog rose steadily higher, until he could see nothing but its ephemeral substance suffused with the silvery-green light of the forest.

Then from somewhere far below him he heard a myriad voices drifting up towards him, growing steadily louder.

Some of them spoke in unearthly tongues he could not begin to comprehend; others were recognisably in his own language and various other speeches of the Known World. All dripped with malice. Some mocked his very will to live, while others warned him of a dreadful fate he was doomed to share with them.

As he stumbled on blindly he felt panic rise within him as if in kilter with the awful voices, which had by now risen to his level and had begun to cohere about him with a horrid malignity.

And suddenly he was running, his heart pounding wildly in his chest, cold sweat pouring off his wiry frame in icy torrents, his breath coming in ragged gasps.

On and on he ran, the voices growing louder and more coherent, and yet there was no reassuring solidity of rock beneath his feet, only the springy surface of the groaning bridge as it bobbed up and down maddeningly. Finally, after what seemed an age, he fell to the walkway, his heirloom blade slipping from his hand and disappearing into the ravine.

In between his choking sobs he heard the voices chorus their command, its words now clear as cold crystal:

So far have you strayed
From the mortal vale
Now nothing remains
Come down and join us!

Our spirits shall wander
These cursed eaves
Until time ceases
Come down and join us!

Kingdoms shall fall
Loved ones perish
Our shades linger on
Come down and join us!

Twixt heaven and hell
The faerie bell tolls
Hearken to its knell
Come down and join us!

Come down and join us!
COME DOWN AND JOIN US!

Again and again the preternatural chorus repeated the words, their dark sibilance penetrating to the core of Vaskrian's soul. He felt his courage draining out of him like lifeblood from a mortal wound; staggering to his feet he clutched at the rope bridge and prepared to haul himself over into the void below.

And then a sudden thought entered his fevered mind. He had a vision of Sir Rutgar, standing in the castle courtyard and mocking him. All of Rutgar's friends were standing around him and laughing too. Next to them Edric, his nose bruised and swollen, exchanged knowing sneers with Derrick, who turned a hideously burned face towards Vaskrian, staring blindly at him across a lop-sided grin.

A hot torrent of anger coursed through him. It rose, quickly building to a rage. Before he knew it he was screaming into the thick fog, cursing the forest and its inhabitants, insanely challenging them to return his sword and take him on in a fair fight.

The chorus stopped, voices falling off again into a discordant cacophony that cursed him from beyond the grave.

The fog began to retreat downwards. Glancing about desperately Vaskrian saw he was halfway across the bridge, exactly where he had been before the white mist enveloped him. He was about to make a dash for the other side when suddenly there came a great rumbling and shaking that nearly knocked him off his feet.

Looking back towards the outcropping he saw with horror that it was crumbling away, great chunks of grey rock tumbling into the bed of fog to be swallowed up by the chasm below. The ghost of Sir Mablung had vanished altogether.

With a mighty crack, the outcropping split in two, the foremost half plunging into the ravine – taking the rope bridge with it.

Desperately Vaskrian grabbed hold of the bridge as it swung wildly downwards towards the far side of the chasm. Gritting his teeth, the squire braced himself as the bridge slammed into the rough unyielding rock. The thick boards of the walkway and his brigandine shielded him from the worst of the impact, but even so it was all he could do not to let go as his body jarred painfully to a halt.

The enormous chunk of rock attached to the other side of the bridge dangled ominously for a moment or two, before plummeting into the ravine. With a tearing sound that was strangely wet nearly half the bridge went down with it – another man's height and Vaskrian would have shared its fate.

Yet even so he was far from out of danger, for he now found himself smothered again by the hateful fog. As he clung to the mangled rope bridge for dear life the voices began once more to afflict him.

This time they spoke in a hideous medley of accents and dialects, some long forgotten. Over and over again, they hissed the last words of their eldritch chant: *Come down and join us! Come down and join us! Come down and join us!*

Beneath them he could hear the gurgling of the river, only down here it was louder. It sounded like a hundred men choking to death.

Shutting his eyes tightly Vaskrian began to pull himself up by the bridge's ropes, praying the remaining fixtures would hold his weight long enough to make the climb.

One hand at a time, he yanked himself up. As he did he fixed his mind on thoughts of his past life – anything that would not remind him of the awful place fate had brought him to.

Come down and join us! He thought of the day he had fought Rutgar in the castle courtyard the previous summer. Bright sunlight glinted on their full armour as he parried his arch rival's crude strokes effortlessly...

Come down and join us! Two summers ago. He was lying naked in a hay bale with Adisa, the tanner's daughter, his first love. The warmth of her ample body was like a second sun, meant only for him. She kissed him softly on the neck and ran a coarse hand appreciatively across his toned chest...

Come down and join us! Last summer again. He was riding to Linden with Sir Branas. Mounting the crest of a hill overlooking the fabulous white castle, his heart leapt as he saw hundreds of tents pitched, their varied pennants a riot of colour in the morning breeze. Among them he recognised the standard of the White Valravyn...

Come down and join us! He was eight years old. His father had just pressed a wooden sword into his hand for the first time. His face, stern yet kindly, was intent as he showed his only son how to grip the hilt properly...

Come down and join us! He was fourteen years old. He had just been squired to Sir Branas and was in the stables at his manor house Veerholt in the eastern marches of Efrilund. He hummed a cheerful tune to himself as he fed his prickly new master's charger. Its glossy chestnut coat was smooth to the touch as he stroked its neck...

Come down and join us! Winter just gone. It was the Year's End feast at the Jarl's castle. Thoros was singing a merry tune, about the misadventures of a fictional wizard who tries to save the world... the great hall was a riot of debauchery, everyone was drinking and laughing. His guvnor was so drunk he could barely stand...

Come down and join us! A rest-day in spring, he couldn't remember which year. He was riding a swift courser across the fields and meadows of his master's estate. He spurred the horse into a gallop, the cold brisk wind flinging his long hair in a steady stream behind him. The green sward shot past him as he rode at a breakneck pace. He felt high-spirited and free. Anything seemed possible, his whole life was in front of him...

And suddenly he was hauling himself over the knuckled lip of the ravine with aching arms, his breath tearing from him agonisingly. Rolling over onto his back he stared sightlessly up at the hideous branches, exulting in the solid feel of cold hard rock beneath him. From the chasm below the sibilant voices could still be heard, their malice subsiding into resentment as they repeated their mantra ever more weakly: *Come down and join us, come down and join us, come down and join ussss...*

Gazing defiantly up at the branches, which now seemed to writhe with displeasure, he silently mouthed a single beautiful word.

'No.'

⇒ CHAPTER IV ⇐

Riding the Nightmare

S ir Branas was slumped against the bole of a thick oak tree
when the two monks found him at a crossroads. He was
weeping, his eyes staring sightlessly before him as he mouthed
unintelligible words. The tears streaked a bearded face that looked
even more haggard than usual in the eerie light. Horskram and
Adelko tried to lift the knight to his feet, but he sullenly resisted
all their efforts.

'It's hopeless!' he cried in despair. 'Alas, I'll never see her again.
Oh, my poor Etta, I'd always hoped to meet you in the Heavenly
Halls, but now I know I shall not. Our shades are doomed to rot here
in Tintagael till the end of time!'

'Ghosts don't rot – only corpses,' Horskram corrected him
firmly. 'And Tintagael hasn't sundered our spirits from our bodies
yet – heavens, man, don't give in! The Fays are playing tricks with
your mind!'

'I saw her!' the old knight replied, his eyes suddenly focusing
with an unsettling intensity. 'I saw my Etta, as radiant as the day
I married her, thirty years ago! They told me I'd never see her
again... we're doomed! Ah, what a curse you have brought upon
us, Horskram! At least against the brigands we might have been
spared our souls – you have condemned us to eternal damnation!'

'There will be no damnation if we keep our wits about us
and survive!' snarled the old monk, growing angry now. 'So pull
yourself together – we haven't fallen foul of Tintagael yet! Curse
you, Branas, show some fight! Or is the bold sir knight nothing
but a craven?'

Just at that moment the trio were distracted by the sound of
someone approaching. Lurching out of the gloom came Vaskrian,
looking wild-eyed and exultant, clutching a long dirk. His sword
scabbard was empty at his side.

'It's you! You're all alive too!' he exclaimed breathlessly. 'They tried to get me on the bridge – they almost had me too, but I survived them!'

'Good!' replied Horskram briskly. 'See if you can impart your master with some of your youthful courage then – the forest has poisoned his mind, and I'd rather not risk angering the Fays with another Psalm of Fortitude unless I absolutely must!'

The old knight had resumed his piteous lament. 'Oh Etta... Etta, I shall never see thee again... Reus has forsaken us!'

'That's his wife – she died of consumption three years ago,' said the squire sadly, lowering his voice. 'When he's had too much to drink he often says the only thing that allows him to live without her is knowing they'll meet again in the afterlife... he loved her so.'

'Then if he loves her, he must pull his mind from this black abyss – if he succumbs to this madness his fate will be sealed!' said Horskram unrelentingly. 'Branas, hear me if you will – we can escape this forest, but we must not let our minds fail us. All of us have been tested – you must pass yours, or else the worst you fear may prove true!'

The old knight merely shook his head and groaned again.

'Wait,' said Vaskrian, addressing the monks in a low voice. 'Let me try and talk to him... after all he knows me best.'

Sheathing his dirk and kneeling before his master, the squire looked him square in the face. 'Sir Branas – can you hear me? The monk is telling it true – not half an hour ago I was ready to throw myself off a bridge into... I don't know what! But I survived, and so will you. Etta's waiting for you – you'll see her again one day, just come back to us... In the Redeemer's name, come back to us!'

Something in his plaintive tone must have caught the old knight. Slowly, ever so slowly, he regained a semblance of lucidity and stared back at Vaskrian with eyes not quite bereft of hope.

'What... what did you see?' asked the old knight in a faraway voice.

'I saw one of the Thirteen, he said I'd never escape the forest. But I didn't believe him – and I passed where he failed!'

A cunning look entered Vaskrian's face then.

'You wouldn't want to be outdone by your own squire would you?' he asked pointedly.

The old knight's eyes narrowed. 'Outdone...? By a common rakehell like you? That'll be the day!'

Some of the usual prickliness had returned to his voice.

'Then in Reus' name, do as Horskram bids and get up!' yelled Vaskrian, standing up. 'Or must I find a braver knight to squire for when we escape this cursed place?'

His ploy worked like a charm. 'Why, you insolent cur...!' growled Branas. 'I ought to have you horsewhipped for such presumption! I'll show you who's the real true knight around here...!'

Lurching to his feet the old warrior drew his sword; the blade caught the silvery light of the forest strangely as the trees shifted and rustled menacingly about them.

'That's the spirit, Branas!' cried Horskram, stepping in. 'A true knight never dies until the last blow strikes the life from his body, eh? Now, let's get going – we'll take yonder trail and get ourselves an audience with the Fay Folk. We've played their games for long enough, I think!'

Just then there came a new sound to assail their beleaguered senses – a myriad howling of fell beasts that drew nearer by the second.

'So the games aren't over yet!' cried Horskram with a mad levity. 'So be it! They'll not find us such easy prey as they could wish for! Run! In heaven's name, run!'

✣ ✣ ✣

The howling sounds grew in number as the four of them dashed along another winding trail. To Adelko's ears they sounded like a pack of wolves, though he knew better by now than to expect anything so mundane. His sixth sense told him there was an unnatural intelligence to the wolfen calls.

It was hard to tell how long they had been running before they burst into another clearing. There was a log hut in the middle: the flickering flames of a fire could be discerned through its single window.

Without a second thought Horskram flung open its sturdy door, making sure all of them were inside before slamming it shut. It had a rough makeshift bolt which the old monk drew across with trembling hands.

Breathing heavily the four of them clustered about the window and peered out of it fearfully. The sylvan light of the forest had gradually dimmed during the chase; the clearing was bigger than any of the others they had yet passed through, the forbidding trees at its edge only dimly visible in the failing light.

A few seconds later their pursuers sloped into the clearing. Adelko counted at least twenty, each lupine form the size of a Great Northlending wolfhound. Hairless and skinless, their muscles quivered horribly as they stalked into the firelight. Red forked tongues lolled around huge white fangs that protruded from distended muzzles. Where the eyes should have been a single yellow orb glared balefully.

'Hounds of hell sent to devour us!' breathed Horskram. 'But they will not chastise us so long as yonder fire lasts – look around, is there any more firewood in this hut?'

'Why do they fear the flames?' exclaimed Branas, who seemed to have recovered his wits if not his composure. 'Surely their hellish bourne is hotter than any earthly flame!'

'That's precisely why they fear it even as it attracts them – it reminds them of the realm they have escaped!' replied Horskram impatiently. 'Don't let your eyes deceive you – each one of those awful carcasses holds a lesser spirit of evil! Naked flame will draw them but they will shun earthly heat! We must keep them at bay at all costs – that fire is close to burning out. Is there any more wood?'

'There's some here!' replied Vaskrian excitedly, reaching into an old pail of charred iron and flinging a couple of logs on to the firepit at the heart of the hut's single room.

Grabbing an old poker from a corner Horskram stoked the blaze into life; the hellhounds howled resentfully as the light from the thickening flames grew stronger. Adelko could see them slinking back towards the edge of the clearing, retreating before the advancing glow. Settling down on their haunches they fixed the hut with baleful cyclopean eyes, waiting in the still silence without. Now not even the rustling of the trees could be heard.

'So what in Reus' name do we do now?' Branas' voice shook with fear. Despite the fire's warmth Adelko found himself shivering.

'We examine our refuge,' replied Horskram, looking scarcely less troubled.

A cursory search of the room revealed half a dozen rough wooden pallets, a pail of stagnant but potable water, and an old cooking pot. Inside the last of these, much to their surprise, they found a couple of skinned coneys and a hunk of mouldy but edible bread. Outside the awful hounds had ceased their howling. Were it not for the twenty odd points of yellow light clustered about the edge of the clearing there would have been no sign of their presence. Adelko could swear that not one of the eyes ever blinked.

'This feels like another game to me,' replied Horskram, shaking his head uneasily. 'It is all too easy – chased by yet another grave danger we suddenly find ourselves with food, water, shelter and a fire. I smell a faerie trap.'

'But what choice do we have?' demanded Sir Branas. 'If we venture back outside, yonder fiends will devour us – you said as much yourself!'

'I didn't say we had any choice,' replied Horskram darkly. 'But we should be on our guard – and not only against what awaits outside... I don't think this food is safe to eat.'

Adelko groaned inwardly. A cursed forest was hardly the place to work up an appetite, but even so he felt famished and exhausted. And a bit of food might at least raise their spirits and keep up their strength.

'I don't see anything wrong with them!' retorted the knight, who was clearly of the same mind. 'Vaskrian – inspect yonder coneys. Do you notice anything?'

'I already have, sire,' replied the squire. 'I don't see anything wrong with them either... and a bit of food might do us good after all.' Seeing Horskram turn beady eyes on him he looked momentarily abashed before adding: 'Who knows? Perhaps they were put here by a good spirit to help us.'

'Good spirits are angels,' snapped Horskram. 'And I can assure you there are none to be found in Tintagael.'

'Which you brought us into!' Branas reminded him. 'I'll have no more discussion of this – you may be a learned friar, but I'm a knight of noble blood, and if I say these coneys are good to eat, then they're good to eat! Vaskrian, cook them up – if tonight is to be our last, at least we'll meet our maker on a full stomach.'

'This is rank foolishness!' protested Horskram.

'Nay, master monk,' said Branas, his eyes narrowing, 'this is a craven knight showing his mettle! You tell me to show some courage, and now you're frightened of a couple of dead rabbits! A pox on that! Vaskrian, cook them up!'

✢ ✢ ✢

An hour later and they were feasting – if you could call it that – on stewed coney and mouldy bread, washed down with foul-tasting water. Under the circumstances it seemed a fine enough repast to Adelko. For their part, the old knight and his squire ate greedily. Only Horskram did not partake, stubbornly heeding his own counsel, though he did take a few mouthfuls of water.

Outside, the forest remained ominously quiet. Once or twice he got up to peer through the narrow crooked window; the pinpricks of light remained exactly where they had been, unblinking in the stygian gloom.

Perhaps this is night-time in Tintagael, thought Adelko uneasily. Then he wondered just how long they had actually been in the forest – it already felt like a lifetime. Even time seemed different in this place.

As the meagre but welcome meal settled in his stomach and the warmth from the fire gradually seeped into his bones, he felt himself nodding – blinking and starting, he saw the others doing the same. Even Horskram's head was drooping on his shoulders.

One by one, they all crept over to a pallet and rolled themselves up in their travelling cloaks...

✢ ✢ ✢

Adelko's sleep was troubled by strange dreams. He was back in Narvik, helping his Aunt Madrice clean the kitchen. She turned to look at him with black eyes, only now they were sinister as they had never been before.

'You're never where you should be, are you Adelko?' she accused him. Her voice was sharp and cruel – quite unlike the gentle tone he always remembered. 'One day you'll go off wandering again – only this time *you'll never come back*!'

She glared at him and spat. Her spittle was vile, a strange silvery-green colour...

The dream shifted, and suddenly he was back on the Brenning Wold, riding with his master through the rain – only this time they were heading the wrong way, back north towards the Highlands.

He kept asking, 'Why are we going the wrong way, Master Horskram?' But his mentor never replied, and would only stare ahead as he nudged his rouncy onwards. The sky above was tinged with a luminous silvery-green colour; the skeletal trees scattered across the bilious green hilltops looked sick and ghastly in the unnatural light. Then they reached the crossroads, where they had found the two hanging corpses. They were still there, only this time their faces were a luminous deathly blue. Nudging his rouncy forwards Adelko peered up at one of them, the tar dripping off its mangled rictus. Behind him he heard his master speak in leaden tones: 'They were too curious, young Adelko, and they paid for it... as you will.'

The novice was just about to turn and reply when suddenly the eyes of the corpse he was looking at flicked open, two bloodshot red orbs with no irises and points of night for pupils transfixing him with an awful stare –

✢ ✢ ✢

Adelko sat bolt upright in a cold sweat, panting feverishly. His side was throbbing painfully. Looking about the hut he could see his three companions were still sleeping. The fire had nearly burned down.

Of course, the *fire*...

He was just about to get up and throw a couple more logs on when suddenly he noticed something at the periphery of his vision.

Standing in a darkened corner of the hut was a female figure wrapped in a ragged black mantle. The throbbing in his side increased as it stepped forward slowly into the light. Beneath its cowl the face was hideously deformed, as if badly burned. Two red eyes fixed him malevolently; its broken mouth was peeled back in a leer to reveal a single pointed tooth. The right hand was stretched out towards him, a gnarled claw – in place of the left was a single wicked talon of yellow bone that dripped with blood.

The pain in his side intensified. Looking down he saw his habit was slashed open – pulling at the rent he gaped in horror as it opened to reveal a great gash in his side. Between the suppurating lips of the dreadful wound he could see his blue-green entrails bubbling as they spilled out on to the floor...

⁜ ⁜ ⁜

Adelko woke with a scream. Horskram, on the pallet next to him, sat bolt upright. Scrabbling to his feet the novice clutched at his side, where he could still feel a dull pain. His habit was untouched, but reaching beneath it and running his hand along his side he felt blood. Looking around the hut wildly he grasped his quarterstaff in a panic.

His master sprang over to him and pinned his arms. 'Adelko!' he cried. 'What is it! What did you see?!'

'B-behind you, she's in here with us!' shrieked the terrified novice. Horskram whirled around to look at the corner where Adelko had seen the horrendous apparition.

'There's nothing there!' he exclaimed. Adelko looked again. He was right. There was nothing in that corner but the deepening shadows in the dying firelight. Outside the hellhounds suddenly started up an awful baying, as if mocking their prey.

'The fire!' cried the adept, quickly seizing two more logs and tossing them into the pit. As he stoked it back into life the baying subsided into a resentful growling.

By now Vaskrian had awoken, blearily blinking sleep from his eyes and shuddering. 'I had the most frightful dreams,' he began, before he broke off, looking confused. 'I can't remember what I saw...'

'Never mind that for now,' said Horskram. 'Wake Branas up. Adelko, tell me everything you saw!'

Adelko quickly blurted out his story – when he reached the part about the wound he pulled open his habit to show his master. The cut was there – hardly a serious injury and not nearly enough to disembowel him, but real enough.

Horskram was about to treat it when suddenly Vaskrian lurched back with a horrified yell.

'What is it?' exclaimed Horskram, but the squire could not speak, and would only gibber and point feebly to where his master lay sprawled across the pallet he had bedded down in.

As the reviving flames of the fire grew stronger they revealed Sir Branas. The old knight's eyes were fixed sightlessly in death, staring up at the ceiling, his mouth open in an agonised scream none of them would ever hear. His sky-blue tabard and mail cuirass had been ripped open from neck to naval. The mangled flesh beneath it was a bloody mass of butchered intestines. Even in the half light of the fire it was possible to see a gaping hole where his heart had been...

Adelko wretched, the half-digested remains of stewed rabbit and bread pouring from his mouth in a thick, ugly stream. Horskram uttered a cry of woe before making the sign. Vaskrian sank to the floor, sobbing uncontrollably.

Outside, as if sensing their distress, the hellhounds started baying again. This time the sound had a malevolent gleefulness to it.

It was some time before the three survivors pulled themselves together. Stepping over to the mangled corpse that had been Sir Branas, Horskram dolefully recited the Psalm of Death's Awakening. As he intoned the final line, the hounds' baying rose to a fever pitch.

Doing his best to ignore the infernal clamour the adept bade the two shaking youths sit down, after first covering the old knight's pitiful remains with his cloak.

'Our troubles have multiplied,' he said grimly. 'We have strayed – or rather been chased – into the dwelling of a Hag.'

'A Hag?' asked Vaskrian, his tear-streaked face tortured by confusion and sorrow.

'Another wicked spirit in the service of the Fallen One – far more dangerous than yonder hounds of hell,' replied Horskram. 'It is a thing of nightmare, but every Hag has an earthly bourne – this hut being one. Once the unwary stray into it they fall under her spell. She waits for her victims to fall asleep before entering their dreams to kill them. The Hag desires nothing but to feed off the life-force of the living – and this she does by torturing them in their dreams. By and large, what happens to a Hag's victim in his nightmare happens to him in real life, and thus his fate is sealed.'

Adelko gaped. He'd heard Madrice whisper tales of hags, and had been taught about them at the monastery too – but they were very rare, and the adepts said that most Argolians could live their whole lives without encountering one. But something else was on his mind now.

'But, my wound... why didn't she kill me too?'

'You are much more psychically attuned than the average mortal, as befits a member of our Order,' explained Horskram. 'That can be used against you as I alluded to earlier, for it makes us more receptive to communication from the Other Side, but it can also protect you. I can only hazard a guess that, in this case, your training and natural spiritual resilience were enough to mitigate the Hag's powers over you. Poor Sir Branas was not so fortunate.'

'But... what about me?' asked Vaskrian in a wavering voice. 'I dreamed bad dreams too... though I still don't recall them.' He broke off and shuddered again – clearly he had no wish to.

'Doubtless the Hag chose to focus its diabolical energies first on young Adelko and your unfortunate master – I certainly was not troubled. Presumably when we go back to sleep it will renew its assault on Adelko in a bid to finish him off before turning to deal with the rest of us. If you experienced some bad dreams that you cannot fully remember that is probably a portent of things to come – are you quite sure you can remember nothing?'

The squire shook his head, blinking feverishly.

'That is a pity,' replied Horskram, staring into the fire. 'It would have helped us to know what you will be faced with again.'

Vaskrian stared at the old monk in puzzlement. 'What do you mean *face again*?' he demanded.

Horskram sighed. 'There is no way out of here – not until we confront this evil and destroy it. I strongly suspect that is why the Fay Folk have led us here... You see, one must never assume that the malicious denizens of the Other Side are always on good terms with one another. When I said that hags lair themselves in an earthly bourne I was not being specific enough: they must do so in a place where the rent between worlds is wide. Otherwise a hag would be as commonplace as a banshee, and could manifest itself anywhere. Thank Reus 'tis not the case.'

Horskram made the sign before continuing. 'But while Tintagael is just such a place, in making its lair here this Hag is encroaching on territory that the Fay Folk believe rightfully belongs to them. In short, they don't want it here any more than we do.'

'So... why lead us into its clutches?' asked Adelko.

'Because by now I think our faerie friends have realised that we are no ordinary wayfarers, and have probably begun to suspect that we may have the power to rid them of an unwelcome interloper. Probably she has been here for centuries, robbing them of what they consider to be their rightful prey – their sport, not hers. If my hypothesis is correct, the Fays are hoping that we can despatch the Hag, in which case...'

'What?' Adelko was beginning to find his master's desultory pauses rather maddening.

'... it's almost certain they will at least grant us an audience, and possibly let us escape the forest.'

'But what about Branas?' demanded Vaskrian sorrowfully.

Horskram shook his head sadly. 'He is gone. The best we can do for him now is to destroy his malefactor and try to bargain our way out of Tintagael. If we succeed in the first we can give him his Last Rites – that way his soul at least may reach the Heavenly Halls.'

'You mean – if we don't, he'll stay here, a ghost forever, just as he feared?'

'Or worse,' replied Horskram grimly. 'He will be doomed to relive the nightmare that killed him, here under the eaves of Tintagael, until the end of time. There shall be no respite for his poor soul. That is not the least of reasons why we must succeed in our next undertaking.'

'And what does that involve?' demanded the squire in a voice still shrill with fear.

Horskram turned from the fire to stare flatly at him. 'You must go back to sleep.'

✠ ✠ ✠

'No, I won't do it! You're asking me to give my body and soul to... to that... *thing*!'

Frowning and taking a deep breath Horskram patiently explained it to the squire for the umpteenth time as Adelko put another log on the fire. The awful hounds had not stopped their baying. Even so, he noticed he was beginning to feel drowsy again.

'Only by luring the Hag with the promise of another victim can we expose her,' Horskram said with renewed urgency. 'In order to feed on a mortal's life force she must be half in our world, half in hers, so as to kill him with her dream magic.'

'But you said yourself, I'm the most vulnerable! You and Adelko have psychic powers – why don't one of you do it?!'

'Because, as I've told you several times already, both of us need to be awake to destroy it. We both need to deliver the recital in order to... oh heavens, sirrah, will you do it or not? If you don't we are all assuredly doomed in any case – the Fays will keep us here until the firewood runs out and then...' he gestured meaningfully towards the window. 'I have performed this operation once before, and it was successful. I do not intend to fail at the second trying – now will you trust me or not?'

The young squire's shoulders sagged. He was fearless in the field, but their tussle with the forces of nightmare had left him enervated and terrified.

'I suppose I'll have to,' he said mournfully after a long pause. 'But how do you expect me to sleep anyway? After everything that's happened!'

'Oh believe me,' said Horskram, stifling a yawn. 'The Hag's magic will take care of that. In fact I can assure you that your task will be the easiest of all. Just lie down – well away from poor Branas's remains if it pleases you better – and you won't be long awake. Now is the time.'

With the greatest reluctance the squire picked the pallet furthest away from his erstwhile master's mangled corpse and rolled himself up in his cloak again.

'Lie upright!' Horskram cautioned him. We must be able to see your face clearly throughout the operation!'

Vaskrian did as he was told. Within a few minutes he was fast asleep, his breathing deep and regular.

Watching his chest rise up and down beneath his soiled travelling cloak Adelko felt his own eyelids growing heavy...

'Adelko!' His master nudged him fiercely. 'I didn't say you could sleep as well! Don't nod off – we're all dead if you do!'

For all his alacrity the old monk looked exhausted; his eyes were hooded with fatigue and blinked spasmodically.

'We don't have much time – soon the Hag's magic will begin to take hold of us again, and we won't be able to stay awake however much we want to! We must hope the Hag is tempted to strike soon – for only when she does will she be vulnerable to our invocation. Get your scripture book ready – you know the chapters you are to read?'

'Yes... yes,' replied Adelko, doing his best to shrug off his drowse. Even as he produced the *Holy Book of Psalms and Scriptures* and turned to the relevant page, he found himself glancing sidelong at the pallet next to Vaskrian. How much easier it would be to give in, relent, and slip into numb, comforting sleep...

Reaching into his habit Horskram produced his circifix and phial of holy water. Placing the latter down on the rushes next to his foot he stepped lightly over the sleeping squire, gently touching his forehead and chest while intoning the Psalm of Protection.

'Won't that scare her away?' Adelko had to ask. Besides, asking questions kept him awake.

'Would that it was so powerful against the likes of a hag,' replied his master. 'It will bolster his strength but momentarily I fear, and purchase him vital moments. We cannot attack it until it starts attacking him through his nightmare – I want him to emerge from this ordeal as unscathed as possible.'

Adelko gaped. 'But, you said he'd be perfectly safe! You mean before we can destroy it we have to let it hurt him?'

'Do you think he would have consented to succumb willingly to its powers if I had not withheld the complete truth from him?' asked Horskram drily. 'Another half hour of that ridiculous debate and we would all have been fast asleep again, doomed to share Sir Branas's fate.' The old monk stifled another yawn. 'Now, be silent and stay alert. We must pray that it comes quickly, before we do fall asleep again!'

✣ ✣ ✣

Time slid by immeasurably. The hounds outside continued their baying, only now Adelko was grateful for it – at least the hideous howling gave him something to focus on, to keep deadly sleep at bay. Horskram's face remained a mask of intent, his gaze never wavering from Vaskrian's sleeping face. The squire seemed untroubled, sleeping the deep slumber of an innocent babe, and the novice began to fear that the Hag had anticipated their trap...

Then again, perhaps that meant she wasn't coming back; he could drift off peacefully too...

Adelko was dimly aware of Vaskrian suddenly spasming on his pallet, his face grimacing with some unseen pain.

'Now!' hissed Horskram.

The command cut through Adelko's fugue like a flaring torch across a darkened room. Fixing the page with eyes that ached he began to read the first words of the Psalm of Revealing: 'Oh spirit of evil, that hath walked overlong in the shadows of innocent men, come forth into the bright light! Skirt no longer the shores of this troubled bourne, but place thy cursed feet upon its soil, that thy wickedness may be revealed for all honest souls to witness!'

Heeding his cue, Horskram took up the prayer in his strong baritone: 'Nyx, for too long hast thou poisoned the fruits of blessed Oneira, turning dream into nightmare to trouble the restful sleep of mortals, blighting their peace of mind with fear of darkness and death!'

Reading with lips that trembled Adelko declaimed: 'Relinquish thy diabolical servant now, for it is the power of the Redeemer that compels thee to give her up to the holy light! The light is the eternal spirit of mortalkind, assailed through the ages but never forsaken!'

Horskram intoned: 'It is the love of Palomedes for the sinners he saved through pain and sacrifice; it is the essence of the Almighty, one and indivisible; it is as the burning of a thousand suns; it is as the bright wings of the Archangels, before whom all servants of Abaddon quail and tremble! Release thy servant, give her up to the holy light that she may face the justice of her deserts, for it is the power of the Redeemer that compels thee!'

'IT IS THE POWER OF THE REDEEMER THAT COMPELS THEE!'
both monks shouted together.

Outside the howling had reached an excruciating pitch. Adelko's
ears rang painfully as though a helm had been struck right next to
him with a heavy sword.

The two Argolians repeated the passage several times over, each
time finishing with the final declamation. Vaskrian continued to writhe
on his pallet, although as they continued his convulsions grew weaker.

On the fifth or sixth intonation Adelko began to discern a shape
taking form above the squire: a shimmering apparition of negative
black light that gradually coalesced into a mutable form. Reaching
down Horskram took up the phial of holy water as the loathsome
Hag came screeching into the mortal world.

She looked much as she had done in Adelko's dream, a hunched sick
figure garbed in shredded black. Stooping over the still sleeping squire
she brandished her yellow talon, which glinted horribly in the firelight...

'Now, Adelko! Read the passage!' cried Horskram.

In a stuttering voice Adelko declaimed: 'Slave of Nyx, turn and face
thy doom, that we may look upon thy hideousness before expunging it
forever with righteous wrath! Unshielded by the stuff of nightmare, you
are undone! The mortal vale you have blighted shall be thy grave – thy
cankerous presence shall be cleansed from the good green earth forever!'

With a horrible scream the Hag obeyed Adelko's command,
turning to face the two friars. She was indeed hideous – every bit as
loathsome as in his dream.

Unstoppering the phial Horskram flung a stream of water at
the Hag's leering face, while intoning the final words of the Psalm:
'Taste now the just fruits of your malfeasance! Drink deeply of our
streams, consecrated in the light of the Redeemer by his faithful
servants, as you have drunk so deeply of mortal blood! Let this be
the last of the Almighty's creation that ever you touch! Let it sunder
you forever from the realm you have no right to encroach upon!'

The stream hit the Hag in the middle of the face. Adelko had
expected another scream, but instead she merely groaned; a deep,
sorrowful sound that smacked of resignation. Her face collapsed,
sloughing off her skeletal frame in vile gobbets of greenish matter.
Stepping in closer, Horskram let fly with two more splashes, a second
in the face and another to her scrawny chest. A vile putrescence filled
the hut as fumes hissed and steamed off the Hag's shrivelling form,
which was melting like a waxwork figurine in a fire. Both monks
gagged and wretched, throwing up watery bile as the Hag expired.

When they had both recovered they cautiously approached her shabby black mantle, lying on the rushes in a crumpled heap. Taking up his quarterstaff Horskram gingerly moved it aside, but all that remained of the apparition was a fast-congealing puddle of slimy ooze. Outside, the hounds had stopped their howling and fallen back into ominous silence.

Stepping over to Vaskrian, Adelko placed his ear close to him... he was still breathing. Making the sign, he pulled back his cloak.

'Careful,' cautioned Horskram. 'We don't want to wake him suddenly. He has survived the Hag's assault, so he should be allowed to return to normal sleep. That way he has more chance of forgetting whatever horror she chose to visit on him, which will be just as well for him.'

'But... what if he's hurt?' asked Adelko fearfully, remembering his own experience. Horskram had bandaged the cut in his side with a fragment of Branas's cloak, but it still stung painfully.

'Well, he doesn't appear to have been lacerated,' frowned Horskram, after examining him gingerly. 'I think we acted swiftly enough to preserve him from the worst. Good work, Adelko, very good work.'

His master clapped him on the shoulder with a wan smile. Despite his exhaustion Adelko had enough energy to feel a surge of pride – before remembering that was a sin and suppressing it.

'So what do we do now?' he asked.

As if in answer to his question, they suddenly became aware of a light from outside. Stepping over to the window the two friars peered out of it timorously. The old sylvan glow was returning to the forest, growing steadily stronger. Gazing about the clearing they could see no sign of the hellhounds.

'It is as I fathomed,' said Horskram. 'The Fays have set us a task, and we have performed it for them. Now we must hope they will be in a generous mood.'

⤖ CHAPTER V ⤖

A Theft And A Betrayal

Balthor Lautstimme's face was grim as he dismounted in the courtyard of the outer ward with the half dozen knights the Eorl had sent with him. His unruly ginger hair made for an odd contrast with his neatly trimmed beard, although both were tainted with the dust and dirt of the road.

Urist Stronghand knew from the look on his old rival's face that they had been spent in vain. Nonetheless he kept to protocol as Sir Balthor approached him with a curt nod. 'Graukolos salutes your safe return, Balthor – how did you speed on your mission?'

The nod quickly changed to a perfunctory shake of the head. 'Nothing,' replied the other knight. 'We made a good clean sweep of the area, for miles around the castle, but no one has seen or heard of anything untoward in the last three days. It would help if we knew how to describe what we were looking for.'

Sir Urist's frown deepened as he studied his rival's face in the torchlight. Both men were powerfully built, although Balthor was slightly shorter and somewhat thicker about the shoulders. Urist felt a twinge in his thigh, the way he often did in the presence of the man who had unhorsed him so spectacularly and put an end to his run as Dulsinor's greatest knight.

Truth to tell, Urist rarely troubled himself about such trifles – he was still Marshal of Graukolos, with duties to perform and sons to raise – but no true knight, however humble, could ever set that kind of defeat aside altogether.

'Few men have ever looked upon such a thing,' replied Urist in a subdued voice. 'And it were better that fewer still did. We had best go and give your news to the Stonefist, though it will please him ill to hear it.'

'For myself I ask nothing, but my men have been long on the road today and are hungry,' put in Balthor. There was an abrasiveness in his voice that Urist disliked – indeed, he had never liked the way his rival spoke to him.

One day perhaps he would remind him that, whoever couched the better lance, he was still in charge of Graukolos.

'Yes, of course,' he replied flatly, meeting Balthor's steely gaze. Though it was dusk, the ward was still a hubbub of activity. The resident craftsmen and artisans were packing up their stalls for the night, while the master of stables Orick and his assistants were busy seeing to their horses. A handful of servants were scurrying around as well, the mighty walls of Graukolos making ants of them beneath the deepening blue skies.

Sir Urist beckoned to one. 'You there! Take these men to the Great Hall and put in a word at the kitchens – they are to be fed immediately.' Turning to Balthor he added: 'Now, sirrah, if you will, it is time we spoke to the Eorl – as you well know, Wilhelm is a man who insists on hearing bad news at once.'

The two men crossed the outer ward in silence. To either side of them the walls loomed, the height of twenty men and tall ones at that. The thick oak beams of the stables ran the whole length of the courtyard: home to more than two hundred horses, a muffled cacophony of whinnying and stamping could be heard from within, along with the hollering of the craftsmen and clamour of the kitchens on the opposite side of the ward. Steam filtering from the window slits of the latter mingled vaporously with smoke from the torches, whose yellow light flickered playfully across the grey corbels that supported the upper level above the kitchens and pantry where the scullions and other servants slept.

A partition wall divided the outer and middle wards. This was guarded by a gatehouse, although its double doors were nearly always left open except in times of war. The partition was a third of the height of the main walls; Goriath Stonecrafty had built it with the eventual lords of Graukolos in mind, so they could look across their vast grounds and view arrivals at a glance from the donjon in the castle's eastern wing.

Two great long-axes stood to either side of the yawning entrance. Atop these a pair of buttresses that reinforced the corners of the upper section of the gatehouse sported two carved warrior angels, their stone greatswords pointing inwards to form a stylised gable atop the gateway's curving arch. The gatehouse summit was slung with shields, each one bearing the Markward coat of arms. There was one for every Eorl of that noble house who had reigned over Graukolos: nine black fists clenched pugnaciously at the lowering skies.

A pair of men-at-arms stood to either side of the gateway, their iron-rimmed shields and polished hauberks catching the light from the torches in the tunnel behind them. Balthor and Urist passed through this before emerging into the middle ward. This was a similarly sprawling affair, and the northern portion was given over to the training yard. Even now, with the day nearly done, men were fighting, their blunted swords gleaming dully in the torchlight.

Glancing over, Sir Urist recognised the combatants. Sir Agravine and Sir Ruttgur, good knights both. The younger sons of landed vassals, they'd taken service in Wilhelm's household as his sworn swords and lances. When the day was done they would take their rest on the floor of the Great Hall directly south of the yard along with the rest of the Eorl's knights.

About a hundred were landless bachelors like Agravine and Ruttgur and served the castle for life, but the other forty changed each month: these were vassals of the Eorl, men like those who had fathered the two worthies now striking at each other in the dust, come to pay feudal service to their liege in return for the lands he had given them.

A dozen or so men-at-arms and knights were watching Ruttgur and Agravine fight, every now and then cheering on a favourite. Urist allowed himself a half-smile as he saw Ruttgur press Agravine back towards the wall of the armoury on the far north side with a relentless salvo of fierce strokes. Though Agravine was the more personable and courteous of the two, and therefore more popular, Urist had often mused that in times of strife he would wish for Ruttgur at his back the sooner.

Both knights were young and relatively new to the garrison, having been spotted at the Chalice Bridge Tourney the previous year. Both couched a solid lance but it was Agravine's flourishes that had won the crowds over, saluting and bowing in the saddle after a successful tilt with an elegance that a Pangonian might envy.

Neither had made it to the final, both knights being dislodged in the penultimate round by Sir Balthor and Sir Corus, a mountain of a man who served Lord Rothstein, the baron giving the tourney.

But Urist had been quick to recognise potential when he saw it, not least because he had gone down before Ruttgur in a previous round. Their performance in the melee the next day had shown them to be doughty enough at close quarters as well – the Marshal of Graukolos had put in a word with the Eorl and had them taken into service, before another lord did.

Balthor for his part had been quick only to boast of his eventual win over Sir Corus in the joust – despite losing his prize money to a ransom in the melee the very next day. His vanquisher had been none other than Corus himself, who had been only too pleased to have his revenge, knocking Balthor from his horse with a great iron mace and breaking several of his ribs in the process.

Balthor didn't boast too loudly of that part of the tourney to the damsels and serving wenches at Graukolos, Urist noticed. But then that was typical of the man.

'They fight well,' grunted the flame-haired knight as they passed the sparring bachelors, heading towards the gatehouse guarding the inner ward. 'I see your trust in their abilities wasn't misplaced – although to be fair you did have first-hand experience of young Ruttgur's prowess.'

The Marshal of Graukolos was in no mood to be baited by its best – and most pompous – knight. 'I did indeed,' he replied levelly. 'As you did with bold Sir Corus. A pity he is already sworn to Lord Rothstein, else I would have approached him on the Stonefist's behalf too – for that swing of his that sent you tumbling in the melee alone.'

Balthor at least had grace enough to smile at this. 'Aye, it was a painful reversal of my good fortunes that week, 'tis true – though had we not been ambushed and taken unawares I feel the outcome of that skirmish would have been very different. What was Rothstein thinking, putting that oaf Sir Reginal in charge of tactics? The man can't plan a mock battle any more than he can a real one.'

'True enough,' Urist had to allow. 'Perhaps his being the younger brother of our gracious host had something to do with it...'

Balthor snorted, only half laughing now. 'Yes, well, thankfully he has enough sense not to make that great fool his marshal in real life!'

'No indeed,' replied Urist flatly, deftly concealing his feeling of triumph. 'As I recall, he has given that duty to Sir Corus.'

Balthor's sudden scowl was not pretty as Urist glanced sidelong at him. It reassured the older knight to remind himself why Balthor would never take his position as marshal – even if he had already taken some of his glory from him. The man could certainly fight: sword, spear or axe, there were few that could live with him on the field of battle. But when it came to tactics, the art of thinking one step ahead in the abstract, Balthor was little better than the hapless Reginal.

They drew level with the final gatehouse. Above them the walls of the keep loomed, stonily impassive and impossibly high. Urist had only seen one building that was taller, but that had been built by an ancient race of wizards who had enslaved demons and Gigants and used them as builders.

The Watchtower of Mount Brazen they called it, and it nestled like a great stone weed in the foothills of the Great White Mountains. He had seen it in his youth, when the House of Markward had ridden off to war against the Eorl of Ostveld, whose lands lay to the south-east, after getting wind of his plans to lay siege to Graukolos in the hope of capturing the great prize. It had been a resounding victory: they had turned the tables on the enemy and caught them unawares with devastating effect.

Yet even still Urist had never forgotten the dread spectacle of that blood-red tower and its peculiar stones, looming like an ill omen over the field of battle. He'd seen it from leagues away, but there had been no mistaking its size even at that distance. And that was long after it had been broken by the wrath of the heavens... who could say how high it had been before?

But that was aeons ago, if the loremasters told it true. The walls of Graukolos Keep were altogether a less alien and more appealing sight – but it was said the castle also had its roots in magic of some kind. The loremasters claimed its builder Goriath had been a warlock himself, using his scrying arts to peer into the distant past and relearn the long-forgotten stonecraft of the ancients. Nothing so blasphemous as the dark arts of the Priest-Kings of legend to be sure – but even so, his knowledge must have come from some lost era. How else could anyone have built such a monstrous castle six hundred years ago?

That had been a benighted age, when petty kings ruled in Vorstlund, sulking behind the crude walls of their mottes and baileys whilst the peasantry toiled from dawn till dusk through miserable lives that were mercifully short. Even the great masons of the renowned Pangonian King Vasirius had been hard put to rival Stonecrafty's monolithic achievement four centuries later.

Small wonder Urist felt a lingering and deep sense of pride as he stepped up to address the inner gatehouse garrison. Graukolos was a seat fit for a king, and its lord and master had entrusted him with its security. Next to such an honour, his tournament trophies frankly seemed like baubles.

The gatehouse garrison was a forty-strong force of men-at-arms led by Brigmore Stoutgirt, captain of the guards. He was several years older than Urist but as a commoner he deferred to the Marshal.

'Sire,' said Brigmore curtly, acknowledging him with a deferential nod before motioning to the guards to raise the portcullis.

He was a man of even fewer words than Urist, and the Marshal liked him for that: he got on with his job and he did it well. A family man with a strong sense of duty – the common folk threw up a few good apples once in a while, and Brigmore was one of them.

Urist knew that he blamed himself for the theft, and had taken pains to reassure him to the contrary. It was clear that no earthly powers could have prevented such an unearthly break-in, and it was hardly Brigmore's fault the common soldiers had been too afraid to guard the Werecrypt. It did not take a perfect or an Argolian to see that some devilish work was afoot.

The archway of the inner gatehouse centred on a huge boss. Carved of the same slate grey stone as the rest of the castle, this depicted a mighty fresco of Ludvic the Builder, fourth king of the House of Tal that had founded the Old Kingdom of Dulsenar. Ludvic had ruled what was now the Griffenwyrd of Dulsinor more than six hundred years ago, and took his epithet from the mighty castle he had commissioned.

That was the way of things, Urist reflected wryly to himself and not for the first time: lesser folk did the toil, but it was the scions that ruled them who were honoured for the fruits of their thankless labour.

Or at least, that was the way the scions of the House of Tal had intended it to be – but in truth Goriath Stonecrafty was far better remembered than the petty king he had served.

Two pairs of crossed long-axes hung on either side of Ludvic, portrayed as a bull-necked giant of a man clad in crude old-fashioned mail and resting two broad hands on a mighty war-hammer. If the old histories were to be believed, Ludvic had been as renowned for breaking things as for building them. But then, Urist supposed, King Ludvic the Breaker didn't carry quite the same legacy.

Above the frescoed boss was draped a great silken cloth the height of several men, pinned at each corner with a shield. All five bore the Markward coat of arms.

In far-gone days it would have been the arms of Tal standing proudly on display, but it had been nearly three centuries since the red heron had flown from the walls of Graukolos, when the last scion of that once-great house breathed his last on the sword of Ranveldt Longyear, first Eorl of the House of Markward and Wilhelm's ancestor.

Above the great coat of arms the huge keep stretched towards the firmament, its crenelated parapet biting the darkening skies with broken teeth. Torchlight glinted on helm and hauberk as more of Brigmore's men patrolled the walkways high above the courtyard. Higher still loomed the westernmost turrets of the inner ward. The summit of the one to Urist's right shone yellowy green in the light emanating from the keep's many window slits.

The creeping ivy was the Lady Adhelina's unique touch. Her knowledge of the natural arts had more practical uses though: the Marshal of Graukolos had lost count of the number of brave knights and men-at-arms whose lives or limbs she had saved during the last war.

Thinking this he felt a twinge of pity for the heiress of Dulsinor: being married off to the likes of Lord Hengist was poor reward for her services, for all that he was rich and powerful. But duty demanded it – and duty was everything.

With a metallic screech the portcullis ground to a halt above them. The clash of arms could no longer be heard from the training yard; the two gallants had called it quits with the oncoming of night.

Thoughts of swordplay would be rapidly giving way to contemplation of a hearty meal and a few stoops of wine to wash it down.

The inner ward gatehouse ran twice as deep as that of the middle. As well as the obligatory murder holes lining the ceiling of its main tunnel there were doorways from which the garrison could sally forth to fight intruders if need be. In the rooms beyond, off-duty soldiers would be idling or playing at dice as they awaited the tolling of the bell in the barracks mess hall to summon them to supper.

With another curt motion Brigmore signalled for four guards to accompany the two knights into the last courtyard. Secure as they were in peace-time this was hardly necessary, but Brigmore and Urist were both sticklers for protocol. Flanked by their honour guard the Marshal of Graukolos and Dulsinor's greatest knight entered the gatehouse.

✛ ✛ ✛

Observing the two knights from her lofty perch, Adhelina heaved a sigh and turned back to face her room. All about her everything seemed the same: an abundance of herbs and poultices hanging up to dry, filling her expansive chamber with a pungent aroma but making it seem much smaller than it really was. A riot of good green colour, just the way she liked it; a smile from the archangel Kaia to cheer the cold grim stone of Ezekiel.

And yet things were not as they had been – indeed never would be. As if her own personal troubles had not been enough, now this calamity had befallen the castle, and her father was at loss as to how to deal with it. It certainly did not make him more receptive to her entreaties that he delay her nuptials.

Turning back to gaze languidly across the torchlit courtyards of the middle and outer wards, Adhelina cast her mind back across the events of that fateful night.

The rumours had spread quickly enough, as she had known they would. There had been a break-in of some sort, and a theft – that was about all they agreed on. That and one other thing. Some devilry was behind it – how else could any common thief break into the most unassailable castle in Vorstlund? Though most of the assembled nobles had been far too drunk to notice anything untoward, the two-hundred strong garrison of common soldiers would not have all been off duty.

The Lanraks had packed themselves off that day with all due pomp and ceremony, the future Grand Herzog of Stornelund-Dulsinor still reeling from too much wine and struggling to stay upright in the saddle. The Eorl of Dulsinor and his household had seen them off with all due courtesy nonetheless, but his only daughter had marked the troubled frown that creased his rugged face.

By then the rumours had had more time to embellish themselves. It was a great war-chest of golden treasure that had been stolen, remnant heirlooms of a vaster hoard gifted to Oberon the Wise, the last petty king of Dulsenar, who had bent his knee to King Gunthor of Vorstlund without bloodshed. It was a great tome written by Goriath Stonecrafty, in which he had laid down the secrets of his masonry, and many other hermetic arts he had learned. It was the heart of Ludvic the Builder, preserved by the sorceries of Goriath – legend had it that so long as the magic organ stayed buried beneath the walls of Graukolos the castle would never be taken, hence its theft portended a great calamity.

Adhelina knew better than to believe such tales. She was far too well-read not to know the truth of the matter, and besides that as the heiress of Dulsinor she had been made privy to many of the castle's secrets by none other than old Berthal himself.

Her feverish reading of the past few days had well reacquainted her with the truth, which was potentially more frightening than all the superstitious rumours put together.

The fragmented shard of the world's most powerful artefact had never been a welcome inheritance, but like the cares of rulership it came with the castle, a responsibility that could not be shirked.

Yet shirked it had been nonetheless – and during her father's tenure to boot. As was to be expected, Wilhelm's common soldiers would do virtually anything their liege told them to – but they would not stand guard in the Werecrypt.

It had never been the most salubrious of duties, sharing the silent vaults with the noble families of Dulsinor that had been laid to rest in them for centuries. But for generations the authority of the liege and the honour attached to the service had seen it performed without question.

That was until several years ago, when things began to change.

Sentries coming off duty from the Werecrypt would return to the barracks pale-faced and trembling, going to bed and board with troubled eyes that told a fearful yet wordless tale. Many would wake screaming in the dead of night for weeks after their service, until finally Wilhelm had quietly ordered the duty dropped, for fear of mutiny.

Whatever was stirring in the bowels of the Werecrypt, it clearly inspired more fear than the iron laws of mortal men.

With equal discretion, her father had summoned an Argolian friar to investigate the matter. The monk had remained in the castle a single night, holding vigil in the Werecrypt before seeking the Eorl's solar for a private audience at dawn. Then he had ridden back to his monastery, to be heard of no more.

As far as Adhelina knew, since then no one had set foot in the mausoleum – indeed normally there would have been no reason to until she, her father, Berthal or any of his family members died. It was only the peculiar custom of the castle, bound up with some older tale of legend known to few, that dictated a sentry guard at all times in the Werecrypt.

After the duty was dropped the afflicted soldiers had gradually shrugged off the pernicious curse and returned to normal. But not one of them could ever hear the name of the Werecrypt mentioned again without blanching.

If the nature of the 'treasure' they had used to guard had been more widely known, Adhelina reflected grimly, her father might not only have faced a mutiny among his superstitious soldiers.

Turning from the window she picked up the weighty tome she had asked Lotho to procure from her father's solar. She knew he wouldn't · mind: he never had the patience for reading and was in any case too concerned with the present evil to be overly concerned with its antecedents.

The more fool him. An inscription in Decorlangue embossed on the musty leather cover in spidery letters proclaimed the title: *A History of the Lords of Graukolos, Past, Present, and Those to Come*.

The whimsical last part of the title referred to the book's unwritten pages, those that Lotho and his descendants would write about her father, her and her future offspring – assuming she had any. Castle custom dictated that a lord's life would only be written in the great tome once it had come to an end. She presumed Lotho kept notes, to aid his wine-sodden memory or his successor when her father's time came.

Sitting down at her desk as Hettie busied herself with tidying up her chamber, the heiress of Dulsinor turned to the page she had marked with a scrap of cloth.

The ink was old and faded, written by a hand that had rotted in the grave some four centuries past. The heading read: *The Reign of Ludvic, Second Jarl of Freiholt-Dulsenar, called by some 'the Stone-Cursed'*. Drawing a tallow candle nearer, she began to read the words again:

✤ ✤ ✤

And though Ludvic was blessed with an unusually long life, perishing only in his ninety-fifth year, his reign has been marred by a great evil, that some say brought sorrow to all his days thereafter.

For it was ordained that into his path should fall one of the most diabolical artefacts crafted in any Age, namely a fragment of what loremasters and perfects have dubbed the Headstone of Mammon, greatest of the devil-worshipping Witch-Emperors of antiquity. And how this accursed anti-relic was broken by the Northlandic hero Søren and brought thereafter to the mainland other tales tell, and it will suffice here merely to recount how one of the four shards came into the realm of Vorstlund.

By most accounts the fragment was discovered by a merchant, one Manfried of Wernost, returning to his homeland after a voyage of trade to the northlands. Becoming lost in the Argael Forest, he and his party of hired swords stumbled upon a secluded clearing, overgrown with choking weeds. Amidst these they found the skeletons of other warriors, their armour and weapons long rusted. It appeared that they had killed each other in battle, though strangely their apparel and equipage were similar enough to suggest they all hailed from the same region of a foreign land, perhaps Thraxia or Northalde.

Searching the clearing for booty Wernost and his men are said to have come upon a shard of peculiar stone, the size of a man's torso and covered with strange markings that seemed to catch the fading light unnaturally. If the most reliable accounts are to be believed, Manfried appears to have been unusually wise for one of his class, and sensing he had stumbled upon an artefact of unusual provenance he decided to bear it to the fortress dwelling of Alaric the Prescient, then ruler of Upper Thulia, whose thrice-cursed name still justly redounds in notoriety to this day.

At the time, that noble was held to be a man of unusual learning; for as well as keeping a library of more than a hundred tomes it was whispered that he had, using ancient lore unknown to latter-day men, constructed an observatory in the summit of his tower, from where he would stay up late into the night scouring the firmament in search of secrets only the stars can tell.

And upon receiving Manfried and his retinue and learning of the purpose of his visit, Alaric offered the former two hundred gold regums for his prize. Being primarily motivated by profit and perhaps secretly glad to be rid of the mysterious burden, the merchant readily agreed, and departed the following morning without further ado.

What little is known is that Alaric installed his new possession in his observatory, from whence over the next ten years peculiar sounds were said to be heard almost nightly, and a series of malign and baleful events befell the lands around. Peasants and wayfarers frequently went missing, and werewolves and revenants were said to multiply in number, howling on moonlit nights and stalking the woodlands of that unhappy region. Rumours abounded of abductees meeting a grisly and horrible fate in the summit of Alaric's fortress home, further evidenced by the discovery of a hecatomb of corpses in varying stages of decay in a cave overlooking a stream not two leagues from his castle.

During this time it is said Alaric was seen less and less by his vassals; when he did appear none could miss his increased pallor and sunken eyes, and the superstitious say he began to resemble the dead more than the living.

Finally, word of his rumoured demonology spread so far that the neighbouring earls of Vorstlund, of whom our most worthy late Ludvic was one, resolved to meet and determine how to proceed against their blasphemous neighbour.

Message was sent to the Supreme Perfect of the True Temple in Rima, who swiftly sanctioned a provincial holy war against Alaric. Ludvic and two other barons, Otho of Hyrlund and Ormrick of Dreylund, made plans for battle and laid siege to Alaric's castle.

There have been many tales told of that ghastly conflict, during which Alaric confirmed all rumours of his delvings into the Other Side, conjuring up a host of fiery anti-angels to do his bidding. And it is told how these awful servants cut a swath through the tripled ranks of his antagonists, slaying Otho and grievously disfiguring Ormrick.

Indeed, it might have been a black day for all godly men had not Ludvic worn the Wheel of Saint Albared about his neck. And that relic, given to Ludvic's grandfather Albaron the Pious by temple perfects in return for generous donations, saved him – for none of the devils torn by Alaric from the flaming pits of Gehenna would come near it.

And so Ludvic mounted to the summit of that ensorcelled tower, and there he met Alaric in mortal combat and slew him, casting his body over the battlements. At Ludvic's pious behest the victorious raiders burned Alaric's castle to the ground, destroying everything within.

Everything except one thing. For as the smoke and fires of war cleared against a smouldering dawn, the surviving warriors saw a fractured piece of unearthly stone sitting atop the ruins, the eldritch and unfathomable glyphs carved on it glowing with a sinister light.

Loath to take it into his possession yet fearing to leave such a diabolical heirloom unguarded, Ludvic brought it with him back to Graukolos, where he placed it in a great casket bound on all sides with iron – said by the wise to be the only metal that has any chance of abjuring sorcery. He placed it in the lowest vault of his castle, forbidding any – family, friend, vassal or servant – to enter it under pain of death. And atop the casket he fixed the relic that had saved his life, trusting in the power of the Redeemer to keep the ancient evil in check.

And may the Almighty grant our prayers that it does so forever!

✣ ✣ ✣

Adhelina paused to accept a cup of watered wine proffered by Hettie. The rest of the life of Ludvic dealt with other matters of his reign that had nothing to do with the fragment. But all the same she knew full well that the prayers of the long-forgotten amanuensis had gone unanswered.

Two centuries later the Wheel of Saint Albared had been needed again, this time to deal with the sorcerer Aracelsus, whose black arts had blighted Vorstlund's southern fiefdoms. And though Sir Wolfram of Gottingen, the pious hero who took the relic, was successful in his quest and made an end of that warlock, the sacred rood had been destroyed in the process.

Even then, the stone's power had seemingly continued to lie dormant – as though its long exposure to the saintly circifix had subdued its malign influence. At least, that was what her father and all his ancestors as far back as Ranveldt had hoped.

And so it had proved – until now.

Closing the book gently, Adhelina took up her cup once more and drained its contents. Then she rose and motioned for Hettie to open the door for her.

'I must see my father,' she said in a subdued voice. Her oldest friend looked at her, the pity in her pretty hazel eyes speaking volumes. She said nothing, but pursed her lips before walking over to the door and undoing the bolt.

The castle corridor was cold as she passed out of the warmth of her chamber, and Adhelina shivered in the chilly breeze wafting through the windows as she made her way down to her father's solar. Outside the stars were gradually blinking into life across the darkening skies.

Reaching the door she rapped loudly on the knocker, its sharp report sounding loudly in her ears. It was opened by Berthal, who was apparently just leaving. She stepped aside for him but just as she was about to enter she found the door closing, pushed timorously but firmly by her father's page boy.

The seneschal looked at her kindly as the oak door closed in her face with a decisive *thunk*.

'I am sorry, my lady, your father is granting audience to Balthor and Urist in his private chambers – he has left strict instructions not to be disturbed.'

Adhelina fixed the seneschal with eyes that made the flaming torches next to her seem like mere tapers. 'When will he be done with them, do you know?'

Her voice sounded curt and abrasive; she could not find a soft tone now, not even for Berthal. But the old steward merely shook his head.

'I am sorry my lady, your father won't be admitting anyone else tonight. He has... pressing matters to attend to, I am sure you will have heard the rumours by now.'

Yes, she thought to herself bitterly, *I've heard them and I understand them better than most.*

Berthal took a deep breath and let out a sigh. He paused and then seemed to make up his mind to say something more.

'I wouldn't trouble about them too much if I were you, my lady,' he said. 'Matters are all in hand, I can assure you. And you have your nuptials to prepare for. Think on that, my lady. Good night.'

The seneschal bowed before descending the stairs towards the exit far below.

Left alone, Adhelina stepped over to the window overlooking the middle courtyard. The training grounds were deserted; all the knights would be in the Great Hall for the evening meal. The outer ward was also still – the craftsmen would be wending their way down the hill on which the castle had brooded for six centuries towards their homesteads, where their wives and families would greet them with food and drink. All about her was a hubbub, as the clamour of Graukolos filtered out through its multitude of windows, borne on gathering winds that swirled her lustrous tresses and whipped her samite dress about her handsome frame.

Raising her eyes from the castle precinct to the limitless skies above, the heiress of Dulsinor resolved to abandon her inheritance forever.

⊱ CHAPTER VI ⊰

The Faerie Kings Speak

They disposed of Sir Branas's remains as best they could. At Horskram's insistence they built a funeral pyre using wood from the hut, for a body so polluted had to be given to the fire. In accordance with custom they laid him out in full harness with his sword across his breast. His ghastly wound they covered as best they could with his cloak.

At the signal from Horskram his erstwhile squire lit the pyre, blinking back tears as he did. Northlendings ought to be stoical at funerals, but Vaskrian struggled to contain his emotions.

Adelko silently mouthed the Last Rites with Horskram, as he implored the Almighty to forgive the dead knight his sins and admit his shade to the Heavenly Halls.

They were a crucial part of any Palomedian funeral. The scriptures taught that shriven souls crossing over to the Other Side faced a harrowing journey. Drawn across the Sea of Second Sleeping by an irresistible force, they eventually found themselves on the shores of Azhoanarn, Island of the Dead. There they would be taken by un-angels across the Bourne of Night's Awakening to the Plain of Azrael, where the Archangel of Death would weigh their sins. Those found wanting would be chained to a vast galleon wrought of tarnished iron, and sent to the City of Burning Brass in Gehenna.

But those who died without receiving the Last Rites were doomed to wander lost in Azhoanarn, along with the pagan idolaters who had worshipped angels and demons as gods before the Coming of the Prophets. Certain of the Unseen might pay them a visit – religious scholars disputed whether the old 'gods' still had a hand in their worshippers' afterlife – but the blessed light of the Heavenly Halls would be barred to them until the Day of Final Judgment.

Shrewd scholars had pointed out that an unrepentant sinner might prefer such a fate to the City of Burning Brass – but the sages agreed that Azhoanarn could also be a dreadful place for wicked souls. And when the Day of Final Judgment came, they would get their comeuppance anyway.

In all honesty, Adelko found the conflicting accounts of what happened to a soul after death inconclusive at best. Even the scriptures were vague on the matter. And the dead weren't in the habit of returning to confirm or deny theories.

Horskram closed the prayer in his sonorous voice: 'May this humble spirit be taken in by Reus and commended to eternal rest by the guidance of Palomedes, the One True Prophet. Forever and anon, amen.'

All three made the sign of the wheel. The thickening flames curled around Branas's corpse in a fiery embrace. Overhead the looming trees shifted and cracked uncomfortably, but did nothing to menace them. Perhaps the Fays were indeed mindful of a service rendered, as Horskram hoped. Adelko hoped so too – it had cost them dear.

They stayed like that for a while, heads bowed in silence and hands splayed across their chests. Presently Horskram spoke again. 'We can do nothing more for him. It is for the Almighty and the instrument of His will Azrael to decide his fate now.'

'What about the Fays?' asked Adelko. 'Might they not hinder his spirit on its journey to the Other Side?'

'I don't think so,' answered Horskram with a slow thoughtful shake of his head. 'Branas perished not by their magic, therefore by rights they should have no power over his shade. But come! Let's speak of it no more – we must be going on our way. I sense our gracious hosts are anxious to meet us in person.'

'Can't we stay until his pyre burns down?' asked Vaskrian in a miserable, faraway voice. 'It's a shame to leave him, seeing as how none of his kith and kin could come to his funeral...'

His eyes were glazed, his face pale. He hadn't fully recovered from his ordeal and seemed not to be completely aware of where he was. In hushed tones Horskram had told Adelko it would probably go better for the squire if he remembered as little as possible – even in defeat the magic of a hag could wreck a victim's sanity.

'We must needs press on,' Horskram told him gently. 'It is not safe to stay here over long under the trees while a fire is burning, even one so necessary.'

As if echoing him, a queer groaning sound began to emanate from some of the trees. Adelko could swear he saw lichen creeping across one or two.

He quickly added his voice to his mentor's: 'Yes I think Master Horskram's right, Vaskrian. There's a clear trail over yonder for us to follow, and it's obvious these trees don't want us here any longer. Branas's soul will find his way to the Plain of Azrael for judgment now we've given him the Last Rites, so don't you worry.'

It was difficult to sound reassuring under the circumstances, but somehow he managed it. Vaskrian nodded absent-mindedly, allowing himself to be led out of the clearing by the two monks after they had gathered up their belongings.

The new trail appeared no different from the others at first, but before long it began to follow a gradually steepening incline. As they followed it ever down deeper into the forest the gnarled branches of the trees parted to make way for them; no longer did tangled briars curl up out of the sedge and try to trip them up. At last Tintagael seemed to be bending to their will.

But if so it was an illusory concession of power, for still the forest commanded the direction they must take. At least the way was becoming easier: looking down at his mud-caked boots Adelko noticed that where the soil had been damp and clammy it was now dry and firm.

✥ ✥ ✥

After another indeterminate length of time the path gradually straightened out altogether. The gradient subsided and they found themselves following a level broad track not unlike a highway. The trees on either side became more orderly, and now stood serried ranks of trunks, uniform as pillars in a great hall of men. Even the branches seemed to jut out at regular intervals, forming an arched tunnel of wood and leaves. It felt every bit as unnatural as the forest's previous incarnation, but somehow a little more reassuring.

The path terminated in a vast rectangular clearing. Its floor was covered in emerald sward; every blade of grass seemed perfectly ordered and sparkled with an impossibly bright lustre. Overhead the trees repeated their trick of intertwining to form a ceiling, only this time, as with the new path, it was ordered far beyond the wild design of nature. Adelko almost fancied he was gazing up at the rafters of a building, the height of several tall men above his head.

From the four sides of the clearing the distended branches converged and tapered to meet at a central point, resembling the ceiling of some great temple. From regular intervals hung what seemed at first glance to be apples, each one kindled with a strange green glow that enhanced with the sylvan light of Tintagael. The faces of his two companions shone luminous beneath the glowing fruits.

The trees on the far side of the clearing were twisted around one another in what looked like a tangled riot of boles, branches and twigs. As Adelko studied these against the intense light he realised they were great chairs, constructed from the defiantly unnatural flora of Tintagael.

Gradually he became aware of humanoid forms coalescing on the arboreal thrones. It was as though the sylvan mists of Tintagael had taken on a denser substance, still translucent but more solid. They resembled androgynous human figures, impossibly beautiful: at once unearthly and familiar.

As their spectral gossamer frames caught and trapped the light, the illusion (for surely it must be such?) of fine apparel could be discerned: rich robes infinitely far from any finery a mortal king might display. Though seated they appeared taller than mere men by at least a head.

'So the self-appointed masters of Tintagael show themselves at last,' breathed Horskram.

Though he had not spoken loudly, a shimmering chorus of eerie voices drifted across the clearing as if in answer. The phantasmal figures opposite them did not move; not so much as a flicker graced their ghostly lips. In keeping with the ways of their immortal kind, they spoke in rhyme, though their grasp of the Northlending tongue was strangely perfect:

> *Travellers three from mortal bourne,*
> *Beneath our eaves of hope forlorn!*
> *One comrade slain, and one near lost,*
> *Life's flame gutters 'Neath death's hoarfrost!*
>
> *The woods you sought in fear of steel,*
> *Yet wounds 'Neath woods are harder healed,*
> *What perils did you hope to flee,*
> *To seek the silence of the trees?*

As abruptly as they had commenced, the voices fell silent. Adelko glanced uncertainly at Horskram. Vaskrian stared ahead wordlessly, seemingly at nothing.

'What do they want?' hissed the novice.

'Even now they are testing us,' replied the adept in a low voice. 'Fays speak in riddles as oft as not. But if we're to survive we must play their game.'

Clearing his throat he addressed the spectral kings and queens in a loud, clear voice: 'It is true as you say that we lost a comrade, but false to say that we gave up hope – for those who hold to the Redeemer shall never forsake it, in life or death.

'As for yon squire, I shall take care to see that his wounds are indeed healed, for his spirit is strong.

'As to the dangers we fled, you know well enough we were pursued by armed brigands belonging to our earthly realm – but it is also true that the girdle of Tintagael has provided us with welcome concealment from other far deadlier foes, though it is bought at a dear price.'

A sussurant laughter filled the clearing, crystal clear yet disembodied. Though it set Adelko's hackles rising he sensed the Fays seemed pleased by his master's response. They answered:

Oh mortal wise beyond your time,
Gifted with reckoning sublime!
The Vylivigs salute your mind,
So far above your meagre kind!

Your Order has ne'er seen your like,
Brave monk your time shall come to strike,
Forces of darkness are abroad,
Not all shall take an open road!

Two enemies have brought you here,
Where fay folk rule in sylvan fear,
Yet fear is felt by those a 'feared,
Our doom pronounced by ancient wyrd!

For all shall dread the coming night:
Both mortal-kind and faerie sprite
Shall quail before the rising fire,
As worlds make a funeral pyre!

Horskram frowned. 'Spare us your flattery,' he replied coldly.
'Although you have guessed aright – it is two foes and not one that pursue
us. But what is this coming darkness and hellfire of which you speak? You
are not the first of the spirit world we have encountered lately to tell of
such conflagrations. We have helped you, as you bade us do – yon Hag is
despatched. Our part of the bargain is fulfilled – now repay us our labours
and set us on a free path out of Tintagael unmolested!'

The faerie voices seemed to reply all at once. A susurration of conflicting
whispers rose and fell for a while before finally subsiding into coherence:

Tic true we tested you before,
Mere torment is no fitting sport
For such troubled age of mortals,
When dark powers strain the portals!

For the rent 'twixt worlds grows wider
To tear asunder the great divider,
So faerie kind seek mortal aid,
For which their own they gladly trade!

Horskram's face showed his growing consternation. 'Powers of darkness grow apace, this much we have fathomed ourselves,' he declared. 'But what and who moves them? And what aid do you speak of? If you would aid us, then set us free of this accursed forest!'

The spectral figures laughed again. Thus far they still hadn't moved – but now Adelko could see their glinting forms starting to stretch, growing longer and thinner, whilst their shimmering colours began to coalesce into a glowing green light that grew steadily more intense. The disembodied voices spoke again:

> Freedom from faerie realm we'll give,
> But who can say how long you'll live?
> Bloody strife bars the southern way,
> Night's terror haunts your waking days!

> So take the eastward road in need,
> Seek the sanctuary of your creed,
> The warrior prophet's blood was shed
> That mortal man might thrive instead!

> This is our counsel: heed it well!
> To stop the yawning gates of hell,
> A crooked path you now must tread:
> Gloom gathers on the road ahead.

> So keep your wits about you all,
> Many are the Fallen One's thralls,
> And though trees may offer refuge,
> Yet others conceal subterfuge...

While the disembodied voices were chanting through the final four stanzas, the light suffusing the faerie kings had grown to an almost blinding radiance, until it seemed to Adelko that they were actually made of it. Gazing on their lucent forms, now stretched to unnatural proportions like a corpse on a rack, the novice felt a queer chill pass through him. It fell short of the sheer horror he'd felt at times since his adventures began, yet he had no doubt that he was in the presence of something altogether alien, only now revealing its true form.

The lambent figures pointed at them with spidery fingers; their features were similarly distended and no longer looked beautiful. Nor did they even look ghastly: they simply defied mortal description. Their eyes were points of deepest night, falling forever back into a nebula of bright bilious green. Worst of all, Adelko felt his thoughts were being *watched*, as though his very soul had been laid bare to the scrutiny of soulless beings. He heard the voices return, whispering to his subconscious; he thought of the first devil he'd encountered, back in Rykken a hundred years ago, but this was different: somehow he felt these voices were *encouraging* him, though to what deed he could not say. But the good wishes of the treacherous Fays unsettled him almost as much as the psychic assault of any demon.

The light grew relentlessly brighter still, forcing his eyes shut. Adelko could now hear two words, overlapping one another and repeating over and over again: *sssanctuary-sssubterfuge, sssanctuary-sssubterfuge, sssanctuary-sssubterfuge, sssanctuary-sssubterfuge, SSSANCTUARY-SSSUBTERFUGE, SSSANCTUARY-SSSUBTERFUGE, SANCTUARY-SUBTERFUGE!*

✢ ✢ ✢

With a great *crack* all the lights suddenly went out, the voices dropping away into still silence. After a moment of darkness the companions found themselves surrounded by a thick dank mist, of a colour so ordinary it made Adelko feel even more anxious. But there was nothing ordinary about the speed with which it parted, and as the tendrils fell away and dissolved into nothing another bright light washed over their eyes, accompanied by a warmth that none of them had felt for a seeming age.

They were in a clearing surrounded by birch trees. The skies overhead were a perfect blue, and the sun was shining brightly.

Blinking in amazement, the three of them gazed about them. There was birdsong in the air and the trees looked perfectly normal, their leaves budding as the full bloom of spring was on them. They might have been standing in any stretch of wood in Northalde.

Over to their left was a trail. No trees parted suddenly to reveal it: it looked as if it might always have been there. The grass and weeds at their feet waved gently in a breeze that rustled the leaves on the trees. But there was nothing sinister or untoward in the sound they made.

Turning around, Vaskrian stared at the two monks. His eyes were wide and glazed, his mouth half open like a village idiot's.

'I had the most strange and terrible dreams...' he said, repeating his words in the Hag's hut before his voice trailed off.

'So did we all,' replied Horskram gently. 'But now they are over – for the time being at least. Let us be gone from this place, it is past time we were leaving.'

✢ ✢ ✢

They took the path set before them. Vaskrian wandered in a daze, and seemed barely to register his surroundings. But to Adelko the dappled sunlight and clean fresh air were like a draught of water to a man in a desert after the horrible hues and strange smell of the haunted forest.

They followed the path for several hours. Adelko began to feel very footsore and weary – how long had it been since he'd slept? There had been the Hag's lair, but that hardly counted as real sleep. He felt his eyes begin to droop as he mechanically placed one mud-caked foot in front of the other...

And then suddenly there were no more trees. The three survivors of Tintagael found themselves standing on a rough sward that stretched out before them, dipping at a gentle incline towards fields and meadows that stretched as far as the eye could see, dotted with hamlets and orchards. The sun was low in the sky now, dipping over their heads behind the forest. Turning to follow it Adelko was shocked to see oak trees looming up behind them, looking every bit as dark and forbidding as the ones that had parted to let them into the forest, seemingly an age ago now.

But even that wasn't quite the final scare Tintagael had in store for them.

'Look!' gasped Vaskrian, his wits suddenly returning to him.

He was pointing agitatedly to the south, a look of fear and wonder on his face. Turning in that direction, Adelko stifled a cry of horror. Grimly Horskram made the sign.

'From thence flows all the wickedness we have lately suffered,' he said in a subdued voice.

The dying rays of the sun revealed a sight Adelko felt sure he would remember for the rest of his days.

Though a shattered ruin for five millennia, the Watchtower of Tintagael still made for fearful viewing. Only five storeys had survived the wrath of the Archangels, yet it was still higher than most castles. Its octagonal structure bore witness to its age-old destruction in the form of a broken crown of smashed stonework that cut jaggedly against the blood-red sky. Each storey was slightly smaller than the one just below it, giving the remains of the gargantuan edifice a curious tapering effect. The lowest one alone was many times the size of the keeps Adelko had seen on the Wold, and he could only wonder how big the tower had been before it was broken. Strangest of all were its huge stones: no ordinary rectangles or squares, but a myriad of bizarrely interlocking geometric shapes. Adelko tried to follow them with his eyes, but they made his head hurt: there was something unnatural about them, as though they had been wrought in defiance of any earthly craft. And they were impossibly big, each larger than a man, leaving him gawping at the thought of the mighty engines that had laid them – if engines indeed their builders had ever used. Even their varied colours were peculiar, and teased the eye with the same malignancy as the trees of Tintagael, veering maddeningly between shade and tint but never quite finding a place in the spectrum. Seemingly set at random intervals with no thought to precision or order, dozens of windows gaped at them: some were round, some octagonal, some oblong, while others like the stones were shapes Adelko had never seen before, their peculiar angles spurning mortal symmetry with a horrid indifference.

The Watchtower of Tintagael was entirely alien, as much as the Fay Folk had been.

It stood about a hundred yards away from them, near the edge of the forest. The ground about the tower was scorched black: nothing had grown there for five thousand years, and nothing ever would. Vast fragments of its hideous stonework were the only things to grace that lifeless threshold, their presence offering scant comfort for mortal eyes.

A steadfast aura of evil emanated from the awful ruin, so intense that it somehow made the thought of their recent travails pale into insignificance.

'Come nightfall that cursed precinct will be wailing with the banshees of the dead, and other worse things,' said Horskram in a voice that suddenly sounded dry and brittle. 'Let's not tarry here. If we follow yonder incline we should be able to put the sight of Tintagael behind us, tower and forest both, before we rest.'

Exhausted as they were, neither youth disagreed.

✣ ✣ ✣

Setting off with renewed vigour, they marched for another hour as twilight's deep purple followed fast on the red heels of sunset. Only then could Adelko bring himself to look back, but when he did he mercifully saw only the rising ground they had just descended, and shortly after that he could see nothing at all except what moon and stars cared to reveal. At that point Horskram called a halt.

His voice was thick with fatigue as he said: 'We have left Tintagael safely behind us, we should sleep now. Tomorrow morning I should think we will wake to find ourselves on the skirts of the King's Dominions once more, though we have emerged some leagues due south of where we entered the forest. But we shall speak more of that on the morrow.'

The old monk cast himself down on the grass to sleep without another word. The other two followed suit.

As he did so, Adelko noticed a few birches over to the right, their branches waving gently in the moonlight. He supposed they might offer some shelter, should the weather turn foul in the night.

On second thoughts, he reflected shudderingly, open countryside would do just fine, rain or no.

⇒ CHAPTER VII ⇒

All At Sea

B raxus ran his slender fingers across his harp, trying to ignore the pitching of the ship as the waves rolled it erratically on its course. His cramped cabin creaked in time with the surf, an accompaniment he could well have done without.

It didn't help that the piece he was rehearsing was Maegellin's *Lay of High Firth*, which told of the trickster hero Bendigedfryn's tragic death on the slopes of that name a thousand years ago. It was one of the more complex pieces in his repertoire, and on dry land he could play and sing it without effort. Now he felt as if he could barely play it alone, never mind the rest. He tried some vocals in his high, clear alto, but they didn't sound right. He still felt queasy.

He didn't like the sea. He knew half a hundred songs that told of his ancestors' journey from the reclusive Island Realms to the north and west, after the Wars of Kith and Kin had seen the brothers Curufin and Orbegon exiled with their tribes. For centuries bards had sung of their fraught journey across the spirit-haunted Sea of Tanagorm to found new kingdoms on the mainland. He supposed that meant his people had been a seafaring folk once, but that had been long ages of men ago. Put him astride a horse rather than a ship, any day.

Or better still, put him astride a hot wench. That was another thing he hated about the sea – no women allowed aboard ships. Who in the Known World had dreamed up such an evil custom? Something about bringing bad luck, and Conway, captain of *The Jolly Runner*, the small merchant cog they'd chartered at Port Grendel to take them to Strongholm, was little different from any other sailor.

He'd had a good mind to look up Siana when they were in town, the ample-bosomed daughter of a local tradesman he had lain with on occasion. So far as he knew, he had not gotten her with child yet – another bonus. And what she lacked in true beauty she more than made up for with enthusiasm.

He hadn't had time to see her, a shame. He had bedded plenty of high-born ladies who weren't nearly so pleasing beneath the sheets. But then that was often the way with common wenches – they had an earthy spirit that made them catch fire when their passions were aroused.

Grimacing as the ship lurched and creaked again, he set aside the Thraxian harp. His amorous thoughts were only frustrating him. There would be no women, high-born or low, until they reached Strongholm. That thought appealed to him, though. He'd never bedded a Northlending before. Yes, he wouldn't mind that – their blonde goddesses were famed far and wide for their beauty. A little on the cold side, mind, from what he'd heard – but then what was life without the spice of a challenge now and then?

At any rate, he would see to it that he took ample reward from this fool's errand. Which is what he'd decided this was, on further reflection. Getting to his feet groggily he lurched past his lute and mandola towards the stubby pine door. He'd insisted on bringing all his instruments – if his father saw him as nothing better than a messenger now, he was damned if he was going to make the journey a joyless experience.

Of course the old man had been quick to justify his decision, even praising him for once. He was likeable, a real charmer, and he spoke the Northlending tongue fluently (he had always had an aptitude for languages as well as music – his memory for lyrics was prodigious, so perhaps that was no surprise). He was, next to his father, the most high-ranking noble in Gaellentir. In short, the perfect envoy.

But Braxus knew better. This assignment was really intended as a punishment, for his lack of success against the highland raiders.

Was it is his fault if they were up against the most determined and canny leader those savages had had in generations? He had protested that his place was in Dréuth, fighting with his brothers in arms to defend his people, but would the old man listen?

Emerging onto the see-sawing deck the young knight felt his mood blacken further. Nothing he ever did was good enough for the old man, nothing. They had never seen eye to eye and never would.

At least he'd convinced his father to let him bring Vertrix. Braxus had squired for him during his training for knighthood, and the old vassal had taught him many a useful thing. And he'd always seen the good in him, unlike the old man, never doubting his skill or courage on the battlefield. When he did admonish him, it had always been done gently, in the manner of a master instructing a wayward but able pupil in need of occasional guidance.

Though it pained Braxus to admit it, and he would never say so out loud, Vertrix was in many ways the father he had never had.

The old knight was standing at the port side of the deck gazing out to sea. Sir Vertrix turned to favour him with a smile as he drew level with him. 'Finding your sea legs at long last, Sir Braxus?' he asked.

'Hardly,' replied Braxus with a frown. 'But better up here than down below. At least the bracing air will do me some good.'

'Ah, it's not so bad once you get used to it,' offered Vertrix. He was nearly sixty, though like many active men of service who had been lucky enough to survive that long he wore his winters well. Braxus was not aware that the old sworder had ever been to sea that much though. Perhaps it just came naturally to him – few things seemed to unruffle him.

'Where are the others?' he asked.

'Sir Bryant and Sir Regan are below decks playing at dice. Their squires are with them I think. Gormly's tending to Paidlin in their quarters – poor lad was sick again just now.'

Braxus rolled his eyes. His hapless squire was an even worse sailor than his master. 'I wondered where he'd got to,' he replied. 'Will he be all right, d'you think? Shall I check on him?'

'Nah, leave him be for now, sire,' replied Vertrix with a wry smile. 'Reus knows he'll have to learn to toughen up if he's ever to be a knight. And last I heard, seasickness never killed anyone – although they might wish it did at the time!'

Braxus grimaced again. He had certainly felt that way on their first two days out of Port Grendel. It was their fifth day at sea now, and he was only just beginning to feel his guts were mostly where they should be.

'All right, so. I'll look in on him later. Have you spoken to the captain today? How are we faring?'

Vertrix nodded across the deck. 'Think he's just about to tell you himself.'

Striding across the shifting boards with a carefree ease that Braxus could only envy, Captain Conway called out a cheery greeting as he drew level with the knights.

'Top of the mornin' t'ye, sires!' he exclaimed, his snaggled teeth cracking an ugly grin. 'And how are the Tyrnian Straits agreein' with ye this fine day?'

'Good day, captain. They're not,' replied Braxus curtly.

The grin did not leave the captain's face as he stroked his rust-red whiskers. A grizzled old sea dog of about forty winters, he hailed from Port Craek in Garth province. Like most of his kind he had been pressed into the sea from an early age: water was like soil to him.

'Ah well, just be thankful we're not sailin' north, towards the Island Realms of our far ancestors,' he said for the third time since they had boarded his ship. 'I've been that way a few times, when I was a boy, and let me tell ye, ye haven't seen anythin' until – '

'No, I've not,' Braxus cut him off. 'But I've *heard* all about it from you – twice already. If it's all the same to you, captain, I'd rather not hear about what the ghosts of drowned mariners, capricious Mermaids and sea spirits are wont to do to unfortunate sailors. I feel queasy enough as it is. Can you tell us how long till we reach the Farov Isles?'

The captain's grin twisted into a strange sort of grimace, his usual expression when asked a question requiring a straight answer.

'Well, let me see, hmm, the Farov Isles...' he mused, as though he had never heard of them before. Braxus and Vertrix exchanged half amused, half impatient glances as the captain went on. 'Well the winds ain't blowin' too rough, and I've got yon swabs runnin' her tightly enough, so I reckon, give or take, we should be there in another two days, maybe three. Course, that's assuming we get through the Pincers all right – we'll run into choppy waters there and no mistake. If y'think this is bad, just you wait!'

Favouring his charges with another gap-toothed grin, Conway ambled off to bark some more orders at his men. Braxus felt his heart sink into his ailing guts. Now he wished that for once the captain had been a little less direct.

So far their journey had been relatively trouble-free. Braxus was in a pessimistic enough mood to doubt whether that would last.

They had set out from Gaellen just over a week ago, taking a low-lying sloop across the still waters of the Cuchlain before reaching the Burryn River at its north-west tip. Even without having to pass between the crags of the Brekken Ranges, infested with highlanders, it was a daunting enough journey. Those lands were ill settled – it wasn't hard to see why Slánga and his fellow chieftains were so determined to extend their boundaries.

Reaching the fork where the Burryn met the Rygar they had caught a glimpse of the northerly reaches of the Liathduil Forest as it stretched up to meet both rivers. The southern woodlands were well enough, but few ventured into its more northerly stretches, long said to be the haunt of Fays and other malignant spirits.

Just before that they had caught a glimpse of Hell's Fortress. That was the nickname given to the blackened ruins of the vast and ancient tower that had stood since the Dawn of Time at the summit of the loftiest peak in the Brekkens. The perfects and friars said it had been built by an ancient warlock-race that had ruled all the Known World long ago, before even the coming of the Exiled Tribes to the shores of Thraxia. There were said to be many others like it, scattered across the latter-day realms of lesser men. Even the Island Realms had one, built aeons ago before the Moon Goddess had visited the shores of Skulla during the First Age of Darkness.

It wasn't a piece of history Braxus cared for. In the histories he had learned wizards came to grief more often than not, or else served mortal kings:

like Orthan, the witch-druid who had advised High King Celtigorm in the days of Bendigedfryn and his ilk.

There was little left of Hell's Fortress – the well travelled said the warlock-kings' other towers were mostly better preserved. Even so, gazing on its gigantic shards as their sloop plied the waters of the Burryn, Braxus had felt a chill run down his spine. It had been dusk, yet the ruin had been suffused in an unearthly orange light of its own, as though the sun were setting behind it, to the east. Naturally, the highlanders shunned it like the Red Plague, although in times past it was said they had practised human sacrifice beneath its shattered walls.

Gazing out to sea he shuddered at the thought. Who knows, they might even be reviving that custom. He wouldn't put it past Slánga, and would be genuinely surprised if the idea hadn't already occurred to his sadistic and devilish lieutenant Cormic.

At least they had not come under serious attack on the way to Port Grendel. A handful of highlanders had appeared on the slopes of one overhanging crag to hurl a clutch of axes and spears at them, but they had been too far away to pose any real threat. Thank Reus those savages hadn't learned to use longbows yet. Thinking this, Braxus felt uneasy again: that was another thing he wouldn't put past Slánga.

That was why, he supposed, his mission was so important. All the same, he could not help but doubt its chances.

Having had time to mull over his father's plan, he had concluded it was unlikely the King of the Northlendings would come to their aid. Surely the cost of a war would outweigh the trading concessions they were offering? In the short term at least – and it was a risky venture. If it failed, the Northlendings would lose much and gain nothing. Freidheim was a wise king, they said. This did not sound like an offer that a wise king would accept.

But then, as his father had said, what choice did they have?

Leaning down heavily against the rail, the young knight stared at the slapping grey waves, and brooded.

⁘ ⁘ ⁘

Captain Conway proved true to his word, and the Pincers were every bit as rough as their cruel name suggested. In fact, Braxus thought it a most apt name for two horns of land that jutted out from the northernmost tip of Northalde and curved inwards to cradle the most ship-hating, capricious, vile-tempered stretch of sea put on the Almighty's good earth. That ordeal lasted for two days, during which the roiling surf made him sick on more than one occasion.

His poor squire Paidlin fared even worse. Twice they had to take him up and lash him to the rail, trusting to the cavorting winds to assuage some of the pain they had done so much to cause. For a while Braxus feared the lad really would die of seasickness. Even Vertrix looked pale, and the four knights and their squires picked queasily at their grubby food at mealtimes.

Their cordial captain could not have been more different. Blithely holding court at his table, he refilled one cup of grog after the next as he regaled them with one far-fetched yarn after another on the last evening of their journey before reaching the Farov Isles.

'Did I ever tell ye about the time we saw a Sea Gigant's hand emerge from the waves off the coast of Caercilly?' he enquired jovially over his sixth cup. 'The size of a house it was, the fingers were like chimneys, only a bilious blue-green they were, much like the colour of a shark's innards, heh heh!'

Paidlin heaved, pushing back his seat and fumbling for the wooden bilge bucket that had been placed next to him.

'Ah cap'n, lay off talkin' so,' admonished the mate, Cullen. A wiry fellow in early middle age with spiky tufts of black hair, he was thankfully less given to garrulous tale-telling than his boss. 'You'll make the poor boy sick with all your stories – and they've already heard this one yestere'en.'

Conway fixed his mate with a squint-eyed glare. 'Reus damn ye, Cullen,' he hiccoughed. 'This is *my* ship, and I'll damn well tell tales whenever I see fit! I'm a man o' the sea, and the ocean is my kingdom!'

Downing his grog he launched into a completely different story. 'Anyway, as I was sayin' before I was so *rudely* interrupted,' he slurred, 'we were becalmed on the Tanagorm. A foul and dreadful sea that, full o' water spirits that'll drown ye soon as look at ye! But 'twas the spirits o' th'air that were our worst enemy that time...'

He paused again to refill his cup unsteadily. Even without his drunkenness to unsettle him the ship was still tossing, although the seas had calmed somewhat since they'd left the worst of the Pincers behind.

Cullen glanced at Braxus and rolled his eyes. The knight did his best not to smile as Conway continued: 'Fifteen days we stayed rooted to the same spot! Miles out to sea, with barely enough provender to last us a week! We were reduced to eating rat meat and drinking our own – '

Paidlin lurched sideways, aiming for the bucket and only partially succeeding. The bile spattered over its side as he choked up the scraps of a meal he'd hardly touched.

Braxus seized his opportunity. 'Thank you for another most entertaining evening, captain,' he said pleasantly. 'But I think I'd best see my squire safely to bed.

Vertrix and the rest of you – that goes for all of you, too. We'll be back on dry land for a while tomorrow, so let's try and get a good night's rest.'

The others lurched to their feet gladly, hurriedly thanking the captain and his mate before beating a hasty retreat. As Braxus closed the door behind them he caught a last glimpse of Cullen staring reproachfully at Conway, who was staring off into space and mumbling something about wyverns.

He was no seafarer, but it seemed to him for all the world that someone was in line for a promotion.

⁘ ⁘ ⁘

It was when they finally put in at the Farovs that they had their first real piece of bad news. *The Jolly Runner* was in Caldeshavn, the islands' only town, to pick up supplies and offload some of its cargo. Most of it was mead and furs – the very trade his father hoped to expedite under terms of the agreement now stashed in the hold with all his other belongings – and most of it was bound for mainland Northalde. But the hardy islanders were never ones to say no to a warm cloak and a no-less warming drop of Thraxia's finest. Given they lived in a place where the winds blew fierce and raw most of the year, one could hardly blame them.

Gazing at the sparse hills that ringed the shoreline as the *Runner* approached the dock, Braxus thought it an ill place to call home. The Farovians were for their part a tight-knit bunch, even more reclusive than the highland inhabitants of mainland Northalde.

Musing on the latter, he wondered at the strange games the Almighty played. The Northlending highlanders were mostly a pacific folk, devout Palomedians who shunned war unless absolutely necessary. The King of the Northlendings had even granted them rule of their own lands, so long as they contributed in times of war and didn't trouble the lowlanders. True enough, their stock wasn't as pure as their barbaric cousins to the west, but they did share a common ancestry. That was about all they shared, luckily for the Northlending lowlanders.

The envy he felt towards this peaceful arrangement was soon dispelled.

He was sitting in Caldeshavn's only tavern by the waterfront with Vertrix, Bryant and Regan and their squires, enjoying the first barrel of mead that had been brought in off *The Jolly Runner*.

Spirits were high. It was good to be back on dry land, even if it was only for a day, and a drop of Thraxia's finest beat the living circles of hell out of Conway's tarry grog. Even Paidlin was starting to look lively again, enthusiastically playing at dice with the other squires while their knightly masters sat at the next table, sparring and jesting over their stoops.

'Braxus, I thought we'd be dumping you with the cargo here in Farov, the way you looked!' laughed Regan. He was a lithe dark-haired man in his mid twenties, a couple of years younger than Braxus. A rakish fellow with devilish charm to match, he shared his passion – and aptitude – for wenching.

'And let you have all the fun with those Northlending beauties when we get to Strongholm?' Braxus shot back. 'Not on your life, Regan! You've yet to match my total, and I'll not see it passed, by Reus I won't!'

Regan laughed again good-naturedly. 'I'm close though, Braxus, after that brown-eyed beauty up in Lindis, I'm very, *verrry* close!'

'More like you've just got your sums muddled again,' said Bryant, deadpan as always. A tawny-haired fellow with a plain but honest face, he was a good man to have along – sense of humour drier than a Mercadian white wine. 'And incidentally, horses don't count,' he added.

They all burst out laughing at this, Regan included. Seeing their tankards were nearly empty, Braxus turned and hollered for the tavern keeper, who was already glaring at him. They had been speaking in Thrax, but even so he felt sure the stocky townsman disapproved of their brazen banter.

But Sir Braxus did not care over much what a foreign commoner thought of him. Addressing him in flawless Northlending, he said: 'Another four stoops of mead if you please, and four small ones for our faithful squires if you will.'

If Farovians believed in deference to their betters, they hid it well. 'We don't serve halves,' replied the tavern keeper bluntly.

'Fine,' replied Braxus, unfazed. 'Eight more tankards then.'

The tavern keeper nodded curtly, before motioning to the only serving wench to fetch the order. She was a flat-chested, shapeless thing, nothing like the Northlending beauties he'd heard about. But then Farovians were a breed apart; it was said their ancestors had arrived on the isles centuries before the Northland reavers settled the mainland, and there their descendants had stayed ever since.

Braxus knew enough about the islands to know that what kept them going was the unique thoroughbreds they reared. Farovian destriers were famed throughout the Free Kingdoms for their quality. The Northlendings were just as famed for guarding them jealously; a strict royal monopoly was kept on the fine horses, with their use reserved solely for the greater noble houses of Northalde and the elite Order of the White Valravyn.

Shame that. Farovian horses certainly interested him more than Farovian women, but it didn't look as if they'd get a chance to see any during their brief stay.

His fluent command of the local language must have done something to abate the tavern keeper's reticence, because just as the wench was setting down their drinks he sidled over and asked: 'Heading down south to the mainland are you?'

Braxus looked up at him over his fresh tankard, surprised at his sudden friendliness, if you could call it that.

'Aye,' he replied cautiously. 'We're knight errants, seeking employ in Northalde. We're sick of fighting highland tribes – we want something more challenging for our trusty blades.'

It was a simple cover story they had rehearsed well. No one could know about their mission – even their squires had been kept in the dark.

The tavern keeper's reply surprised him. 'Well, you've picked just the right time, I'd say. There's war brewing in the kingdom.'

Braxus blinked. It took a few moments for the words to register.

'Braxus, what's he saying?' asked Regan, seeing his look of surprise. Apart from Vertrix, none of the others spoke Northlending. The old knight's face looked grave in the weak candlelight, which did little to augment the poor light from outside.

Holding up his hand for silence, Braxus pressed the tavern keeper. 'War you say? Where – and with whom?'

'Not rightly sure yet,' replied the tavern keeper indifferently. 'We don't get a great deal of news up here. As far as we can tell it's the southern barons up to something again – there's been talk of civil war. Same thing as fifteen years ago – sure it'll all end in much the same way, the King'll see to 'em and no mistake. Still, it's lucky for you knights – doubt you'd have had much joy of your trade six months ago. Now it seems there'll be fighting aplenty.'

Farovians were men of few words. The tavern keeper had just exhausted his daily stock. Without another syllable, he turned back to supervise the loading in of more barrels. He'd just bought enough to last a year, and his sons were busy rolling them in through the tavern's crooked entrance.

Braxus leaned back against the cold stone wall. This wasn't good.

'Did I hear that right?' asked Vertrix, speaking in Thrax. His Northlending wasn't as good as Braxus's, but all the same there was more hope than anything else in his voice.

'I'm afraid so,' replied the knight, translating the tavern keeper's information for the benefit of the other two.

'Well that scuppers another fine quest,' remarked Bryant dourly into his mead. 'There's as much chance of Regan swearing an oath of celibacy as there is of King Freidheim aiding us now.'

'If I could persuade him by swearing one I would!' exclaimed Regan, though no one believed him.

'All right, knock it on the head, you two,' growled Vertrix. 'This is no time for japes. Palom's blood, what do we do now, Sir Braxus?'

All three knights were looking at him expectantly. Braxus suddenly felt queasy again as he thought of his father scowling at him in his solar.

'All right, peace a minute,' he said. 'Let me think for a bit.'

He took a few more slugs on his mead while the other knights did the same, uneasily making small talk. Behind them their squires continued to shout loudly over their game of dice, the mead fuelling their excitement. Vertrix turned around and told them all sternly to pipe down.

And that's when the idea occurred to him. Bold, and not in the original plan, but it might just work...

'The way I see it, we've no choice but to press on,' said Braxus, breaking his silence. 'Even if we wanted to turn back, there's no saying how long it'll be before another cog passes this way. And I for one am not running back to my father empty handed after falling at the first hurdle.'

'Fair enough,' put in Regan. 'But if there's a war on, what chances are there of persuading the King to help us? Reus knows they were thin enough to begin with!'

'True,' Braxus allowed. 'But for starters we don't know how serious this war is yet. They don't get a lot of steady news on this godforsaken rock. So it's best not to get too discouraged until we've struck the mainland and had a chance to learn more.'

The other knights nodded slowly. They seemed half convinced at least. Certainly none of them wanted to stay on the Farovs any more than he did.

'But something else occurs to me,' he continued, getting excited now. 'If it's true what they say that the southerners are rebelling again, why then that puts them almost in the same position as us! Oh the King might well crush them this time around, but who's to say they won't come back for more again – and again? Sounds to me that now's the time to propose something that would've been unthinkable to our forefathers...'

He let his voice trail off. The other three stared at him expectantly. Taking another sip of mead he came straight out with it: 'A standing military alliance between the Kings of Thraxia and Northalde – once we've dealt with that bitch who's ensorcelled our Cadwy of course.'

Regan and Bryant exchanged uncertain glances. Vertrix frowned into his mug. He'd fought the Northlendings at Corne Hill, when he was a fresh-faced squire. Clearly any kind of permanent alliance with his age-old enemies was a bitter draught to swallow.

'I don't know about any military treaty, Sir Braxus,' he said slowly. 'That wasn't what your father authorised you to sue for.

You can only speak for him and the other lords of Dréuth.' He lowered his voice, mindful of their squires sat behind him. 'What we're asking for, technically it's still treason – despite all the circumstances! Anything beyond that is speculative.'

Braxus flung his arms in the air in frustration. 'Why, the whole damn thing is speculative, Vertrix!' he cried, before remembering himself and lowering his voice again. 'For all we know the King might not even honour the contract terms we've negotiated in his... temporary absence. How do we even know for sure he'll come to his senses once Abrexta's dealt with?'

They all fell silent, gazing uneasily at their mead. He had just spoken the thought all of them had been afraid to give voice to.

Braxus felt a sudden twinge of anxiety. He was losing them, and he needed them right behind him.

'All right look, we're probably getting ahead of ourselves anyhow,' he persisted. 'But for now one thing is clear to me – we press on regardless. Let's see how this plays out, we don't know what lies ahead. We have to try – what other choice do we have?'

'None,' replied Vertrix ruefully, draining his flagon. 'No, you're right Braxus – we need to take this thing by the horns, and see if we can't bend it to our will. Whatever you decide, I'll be with you.'

As one, Sir Regan and Sir Bryant voiced their assent. Braxus gave an inward sigh of relief. He felt as though he had just hurdled the first major obstacle in their mission: well, that and the seasickness.

Finishing his own mead, he allowed a slight smile of satisfaction to creep across his face. Perhaps he would make a good envoy after all.

⤝ CHAPTER VIII ⤞

Storm Clouds Gather

Vaskrian woke to find his horse nuzzling him. It was another clear bright day, and the sun was directly overhead. That meant it was noon – they had overslept. It was only when he was pulling himself up off the green sward that he remembered with a shock that their horses had been lost in the forest.

The forest... he tried to recall it. It all seemed so vague somehow. He remembered meeting a ghostly knight (hadn't he claimed to be one of King Thorsvald's Thirteen?) and then there was a perilous bridge crossing – he'd survived that, though he had lost his father's sword. But he had lost something else too, what was it?

The recollection came to him suddenly, borne on a surge of grief. Of course, his master: prickly old Branas. What had happened to him? Try as he might he couldn't recall... he only remembered lighting his funeral pyre, then some half-glimpsed memory of tall sylvan figures that looked like elongated spectres... They had definitely lost their horses though, because much of the time they had been on foot... hadn't they?

Yet here they were – his courser and the rouncies belonging to the two monks at least. Of his dead master's charger there was no sign.

Adelko and Horskram were beside him, both snoring softly. Nudging them awake with his travel-stained boots the squire pointed at their steeds. 'Now what in the Known World do you make of that?' he asked.

Adelko sat up slowly, yawning and blinking away sleep before putting on that goggle-eyed look he seemed to get whenever he was perplexed. Horskram harrumphed and cursed them all (including himself) for oversleeping, before getting up to inspect their steeds.

'Well,' he said, running a hand thoughtfully over his beard, now bristling and unkempt after days on the road. 'It seems as though the Fays have proved true to their words, however cryptic. They are indeed trying to help us – not only have they returned us our steeds, I think they've seen to it that their sojourn in the faerie kingdom was beneficial!'

It was true. Where before there had been two tired old nags of rouncies there now stood two healthy, robust animals: their brown pelts were rich and glossy, their limbs seemed fuller, their eyes keener. Both steeds whickered impatiently to be off, as if well-fed thoroughbreds.

Vaskrian's courser had undergone a similar subtle transformation. Yorro had always been well-kept – he had seen to that diligently – but he seemed a little taller and stronger than before, and the hair that glistened on his flanks was now as fine as that of any rich knight's palfrey. As Vaskrian reached out to pet Yorro, he whinnied and stamped, as if demanding to be ridden into battle.

'Well, Yorro, you're looking better than ever!' exclaimed the squire. Hearing his name Yorro tossed his head and whinnied even more loudly, his glinting mane catching sparkles of noon sunlight.

'Can we really trust steeds tainted by faerie magic?' asked Adelko tremulously. 'Surely it would be a grave sin to ride such mounts!'

Typical. They'd just survived Tintagael and now the novice had to find something else to be frightened of. He reminded Vaskrian of Festius, the glum fool in Maegellin's satire about a jester who always saw the worst in life. But Vaskrian was far too pleased to have his horse back to brook any Festian mutterings about it.

'I don't see any sin in it!' he retorted. 'Yorro's still Yorro... he's just, well, a bit different is all. And I don't see any magic to it either! His hair is glossier and he looks a bit sprightlier, but where's the harm in that? It's the same with your steeds, and Reus knows they needed sprucing up more than Yorro did!'

Adelko was about to protest when Horskram interjected.

'For once I am inclined to agree with a layman on this matter,' he said, measuring his words carefully. 'For my part I do not believe our horses have been bewitched – for one thing they would not bear us if so. And there is one way to be sure...'

Pulling his circifix from his habit the monk presented it to each of the horses in turn, intoning a simple blessing as he did. He made for an amusing sight doing this, but he proved his point.

'I think we can rest assured that we have not been given possessed steeds,' he said finally. 'But it is true that the Fay Folk can alter the nature of things in this world somewhat, as their sorcerous sway over Tintagael Forest proves in abundance. And whilst I would not normally hold with using mounts that have been so influenced, our need is great and I am now genuinely persuaded that the Fays are trying to help us. Now, what I – '

He was interrupted by Vaskrian.

'Look!' he exclaimed with a cry of joy. 'They returned my father's sword! They've given it back to me!'

He drew the blade from its sheath: he'd been so preoccupied with the horses and trying to recall what had happened in the forest that he hadn't noticed it hanging at his side.

It soon became obvious that his sword had been touched by the Fays too. In shape and form it still resembled a common serjeant's sword, but the Kindred had given it a straighter edge and sharper blade. The balance felt better too; trying a few practice cuts it felt as easy in his hand as the best-forged blades of Strongholm steel.

'They've enchanted... I mean improved my blade as well!' he said, trying a florid swipe that had Adelko flinching backwards. 'I'll thank them by slaying a few brigands with it!'

'Perhaps you should thank them for driving your erstwhile master into a situation that killed him too,' replied Horskram, more sadly than anything else. 'Make no mistake – the Fays are only helping us out of self-interest. Whatever coming evil we are facing, they fear it as much as any mortal. Which makes me fear it all the more... I must meditate upon their words, one or two things have already become apparent. Now sheathe that thing and let's have a bite to eat – I hope they haven't meddled with our provisions as well!'

✧ ✧ ✧

To Adelko's relief it was not so, and the hardened cheese and bread, washed down with a few mouthfuls of water, tasted delicious. They ate ravenously, each taking at least twice what they would normally eat. Even Horskram, usually so frugal, did not stint. How long had they gone without eating, the novice wondered.

After their meal both youths lay down in the sun to digest. Adelko felt its warmth against his face, pleasantly offset by a chill easterly breeze...

Horskram nudged him in the leg with his quarterstaff.

'Best let me have another look at your wound,' he said gruffly. 'Then we must be off, we've lost half the day and we'll struggle to make the crossroads by nightfall, swifter steeds or no!'

Vaskrian frowned and sat up. 'What are you talking about? We've emerged south of the crossroads – all we need to do is find the southern road and we can continue our journey. The Vyborg can't be more than a few leagues south of here – we could probably make Linden by nightfall, I'm sure they'll remember me. We might even get lodgings in the castle if we're lucky.'

Horskram frowned and shook his head. 'I hardly think turning up at Linden and proclaiming poor Sir Branas's passing and all our troubles besides will help our cause,' he said. 'And in any case, we aren't heading south – our road now lies east.'

The pair looked at him askance.

'*Bloody strife bars the southern road*, the Fays said,' he reminded them patiently. 'They're probably referring to the war stirring down south – if what the guard at the Rymold told us is true, the Jarl of Thule and his allies will be up in arms.'

'But I thought our Order takes no part in earthly wars?' Adelko protested. 'Surely they'll let us pass?'

'You underestimate the suspicions of powerful men,' replied Horskram. 'For all Krulheim knows, we could be spies – and not all the southern barons are friends to our Order. Though I hate to agree with such malicious sprites, the Fay Folk are probably giving us good counsel. Eastward is our best way now, for two reasons. We may be able to take a ship at Strongholm to take us to Meerborg – from there we can ride or take a river barge to Graukolos, which is our next major destination ahead of Rima anyway.'

'But ship berths are costly, and you said you don't have any money left,' protested Vaskrian. 'And poor Branas kept all his on his charger. I only found a few silver marks on his purse when we... gave him his funereal rites.'

'I've already thought of that,' replied Horskram. 'There is another monastery belonging to our Order, in Urling at the foot of the Staerk Ranges – we could stop there on the way to the capital and secure funds from the Abbot, or failing that the King himself is not unknown to me.'

'But wouldn't asking either of them to help us mean breaking with our secrecy?' asked Adelko.

'Secrecy, secrecy,' echoed Vaskrian, getting exasperated. 'All I ever seem to hear from you Argolians is secrecy! You won't tell me what's really going on – that much is clear – but what could be so terrible that you won't even tell your own kind, or our King? It can't be any worse than what we've just faced!'

'I will not speak further of such things now,' said Horskram, favouring the squire with a dark look. 'As for your involvement, my deepest condolences on behalf of our Order – it was never my intention that you or your master should come to harm. But what the Almighty has written cannot be unwritten, as the Redeemer sayeth. I can put in a good word for you at Strongholm, or any other suitable place we come to, in the hope that some brave knight will take you into service to replace the living you have lost. Unless of course you wish to return by your own way to Hroghar – though I cannot guarantee that your journey home would be a safe one.'

Vaskrian shook his head emphatically. 'Sir Branas swore an oath on behalf of us both, I'm still bound by it even though he's... gone. I'm coming with you, as far as Strongholm at least. If you can find me another guvnor once we're there, so much the better.'

With a flourish he drew his sword again, giving it a couple of twirls for good measure.

'And let's face it, now poor old Branas is gone you're going to need this more than ever,' he said, his face suddenly cracking a grin. 'Vaskrian, esquire of Hroghar, is officially at your service!'

Horskram smiled sardonically and rolled his eyes. 'Heavens! Well that's all our troubles dealt with in a trice!'

Adelko couldn't help smiling himself. The squire was obviously slightly unhinged, but he was high-spirited too. He supposed friends like that were good to have around in dangerous times.

※ ※ ※

Vaskrian saw every reason to feel high-spirited. Though he genuinely mourned old Branas, and memories of the forest were a lurking chill of horror at the edge of his recollection, he could see prospects in this venture. The older friar clearly knew some very influential people (the King, for Reus' sake!), and a journey to the capital he'd never seen seemed a far more cheering prospect than a lonely trip back to Hroghar, Rutgar's barbed jibes and a blood-feud with Derrick's family that would probably see him finished without Branas's protection.

He was duty-bound to tell the Jarl about Sir Branas, but he could always send word from Strongholm – with the country preparing for war there would be plenty of messengers knocking around. Yes, better to do it that way – telling the unlikely story of the old knight's death in a haunted forest to Lord Fenrig in person didn't seem like such a good idea.

Far better to journey on into perils that held some chance of reward.

Sheathing his sword, Vaskrian set about preparing his horse with a cheerful hum.

※ ※ ※

'You said two reasons for heading east – what's the second?' Adelko asked his mentor as he tended his wound. It was still there, a nasty gash across his right side, but the pain had ebbed considerably and mercifully there was no sign of infection.

'The second just occurred to me while we were breaking our fast,' replied Horskram. 'And I must confess I felt rather a fool for not having thought of it before. I should have recalled the *Gospel of St Alysius*, and in truth I'm shocked that it would take the soulless faerie kindred to remind me of its relevance.'

His mentor said nothing more for a while, as he washed the makeshift bandage with water from his skin and fastened it around his waist again.

Adelko frowned as he tried to make sense of the titbit Horskram had thrown him. St Alysius had been one of the Redeemer's Seven Acolytes: the first of Palomedes' rebel soldiers to follow his example and put aside the sword, seeking victory over the pagan unbelievers with preaching and prayer rather than war and strife. The Redeemer's lieutenant, Antiochus the Red-Handed, had betrayed him soon after, giving him up to the soldiers of the Old Thalamian empire through treachery; not long after, the Redeemer had been broken on the Wheel in Tyrannos, relinquishing bodily life without a fight so that all the faithful might follow his example and be saved.

The fate of Antiochus, who as punishment for his sins was stung to death by hornets possessed by divine wrath, was well documented, as was the fate of the other Acolytes. Most of them had travelled east and west, spreading the Creed throughout the vast dominions of the Thalamian Empire.

But on the fate of St Alysius few scholars agreed. Even the Gospel dedicated to his doings after the Redeemer's sacrifice was vague and shrouded in mysteries, written in tantalising couplets that offered recondite truths obscured by dense imagery and rich symbolism.

Most did agree that he had been one of the last Acolytes to leave Tyrannos, lingering there at great risk to his life. Common consensus also had it that he had taken with him a vessel containing drops of the Redeemer's blood, which he had caught as they flowed from the cruel wounds inflicted on him by the torture-master of Thalamy at the Emperor's behest.

Religious authorities disagreed wildly as to what happened next, but one popular legend had it that Alysius headed north, journeying hundreds of miles through the imperial heartlands and barbarian forests and wildernesses beyond, until arriving at a port overlooking the Wyvern Sea he finally took ship and crossed over into the far north of Urovia...

That was interpreted by some scholars to have been present-day Northalde, though it would have been long before the reavers came and settled there. Not even the Headstone fragment that was the cause of all their troubles would have been brought there yet – Palomedes and Alysius had lived three hundred years before Søren. The lands about them would still have mostly been occupied by Westerling tribes, the descendants of exiled clans from the Island Realms who had fled to the mainland after the Wars of Kith and Kin a thousand years before.

But he was allowing history to distract him, he reflected as he mounted his horse – just what was his mentor getting at?

The Fays had referred to the Redeemer's blood being shed for mortalkind – that was clearly what they meant by *warrior-prophet*... The legend also claimed St Alysius had been buried, with his treasured relic, in a tomb on the site of Strongholm. Centuries later, when that city was founded by the ill-fated King Olav, St Alysius' resting place was all but ignored, and a pagan princeling built a hall atop it.

But in time the Creed came to the old kingdom of Nylund, which was later absorbed into Northalde. When the newly ordained perfects had learned of the tomb's existence, they had destroyed the mansion and laid the foundations of the High Temple over it, that the centre of the realm's faith might be built on the blood of the Redeemer and the bones of his bravest acolyte.

Or so the perfects of the Most Holy Bethel of St Alysius liked to claim. Adelko had heard that rumour spoken of before at Ulfang – but he'd also heard several of the adepts there disputing its veracity.

But more to the point, what did such a thing have to do with their mission?

He voiced his query as the three of them nudged their steeds into a north-easterly amble towards the highway.

'So you have worked out one puzzle – that is good,' replied Horskram, who liked to test his novice's faculties whenever possible. 'Now you must think on the answer to the next. Assuming the legend of St Alysius is true, and the Arch-Perfect's seat in Strongholm holds nothing less than the blood of the Redeemer, what could it mean for us?'

Adelko thought long and hard about that while his master waited patiently and Vaskrian heedlessly whistled a marching tune beside them. Then, unbidden, the words of the Fays came back to him.

Seek the sanctuary of your creed.

'Sanctuary!' he gasped aloud, the realisation suddenly dawning on him. 'Of course, if we manage to get to Strongholm, the blood of the Redeemer will shield us! No lesser denizen of the Other Side would dare come near such a powerful relic! Even... even a greater demon might have pause before the remains of the True Prophet himself!'

'Well done,' replied Horskram crisply. 'I am glad to see our recent ordeal has not sapped your intellect. Indeed, now I'm sure you can appreciate my embarrassment at having overlooked the High Temple before.'

'Yes but... this is all assuming those stories are true, isn't it?' said Adelko anxiously. 'I remember a lot of the adepts saying that they doubted the legend...'

'As I'm sure you are becoming aware, there is not always a great deal of love lost between the Temple and our Order,' said Horskram. 'Since... certain events, there has been much suspicion on either side. I will not detail them now, but suffice to say that many in our fraternity feel it is in their interests to denigrate any claims to sanctity made by the mainstream clerics, and vice versa. But having read much on the subject myself, I am inclined to believe the legend is true – though there can be no doubt that if the blood of the Redeemer is indeed kept below St Alysius' Bethel it has been a jealously guarded secret for centuries.'

'So... why do you believe it, Master Horskram?'

The adept's response surprised him. 'Doubtless, young Adelko, you have found occasions to read Gracius' *Lays of King Vasirius and the Knights of the Purple Garter* when you should have been reading Scripture?'

Adelko flushed, feeling suddenly guilty. But Ulfang library contained hundreds of texts from far and wide, and not all tomes could be religious. And the stories of the Pangonian King who founded the Code of Chivalry more than a century ago made for a gripping read.

'Ah, yes, I suppose so...' he replied hesitantly.

Horskram only smiled. 'Have no fear, for in this case your extra-curricular reading should serve you well – are you familiar with the tale of *Sir Alric the Pious and the Holy Bloodquest*?'

Adelko nodded, his enthusiasm returning. 'Why of course, it's one of the best stories of the Age of Chivalry... the King was cursed by the White Blood Witch, and only the blood of the Redeemer could heal him. But only his purest-hearted knight could ever find such a relic, and that's why all the others failed where Alric succeeded. They say he was, um... virginal, and he'd never even killed anyone – '

'What sort of a knight is that?' snorted Vaskrian, suddenly paying attention. 'Never mind Alric, everyone knows Sir Lancelyn of the Pale Mountain was King Vasirius' greatest knight! Well, for a Pangonian he was quite good anyway...'

The squire's voice trailed off as Horskram fixed him with a stare that would curdle milk.

'Anyhow, they say he journeyed for a year and a day until he found what he was looking for,' continued the novice. 'But none of the lays I've read specifically say the blood was kept in Strongholm...'

'No, none of them do,' agreed Horskram. 'That's because most Pangonians are notoriously indifferent to foreign countries, and their poets are no different. But Gracius' description of the remote northern city shrouded in mists, where the perfects guarding the Redeemer's blood lived, is strikingly reminiscent of our capital. Of course that could just be coincidence – many cities of the world are built by the sea and have high stone walls after all – but the apparent similarities are worth bearing in mind in light of one other important consideration.

'In the seven centuries since Strongholm was founded, there have scarcely been any diabolical incidents there. Possessions, hauntings, manifestations, reports of witchcraft... our capital and its environs have been an oasis of calm, as far as such things go. When there have been incidents, they have only been of an extreme nature – a greater demon or the shade of one especially powerful or wicked in life, a mighty warlock... something or someone powerful enough to contend with the blood of Palom. That above all else persuades me that the legend is true. I believe that the perfecthood at the Bethel of St Alysius have worked hard through the centuries to convince the rest of the True Temple, from here to Rima, that the tale of the Prophet's Bloody Chalice is nothing more than a myth.'

'Why would they want to do that?'

'Think on it, Adelko, green as you are the answer is ready and waiting. The head of the True Temple has his seat in Rima. How do you think the Supreme Perfect, sitting on his marble throne in the greatest Urovian city west of the Great White Mountains, would feel knowing that arguably the most potent relic of the Creed was sitting, not beneath his plush floors, but those of a distant northern priesthood in a realm regarded by haughty southerners as little better than a collection of barbarian tribes?'

'Barbarians?' broke in Vaskrian. 'Pangonian swine, fie on them! Those effete southerners are no match for stout Northlendings in the field, that's the only reason they call us rough!'

'Yes, thank you, Vaskrian, for your cultural observations,' replied Horskram dryly. 'But I believe my novice and I were holding discourse about the politics of our great mother Temple. Now if you'd be so kind...'

'Alright, I know when I'm not wanted,' replied the squire. 'And I know a dull conversation when I hear one! If you don't mind, Yorro and I will keep our own company for a bit.'

He nudged his courser ahead of them, leaving the two monks to continue talking.

'I see...' resumed Adelko. 'So, you're saying that it's not just the Temple perfects and us who don't trust each other – the perfects don't trust each other either?'

Horskram sighed. 'I'm afraid so, and sorry to say that if I were to tell you everything I know of the machinations of Temple politics we would still be talking long after sunset. We shall speak of such things further, when the time is right, but not now.'

The last thing Adelko wanted to hear about was more Temple politics – he'd been traumatised enough lately as it was. There were a couple of things playing on his mind though.

'But this... thing that's chasing us – can it really be stopped by the Redeemer's blood?'

Horskram pursed his lips. 'A more powerful entity would probably have killed us at Landebert's hut, as we discussed before. Once we get within the Strang Ranges that encircle the lands that feed Strongholm, the relic's power should be enough to protect us.'

'But what then? We can't just cower behind the walls of Strongholm – we have to get to Rima don't we?'

'Indeed we do. Which is why, when we reach the capital – assuming we do – I must find some way to persuade the Arch Perfect to do the unthinkable.'

'Which is?'

'To do what has not been done for anyone save pious Sir Alric more than a hundred and fifty years ago – to let me take a part of Strongholm's great relic with me to Rima, for our protection.'

Adelko stifled an incredulous laugh. 'But... with all due respect Master Horskram, from what you've just told me, His Holiness will never do it. Even if he is a great friend to our Order!'

'He is not a great friend to our Order,' replied Horskram flatly, before nudging his horse to catch up with Vaskrian's.

✣ ✣ ✣

The three of them continued riding, stopping only at a stream to refill their waterskins before reaching the highway around mid-afternoon. They passed many people as they took it north: knights and men-at-arms heading south towards the war, travelling merchants and artisans fleeing the same, yeomen farmers with wayns heading in both directions with much needed victuals, freeswords and archers looking to sell their services, and one or two black-robed mendicant perfects, calling on those about to shed blood to give money to atone in advance for their mortal sins.

Toward dusk they overtook a ragged group of peasants. They had a look of abject misery and carried sorry-looking bundles on their backs. Adelko guessed they were all the poor folk owned.

'What takes you north?' asked Horskram as they drew level with the sorry band.

The nearest one squinted up at him. He had a rough bloodstained cloth over one eye and one side of his face was pock-marked from the ravages of an old illness. His mouth was set in a perpetual grimace.

'We're from Salmorlund,' he replied in a thin reedy voice. 'Our village was set upon by the Jarl of Thule's men – or should I say *Prince* of Thule, as that's wot he's taken to calling himself now – ten days ago. They swept across the river by night, commenced to burnin' everything and slaying everyone in sight. We're all that's left of our village, aye and I daresay those for a few leagues around will tell a similar tale.'

'May the Redeemer console you for your losses and the Almighty wreak just vengeance on those responsible,' replied Horskram. 'But what of the border defences? What of His Royal Highness Prince Wolfram?'

The one-eyed peasant glared and spat. The two yeomen walking nearest him, a middle-aged woman with a pale tear-streaked face and a bearded yeoman missing an arm, shook their heads dolefully.

'Well now, a poor peasant as I am don't dare speak ill o' the King's son and heir,' continued the one-eyed yeoman sourly. 'But let's just say the Lord Warden of the Southern Reaches was too busy tourneying away up north to fight a real war on his back doorstep. By the time he'd heard of Thule's uprising and set out with his knights it were too late. It was left to Lord Kelmor to defend Salmor on 'is own.'

The future king's love of glory on the field was well known. The news made for bitter irony.

'That is regrettable,' said Horskram. 'But it should have made little difference who was left in charge – why did the Jarl of Salmorlund not send men to protect your village?'

'His lordship Kelmor was pinned down in his castle – too busy resistin' a surprise attack that turned into a full-blown siege overnight to help the likes o' us,' continued the one-eyed peasant. 'And looks like Thule's got men to spare for ravagin' us poorer folk in the meanwhile. By the time they came down on us, killin' and burnin', we heard that he'd taken Blakelock too – aye, sent the Lord Warden headin' for the hills, he did! Fact o' the matter is, master monk, until His Majesty musters a proper army, folks down south are outnumbered. Krulheim's got every baron south of the river on his side.'

Horskram tugged fretfully at his unkempt beard. 'Where are you headed now?' he asked. 'You have travelled far from your homes.'

'Not far enough, master monk. We're headed north of the Rymold – rumour has it Krulheim means to march on the capital, when he's done with the southern reaches o' the King's Dominions. They say he wants these lands for himself, and Strongholm for his seat. He means to avenge his father good 'n' proper, and he's got the strength to do it, they say – mark my words, master monk, there'll be a siege o' the capital before the next winter sets in, that there will.'

✛ ✛ ✛

They reached Ryosfal shortly after dusk. By that time they had fallen in with a motley assortment of freeswords and craftsmen, making their way to join the King's muster. The sight of blacksmiths heeding the call to war put Adelko in mind of his father, far away up north in Narvik.

He would probably be too old to be sent south with the Highland clans – assuming he was even still alive. That brought on a twinge of homesickness that he struggled to suppress.

The ancient town stood where the north-south road met the east road for Strongholm. Colloquially known as the king's highway, it had no westerly branch: that way led only to the borders of Tintagael, where no sane man would ever dare venture.

Pushing the thought of their recent mad adventures to one side, Adelko guessed that they must now be a day's ride south of where they had been chased off the road into the dreadful forest. Recalling that incident had him wondering: what had become of the brigands since? He supposed they had to be somewhere in the vicinity, and with so many freeswords on the roads they would blend in easily enough. The thought did as little to settle his mind as the oncoming night – he began to remember why they had entered Tintagael in the first place.

With a population of nearly two thousand souls, Ryosfal was the biggest sort of town, but even so all the inns were full, crammed to the rafters with craftsmen, freeswords and refugees.

'We must seek shelter the old-fashioned way, and beg a floor and bowl of soup for the night,' said Horskram, referring to the time when the craze for new-fangled inns had not spread across the Great White Mountains from the Empire, which seemed to have the knack for coming up with such novel ideas.

The first couple of houses they tried turned them away, having already taken in wayfarers. The third opened up for them, but taking one look at Horskram's grey habit, the householder spat and cursed: 'Argolians is it? I'll not shelter the likes of you heretics under my roof, meddling with demonspawn and all – begone, before I call a perfect and have a real man of the cloth send you on your way!'

The surly townsman slammed the door in their faces without another word.

'What did he mean by that?' asked Adelko, aghast. 'We don't meddle with demons – we fight them! And we're certainly no heretics – why would he say that?'

'Because he's been listening to the wrong kind of perfect,' replied Horskram flatly. 'Never mind that for now – let's try another house. These are all well-to-do, as far as towns go – there's bound to be somebody left who can spare us a floor and some stabling space.'

The fourth house they tried did not even answer, but when Horskram knocked on the varnished pine door of the fifth it was opened promptly enough by a bent-backed servant of about forty winters. She gazed at them suspiciously as Horskram humbly requested food and lodgings,

and looked about to turn them away when a deep-throated voice came
from behind her.

'Did I hear rightly, an Argolian friar seeks my roof for the night?
Maddie, stand aside – I'll not have it said I turned away the Order
from my door in need, though there's many round here as would!'

The speaker stepped from the house's interior into the light shed
by the serving maid's candelabrum. He was a short, stocky man, with
cropped greying mousy hair and a plain-looking face, some fifty winters
old. His clothes were of simple design but well kept and cut from the
finest wool. Holding out a stumpy-fingered hand adorned with rings
studded with semi-precious gemstones for Horskram to shake, he said:
'My name is Arro, wool merchant, at your service. Perhaps you'd do
me the honour of introducing yourself and your companions?'

'Of course,' replied Horskram, betraying no sign of his dislike
of merchants or consternation at having to give their names. 'I am
Horskram of Vilno, this is my novice, Adelko of Narvik, and this
is Vaskrian, esquire of Hroghar. We would be most grateful if – '

'Aye, I know what you need,' interrupted the merchant. 'Bed and
board. I heard plain enough when you were talking to Maddie just now.
Step inside, I just wanted names is all – can't be too careful nowadays,
with all these rakehell freeswords and Reus knows what other vagabonds
roaming the land.'

Presently the four of them were sitting in Arro's spacious main
room, which boasted the kind of rude opulence typical of a bourgeois
townsman. He clearly thrived at his trade, because he had enough
chairs for all of them to sit on, a luxury that few landed knights
could boast. A low oak table by the hearth had been set by Maddie
with a large earthenware flagon of red wine and four pewter cups.
Among the numerous hangings and curios adorning the crowded
walls, Adelko noticed three small tapestries arranged in a triptych
depicting scenes from the Scriptures. That surprised him – he had
been led to believe by Horskram that merchants were an ungodly lot.

He soon had the answer to that riddle. On his second cup Arro
candidly let it be known that his younger brother had taken holy
orders with the Argolians, and that he had always been a friend to
the Order. Anything he could do to help the good friars, anything at
all... Maddie was cooking up a hearty stew even as they spoke, and
there would be blankets aplenty and space on yon rug. He would
see to it that the hearth was kept burning all night.

Horskram thanked the merchant levelly and pressed him for
more news of the impending war.

'Hmm, not much more I can tell you besides what you already know,' frowned Arro, stroking his broad chin thoughtfully. 'They're said to be sore pressed on the southern borders, sounds as if Thule and his lot are making swift progress – you've heard about Blakelock, well they've got Rookhammer surrounded as well now. Once they take that and Castle Salmor there'll be no stoppin' them – I'd say Prince Wolfram will be under siege at Linden before too long at this rate. But it's not all bad news – the recruiting serjeant I spoke with t'other day said Freidheim plans on marching south to meet the rebels next month.'

Horskram frowned. 'Next month? But that's weeks away – by my reckoning it can't be later than the 8th of Samonath...'

Arro looked at him incredulously. 'Begging your pardon, master monk, but either my wine's too strong or you've been preachin' in the wilderness over long – why it's the 20th, or I'm a Thraxian!'

Horskram gaped and shook his head. 'But that can't be – we set out from Ulfang Monastery on the 24th of Varmonath. By my reckoning we've been on the road for a fortnight, and I always keep strict track of the time. Our way has been... compromised, but I can't have miscounted by twelve days!'

Arro was shaking his head ruefully. 'Oh but I'm afraid you have, Master Horskram. Now I'm no scholar as you are,' he went on, raising a broad hand in acknowledgement. 'But in my trade, him as don't keep track o' the days is as like to come a cropper as him as don't keep track o' his pennies. If you want I can show you all me ledgers, they're bang up to date, and as I said before – today is the 20th, or I'm a knight about to ride off to war wit' King Freidheim and all his men!'

Horskram seemed about to protest but suddenly stopped short as the realisation dawned on all three of them. Adelko felt a chill creep down his spine as he recalled the timelessness of the cursed forest. No wonder they had all been so ravenous at lunch that afternoon.

Horskram stuttered a feeble excuse at the quizzical merchant and did his best to dissemble, just as Maddie arrived to announce that supper was ready.

The four of them ate in the same room. Like their kindly host the stew was simple but wholesome, and each of them had more than one helping. Adelko felt no monkish pangs of guilt as he tucked in – after all they had a fortnight's eating to catch up with.

When they were done Arro bade them good night and left Maddie to bring fur blankets and stoke up the fire. Outside it had begun to rain. Northlending weather remained as changeable as ever at this time of year. In a strange way that seemed comforting.

Listening to the pattering of drops against the horn windowpanes as he settled down for the night, Adelko turned to Horskram and whispered: 'How can it be that we were in the forest for so long? I only remember one night as such... at the Hag's hut. Surely it was two days, not two weeks!'

'It is possible we walked in our sleep,' mused the adept. 'Or simply that time passed in the forest is not the same as time passed in the outer world. I do not really know, to tell you the truth. All I know is that time is against us, more even than I thought before. Go to sleep – we'll need to make the most of it tomorrow!'

Vaskrian was already gently snoring beside them. Turning over the two monks followed suit, quickly drifting off to sleep.

That night Adelko dreamed again. This time he was back in Narvik, returning from a long journey. Only somehow he had become lost in a vast forest, and a hundred years had passed without his knowing, and all the faces that greeted him as he rode into his home village were strange ones.

⇥ CHAPTER IX ⇤

The White Raven Flies

They had been on the king's highway for several hours out of Ryosfal when they heard the sound of many horsemen closing on them from behind at a gallop.

Adelko stiffened in the saddle; the road leading out of town had been clogged with wayfarers also heading to the capital, but with most of these on foot the trio had soon found themselves alone on the highway.

The sound of swift horses brought thoughts of slavering brigands back to his mind with an unpleasantly sharp clarity. Next to him Vaskrian wheeled his steed around, his hand flying to his sword hilt in evidence that he was thinking much the same thing. Horskram bade them stand their ground.

'If it's our old friends from the Far Northlands we won't outrun them,' he said. 'Their chargers are swifter than our rouncies, though Vaskrian's courser might outrun them.'

'But,' Adelko protested, 'our horses are different since... the forest. I can feel it when we ride them...'

Horskram scowled. 'I'll not trust my life to faerie magick until all else fails! But let us get off the road – yonder trees may give us some cover.'

Adelko glanced over doubtfully at the half dozen yew saplings languidly stretching towards maturity a few paces off the highway. Squinting back down the road he could see the outlines of a company of horsemen approaching. Judging by the glint of weak sunlight on their frames they had to be knights – or heavily armed mounted serjeants at the least. Or brigands contracted by an unknown enemy to kill them.

Cultivated farmland stretched flatly to either side of them – there was nowhere else to hide. Hurriedly they nudged their horses over to the trees, dismounting so as to be less obtrusive.

Vaskrian as usual took some persuading, deploring the monks for cowards – until Horskram took his reins in a vice-like grip and urged him off the road in an icy voice. Even the hot-headed squire knew better than to tussle with a man of the cloth. Or an angry one, at least.

By the time they were off the road the horsemen were clearly in view. To Adelko's relief they were not brigands, but heavily armoured knights, about a dozen strong.

Leaning forwards Vaskrian peered at them intently. Adelko followed his line of sight. He was scrutinising the banner that one carried. The heraldic coat of arms on it loomed into focus: a white raven taking flight over a pair of crossed lances picked out in the same colour, on a jet black background.

'They're knights of the White Valravyn!' yelled Vaskrian. 'They'll help us!'

'No, you fool, leave them be!' cried Horskram.

But it was already too late. Vaskrian stepped back on to the highway, his arm raised in a gesture of parley. In what seemed the blinking of an eye, the knights closed the distance and pulled up their snorting chargers, facing the squire in a semi-circle. They did not lower their spears, but all glared at him suspiciously.

To Adelko they seemed a fearsome bunch: long-limbed, keen-eyed and broad-shouldered. Though dressed in full armour from neck to knee none wore a helm; their long hair ruffled in the mid-morning breeze. Their complexions were for the most part fair, their locks flaxen – noble Northlendings in the King's Dominions had kept their Northland ancestry purer than most.

⁜ ⁜ ⁜

To Vaskrian they were a glorious sight. Though stained by caked mud and dried blood their mail was of the finest quality, their black surcoats fashioned of rich wool and depicting the same coat of arms as the banner, whilst their cloaks were chequered black and white. Their dappled grey Farovian destriers were caparisoned in a like manner, armoured only in boiled leather to allow for greater speed. Each knight carried a shield of iron-shod oak besides his long ash spear, and a stout sword was girt at the belt of every one.

The apparent leader, a doughty-looking fighter of some forty winters with neck-length dirty blond hair, a rugged beard and pale grey eyes, addressed the squire sternly. 'What business do you have, obstructing the Order of the White Valravyn? The country is at war, and we ride urgently on the King's errand – speak swiftly, and your reasons for stopping us had best be good ones!'

Vaskrian faltered. It had seemed like a good idea at the time to stop them. But now he had, he wasn't sure what to say. *We've just been adventuring in Tintagael Forest after being pursued by a demon and a pack of Northland brigands* didn't seem like a good place to start.

'I... forgive me, sir knight,' he mumbled, suddenly feeling like the fool he probably was, 'er, that is to say...'

The leader knight's face darkened, his countenance more angry than stern now. 'Well, spit it out lad – you've taken the trouble to stop us. What is it that ails you, besides a twisted tongue?'

Several of the other knights were exchanging bemused glances now, whilst one or two muttered darkly and sneered. One of the latter caught Adelko's eye – well built like all his fellows, his wavy blond hair had a reddish tinge to it. Unlike the rest of the company, his beard and moustache were finely trimmed and well-kept; his green eyes had a malignant gleam to them that he thought went rather too well with the cruel twist of his otherwise handsome mouth.

By now Horskram had stepped on to the road. Clearing his throat pointedly the old monk addressed the whole company, but kept his eyes fixed on their leader.

'Greetings, knights of the Order of the White Valravyn, protectors of the King's Dominions, keepers of the peace of his realm, justiciars of royal law,' he declaimed, drawing on protocol. 'Horskram of Vilno, adept of the Ulfang chapter of the Argolian Order, salutes thee! He also offers his humble apologies for the rash actions of yon squire, bound by oath to his service until circumstances dictate otherwise.'

The leader knight raised his eyebrows. He looked somewhat taken aback. 'Two Argolians and a squire without a knight, travelling as boon companions,' he mused aloud. 'Now that is an unusual band of wayfarers – even in wartime! There's more to this than meets the eye I'll warrant – come now, sirrah, let us have your story, and have it quickly.'

'I regret that I cannot divulge all its details,' replied Horskram warily, 'but suffice to say that my novice and I are on urgent monastic business – it is imperative that we seek an audience with the Arch Perfect at the High Temple in Strongholm. Vaskrian of Hroghar here is accompanying us for our protection in these troubled times, though we would be grateful for an armed escort if you would be willing to let us accompany you. Are you headed for Staerkvit Castle, pray?'

The leader knight's eyes narrowed at this. 'He who answers a question with a question wishes to avoid being questioned, methinks... now why might that be, I wonder? You tell us next to nothing of yourself, then request an armed escort! Since when were humble friars so audacious?'

The knight with the cruel mouth spoke up. 'Sir Tarlquist, we should not be allowing this Argolian churl to bandy words with us at such a perilous time! Who does he think he is, I wonder? Perhaps a spell in the dungeons of Staerkvit would teach him a lesson.'

Hearing this another knight with rich neck-length golden hair teased his Farovian charger forward a step or two. He was even taller and more powerfully built than the other knights; well-made as they were, they looked like ordinary fighters next to him.

'Sir Wolmar, those are unmannerly and ungodly remarks both,' he said. 'A knight of the Order should know better than to chastise and threaten a man of the cloth. The Argolians have ever been friends to the realm.'

Unlike the other two knights he was clean shaven; a pair of grey-blue eyes burned with a singular intensity in his ruggedly handsome face.

'That's not the way I heard it,' snarled the knight called Wolmar. 'I heard that the Argolians are heretics who practise dire sorceries in the privacy of their monastic retreats – perhaps that is the business they ride to now in such great secrecy!'

'Enough!' barked Sir Tarlquist. 'I'll have no squabbling – now, master monk, if you please, a little more candour would not go amiss. Your young swordsman friend was certainly eager to attract our attention – why would that be, pray? And where is your knightly master?'

Sir Tarlquist turned his flinty eyes on Vaskrian as he asked the last question – but the squire had eyes only for the golden-haired knight who had spoken before.

'I don't believe it!' he exclaimed, gaping in delighted astonishment. 'But you're... Torgun! Sir Torgun of Vandheim!'

'I must confess I am not used to being recognised by strangers without my own coat of arms,' replied the golden-haired knight mildly. 'Have we met? If you have squired for me before and I have forgotten, pray forgive the oversight on my part...'

'No, no, nothing like that!' blurted Vaskrian. 'I saw you joust – at Linden Castle last summer! You were... magnificent!'

'Why look, Sir Torgun's found himself another damsel admirer,' sneered Sir Wolmar, getting a few chuckles from among the other knights. A few chuckles – but more glares, Adelko noticed. Clearly this Wolmar was not universally liked. The novice already knew which camp he belonged to.

Vaskrian was too excited at meeting his hero to pay Sir Wolmar any heed, and was virtually re-enacting Sir Torgun's victory over Sir Brogun in the jousting final for the benefit of the monks, much to the knights' amusement. Even stern-faced Tarlquist could not help smiling.

Sir Torgun merely nodded in modest acknowledgement. 'I am pleased you enjoyed the event,' was all he said, though a slight smile played on his lips too.

'All right, that's enough reminiscing,' said Tarlquist. 'There's a real war on, in case anyone's forgotten – and I'd still like to know more about *your* story, lad. What of your knightly master?'

'He...' Vaskrian paused, feeling Horskram's icy stare on him. 'He's dead.'

Horskram rolled his eyes to the heavens. Adelko stood silently, unsure what would happen next. The knights seemed unperturbed – after all, warriors died all the time.

'Aye?' replied Tarlquist patiently. 'And how, pray tell, did he meet his end?'

'In... in Tintagael Forest,' blurted Vaskrian. Adelko felt his heart sink. Horskram was staring at the squire aghast. Several of the knights gasped; some made the sign of the Wheel.

'Tintagael?' gaped Sir Tarlquist. 'What is this madness you speak of? None have ventured there for years – and no sane man ever would!'

Turning his eyes on Horskram again he glared flintily at him. 'Tell me, is this true?'

The adept took a deep breath and let it out slowly. He met the knight's gaze.

'It is true,' he said.

'What did I tell you?' Sir Wolmar snarled. 'They are black magicians, in league with the Fallen One – for all we know they've been sent by the rebels to wreak havoc behind enemy lines! We should hang them forthwith!'

'You've no way of knowing that,' replied Sir Torgun evenly. 'And in any case – innocent until proven guilty, that is our way! These men deserve a trial at least!'

'Trial?' replied Wolmar, incredulous. 'They've just condemned themselves out of their own mouths!'

'Which is what you do every time you open yours,' interjected another burly knight with thick blond curls and a scar running down one of his ruddy cheeks.

'Meaning what, exactly?' snarled Sir Wolmar.

'Meaning you condemn yourself for an unjust fool every time you speak,' replied the ruddy-faced knight. 'Torgun has the right of it – our Order has never hanged a man without trying him first!'

'You dare speak to me that way!' retorted Wolmar. 'Check your words, Sir Aronn, or I'll see to it you're reprimanded!'

'If you think you'll be able to pull strings because of who you are then you're wrong,' growled Sir Aronn. 'I was in the Order keeping the King's peace when you were still a page boy – His Royal Highness won't forget that, even if you have! All men are equal in the Order, save for those of higher military rank – or had that slipped your mind?'

The knights degenerated into a heated argument that lasted several minutes. Wolmar and Aronn continued to bicker at one another while the rest of the company argued over what to do with the trio. Some including Torgun were for trying them on the spot; a couple advocated handing them over to their fellow Argolians to be tried for witchcraft; a few were simply for leaving them and pressing on.

With some difficulty Tarlquist silenced them, before addressing Horskram again.

'Well, master monk, what more have you to say for yourself? As you can see we are quite at odds as to what to do with you.'

'I can only tell you that we are being pursued by a great evil,' Horskram sighed. 'Believe me, sir knights, there *are* dark forces abroad, but we are not the cause – rather we are the victims of such. If I were to tell you our tale in its entirety perhaps the hairs on your noble heads would turn as white as the Valravyn itself – but you have my sworn oath, by the Redeemer's own blood, we are no black magicians! In fact quite the reverse.'

So saying, Horskram made the sign and intoned a curt blessing on them all.

If this mollified Sir Tarlquist, it did so only a little. He continued to glare at the adept as he said: 'You offer assurances, yet still your story is shrouded in mystery! Very well, keep your secrets – for now. There is nothing apparent to suggest that you yourselves mean any harm – but I cannot in fairness allow you to continue through the King's lands unchecked until you have been examined further. You are to surrender your weapons and come with us to Staerkvit – we'll see what the High Commander has to say, although Reus knows he's sore pressed as it is! Unhappy day, that you should stray into our path now of all times!'

Sir Aronn protested. 'But, sire, with all due respect, they'll only slow us down! We have to report back to Prince Freidhoff as soon as we can!'

'I know my duty, Sir Aronn, and I haven't forgotten the urgency of war either!' Sir Tarlquist shot back testily. 'Their horses look swift enough, and we'll ride them hard, so don't you worry! Since you're so concerned for our speed, you can tether our learned friar's mount to your own horse and make sure he keeps up.'

Turning, he addressed two more knights. These were identical twins, save for their hair – one had jet-black locks where the other's were snowy white.

'Doric! Cirod!' he barked. 'Tether the other two to your own mounts. Make sure you take all their weapons too – and that includes the monks' quarterstaves. I've heard they can crack a man's skull like an egg with those iron-bound beauties if they're so minded.'

Horskram bowed his head in obeisance. 'Have no fear, sir knight, you will find no resistance from us – all we craved was an armed escort as far as the road to Staerkvit, although we hadn't intended being taken to the castle itself as captives. But if such is your will we cannot in all rightness refuse the King's Law. Might I at least know the full name of my captor?'

'Take caution, sire,' interjected Sir Wolmar, 'I've heard tell an enchanter needs only learn the name of a man to have him in his thrall forever!'

'And I've heard tell far too much from you for one day!' Sir Tarlquist growled back. 'Now be silent and leave me to make the decisions!'

That exchange seemed to make up his mind. 'I am Sir Tarlquist of Gottenheim, Commander in the Order of the Knights of the White Valravyn,' he said. 'And between here and Staerkvit, I'll be giving you the orders – I hope that's understood.'

'Most eminently,' replied Horskram courteously as he surrendered his quarterstaff, before turning to give Vaskrian a look that Adelko thought almost as terrifying as Tintagael. The squire was too busy staring at Sir Torgun to notice.

✣ ✣ ✣

True to Tarlquist's word, they rode swiftly, and around mid-afternoon the land began to rise steadily again. Vaskrian had seen enough of maps to know they were approaching the Strang Ranges, a girdle of wooded ridges that surrounded the coastal arable lands that fed Strongholm. Their steeds had little trouble keeping up with the knights' Farovian destriers. Vaskrian had to marvel at this, for the dappled grey steeds were the mightiest of great horses, famed far beyond their island home for their speed and endurance.

There was little hope of conversation above the thundering of hooves, but from the knights' bloodstained apparel and grim faces it was obvious they had been in a battle. Vaskrian knew enough of war to read their grim expressions and guess that the outcome hadn't been a good one.

They soon reached a junction. The king's highway continued to plough on steadily through the ranges; another path, narrower and meandering, struck due north. The knights took the latter road, riding two at time. Soon it began to climb steadily as they pushed on into the highest part of the ranges.

They had left the lush meadows and fertile farmlands far behind them; the trees and bushes that now teemed to either side of them were a riot of unkempt nature. Birds flew from crooked trees in alarm at the boisterous sound of the approaching knights, who rode on regardless, their unshorn locks and chequered cloaks streaming behind them. All the while the road zigzagged upwards, heading steadily north.

It was drawing towards early evening when Vaskrian caught his first glimpse of the white walls of Staerkvit. The trees had thickened;

the first flash of sunlight on silvery stones was quickly replaced by a flurry of green as they rode through another copse. As they emerged from it the ranges began levelling off and he could see it clearly.

Perched imposingly beside a sparkling lake nestled between tree-lined ridges, the castle was every bit as impressive as he had heard. His heart leapt – he'd often dreamed of visiting the lofty headquarters of the Order of the White Valravyn, though he had never imagined he would do so as a captive.

Its square curtain wall stretched high up into the firmament, enclosing a single keep that stood at least thirty men high. A square turret stood at each corner of the outer wall, whilst its mighty gatehouse was topped with crenelated machicolations that loomed menacingly over the only entrance. The castle's founders had chosen their spot well, for the promontory of rock on which it rested meant that it was surrounded on three sides by the lake.

The Silverwater men called it, for the glossy sheen that coated its surface in high summer – although some said the real reason was bound up in the legend of the White Valravyn itself, some creature of fable that had given the Order its name.

Men-at-arms and archers lined the outer walls. Each of the four turrets sported a mangonel, with another two positioned on the gatehouse battlements. Atop the keep a mighty standard proclaimed the Order's coat of arms; another great cloth slung across the gatehouse bore the same device.

It wasn't the most beautiful castle Vaskrian had seen, but it was undoubtedly the tallest and strongest. Even the walls of Linden would have looked somewhat mean next to the impregnable seat of the White Valravyn.

Just before the approach to the gatehouse a fast-flowing river sluiced through the gnarled ranges, pouring its waters into the lake. A small sturdy bridge of white stone traversed this, so narrow that it could only be crossed single file. It was guarded at either end by two smaller gatehouses. Between the bridge and the castle and lake lay only a narrow strip of uneven, rocky ground – a besieging army would have its work cut out for it.

Staerkvit certainly lived up to its reputation – it enjoyed peerless defences. That meant no chance of their being rescued. Not that anyone would try anyway.

Thinking on this, Vaskrian bit his lip in a rare moment of doubt – just what had he gotten them into?

Glancing over at his blade where it was tethered to Cirod's saddle he felt a twinge – he'd hated to surrender his father's sword, especially after being so unexpectedly reunited with it...

but even he knew better than to resist the best knights in the land when they outnumbered him a dozen to one.

Besides, he didn't really want to fight them – on the contrary, he wanted to *be* one of them. Surely their commander, the King's brother no less, would hear them out when they got to the castle. They couldn't really think they were witches or enemy spies – could they?

The bridge was guarded by a squadron of footsoldiers dressed in mail and the chequered livery worn by common serjeants of the Order – only knights were permitted to wear the symbol of the Valravyn on their surcoats.

The serjeants were led by a single knight, who hailed his fellows: 'Sir Tarlquist, well met! What news from the south?'

'Grim news,' replied Tarlquist curtly. 'We are all that remains of the sortie sent to relieve Salmor. The castle is as good as lost. Now step aside, we must speak with His Royal Highness at once!'

The crestfallen knight complied at once, motioning for the oak door guarding the bridge to be opened. The sentries blew a series of sharp notes to signal their approach, and soon they were beneath the walls of Staerkvit, waiting for the drawbridge to open and the portcullis to be raised.

Vaskrian's head was awhirl with frantic thoughts. Castle Salmor all but taken: that meant Thule's forces would be able to sweep north into the King's Dominions. If everything they'd heard about the size of his army was true, it would encounter no stiff resistance before Linden.

The words of Arro the wool merchant came back to him: *Once they take Rookhammer and Salmor there'll be no stopping them...*

Salmor was more than a hundred miles away, so even riding at full tilt their captors must have spent at least two days on the road – from what he'd heard, Rookhammer was a good deal smaller than Linden and Salmor, and wouldn't resist an army for long.

The thought made him angry – what were they doing, stuck up here in the ranges? They should all be riding south, to show the rebels who was really in charge! He'd love to be down there right now, cutting southrons to pieces and covering his name in glory... well, future glory at any rate.

His thoughts were interrupted by the screeching of the portcullis grinding to a halt. Riding over the drawbridge and under the massive gateway the knights and their captives emerged into a great courtyard.

Though it was a hive of activity, there were none of the usual signs of civilian castle life: no artisans or traders with their stalls, no troubadours tuning their lutes or practising for a feast performance. The castle had a thoroughly military air about it: dozens of knights practised their swordsmanship and tilted at targets, their martial sounds mingling cacophonously with that of the overworked blacksmiths, armourers and bladesmiths as they all prepared for the coming war. Drovers and draymen were busy preparing food supplies for the impending march, loading horses and carts with kegs of ale and wine and barrels of cured meats and hard cheeses.

All in all, Vaskrian liked what he saw.

Noticing the new arrivals after they had reined in their horses and waited patiently for several minutes, a bald bull-necked knight of about fifty winters strode over to greet Tarlquist.

'What news?' he inquired bluntly. His face darkened as the Commander told him.

'Those are ill tidings – the High Commander will want to know directly,' he replied. 'And who are these?'

'Prisoners,' replied Tarlquist. 'The friar is from Ulfang – says he and his novice have been fleeing some great evil, but he won't say what. And this young tough says he's a squire – claims he lost his knightly master in Tintagael Forest, of all places, and that he's sworn to accompany the Argolians as far as the capital.'

'*Protect*,' corrected Vaskrian. 'I've sworn to protect them, not accompany them.' His impromptu visit to the Valravyn's legendary headquarters was doing a good job of raising his spirits, captive or no. He went to lay a hand on the pommel of his sword for emphasis, before remembering he didn't have it.

Tarlquist narrowed his eyes at the squire and shook his head. Horskram gave him a look to curdle manna from heaven. The old monk took everything far too seriously – he certainly wasn't much fun. Or very grateful, come to think of it.

Tarlquist continued: 'The older friar wants an audience with the Arch Perfect in Strongholm – some supernatural business he won't explain.'

The bald knight fixed the trio with an inscrutable stare. He wasn't pleased to see them – Vaskrian could tell that much at least.

'I see,' he said. 'And what are your names, pray tell?'

'I am Horskram of Vilno, adept of the Argolian Order at Ulfang monastery,' replied the adept. 'My companions are Adelko of Narvik and Vaskrian of Hroghar. Our Order has ever been a friend to yours, in times of peace and war alike, but I regret I cannot divulge the nature of our business save to say that it is grievous perilous.'

'Really?' replied the knight, glaring now. 'I am Sir Toric of Runstadt, Deputy High Commander of the Order – will you divulge details now?'

Horskram shook his head regretfully. 'With all due respect, my lord, secrecy is of paramount importance, the fewer that know of our mission, the safer – '

'They are in league with dark forces, as I've been saying all along!' interrupted Sir Wolmar. 'How else could any man venture beneath the eaves of accursed Tintagael and live to tell the tale?'

Vaskrian shot the knight a black glance – he had been wondering when he'd stick his lance in where it wasn't wanted again.

Fortunately the Deputy High Commander didn't seem much more impressed by Sir Wolmar, judging by the look he gave him. But he spoke courteously enough as he replied: 'Doubtless their tale is a strange one, Sir Wolmar, yet still it remains to be seen whether they're in league with dark forces... or if their frightful tale even be true.'

Turning back to face Horskram the deputy marshal of Staerkvit squinted at him, his ugly face pinching up in a manner that didn't bode well.

'Secrecy ill becomes a friend to our Order,' he said. 'If you will have it so then I must refer the matter to the High Commander. Prince Freidhoff will decide what to do with you – but I should warn you that he is a busy man these days, as no doubt you will have fathomed.'

Turning, he barked an order at a group of soldiers dressed in chequered tabards: 'Take these three to the dungeons, upper level – they're to be well treated and fed properly. Stabling shall be found for their horses – such fine-looking mounts should not go wanting either. Tarlquist – you, Torgun, Aronn and Wolmar come with me. The High Commander will want to hear your news right away, bad as it is. The rest of you are free to seek victuals and rest – see that any wounds among you are treated as well, I'll have no chivalrous heroics of fortitude in times of war. Dismissed.'

The three of them were marched across the courtyard in the fading light towards the huge keep, through an iron postern gate and down a winding flight of stairs into a dank torchlit chamber. At a table in one corner sat three more guards in chequered livery. They looked every bit as upright as the soldiers escorting them and a far cry from the slovenly gaolers at Hroghar, which Vaskrian supposed was something to be thankful for.

The serjeant in charge of their escort approached the gaolers and muttered: 'Three prisoners. Upper floor, full victualling. No chastisement. Well,' he added, favouring the three captives with a cold-eyed stare, 'not yet, at any rate. They're to stay here until the High Commander calls for them.'

The escort stayed only long enough to see the captives safely manacled, before leaving them to be escorted to the cells.

These were located in a long corridor just off the gaolers' room. Many were occupied. From what Vaskrian knew of the Order these would be lesser criminals awaiting trial or serving out their sentences. Most of them looked seedy enough. Some leered at them as they walked past; one or two even called out, mocking the friars' habits. But most barely even acknowledged them. The lower dungeons would be where the more serious criminals were kept, though not for very long – the King's justice was known for its impartiality, but heinous crimes were usually punished as harshly in the Dominions as they were anywhere else.

Horskram's face was grave and unyielding in the flickering torchlight as they trudged down the corridor. He had not said a word to either of them since they had been taken by the ravens, and Vaskrian wasn't keen to risk the testy old monk's wrath. Adelko looked nervous and afraid – but then he had not seen fifteen summers, and he was a monk to boot.

Vaskrian felt more frustrated than anything else – why should they be held prisoner just because they'd fallen victim to some nameless power of darkness?

Thinking on this as the gaoler ushered them into a cell with nothing in it but straw, a long wooden bench and a chamber pot, he felt a sudden shiver run down his spine. Something told him that power wasn't done with them by a long stretch.

Settling down on to the bench with his fellow captives, Vaskrian pushed the thought away and resigned himself to waiting for the King's justice.

⊰ CHAPTER X ⊱

A Marriage Contested

H ettie sat very still, trying to absorb everything she had just heard. Her mistress was standing by the south window, stock still but for a hand that fingered her strawberry tresses idly, gazing across the fields and orchards of the land she had sworn to leave forever.

Presently her oldest friend turned to look at her with a wan smile.

'Well, dearest Hettie, what say you?' she asked gently. 'I make the declaration of my life, and you repay it with silence.'

The voice was sad yet playful, but also expectant – Hettie knew her mistress wanted her to say something.

That was fair enough, but what did you say to a revelation such as this? Come to think of it, Hettie knew exactly what one should say.

'My lady, it's... madness.'

It was the closest she could get to summing up her thoughts on the spot. In fact, perhaps that said it all.

Adhelina smiled sardonically, seeming unperturbed by her lady-in-waiting's frank answer.

'I'd thought you'd say as much,' she returned, walking slowly from the window to sit opposite Hettie at an old walnut table. On it rested two earthenware cups of the herbal tea her mistress was fond of preparing – the heiress of Dulsinor preferred not to drink wine during the day, although truth to tell Hettie could have done with a stiff drink right then and there.

The table itself was a lovely old antique – the two women had shared many a silly adventure over it as girls, playing at dice and pretending to be idling soldiers, experimenting with some of Adhelina's less orthodox concoctions, strange poultices that had made them giddy and light-headed and had them in fits of laughter for hours.

But they had never shared anything potentially as explosive as this over it. Taking a deep breath, Hettie prepared to remonstrate as best she could as Adhelina poured them a refill from the earthenware pot resting by the two wooden cups and an old map of the country next to it. Her mistress disliked drinking her tea from silver chalices – said it interfered with the flavour.

'It's madness, Adhelina,' she repeated, doing her best to sound calm and making a point of using her mistress' given name. 'Even if you get to Meerborg, what will you do then?'

Adhelina sighed exasperatedly. 'I told you already – I'll take a ship. Meerborg is the greatest of the Vorstlending ports, it services many destinations. From there I'll be able to get to the Empire.'

'The Empire!' Hettie's heart skipped a beat. 'What ever will you do there? Full of strange people, that place – the perfects say they're in league with the Archfiend himself, what with all their clever contraptions and such... it isn't natural. And anyway, they're heretics – they don't worship the Redeemer in the way that good Palomedians ought to.'

Hettie made the sign of the Wheel. She wasn't usually that pious, but right now these commonplace objections to Imperials seemed as sensible a way as any of getting her beloved mistress to reconsider her sheer folly.

'Yes, well, that is indeed what our goodly Father Tobias says,' Adhelina replied wryly, her mouth curling with distaste. Her dislike of the sanctimonious perfect was well known, to Hettie at least. 'But I've read different things about them – they're, well, a bit more civilised than we are. They have more respect for women too. Oh Hettie, don't you see, with all the jewels and plate father has lavished on me since I came of age, I've enough to live modestly but well, at least for the foreseeable future!

'In the Empire 'tis said a woman can live independently, so long as she has the means to do so, with no questions asked. I could take up residence in one of their great cities – perhaps even Ilyrium itself! I could study the great philosophers and poets... who knows, perhaps even become a true sage!'

Hettie frowned as she tried to think of another way to put her high-spirited mistress off the foolish idea. Then she had it.

'But they've no knights,' she opined cautiously. 'The Code of Chivalry doesn't exist over there – they have a, oh what do you call it, a standing army, of professionals. Legions they call them – I remember my father used to say they don't fight for honour, or a liege lord, they just fight for pay, like any common mercenary, only they call it serving their Mother Empire, or something ridiculous like that! Why, my lady, imagine that, serving something so big and, well... remote as that – with your life! You're a Vorstlending, and we don't hold with grand empires – why, we couldn't even abide a king! Everything I hear tells me they're queer folk out east – you've no business taking up with their sort.'

Her mistress pursed her lips, deep in thought. Hettie's heart began to lift – was she getting through to her?

Adhelina took another sip of tea and said: 'Well, perhaps you may be right, Hettie, though to tell the truth at times I'm not sure the Code of Chivalry exists over here anymore... oftentimes I wonder if our household knights are any better than mercenaries themselves.'

Hettie's eyes widened. She was genuinely shocked. 'My lady! How can you say such a thing! And my poor father...'

Adhelina's face softened. 'Oh Hettie, I don't mean all of them! And certainly not your father – why Sir Gunther was as humble and loyal a bachelor as any lord could ask for! If only all my father's knights had his virtues! But alas, they do not – most of them fight for little more than land, glory or spoil. I sometimes wonder if the courtly knights of King Vasirius ever existed... perhaps I should go to Pangonia and find out.'

'Yes, why don't you?' Hettie couldn't resist putting in. 'At least that would be better than going to the Empire!'

Adhelina shook her head decisively. 'No, it wouldn't do, Hettie – to make good my escape I shall need to put out to sea as soon as possible. The longer I journey on land the more chance I have of being caught. And it's precisely because the Imperials are deemed so queer, as you put it, that going to the Empire makes the most sense! The Great White Mountains separate them from us – the only contact the Free Kingdoms have with them is through trade, via the northern ports. They guard their borders jealously, and are strong enough to resist any summons from a western lord – anywhere else in the Free Kingdoms and there's always the risk that someone might find out who I am and have me sent back, for a fee or a favour.'

Hettie remained unmoved. 'Yes, well I've also heard that the Imperials guard their secrets as jealously as their borders. How do you know you won't be arrested as a spy?'

'I don't,' admitted Adhelina. 'But I have to try. Oh Hettie, it wouldn't be forever, don't you see? I've enough jewels and finery in this chamber to live modestly for years if I spend wisely – if I stay away long enough, my father will give me up for dead and entail Graukolos and all its desmesnes to someone else, a more worthy heir than I. Why, Hettie, Dulsinor will always endure – and I was never meant to bear its burdens!'

Faced with her mistress's flashing eyes and the determined set of her handsome face, Hettie felt her resolve begin to crumble. She had known her dear friend too long not to tell when her adamantine will was set on something. But she had to keep trying.

'You are cruel to inflict this pain on your sire – he's suffered enough in his life as it is,' she said, partly meaning it. For all his temper and rumbustious habits, the Eorl of Dulsinor was at heart a good man, she felt. He could be fierce and deadly towards his enemies, ruthless even, but for more than thirty years he had ruled his lands with an even hand – and he loved his only child with a deep and abiding passion.

Her mistress stared at her reproachfully, and for a moment Hettie feared she had overstepped the mark. But then she said: 'You are right, Hettie – it is cruel, what I plan on doing to father. But then what he plans to do to me is crueller still! I have my whole life in front of me, he has had much of his, aye and triumphed throughout for the most part! I wouldn't hurt him to preserve my freedom for all the world if it could be avoided – but Reus knows I have tried and tried, and he will not have things otherwise! He has left me with no choice.'

'But, you don't even speak the language!' Hettie wailed. She was reaching the end of her stride, like a panting courser with no energy left to run. She felt her spirited assault on her mistress' madcap plan faltering.

'Oh but I do, Hettie,' replied Adhelina, turning back to face her with a sly twinkle in her eyes. 'I've always been good at learning languages, you know that. Why, I taught you to read - '

'Oh, I recall. What a fun summer that was,' interjected Hettie, rolling her eyes. Even now she found time for their old humour.

'You'll thank me for it one day,' retorted Adhelina with the air of an old sage. 'And anyway, as I was saying – I also learned to speak Imperial tolerably well, it's not that different from our tongue as you might think actually, in fact it's related to - '

'My lady, please, spare me the discourse on philology,' sighed Hettie exasperatedly. 'Learning to read was quite enough, I pray you!'

'Clearly it has done you no harm, if you know what "philology" means,' retorted Adhelina again. She was smiling now.

Meeting her eyes Hettie felt sure that she could never be parted from her dearest friend. And by the looks of things her dearest friend could not be dissuaded. And that meant...

'Oh my lady, you do not fully realise, I think, what it is you ask of me!'

Adhelina's smile turned into a beam. 'Then you'll do it? You'll help me to escape!?' She lowered her voice instinctively as she said the last word. That didn't stop Hettie from feeling terrified at the prospect of what they were contemplating.

But she spoke the abject truth when she said: 'Oh my lady, dearest Adhelina, of course I will! For don't you know that I had rather go to the gallows than be parted from you? My father served yours loyally with his life, and I'll do the same for you – you know that full well! And that means if I can't talk you out of this reckless nonsense – well, I suppose I'm coming with you!'

'Oh Hettie, I knew you would! I knew you would!' exclaimed Adhelina, reaching over the table impulsively to hug her and nearly knocking over the cups and teapot.

For the next few minutes her mistress was all of a babble – the excitable and strong-willed girl of their childhood – as she pulled the map across the table to explain her plan in detail.

'Meerborg lies about a hundred miles north and east of here, as the raven flies,' she said, pointing to a stylised image of what Hettie supposed was meant to be a cityport nestling against a sea of blue on the old hide map. 'If we ride swiftly we should be able to get there in three days, although we may have to detour if getting off the main road gives us a better chance of shaking off my father's knights when he sends them after us.'

Adhelina paused and bit her lip thoughtfully. 'I'm not sure yet which of those will prove the best course – I'll have to think on it.'

Hettie's mind – when it was not reeling at the thought of her liege lord's best warriors tearing frantically up the highway in search of them both – was on more immediate concerns.

'Yes, that's all well and good for when we're out of the castle,' she said. 'But how do we get *out* of it? You mentioned something about a secret tunnel just before you started on the map...' Her mistress was difficult to keep up with when she was in one of her wood moods.

The smile returned to Adhelina's full lips. 'Yes! Old Berthal told me all about it when he taught me the castle's secrets! The loremasters say that when Goriath built the castle, he realised that he'd made it so impregnable it might one day prove the undoing of the very masters it was meant to protect. After all, castles under siege have been known to be starved into submission, without a single wall being taken by force. So he designed a safeguard...'

'Which was?'

Adhelina reached for a second map. This one was made of parchment, and depicted the castle grounds from an aerial view. It seemed odd to Hettie – why would anyone want to draw a building from a bird's eye perspective? She had heard tell of ancient maps, drawn by the sorcerer kings who had once ruled the Known World, as they gazed down on it from their flying carpets... she shuddered. She didn't like the map, and told her mistress so.

Adhelina only laughed. 'No! Dear, superstitious, and frankly rather silly Hettie – it isn't a wizard's map!' she chided. 'It's an engineer's plan – this one is actually an old copy of the original made by Goriath when he built this place. I found it in father's library – you know he never uses it much, I hardly think he can even read. Anyway, engineers use these when they want to design the castles and manors they are going to build, so they can work out how to build them... do you understand?'

Hettie stared at her mistress blankly. She did have some peculiar interests.

Adhelina shook her head. 'Never mind,' she said. 'Just look here – do you see the part that says Inner Ward?'

Hettie nodded. That much she could understand at least, thanks to her mistress's girlish attempts to play the old loremaster when they were younger.

'Well,' Adhelina continued. 'Have a look here, do you see where it says Lord's Quarters?'

Peering closer, Hettie nodded again. She was beginning to get the hang of this – her mistress was pointing to what must be the south wing of the Inner Ward, right next to the turret where they lived.

'So, inside on the ground floor as you walk in, there's the staircase leading up to father's private chambers,' Adhelina explained. 'As you know he doesn't use them much nowadays, he just has his own bedchamber at the top of the west wing, next to his solar. Anyway, you remember how under the staircase there's a rude sort of fresco, statues of the old kings of Dulsinor, the really old ones, from back when the Griffenwyrd was called Dulsenar and it was a petty kingdom in its own right?'

Hettie had to think a moment. But she remembered well enough – her duties rarely took her to that part of the castle, but the statues were distinctive. Old and brooding they'd always seemed to her, graven milestones marking the passing of a fallen age.

'Yes,' she ventured. 'There were four of them, weren't there?'

'That's right! One for each of the petty kings who reigned before and during the time the castle was built – Ludvic the Founder, Alaric the Reckless, Ulmo the Besieged and lastly good old Ludvic the Builder himself! Well, Berthal told me that one of them is actually a secret doorway – '

Hettie couldn't resist interrupting. 'Oh let me guess – King Ludvic the Builder himself!'

'No!' said Adhelina, shaking her head, her eyes sparkling. 'That's the clever part! It's neither of the Ludvics – the ones you'd most expect it to be. It's old Ulmo!'

'That doesn't make much sense!'

'No, it does when you really think about it,' countered Adhelina. 'The secret tunnel was only meant to be used as a last resort, when all was lost, allowing a lord, his family and closest retainers to flee the castle under siege... Well what better scion to guard that escape route than Ulmo the Besieged? The sages say he resisted his foes for more than a generation before they packed up their armies in despair and went home. He ruled Dulsenar in peace for the rest of his days after that.'

Hettie nodded again, hoping her mistress wasn't about to launch into another impromptu history lesson. 'I see, yes – that does rather make sense, I suppose. So... how does this secret door open?'

'There's a catch hidden on the statue – or rather it's part of the statue itself. Very few know about it, but Berthal told me because he said as the future mistress of Graukolos it was important that I know the escape route. The secret door opens onto a flight of stairs that wind down, deep below the castle into the very bowels of the hill on which it stands.'

Hettie nearly shuddered. Her mistress' dramatic figure of speech wasn't welcome. She did not like the idea of going deep underground – the ill rumours circulating the castle about the theft of some ancient artefact kept below the Werecrypt had heightened her natural fear of strange places. Strange, dark places all the more so.

'Don't worry!' exclaimed Adhelina, seeing the troubled look on her face, before lowering her voice again. 'Goriath knew a great many things – some say he was the greatest engineer the Free Kingdoms have ever known. If he built an escape tunnel, it'll be safe to use. We'll need to bring tapers to light our way, that's all.'

Hettie frowned disparagingly. She too had heard that the Stonecrafty knew a great many things – including blasphemous pagan sorcery. And there seemed to be enough rumours of that emanating from the Werecrypt as it was.

Heedless, her mistress continued. 'The tunnel exits around here,' she said, pointing to the southern edge of the great hill on which the castle rested as it was marked on the map. 'From there we should be able to get away in the dead of night without anyone seeing us.'

Hettie nodded slowly. Her mistress seemed to have thought everything through. But then one other crucial thing occurred to her.

'What about horses?' she asked flatly. 'I'm supposing we can't get those down the tunnel, even if we could get them from the stables without anyone asking questions. And we certainly aren't going to get very far on foot.'

Her mistress looked up again from the map. Her eyes were gleaming again. A look of devilish cunning crossed her face as she replied: 'Well, my dearest Hettie, that is precisely where you come in...'

⁜ ⁜ ⁜

Sir Urist's face was tight and drawn as the herald announced the latest arrivals to the castle. He knew already by their names and provenance that they would not come bearing glad tidings.

But then what tidings had been good of late?

He had stood, stony-faced, as his rival Sir Balthor had delivered his report to the Eorl in his solar three nights ago. The shadows had lengthened, making the menagerie of animal heads look like dread beasts as they loomed over them from the cold grey walls in the torchlight.

Balthor and his men had searched everywhere they could within five leagues, asking tradesmen at Merkstaed, monks at Lothag, and peasants and vassals alike in the scores of villages and manors that dotted the lands about the castle.

All to no avail. The only thing out of the ordinary had been a few reports of an indefinable *presence*, some strange shadowing of the soul claimed by those living near the Glimmerholt.

That would have been nothing so unusual in the peasant folk – fearful villagers tended to shun the woods, which they claimed were the preserve of nature spirits and other devils of the earth and soil.

But even one or two knights living in the area had mentioned a similar thing – and the Eorl's noble-born vassals were usually quick to dismiss any superstition that got in the way of their hunting privileges.

Of the fragment itself, not a whisper. No one had seen any signs of earthly thieves making off with what might have been a clandestine booty. But then what earthly thief could have pulled off such a theft, Urist wondered?

Sir Balthor and his men had overtaken and searched several groups of wayfarers during their three-day search: a few parties of merchants and one band of wandering freeswords who had almost made trouble, then thought better of it when they realised they were dealing with the greatest knight in Dulsinor (that was Balthor's version at any rate – did the man never pass up an opportunity to sing his own praises?). But busy (and valiant) though they might have been, the Eorl's trusty knights had returned empty-handed and none the wiser.

After that there had been nothing left to do but despatch a messenger to Strongholm to warn the King of the Northlendings that some unknown entity had apparently taken a determined and highly illicit interest in dangerous ancient artefacts.

Urist knew it was the only thing Wilhelm could do to make amends for his laxness. A sister fragment was kept somewhere in the far reaches of Northalde, under the watchful eyes of the Argolian monks. There were said to be one or two others that formed part of the same set, but no man in the Griffenwyrd knew where in the Known World they might be, assuming they even existed. And if even the learned Father Tobias could not say, who else would know?

What Urist and Tobias did know was the old legend that said the stones would wreak ruin on the world if reunited. Wilhelm knew it too, and that didn't sit well with a lord whose age-old duty had been to help prevent the calamity from ever happening by guarding the fragment in his trust.

Lesser scions might have dismissed it as a mere fairy tale of yore, hardly worth fussing about. But Wilhelm – and Urist near loved him for it – was a good Eorl who took all his responsibilities seriously. If his ancestors had sought fit to believe the old stories and act accordingly, he would not be one to disagree.

And yet Wilhelm had been unable to maintain the guard on the Werecrypt – and now the thing was gone, on his watch. Damned superstitious soldiers – but could one really blame them? Superstitions weren't always ill-founded, after all... It had long been whispered that Hardred the Melancholy, the Second Eorl of Dulsinor, and his successor Weregrim the Mad had both incurred torment for daring to venture into the forbidden chamber that lay beneath the Werecrypt, both victims of their own curiosity. Weregrim had abdicated a hundred and fifty years ago and gone tearing off raving mad into the wilderness, foreswearing the realms of men. He'd died some years later in a priory, it was told, ranting on his deathbed of dark kingdoms to come. Since then the Eorls of Dulsinor had learned to be less curious.

Recalling his liege lord's troubled mien after he had sent the messenger on his way, Urist suppressed an anxious sigh. They could only pray that the Argolians and other guardians, wherever they were, had proved more vigilant...

They might not find out any time soon. A day ago word had reached them of a fresh civil war in Northalde – the old southron pretender's heir was up in arms, prosecuting the same grievous cause as his father Kanga had during the War of the Southern Secession.

That was what came of trying to keep a kingdom together, Urist reflected. More trouble than it was worth – far better to call a spade a spade, as the Vorstlendings had done for two centuries now. A shaky coalition of rivalrous baronies, that was all a kingdom was at heart.

The war in Northalde meant there was less chance of Wilhelm's messenger being listened to, assuming he even got to Strongholm now. Word had also come from Meerborg that her erstwhile trading partner Urring was hosting a war fleet – what with all the galleys being mustered to the rebel cause, there would be nary a berthing space for an honest merchantman.

In light of all that, perhaps more pressing – and earthly – problems were welcome, thought the Marshal ruefully as Sir Malthus

of Gorr, knight of Upper Thulia, and Sir Ugo of Veidt, knight of
Ostveld, strode purposefully into the Great Hall.

Four winters had passed since the two neighbouring
Griffenwyrds had made their last bloody foray into Dulsinor, burning
and slaying where they could until checked by the Stonefist's forces.

On that occasion he had punished his enemies harshly, making them
pay dearly for their warlike presumption. The Eorl of Ostveld he had
beheaded with his great war-axe as he knelt bleeding in the dust on the
banks of the Graufluss; the Eorl of Upper Thulia had suffered the ignominy
of seeing half his best knights slain, including his two sons, before Balthor's
lance had driven him from his charger and sent him hurtling to the ground.
The fall had left him crippled, and now he had to be carried in a palanquin
wherever he went, just like the effete electors of the Empire were said to
do. A sore blow for any haughty liege to bear.

Perhaps not being a kingdom made little difference after all:
barons always found a reason to go to war. But then that was good
for the knights who served them – internecine warfare had made
Urist the man he was today.

The Lanraks had ridden to their aid on that occasion too, and Sir Urist
felt it was little coincidence that clandestine talk of uniting both houses
had begun in earnest shortly after. Storne's crafty steward Albercelcus was
always one to smell an opportunity – and he always made sure that any
aid from the House of Lanrak came with a hefty price attached.

But in this case, Urist felt, the burden of cost would fall on their
neighbours in Ostveld and Upper Thulia.

Hence this visit.

Both men, stalwart vassals known to Urist and many of the
knights gathered about the hall, kneeled before the Eorl's high chair
before he bade them rise and speak their minds.

As one they informed him of the purpose of their visit. Their
liege lords had learned of the Stonefist's plans to marry his daughter
to the Herzog of Stornelund, and would have it known by all and
sundry that they both opposed the match on the loftiest grounds.

'Oh really?' boomed the lord of Dulsinor, so all about the hall
could hear him. 'And what lofty grounds might those be?' His voice
was as contemptuous as it was loud. Urist's hopes for a diplomatic
audience began to diminish rapidly.

This question was answered by Sir Malthus, a short, rotund
knight with a toad-like face made all the more ridiculous by his
finely trimmed black beard and mustachios. He was not pretty, but
no one doubted the strength of his thews.

'You know full well what authority we speak of,' he spluttered indignantly. 'This proposed union breaks with the Treaty of Lorvost, agreed more than two hundred years ago. No single lord must be allowed to gain more strength than the others, so as to preserve the balance of power in Vorstlund and ensure it never falls under the tyranny of monarchy again!'

'That's the right of it,' pitched in Sir Ugo, slightly taller than his ally but somewhat less brawny. He was no less ugly; an unkempt mop of sandy brown hair did little to conceal a battle scar that disfigured his already lumpen features. 'Nine lords to rule over the realm in peace, so it was agreed ten generations ago! Six earls, two dukes, and one prince! It didn't say anything about a grand duke!'

Wilhelm let a great laugh off the leash. Sir Ugo's wording of the matter was somewhat ridiculous in its pedanticism – although that did not detract from the seriousness of his point. Around the hall several of the Stonefist's bachelors and one or two vassals joined him in laughing; Sir Balthor and his warlike cronies sneered and exchanged knowing glances.

From where he stood at his lord's right hand, Sir Urist kept a straight face; on the other side of Wilhelm the steward Berthal did likewise. A sensible man.

'Aye,' returned the Stonefist when he had finished with his mirth. 'And the Treaty doesn't say anything about raiding and pillaging your neighbouring lords either – in fact you used the very words I'm looking for just now, Sir Ugo – "to rule the realm in peace" you said!'

Raising his huge hand he stabbed a stout finger in the emissary's direction. Ugo flinched slightly as though he were being menaced with a spear as the lord of Graukolos raised his voice another notch: 'Peace! Fie, I've barely known a minute of it with your thrice-cursed liege lords! I would have thought the younger Eorl of Ostveld would have learned some sense after I put his father in an early grave, and as for you Malthus, I would have thought your master of hounds would have learned his place too, after Balthor here made a cripple of him!

'But no! Here we are, back they come for more! The Ürls and the Kaarls, they never know when they're beaten – and still less when they're in the wrong! Thrice in my reign alone they've tried to take this castle and all its lands, and thrice they've failed! Do you think the Almighty might be trying to tell your lords something? He doesn't support their cause – and with good reason!'

Both knights' faces reddened. Urist tensed inwardly. The Eorl's words may have been spoken in anger, but they were also designed to provoke. He knew his liege all too well – as much as he claimed Ezekiel's justice of defensive war he never shied away from provoking attackers either. It was simply in the great man's nature: if he had one flaw it was his pride.

Containing his anger with some effort, Sir Malthus spoke again. 'The Treaty clearly states that what you and the Herzog of Storne are planning is in violation of the terms agreed by all the Vorstlending barons - '

'A pox on your damned treaty!' cried the Eorl, rising from his seat. Standing on his dais he loomed over the assembled notables with a dread presence; it was as if the Almighty had suddenly caused a smouldering volcano to be raised up inside the Great Hall, vast and fiery and fit to explode at any moment.

'A pox on it, I say again!' he thundered. 'It hasn't been worth the ink it was written in for a hundred years – I'm sick of hearing about that worn old scrap of parchment! Now you leave my hall, you take your horses, you ride back to your kennel masters, and you tell them this: the Grand Herewyrd of Stornelund-Dulsinor is a reality, it's going to happen, treaty be damned! Your arch drinkers of lickspittle perjured their chances to abide by its terms years ago – if I wasn't having to defend my borders every other year from their murderous and illegal sorties we might have kept covenant with the wretched thing! As it is they've left us no choice – you can solicit Storne for his opinion if you like, but rest assured you'll find him of the same mind!'

Sir Malthus' black eyes narrowed to gimlets. 'Oh, our lieges already have messengers warning the Lanraks just the same as you, rest assured, my lord. So the Herewyrd of Stornelund won't be our next port of call. Seeing as you are hell-bent on persisting in this course of action, we'll have no choice but to send word to the rest of the High Lords of Vorstlund!'

'Indeed, my lord, it will be interesting to see what the Herzog of Lower Thulia and the Prince of Westenlund make of your intended alliance,' put in Sir Ugo venomously.

That gambit came as little surprise. Westenlund was the most powerful barony in the realm, Lower Thulia a close second along with Stornelund. Of all the High Lords, they stood to lose most from the Grand Herewyrd's creation.

Perhaps, inflamed by the memory of his age-old feud with his two unruly neighbours, the Stonefist had forgotten his potentially more dangerous rivals. Dulsinor had not been to war with Lower Thulia for two generations, and never with Westenlund. The latter was mostly a result of simple geography: the Principality comprised the westernmost lands of the former kingdom of the Vorstlendings, and had little reason to come into conflict with north-easterly Dulsinor.

But the coming alliance of families could potentially constitute just such a reason: Sir Urist knew his liege lord had to tread very carefully.

So did most of the knights assembled in the Great Hall. There was a palpable tension in the silence that followed Sir Ugo's declaration, dangerously coated as it was with false courtesy.

With a deep breath the Eorl of Dulsinor sat slowly back down on his high oak chair.

'Yes, it will indeed be interesting to see what the Alt-Ürls and the Drülers have to say about it,' he replied in a voice that was noticeably quieter and calmer. 'And you can rest assured that the Herzog of Stornelund and I will come to a satisfactory arrangement with them. Now if that is the only matter you have come here to discuss, I think it is time you both took leave of my castle.'

Sir Ugo seemed resigned to the outcome and was about to turn and go. But Sir Malthus wasn't quite done yet.

'So be it,' he said. 'But you may also rest assured, my lord, that the Eorl of Upper Thulia will stop at nothing to see this alliance prevented.'

Lord Wilhelm's face darkened again, his mood turning ugly once more with the swiftness of a summer storm. 'Get out of my castle, now, both of you – get out before I have you thrown out, in little pieces.'

Anxious not to provoke him into making good on his threat, both knights turned to leave. As they did the Eorl's bachelors and vassals fell into excited conversation. It was perfectly understandable: there had been war brewing in the angry words they had just heard, and war always made knights excitable. Above the chattering Balthor could be heard calling loudly for ale.

'A well-played hand, my liege,' said Berthal in a soft voice, 'by no means meek but not too angry either.'

Urist nodded his assent, adding: 'We should send messengers to Storne and confer. It is high time we discussed our strategy for approaching the lords Alt-Ürl and Drüler.'

But the Eorl of Dulsinor seemed preoccupied with something else.

'Nothing,' he said in a rumbling voice, as if to no one in particular. 'The little rug rat said his liege would stop at *nothing* to prevent my daughter's wedding. Aye, and I believe that vindictive cripple would, too...'

With a wave of his huge hand the Eorl ordered both men to leave him. He had some thinking to do, alone.

⇌ CHAPTER XI ⇌

A Shadow On High Walls

'The White Valravyn are a chivalrous bunch – they're bound to see sense and let us go eventually! You'll see!'

Adelko groaned inwardly as he watched his mentor fix Vaskrian with a cold stare. By now he was beginning to share Horskram's impatience with the hot-headed squire – were it not for his recklessness they might well be at Strongholm by now, not languishing in a castle dungeon.

They had been there for two days. At least the food brought to them by their gaolers was passable fare, much to Adelko's relief: in fact it was somewhat better than he might have expected during many a long hard winter in Narvik.

Horskram had said little, but sat brooding sullenly on his corner of the bench. As Vaskrian launched into yet another eulogy of the White Valravyn and how amazing it had been to meet his hero Sir Torgun the old monk's stare froze over.

This time Adelko could not stop the exasperated sigh from escaping his lips. Was there no end to the squire's prating about chivalry? Still, he was a friend, of sorts. That meant he ought to come to his rescue, before the fool got his head chewed off by Horskram.

'Master Horskram, tell us more about the White Valravyn,' he said, deliberately interrupting Vaskrian for his own good. 'After all, we've… time on our hands. I'd like to know something of our captors' history.'

Horskram turned to favour his novice with a frown. For a moment Adelko thought he was about to get rebuked himself, but the adept slowly nodded his head.

'Seeing as we are in the power of these men,' he replied, shooting a piercing glance at Vaskrian, 'it is not unreasonable to want to know more about what moves them, although the founding of their Order is wreathed in legend.'

'Yes, tell us, Horskram,' said Vaskrian, warming to the idea. 'I've heard bits of it, but never the whole thing.' His eyes were shining even more brightly now. Adelko silently prayed he would hold his peace.

Fortunately he did. Clearing his throat, Horskram told them the tale of St Ulred, the hero who had become an avatar after death and inspired the founding of the most prestigious group of knights in Northalde.

Sir Ulred, as he had been known in life, had lived more than a hundred years ago, during the reign of Thorsvald the Hero King. Landless and lordless, he had roamed the realm as an errant, fighting robber knights and brigands and upholding the King's Law wherever he found it breached. There was no shortage of heroes in that era – the Thirteen Knights of Tintagael had lived and died during those times – but Ulred more than all the others had championed the weak and defenceless, putting the concerns of the poor before the winning of a damsel's favour or glory and riches on the battlefield.

'Some say this was because he was of common stock himself and had been knighted in the field for exceptional courage,' explained Horskram. 'Others claim that had happened to his father, who raised his son never to forget his roots. Others still claim he was noble born but had been told by the Redeemer in a vision as a child to put all vanities aside and help the downtrodden.'

'Didn't the same thing happen to you, Master Horskram?' blurted Adelko, instantly regretting his interruption. 'I mean… about joining our Order…' He faltered uncertainly as Horskram stared at him inscrutably.

'Ah, is that what they say about me at Ulfang?' he queried, a gentle smile playing across his lips. 'Well, there may be some truth to that, or there may not – but I was under the impression you wished to hear more of St Ulred, not Horskram of Vilno?'

Adelko lowered his eyes to the rush-strewn floor. 'Pray forgive me, Master Horskram,' he said bashfully. 'Please continue.'

The old monk cleared his throat again and went on.

'Whatever the truth of his origins, the stories agree that Sir Ulred's relentless do-gooding had made him powerful enemies, robber barons who eventually conspired to murder the young knight. Their henchmen took him unawares one day as he was riding through the forest in search of another worthy cause and slew him, leaving his butchered body for the crows.

'His killers could not possibly have known what would happen next. Troubadours and loremasters alike tell it that a Valravyn crossed over from the Other Side. Happening upon Ulred's corpse, it chased off the crows that had gathered around it and devoured his heart.'

Adelko had learned about Valravné at the monastery. They were malicious spirits trapped in the bodies of ravens, who could only escape by eating the heart of an unburied warrior slain in combat. That allowed them to possess the corpse, and rising from the bloody earth the host body would wreak havoc and rapine upon the mortal vale until the Valravyn was expelled by an Argolian or neutralised by a warlock.

'Yet so pure had Ulred's soul been during his life that the Almighty would not permit his body to be so foully used,' continued Horskram, 'and he was allowed to re-inhabit his earthly remains to do battle with the Valravyn for possession of them. And after a great struggle he triumphed over the spirit, casting it out.'

Here Horskram broke off for one of his customary pauses. 'Is that it?' asked Vaskrian incredulously. 'That doesn't sound like the part of the tale I heard!'

Adelko could not resist smiling. His new friend was unfamiliar with his mentor's dramatic style of story-telling.

'No, young gallant of Hroghar,' the old monk replied wryly, 'that is not the end of the tale. For the legend tells how each and every one of his murderers was hunted down and slain by a terrible white knight, with a pale face and merciless eyes, a gaunt cadaverous parody of the man they had killed, his body crisscrossed with blood-encrusted gashes, and a gaping wound where his heart should have been...'

That bloodthirsty narrative put an end to Vaskrian's interruptions, and the adept finished his story without further pause.The revenant of Sir Ulred slew the barons who had conspired against him too, before freeing all the common folk they had unjustly kept imprisoned and oppressed. The legend finished by recounting how, his earthly mission accomplished, Sir Ulred relinquished control of his mortal remains forever. His body crumbled and decayed before the eyes of the peasants he had liberated, and from the stinking pile of morbid flesh a raven white as snow rose to fly far up into the heavens, never to be seen again.

'Thus was born the legend of Sir Ulred and the White Valravyn,' concluded the old monk. 'Inspired by Ulred's devotion to the Code of Chivalry, King Thorsvald established the Order of the White Valravyn to uphold justice and protect the weak, and many of his best knights flocked to join it. The Temple subsequently proclaimed Ulred a saint, and to this day nobles and commoners alike still pray to him as the patron of justice and divine retribution.'

Adelko bit his lip as he mulled that over. Retribution. Divine justice. Protecting the weak. All well and good – but there wasn't much there about showing leniency to suspect witches.

'It is said the White Valravyn have never put a man to death without giving him a trial first,' said Horskram when the novice voiced his fears. 'So have no fear on that count. But as for "seeing sense and letting us go" as our reckless young friend put it, that depends – '

He was interrupted by the sound of approaching footsteps. Adelko's spirits rose a little when he saw Sir Tarlquist with a gaoler and four men-at-arms in tow draw level with their cell.

'Good e'en,' the knight said curtly, addressing Horskram. 'I trust that your needs have been well tended to?'

'As well as can be expected under the circumstances,' replied the adept dryly, 'although yon chamber pot could use emptying, for your prison fare is passing fine.'

Sir Tarlquist allowed a thin smile to crease his war-worn features. 'I did not think the Argolians commanded such earthy humour – but I shall have the gaolers see to it directly. In the meantime, the three of you are to come with me. The High Commander will see you directly.'

Without another word he motioned for the gaoler to open the cell door. Adelko felt a sense of trepidation despite their being temporarily freed. Were they being summoned to an audience – or a trial?

✣ ✣ ✣

Sir Tarlquist remained silent as he escorted the three prisoners around the perimeter of the keep towards the main entrance. It was early evening. The weather had turned foul while they were underground; the darkening wet skies looked grim against the oncoming night.

The castle was already aflame with torch and taper. Statues of various warrior saints were set in alcoves along the walls; the wavering light strafed them with ghostly shadows. Adelko was reminded a little of the refectory in Ulfang, but where St Ionus and his ilk had stared impassively stern patrician figures now glared at them, clutching spears, swords and shields in pitted stone hands. Most of the statues depicted St Ulred; representations of the saintly warrior killing robber knights and the like dotted the keep's walls in a riot of sculpted butchery.

Adelko felt his gut tighten. His sixth sense wasn't ringing but Staerkvit's interior and its glorification of violence made him feel uneasy.

The gatehouse leading into the keep was flanked by four more statues, each several times larger than a man: one was of St Ulred, the other three he recognised as the archangels Ezekiel, Virtus and Stygnos, avatars of just war, courage and fortitude. A fresco straddling the gatehouse lintel showed a raven taking flight from a heart torn in two, symbolising St Ulred's supernatural alter ego.

Two soldiers guarding the gatehouse uncrossed their halberds at a signal from Tarlquist. Passing through a torchlit corridor they emerged into a large antechamber lined with more statues like the ones outside. A great mural covered the upper part of the walls, depicting scenes from the tale Horskram had just told them.

Directly ahead was a closed pair of oak double doors bound in iron.

'That'll be the Great Hall, where the knights eat and the High Commander hears cases,' Vaskrian whispered to Adelko.

'Is that where we're going?' Adelko whispered back.

Vaskrian was about to reply when Tarlquist answered his question by leading them towards a flight of stairs to the right.

'Suppose that means they haven't got a case yet,' said Adelko.

'No – it only mean they haven't decided whether to try us yet,' replied Vaskrian, before being shushed by one of the guards.

Led by Tarlquist and flanked by their escort they ascended many flights of stairs. Adelko's legs ached by the time they reached the summit; their recent lack of use didn't help. The air was dank and cold. Perhaps living in a castle wasn't all it was cracked up to be. At least a peasant's hut was easy to keep warm if you had enough firewood.

Tarlquist led them along a narrow corridor that ended in a door guarded by a sentry. At a nod from the knight they were ushered into what Adelko supposed must be the solar of Staerkvit Castle. This was a sizeable rectangular chamber with a row of south-facing windows. The smaller west wall was taken up entirely with a black and white mural, depicting the Order's emblem in partitioned squares at each of its four corners. The centrepiece showed a stylised knight clutching a sword in one hand and scales of justice in the other, a white raven bursting from his chest.

The middle of the room was given over to an oblong pine table covered with maps. This was flanked by two long benches, with a high-backed mahogany chair of simple design at its head. Half a dozen knights dressed in mail were poring over the maps and arguing. Did they ever remove their armour, Adelko wondered.

He recognised bull-necked Sir Toric, golden-haired Sir Torgun and cruel-mouthed Sir Wolmar immediately; he guessed the other knights were commanders in the Order like Tarlquist.

The sentry announced them. As the knights turned to stare at them Adelko's eyes fell on the one standing at the head of the table, before the chair. Like Torgun he was tall even for a high-born Northlending. He was leaner, but his wiry frame betokened a man seasoned in battle. His short cropped hair was receding, but here and there a reddish-gold lock still graced the grey. A pair of fine mustachios sprouted from his hooked nose; keen green eyes stared intently at the new arrivals while the stern curve of his mouth gave nothing away.

Everything in his bearing said this was a man used to being obeyed, and Adelko knew at once that he was in the presence of royalty: Prince Freidhoff,

High Commander of the Order of the White Valravyn and brother to the King. The man who would decide what to do with them.

Sure enough, the guard announced the Prince and commanded the captives to kneel. Adelko felt there was something about the High Commander that was familiar, though plainly he had never met such an illustrious figure before.

Prince Freidhoff bade them rise impatiently. 'Enough of the regal formalities,' he said in a gravelly voice weighty with authority. 'We are at Staerkvit Castle, not court, so you will address me as High Commander. When I say "you" I mean you, Horskram of Vilno – yon lads shall not speak unless one of us here addresses them directly. Sir Tarlquist, Sir Toric, Sir Torgun and my son Wolmar you are acquainted with – these two are Sir Redrun and Sir Yorrick, commanders in the Order.'

Adelko barely noticed the last two, both tall, broad-shouldered men in early middle age, as they nodded curtly at Horskram, stunned as he was by the revelation. Sir Wolmar was the Prince's son – no wonder his father had seemed familiar!

Peering at them both in the flickering torchlight he could see the resemblance – Freidhoff's mouth was stern where his son's was cruel, his jawline somewhat broader and less aquiline, the curve of his nose more pronounced, but the family resemblance was unmistakeable.

So high-handed, ruthless Wolmar was a king's grandson – that didn't bode well either.

'Well met, sir knights,' replied Horskram courteously. 'And may the Almighty watch over you and the Redeemer bless your days, High Commander – it seems an age since last we met. Pray tell me how fares the Lady Walsa?'

'My cousin fares well enough, as much I hear,' replied the High Commander gruffly, tugging at a mustachio. 'Seems content to drive my brother mad at court with her querulousness, if the tales be true. Far more shrewish than her sister ever was, Reus rest Her Majesty's soul. Still she can hardly pester her lord husband, Willeng, given he's lost his wits and weeps like a babe from dawn till dusk in his seat at Stromlund. Some wasting disease that ruins a man's mind, the Marionites say. A pity you can't cure him as well.'

Horskram shook his head slowly. 'I am afraid I can only save a soul from madness when the servants of the Fallen One are responsible,' he said. 'But I am glad to hear that the King's cousin now resides at Strongholm – possessions there have been few and far between, so she should be safe. Would that Her Highness had never come into possession of that accursed bauble from the Blessed Realm – an Ifrit is a powerful and vindictive spirit when released from the article that binds it! It would have been a tragedy for someone of the blood royal to succumb to such a tormentor.'

'Thanks to your ministrations she didn't,' replied the High Commander courteously. 'But, be that as it may... your latest story, as I have heard it, is a strange one indeed. Tintagael Forest – even that is surely a challenge too great for the mighty Horskram of Vilno?'

'I make no claims to might, High Commander,' replied the adept quickly. 'Only such wisdom and learning as the Almighty has seen fit to bless me with. And I am sorry to say it is true that we fell foul of the accursed forest that the Elder Wizards poisoned – and lost one of our comrades to its horrible magicks.'

Sir Wolmar scowled and appeared about to say something, but his father anticipated him, silencing him with a flick of the hand. Beckoning to a page boy standing in the corner, the High Commander ordered stools to be fetched for the captives. When servants had brought these he bade them leave with the page and the guards, ordering the sentry to shut the door behind them.

The trio were sat in a row opposite the far end of the table facing the High Commander; on either side of it the six other knights sat, their faces turned towards them. The last vestiges of twilight had disappeared outside. Torches flickered in a chilly evening breeze offset by the firepit next to the east wall. Despite this Adelko felt shiverish as seven pairs of eyes scrutinised him and his companions. The interrogation had begun.

⁜ ⁜ ⁜

They questioned Horskram closely. He answered loudly enough, giving a comprehensive account of their journey from Ulfang and the adventures that had befallen them. The part about the Headstone fragment he left out, saying only that an artefact of great importance had been stolen from the monastery by something he suspected was not mortal. He was similarly vague about the supernatural horror pursuing them, although it was true that they knew little enough about the blasphemous devil anyway. Of the Northland brigands he gave a full account, detailing their fight in the clearing by Lake Sördegil and flight thereafter. When he reached the part about their ordeal in the forest, he was circumspect again, saying only that they had been beset by numerous evils, the last of which had claimed the life of their comrade.

When his mentor reached that part Adelko sensed Vaskrian shudder; he wondered if the old monk was being sparse with details as much to spare the squire as to preserve secrecy.

Of their audience with the Fay Kindred, Horskram said little, despite being pressed for details. All he would say was that they had been rewarded with free passage out of the forest after despatching a rival spirit that was hostile to the faerie kings.

At that point Wolmar got to his feet and denounced them all as devil-worshippers, only to be told sternly by his father to pipe down and be seated.

But Sir Redrun clearly shared Wolmar's misgivings, glaring at Horskram suspiciously throughout the interrogation.

'What kind of man of the cloth seeks sanctuary in accursed Tintagael?' he asked several times, to Wolmar's nodding approval. 'Many in the Temple have spoken ill of the Argolian Order – until now I had not been minded to believe them. But they say only a sorcerer of great power could ever hope to escape that place. Perhaps 'tis true what some say, that the Grey Friars are warlocks in disguise! And warlocks are no friends to the Knights of the White Valravyn, or any god-fearing man!'

But the High Commander waved him silent too, and bade Horskram continue: 'You said from the outset you were headed for Rima to speak with the Grand Master of your Order – why did you change your mind and seek Strongholm instead?'

Again Horskram answered as loudly as he could without giving everything away. At least the war offered a convenient smokescreen – it was perfectly true that they had thought it better to take ship from Strongholm rather than risk a journey through the strife-torn southlands.

Prince Freidhoff was quick to disabuse them of that notion.

'The rebels have been mustering a navy out of Port Urring for some weeks now,' he said. 'You'll have as little joy travelling by sea as by land before the month is out. But there was another reason for your journeying to the capital – Sir Tarlquist informs me you were seeking an audience with the Arch Perfect. I wonder what he would make of your blasphemous journey.'

The High Commander sounded more suspicious than outraged. It was often said that the ravens put 'Regis before Reus' – their very existence was founded on a legend shrouded in magic, so they couldn't be all that pious. Adelko sensed Wolmar's insistence that they were heathen warlocks was hardly couched in god-fearing piety either – rather a petulant prince's son had taken an immediate dislike to mysterious travellers who defied him, and wanted to punish them under any pretext. He could feel the malice pouring off him like venom – thankfully his father, though fiercely authoritarian, seemed to be cut from a different cloth.

'I realised after the horrors of Tintagael that we could not possibly hope to make it all the way to Rima on our own,' said Horskram, dissembling around the eerie counsel the Fays had given them. 'So I thought it wiser to seek out the Arch Perfect and consult him while arranging a ship. Though not a member of our Order, he is a wise and powerful prelate and might be able to offer some counsel at need.'

The High Commander glared suspiciously at Horskram. 'He is a wise and powerful prelate who has always been as critical of your Order as he has been of ours,' he replied sternly. 'But of a sudden you wish to breach the divide and make parley with him, as it were... There's more to this than meets the eye, Master Horskram. I know little of Temple matters but I can see that plainly enough.'

The knights went back over Horskram's story in full, painstakingly making him reiterate everything he had said again to try and catch him out. But the old monk never wavered – each and every time the details were the same.

By the time they were done the torches were burning low in their brackets, and Adelko's belly was rumbling painfully. At least in the gaol they had been fed regularly – it must be far past supper time by now. Vaskrian was silent and subdued – the novice had feared he would butt in impetuously as he usually did, but Horskram's recounting of Tintagael seemed to have knocked the stuffing out of him. He gripped the sides of his stool with white-knuckled hands and stared at the floor dumbly.

If the ravens were hungry, they showed no sign of it. At last, leaning back in his high chair with a sigh the High Commander frowned.

'It is evident to me, master monk, that you are leaving in enough details to impress upon us the importance of your mission, whilst leaving out enough to keep us in the dark. Just what is it you are hiding from us – and more to the point, why? Is this supposed to be for our own protection, or yours? What is so terrible that it cannot be shared with the justiciars of the King's Dominions – and need I remind you, I could sanction force to reveal your true story... indeed is there any reason why I should not now do so, as you refuse to speak fully of your own accord?'

That provoked another fierce debate among the knights. Wolmar and Redrun were for having them 'chastised' in the lower dungeons; Torgun and Tarlquist strongly opposed such a course, whilst Aronn and Yorrick suggested starving them for a day or two to loosen their tongues.

'We cannot and should not inflict torment on these men,' said Torgun quietly but firmly. 'Two are friars and one is a man of arms sworn to service – to treat them as common criminals would be a grave injustice!'

'They are warlocks, or spies, or maybe even both,' persisted Wolmar. 'Perhaps you are too dull-witted to see it, but I am not! To the dungeons with them I say – hot irons will quickly reveal their true story!'

'Aye, Sir Wolmar has the right of it,' put in Sir Redrun, a stony-faced knight whose head, shorn clean at the back and sides, was topped with a tuft of straggly black hair. 'He says the Fay Folk let them go free – but only a sorcerer could compel such fiends thus. A true Argolian would never treat with evil spirits!'

'What do you know of the Argolians and their ways, Sir Redrun?' retorted Tarlquist. 'How do you know he treated with them? Do you dare to say pagan sorcery could compel such wicked imps but the holy power of the Redeemer could not? Perhaps it was his prayers that set them free!'

'Aye, perhaps,' Sir Redrun allowed. 'But I'm thinking something else too – perhaps this is all a smokescreen, and there was no cursed voyage to Tintagael, no foreign brigands, no night-tripping stalker... perhaps it's all an elaborate hoax, to put us off our guard! For all we know they could be spies – sent by Thule to learn our true strength and fathom our battle plans.'

'I've said as much already!' chimed Sir Wolmar.

'Both of you are half out of your wits with fear of the enemy, it seems,' said Sir Torgun. The young knight, who could not have been older than five and twenty summers, never raised his voice a great deal, Adelko noticed. But when he spoke everybody, including Prince Freidhoff and Sir Wolmar, listened.

'Thule knows our strength as well as he knows our own,' the tall knight continued. 'He has been planning this assault for months, maybe years – that much is clear. Whatever he needed to know about our forces he will have learned long since. As to our battle plans, those should be obvious enough – even now his army presses deep into our heartlands, and we must meet him in the field before Linden as soon as we can muster an army of our own. I can see no obvious connection betwixt these wayfarers and the rebels, strange as their story may seem.'

Sir Tarlquist nodded his assent. Yorrick looked as though he might be leaning towards their view, but Aronn remained uncertain. 'I still say a day or two without food, just to be sure they aren't keeping anything back that we ought to know about, would do no harm,' he mused aloud.

'I say a pox on that!' snarled Wolmar. 'Monks fast every season! They'll endure that easily, and yon staring squire is clearly a halfwit! The only way to be sure is to put the maiden on them – we'll soon get the full story then, mark my words!'

'I thought you said they were spies and warlocks, now they are monks when it suits you to say so,' answered Torgun, fixing the Prince's son with a cold stare. It was the closest to angry Adelko had seen him get. 'Forgive me for speaking ill of your flesh and blood, High Commander, but it is becoming fast apparent that Sir Wolmar desires only one thing – to inflict pain on these strangers for cruelty's sake alone.'

Wolmar's eyes narrowed, their green irises glinting with cold fury as he glared at Torgun. 'I am serving the realm, not my own vanity,' he replied venomously. 'You would sooner see its enemies walk free than have anyone say your precious knightly honour was compromised by sanctioning a necessary evil.'

At last Torgun grew angry. 'You dare to accuse me of putting my own vanity before the defence of the realm, Sir Wolmar!' he said, raising his voice for the first time. 'Even for you, that is low – were it not for the rules of our Order and your blood royal, I would demand satisfaction in the lists forthwith!'

Wolmar remained unimpressed. 'Satisfaction you can have any time, Sir Torgun of Vandheim,' he spat back. 'Let us remove our surcoats and repair with witnesses to a suitable place – I've had enough of your more-chivalrous-than-thou prating, let's see how well your steel talks instead!'

'Enough!' bellowed Prince Freidhoff, slamming his fist down on the table. 'What foolishness is this to speak of? There will be no clandestine duelling between knights of the Order – its rules are there to be adhered to, not broken at will, and especially not by my own son! Now, silence, all of you, I'll – '

The sound came, sudden and awful and otherworldly, stilling the angry words of mortal men in a heartbeat.

Adelko felt a horribly familiar dread clutch his spirit with icy fingers. He had hoped never to hear that horrid cry again, but on this occasion his prayers were not to be answered. Vaskrian looked up and over towards the solar's windows in the direction of the hideous sound as he broke out into a cold sweat. The knights stared at each other aghast, paralysed by the dreadful call, an avian shriek suffused with an insectoid buzzing. It was loud, very loud – it pierced the ears and transfixed the heart.

Horskram was first to throw off the terror gripping them. Stumbling over to a window he gazed out of it. 'Ye Almighty,' he gasped. 'It's directly above the castle grounds – that's close enough to sense us!'

Adelko, Sir Torgun and Prince Freidhoff managed to shrug off their fear and join him at the window. The rest of the knights and Vaskrian were bent low, clutching their ears and trembling – brave men unmanned by a horror that defied mortal courage.

'What in the name of the Redeemer is that?' cried the High Commander in a choked voice. At the window next to him Sir Torgun said nothing at all, his mouth agape, his face white.

The thing that had pursued them since the Highlands was hovering above the courtyard, on a level with the keep's turrets just above the solar. Adelko was closer to it than he had ever been, and the clouds had parted during their interrogation to reveal a sickle moon and stars. His first clear view of the netherworld demon would leave a chill of horror on his heart forever.

It was huge: its bat-like wings alone were each bigger than a man. Their membranous matter reminded Adelko of bees kept by the journeymen at Ulfang. Its tubular body and tail he had glimpsed at Sørdegil; at this range he could see its scythe-like point was bigger than a sword. Wicked yellow talons sprouted from myriad insectoid limbs, and a carapaced exoskeleton of deepest black served as its skin. A cluster of eyes sprouted from its featureless convex head; but where natural order would have dictated the mindless orbs of a hornet, mammalian pupils glinted with alien intelligence. Perhaps worst of all was its mouth, which opened horizontally to reveal rows of fangs shaped like giant pine needles. A horrid stench permeated the air around it, making Adelko feel as nauseous as he was terrified.

The dreadful thing seemed to be inclining its head towards them, and for an instant he feared it had seen him, when suddenly a handful of arrows flew up to meet it. Most of the shafts glanced harmlessly off its thick hide, but one tore through a wing, becoming lodged there. The demon let out a shriek that set Adelko's gorge rising before turning to descend on the ramparts where a cluster of terrified archers stood trembling.

Their leader must have been a truly courageous and inspiring serjeant, for the courtyard below was a riot of chaos as knights and soldiers ran to and fro or writhed on the ground, overcome by a terror they could not comprehend. The few who hadn't succumbed were preparing to receive its attack on foot as best they could, as their panicked warhorses reared and whinnied helplessly.

Those bowmen who hadn't descended into madness with their comrades on the walls were rewarded for their fortitude with swift ugly deaths.

Adelko swallowed back bile as he watched the demon tear the head off one with a single bite, at the same time as it impaled another with its tail: driving it through the screaming archer's lightly armoured midriff it lifted his quivering body clear of the ramparts before dashing his head into bloody fragments of bone and brain on the battlements. A third archer made to run away, his courage broken. The thing opened its bloodstained maw – what looked like a short suckered tentacle shot out, spitting the same tarry substance Adelko had gagged on in the Laegawood. The gobbet caught the fleeing archer in the back; he gave a piteous scream as he plummeted off the rampart. A thick tendril of smoke rose from his corpse. A fourth archer had collapsed gibbering to the parapet walkway. The fiend put him out of his misery with a rake of its talons as it hovered on wings that buzzed frantically.

Even now the serjeant refused to give up the fight, discarding his longbow and pulling a short sword from his belt. The demon stared at him for a split second with myriad eyes before opening its maw again.

For an instant Adelko thought the horror was going to spit its acidic venom at the serjeant, but instead it caught him a treacherous blow with its tail, transfixing his chest and lifting him up to tear his head off in one fell movement. With a contemptuous flick of its gargantuan tail it sent the headless corpse crashing into two fleeing soldiers in the courtyard below.

With a twist of its body and another hideous shriek the demon descended to attack.

'Redeemer save us!' cried Prince Freidhoff, lurching back from the window. 'Yon horror will slay half the garrison – Torgun! With me – we need to rally the men now!'

The High Commander sprang over towards his son, grabbing him by his surcoat and yanking him off the floor. 'Wolmar, as you honour your blood royal, pull yourself together!' he yelled in his son's ashen face. Whatever his other failings, Wolmar was no coward – stung by his father's words he recovered his courage and staggered to his feet.

Cursing in a manner unbefitting a pious monk, Horskram turned to Adelko. 'We must go with them, they cannot hope to prevail against this horror with cold steel alone – I hope you're in the mood for more scripture!' he cried. 'Here, first help me get yon squire to his feet – he swore to protect us, now he'll have a chance to make good on his oath!'

They pulled Vaskrian up. He was white as a sheet and shivering from head to toe. Adelko felt scarcely better himself. Taking out his circifix and pressing it to the squire's sweat-soaked forehead, Horskram began reciting the rhyming verses that marked the beginning of the Psalm of Fortitude:

> *O Redeemer thy servants shall not quail*
> *Though shadows make cuts across the land,*
> *The faithful shall pass through the darkling vale,*
> *Your light guides our feet and strengthens our hands!*
>
> *The works of Abaddon shall share his fate*
> *As the Cursed City shuddered aeons ago,*
> *The meek shall rise to topple the great,*
> *The proud and the wanton shall be brought low!*
>
> *My faith is my harness, my spirit a sword,*
> *Piety my steed and prayers my shield*
> *In mortal strife let all sins be abjured,*
> *For I shall not yield, I shall not yield!*

The sacred words had the desired effect. His natural courage augmented by the monk's blessing, Vaskrian shrugged off the nightmarish effects of the demonic howlings that now filled the courtyard. Yorrick, Aronn and Redrun were also stirring from frightful madness, their spirits bolstered by Horskram's prayer and Prince Freidhoff's exhortations.

The knights frantically busied themselves rearming from a rack against the wall where they had placed their swords – members of the Order were instructed never to be far from a weapon at any time. Watching them Vaskrian realised he was once again weaponless – the last time he'd seen his sword and dirk they were being handed over to the guards in the courtyard. He wondered grimly if they would be making much use of them now.

Freidhoff flung open the door. Outside in the corridor the sentry was writhing on the floor babbling. Stepping over him the seven knights made a dash for the stairwell, making a great hue and cry. At Horskram's behest they followed, but not before the squire had grabbed the sentry's discarded spear. It wasn't a sword, but it would have to do – at least it was his next best weapon after a blade, although he was more accustomed to using one on horseback as a lance.

The ten of them dashed back down to the antechamber. On the way they found many more soldiers and menials out of their wits, and one or two knights besides.

But not all had succumbed to the terror. By the time they reached the courtyard their numbers had swelled around them. Some thirty knights and footsoldiers stepped out into the torchlit precinct with the two friars, to do battle as best they could. Among them was the castle chaplain, a stern military priest if ever Adelko saw one, dressed in full armour like his fellows but wearing a large iron circifix around his neck.

The courtyard was a scene of pandemonium. Several dozen men and horses lay dead, dying or wounded, their blood spattered in pools and streams across the bailey's dirt floor. Those that had not shrugged off the terror were clustered about the base of the walls or the parapets above, curled up against the cold unyielding stone as they shook uncontrollably.

Those who had mastered their fear had done so only enough to substitute retreat for rout: one cluster of knights and soldiers huddled behind an overturned wayn, another group cowered in the armoury, whilst a third was assembling in the forge. Those who had proved bold enough to stand their ground had quickly shared the fate of the archers on the walls. One young knight screamed pitifully as his entrails dribbled out of his torn midriff and onto the blood-soaked dirt; a serjeant gaped at the bleeding stumps where his sword arm and both legs had been, too stunned even to cry the last of his life away.

Another warrior, a great gory rent where his face should have been, moaned feebly as he tried to crawl away from the demon.

Atop the splintered wreckage of two carts it squatted, a loathsome horror; beneath the shattered wayns a dying horse added its screams to the awful soundscape of pain and suffering. The demon was bent low, its mandibles moving left and right as it feasted on a corpse. It was impossible to tell whether he had been a knight or serjeant in life, for the demon's acidic spittle had robbed his sloughing flesh of all mutable form: acrid smoke rose from the amorphous mass of fused muscle, bone, metal and clothing as it tore off great strips and swallowed them whole. Several of the knights and men-at-arms in their company were sick on the spot; a handful more relapsed into gibbering madness straight away. The rest gripped their weapons with trembling hands, their faces ashen in the yellow torchlight. At this range the creature's stench was overpowering.

They were at least spared the hideous sight of the demon feasting further. The thing turned its blasphemous head towards them, cocking it in a way a madman might have found comical. Adelko could feel its myriad eyes scrutinising their company with a malignancy far beyond any mortal villain's.

'It sees us!' said Horskram in a hoarse voice. 'It knows it has its prey – High Commander, only the power of prayer can hope to abjure this dread thing! You and your men must defend us and buy us enough time to banish it!'

'Very well, Master Horskram!' the Prince shouted above the screams of the dying. 'But you had better have the Redeemer on your side, else we are all doomed!' Turning to a serjeant he barked an order: 'Varo! Take the rest of the footsoldiers and get the wounded into the keep – reconnoitre with the others in the armoury and forge and behind yonder wayn and get them to help you!'

Then, tearing a shield from a nearby corpse he held his sword aloft and addressed the rest of his men: 'Knights of the White Valravyn – shield the monks from yon horror! Let their holy prayers be your succour and your strength! They must not be harmed!'

The order came not a moment too soon. With a dreadful cry the demon launched itself up into the air, its wings buzzing horribly as it curled down in an arc towards the monks with terrifying speed. Desperately the knights scrambled to form a circle around Horskram and Adelko; several of the more quick-witted including Torgun and Wolmar had also availed themselves of shields – they now pressed towards the front, holding them aloft to defend the monks from an aerial attack.

Some fifteen knights met the thing with a ring of steel as it lunged through the half-darkness at them, its talons raking aside the shields of the two foremost as it snapped at Horskram with its maw.

It would have severed his head clean off his shoulders had he not held his circifix aloft at that moment and begun to recite the Psalm of Abjuration: confronted with the sudden spectacle of the holy rood the thing shied back, just as Torgun struck the base of its neck. It was a mighty blow and well placed: the thing shrieked as steaming ichor bubbled from a rent where two parts of its carapace joined. With a flick of its wings the demon lurched upwards again, out of range of the knights' questing swords, circling as it glared balefully down at them with its many eyes.

Pressing their temporary advantage, Horskram continued to recite the same words he had uttered in Landebert's hut on the Brenning Wold, Adelko quickly joining in. Next to them the castle chaplain chorused their words as he brandished a sword, his circifix clutched in his other hand. An ordinary perfect would not be able to channel the sacred power of the words as well as a trained Argolian, but all the same the novice was grateful. Right now they needed all the help they could get.

✣ ✣ ✣

Surrounded by heavily armoured fighters, with only his tattered brigandine and a footsoldier's spear to protect him, Vaskrian felt virtually naked. Though he wasn't pious by nature, he felt the words of the Redeemer warm him as no fire could: they were being recited by initiates of an Order that some said had the ear of the Almighty Himself. He'd never paid much heed to that until now – now it seemed a comforting thought.

Around him the raven knights seemed similarly emboldened, and standing fast amidst their dying and deranged comrades they shook their spears and swords as they uttered the war cry of the White Valravyn, defying the demon to descend again.

But the thing that had pursued Adelko and his mentor across half the realm was not so easily goaded. It reared back, its mouth yawning open to reveal a hideous rubbery tongue. No, not a tongue... With an instinct born of terrifying experience Vaskrian realised what was about to happen.

'It's going to spit venom at us!' he yelled. 'We need more shields!'

A jet of thick tarry substance shot from the devil's mouth, catching one of the knights in the face and chest. The scream he uttered was mercifully soon silenced as his face dissolved, the flesh dripping off his skull as he collapsed to the ground in a quivering heap.

If he'd had his hands free Vaskrian would have made the sign – this encounter was doing wonders for his piety. He watched helplessly as the demon turned towards the monks, seeking another target...

✣ ✣ ✣

Absorbed in prayer, Adelko could do nothing to avert the next gobbet as it came flying towards him. Torgun threw his shield in the way, barging Redrun to one side as he did. The kite-shaped board hissed and steamed as pieces of it sloughed off. Adelko and the knights nearest him gagged, their eyes streaming. Wolmar and Tarlquist launched a frenzied counter attack from either side of the devil, their blades bouncing harmlessly off its thick carapace just as it sent the High Commander crashing to the ground with a sidewise swipe of its tail and speared another knight in the chest in quick succession. He fell to the ground with a cry. In the light of the torches Adelko could see the agonised face of Sir Yorrick, contorted in an ugly grimace of death.

Rearing evilly over the monks and their beleaguered defenders the demon drew back its head and prepared to spit venom at them again. They were saved by a fresh sortie of knights: these were from the armoury and fully equipped, a fact not lost on their seasoned commander.

'All men with shields form a defensive ring with me around the monks!' yelled Prince Freidhoff. 'All those lacking shields get over to the armoury on the double!'

The knights and men-at-arms scrambled to obey his order. A flurry of limbs saw most of the guard around the friars changed – only Torgun, Wolmar and the High Commander remained from the original circle. Another gobbet of acidic spittle went flying through the night air. Another man fell screaming, his flesh and armour sizzling.

Adelko barely had time to register this as he and Horskram ploughed on with their scriptural mantras, reciting the Prophet's thousand-year-old words and repeating the refrain again and again: *It is the power of the Redeemer that compels thee, it is the power of the Redeemer that compels thee!*

Just as they reached the part that said *the penitent shall kneel before His godly grace* they bent their knees to the ground, allowing the knights to defend them more effectively from a standing position. Adelko felt the demon's spittle splash past his face a couple of times as it bounced off the knights' interlocked shields, now woven in a tight upwards-facing circle around them. Beyond this a second ring of knights and serjeants arriving from the forge knelt to protect the interior ring from any treacherous attacks from the demon's tail.

However unused it was to fighting denizens of the Other Side, the Order of the White Valravyn was learning fast.

Yet even so their defence was far from impregnable. The fighters who had dashed over from the forge were less well equipped than their brethren from the armoury, and several gaps presented inviting targets: by the time their fellows returned to bolster the second ring of protection, several more knights and serjeants had perished beneath its lashing sting.

But Adelko could sense that their stubborn defence was beginning to fluster the demon, if such a thing could ever be said to feel flustered, and he could feel its discomfort growing as the Redeemer's words began to penetrate its psyche. Round and round it circled, now spitting another gobbet of spittle, now lashing out with its tail or a swipe of its talons. But its assaults, though still vicious, were steadily growing weaker: the gobbets less copious, the swipes less fearsome.

Sir Toric and Sir Tarlquist had each taken charge of another sortie that crouched in wait around the defensive circle of knights in the middle: every time the winged devil flew down to attack the monks and their defenders, the group nearest would launch a counter strike from behind.

Most of these proved fruitless until, ducking under its lashing tail, Tarlquist thrust a spear deep into a chink in its exoskeleton. The thing screeched and buzzed with rage as ichor bubbled up out of the wound; with an awful speed it turned and lashed out with its razor-sharp teeth. Tarlquist threw his shield up to parry, falling back into the dirt with the force of the blow. The knight next to him was not so lucky. Bringing its tail around lightning-quick the demon lopped off both his legs above the knee. Screaming, he fell to the ground in pieces.

✣ ✣ ✣

Vaskrian found himself in the sortie led by Sir Toric. His muscles tensed as he gripped his spear in both hands, waiting for an opening. Soon he had it. The demon suddenly changed tactics, flying down to grip the double ring of shields with its talons. Its tail arched high, the deadly point quivering directly above the aperture created by the inner circle...

Grasping his spear he launched himself forwards, striking at the point where its body tapered off into its tail. It proved an inspired move: here the exoskeleton was less thick, and the thing screeched again as his spear-point pierced deep into its foul-smelling hide. Flinging its head upwards it aborted its lethal attack on the Argolians.

I'll stay true to my vow yet, he thought feverishly as he yanked his spear free of the hissing wound. He had no time to appreciate his skill and daring. The demon lashed out with a sideways flick of its tail, sending him flying across the courtyard into a serjeant in the next sortie. The pair of them collapsed in a heap on the ground, both too stunned to move. Vaskrian felt a stabbing pain shoot up his side as he groaned in the dust.

Just then Sir Toric and his men threw themselves at the demon, whilst knights and serjeants in the outer ring nearest it risked breaking ranks to launch a rear attack. Faced with determined foes on two fronts the thing retreated, flying up to circle above them again.

After that its attacks became less frequent and determined, as the monks' clear voices rang out into the night air, calling upon the power of the Redeemer to protect them. The old chaplain, who had joined Vaskrian's sortie after arming himself with a shield at the High Commander's order, still chanted the words with them.

Other knights and men-at-arms who had succumbed to the demon-fear began to recover their old courage, as if sensing a turn in the tide, and either joined the fray or helped to get the wounded into the keep. And as courage returned to the Order of the White Valravyn, fear – or something akin to it – seemed to grow apace within the demon.

✣ ✣ ✣

Adelko's voice sounded hoarse in his ears and his throat felt raw. Channelling the Redeemer's power was enervating work – it took all a man's spiritual fortitude to recite his words again and again with the proper conviction. They had to break the demon's will soon – how much longer could they keep this up?

Suddenly it gave vent to another blood-curdling shriek and flew up into the night sky. This time it wasn't circling for another attack: soaring high above the battlements, it vanished into the blackened firmament as abruptly as it had emerged.

He longed to stop right then, but knew they couldn't risk it yet. It might be a trick – the thing had shown evidence of possessing an alien intelligence. The knights and soldiers about him remained stiff and tense, refusing to break formation as he and Horskram continued to recite scripture without missing a syllable.

They continued like that for a while, and the demon did not return. Gradually they brought the mantra to a close. Adelko could feel a palpable wave of relief washing over everyone, the panicked horses and oxen subsiding into fidgety silence as knights and soldiers embraced one another. Some even whooped and cheered.

Overcome with exhaustion, Adelko collapsed to the ground with his mentor. As he stared up at the stars in the firmament he felt joyful and relieved: once again they had prevailed. The denizen of the Other Side sent to kill them had been repulsed.

But even then a nagging and unsettling question gnawed at the back of his mind. *For how long?*

⇒ CHAPTER XII ⇒

The Road To Sanctuary

They counted the cost of victory beneath a sad but welcome sunrise. Some twenty knights and men-at-arms had perished, with a like number wounded. Half the latter were beyond saving and several others would be maimed for life. Vaskrian was among the few casualties lucky enough to have escaped with light injuries.

'Just a few scratches,' he said breezily as they took him to be treated by the castle chirurgeon for a couple of fractured ribs and minor cuts and bruises. 'Nothing a true warrior like me can't handle.'

He was putting a brave face on things – and wasting no opportunity to assert his knightly fortitude – but Adelko could sense his friend was just as tense and drained as he was. This time there was no convenient faerie magic to cushion the squire's memory from the horror he had just grappled with. Nor his own for that matter.

The demon had also put an end to around a dozen horses, including several Farovian destriers. A like number had been struck blind or driven so mad that they would never consent to be ridden again.

'Such is yon demon's baleful influence on the animal kingdom it mocks so grotesquely,' muttered Horskram darkly. Adelko recalled Landebert's story back in the stone hut. Not for the first time on their journey, nor he suspected the last, he suppressed a shudder.

Much of the garrison were still in shock as they went about cleaning up the wreckage left by the devil's assault. The corpses were placed in a corner of the courtyard and covered with tarpaulin. It was normal practice to send the remains of noble-born knights back to their families, whilst the ordinary soldiers were given plots in the graveyard not far from the castle.

As the ashen-faced men used the wreckage of shattered wayns to make a funeral pyre for the slain horses, the chaplain intoned a prayer for the souls of the dead. Adelko hadn't found time to thank him for his spiritual aid. It probably hadn't made all that much difference truth be told, but the man's bravery and piety deserved recognition.

In spite of his better instincts, he found himself hoping that the victims' shades hadn't been dragged back to Gehenna with their preternatural killer – the Argolians generally taught that a shriven soul was entitled to fair judgment in the afterlife regardless of demonic interference, but the superstitions of his people claimed otherwise, and old beliefs died hard. Making the sign and intoning a prayer of his own for the dead, he resolved to place his trust in the Almighty's power. After all, it had just saved them yet again.

Some of the men had not recovered from the terror inflicted by the demon's presence. The worst of these – mostly menials and less experienced knights and soldiers – were confined to the upper dungeon cells under close watch until their damaged minds could recover. Adelko wondered what the regular criminals and vagabonds would make of their new fellow inmates, and if they even had an inkling of the calamity that had befallen the castle the previous night.

His reverie was interrupted by Vaskrian, who came striding across the courtyard from the keep to speak to him. His torso was swaddled in tight bandages. If he felt any pain he showed no sign of it.

'How are you?' asked Adelko.

'Fine,' replied the squire. 'The chirurgeon gave me a poultice for the pain – not that it was so bad in the first place. Says I'll heal in time, fractures aren't serious.'

He still seemed tense beneath his veneer of hardiness, but Adelko did not press the matter.

'Horskram said to bring you,' Vaskrian continued. 'Says the High Commander wants to see us in his solar again – I suppose they want to finish questioning us.'

'I wonder what they'll make of Master Horskram's answers now,' replied Adelko, feeling suddenly very weary. It had been a long and sleepless night. Turning his back gratefully on the blood-spattered courtyard the novice followed the squire back inside the keep.

✠ ✠ ✠

The solar was the same as they had left it, only this time the south windows afforded a daytime view of the courtyard, its white walls, and the wooded ridges beyond. The same knights were assembled around the sturdy table – all save Sir Yorrick, who now lay with the other corpses of the slain. Horskram was there, gazing broodingly out of the windows from the same seat he had occupied the night before.

The grim faces of the surviving knights looked pale and drawn in the morning light as the High Commander bade the two youths resume their seats next to him with a curt gesture. The sentry – a different one from last night, older and more grizzled – closed the door behind them at Prince Freidhoff's bidding.

Turning a stony gaze on Horskram the High Commander cleared his throat. 'Thirty of my men lie dead or dying, and we have not even ridden off to war,' he began. 'Many more are out of their wits, babbling of a horror which I myself can scarcely begin to comprehend, though I have witnessed it with mine own eyes. You have intimated that this... creature is bound up with your own quest, details of which you are chary of revealing. My son presses for the harshest means of chastisement to persuade you to divulge said details. Hitherto I was not minded to agree with him – for he is young, impetuous and headstrong.'

Sir Wolmar, who was scowling at the three of them, made as if to protest this last remark, but his father held up a gauntleted hand. 'He is young, impetuous and headstrong,' he repeated firmly. 'But in light of what has just occurred, I will not hesitate to heed his counsel if you persist in your obstinate secrecy. The choice is yours, Master Horskram: either you finish your story here in my solar, or you finish it in the lower dungeon.'

For one fearful moment Adelko thought that his mentor would not yield, that he would stubbornly condemn them all to iron and fire below Staerkvit, with Wolmar leering on sadistically.

He breathed an inward sigh of relief when the adept nodded slowly and replied: 'I had hoped to conceal the true reason for our journey from you, for the fewer people that know of such a calamity the better. But after last night I realise I cannot reasonably hope to prevail upon you to let our secret go unrevealed.'

And so he told them everything, about the evil spirit at Rykken, the fragment and its theft, of his suspicions of demonic interference and black magic, of the warlock Andragorix and his struggle with him in Roarkil several years before, of the tale of Søren and Morwena long centuries ago and what the reuniting of the Headstone might mean for the world. And he told them of his fears of revealing the theft and what it might portend for the Order of St Argo if the mainstream Temple got wind of it: the very Temple that he now sought an audience with, so he might beg a drop of the Redeemer's blood to protect them on their journey to Rima.

When he was done the High Commander leaned back in his chair, considering all that had just been said. None of the knights said a word. Aronn and Torgun sat wide-eyed as if barely able to take in all that they had heard. Toric frowned, deep in thought, his ugly face a picture of consternation. Redrun stared down at the table, expressionless. Even Wolmar was speechless, though Adelko thought his green eyes still

glinted malignantly. Tarlquist was staring at Freidhoff anxiously, as if
the two shared some unspoken thought.

Even Vaskrian looked impressed, although it was hard to tell what the
squire really made of the gravity of their situation. So far he seemed to have
treated their predicament as one big adventure, ripe with opportunities for
an ambitious young hotblood. Adelko supposed that if Tintagael and last
night's encounter didn't change that perception, nothing would.

At length the High Commander spoke again. 'Your tale is a dire
one,' he said. 'So much so that I am inclined to believe it. Indeed,
all the more so given the battle tidings I have received of late – and
I begin to suspect, Master Horskram, that you will not have to look
to your old foe to find your sorcerous mastermind.'

He gave the adept no time to weigh these cryptic words as he turned
to meet Tarlquist's steady gaze. 'Sir Tarlquist,' he said. 'Master Horskram
has been so good as to share information with us, I think it is time we
repaid him in kind – tell our guests what you told me three days ago.'

Sir Tarlquist nodded as though he had been expecting this, and turned
to look at Horskram. 'You will forgive me, master monk, if I withheld the
following details when we first met on the road,' he began. 'But you of all
people will appreciate the value of secrecy when faced with an uncertain ally.'

'Of course,' replied Horskram, nodding curtly and fixing the
knight with a quizzical look. 'Please do not feel you have to explain
such things – but I would hear your story now if it please you.'

With a curt nod the knight let them have it. He told them of their
brave ride to relieve beleaguered Salmor, how they had come upon one
of Thule's armies at dusk and taken them unawares. It sounded more
foolhardy than brave to Adelko – they had been outnumbered tenfold.
But then he supposed such derring-do was meat and drink to the Order
of the White Valravyn.

Vaskrian's eyes shone as he listened. The novice guessed he was
picturing himself as part of that bold sortie, and he seemed to hang
on to Tarlquist's every word.

His rapt expression soon darkened when the knight reached
the part about the ensorcelled moat. Horskram's frown deepened
as Tarlquist described the gigantic forms of knights, fashioned of
naught but water, riding round and round the castle and preventing
Kelmor's forces from sallying forth to aid their rescuers.

'Thaumaturgy,' said Horskram, spitting out the word with
distaste. 'One of the Seven Disciplines of Magick, which gives the
practitioner unnatural control over the natural forces of the world.
This Sea Wizard would appear to have a powerful command of it.'

'After we saw that we knew we had lost the battle,' resumed Tarlquist, finishing his story. 'The rebel host pressed in upon us, and not even our valour and superior skill at arms could hope to win the day without the reinforcements we had so anticipated. The dozen knights you met on the king's highway were those of us who managed to cut our way out and escape under cover of darkness – the best warriors in the land, reduced by foul sorcery to fleeing the field like thieves in the night!' The battle-scarred knight shook his head ruefully.

'Have some cheer,' put in Torgun. 'By my reckoning we left at least two dead or wounded for every one we lost – and those of our number who were captured and not slain will most likely be held for ransom. So not all honour was lost, and we shall see some of our comrades again, I trow!'

Horskram appeared not in the least concerned with knightly honour as he addressed Tarlquist: 'I had no inkling that Thule had allied himself with the powers of darkness. If so then his treachery runs deeper than we could have imagined.'

'Whatever the truth of the matter, Master Horskram,' said Prince Freidhoff, 'it would appear that the troubles of the realm and the troubles of your Order may be linked – assuming this "sea wizard" is behind the theft you spoke of. It would certainly explain why the fiendish thing we faced last night chose to attack us – if Thule has enlisted the services of a warlock who can conjure up such things to trouble us in the heart of loyalist lands, then he will prove a formidable foe indeed!'

The hoary old commander made the sign of the Wheel. Horskram absently followed suit, touching his forehead perfunctorily. But it was obvious to Adelko that his master's mind was awhirl with thoughts, not all of them pious.

'I am not convinced the demon was sent specifically to attack Staerkvit,' said the adept carefully. 'Rather I think it was summoned again – either by this sorcerer or another wizard – to renew its pursuit of us. Whoever wants us dead is evidently versed in Scrying, which we know to be the Fourth Discipline of Magick, and therefore capable of spying on us. But from what we've learned from captured warlocks in the past, it is an unwieldy tool that can often mislead a lesser practitioner. Let us be thankful for that much at least!'

Freidhoff nodded perfunctorily, looking about as interested in the finer points of sorcery as Horskram had in the finer points of chivalry just a moment ago.

'Go on,' he urged. 'What do you make of this then?'

'I think our sorcerous antagonist must have sent his or her unearthly servitor after us again when he or she learned we had survived Tintagael,' replied the adept. 'Such a demon will materialise within a certain radius of its intended target – from there it must rely on whatever unnatural senses the Fallen One has gifted it with to track down its prey. It nearly had us on the Wold, and again at Sördegil, and here last night – the more contact it has with us, the stronger its sense of our psychic spoor becomes, if you follow. But although as you have seen it is dreadfully strong, certain natural substances abjure it somewhat – it likes not stone, and wood seems to confound its senses to a degree.'

'So why attack the strongest castle in the realm?' asked Wolmar. It was the first time he had spoken in a while. His tone was as abrasive as ever. Adelko wished he had kept quiet.

'The Author of All Evil gave his diabolical creations a crafty deviousness in mockery of his own,' replied Horskram. 'Coming on us last night, yon horror must have sensed our presence and realised that the best way of goading us out into the open was to attack the garrison. It knew that two god-fearing monks of the Order would never cower behind walls whilst good men were being slaughtered without.'

Hearing this the High Commander pursed his lips and fixed his steely eyes on Horskram. 'So what you are saying, master monk, is that essentially you and your quest to save your precious Order from being publicly humiliated have brought this calamity on us?'

Now it was Horskram's turn to get steely. 'No, High Commander, what I am saying is that the reason why someone wants us dead is because they don't want word of the theft to spread – as I have just explained, Sacristen was never meant to breathe a word of it to anyone, for fear of the humiliation you speak of. And the reason they don't want the world to know is so they can continue their plans in secret. And if those plans amount to what I think they do it will spell calamity for all of us – the whole realm, aye and the wide world beyond!'

'You speak of secrecy, master monk, yet you yourself sought to shroud your own journey in it!' Wolmar interjected again. 'You're little better than this Sacristen you speak of – you'd rather save your Order from being purged again than alert the world to this terror you speak of!'

'Do not speak of the Purge!' exclaimed Horskram sharply, before collecting himself and adding in a calmer voice: 'I would not have the whole world know of this, 'tis true, but I would tell the right people, those who need to know!'

'Aye, and who would they be?' rejoined the High Commander suspiciously. Adelko began to have a sinking feeling that this might not go as well as he had hoped.

'You know yourself,' replied Horskram. 'The Grand Master of my Order must be told – given the theft took place on an Argolian holding it is his responsibility. The Arch Perfect at Strongholm I had not planned on telling, not before Hannequin anyway, but I see now that I have little choice in the matter if we're to have any chance of reaching the Grand Master in one piece. His High Holiness will certainly not part with what I must ask him to if he does not know the full reason behind my request.'

'And the King?' inquired the High Commander testily. 'The ruler of this realm, where this "Argolian holding" as you put it is situated, to whom you owe your allegiance as a loyal subject? Had you planned on telling him?'

There was a gleam in the prince's eye that only a foolish man would not have considered dangerous.

'Not initially,' admitted Horskram with a sigh. 'As I keep trying to tell you, my original plan was to get to Rima as quickly as possible, alert the Grand Master, and then confer with him as to what to do next. Hannequin is wise and influential – I imagine he will quietly inform the monarchs of all the Free Kingdoms and the most important barons in Vorstlund, not least the Jarl of Graukolos if we haven't told him already by then. The Supreme Perfect of the True Temple in Rima will also need to be informed, though it will pain Hannequin to do so.'

'I can't imagine why,' put in Sir Redrun with a sour sneer. 'His Supreme Holiness has been looking for an excuse to nullify the Argolian Order since... since the event you so dislike to hear mentioned.'

'I don't like hearing it mentioned with good reason,' returned the adept coldly. 'And now is not the time or place for debating Temple politics. As I was saying, my intention was never to keep His Majesty in the dark for ever, but you will appreciate the need for due caution. Heavens, we cannot have everyone knowing of this – we don't even know for sure who is behind it yet!'

The High Commander waved the others silent and sat in contemplation for a short time. Then he said: 'You are right to proceed with caution I think – as you say we do not know enough about the nature of the threat we face to let word spread. It seems to me that this strange and dreadful incident is connected to the traitor Thule and his sorcerous ally, though that too remains to be proven.'

He paused again before saying with an air of finality: 'Master Horskram, I will allow you to continue your journey – for one thing, if it is true that this winged devil is pursuing you then the sooner you are away from my men the better I shall like it. It is hard work enough putting down a treasonous rebellion without having one's best warriors decimated by hellspawn as well!'

'Given that consideration, I would be extremely reluctant to send you to the capital with a ravening demon on your trail, but I will defer to your superior knowledge of such matters and trust your assurances that the reliquary of the High Temple at Strongholm will preserve you from its depredations. If what you say is true then once through the Staerk Ranges you should be safe from it – for the time being anyway. But I will not have my brother, the rightful ruler of this realm, kept in the dark about an urgent matter that concerns his lands, whilst you and your priestly ilk confer, connive, and bicker.'

Horskram seemed about to protest but Freidhoff bellowed: 'Enough! Silence when a prince of the realm is addressing you!'

The adept reluctantly deferred and the High Commander continued: 'I shall send an escort with you to Strongholm, to ensure you stay out of further mischief – Tarlquist, you shall take Wolmar, Torgun and three other knights of your own choosing. See that our guests are escorted safely to the King's palace. I shall write a letter of introduction which you shall bear.'

Turning to Horskram again he continued: 'If His Majesty sees fit to grant you an audience with the Arch Perfect, you may pursue your claim with him then. As for the rest of your journey, that will be up to the King to decide. Now, I have considered your story and I appreciate your argument for secrecy – besides that I do not think it fitting that anyone else learns of this before our royal liege. As such, every knight in this room is to swear an oath not to breathe another word of what they have heard here to anyone, on pain of death, until such time as I or the King release them from that oath. Is that understood?'

The assembled knights nodded their assent. 'Very good,' resumed the High Commander. 'I am glad that is settled. Horskram, I will trust you to keep your two companions silent until His Majesty has been told of this. The rest of you shall swear your oaths here on the standard of the White Valravyn.'

He added: 'Master Horskram – if I could prevail upon you to bless my garrison before you set out, I would be much obliged. The White Valravyn is renowned for its courage and rightly so, but it is not in the habit of fighting devilspawn. The sooner the men put this behind them the better – we've a civil war to fight and frankly speaking an enemy we know how to kill will be more than welcome after this frightful encounter. For all our sakes I wish you Reus' speed on your journey. You will leave at noon.'

✦ ✦ ✦

At midday they were assembled in the courtyard. The intervening hours had not been ill spent and it had been cleared of the previous night's horrible slaughter. Just beyond the castle walls smoke still rose from the ashes of the pyre built for the dead horses; the common soldiers who had shared their fate were being laid to rest in plots dug by their erstwhile brothers in arms, whilst the corpses of the noble dead lay waiting below the keep for their relatives to send for them.

The Argolians' fervent prayers had worked a sacred magic of their own. By the time the sun was overhead and turning the castle walls a silvery white, most of the knights and soldiers had recovered their wits sufficiently to resume duties. The courtyard was thus the same hive of activity as it had been when they arrived at the castle as captives; now they were preparing to leave it as free men, with an honour guard of six of the best swords in the land. Adelko added a silent prayer that it would be enough.

As well as Wolmar and Torgun, Tarlquist had chosen the chequered twins Doric and Cirod and a handsome young knight called Sir Corram to accompany them. Their weapons had been returned to them, and the garrison had gifted Vaskrian with a small target shield and mail byrnie to replace his broken buckler and tattered brigandine. The storehouses had also been generous, and their dwindling provisions were now bolstered with salt beef and pork, bread, biscuit and dried fruits.

That pleased Adelko every bit as much as Vaskrian's new harness delighted him. Their horses had not been neglected either, and had plenty of oats for the rest of the journey.

At a clarion call from the sentinel on the gatehouse parapet the drawbridge was lowered. The sky was clear but for a few clouds, and though the breeze that ruffled the banners on the high walls was chilly it had a bracing quality to it. Passing out of Staerkvit they caught a glimpse of the long lake to either side of them; its glossy waters caught the noon sun with a sheen that justified its sensuous name.

Adelko had resigned himself to an afternoon of hard riding. Horskram and Tarlquist hoped to rejoin the king's highway and break clear of the ranges by sunset; by that time, the adept hoped, they would be close enough to the capital for the Redeemer's blood to protect them. As a denizen of the lower tiers of the City of Burning Brass, the demon was probably not strong enough to approach such a powerful relic without suffering unbearable agony... or so the old monk prayed.

Thinking on this, Adelko felt uneasy. Two demons he had encountered now in his young life, one a bare spirit in a mortal host and another in corporeal form. Neither was considered the deadliest subject of the Kingdom of Gehenna, yet one had proved dreadfully malicious and resilient, the other capable of troubling one of the strongest garrisons in the land – he did not care to think about what the more powerful servants of the Fallen One could do if summoned.

He recalled the words of Belaach in Rykken, the ones the spirit had spoken just after they drove it out of Gizel's body. Horskram had recited them for the knights that morning while giving a full account of their mission.

Hell's Prophet shall reawaken/the Five and Seven and One shall lead the hosts of Gehenna to victory

The Five and Seven and One. The first number referred to the tiers of hell: the first and foremost of which was occupied by Abaddon and his most powerful servants, fallen archangels who had sided with him in the battle for worlds at the Dawn of Time. The second number referred to the Seven Princes of Perfidy – foremost among these entities.

His lessons in counter-demonology at Ulfang came back to him, and he could picture Brother Rothrik teaching them in his soft voice: 'The Seven Princes of Perfidy represent emanations from the seven archangels of virtue, the Seven Seraphim. That is to say, they are at once essential to and distinct from the archangels they originally emanated from at Abaddon's behest. They represent the perversion of these virtues, and thus are a powerful embodiment of the Fallen One's efforts to corrupt and subvert all that is good.'

The mainstream Temple held that the Seven Princes had always been distinct from the seraphim they mocked; but the Argolians taught the more radical doctrine that they had originally been one with them. On the eve of the battle for worlds, Abaddon had sought to corrupt the Almighty's foremost servants, appealing to their darker impulses. The Seven Seraphim had resisted him, but only with great effort and at great cost: in suppressing their darker nature to resist his call they had been forced to divide their essence, casting out all that was selfish and wicked.

And thus the Seven Princes had been born, a dark mirror image of the Seven Seraphim.

'Thus Sha'amiel, avatar of greed and bigotry, is the dark emanation of Logos, archangel of prosperity and tolerance,' Rothrik had quavered. 'Azathol, avatar of vanity and hubris, is the emanation of Siona, archangel of grace and dignity.'

The ageing monk had gone on to list the other five: Zolthoth, avatar of wrath and dark emanation of the archangel Virtus, avatar of courage; Ta'ussaswazelim, who represented cruelty and had emanated from Stygnos, embodiment of fortitude; Chreosoaneuryon, avatar of gluttony and intemperance, the emanation of Euphrosakritos, archangel of merrymaking; Satyrus, avatar of lust and sexual depravity, set against Luviah, archangel of love; and Invidia, personifying envy, the twisted mirror image of Aeriti, archangel of aspiration.

The Seven Princes of Perfidy, led by Abaddon, the original Fallen Angel, who had made mortalkind cunning and clever, and in doing so poisoned the gift of free will bestowed on it by the Almighty in the beginning.

The One.

Abaddon would lead the hordes of Gehenna back into the world he had failed to seize aeons ago, if Belaach's twisted prophecy proved true.

And from everything he'd heard his mentor say about the Headstone, it had the power to summon just such a host if reunited... small wonder the Almighty had seen fit to lay waste to the world He had created, rather than allow it to suffer such an invasion at Mammon's behest.

What would He choose to do if confronted by that possibility a second time? The Temple and Argolians both taught that Reus was omniscient – but in that case, had He always known such an event was destined to come to pass again? And if so, was this all just a test of His creation's wits and moral character? In that case, how important a part would they play in the tumultuous events to come?

As they set off through the Staerk ranges, Adelko made the sign. Just what doom had he unwittingly embraced in Malgar's hut, a seeming lifetime ago, when Horskram had placed the book on the table in front of him and asked him to choose his fate?

Questions. Always so many questions.

✣ ✣ ✣

They retraced their steps back towards the highway, galloping through the afternoon with scarcely a pause except to water their horses and snatch a morsel of food.

Adelko's feelings of unease deepened into trepidation. Though the sun was still shining and by now the temperature was quite warm he felt chilly – his encounter with the demon had not left him unscathed. In his unnerved state he couldn't even tell if it was his sixth sense troubling him, or just the aftershock.

He glanced around to see if his companions appeared similarly troubled. Vaskrian was riding beside him, singing another battle tune, revelling in his shiny new harness. Like Adelko he had only managed to snatch a few hours of troubled sleep, but nothing ever seemed to dampen his spirits for long. Just before them Wolmar and Corram rode together, with Horskram and Tarlquist in front while Torgun rode up ahead alone and the chequered twins brought up the rear.

None of them seemed overly troubled – but then they were all moving quickly and it was hard to tell what everyone was really thinking. Adelko had little choice but to keep his anxieties to himself – perhaps he would seek his mentor's counsel when they paused at the highway.

They were just navigating a steep stretch of hill road, dipping down through a valley crested on either side by trees before rising sharply again, when the novice's fears were realised.

From the trees came an all too familiar *twanging* sound. Quarrels strafed them from left and right. Corram fell screaming, a bolt sprouting from his neck – a split second later Adelko felt a stab of pain across his forehead and something sticky run into his eyes. With a cry he toppled backwards off his horse... a clump of bushes broke his fall and saved him from further serious injury, though several branches tore through his habit and gashed his flesh. Overcome by pain, he fainted.

✣ ✣ ✣

Vaskrian felt a quarrel whistle past his ear and wasted no time in drawing his sword, wheeling his mount around to face the attack. He could see them up between the trees to his right, around half a dozen Northlanders reloading crossbows.

With a great war-cry he spurred his horse up the rocky slope towards them. He was joined by Sir Wolmar, who had a bolt dangling from his mailed shoulder – his fine armour had absorbed the brunt of the impact, although not enough to prevent it drawing blood.

The bolt intended for Horskram had missed him but slashed his horse across the back of the neck. The terrified steed reared screaming and it was all the hardy old monk could do to stay in the saddle. Torgun was already charging up the left bank, his sword drawn and a quarrel protruding from his shield. Tarlquist had been hit in the thigh – gritting his teeth he ignored the pain and joined Torgun on the counter attack. The chequered twins spurred their horses together up the right bank to join Vaskrian and Wolmar.

As the squire reached the top of the rocky bank he could see their assailants clearly. They were the same brigands who had attacked them in the clearing by Lake Sördegil, still relying on the same cowardly weapons and the element of surprise. All were mounted.

Only two of them had managed to reload by the time they reached them. One fired at Vaskrian's face but the squire's quick anticipation saved his life: bringing up his target he caught the quarrel, which glanced off the iron rim of his shield with a whining ring.

In a flash he was on the brigand, bringing his sword down onto his head in a curling arc before he could reach for his axe. The blade sheared through the barbarian's skull, cleaving it in twain right down to the nose bone. He felt a surge of joy as a fountain of blood erupted from the brigand's head. His sword was sharper than ever, and he hadn't even had the chance to run a whetstone across it in the past few days. He could thank the Fays for that.

Yanking the blade free he turned to see Wolmar already on to a second opponent, hacking at him with a blistering savagery. The Northlander had barely had time to draw a crude-looking broadsword and unsling his shield as the knight cut down his comrade, who now lay on the ground groaning pitifully as he tried to stop his entrails spilling from a great gash in his belly just below his byrnie. He would have little joy there – his hand was missing three fingers and his other arm was twisted beneath his torso at an odd angle, broken in the fall from his horse.

The twin knights were fighting on horseback with the last two Northlanders and also looked to have the upper hand, driving them back into the trees with fell strokes that seemed perfectly choreographed.

Wheeling his neighing steed around Vaskrian stared across the narrow valley. Tarlquist and Torgun were outnumbered five to two on the other side, but that didn't seem to bother them – with a mighty sweep of his sword the greatest knight in Northalde beheaded one Northlander whilst effortlessly parrying a second attack with his kite.

Vaskrian recognised the other attacker – it was the one-eyed brute he'd fought at Sördegil. The hulking Northlander squared off against Sir Torgun now, the pair of them rashing together as their horses reared and bit viciously at one another.

The barbarian was a mountain of a man, but Torgun's strength and speed were astonishing: within a few swift exchanges he had slain his opponent, parrying a crude blow before disengaging his blade in a riposte that transfixed the Northlander's throat before he had time to realise he was dead. His single eye rolled up into his head as he slumped off his horse, choking on his own blood.

That was the only chance Vaskrian had to admire his hero's swordsmanship as the remaining three brigands caught his eye. Two including the red-haired leader were charging down towards the monks whilst the third fought with Tarlquist. Adelko was only just regaining consciousness, blood pouring from a cut in his forehead where a quarrel had grazed it. Horskram had been forced to dismount from his horse, which was still rearing in agony. Vaskrian supposed there was a limit to what faerie magic could do.

The two monks looked to be fodder – the squire didn't fancy even the hardy adept's chances against two mounted foes on foot and armed with naught but a quarterstaff.

'Master Horskram, look out!' he cried, spurring his horse down towards the trail to meet the brigand charging Adelko. Alerted, the adept let go of the reins of his horse and turned to face his oncoming barbarian, pulling his staff free from its sheath.

The red-haired brigand was nearly on him now, whooping and swinging his war axe in a dreadful arc above his head. Bearing down on Horskram full tilt, he raised the weapon to strike as the monk crouched in the road, both hands gripping his quarterstaff...

At the last moment Horskram sprang agilely to one side, ducking under the sweeping blade. As the brigand's horse galloped past, the monk whirled and struck its hind leg with all his might. The iron-shod pole snapped it like a twig. With a scream it buckled, bringing down its rider with it. The brigand was not so lucky as Adelko, and falling into the rocky trail with an agonising *crunch* he could do nothing but lie prone as Horskram leapt over him and struck him full in the face, shattering his front teeth. The red-haired warrior writhed in agony, dropping his axe and clutching his bloody mouth as Horskram mouthed a few quick words of repentance for his violent but necessary act.

Vaskrian reached the other brigand in the nick of time, once again saving Adelko from almost certain death by brigandage.

'That's at least two lives you owe me!' he yelled as the two of them fought fiercely, trading strokes. But the brigand had one advantage he lacked. Whatever wonders Fay magic had worked on their horses, it had not made Yorro more vicious. A seasoned courser though he was, trained and accustomed to war, he could not hope to match the Northlander's great black brute of a charger. Lashing out with iron-shod hooves, it forced Yorro to retreat, pulling Vaskrian back on to the defensive. The brigand was about to press his advantage – but at that moment Sir Torgun rode down into the road, his bloodied sword held high.

'Turn and face me, Northland savage!' the young knight cried. Even now he was chivalrous – Vaskrian had to admire him for that. The brigand wheeled his horse around to oblige him.

If a man is going to oblige the best knight in the realm, he had best be fighting for love, or else a mighty warrior himself. The brigand was neither. A lightning strike to his shield arm broke both, and Torgun's second blow was so hard it shattered his sword into fragments before shearing through his byrnie, collar-bone and sternum. A great gout of blood erupted from the Northlander as the knight wrenched his blade free. The brigand's mangled frame slumped off his horse like a sack of offal.

And suddenly it was all over. Looking around him Vaskrian saw another brigand lay dying at the tree-lined top of the slope above, blood pouring from his guts where Tarlquist's sword had pierced him; the twin knights and Wolmar had made corpses of their opponents too, one groaning pitifully from a mortal wound until the High Commander's son drew his dagger and despatched him.

The only survivors were Tarlquist's foeman, whom they dragged down into the road, and the red-haired leader. The former died before they could question him, bleeding his life away as they were tending to Adelko, Wolmar and Tarlquist and saying a prayer for poor Corram.

Snarling fiercely and swearing revenge Wolmar yanked the red-haired brigand up by his braided beard, brandishing his blood-stained dagger.

Torgun grabbed his wrist firmly before he could strike. 'No Wolmar!' he exclaimed. 'Do not sully yourself! He is a vanquished foe!'

Wolmar sneered and was about to reply when Tarlquist interjected with a more pragmatic argument for sparing the leader's life. 'Do as he says and let him live, Wolmar,' he said. 'We need to question him. Put him over against yonder rock.'

The raven knights had already disarmed and bound the brigand. Now they complied with their leader's request. The red-haired Northlander was grievously injured but not mortally so. His mouth was a bloody ruin where his front teeth had been and the fall appeared to have broken his back, but he would live – for as long as they needed him to at any rate.

⁙ ⁙ ⁙

Horskram led the questioning, speaking in the Low Norric tongue. Adelko had studied enough of it at the monastery to be able to follow the interrogation. He'd had trouble understanding the Northlanders when they yelled commands at one another, but his mentor spoke slowly and deliberately.

'You have pursued us since Kaupstad,' he said in a flat voice that betrayed no emotion. 'Why this relentless attempt on our lives? Who sent you and why?'

The brigand gazed upwards and grinned through the bloody stumps of his teeth. His face looked like a ghastly death's head. He appeared to be staring at something else, though his blue eyes were fixed on nothing Adelko could see.

A drool of blood and saliva ran down his chin and into his beard as he turned his eyes on Horskram and replied: 'Blue eye... sees everything, yes, everything...'

'Blue eye? What is this you babble of? No riddles, man – speak clearly and these men can ease your passing!'

'The priest tricked us... gave us jewels, said go kill monks, one young, one old, travelling on the south road...'

'What priest? Where did you meet him?'

The warrior was struggling to speak now, his harsh voice becoming more strained.

'C-Cravern, Port Cravern... where our ship landed... the tall priest met us at the docks, he was from our land, spoke our tongue... *ack*... said he'd give us more when we were done... *ack*... cursed, they were *cursed*...'

The red-haired mercenary was twitching spasmodically now. The knights and Vaskrian, unable to follow the exchange, were looking at each other in perplexity. Horskram pressed on with his questions, his face growing more intense.

'What was cursed?' he demanded.

'The jewelled necklaces he gave us,' gasped the brigand. '*Cursed*... oh Lord of Oceans, help me...'

A torrent of blood suddenly washed down over the neckline of his mail shirt. Wrenching the byrnie downwards Horskram gasped – about his neck a chain of silver, previously concealed by the shirt, was contracting with an unnatural will of its own, tearing through skin and choking the life from its wearer. At the end of it a pearl-shaped gemstone pulsed with a blue light tinged with a sea-green radiance.

'It's killing him!' cried the monk. 'Quickly, a dagger to cut it free!'

But it was too late. The enchanted necklace finished its evil work, contracting horribly about its victim's neck with an agonisingly drawn out crunching sound. The red-haired killer writhed and twitched violently, his upper body twisting and turning as his face turned blue, then black.

As he quivered his last Adelko saw that the gem had gone through the same change of colour. Before his eyes the strange jewel sloughed and steamed, dissolving into an ugly puddle of tarry ichor that mingled nastily with the dead man's blood.

Horskram stepped back with a shudder and made the sign. In a shaken voice he muttered a quick prayer.

At his behest they searched the rest of the Northland mercenaries – besides a quantity of gold and silver they found a silver necklace around the necks of every one. On the end of each chain steamed a tarry black gobbet of foul-smelling ichor.

'A Northland priest hoodwinks reavers from his land into trying to kill you,' said Tarlquist after Horskram had translated the interrogation for him. 'It seems as though Thule's rebellion and your own troubles are linked after all.'

'As I keep saying, they will be more than just our troubles if what I think is afoot is allowed to come to pass,' replied Horskram, frowning. 'But as for what you say, it certainly seems as though this Sea Wizard was behind these killers – indeed only a powerful enchantment could have induced such men to pursue us so deep into the heart of the realm, for the mere promise of gold would not likely have compelled them to undertake so dangerous a mission. Were it not for the smokescreen afforded by civil war I doubt they would have got this far.'

Yet still he continued to frown, as though unsatisfied.

'Something troubles you, Master Horskram?' pressed Sir Tarlquist.

'Nay... 'tis no matter,' replied Horskram, shaking his head. 'I am quite confident that yon cursed jewels were the "blue eye" the leader spoke of before he died – I have heard tell of warlocks who use such devices to communicate with their servants across great distances, and to keep control of them as well. Such glamours work a powerful charm on the greedy and the foolish – doubtless these Northland brigands would have been quick to accept such spoil when they met this priest at Port Cravern. Merchant ships carrying goods from the Northland Wastes and the Empire often employ their kind as bodyguards – to ward against their very kindred who ply the Sea of Valhalla as pirates, as often as not.'

'The Northland reavers have ever been the curse of the northern seas,' said Tarlquist ruefully.

'Our ancestors were Northland reavers – it was such who founded this kingdom,' Horskram reminded him. 'But enough of this – we have survived another foe and have a better idea of who we're up against, though to my mind many questions remain unanswered.'

✤ ✤ ✤

No more was said, and they busied themselves with the aftermath of battle. The horse whose leg had been broken by Horskram was still whinnying pitifully until Vaskrian reluctantly put him out of his misery – good vicious warhorses were prized by knight and squire alike.

The rest were theirs for the taking. The rules of the Order dictated that a portion of all spoils be donated to the White Valravyn, but even so there would be enough to make it a good day's work, all the more so given the contents of the horses' saddle bags.

'It was definitely them who looted the bodies of the merchants and their bodyguards back at Sördegil,' said Vaskrian, his eyes shining nearly as brightly as the plate, coin and semi-precious stones they had just found. There were also bolts of silks and other valuable cloths in the bags. 'I've never seen so much treasure! This beats melee prize money at a tournament any day!'

'You'll still only get a squire's share, so don't get too excited,' Tarlquist reminded him gruffly. 'But you fought well, so you won't go away empty-handed,' he added, clapping Vaskrian on the shoulder when he saw his face fall.

The silver necklaces they threw on a fire at Horskram's insistence – such items were cursed and should not be kept or left for others to find. His steed was thankfully not grievously harmed; like Adelko, Wolmar and Tarlquist it would recover in time from its injuries.

The same could not be said for Sir Corram. They wrapped his body in his chequered cloak and lashed it to his horse.

'We'll take him to the next village and have a yeoman deliver his remains back to Staerkvit to await proper burial,' said Tarlquist, shaking his head sadly. 'This is bad, very bad – the best knights in the land dropping like flies, and we haven't even engaged the enemy yet!'

'We just did engage the enemy, if our surmise is correct,' Horskram said darkly.

The corpses of the Northlanders they left for the worms and crows. They divested them of their mail shirts, which were of decent quality, and piled these alongside their shields and weapons.

'Someone from the Order should be along presently,' said Tarlquist. 'They'll know what to do with these – doubtless the levies and other conscripts may find a use for them. Every bit helps when there's a war on.'

With that they were off again, Cirod leading Corram's horse as he had done Vaskrian's on the journey to the castle. The squire was glad to have avoided the young knight's fate – Corram could not have been more than a few summers older than he was, and Torgun especially was clearly much grieved by his companion's unchivalrous death.

'Corram was a good knight,' he said dolefully as they remounted. 'He deserved better than to die by such an ungodly and cowardly weapon!'

'At least his soul won't seek the Heavenly Halls unavenged,' put in Wolmar grimly. It was first thing the princeling had said that Vaskrian could warm to.

✣ ✣ ✣

The afternoon shadows were lengthening by the time they reached the highway again. It was bustling with traffic, and they overtook a motley of knights, soldiers, mercenaries and craftsmen making their way towards the King's muster.

The number of refugees had increased. During their enforced stay at the castle, word had reached it that Thule's men were ravaging the southern reaches unchecked, having taken Rookhammer, the last castle before Linden, after a week-long siege. The Young Pretender had slaughtered the entire garrison, mounting the heads of the castellan and his family on spikes as a warning to the defenders at Linden. Loyalist forces who had managed to avoid capture were now gathering there under Prince Wolfram's banner, in anticipation of the coming assault. No quarter would be asked or given.

To the left and right stretched rich arable lands dotted with sturdy farmsteads and lush orchards; the heartlands of the King's Dominions, as yet untouched by war, enjoyed a prosperity that left its stout yeomanry well fed and industrious.

Even so, with his heightened intuition Adelko could see in his mind's eye a brooding shadow of war, dark clouds edging the clear firmament with promises of storm and thunder. And though his bandaged head stung and they now rode at a breakneck pace, the peasant militias training in the fields with pitchfork and wood-axe were not lost on him.

✢ ✢ ✢

As the sun was setting they reached a prosperous-looking village. Sir Tarlquist spoke with the headman and explained their need in terms that were courteous but brooked no argument from a commoner. The headman, a plump tremulous fellow, barely had time to nod and stammer his compliance before Tarlquist was barking an order to his men to be off again, leaving the dead knight and his steed in their wake.

It was dark when they arrived at Sir Albrik's manor, a couple of leagues from the village. Its lord was away – he had obeyed the King's summons and ridden off to the muster at Strongholm in full panoply of war several days ago. It was left to his wife Lady Selma, a timid young thing, to show them hospitality.

Her name reminded Adelko of Silma, the girl his eldest brother Arik had courted and probably married by now. That put him in mind of the home he had left so long ago, and a pang of homesickness suddenly washed over him. He felt then a profound longing – for the life he had deserted, one he would now never know. A simple existence of hardship and reward, love and bereavement, family and familiarity.

As he sat around the table in the hall eating and drinking by candlelight with knights, squires and ladies, he felt the pang subside – this was after all everything he had dreamed of doing in his remote childhood.

The white ravens were in high spirits after their victory over the Northlanders and the unexpected booty, and their ebullience carried over into optimism for the coming war – a chance to uphold the King's justice and cover themselves in glory. Vaskrian was all agog as Sir Torgun condescended to talk to him during the meal, taking time to praise his swordsmanship and advise him on one or two areas of improvement. Even Horskram seemed unusually light-hearted, perhaps buoyed by their recent triumphs and the knowledge that they would at least be safe for a while from the dreadful demon.

And so Adelko joined in the fun, embracing a welcome respite from danger and gladly accepting the serving girls' offers of more food and ale as he listened to the knights' stories of battles and victory and hardships overcome.

They continued thus until the Wytching Hour, when Horskram intoned a blessing on the house before the guests sought the pallets laid down for them in the hall by Lady Selma's servants.

But warmed by drink as he was, Adelko found his thoughts returning once more to Narvik as he drifted off to sleep. One by one his loved ones appeared before him: his father Arun, his brothers Arik and Malrok, his Aunt Madrice. But their faces appeared unclear to him in his dreams, and when he awoke next morning he struggled to remember what they looked like.

⚡ CHAPTER XIII ⚡

Salt In The Wounds

They were two days out of Caldeshavn when they spotted the longship. At first no more than a dark scratch on the blue horizon, the tell-tale square sail and sharp prow coalesced into view, along with the bristling oars propelling it towards the *Jolly Runner*.

Reaching into a large leather pouch at his belt, Captain Conway produced a curious-looking item. Fashioned of brass, it was cylindrical in shape. Tugging firmly on it he nearly doubled its length before putting it to his eye, squinting into it.

'Aye, Northland Reavers, sure enough,' he said, showing less fear than he ought to. 'A good forty of them, I'd say. Hungry for our spoil, heh heh!'

Pushing the brass cylinder back to its original size he turned to Braxus. 'Freesail buccaneers, they must've got wind o' Freidheim's war – takin' advantage of the distraction to prey on merchant shipping. Cullem! Bring her round – we'll tack into the north-easterly wind and see if we can't outrun her first. Take us out of our way a bit, but then so will a skirmish on the high seas! And if we can't outrun her, well...' He fingered the hilt of his cutlass. 'We'll just have to give 'em that skirmish!'

Conway grinned crookedly. He was the only sailor on board that did not look perturbed.

Braxus turned to Vertrix and barked an order of his own. 'Fetch Regan and Bryant,' he said. 'And get the squires up here too – all fully armed. Don't bother with armour, there's no time. We'll need every sword-arm on deck if that lot catch up with us.'

Vertrix nodded and strode off towards the hatch leading below decks, his dirty-grey hair streaking behind him in the wind.

Turning back to face the captain Braxus looked at him quizzically. 'Forty? You're sure? How can you tell at this distance?'

Conway favoured him with another grin. 'This here's a looking glass,' he beamed, holding up the brass cylinder. 'Won it off a sea captain of an Imperial dromon in Port Cravern two years ago. It'd be his head if the

authorities over there ever found out he'd gambled away such a precious
thing, for they guard their secrets carefully! But then old Sagitus always
was a fool for the dice! Here, take a look for yourself!'

The captain proffered the cylinder as the crew brought the cog
round hard to take the wind full in its sails. It was blowing up a
fair gust today, but even so Braxus doubted it would be enough to
outrun a swift longship manned by forty strong Northlanders.

But for a moment their impending danger was forgotten as he
fumbled with the strange article.

'Aye, that's it,' said the captain as he clumsily extended it, keeping
one eye on the looking glass and the other on the approaching longship.
'Now just put it to your eye, no the other end – that's it...'

Holding up the looking glass and pointing it out to sea in the direction
of the longship, Braxus got the shock of his life. Where before a growing
but still distant outline had been, now a vessel loomed before him,
crammed with hardened Northlanders dressed in studded leather jerkins,
with axes and swords on their backs. He was so stunned he almost let go
of the looking glass.

'Watch it!' bellowed the captain. 'I could sell that for a hundred
gold regums in Meerborg, if I had a mind to! You drop it, I'll throw you
overboard after it!'

Braxus turned from the looking glass to favour the captain with
an icy stare. Here on the high seas, where his ship was his realm,
the commoner had forgotten himself.

Realising the same thing, Conway faltered. 'Begging your
pardon, sir knight, I – I meant no offence... just that that glass is
very precious to me, is all. Hard to come by, you see...'

Pursing his lips, Braxus let the slight pass and turned back to look in
the glass again. There was no honour to be had in chastising a common
sailor after all. And by the looks of things they would soon be needing
every able man on deck. The glass was a strange and miraculous device,
typical of the sophisticated Empire, but it seemed to be telling a plain
enough message. Forty reavers. The captain had been right.

'How do you propose to fight them if they do catch us?' he asked
bluntly, handing Conway's precious looking glass back to him. 'I've
got seven good fighters with me, and you and your mate look as if
you've seen some action in your time, but...'

'Them?' laughed the captain throatily, nodding towards the
scampering crew as they scuttled up the rigging and ran to and fro across
the deck. 'Don't you worry, sir knight – they may seem a timorous bunch,
but they've seen their fair share o' bloodshed too! We fought to a man in

the War o' the Cobian Succession – why d'ye think I take no mercenary
guards on these jaunts? We're more than capable o' defendin' ourselves
– though it's bad luck alright to have reavers on our tail. Aye, very bad
luck indeed!'

The captain turned back to bark more orders at his crew. As if
that would make the wind blow more swiftly.

Squinting out to sea at the longship with unaided eyes, Braxus
chewed thoughtfully on the captain's words. The War of the Cobian
Succession. That had been fought just over five years ago, when the Free
Ward of Cobia on Thraxia's southern border had had a succession crisis.
That had prompted King Cullodyn to step in and claim it for himself,
and satisfy a long-cherished Thraxian ambition to annex the horn of
land that had steadfastly refused to join the kingdom for generations.

The war had mostly been fought at sea. It had lasted nine months and
ended in a disastrous and humiliating defeat for the Thraxian navy. This
did not bode well.

Braxus sized up the crew while he waited for Vertrix to return
with the others. Like most cogs the *Runner* had a standard crew of
thirty – ten less than the Northland longship. One advantage of
rowing instead of sailing was that you needed more crew to take to
the seas in the first place. Very handy if it came to a fight.

But the problem wasn't just one of numbers. The crew of the *Runner*
did look a likely enough bunch, their sinewed bodies hardened by a
tough life on rough seas. But Northland reavers were something else,
berserker bloodthirsty and strong as oxen. The Treaty of Ryøskil, signed
three generations ago after Thorsvald the Hero King of Northalde
defeated the last alliance of Northland sea princes, had kept the
Northlanders mostly quiescent, but that didn't stop the odd privateer
turning freesail to try his chances.

The captain had summed it up nicely. It was bad luck for them,
very bad luck indeed.

Vertrix emerged with Regan and Bryant. They had partially disobeyed
his orders, pulling on mail byrnies, but that was to be expected. Behind them
came their squires, including Paidlin. The poor lad had just about found
his sea legs at long last – now he would have to find his battle courage too.
A distant cousin, he was fourteen summers, the youngest of their party.
Braxus bit his lip momentarily as he caught him trying to look brave and
hardy, even though it was obviously not the raw wind making him tremble.

Vertrix handed Braxus a target shield to complement his sword. He
normally used a heavier kite when on horseback, but this made more
sense under the circumstances. Good job the grizzled old knight had

insisted on bringing extra arms. All Braxus had been thinking about when they were preparing to leave was how many instruments he could fit in the hold.

'All right boys,' he said evenly as the other seven gathered around him, faces set grim and weapons ready. 'The good captain here is going to try and outrun yon reavers – give them a merry chase and tire those brawny arms of theirs at the least. But it doesn't take a seasoned sailor to see that we're not likely to outrun a well-manned Northland longship on a day like this, gusty as it is. So it's a fight we're looking at most like, and I don't plan on losing a single one of us before we get to Strongholm!'

He couldn't help but catch Paidlin's eye as he said this. The poor lad was plainly terrified. He had never been in a real fight, let alone killed a man. Out on the sea with a deck heaving beneath his feet was not a good place to start learning.

'Not a single one of you,' he repeated, as if to reassure himself. 'Now, most like they've reckoned on piecemeal crew resistance – and our trying to run will only convince them of that. They won't be expecting a bunch of Cobian War veterans and eight trained swords from Dréuth. So we've a small advantage of surprise – when they pull up alongside us, wait for them to board, then hit them hard, and hit them fast. Don't ask any quarter or give it – we're not tilting at fellow knights on the plain now, these berserkers are barbarian scum no better than Slánga's lot. They'll gut you without thinking twice about it if you give them half a chance.'

Catching Paidlin's eye again he nodded curtly at him. 'Never fear lad, this is what you've been training for every day except Rest-days since you had ten summers,' he said, doing his best to sound confident. 'Just stick by my side and remember everything I've taught you these past six months, and you'll make out just fine.'

Paidlin smiled then. A fresh, naive smile it was, full of hope and courage found unexpectedly in fearful times. The only kind of courage there was, come to think of it. Bravery came all too easily in sight of hearth and home.

'Alright,' he continued, sweeping his eyes across the rest of them one last time. 'Take up positions – we flank the port side. If there's any fighting, I mean to see that we're first in! Looks like they've no bows of any sort, but have your shields up and ready just in case.'

The last words were meant for the less experienced squires rather than Vertrix and the other knights, plainly already relishing the latest chance to test their mettle and add some more glory to their names. And they certainly were not meant for Gormly. Squire or no, he was arguably the best fighter of them all besides his master Vertrix and maybe Braxus. He had served as a serjeant in Braun's garrison for more than twenty summers before unexpectedly seeking knightly service. Couldn't ride worth a penny, and didn't carve meat too well, but in every other respect he was a perfect second for any knight.

Across the deck Captain Conway had evidently been giving his crew similar instructions and encouragement. Some of the men still looked afraid, but that didn't stop them arming themselves with a motley array of weapons as they took up their own positions – hand axes, short swords, the odd cutlass like the captain and his mate, plenty of dirks and one or two iron-shod cudgels.

Crude weapons, and Braxus wasn't sure they would last long against a Northland war-axe. But then each man to his own. If this lot had managed to survive one of the worst-led naval conflicts in the Silver Age, they had to be made of some fairly stern stuff.

✵ ✵ ✵

Gradually the *Jolly Runner* slowed as the crew forsook the sails to fight. The longship was by now plainly in view, looking glass or no: its single sail sported a stylised black carrion crow feasting on a ship broken in twain. The standard flag used by Northland pirates, it was mainly intended to intimidate victims into immediate surrender. But from what Braxus knew of reavers, they preferred to whet their appetites for spoil with a good fight first. Clutching his castle-forged blade, he grimly hoped that today they would get more of that than they bargained for.

As the longship drew up alongside the *Runner* one of its crew stood up in the stern. Clearly the leader, he sported a tarnished mail byrnie gilded with what looked like silver. Plunder from a rich cargo, probably. He wore a close-fitting helm fashioned in the style of the Northlanders (no horns – why tapestry weavers and bards insisted on portraying reavers with horned helmets Braxus could never fathom, a ridiculous notion with no basis in reality). A broad round shield was slung across his left arm; in his right he clutched an ugly-looking broadsword. He was a head taller than Braxus, and built like a warhorse.

That'll be my opponent – a good knight never shies away from a challenge, Braxus thought ruefully to himself as the reaver barked a guttural command in thickly accented Northlending: 'You haf one chance to surrender. You are slaves, or you are dead – you choose.'

Simple but effective, Braxus supposed. The captain understood enough of the Northlending tongue to get the gist too.

'And ye've one chance to turn around and go back to whatever frozen hole spawned ye,' he replied, brandishing his cutlass in a way that looked more comical than threatening. 'I've four knights of Thraxia and thirty war veterans on board, so don't think ye'll find us easy fodder!'

Glancing sidelong at Braxus as he quickly translated, Regan rolled his eyes. 'Well there goes our element of surprise,' he observed drily.

'Yes, I'd so been looking forward to taking advantage of that,' put in Bryant, drier still.

The reavers' captain laughed, a barking sound that seemed to scrape at the tangy air between them.

'Oh, goot, goot,' he bellowed in between chuckles. 'Ve like it ven der little men from mainland make us sport ja?' He bellowed again, this time in Norric, and his men strained at the oars again, expertly closing the remaining gap between ships and bringing theirs alongside the *Runner*.

Raising his sword and shield, Braxus tensed as he took up a fighting stance. The parley was over. Battle was nigh.

With blood-curdling war whoops the reavers forsook oars for blades as they launched themselves towards the deck of the *Runner*. The longship was a war-worthy craft, its freeboard nearly as high as the cog's, but even so those aboard the *Runner* had a slender height advantage.

Braxus took the first reaver in the guts as he leapt across the rail at him, his axe biting heavily into his shield. His cry of battle-rage turned to one of agony as he slumped to the deck. Even then he was not done, and picking himself up with another strangled scream he hurled his burly frame at the knight, the mindless assault of a dying man. Braxus darted nimbly back before closing in again lightning quick, driving the point of his sword through the reaver's unprotected throat.

He had no time to savour his opponent's gurgling death throes. Another reaver came at him hard on the heels of the first. For a while they fought ferociously, trading blows and blocks with sword and shield. Braxus felt the deck lurch beneath him several times; the gusty weather was bad enough on its own and the crowding of men on the port side didn't help.

The seasoned reaver was used to it. Braxus was not. The ship lurched again just as he was thrusting his sword at a gap in his foe's defences. It caught him off-balance and forced him onto one knee. The reaver leered at him as he brought his sword down towards his head. Flinging up his shield he caught the blow. Dropping his sword and unsheathing the dirk at his boot in one fluid motion, Braxus brought it down hard on the reaver's unarmoured foot, pinning it to the deck. The reaver screamed in pain as, lurching upwards, Braxus barged him with his shield, forcing him to fall backwards, his pinned foot twisting agonisingly against the cold unyielding metal. Reaching down he swiftly snatched up his sword and hacked savagely at the reaver's neck, just below the helm. A fountain of blood erupted from the wound as the Northlander slumped awkwardly to the deck, which lurched again, pulling the dirk free of the boards.

Not the most chivalrous way of despatching an opponent – but then you could hardly be expected to play by the rules fighting at sea with a rolling deck beneath your feet.

Braxus took advantage of the brief respite to take in how the others were faring. As he had feared, the sailors were getting the worst of it. Most of the reavers had fought their way onto the deck of the *Runner* by now, and the melee was spreading towards the middle of the ship. Ten of Conway's men lay dead or dying, the others were hard pressed. Vertrix had slain one reaver – no, make that two: his second man turned a red pirouette of spurting blood before collapsing to the gore-spattered boards in a twitching heap. Regan and Bryant were fighting back to back, a sensible move seeing as they were outnumbered two to one.

Their squires had followed suit – but then Conric and Heiran were fairly seasoned fighters by now, just a year or two away from knighthood. Gormly had already killed two reavers, butchering them like slabs of meat with the great two-handed axe he liked to use. He was pressing another one hard as he fought stolidly by his master's side, his face never changing expression.

But where was Paidlin? A scream of agony soon answered that question. Turning around he saw the young lad hit the deck, a great gout of blood welling up from his thigh. A grinning reaver stood above him, scarlet axe raised to deliver the death-blow as the youth writhed on the deck.

With a roar Braxus charged the reaver, hurtling into him, his shield bludgeoning aside the blow meant for his squire. A red mist came over him then – afterwards he remembered only a flurry of grey blurs as his sword went up and down, left and right. And then he was standing over the mangled corpse of another reaver, his breath coming hard in ragged gasps.

Just went to show Thraxians could do berserker rage too, when called for.

Paidlin was moaning pitifully, squirming about and clutching at his spurting leg, which looked to have been half severed. But Braxus had no time to tend to him. Regan and Bryant had evened up the odds, bringing two more buccaneers low, and Vertrix and Gormly were stepping over fresh corpses to help Conric and Heiran.

But the wider skirmish was being lost.

More than half of Conway's men were down. The doughty captain was backed up against the mast, doing his best to fend off the cruel strokes of the chief buccaneer. Tough as he was, it didn't look like a fight he could win by himself.

He would get precious little aid from his men. Some fifteen reavers were dead or on the way to being, but that still left twenty five. To his right the mate Cullen was struggling against three attackers. One of them had blood pouring from a deep cut in his head and clearly wouldn't last long, but even so his chances didn't look good either. On top of that Cullen was injured too – his bloodied left arm hung limply at his side.

The rest of the crew were just about holding their own – for now. That gave Braxus a chance to save either the mate or the captain.

He should save Conway. He ranked the highest, and if they could bring down the reaver's leader it might just turn the tide. It made sense.

Then Conway's drunken boastfulness flashed through his mind, along with Cullen's long-suffering eye-rolling...

Roaring another battle cry Braxus trampled over corpses and thrust his sword deep into the side of one of the reavers pressing Cullen. The mate had just enough time to spare him a grateful glance as the wounded reaver turned on Braxus with a snarl. Braxus went back on the defensive, letting him come. He'd lost a lot of blood, half of it seeping into his eyes, and the lunge was wild and unsteady – as he had known it would be. Sidestepping, Braxus cut downwards in a vicious swipe that took the reaver's sword-arm off at the wrist. He expired in a fainting heap.

Cullen found renewed energy. Pressing his reaver hard he caught him a tidy thrust in the midriff. It was a street fighter's move, a canny move and a lethal one. The reaver slumped to his knees making an odd belching sound as he dropped his axe and clutched at the cutlass stuck in his guts. Braxus took his head off his shoulders.

'Don't worry,' he said, flashing the goggle-eyed mate a grin as blood showered both of them. 'That one still counts as yours.'

A flicker of motion to his left. He turned just in time to parry the first blow, and the next. The captain of the reavers was on him, lashing frenziedly at him with a sword slick with Conway's blood and brains. Braxus took a couple of steps back, tripped on a corpse and fell flat on his back.

He remembered then what Vertrix had told him once, more than ten summers ago when he still squired for him. *No matter what befalls you on the battlefield, never lose your composure. There's always a way to turn a bad situation around. Don't die till you're dead!*

Braxus had no intention of dying, not by a reaver's hand anyway.

The barbarian captain straddled him, raising his sword high. Desperately Braxus made as if to lunge at his midriff with his sword. The captain brought his shield in to ward off the coming blow...

And screamed as Braxus kicked him hard in the groin.

The shock was enough to put his swing off, and the captain bent over double as his blade bit the deck. Lurching to his feet Braxus was just about to press his advantage when the captain's back arched spasmodically, a red curved sword-tip sprouting from his mailed chest.

Braxus blinked as his assailant slumped to the deck, revealing Cullen, a vicious snarl on his face as he yanked his weapon free.

'That's for Conway, Northland scum – looks like that fine mail wasn't so fine after all.'

Braxus glanced about him. All of a sudden, as was so often the case in battle, the tide had turned. The remaining reavers were fleeing back to their ship, Vertrix and the other knights hewing down a couple more for good measure as they pursued them to the rail.

Leaning on his cutlass and breathing heavily, Cullen motioned with his head to the corpse of the reavers' captain and grinned sardonically.

'Don't worry,' he said. 'That one still counts as yours.'

✜ ✜ ✜

The cost of victory was not cheap. Of the casualties on their side, eleven including Conway were dead and three more soon would be. Vertrix and Bryant and all the squires barring Gormly had taken light injuries, but Paidlin was in a bad way.

'Most like he'll lose that leg,' said Vertrix quietly after Gormly had bound up the wound and put it in a makeshift splint. Bereft of any kind of opiates aboard ship, they had left the unfortunate squire writhing in agony below decks to take the air before sunset. 'Gormly's an experienced field-dresser, but without a proper chirurgeon to see to that wound it'll fester. We're still five days out of Strongholm, probably more now we're left with a skeleton crew. That's all it'll take, mark my words – I've seen it before.'

'So have I,' snapped Braxus, 'in case you'd forgotten all the years that have elapsed since I was your squire.'

He regretted the harsh words instantly. The surprised look of hurt on Vertrix's face did little to allay his guilty feeling.

'I'm sorry Vertrix,' he said, laying a hand on the knight's uninjured shoulder. 'I had no right to say that. Please forgive me. I'm just... dammit, Paidlin was my charge! He wasn't supposed to get into a vicious fight like that for another year at least! He wasn't ready – yet another miserable failure of Braxus of Gaellen, good-for-nothing son and heir to Lord Braun!'

He slumped miserably over the rail of the deck, where but two hours ago all had been pandemonium and bloodshed. He could still smell that blood in his nostrils.

'Now don't take on so,' replied Vertrix softly, laying his own calloused hand on Braxus's shoulder. 'You think too much of what the old man says. You know he really cares for you at heart, just has a funny way of showing it sometimes, that's all.'

'Funny indeed,' muttered Braxus. He didn't see what was so funny about it.

The surviving crew had done what they could to clean up the mess. They had tended to their wounded as best they could; the bodies of the slain were wrapped in tarpaulin and lined up, ready to be committed to the ocean deeps. Cullen, his arm in a crude sling, was preparing to say a few last words for the dead.

Glancing at the new captain of the *Jolly Runner* Braxus reflected that his premonition had come true after all – somebody had been in line for a promotion all right. And in a way he'd helped to bring it about. He felt his guilt intensify. Conway had been a boastful old sot, ebrious and opinionated, but he had been a decent enough sort after his own fashion, and undeniably brave.

Another victory, another failure. Why did the two always seem to go hand in hand? He had been raised to believe that battle was the crowning glory of knighthood. If that was true there was little joy in glory, it seemed.

The bodies of the dead reavers had been piled up in an unceremonious pile. Cullen would have had them thrown overboard already but Regan, relentless opportunist that he was, had insisted on keeping them on board for searching before getting rid of them.

With his own squire's injuries tended to, he emerged from the hatch and breezed across the freshly cleaned deck towards Vertrix and Braxus, looking for all the world as if he had just had a tumble with two wenches, not a tussle with two score reavers.

'Well, my hearties, as the seafaring folk say!' he declaimed, grinning broadly. 'To the victors the spoils – and we, I believe, are the victors! I'm going over to search yon Northlanders – a grisly job, but someone's got to do it. I'd delegate it to Conric but his arm's a bit sore right now, poor fellow!'

Braxus managed a wan smile in the setting sun. 'Of all of us, I feel you're the best fitted for such a daunting task,' he replied, trying to sound cheerful. 'Be careful you don't cut yourself on their horned helmets.'

Regan gave a short bark of laughter over his shoulder as he turned to his task. 'Only in the lays, my friend, only in the lays – you of all people should know that!'

Braxus turned back to look at Vertrix. 'Speaking of which, I'd better get the harp up here and play a dirge or two, to see those poor men off. They fought well and bravely.'

Vertrix nodded. 'Aye, and when you're done with that, you take it back below and play us a dozen or two merry ditties. Reus knows, unless Regan finds the barbarian treasure horde he's hoping for, we're in need of some cheer, and I for one intend to spend this evening getting wood drunk! Conway's black grog has never seemed more appealing, Almighty rest his soul!'

Braxus was just about to reply when Regan called over sharply.

'Braxus! Vertrix! Come here, you'll be wanting to see this!'

Both knights exchanged a raised eyebrow and strode over to join Regan. Naturally he'd gone for the leader's body first, wasting no time in pulling the silvered mail shirt off him – damaged or no it was probably worth a fair price. He had used his dirk to tear open his undertunic, perhaps hoping to find a bauble of some kind.

What he had found was altogether less welcome.

'Is that what I think it is?' asked Braxus, staring at the dead reaver's blood-soaked chest.

'Aye, it is,' said Vertrix, nodding slowly.

The sight of them clustered around the corpse of the man he had slain must have caught Cullen's eye, for at that moment he drew up alongside them. Peering over their shoulders he stared at the marking on the reaver's chest. His deadly thrust had obscured part of it, but even so it could still be seen clearly enough in the light of the sinking sun: two valkyries suspended above a high-prowed ship, their swords raised high.

Cullen blinked. 'What's that?' he asked, none the wiser.

'It's a Seacarl's tattoo,' said Vertrix quietly. 'Only the Northland nobility are allowed to have them.'

Cullen blinked again, still none the wiser. 'What does that mean?'

'It means,' said Vertrix slowly, 'that these were no ordinary freesailors. These are made men, beholden to the sea princes of the Frozen Wastes.'

'And that means,' said Braxus, finishing for him, 'that after more than eighty years of relative peace on the Wyvern, the Northlanders have broken the Treaty of Ryøskil. They're going to war with the mainland.'

⇥ CHAPTER XIV ⇤

In The City Of Kings

A delko and Vaskrian exchanged excited glances as they caught their first glimpse of two things they had never seen before in their young lives: Strongholm, and the sea.

A few leagues before reaching the coastline the plains dipped at a slight gradient, and following the king's highway they could see a thin blue roiling strand on the horizon. As they drew nearer they began to discern the grey walls of the capital, looming high and proud from their perch overlooking the Strang Estuary. Here the waters of the Vyborg reached their final destination, plunging into the salty vastness of the Wyvern Sea.

There legend had it the Tritons and Seakindred had made one of their many underwater realms, long ago in the Dawn of Time. Back then the Wyrms that gave the sea its age-old name had made sport across its tumbling waves, before their once-mighty race was withered to extinction by the slow passing of millennia. Or so the sages told.

Adelko had little time to ponder the unfathomable fastnesses of the ocean deeps, for soon they were drawing near to the city, and gazing on the double unicorn banners that fluttered from every turret of its crenelated walls he found plenty more recent history to occupy his mind.

Though it seemed mighty indeed to his raw eyes, the novice had read enough to know Strongholm was small compared to the sprawling cities of the Sultanates of Sassania or the venerable metropolises of the Urovian New Empire. It probably sheltered something like twenty thousand souls, a fraction of the populations of Ilyrium or Ushalayim. Or Rima for that matter, the Pangonian capital that was their destination.

But still, it was impressive enough. And besides that, it was *his* capital. Remote as his upbringing had been, Adelko felt some sense of civic pride as he looked upon his kingdom's first city for the first time.

Much of Strongholm's compact walled area was given over to the citadel, where the King's palace overlooked the great harbour built by the First Reavers who had founded the Three Old Kingdoms that would later become one. The citadel perched on a high hill overlooking the harbour and the rest of the city, a warren of narrow crooked streets flanked by overhanging buildings mostly wrought of stone. A far cry indeed from the wattle village huts of his childhood.

The approach to the West Gate was clogged with traffic, and noon was long gone by the time a harried looking sentry waved them through. Riding under the great stone archway and into King's Approach, the city's main thoroughfare, the two youths marvelled together at the cobbles paving the streets, unknown to the dirt trails of the villages and towns they had visited.

As they rode deeper into the city to be swallowed up by its tumult, Adelko found his senses under assault from all directions. The streets were thronged with every kind of humanity he could have imagined: hawkers, harlots, tradesmen, mercenaries, beggars, drunkards, watchmen, town criers, preachers, refugees and other wayfarers like themselves all clamoured for a meagre stretch of space.

Accustomed as he was to the silence of the country, he found the noise overwhelming. The reek was no less intense, though by a fortune of Strongholm's location this was offset to some degree by a constant sea breeze.

As he narrowly avoided being spattered by a washerwoman emptying a tub of nightsoil out of a window above him, the young monk found himself thanking the Redeemer for small mercies.

The city was intoxicating, although Adelko thought its blandishments somewhat uncouth; Vaskrian almost trampled on a lolling drunkard on the corner of Tavern Street as they drew near the citadel, and the novice did his best to ignore the brightly painted wenches who leered and cooed at him out of gaudily painted shutters that were half open. He was ashamed to admit that their warm smiles and enticing bodices, half undone, were not completely lost on him. Although to tell the truth they scared him more than anything else. Girls. Even now he still wasn't sure what all the fuss was about.

'Pay scant attention to this filth, young Adelko,' his mentor counselled prudishly. 'As we often teach, cities are a repository of moral degradation and iniquity! A necessary evil, unfortunately, to the governance of realms – you would do well to consider this brief sojourn another test of your faith and spiritual fortitude.'

'Indeed, Master Horskram,' replied the novice breathlessly – although he couldn't honestly say he found busty whores or belligerent tradesmen nearly as much of a drain on his fortitude as half the horrors they had encountered on their journey.

When they reached the walls of the citadel, Sir Tarlquist produced a parchment scroll bearing the High Commander's seal. The serjeant glanced at it before ordering his men to open the gates and let them in without question.

Inside the citadel the streets were somewhat straighter and better kept – and far less busy. Here only the wealthiest nobles, merchants, master craftsmen and perfects could afford to live. As they made their way towards the palace Adelko caught sight of a round colonnaded temple on the other side of the citadel precinct. Each of its pillars featured a bas-relief carving of the Redeemer's Seven Acolytes and the Seven Seraphim. Atop the temple's central dome loomed a great stylised wheel. To this a life-sized statue of the Redeemer was affixed, his hewn limbs twisted about the granite spokes, his carved face a stone mask of agony.

Seeing this, Adelko made the sign – though somewhat primitive, the graven image was curiously potent in its portrayal of Palom's suffering and sacrifice.

The palace itself looked more like a fortress. It had been built by Olav Iron-Hand not long after he arrived from across the sea to take the throne of the Old Kingdom of Nylund, and its crude but bluntly efficient masonry served as testimony to the simple hardy craft of their Northland ancestors. Since then the Northlendings, as the descendent peoples of Northalde had come to call themselves, had gentled somewhat, absorbing foreign influences from the more southerly Free Kingdoms. Through long centuries, as the mainlanders exchanged longship and war-axe for warhorse and lance, sporadic rapine and pillage for more codified if scarcely less brutal forms of war, they had become sundered from their Northland ancestors, in some cases mingling with the Westerling tribes they had conquered.

The sturdy oak gates of the King's residence were approached by ascending a great flight of broad stone steps that led into an outer courtyard surrounded by ramparts that overlooked a wharf teeming with war galleys. Everything spoke of a strong martial character, from the ships in the harbour below swarming with sailors to the heavily armed guards lining the thick crenelated walls of the palace and courtyard. Though he could be wise and just in peacetime, King Freidheim was not an unwarlike ruler.

A distinct blot on the landscape they had seen on their approach to Strongholm further bore this out: the unmistakeable signs of an army camp, where the loyalist forces were mustering for the coming war.

✠ ✠ ✠

Vaskrian felt his heart thumping with excited expectation as they mounted the steps and crossed the flagstoned courtyard to the palace gates.

The sea breeze whipped at his hair and cloak; its salt tang stirred his breast as no beckoning harlot in the streets down below could. He felt his ancestors' yearning for the ocean tugging at him. But more alluring still was the spectacle of the royal seat they now approached.

The gates were guarded by soldiers in chequered cloaks. The White Valravyn was personally responsible for the King's safety, and all knights and soldiers on duty at the palace were hand picked from the Order's ranks.

Their serjeant scanned the sealed parchment proffered by Tarlquist before motioning for the gates to be opened and favouring the knight with a curt nod.

It was not a deferential one, Vaskrian noted: here at the heart of the realm a common soldier's duty to King and country superseded all other hierarchies. It was this complicit understanding that had ensured the security of Northalde's rulers since the Order's founding: before then rebellious nobles had been known to murder a rightful liege after using nothing more than their rank to get past his guards.

But that was long ago, and no king now need fear such an attack while the White Valravyn protected him – custom also dictated that a dozen of its best knights personally guard him, night and day. If Thule wanted to kill the King, it would take a successful war to do it. And his loyal subjects would soon see about that!

⁜ ⁜ ⁜

If Vaskrian could have read his friend's thoughts, he would have known that Adelko felt less sure of the impending war's outcome. The novice had read enough of the world's histories to know rebellions could and did succeed, often in the face of all expectations – and with bloody consequences for those on the losing side.

They were ushered into the palace's inner courtyard, a surprisingly small cobblestoned affair that seemed a ruder version of the elegant plazas he'd read about in musty old tomes at Ulfang that treated of Rima and the great cities of the far-flung Southlands.

Stable boys came to take their horses. They were dressed in royal livery, purple cloaks and tunics embroidered with the clashing unicorns of the House of Ingwin picked out in silver thread.

A tall man with silvery grey hair dressed in purple robes of ermine also bearing the royal coat of arms walked across the courtyard from the keep to meet them. He was accompanied by four more knights of the Order.

Drawing level with them he bowed stiffly.

'Sir Tarlquist and Sir Wolmar, welcome both,' he said in a dry, distinguished voice. 'Strongholm is gifted by your presence – and yours, Sir Torgun. His Majesty's men are always glad to have their greatest knight among them.'

'All knights who serve the Order and their King are great,' replied
Sir Torgun humbly.

From the corner of his eye Adelko caught Wolmar scowling. He
wouldn't put jealousy past the vindictive knight.

'And all are just as pleased to be received by their royal liege's right
hand,' said Tarlquist, continuing the formalities. Proffering the letter
of introduction, he added: 'Lord Ulnor, if it please you, we seek urgent
audience with His Majesty, for we have tidings of the war and other
pressing business to discuss with the King.'

Lord Ulnor, Seneschal of the King's Dominions and one of the most
powerful men in the realm, raised bushy brows and fixed Sir Tarlquist
with keen eyes that were the colour of summer skies. They reminded
Adelko of his mentor's, yet where there was wisdom and knowledge in
those of the old monk he thought he detected a more cunning intelligence
in the steward's. That made sense. Horskram had spent most of his life
grappling with spirits; Adelko fancied Lord Ulnor had most likely spent
his grappling with the wiles of mortal men.

Not a man to cross, in other words.

'And what other business could be so pressing in times such as these?'
the haughty steward demanded, drawing himself up to make himself look
even taller. He carried a cane of polished walnut fashioned to look like a
hippogriff rearing in full flight, although it seemed to Adelko as though
he merely carried it for show and didn't really need it – though he must
have seen well over seventy winters.

'I fear these are matters for the King's ears only at present,' answered
Tarlquist nervously. 'Though no doubt he will make a full disclosure to
his most trusted advisers once he has been informed of our news.'

The seneschal held the knight in his cobalt eyes for a second or two
longer, his wan smile and taut face giving nothing away. 'Very well,'
he replied. 'And would you do me the honour of introducing your
companions? The chequered twins are known to me – you needn't trouble
with them.'

Pointed as it was the question had to be answered. When Tarlquist
had done so Ulnor nodded. 'Ah Master Horskram, I must be getting
old, failing to recognise you straight away. I did think your face looked
familiar – a healer of the blood royal is ever welcome at the King's seat.
The Lady Walsa shall be delighted to learn of your presence I am sure.'

'And I will be delighted to speak with her – and all of His Majesty's
kin,' responded Horskram with a courteous bow. Over the past few weeks
Adelko had realised that his tetchy master could certainly curb his crabby
nature and turn on the manners and charm when it suited him.

'Very good,' said Lord Ulnor, before motioning for the travellers to follow him. 'Let us go now. The King's Court is in session, so you may have to wait a little while – though when I tell him your news is urgent and comes from his brother I am sure he will admit you directly. And in the meantime I will see to it that you are brought refreshments – the road to war makes hungry men, as the old battle proverb has it.'

Adelko liked the sound of that – he had yet to be feasted by a king, and it was an experience he was keen to relish. They were taken through a single brass-bound door fashioned of pine and down a long, wide corridor lined with guards, before emerging into a large antechamber. At the far end loomed a pair of double doors fashioned from the same materials.

At its centre was a great bronze relief portraying a bust of Thorsvald, the Hero King, divided straight down the middle by the double doors. Its peculiar design had led one of his vanquished foes, the Wolding robber baron Lord Jale, to famously remark that the only way of cleaving the Hero King's skull in twain was to seek an audience with him.

But that had been well over a century ago, and the Wolding barons were long since cowed as a political force, if still fiercely independent and scarcely obedient to royal law. The latter meant there was never a shortage of skirmishes with Wolding knights – Adelko had heard Torgun and several others including Vaskrian speak of fighting them during the evening meal at Lady Selma's. But full-blown war was another thing. That was a Southron problem nowadays.

They were shown to a wooden bench running the length of the antechamber's east wing, where a row of great arched windows looked out onto the harbour, its teeming warships and the roiling seas beyond.

A gaggle of people thronged the chamber. Some were merchants, tradesmen and other city dwellers, but there were also many who were clearly from out of town: groups of ragged peasants stood or sat about the chamber, many of them caked in mud and dirt from the road. Many more bore the ugly signs of war: here and there a bloodied bandage told of a lost eye or severed limb, and many of the low-born women wept openly. Looking on their inconsolable faces, Adelko did not like to dwell on the cause of their grief – young as he was, he knew full well some of the worst wounds of war need not always be inflicted with cold steel.

The guards on duty had cleared a space around them to separate the important guests from the more ordinary petitioners. Many a liege would have simply ordered noble arrivals with urgent news brought through immediately, but King Freidheim insisted on hearing out those he had already admitted to court without interruption.

As liveried servants brought a small mahogany table to them and set this with a roast chicken, small tomatoes, chopped parsnips, a wedge of cheese, a loaf of bread and a jug of watered wine with silver trenchers and goblets, Adelko found himself thanking the King's sense of justice for the delay.

But surrounded as he was by the poor, destitute and hungry, he could barely manage more than a few morsels for guilt, famished though he was. He was grateful when Horskram, clearly thinking much the same thing, bade the guards surrounding them distribute the rest of the food among the poorer folk after he and Vaskrian had also taken a few bites. The knights had a table of food set before them as well; at Tarlquist's behest they did likewise.

'You set us all a worthy example with your Palomedian charity, master monk,' said Tarlquist, wiping his mouth before taking another sip of watered wine.

'It will make little difference to their ruined lives, I fear,' replied Horskram unsmiling. 'But I do as the Redeemer would have me do – indeed, 'tis all one can do when faced with adversity and temptation alike.'

Tarlquist nodded as if weighing these words. 'Indeed,' was all he said, before turning in his seat to gaze out of the window.

✢ ✢ ✢

Vaskrian followed his gaze. A couple more warships could be seen making their way across the choppy seas of the Strang Estuary to join the rest of the fleet in the harbour, a motley array of cogs and galleys. Some would be independent contractors, seaborne mercenaries who were little better than pirates in peacetime, but suddenly very useful when war beckoned – if one could afford them. The rest would be seafaring vassals of those loyalist lords who owned coastal demesnes. He searched for Lord Aesgir's standard amongst the bristling sails, but couldn't make it out. Perhaps he had not arrived yet. He would though – like the other lords of Efrilund, including his own liege Lord Fenrig, he was loyal.

The latest arrivals looked to be from Vandheim, the coastal jarldom where his hero Sir Torgun hailed from. Vaskrian glanced at the blond knight to see if he had registered their arrival, but he was staring grimly at the huddled refugees, a mingled look of sorrow and anger on his rugged face. Beside him Sir Wolmar affected a dandyish boredom, as though he had seen it all before. The chequered twins sat stiff and silent, saying nothing. Vaskrian wondered how their hair colour had come to be so different, when they were identical in every other way. In some lands it was said that people applied dyes to their hair in the way that a tailor would to wool and cloth, but such an effete custom was unknown in the Northern Kingdoms.

Quite right too – what kind of nancy would colour his hair? Doric and Cirod were real men, there had to be some other explanation.

He turned his attention back to the ships. The new arrivals at harbour would have come in answer to the summons put out by Prince Thorsvald, the King's younger son and Sealord of the Eastern Reaches: it was his job to muster the ships commanded by loyal barons to fight the rebel navy for mastery of the Wyvern Sea.

Vaskrian silently hoped the King's second son would make a better fist of his duties than his first: half the southern Dominions seemed to have fallen before Prince Wolfram had made a stand at Linden.

He didn't like to think how demoralising that must be for the loyalist forces struggling down south to defend the realm from further invasion. He didn't like to think ill of the heir to the throne either, but it was common knowledge that Wolfram was too reckless by far – though no one doubted his courage.

Then again, that was what most folk said about *him*: that he was reckless and hot-headed. But he was just a lowly squire and a commoner to boot, so what did it matter how he behaved?

He felt the old familiar bitterness welling up inside him, and did his best to suppress it. Now wasn't the time for self-pity.

At least it looked as though his fortunes might improve, here on the threshold of an audience with his King and a full-blown war coming hard on its heels. His service to the monks was done – he'd got them to Strongholm in one piece. Judging by everything he'd seen and heard, they were fighting some great supernatural evil, something you couldn't kill with sword or spear. Not easily at any rate.

He chose not to dwell on it. He didn't like the idea of things he couldn't fight. Best to let the Argolians deal with their sorcerous quest in their own way – that was their job after all.

He preferred to focus on the coming war, something he could understand. Something he could profit from. Surely he would get his chance to distinguish himself, to prove to them all that his self-belief was justified…

Just give him that chance, and he'd show all those bluebloods his true worth.

He was just about to ask Sir Tarlquist something about the royal war fleet when he was interrupted by the sound of silver trumpets blowing and the herald calling out: 'The King will now see Sir Tarlquist of Gottenheim, Commander in the Order of the White Valravyn, and his entourage!'

⚜ ⚜ ⚜

Adelko hardly had time to draw breath before the chequered guards that had sequestered them from the common mob were escorting them through the crowded chamber towards the double doors.

The herald, a shortish heavy-set man in early middle age, stepped up and addressed their party in a stentorian voice: 'You will approach the King and kneel at the foot of his dais! You will not speak if he does not address you directly – unless he gives you leave to speak freely! You will rise only when he bids you! You will not turn your back on him, unless it please him that you do so! You may meet his eyes once he begins discourse with you, but not before!'

Adelko had the distinct impression that the unsmiling herald's words were aimed at himself and Vaskrian – doubtless his mentor and the raven knights were familiar with court protocol. The authoritarian instructions did little for the young monk's nerves as the herald stepped aside and motioned for two liveried pikemen to open the doors.

As the bronze face of Thorsvald V parted to reveal a first glimpse of the royal throne room, Adelko steeled himself and prepared to meet his King.

PART THREE

⊷ CHAPTER I ⊷

The Priest And The Pretender

From where he lurked in the shadow of a tent the urchin could hear the sounds of war subsiding for another day. No one in that vast camp knew his name, and most likely none would ever ask it.

Not even the strange and frightening foreigner who approached him now, his sea-green robes dully catching the fading light of the sun as it dipped ever closer towards the western mountain ranges. The flat plains that lay south of the Vyborg River allowed the eye to roam far and wide across the lush green earth of the King's Dominions; they also made Linden Castle, a mighty holdfast situated atop an incongruous knoll, difficult to assail.

Even the urchin knew that: the past ten days' blood and toil had told him that much.

The foreign priest who had commissioned his services drew level with him. In his miserable ten summers' existence as a beggar and cutpurse on the filthy streets and side alleys of Lindentown, the urchin had seen and endured much that might have made grown men quail – yet even so his new employer sent shivers down his spine.

Small wonder, the ragged boy thought as he looked timorously up at the tall, lean Northlander who stood before him, staring down at him balefully with his one good eye. But it was the other one the urchin feared most – though it was cloudy and sightless, he could not shake the feeling that it was seeing right through him, peering into his very soul.

He didn't like that, not one jot.

The 'sea wizard' they called him, but the urchin had heard him called other things too: warlock, devilspawn, cursed. Staring at the strange fish-like scales that covered the blind half of his face, he could well believe it.

'Do you have it?'

The voice was thickly accented but the warlock-priest or whatever he was spoke fluent Northlending. He spoke it better than the urchin if the truth be told, but then he supposed he was an educated man this priest, pagan or not.

'Course I do,' replied the urchin, trying to sound confident. 'Where's me money?'

'You'll get your money – I want a look at it first.'

This time the words were spat out with contempt – well, the urchin was well used to the distaste of his betters. The Northlander was a paying customer, so what did he care?

Reaching inside his mildewed jerkin the urchin produced a folded scrap of cloth and handed it gingerly to the strange priest. His hands were ice-cold as he took it from him and opened it up. Gazing at the contents he nodded, wrapped the cloth again and put it in the deep folds of his glaucous mantle.

'And you are sure he didn't notice?'

The urchin felt himself swell with a rare sense of pride. 'What did I tell you, mister? Been doin' this since I was old enough to walk – 'e didn' notice a thing, just turned over in 'is sleep is all. Can't say as I ever 'ad to nick – '

The priest cut him off sharply. 'That is enough. Your opinions are of no interest to me.'

Reaching into a leather purse at his belt – a peculiar affair, fashioned of knotted hemp interwoven with dried seaweed – he produced two silver marks and pressed them into the urchin's outstretched hand.

'And you are still willing to do me the other service?' he asked. 'The one we spoke of before?'

The strange warlock's voice betrayed no emotion as he asked this, but all the same the urchin felt a wave of unease come over him. He'd mulled this part over but he still wasn't sure...

'Five silver marks, you said?' Even now, with all that money on the line, it didn't seem quite right.

But the priest was inexorable. 'I sense your reluctance,' he replied in the same flat voice. 'Shall we make it ten? Perhaps that will put your mind at ease.'

The urchin wasn't sure about that, but it did settle the matter. Ten silver marks was a *lot* of money. 'Done,' he said, before he had a chance to regret it.

'Wait here,' said the priest.

He was not long gone. During that time the urchin contented himself with loitering beside the tent, glancing from the two silver pieces that glinted in his palm to the serjeants and other soldiers passing to and fro.

The booming sound of the mangonels firing pellets at the outer wall of Linden had stopped as the sun began to draw level with the mist-wreathed Hyrkrainians. The camp became increasingly busy with the bustle of knights and men-at-arms returning from the battlefield;

their clamour mingled with the groans of the wounded being brought back on stretchers, whilst the chirurgeons, cooks, whores and washerwomen began to prepare for another working night servicing a besieging army.

There'd be a fair number of his own kind working the camp too – just as he had been before the serjeant he was robbing had caught him running a blade along the bottom of his money pouch. He'd nearly robbed the urchin of his life on the spot for that – but the strange foreigner had suddenly stepped in and ordered the man to release him and sheath his steel.

The serjeant had been a burly fellow and battle-scarred, but he'd gone pale at the sight of the Northlander. After that no one had dared lay a hand on him – but it also meant he had a guvnor now, a benefactor who expected to be obeyed.

It had occurred to him to run – to flee back to town and hide himself amongst the ordure of his old familiar haunts. But somehow he couldn't quite bring himself to do it – the promise of pay and a peculiar sense of adventure stopped him.

Or that was what he told himself it was anyway.

Towering over him again the Northland priest blocked out the sun's dying rays. He handed the urchin two items and told him to cover them up immediately. Wordlessly the urchin obeyed.

The priest's voice was dark and hushed now, a mere shadow of a whisper. 'You remember what I told you to do with these?'

The urchin nodded, his gimlet eyes meeting the priest's with difficulty.

'You wait until the last of the sun's rays disappear over yonder mountains, and not before, then you do it just like I told you – do you understand?

The urchin swallowed nervously and nodded again.

'Very good,' said the priest, slightly more loudly this time. 'If you serve me well in this, you shall have your reward directly. You are to stay here when the work is done – I will meet you with the rest of your pay. Is that clearly understood?'

'Y-yes,' the urchin stammered. He felt as though he could barely speak.

Without another word the priest spun on his heel and walked towards the pavilion at the other end of the clearing formed by the ring of tents. It was only then that the urchin really noticed the three-pronged trident he carried, its points curving inwards so their tips nearly met. It was fashioned of a strange silvery-blue metal and covered with peculiar markings, which seemed to move when its owner did.

✢ ✢ ✢

Krulheim son of Kanga, self-styled Prince of Thule, prepared to address his war council. It was dark in the tent; the inchoate light of the braziers that had just been lit was only beginning to augment the fading light outside. Around a pine table topped with a model of Linden Castle and other crude representations of the armies and lands surrounding it stood his allies: men of power who thirsted for more of it, and had chosen to gamble everything they owned – including their heads – on a chance to further their worldly ambitions.

Sir Jord, Marshal of Thule and de facto commander-in-chief of the rebel forces (although that title officially belonged to his liege lord), was first to speak.

'The palisades are finished, Your Highness, so our mangonels should be able to harass them with impunity from now on. We are building a covered way to protect our vanguard for when we assault the outer bailey walls, and our engineers are constructing belfries too. Those should be ready within a tenday.'

'A tenday?' Lord Aelrød, a tall, wiry man in middle age, spoke up. As the Prince of Thule's most powerful ally, he felt it behoved him to voice his opinion in all matters. It was a duty he adhered to far too often for Jord's liking. 'Why wait so long? The covered way will be finished by then – that means we can take a battering ram to the outer gates. Why, we'll be storming their inner walls by the time the belfries are completed!'

'I was coming to that, Lord Aelrød,' said Sir Jord, doing his best to conceal his impatience. The Baron of Saltcaste was a titled lord, whilst he was but a landed knight who served the Jarl of Thule as marshal – and until very recently he had not even had his modest holdings to call his own. All that meant he had to defer to Saltcaste – but that didn't change the fact that the man's knowledge of battle tactics was clearly inferior.

The Marshal continued: 'The covered way will indeed be finished before the siege engines – in a week's time by my reckoning. That means we can begin to storm the gates before we send the belfries up to harry their walls as you rightly observe, my lord – but in the meantime we can also begin sending squadrons of foot up the sides of the hill to mount escalades here and here...' He moved pieces across the table to demonstrate.

'Our archers will provide them with covering fire from the palisades – that should keep their crossbowmen pinned, but each detachment will have extra soldiers with them armed with kite shields just in case. These can then of course join their comrades in the escalade should it prove successful.'

The thick-set Marshal said this last part rather as if he were explaining the basics of siege warfare to a green squire, which was exactly what he felt he was doing at times. Lord Aelrød was a canny politician and not unskilled with sword and spear, but like many of his kind he seemed to believe that knowledge of the battlefield came with blue blood. It was attitudes like that which led to blood of all hues flowing all too often.

'You have excelled yourself and left no stone unturned as always,' said the Prince of Thule, nodding. Somewhat shorter than the Northlending average but powerfully built with broad shoulders, Krulheim was handsome enough in a rugged sort of way. His grey-green eyes burned keenly with an unquenchable fire. His brown wavy hair tumbled about his shoulders in ringlets and his incipient beard and moustache looked bristly and sparse by contrast.

He had begun growing the latter at Jord's insistence. 'Look like a king, and men will respect you as one,' he had told him. Right now though it made him look more like what he was in reality – a self-styled prince, a pretender to a throne that was far from won.

Thinking this the Marshal reflected that perhaps his liege had been wise after all to stop short of having himself crowned King of Thule – Krulheim had insisted that he would only bequeath himself this accolade once he was sitting on the Pine Throne in Strongholm Palace, a conqueror.

The Pretender continued: 'But what of their supplies? Have we an inkling as to how much they have? Freidheim shall not be over long in mustering an army, I trow – we were best to be meeting it from within Linden's walls.'

Jord shook his head frowning. 'Linden will be well victualled, make no mistake, Your Highness,' he replied. 'Do not hope to starve them out before the capital comes to their rescue – though we have taken pains to ensure there will be no other relief. Lord Magnus and Lord Johan – if you would both be so kind...'

The first of these two, a flint-faced man with dark close-cropped hair, nodded curtly before speaking. 'My forces ravaged the lands for leagues about, Your Highness, and we have occupied those that feed the castle. Lindentown, as you know, has surrendered, and its provisions have been given over to us for our use. The river is secure – we guard it night and day. There'll be no midnight forays for extra food and drink – whatever the garrison has stored, it's all they've got.'

The second baron, a huge fat man with an unkempt mane of dirty blond hair and an unshaven face flushed red from too much wine, slurred his way through his own battle report.

'Indeed, Your Highness, be assured – we have burned and ransacked every village and poisoned every well within five miles of this place. That should make trouble for any relief army seeking provisions, and we've got scouts roaming the riverlands and sentries posted all about the vicinity – if anyone comes within a country mile of us, we'll know about it.'

Lord Johan slapped his mailed belly, as though his words signified a great victory in themselves.

The Pretender nodded again and was about to say something when he was interrupted by a commotion outside the tent. The dozen or so men gathered about the table turned to look as Father Pretchon, Superior Perfect of the Temple of Urring, strode in. A slight man in early middle age with blood-red hair, his eyes burned with a fire not unlike Krulheim's. Only where that lord's smouldered with the fires of unwreaked vengeance, those of the priest blazed with the zealotry of the Creed.

Krulheim's voice was conciliatory as he said: 'Pretchon, what mean you, barging past my sentries? This is a counsel of war, which methinks a perfect of the cloth should not be party to.'

'It is in the name of the very Creed that I come here now!' exclaimed the perfect in his thin reedy voice. It grated so on Jord: he knew how important it was to have the blessings of the Almighty invoked on any army before battle, but the priest's fanaticism irked him to the marrow.

'This heresy must stop!' continued the perfect, his pallid face looking even more wan in the disappearing sunlight. The braziers were beginning to burn more strongly now, but this did little to bring colour to Pretchon's pinched features. 'Only just now have I learned of the dire means by which Castle Salmor was won! Your Highness – do not, I implore you, surrender your cause to the forces of darkness! Though it be just in the eyes of the Lord Of Heaven, this unholy alliance shall put your immortal soul beyond His aid! Aye, and those of them that choose to follow you in this iniquity!'

The perfect paused to let his words sink in, gazing around the table at the assembled barons and lordlings, his fevered eyes catching the flames from the braziers with fearsome effect. Several of them flinched, and even Jord, loyal to Thule as he was, felt himself tensing.

For some time now there had been mutterings in the camp. Many of the men were beginning to voice a similar opinion to the pious perfect – that Krulheim's alliance with the foreign wizard was a step too far. Now it was obvious that even some of the highest lords in Thule's host, who stood to gain most from a successful rebellion, were uneasy at the thought of the price they might pay in the life hereafter for putting themselves in league with a pagan sorcerer.

But Krulheim betrayed no such misgivings. A wan smile flickered across his face as he said: 'Father Pretchon, be of good cheer – Ragnar of Landarök is here to help us win what is rightfully ours. You know he has prophesied our victory – surely it could not be so if the Almighty were not on our side.

For years now the northern lords have taxed us unfairly, and with many an unjust tithe have our people been burdened. Nowhere is it written that a lord may not carve out his own kingdom – so long as he does obeisance to the Creed...'

'Aye, so long as he does obeisance to the Creed!' echoed Pretchon, stepping forward and shouldering past the nearest lordling to lean across the table, fixing the Pretender with a venomous glare. 'That was precisely what was agreed, when we planned this rebellion! 'Twas all well and good – until you solicited the diabolical services of this pagan witch!'

'I presume you are referring to me?'

The voice was thickly accented and unmistakable. The assembled barons had looked unsettled in the presence of Pretchon; they looked decidedly afraid as Ragnar of Landarök, whom some men called the One-eyed Tamer of Oceans and others simply called the Sea Wizard, strode into the pavilion with a measured tread.

Pretchon rounded on him unabashed. 'Poltroon! Idolater!' he spat. 'You dare to come to this god-fearing land with your pagan filth! Begone I say, back to your own benighted bourne – before I have you hanged for your sinful crimes!'

'And what crimes are those, pray tell?' replied the foreign priest in a hushed voice. 'As I believe your liege lord was just pointing out, I am merely helping a future king secure what is rightfully his. All I ask in return is the right to establish a temple of my own here, so that its people may choose to return to the worship of their ancestors – if they so wish.'

'You would have them throw away their immortal souls!' gasped the perfect in a horrified voice. 'Abandon themselves to eternal perdition – this is blasphemy! This... lord of oceans you and your savage kind worship as a god is naught but an un-angel! He does not even sit at the side of the Almighty's throne – even to worship one of the Seven Seraphim as a deity would be a gross heresy, but this... this is unspeakable!'

Ragnar's face darkened. The scales covering the one side of his face glinted in the brazier-light. They were a grey-green hue, similar to the robes he wore. Outside, the last of the sun's rays were disappearing beyond the far-off peaks.

'You should learn to speak more respectfully of Sjörkunan,' the pagan priest said gravely. His voice was still hushed, but now there was a deathly silence in the air that made his words seem to resonate more loudly. 'You would find him a most powerful deity, if only you would open your heart to him – aye, him and others besides. No man can hope to live upon this earth and defy the elements – let you and all your kind speak of this One God how so ever much you will, it is not He who governs the forces and powers of this world from his far-flung heavenly throne.'

Pretchon said nothing, only staring at him with a contorted look on his pinched face. Krulheim seemed about to say something in protest at what was undeniably blasphemy, but the pagan priest was quick to forestall him.

'But be that as it may,' he said, raising his gnarled hand in a gesture of acknowledgement. 'I make no attempts at conversion – let each man here believe as he will. I shall not proselytise, nor shall I preach. No man in this army, no subject of this realm, will I induce to abandon any faith that has sustained him to this day. But perhaps there shall come a time when others seek me out of their own free will.'

Krulheim closed his mouth, apparently mollified if not entirely reassured. Aelrød frowned and looked away, as did many of the other barons including Magnus. Jord scowled – he did not care for the pagan foreigner and his sorcerous ways any more than Pretchon if the truth be told, but he obeyed his liege's will in this as in everything. That was enough for the Marshal to hold his tongue – though he was surprised that the zealous perfect had not launched into yet another fire-and-brimstone diatribe.

He was just thinking this when the perfect made a horrible choking sound.

Turning to look at Pretchon, Sir Jord saw he was still staring at his rival with a contorted look on his face. Only what he had assumed a moment ago was an expression of righteous rage was now revealed for what it was.

It was an expression of profound agony.

Another choking sound escaped the perfect's drawn lips, from which a thin drool dangled as he bent over double to grasp the edge of the table. This was followed by a high, thin cry as the perfect pitched over, falling to the ground where he began convulsing horribly. He grasped frenziedly at his black habit and white scapular, his chalky hands tearing the thin cloth as he clutched at his chest. Knights and lords gathered around him and exchanged stupefied glances as they began speaking all at once, taken completely by surprise and at a loss as to what to do.

Only Pretchon's Northland rival remained unperturbed, standing as still as a frozen stream in winter while the others rushed to and fro.

'Send for a chirurgeon, for Reus' sake!' cried the Prince of Thule.

It was a futile command. The hapless perfect gave a final elongated cry, his body convulsing one last time as his zealous eyes froze over in the sightlessness of death. More than once Jord had seen a man run through with a spear die in a like manner, though not a speck of blood stained the rushes on the tent floor.

'Well, it seems as though your god has spoken,' said the Sea Wizard, his cloudy eye pale and pitiless in the flickering firelight. 'I shall leave you all to meditate on the ramifications of this occurrence, as rest assured will I.'

Without another word, the priest swept out of the tent, leaving a gaggle of stunned nobles in his wake.

✣ ✣ ✣

The camp was gradually becoming suffused with the scattered light of cooking fires. The urchin shivered in the chill breeze that had begun to billow the tents about him. His surroundings were noisy, but he could have sworn he'd heard a strangled cry coming from the pavilion as he was performing his duties. He didn't like this, not one bit – the sooner he was done with the frightening priest the better. It was almost a relief to see him emerge from the tent and walk over to where he skulked, though the boy shivered again as he drew level with him.

It was probably just a trick of the light, but the Northlander seemed to have grown even taller – he felt his presence looming over him. Though he scarcely had the words to describe it thus it felt like the first frost of winter, only it was a winter that chilled the soul not the body.

In his strange flat voice the priest said: 'You have performed your task satisfactorily. Give me back the things I gave to you, and you shall have your reward.'

By now the urchin was too afraid to hold out for his money first. With hands that trembled he pressed the desired articles into the priest's icy hand.

Reaching into the folds of his sea-green robes the Northlander pulled out a peculiar-looking blue gem on a silver chain. It sparkled like hoarfrost in the twilight.

'Th-that isn't the price we agreed,' said the urchin nervously. Yet all the same, he found his eyes drawn to the blue bauble, which was tinged with a grey-green colour at the edges.

'It is worth many times more than the price we agreed,' replied the priest. 'An extra reward for performing so well. It has special properties. Put it about your neck, boy, and I promise you shall never feel the cold again.'

Robbed of all volition, the urchin took the necklace and did as he was told.

✣ ✣ ✣

The priest did not wait to observe the last of the urchin's death throes, but turning swiftly he walked across the clearing towards his own tent. As he did so he put the two items the cutpurse had given him back into the deep folds of his robe.

One was a sharp needle. The other was a tiny effigy of a priest dressed in black and white robes, with a lock of blood-red hair attached to its head.

⇒ CHAPTER II ⇐

A Clandestine Trip To The Market

'I'll give you ten regums for it, and not a penny more,' said the hunchbacked merchant, his crooked teeth glinting in the lantern-light as he scrutinised the gem-studded gold brooch.

'Ten regums?' spluttered Hettie from behind her shawl. 'It's worth twice that at least – give me twenty, that's a fair offer.'

The jewel merchant laughed at this, his teeth glinting again. Hettie had seen a few gold teeth in her time, but she had never seen this many in one mouth. She wondered if perhaps the merchant's body was his strongbox. His bodyguards had better be handy swordsmen if so.

'There is barely gold for two regums in the brooch,' he said, as if explaining patiently to a petulant child. 'I am already being generous with my offer. No, I'm sorry, madam – it's ten regums or no deal.'

'You're patently ignoring the fine workmanship – made in Meerborg that was, look how detailed the horses and stags are. Not to mention that it's studded with rubies and emeralds – d'you take me for a complete fool, sirrah?'

'Hmm, no doubt it was made for a fine high lady,' replied the merchant, the glint transferring from his teeth to his eyes. 'Who did you say she was?'

'I didn't,' replied Hettie. 'A wealthy jeweller's wife from the Free City if you must inquire. She has run into certain financial difficulties but would rather nobody knew, hence she has sent me here to Merkstaed for secrecy... I'm sure I need say no more on the matter.'

The gem merchant was nodding. With his crooked back and dark brocade gown he looked positively sinister in the cramped interior of his little shop, which was festooned with wooden shelves crammed with an assortment of jewellery, most of it worth considerably less than the piece they now haggled over.

Outside the shop's single entrance just behind Hettie loitered a pair of freeswords. The merchant was new to town, having set up shop in Merkstaed last spring after the original owner Otho died of the pox.

That was good. This newcomer was far less likely to recognise Hettie's voice and see through her disguise than poor old Otho.

'I see, yes,' the merchant was saying. 'But that rather puts you at a disadvantage in terms of bargaining. You wish to make a sale without causing your mistress any... inconvenience. Or to put it another way, I am providing you with a conveniently inconspicuous sale. But as I am always fond of saying, convenience costs money.'

Hettie fixed the loathsome merchant with a disdainful stare. 'Meaning what, exactly?'

'Well... you say you cannot make the sale in Meerborg. Here I am, the nearest alternative. To seek out another buyer for the brooch you would have to ride many leagues further south of here. So, unless you wish to greatly extend your journey, you are not in a very good position for bargaining. And therefore I say – ten regums, and not a gold piece more.'

Hettie sighed. She had rather suspected it would turn out like this.

'Very well,' she said with an air of faint resignation. 'How about fifteen? You'll sell it for more than twice that – a precious piece of work as fine as that, why you might even persuade the heiress of Dulsinor herself to purchase it next time she comes to town!'

Hettie caught her breath as she said this, shocked by her own impulsiveness. But the ruse was a good one, though bold. Throw the weaselly merchant off the scent as much as possible. He could not be allowed to suspect anything.

Sitting back in his walnut chair the merchant held the brooch up to the light again: common security dictated that a store such as his should have as few entry points as possible, and the shop had no windows. After a couple of moments' further scrutiny he turned his flashing eyes and teeth on Hettie again and said: 'Well, Reus loves a trier, as they say. I have taken rather a liking to you, persistent as you are. Twelve regums shall I give you for this brooch – that, and my solemn oath to remain silent on the matter of this transaction, as per your wishes.'

Hettie returned his stare. 'Twelve gold pieces? For that you'll swear secrecy – on the Redeemer's wounds? Not a soul you'll tell how you came by this brooch?'

'Not the truth of it surely,' replied the greedy merchant, nodding enthusiastically. 'If pressed by a future buyer for its origins, I shall say that I brought it with me from my home city of Westerburg, where the jewellers' craft more than rivals that of Meerborg.'

Hettie nodded. 'Twelve it is then – though this is daylight robbery methinks.'

'Call it lantern-light robbery,' responded the merchant with an oily smile. Hettie showed exactly what she thought of his sense of humour by not laughing.

✢ ✢ ✢

With the transaction done and her first errand completed, Hettie stepped back outside into the busy street and adjusted her shawl and hood so most of her features were concealed.

She felt dreadfully self-conscious: Merkstaed was a bustling town of more than two thousand souls, and she only visited it once a month or so, but nonetheless she felt sure that somebody would recognise her sooner or later. Either that, or someone might pause to ask what a lady was doing going about with her head and face covered on an overcast but dry spring day.

But she need not have feared: the tradesmen and women of the busy riverside town were far too preoccupied with earning their daily bread to give any concern to a lone woman, even if she was somewhat outlandishly dressed. After all, Merkstaed was no stranger to strangers: sometimes you even got a foreigner or two passing through, usually travelling to or from the Free City, a bustling port in its own right.

Pushing her way up the filthy muddy street towards the river, Hettie turned her attention to her second errand.

Merkstaed's horse market came to town once a month – most if not all of the dealers would be from out of town, another good thing.

The price of that advantage had been time – the horse market was held at the beginning of every month, and so they had had to wait more than a week to put this part of their plan into action.

The paddocks were set up in a series of enclosures overlooking the Graufluss. Already the area was thronged with potential buyers, haggling furiously with the tradesmen. Half the horses there were worthless old nags scarcely worth her attention, but Hettie's eye soon settled on something more appropriate to their needs.

Her father had taught her everything she needed to know about horses when he had taught her how to ride them, and Hettie prided herself on her equestrian knowledge being as good as any knight's.

If the two roan mares that had caught her attention were agreeable to her senses, the grubby outrider selling them was far less so, and she was forced to endure his foul habit of spitting gobbets of phlegm every second sentence as she hammered out a deal with him.

He drove hard, but she drove harder still: another thing Hettie prided herself on was being nobody's fool. What she lacked in her mistress's intellectual acumen she made up for with worldly-wise, good old-fashioned common sense.

'All right, all right, three regums each I'll let them go for, plus another half a regum for all the necessary accoutrements,' said the horse trader at last with an exasperated sigh, scratching his chest and ejecting yet another gobbet at a nearby rat that sent it scampering away through the muddy yard. 'Good mixed stock these rouncies,' he continued as Hettie reached for her money purse. 'Sturdy Vorstlending thoroughbred, foaled on the plains down south – better than those overrated Northlending nags you keep hearing about, these beasts are hardy to the core – '

'Spare me your after-sale tittle tattle,' said Hettie, cutting him off as she pressed seven regums into his meaty hand. 'And I'll be wanting my change, thank you.'

The horse trader gave her an offended look as he took the proffered coins and reached for his own money pouch. 'Why of course, madam, what d'ye take me for, a common vagabond? Hoi, Arlus! Get thee over here now, and see to this lady's order!'

A ragged and no less filthy-looking boy of about twelve summers bounded over to see to his guvnor's needs. Where the tradesman was a bloated sack of a man, his apprentice was scrawny and half-starved. Hettie guessed he was not well treated.

'Me cousin's son,' offered the trader as if by way of apology. 'Nary a more fool boy as you'll come across, still 'e does as he's told, I suppose.'

Hettie nodded perfunctorily. She had no wish to get any deeper into conversation with this man – apart from the fact that he repelled her, the fewer reasons for him to remember her, the better.

While Arlus was bridling and saddling up the horses and fixing bags to the saddles, the merchant pressed six silver marks into her outstretched gloved hand. Hettie took her change and paused a moment, biting her lip and weighing up her options.

She decided she probably didn't need to bribe the horse dealer into silence and put the coins away: he hailed from the far south of Vorstlund and led a peripatetic existence by the sounds of it, travelling for most of the year. If anything a proffered bribe might only arouse his suspicions.

'And where will ye be wanting these horses delivered to?' asked the horse trader once they were ready.

'I'll send you word of that presently,' replied Hettie, adjusting her shawl again. 'You'll hear from me before sunset.' Without another word she turned on a muddy heel and set off on her third and final errand.

✛ ✛ ✛

Merkstaed had three inns. The custom had been brought over from the Empire several generations ago and had caught on quickly; it was a fairly simple concept that promoted convenience after all, and much less difficult to mimic than some of the other wonders of that mighty and mysterious realm across the Great White Mountains.

And a good job too, Hettie reflected, for once mindful of her mistress's numerous history lessons: in many parts of the country it was still the custom for wayfarers to seek shelter and lodgings with ordinary townsfolk. That would have most likely scuppered their plans, for most ordinary tradesmen would have raised an eyebrow at being asked to keep a pair of horses for longer than a night or two.

But amid the bustle of a busy inn, there was always a chance an ostler could be bribed into keeping a pair of horses for a while. An innkeeper would be too busy tending to his side of the trade to notice, so long as the bribe was enough to pay for the horses' victualling and stabling too.

That was what Hettie and her mistress were hoping anyway. Their plan had seemed a devilishly cunning one when they had sketched it out over another round of herbal tea in Adhelina's high chamber at the castle a week ago.

But as Hettie made her way through the main market square, now a roil of noonday vendors, travel-stained wayfarers, loitering mercenaries and common prostitutes, she felt a stab of doubt. She had decided to try the *Flying Fish*. The newest of the inns at Merkstaed, it had been built only a generation ago and was therefore the least established of the three. It would still be busy enough that two ownerless horses should not attract attention if kept discreetly, but not so busy as to be unable to spare the space.

All the same, Hettie felt increasingly anxious as she pushed her way free of the throng and up a narrow winding road that ended with the inn.

As a privileged resident of the castle she had never had any reason to set foot there, so it was unlikely she would be recognised... yet people at inns did so love to gossip. It was a perk of the trade after all, a chance to hear and give news of the wider world. Would even a bribe secure complete silence?

Her misgivings increased when she made her way around the side of the inn courtyard and sought out the ostler. He was a stocky youth with a mop of lank, sandy hair, his pasty face blemished with an unsightly crop of pimples and a perpetual smirk that Hettie did not think boded well.

Self-consciously adjusting her shawl again she did her best to sound like the noblewoman she was as she addressed him peremptorily: 'Ostler, might we have a word to one side?'

The smirk did not leave the ostler's face as he replied: 'Well, I see no one else in the yard at present, but if m'lady wishes a word *to one side,* who am I to refuse?'

Hettie did not care for the sarcasm in his voice any more than the suggestiveness of his words. Nevertheless she thanked him cordially as they removed themselves to a corner of the yard.

'I would have you keep two horses for me in yonder stables,' she said, meeting the ostler's eyes. They were a pale watery colour, curiously bland and unpleasant to look at.

'Aye, m'lady,' he smirked. 'This is an inn, and these are stables – you needn't have taken me to one side to ask me that! And where are these beasts, pray tell? You have the look of one who has trudged here on foot: aye, and taken the long way about if I'm any judge!'

He was staring at her boots and lower skirts, which were both caked with mud. Hettie cursed inwardly but quickly regained her composure.

'My horses are elsewhere, but I can have them brought to you directly. I need them to be kept here, to be fed, watered and tended to, for the next fortnight. Do you know how to keep the calendar?'

The youth did not leave off fixing her with a cold-eyed stare as he replied: 'I don't, not personally. But I knows well enough from the merchant folks as stays here the date, if you follow m'lady.'

'Very good. In that case you'll know that today is the 1st of Varmonath. On the 15th I shall return to collect my horses, and if you have kept them well you shall be rewarded handsomely.'

The ostler's expression did not change. 'I see,' he replied. 'I take it there's more to this than just a matter of fourteen days' stabling and victualling then?'

'There is,' confirmed Hettie. 'You must not let on to anyone, not even the innkeeper, that you are keeping my horses. Of course I will pay in advance for the cost of keeping them, plus another sum... to ensure your silence on the matter. Finally, a third sum will be paid to you for the inconvenience when we arrive to collect the horses.'

'We?'

'Of course. One rider hardly needs two horses.'

'Mm-hmm, I see... And what is this inconvenience you speak of?'

'When we arrive to collect our horses on the 15th, it will be well after sunset... close to the Wytching Hour. I will ask that you remain alert, which will mean giving up a good night's sleep.'

The ostler's eyes narrowed another fraction. Keeping horses in secret was suspicious enough, but as far as most ordinary townsfolk were concerned, riding around in the dead of night was the preserve of outlaws or worse – very few folks had any business being abroad at the Wytching Hour, fewer still any good business.

Hettie held her breath behind her shawl. This was precisely what she had feared. That the ostler could be bribed for his pains, she doubted not: townsfolk loved money more than any good Palomedian ought to. But the suspect nature of the situation might prompt him to report her to the watch – the prospect of a veiled woman asking him to keep horses in secret so she might collect them in the dead of night two weeks hence was almost too suspicious for him not to.

These thoughts went galloping through Hettie's mind as the ostler continued to stare at her for moments that seemed like hours.

Then, still smirking, he asked: 'Well, how much?'

Hettie felt a sense of relief wash over her.

They did not take long to agree terms. The ostler was greedy, but in a small-minded way; his sort were not used to seeing more than a few coppers a week besides bed and board, and the prospect of silver, let alone gold, in his hand seemed enough to induce him to do Hettie's bidding with no further questions asked.

He did not even comment on her secretive appearance – but then her whole manner was secretive, her needs clearly motivated by the wish to go unremarked. And of course the date of their departure was risky – just a few nights before the wedding, which had by now been announced to all and sundry by the town criers. But the prospect of an heiress defaulting on a marriage was unthinkable to most ordinary folk – and most high-born ones too come to that. She could only hope that would keep the ostler from joining up the dots.

In the end it was agreed that besides the cost of keeping the horses she would pay the ostler five silver marks now, and another five upon collecting them. He seemed content enough with the arrangement, nodding agreeably when she told him Arlus would be along with the horses shortly.

That the horse dealer's assistant would know where they were being kept did not trouble Hettie overly – the horse market would be finished in three days, after which he and his master would leave town.

She only wished she could feel as sure of the ostler, in spite of everything.

His sleeping quarters were located in a corner of the stables, allowing him to be alerted at night without waking up any of the inn's other occupants – everything in this part of the plan seemed settled with her third and final errand.

Yet as Hettie turned to leave the yard she still felt anxious; turning once to look back she saw the ostler still standing in front of the stables, his hands tucked into the rude pockets of his breeches, the same smirk plastered across his pallid face.

✣ ✣ ✣

On her way back up the hill to the castle Hettie ducked behind a tree when she felt sure there was no one else in sight. Removing her cloak and shawl she stuffed these inside a bag she had brought for the purpose, extracting in turn her more familiar russet-red mantle.

The latter was a gift Adhelina had given her four years ago for her fourteenth birthday, when she had come of age. It was made of the richest wool and lined with pretty silver sequins and quite valuable – Hettie was rarely seen about the castle without it.

She fastened it about her neck with a silver clasp fashioned to resemble two embracing cherubs. It felt good to be one's true self again – really all this subterfuge was too much for an honest girl to bear, but she supposed it was sadly necessary. Her mistress's mind was set on this course of action – and Hettie would follow her to the ends of the earth if need be.

Stepping back on to the road, she continued her steady trudge back up to the castle.

⚔ CHAPTER III ⚔

The Harpist On The Roof

Adelko and Vaskrian had just reached the top floor of Strongholm Palace when they heard the plangent notes of a harp from somewhere above them.

'Where d'you think that's coming from?' said Vaskrian, his eyes lighting up.

'It sounds like it's coming from up above us,' replied Adelko, casting his eyes to the ceiling, 'it must be the roof.'

'Let's go and find out!' said Vaskrian with a grin, tugging at Adelko's habit and bounding off down the corridor.

The squire had good reasons to be cheerful. They had been staying in the palace for a week, and already he had found his own personal paradise in the well-equipped royal barracks.

Better still, he'd secured himself a new position. Lord Visigard, the Royal Marshal in charge of the capital's security, had pressed him into the King's Army. Sir Ulfstan of Alfheim was a respectable vassal who hailed from the plains north of Strongholm: his old squire had been recently knighted, opening up a vacancy for a promising young sword.

A warm bed and three square meals a day were enough to keep Adelko in high spirits of his own. And then there was the palace itself: it was by far the largest building he had ever been in, and he'd longed to explore it.

He hadn't had the chance to do that properly until today: Horskram had insisted on confining him to the chamber they shared during the day, so he could resume his long-delayed instruction in lore and scripture.

Both he and Vaskrian had been left at a loose end that afternoon: Horskram was conferring with the King and his advisers, while Sir Ulfstan was visiting a house of ill repute in the low city (perhaps he wasn't so respectable after all). They had decided to explore the palace together, to while away the hours until feasting time after sunset.

It had proved time well spent. The palace's vaulted corridors and grand chambers – festooned with a rudely splendid assortment of arms, tapestries, skins, furs and the odd statue and rough-hewn fresco – had given the pair plenty to marvel at. If this was what the Northlending King's residence looked like, Adelko could only wonder what the palaces of richer realms like Pangonia and the Sassanian Sultanates must be like. Perhaps he'd get to visit the famous White Palace at Rima too, if they ever got there.

A few servants had scowled at them suspiciously, but the King had let it be known they were in service with Master Horskram, a cherished friend to the House of Ingwin. The exorcism he had performed on Lady Walsa, Freidheim's cousin and sister to his late wife Queen Weirhilda, had placed him in high standing with the royal family. Privilege by association was always worth taking advantage of – commoners didn't get the freedom of their king's palace every day.

Adelko followed Vaskrian, struggling to keep up – he'd never been a fast runner and wasn't nearly as athletic as his older friend. But something in that music was having the same effect on him as the squire.

He hadn't heard anything quite like it before – even through the ceiling, the notes were alluring and stoked up mixed emotions in his breast. He felt euphoric and melancholy at the same time. Feasting-time in the Hall of Kings also meant jugglers, musicians, dancing girls and other ribald entertainments, but Northlendings didn't play music like this.

A few minutes of scurrying up and down corridors brought them to a narrow flight of stairs leading up to the roof. The music was louder now; above the melodious strings they could hear a dulcet voice begin to sing. As they ascended the stairs, Adelko tripping clumsily on his habit, it grew louder still; other voices could be heard singing in harmony with the leader.

'Come on!' hissed Vaskrian, grabbing Adelko and hauling him back on to his feet.

They emerged on to the windswept roof of the palace. Perched against its crenelated walls lounged a handsome knight, playing a harp and singing in a high clear voice. Another half a dozen men of similar appearance loitered around him, joining their voices to the chorus with gusto.

The leader knight was tall and slim, his lithe body well made despite his lack of bulk. His long auburn tresses swirled about him; grey-green eyes sparkled in acknowledgement as the two youths approached him. He was sumptuously dressed in black velvet breeches and doublet trimmed with gold lace arranged in pleasing arboreal patterns. Around his slender waist was a girdle of dyed green leather with a gold clasp fashioned to resemble two interlocking daggers. A real poignard hung from this, its hilt and baldric chased with damascened silver that offset the rich bark-coloured leather of the scabbard. His boots were of the supplest doe-skin and a rich green colour.

Three of his companions were similarly attired, though somewhat less splendidly, while the other three were more plainly dressed in similar colours. Most of them had the same pale complexion and auburn hair as their leader. One knight was considerably older than the rest, with greying hair; another had raven-black tresses and looked almost as handsome as the knight playing the harp.

Several of them bore signs of injury: Adelko could spot the tell-tale bulk of bandages beneath the rich clothing. His own head injury had healed somewhat, though his swaddled forehead still throbbed. He suddenly felt self-conscious: what must he look like, a pious monk with his head all trussed up?

The flamboyant knights did not cease their song. Adelko recognised the language as Thrax. He wasn't quite fluent, but he knew enough to follow the words:

From far across the field
The sun reached for the sky
The sad knight raised his shield
As he prepared to die
His coat of mail was stained
With blood from head to toe
His heart forever pained
By thoughts no swain should know

High above the clouds
The mountain castle loomed
The damsel wept aloud
She knew her love was doomed
Her face was streaked with tears
Her soul it knew remorse
Her brave knight knew no fear
His life had run its course

At this point the rest of the company joined in on what Adelko supposed must be the chorus:

So be wary ye knights and ladies
Put not glory before love!
Make peace ye knights and ladies
Forsake the eagle for the dove!

The lead knight began the next verse alone again, plucking the strings more quietly than before, muting them with his palm so they carried a hint of underlying menace:

Out across the plains
The battle-wounded wailed
The sad knight fought for shame
Of the lady love he'd failed
On the left and right he slew
Till corpses piled in mounds
Though glory was his due
Ease of heart he never found

Now from her silver tower
His tearful mistress croaked:
'Gwinian come to my bower,
Forget the words I spoke!'
But her words had cut too deep
The wound could not be healed
Except by gift of sleep
Earned in slaughter on the field

Once again the other Thraxians joined in with the chorus:

So be wary ye knights and ladies
Put not glory before love!
Make peace ye knights and ladies
Forsake the eagle for the dove!

This time, when the lead knight resumed solo, he plucked the strings and let them resonate, so that each note seemed to hang in the air in defiance of the billowing wind that swirled about the citadel summit. He raised his voice another octave; it cut across the keening gusts like lightning piercing thunderous clouds:

At last he met his end
A spear shaft pierced his breast
He fell dying to the ground
Gasping: 'Now I'll have my rest!
'When Rowena you next see
'Will you tell her of my valour
'Will you tell her I was worthy
'To be her paramour!'

He brought his voice low again, the strings barely audible now as he delivered the last verse in chilling tones:

They brought Sir Gwinian home
Wrapped in cloth of white
People wept high and low
As candles flared by night
Rowena fled in sorrow
Back up to her high room
And stepping from her window
She embraced her lover's doom

Again the other Thraxians joined in on the final chorus with an even greater gusto than before. This time Adelko felt confident enough of knowing the words to do the same:

So be wary ye knights and ladies
Put not glory before love!
Make peace ye knights and ladies
Forsake the eagle for the dove!

The lead knight finished the last phrase with a grand flourish, drawing slender fingers across the strings, plucking extra notes to add resonance. The final chord seemed to hang in the air for an interminable length of time, before being swallowed up by the wind.

Without knowing quite what else to do, Vaskrian and Adelko filled the silence with enthusiastic applause.

The foreign men smiled at this, none more broadly than their leader, who ran his fingers gently across his harp again as he said in accented but fluent Northlending: 'Oh ho! It seems we have garnered ourselves an audience, and a right mismatched one too by the looks of it – a monk and a man of arms, unless I'm very much mistaken!'

His accent carried the singsong lilt of the Thraxians, whose tongue was almost as melodious as their legendary music-making.

'I'm Adelko of Narvik, a novice of the Order of St Argo,' replied the novice. He felt clumsy of speech, even though they were speaking his native language.

'And my name is Vaskrian of Hroghar,' put in the squire, 'in service to Sir Ulfstan of Alfheim, lately squire to Sir Branas of Veerholt, Reus rest his soul.'

The knight's cheerful countenance darkened momentarily. 'It sounds – and looks – as if you've had yourselves a dangerous journey to get here,' he said. 'Strangely comforting to learn we aren't the only ones who got into a scrape on the way to Strongholm!'

With a florid sweep of his arm he motioned them to sit beside him.

'Come!' he said. 'You've been lured up here by our sweet tune, now linger a while and tell me your story. Apart from Sir Vertrix here,' he indicated the grey-haired knight, 'my countrymen speak little of your tongue, but I would fain hear more of your travels and what brings you here. I am Sir Braxus of Gaellen, knight of Thraxia and son of Lord Braun of Gaellentir, a fair land of fairer folk that lies across the Hyrkrainian Mountains.'

The flamboyant knight inclined his head courteously. Vaskrian and Adelko bowed low. They were in the presence of a high-ranking nobleman, albeit a foreign one.

Sitting next to Braxus, Adelko gazed over the rampart overlooking the harbour. Since they had arrived many of the ships had put out to sea – even now the roiling blue dunes of the Wyvern would be stained red with the hues of war, as the loyalist fleet led by Prince Thorsvald clashed with the mighty flotilla assembled by Krulheim. No sign of that aquatic struggle yet besmirched the Strang Estuary, whose peaceful waters were for the moment troubled only by the mustering North Wind.

Sir Braxus handed his harp to the raven-haired knight.

'Here, look after this would you, Regan – only don't try playing it! I still haven't forgotten the time you murdered the *Ballad of Curulaîn and Magwyn* at the last Feast of Palom's Ascension!'

Sir Regan flashed his leader a rakish and unabashed grin. 'Well it's a murder ballad after all, so I only thought it fitting!' he chuckled in Thrax. Adelko couldn't help but smile. He had to admit, Thraxian knights were a lot less stiff than Northlending ones. Vaskrian, completely ignorant of their tongue, stared blankly.

Turning back to look at the youths Sir Braxus shook his head and smiled wryly. 'Grand fellow, Regan – a trusty sword and a passable tenor,' he said in Northlending. 'Couldn't play the strings to save his own mother though, bless him!'

Vaskrian could join in on that joke. The butt of it seemed oblivious, and had turned back to speak with Vertrix and the fourth knight. The other three Thraxians, presumably squires, were already talking amongst themselves.

'Now,' Braxus continued, fixing the pair with keen eyes. 'Tell me your story, and I'll tell you mine. We've been all but ignored since we got here, and it's nice to meet some fellow outsiders who aren't complete strangers to this country like us.'

Adelko and Vaskrian exchanged uneasy glances. The young knight was friendly and charismatic, but on their first night at the palace Horskram had given them strict instructions to keep their mission secret.

And you didn't want to get on the wrong side of Horskram, especially not lately. He was even crabbier than usual. Several times that week the adept had thumped his tanned fist down hard on the table when Adelko had made a few forgivable errors at the lectern.

Licking his lips nervously he did his best to dissemble. Leaving out the details of the Headstone fragment, and skirting around their more diabolical encounters, he told their story as best he could to Sir Braxus, who scrutinised them both and stroked his well-kept beard and moustache thoughtfully throughout.

When he reached the final part about their audience with the King, Adelko waxed lyrical to make up for his previous reticence.

That wasn't too difficult – the memory was a powerful one, and still fresh in his young mind.

The royal guards had pulled back the doors to split old Thorsvald's head asunder, revealing a large rectangular chamber. To one side a row of tall windows looked onto the harbour, while a great tapestry ran the length of the opposite wall.

It depicted great victories won by the House of Ingwin: the Hero King's crushing defeats of the Woldings and the Highlanders, Adelko's ancestors; the successive struggles against the Thraxians in what would later become known as the Border Wars, culminating in Freidheim's triumph at Corne Hill nearly half a hundred years ago; and last of all his defeat of Kanga, father to the present pretender, at the Battle of Aumric Fields.

Beyond that a stretch of canvas lay blank and bare, inviting future history to stitch its deeds across its waiting surface – deeds soon to be wrought, for good or ill. Above them the rafters of the high hall were strewn with banners bearing the royal coat of arms; a riot of dancing unicorns seemed to swirl about the oaken beams in the brisk sea breeze.

Before them a thick carpet of horsehair stretched to the foot of the dais where the King sat flanked by his advisers on the Pine Throne.

That had been built by Manfred the Ready, when he succeeded the unfortunate Olav Iron-Hand. After destroying the cursed throne that had brought such ruin on his predecessor, he had decided a more humble perch for his regal buttocks might be wise. Manfred had ordered wood from the longship that had brought him over the Sea of Valhalla used to forge a seat that would last – and not destroy its owner.

But it wasn't the Pine Throne – nor even its royal occupant – that drew the eye as they trudged up the horsehair carpet, flanked on either side by a throng of curious knights.

Looming over the royal seat was the most impressive – and grisliest – hanging Adelko had ever seen.

A macabre collection of giant femurs, tibias, ribs and other skeletal parts was arranged in a crude sunburst pattern centring on a huge skull the size of a man. Adelko felt his spine tingle as its yellowed teeth parted in a silent rictus of welcome, its cavernous eye sockets staring hollowly at the new arrivals.

The Giantslayer's Gift, they called it. He'd read about it in Ulfang's library – the macabre hanging was fashioned from the remains of the Gigant, Horg, who had descended from the mountains during Thorsvald's reign to wreak havoc on the lowlands.

Legend told how Sir Valkryn, greatest of the Thirteen Knights, had put an end to Horg's rampaging. On the foothills of the Hyrkrainians he had driven his dagger beneath the giant's big toenail, inflicting a tiny but agonising wound and causing Horg to topple and strike himself senseless against a hill. As Horg lay out of his wits, Sir Valkryn had driven his sword deep into the corner of his eye, piercing the monstrous creature's dull brain and killing him.

Not the most chivalrous way of despatching an opponent – but then one had to make some allowances when faced with an opponent many times one's size with concrete for skin, and few thought Valkryn any less a hero for his cunning tactics.

Braxus nodded enthusiastically, caught up in Adelko's skilful interweaving of history into his story.

'Aye, that tale is well known in our country too,' he mused. 'Other tales say the cause of Horg's rampaging was the elementalist Yabra, a descendent of the White Blood Witch who troubled Pangonia during its own age of heroes. You are well informed, it would seem – but then I should expect no less from an Argolian novice.'

Adelko suppressed his un-Palomedian feelings of pride as the knight continued: 'I know several songs in our tongue that tell of your Thirteen Knights and their exploits. After Sir Valkryn killed Horg, he gathered together Sir Damrod of Linden, Sir Wolfram of Salmor and Sir Kalla of Thule, and they braved the mountains in the dead of winter to seek Yabra in his eyrie. They slew him after defeating his guardians, demons conjured from ice – they say that since then no giant has ever descended to trouble the dwellings of men on either side of the Hyrkrainians. So despite all our differences, we can at least be thankful to the Northlendings for that!'

Adelko's sixth sense registered a deep-seated tension in the knight at the mention of mountains. And when he had mentioned his highland upbringing the handsome face had briefly contorted in an ugly scowl. He had better tread carefully – charming or not, Braxus didn't seem like a man you wanted to cross.

'Most loremasters agree there are probably less than a dozen Gigants left in the entire range,' Adelko said nervously, before deciding to get off the subject of mountains. 'They learned to fear us long ago, thanks to the Elder Wizards. The sages say they enslaved the Gigants, and used them to build their palaces and watchtowers.'

Braxus raised an eyebrow at this. 'The Priest-Kings of Ancient Varya, you mean? I certainly don't know any songs about those times – a race of devil-worshipping warlocks, I've heard, half demon, half man! They nearly brought the entire world to ruin if the legends be true.'

Adelko faltered – he hadn't meant to get on to this subject at all.

'Accounts vary,' he stammered, before changing tack again. 'Anyway, you'll know that Valkryn brought back Horg's corpse and had his bones stripped clean. Then King Thorsvald had them mounted in the Hall of Kings, so everyone could see his greatest triumph.'

Braxus grunted noncommittally. 'See it, you say? Be awed by it, more like,' he said grudgingly. 'Few kings have ever boasted a giantslayer among their knights – Sir Lancelyn of the Pale Mountain who served King Vasirius of Pangonia is the only other I know of.'

Vaskrian's eyes lit up at the mention of the legendary knight, still believed by most to be the greatest that ever lived. He was about to say something but Braxus cut him off.

'But come, you were talking of your audience with the King, the very man we've come here to speak with ourselves. I'd hear more of what he had to say. Pray continue!'

Adelko nodded and went on with his story.

Their ceremonial entrance done, another herald next to the throne had bellowed: 'Freidheim II, Lord Protector of the Realm, First Scion of the Kingdom of Northalde, Seventh King of the Lineage of Ingwin, bids thee all rise!'

⁜ ⁜ ⁜

Adelko got to his feet. In keeping with the first herald's instructions, he kept his eyes on the horsehair carpet as his King addressed them: 'Welcome, travellers, to my hall. All of you are known to me save yon youths. What are your names?'

Adelko raised his eyes, glancing sidelong at Vaskrian as he did. The squire seemed momentarily lost for words, before answering haltingly. Adelko did likewise, though he suddenly felt very small and struggled to keep his composure. He hadn't expected the King to take any interest in him. He was peripherally aware of the knights of the court staring at him, but the scrutiny of the man before him was far more arresting.

He certainly dressed like the King of a realm founded by sea princes. His electrum crown had been fashioned to resemble a flotilla of longships and warlike mariners, the details picked out with aquamarines; his robes of office were the colour of the waves and decorated with stylised ships of mother-of-pearl.

But King Freidheim would have been a presence without his regal paraphernalia.

Like Horskram, he was robust for a man of his winters, his brawny arms knotted with muscles that had not yielded to time. His kingly beard was an iron-grey colour that matched his keen eyes and shrouded a broad, perfectly proportioned face. To call him handsome would have been to miss the mark: *well wrought* was nearer the truth.

Adelko knew some clerical scholars argued that kings who ruled over Palomedian realms were divinely inspired; Reus touched such fortunates in the womb, endowing them with gifts. Many of the Palomedian rulers he had read about seemed hardly to warrant such a contention, but in Freidheim II he found the argument convincing.

'And how was your journey to my city, Adelko of Narvik?' the King pressed. 'How smooth the way, in this grievous time of war?'

His voice was manly without being harsh, but it resonated with the manifest confidence of one who expects to be obeyed. Adelko could sense a lingering sadness too. He didn't have time to puzzle that over – he was far more baffled as to why his King was taking such an interest in him. Along with Vaskrian he was the least important person in their retinue.

It took him a few painful seconds to gather his wits and answer.

'It... was not without its hardships, Your Majesty,' he stammered, struggling to meet his monarch's eye. 'We ran into some dangers... but we're very pleased to be here now...' His voice trailed off. He knew he shouldn't divulge too many details about their mission – but how did you refuse to answer your King?

Some of the knights and ladies tittered, amused by his meek attempts at politesse. Adelko felt his ears burning.

'Silence!' boomed the King, raising his voice and sweeping the hall with an iron glare. He got it instantly; Adelko fancied he could hear the roaring waves of the Strang Estuary grow louder as Freidheim's voice crashed through the chamber with an elemental force.

'I'll not have an honest man mocked in my hall!' he roared. 'Yes indeed, you can always count on a youthful tongue for an honest answer!

I daresay your response, when you give it Master Horskram, will be considerably more guarded than your novice's – though you are a welcome guest. You are all welcome guests!'

The King was the soul of affability now; Adelko was stunned by how quickly he seemed able carry his voice from one intense emotion to another with the utmost conviction.

'And now,' continued Freidheim, his voice suddenly becoming flatly neutral, 'Sir Tarlquist, the latest news of the war. Horskram, I shall want to hear what brings you to Strongholm afterwards – in private, as I'm sure you will prefer. I don't doubt you'll have strange and unsettling tidings, as usual. Not lightly do you visit my halls.'

Horskram acquiesced with a courteous nod, saying nothing. Sir Tarlquist did all the talking after that, omitting the demonic attack on Staerkvit by prior agreement – the last thing needed now was a superstitious panic sweeping the capital on the eve of war. Sir Torgun kept his counsel, managing to look even meeker than Adelko felt. The novice wondered if the knight was happiest saying nothing. As for Sir Wolmar, even he seemed to know to keep quiet in the presence of his uncle the King.

The hall erupted with cries of anger when Sir Tarlquist recounted the fall of Salmor and Rookhammer: the White Valravyn's attempt to save the former foiled by sorcery, the latter's entire garrison put to the sword.

'And so does the traitor of Thule repay my kindness in sparing his life seasons ago, when all my advisers, kith and kin counselled me otherwise!' the King thundered after Tarlquist had finished, his rage waxing dark and terrible. 'Thus does the Almighty punish proud fools who refuse to besmirch their precious honour for the greater good! Alas, that I should be played a gull to the better angels of my conscience!'

His voice had become sorrowful; keen as his sixth sense was, Adelko fancied he could literally feel the monarch's pain. 'And so it may rightly be said that this tragedy is my doing!' he continued, before reverting back to white-hot anger in the blinking of an eye: 'Yet here and now do I vow that blood shall atone! Krulheim shall not be allowed to escape justice! No, nor this idolatrous foreign hedge wizard, who thinks it clever to unman brave knights with sorcerous chicanery! Tell the heralds without – one hour more I shall linger to hear petitions, and only those made by victims of this cruel civil war! Then let the hall be cleared, let every knight and man of arms go look to his weapons – for we shall not be long in riding out to meet this impostor! Thule marches on Linden, does he? Well we'll meet him there, and send him to Gehenna where he belongs on a tide of his own blood!'

A resounding cheer filled the hall. Even Adelko, unmartial as he was, found himself joining in without thinking. Only Horskram remained silent, keeping his usual alert composure.

⁜ ⁜ ⁜

'And that was our first meeting with the King!' finished Vaskrian, having interrupted Adelko a couple of minutes earlier so he could re-enact Freidheim's speech-making – it was already clear to Braxus that he was the enthusiastic type when it came to military matters. 'We haven't seen him since – well, except at feast times, but he's so far away up the other end of the hall, we don't *really* get to see him...'

Braxus continued to scrutinise the pair of them as they lapsed into awkward silence. It was painfully obvious the youngsters were concealing plenty.

'You make a meal of your first encounter with your King,' he said at last, 'but stint on details of your journey to meet him... Well, I'm sure your master is as wise as they say the Argolians are in swearing you both to secrecy.'

Adelko glanced nervously at Vaskrian. The young monk might have known many things that Braxus didn't, but lying well certainly wasn't one of them. His mentor, this friar Horskram, had evidently given him strict instructions. But then the Argolians were well known for being a secretive bunch.

Ignoring the guilty looks on their ingenuous faces the knight continued: 'Your Order is not unknown in my realm – fear not, I will respect the learned friar's wishes by prying no more into your business. It's clear to me that he doesn't want you sharing it with too many people.'

'Thank you,' said Adelko, looking plainly relieved.

Braxus saw no reason to pry further in any case – he had already learned the most valuable thing he could from them, namely the state of mind of the king they had come to petition. And what he'd learned didn't put him in an optimistic mood.

'And what about you, my lord, if I may make so bold?' said Vaskrian. 'It's always good to hear a knight errant tell his story...'

Sir Braxus laughed. 'If it's knights' tales you're after, then you can begin by addressing me as one – "sir knight" will do, I shan't be a lord until I inherit my father's lands and title.'

Vaskrian looked puzzled at this. 'But in Northalde the heir of any baron is called "lord" – as a courtesy title, if you will.'

'Pah,' snorted Braxus. 'Where I come from we don't stand on ceremony half so much as you Northlendings. We call a man what he is – at present I hold no lands, command no men but these, my fellow emissaries. I am trained to arms, and deeds of courtly love... and feats of both have I accomplished many, of that I can assure you! But until I inherit my father's estate I am what I am – a knight, no more, no less.'

Vaskrian chewed his lip, clearly thrown by this casual rejection the world order he had grown up in.

Looking at him brought a stab of guilt to Braxus's heart. The Northlending squire reminded him a little of Paidlin. He was a couple of years older and looked a lot tougher – but then Paidlin might have looked like that in two summers, given the chance.

The amputation had been taken care of quickly and cleanly by the King's chirurgeon, as befitted the squire of an honoured guest at court. That had saved his life – but the poor lad's career was over before it had begun.

Adelko took advantage of his temporary silence to interject: 'You said "fellow emissaries", my – sir knight... what message do you bring from your land? Will the Thraxians be supporting the King's cause against the rebels?'

Braxus laughed again. You had to relish the irony. 'Why no!' he said, trying not to sound too exasperated. 'In fact, I was sent here for virtually the opposite reason – I come on behalf of my father, who would seek your King's help with a planned uprising against our own.'

Both youths gaped at this. 'But that makes you a rebel and a traitor,' said Vaskrian hotly. 'You're no different from Thule!'

He looked genuinely angry, as if he were about to challenge him to a duel of honour right there and then. Brave lad. Foolish, but brave – you had to give him that.

Braxus merely chuckled again, although this time his mirth carried a bitter tinge.

'That, I would say, all depends on the nature of the sovereign one seeks to oppose,' he said ruefully. His retinue were mostly talking among themselves in Thrax, but Vertrix was listening, a grim expression on his face.

'Our last King, Cullodyn son of Morwyn, was a good man,' sighed Braxus. ''Twas he who turned the truce with Freidheim after Corne Hill into a lasting peace. Morwyne was cowed after the hiding you dealt us there, but ever in his heart he hated you, and would have continued the Border Wars if he'd felt able to. Cullodyn, he was cut from a different cloth – he saw the folly of making war on a powerful neighbour when so much of his own kingdom remained unpacified. He spent the entire thirty years of his reign fighting the highland clans, who still dispute the crown and wish to see the Kingdom of Thraxia broken up. You see, our problems are similar to yours.'

He caught the young monk frowning. But then he was of highland stock. True, the Northlending highlanders were of mingled blood and had embraced the Creed long ago, but they could still trace their ancestry back to Slánga's forebears.

Well, the novice would just have to weigh his loyalties in his own time. They had asked to hear his story, and now he was giving it to them.

'But now we have another problem,' he continued. 'When Cullodyn passed four years ago he was succeeded by his nephew Cadwy. At first we thought he'd be a decent king like his uncle – he'd distinguished himself in the wars against the highland clans, and promised to be as wise in rule as he was cunning in the field.'

'So what went wrong?' asked Vaskrian.

'A southland witch called Abrexta the Prescient is what went wrong,' replied Braxus, before telling them of the troubles her sorcerous meddlings had plunged the realm into.

They looked a little more sympathetic after that – at least they weren't still accusing him of fomenting treason. These Northlendings were a serious lot but give them their due, they did have a strong sense of justice.

A lowly novice and squire – perhaps he was a fool to even care about placating such. But they were listening to him, which was more than could be said of the high-born nobles and influential courtiers who had snubbed them since they arrived. Perhaps they should consider themselves fortunate just to be lodged at the palace, he reflected bitterly.

'Now, we're not trying to kill our King, or even depose him, you understand,' he continued, doing his best to reassure them further. 'But we need to act to save the kingdom, and the only way we're going to do that is by taking the capital and putting that witch to the sword – her, and whoever's put her up to this! Personally I think the southerners are behind it – they're every bit as troublesome as yours, and this Abrexta hails from their lands. Well, we'll find out. But first we need to storm Ongist so we can get her away from the King, and to do that we need an army. Even without having to worry about fighting Slánga's lot we still don't have enough men to do it without getting help. Help from your King.'

Vaskrian frowned. 'Begging your pardon, sire, but I think our King's got his hands full dealing with his own problems.'

Braxus returned the frown. 'Aye, that seems to be the case. We arrived here three nights ago, and so far he's been too busy even to hear our plea.'

'How did you hope to convince him in any case?' asked Adelko. It was a shrewd question. He might have added: *Why would the King of the Northlendings help a country he and his ancestors fought for generations?* The young knight had been asking himself the same question all the way from Port Grendel. He still had mixed feelings about his father's master plan. But then he had mixed feelings about everything that concerned the old man.

He sighed again. 'A pledge to grant favourable trading terms once the King is restored to his wits and Abrexta and her nest of traitors rooted out,' he replied. 'Plus an annual surfeit of Thraxian furs and mead, and a certain sum to be paid out of the treasury once order is restored. Then there's the possibility of mining ebonite in the Brekkens, if we should succeed in crushing the highlanders utterly. That black metal is harder than steel, they say – though to be honest none have ever learned to smelt it since the times of the ancients. Still it's an extra incentive, if you will. The rewards we offer are all speculative, of course.'

He felt his spirits sinking like a scuttled man o' war. The more he spoke of it the less likely to succeed his suit seemed. In fact one might have more joy trying to forge something out of ebonite.

'Perhaps we have come here on a fool's errand,' he said sourly, giving free rein to his gloomy thoughts. 'But there seems little else we can do under the circumstances.'

⊹ ⊹ ⊹

The Thraxian knight lapsed into a moody silence. His jocularity erased by his storytelling, he gazed across the battlements at the rolling surf with sad eyes.

'Our King is a just man – he will hear your plea at least,' said Vaskrian. The knight grunted noncommittally, looking none the happier.

Adelko bit his lip and said nothing. Part of him sympathised with the highland rebels. True, the tales Braxus told made the Thraxian clans sound completely different from the god-fearing, peaceful folk he'd grown up with: the way he put it, the men that followed Slánga were little better than bloodthirsty savages.

But then that was *his* side of the story. If the young monk could have sat and talked with this Slánga, what kind of picture would he have painted of the lowland knights – who kept his people confined to the ragged ranges while they squabbled and fought over the country's rich lowlands?

Thinking on this and the troubles of his own realm, Adelko reflected how fragile a thing a kingdom was. Loremasters told how the Urovian New Empire was made up of seven older kingdoms that had been pacified and united during the Hundred Years Conquest – yet in this corner of the world kings struggled to rule a single realm.

Rebellion and war, bloodshed and treachery – was it worth all that to keep a kingdom together? His own people had lived meagrely but stably in small, tightly knit communities for centuries – why couldn't the rest of the world follow suit and learn from its more humble occupants?

Adelko recalled Horskram's words on the road to Kaupstad, about wars being fought time and again for the wrong reasons. He felt he was beginning to understand his mentor's world weariness better.

It was not a feeling that he relished.

⊰ CHAPTER IV ⊱

A Realm Divided

Lord Visigard's face was set grim as he gave his liege the latest news of the muster. Princess Hjala Ingwin, the King's only daughter, watched him keenly as he did.

'The White Valravyn has commenced marching and will be outside the walls of the capital in full panoply in two days' time,' said Visigard stiffly. The old raven didn't look nearly as self-important as he normally would giving such news, Hjala reflected. Rather he had the look of a man who was grateful to be giving such news at all.

Hjala knew all too well why that was, but of the strange and terrible incident that had disrupted the Order's war preparations nothing was said.

They were in the King's solar high up in the palace, although its spectacular view across the city was the last thing on the princess's mind. Hjala had plenty else to think about. She had also been present when Sir Tarlquist and the monk Horskram had told her father of the dreadful attack on Staerkvit a tenday ago. It had been decided on the spot that the less said about it on the eve of war the better.

And a good job too, the princess reflected as the Royal Marshal droned through his report: for what her aunt Walsa would have had to say about it alone.

'The barons of Efrilund have also begun marching,' continued Visigard. 'Lord Vymar of Harrang and Lord Fenrig of Hroghar will travel overland with their men, while Lord Aesgir of Sjórvard brings troops and supplies south by sea.'

Lord Toros of Vandheim had already done likewise: his knights and soldiers were encamped with the Royal Army and the Jarl of Stromlund's forces outside the city. As usual, the problem lay with the Wolding barons, who were procrastinating as they always did on the eve of any conflict, in the hope of extracting some petty concession or other.

The latest news of them made matters only worse.

'The Woldings are refusing to let the Highland chieftains pass through their domains until they pay a toll for the privilege,' said Visigard, sighing and shaking his head. 'We had to factor that into our bargaining with the hill-land barons.'

Hjala pursed her lips. Highlanders were far from rich and proud as the day was long – there would certainly be no paying of tolls, not from their purses at any rate. They had no other route to the muster, shipcraft being virtually unknown to them. The Woldings were taking full advantage of their feudal privileges to drive the hardest bargain they could with the Dominions.

'Damn the Woldings, curse their wretched hides!' shouted the King, slamming a broad fist down on the solid oak table before him with enough force to rattle it. 'It's always the same with them! I've a good mind to make war on *them* after we're done with the southron traitors – I should have offered the Highland chieftains their lands to help us crush those robber barons years ago!'

'Your policy has ever been to make peace wherever you could, and resort to war only as a final recourse,' Lord Ulnor reminded him crisply.

He said this in a manner that suggested he had long disapproved of such clemency, and would have happily seen the King's angry suggestion played out long ago.

Princess Hjala had never fully trusted the cold-eyed steward and his icy reasoning. The Royal Seneschal stood at her father's right shoulder as she stood at his left, facing Visigard across the table. That was appropriate, she reflected somewhat bitterly. In the presence of the steward and marshal she felt just like a left arm: not useless by any means, but clearly not the most important limb in the kingdom's complex polity. At least she was privy to her father's counsels, she reflected philosophically – that was more than most high-born women could say.

'We have taken steps to... appease the Woldings,' clarified Visigard cautiously, adjusting his girdle. 'They have at any rate agreed to take our part in the war – the passage of the Highlanders is also being negotiated.'

In charge of the security of the capital, Visigard was a rotund, barrel-chested knight of about sixty winters. His voluminous side whiskers cascaded down his ruddy cheeks in a snowy tumble, and his bald pate was a shiny red. Though he was a seasoned Commander in the Order of the White Valravyn, Hjala found him somewhat comical. She didn't doubt his loyalty or efficiency, but his pomposity and appearance made it difficult for her to take him entirely seriously.

'And what has been promised them?' asked the King, his face frozen over with cold rage.

'Nothing, in short, that cannot be renegotiated after the rebellion has been put down,' interjected Lord Ulnor. It disturbed Princess Hjala that the seneschal seemed always to know of every negotiation that transpired in the kingdom before her father did. Fortunate indeed that he had proved as loyal as he was effective, she thought uneasily.

'Very well,' said the King, waving his hand dismissively. 'You are right – now is no time to discuss such lowly matters. The Woldings can be dealt with after the war – in the meantime, how soon can they get here?'

Visigard licked his lips nervously. 'Our emissaries say a tenday at least – perhaps longer.'

'A tenday!' the King spat. 'Why, do they not know that Thule has invested Linden already, that my own son and heir is sorely pressed to defend it against the entirety of Krulheim's traitorous army?! At this rate his men will be marching across the Vyborg by the time ours move a foot towards the fight!'

'The Highlanders are ready,' said Visigard, doing his best to mollify his irate liege. 'They've always had the knack for mustering and moving swiftly – assuming the agreement with the Woldings is concluded in the next day or so, they could be here in a week's time.'

'Aye, and good subjects that makes 'em, even if I do barely have a say in their lives up in that blasted wilderness they call home,' replied the King irritably. 'But it's not lightly armoured clan swordsmen I need to win this war – it's armoured knights, as many as I can get! You know as well as I do how rich the southern fiefdoms are – that means Krulheim and his barons can field a mighty army. The one advantage we might have over him is in heavy horse.'

'Do not be so quick to dismiss the highlanders, Your Majesty,' interjected Horskram from his seat. He was sitting next to Tarlquist by a window overlooking the streets of the citadel. 'Much of Thule's army will not be ahorse as you rightly say, and doughty clansmen have proved more than a match for common footsoldiers ere this occasion.'

Tarlquist nodded his assent. 'Aye, my liege, and forget not my Order, that your very brother commands. Any raven is worth five lesser knights!'

'A little more modesty would become you, Sir Tarlquist, if you consider yourself a true knight,' replied the King, more wearily than acidly.

His only daughter had noticed that tired timbre creeping into his voice – normally such a potent force – more often of late. Her father had proved a mighty monarch, meeting the trials and tribulations of war and peace alike with a steady hand, yet even he was subject to mortal frailty.

Sixty-three winters... and now he had to go to war yet again to preserve his realm. Could he really stand much more of this? Princess Hjala felt a stab of pity –

she knew her father had spent half a century trying to do what was best for his people. How many other kings could say the same? He deserved better than this in the twilight of his life.

'And what of the battle at sea?' the King was asking, in the same weary tone. 'How speeds my other son?'

'The Sealord sends back word of being hard pressed,' said Visigard, his face lengthening. 'Of course when Lord Aesgir is able to join his ships to Prince Thorsvald's that should even the odds up, but as things stand... well, Thule appears to have had Lord Saltcaste impressing seafarers left and right for many months. Along with that he's also enlisted a score of longships crewed by reavers from the Northern Wastes – report has it they aren't hired freesailors either, they're commanded by seacarls loyal to the Frozen Thane Hardrada.'

There was a general muttering at that. A Thraxian cog had put into harbour several days ago with news of an attack by Northland reavers. Those hadn't been freesailors either – the dead pirate leader had been identified as a seacarl, the Northlandic equivalent of a knight. Hardrada and his fellow thanes were clearly weary of several generations of peace and itching for a return to war.

'First the Ice Thanes break the Treaty of Ryøskil, now one of them allies himself to Thule's cause,' said Tarlquist, his scarred face dark and brooding. 'This doesn't bode well at all – what's made them so bold all of a sudden, I wonder?'

Hjala didn't see that there was much to wonder at. In her eyes the answer was simple – fifteen years of relative peace had left the kingdom complacent; now a determined rebel with an army at his back was prepared to take advantage of that. She knew what she would do if she were a Northland thane, nursing an age-old grudge and hungry for mainland spoil.

'So far as we know it's only Hardrada who's broken with the treaty,' sighed the King. 'Let's not concern ourselves with the other Northland princes until we have to – we've plenty to deal with as it is. So, give me the sum, Visigard. By how much are we currently outnumbered at sea?'

'By two to one, my liege.' Visigard's blue-grey eyes sank to the floor like a breached cog.

A silent, uncomfortable pause followed. The King reached for the silver goblet of watered wine at his elbow. 'Have word sent to my son that he is under no circumstances to engage the enemy directly until he is reinforced by Lord Aesgir's ships,' he said. 'Hit and run tactics only – tell him to play for time, and above all don't let Thule's fleet get near the coast! We don't want them landing a sortie on the shores of Stromlund, we've enough to deal with at Linden as it is.'

'No indeed, Your Majesty, and I'm pleased to tell you that your command is already being carried out,' replied Visigard, his chest puffing out self-importantly – as it usually did when he felt he had good news for the King. 'In his latest message your son says this is precisely the stratagem he is pursuing until he is joined by naval reinforcements – or you tell him otherwise.'

It was good to see the unearthly attack on Staerkvit hadn't completely robbed the veteran commander of his pompous bearing, Hjala reflected wryly.

The King nodded. 'Good. Good boy, my Thorsvald. Sensible and keeps his head under fire. I wish I could say the same of my elder – but I trust he has since redeemed himself by stiffening Linden's defences.'

'Well, that brings us to our next matter – assessing our relative strengths in the field,' said Lord Visigard.

The King nodded. Turning to address a bloodied young knight standing just behind Visigard he boomed: 'Sir Bragamor, step forward! You've ridden hard from our last bastion – I believe you have an account of the Young Pretender's forces from my son Wolfram?'

The battle-weary knight obeyed. He was lightly armoured to facilitate speed of travel; his mail byrnie and the helm he carried under his arm were both dinted. His head was bandaged, his face sooty, his surcoat soiled with mud and the odd streak of blood.

'Thule assails us hard,' he said nervously. 'His palisades are finished and his catapults batter our outer walls. Our scouts report that he's constructing siege towers as well. He's also well equipped with archers. Thanks to the foresight of the Castellan of Linden we are well victualled, but even with His Highness's knights to stiffen our garrison we're sorely outnumbered and unable to mount an effective counter-attack. Thule's barons have men stationed about the castle for leagues around – of myself and two companions that were sent here, only I survived, and that barely.'

The knight's head and side of his face were bandaged. His light helm did not fully protect the face, leaving him vulnerable to snipers. 'I lost an earlobe to their archers,' he said with a hint of pride, 'but I was lucky compared to the others. Their shades will be seeking the Heavenly Halls as we speak.'

'They'll have much company in the coming weeks, I warrant,' put in Lord Visigard grimly.

The King's face was a stone mask. Only his eyes revealed the anguish he felt – it was a look Princess Hjala had seen before many times.

'Sir Bragamor, your valour in the face of hardship befits a true knight, and I shall not forget your service to the realm,' said the King, managing a wan smile. 'But now swiftly if you will, proceed to tell us how many men the traitor fields. I want as detailed an appraisal of his land army as it is in your power to give.'

War-wounded Bragamor answered as loudly as he could. When he was done the King sat back and emptied his goblet in a single draught.

'Twelve thousand men!' he repeated, scowling. 'More than a thousand knights plus a like number of squires, two thousand men-at-arms, the same number again of bowmen, and six thousand levied foot. This isn't a rebellion, it's a fully fledged civil war!'

'It is as much as we expected,' commented Lord Ulnor.

The King nodded curtly. 'Well, let's to it then – a summary of our own forces.'

Lord Visigard took a deep breath and began. 'The Order of the White Valravyn including my own garrison here comes to five hundred knights, the same again of men-at-arms, and three hundred bowmen.'

'And that assumes we are willing to empty the palace of guards,' put in Lord Ulnor.

'The regular watch that police the lower city number five hundred,' said Visigard. 'I could have them take over citadel duties as well if need be, to free up the entire Order.'

'If we lose this coming battle the city is doomed anyway,' said the King darkly. 'Sanction it, I do so permit you.'

Visigard nodded and continued with his reckoning. Before he had finished Hjala knew it would not be enough. As a princess of the blood royal she was well read, and her studies of mathematics had not been neglected in her youth. She listened in tense silence as the Royal Marshal eked out the numbers: five hundred knights with vassal holdings in the Dominions, a hundred knights apiece from the Jarls of Vandheim and Stromlund, five hundred archers mustered from the yeomanry of lands ruled directly by the King...

Not enough.

'When the Efrilunders arrive they should each have a hundred and fifty knights and the same again of squires, men-at-arms and bowmen,' Visigard droned on. 'The Highland clan chiefs between them are bringing some six hundred foot, doughty fighters as Horskram here was mentioning...'

Not enough.

'Yes, yes, and what of our own peasant levies and the thrice-cursed Woldings?' asked the King testily. The meagre figures weren't putting her father in the best of spirits. Hjala could hardly fault him for that.

'At such short notice we cannot hope to muster more than a thousand well enough trained to be of any use,' said Visigard. 'As for the Woldings, between them they should be able to bring another two hundred knights and the same again of foot. Don't expect any more. They won't stint on the levies at least – count on them for a thousand of their usual brutalised peasant conscripts to use as fodder.'

'I see,' replied the King, oblivious to Horskram's disgusted expression even if Hjala wasn't. Strange that a former knight should be so appalled by the realities of war, the princess mused. But then the old monk had forsaken the lance for the lectern long ago.

'Ach, I must be getting too old for all these figures,' muttered the King. 'What is our sum total in parts?'

Visigard paused to total an army that Princess Hjala had already calculated.

'More than eighteen hundred knights including the Woldings, and the same number of trained footsoldiers including the Highlanders,' he said gravely. 'Some twelve hundred archers and double that of peasant levies. Some eight and a half thousand fighting men overall including the squires.'

Not enough. Not nearly enough.

'So we outnumber them in horse by five hundred – assuming the Woldings can get here in time – but they overmatch us with archers, and outnumber us greatly overall thanks to their long-prepared levies,' said her father after a brief pause. 'Of trained foot we almost have parity – assuming the highlanders can get down here without further hindrance from those damned hill-dwellers! Master Horskram, you were right it seems about the importance of their contribution.'

Horskram returned his liege's acknowledgement with a brief nod. He looked as optimistic as Hjala felt.

Her father was obviously putting a brave face on things. She knew he had to as King – but she also knew he still believed he could win this war. After all, he had triumphed against superior odds at the Battle of Aumric Fields, and Corne Hill before then...

But he had been younger in those days, full of fire and vigour. His daughter knew the man beneath the crown too well – age had not greatly weakened his body, but it had attenuated his soul. Could an old man, even one like her father, really inspire his men to yet another victory against the odds?

She pushed the question away – she didn't like it.

'Sir Bragamor, tell me,' asked the King, 'there are levies, and there are levies... how well trained and equipped is their yeomanry?'

'From what our scouts tell us they are for the most part well prepared, for conscripts. Most have brigandines and light helms, and are armed with rude axes and spears. Our reports indicate they have received some training, and to a man they are highly motivated – Thule has promised them a lifting of all royal taxes under his reign.'

'A lifting of royal taxes?' roared the King. 'Or a lifting of the taxes Krulheim and his ilk levied on their own peasantry to pay my tribute? I seem to recall levying royal taxes on southron nobles, not their common folk!'

'Nonetheless, as barons it is their feudal prerogative to set taxes of their own where they deem fit to do so,' Lord Ulnor reminded his King, none too gently Hjala thought. 'These past years it has been all too easy for the traitor Krulheim to blame the woes of his people on the capital.'

'Aye, aye,' replied the King, waving a hand irately. 'Spare me the reminders of the exigencies of rulership, Lord Ulnor, I've had plenty enough over the years! And what of the quality of our own levy?'

'Don't expect the Wolding conscripts to be armed with anything more than pitchforks and clubs,' put in Sir Tarlquist. 'And as for training and armour, the royal breath should not be held. I doubt half of them will even have decent clothes.'

'The levied yeomanry from the Dominions at least should be a match for Thule's commoners,' added Lord Visigard. 'And the Efrilunders will hopefully have given some thought to training and equipping their yeomen.'

'Some, but not much,' warned Horskram. 'I have travelled often in the hinterlands, and whilst you will find their knights and soldiers as doughty as any, the Efrilunders don't give much thought to training irregulars. Frankly, they are too preoccupied with gaining their own glory on the battlefield to concern themselves with such matters. Besides that they don't get much trouble nowadays, other than skirmishes with the Woldings and the odd Northland privateer.'

The King sighed, motioning for a page boy to refill his cup from the matching silver flagon next to it.

'And so it goes!' he exclaimed again. 'Peace has made us all soft – while in his bitterness and contumely Thule has silently oiled his machine of war! But still, once the northerners get down here we should comfortably outnumber them with horse at least – '

The door to the King's solar was suddenly flung open by the raven knight guarding it.

'Your Majesty,' he said. 'Sir Torgun is without and brings urgent news from his brother Lord Toros of Vandheim.'

The King's face darkened again. 'Well, better let him in then!' he bellowed. Hjala felt an old twinge of longing as her former paramour entered the room, looking as handsome and well-made and earnest as ever.

'Your Majesty,' said the blond knight, taking a knee to the rushes.

'Up, up,' said Freidheim, gesturing impatiently. 'We have no time for formalities – what is it?'

Raising his huge frame in one fluid motion despite his full armour, Sir Torgun gave them his news. It was no better than the rest of it.

'I was at the muster camp with my brother when a messenger from Stromlund arrived,' he said. 'The seacarls sailed their longships around Prince Thorsvald's blockade while it was being pressed by the rest of Thule's fleet. They've made a landing, some ten miles south of Lake Strom.'

'How many of them?' asked the King, his eyes narrowing.

'They say all twenty longships landed, Your Majesty, and disgorged their entire contents. Some two thousand reavers armed to the teeth are now marching cross country towards Linden. They must have a native of our land with them who knows the way, for they make swift progress.'

'But a Northland longship carries no more than fifty men at most,' interjected Visigard. 'They surely could not number more than a thousand!'

Torgun shook his head. 'The longships were never intended for use in the sea battle it seems – Krulheim had them join with his main flotilla only to make it look so, then turn aside for the coast at the last minute. They must have had extra men hiding in the aisles, two down the centre for every pair of rowers.'

The young knight's demeanour was as calm as ever. Hjala felt her heart quicken despite herself. That was what she had loved about him most – he was strong as steel, yet his manner was soft as silk.

'But that doesn't make sense,' said Tarlquist. 'A longship encumbered by a hundred men could never hope to outrun a Northlending cog!'

'Have you so soon forgotten our own experience of the forces that Thule commands?' asked Sir Torgun. 'We saw at Salmor that his hedge-wizard has some unnatural mastery of the waters.'

'And he is no hedge-wizard if he can harness the spirits of the sea to make ships move faster,' said Horskram, rising from his seat. 'I think young Torgun has the right of it – this tale smacks of sorcery and seems uncomfortably reminiscent of our own recent experiences with Northlanders.'

Lord Ulnor fixed the monk with a cold stare. Clearly Strongholm's master of secrets did not enjoy the presence of another man who had a few of his own. He had been present with Hjala at the private audience granted to Horskram and Tarlquist. It had been obvious the Argolian was holding back salient details. The adept had spoken of a theft from his monastery and a dangerous journey pursued by unspeakable forces linked to the attack on Staerkvit. But he had refused to elaborate until he and the King were alone. The seneschal hadn't been pleased about that at all.

'So, we can add two thousand battle-hardened reavers led by experienced seacarls to Thule's tally,' her father was saying. 'That means their trained footsoldiers will outnumber us by two to one, even with the Woldings and the Highlanders on our side. Their levies outnumber us three to one, and their bowmen nearly double ours. The only advantage we have is in knights, of which we outstrip them by a mere five hundred.'

A grim silence descended on the room. Even the fearsome reputation of the White Valravyn was small consolation in the face of such odds. And many of the Order's younger knights had never experienced a full-scale war before.

Not enough, not nearly enough.

'And how many men does my son command at Linden, Sir Bragamor?' asked the King at length.

'The castle itself is garrisoned with a hundred knights and two hundred footsoldiers, plus fifty crossbowmen,' replied Bragamor. 'Add to that the hundred knights Prince Wolfram brought with him and we have four hundred and fifty men at our disposal – assuming we can relieve them.'

'Well we can at least count on adding those to our tally, if they manage to hold Linden for the next fortnight,' said Visigard. The look on his face suggested he was only half sure that they would. So far the Young Pretender's forces had proved exceedingly adept at siege-craft. Hjala shared his misgivings. And adding her brother's beleaguered forces to their numbers in the face of such odds felt like scraping the bottom of the barrel in any case.

'My Lord Ulnor,' said Sir Tarlquist. 'Though it pains me to suggest such a thing, what about recruiting mercenaries of our own? It would take time, but could you not commission a sortie of reinforcements while we sally forth to save Linden? With His Majesty's leave of course – after all, there are plenty of those barbarian devils in our ports that could be hired into service.'

Lord Ulnor shook his head. 'The Treasury will not stand to it,' he replied in a voice that Hjala noted was strictly neutral. 'His Majesty's policy has ever been to look after the wellbeing of his subjects wherever possible, and he has instructed me to avoid punitive taxes on the Dominions. What revenue we have is already tied up in maintaining the Order and supporting the Temple's charitable works.'

'If only I could believe the Temple always justified the Crown's generosity,' interjected Horskram sourly.

Lord Ulnor shot him a piercing glance. 'Nonetheless, master adept, the Temple *is* the Almighty's true agency on this earth – and my understanding is that you crave some sort of boon from its leader here in Strongholm. Might I suggest therefore that such remarks are somewhat injudicious under the circumstances?'

Horskram scowled, not caring to meet the wily seneschal's eyes. 'Indeed you might,' was all he said, before turning to gaze out of the window.

'Besides,' continued the steward. 'There will be foreign mercenaries in our ports, but scarce enough to make a difference to a full-scale war at such short notice. And even if there were, the loan needed to hire them would take too much time to raise.'

'There shall be no further debts incurred by the Crown,' said Freidheim with an air of finality. 'Not on this upstart's account! The White Valravyn and loyal knights and lords shall uphold the security of the realm, as has ever been the case! Let the muster continue – Lord Visigard, send messengers back up north and tell the Woldings to get a move on. Agree nominally to anything within reason if it gets them here in a tenday – I want a united loyalist army on the move by the 15th of Vaxamonath at the very latest.'

'It shall be as you say,' said Visigard with a stiff bow before leaving, his chequered cloak and Sir Bragamor trailing in his wake.

The King turned to Horskram. 'Master monk, as you see I have precious little time to help you in your peculiar mission – though you have impressed on me the importance of its outcome.'

Hjala caught Lord Ulnor's eyes narrowing at Horskram. Oh, he didn't like being kept out of secrets, not one jot.

Freidheim paused a few moments, as if giving the matter one last weighing before deciding on a course of action.

'You have asked for an audience with the Arch Perfect and leave to make your way to Rima,' he said. 'I shall grant you both, but on my terms. Some days from now we shall hold council on the matter of your strange quest. I shall invite His High Holiness to this council, where you can make your petition to him after giving full disclosure of the details surrounding it. Also present shall be my right hand Lord Ulnor, and my brother whom you have already spoken with.'

Lord Ulnor relaxed visibly. So he would get to learn his precious new secret after all. Hjala sighed inwardly. Men were so predictable in their lust for control. Some might say it was lust for knowledge in this case, but after nearly forty years at court the princess knew it boiled down to the same thing in the end.

'Tarlquist and Torgun and my nephew Wolmar have also had some hand in this affair – I will have them party to this as well,' her father continued. 'Finally, my daughter and my dear late wife's sister Lady Walsa shall be present – the one is as shrewd a counsellor as any despite her gentler sex, and has her letters, which I feel may be of some use in this eldritch matter. The other will simply never let me rest if she hears of her worshipful Horskram on a dangerous mission against the netherworld that she is not privy to!'

Princess Hjala had to smile at this. Her aunt was as fiery and pious an old harridan as any that ever stalked a king about his court. Horskram suddenly looked extremely bashful, but said nothing.

As for her own inclusion in the secret council, she was content but hardly happy. Her father often took her into his closest confidence, but that would never mean taking her word over a man's. Never mind that she was wiser than most men.

The King added: 'Whether you choose to include your novice in the council is up to you, master monk. But I must point out that yon squire you travelled with has since been bound to one of my vassals for the duration of this war. I could permit you to summon him without his new knightly master of course – but such a thing would be in breach of all decorum.'

'I quite understand,' replied Horskram. 'If I may speak freely, Your Majesty, I am already slightly dismayed by the size of this so-called secret council. It will be no harm if the youth Vaskrian is not present – he already knows everything anyway.'

The King's eyes narrowed as he scrutinised the wilful monk. 'Your Order's penchant for secrecy is precisely what got it into such trouble twenty years ago,' he said frowning. 'Oh and that reminds me – the Abbot of Ulfang is too far away to summon to this council, but I will not have the head of the local Argolian chapter kept in the dark about something that concerns his Order so closely. Ulnor, you will send word to Prior Holfaste at Urling Monastery as well as the Arch Perfect. Tell them both they are summoned to court for a secret council. On no account will they breathe a word of the reason for their coming, not even to adepts and senior perfects.'

'I shall see to it at once, Your Majesty,' replied Lord Ulnor, shooting a triumphant glance at the peeved-looking monk before turning on his cane and sweeping out of the chamber.

'Now, if that is all pressing matters dealt with for the time being, I think I will repair next door to eat,' said the King, relaxing visibly. 'I have not had the chance of a meal since this morning and ruling restive realms is hungry work! Hjala, my dear, you shall join me. Private council is hereby dismissed.'

Princess Hjala caught Sir Torgun's eye as he turned to leave with Sir Tarlquist and the irascible old monk. Her heart skipped a beat as he smiled faintly at her... but then his back was to her, his armour jingling as he strode from the room.

She sighed inwardly and forced herself to let it go – the ashes had been raked over the fires of that romance long ago.

Her father sent the page boy to tell servants to prepare food, leaving the two of them alone in the solar.

Getting to his feet and walking over to a window, the King gazed out at the city he had ruled for half a century and sipped at his watered wine broodingly. Hjala walked over to join him as he emitted a sigh that heaved his broad shoulders up and down.

'After all these years of peace, Ezekiel and Stygnos come to test my resolve again,' he muttered. 'Haven't I shed enough blood already? Don't I deserve to see out my wintering years untroubled by yet another war? This is what comes of taking the Code of Chivalry too seriously – I should have killed Krulheim when I had the chance! Everyone near me at the time counselled such.'

His only daughter rested her long, elegant hands on his shoulders. She could feel his muscles, taught beneath the fur cloak he wore over his blue mantle. 'You would not be the King the people love if you had done such an unmerciful deed,' she said softly. 'Krulheim was but a boy.'

'Aye, 'twould have been an evil deed and a dishonourable,' muttered her father glumly, taking another swig. 'I should have disinherited him at least though – now that *was* foolish.'

'Many said at the time that Krulheim would have been far more likely to rebel had you spared his life but taken away his ancestral birthright,' she reminded him in a cool voice. 'It was kill a lordling child in cold blood or spare him and forgive him his father's sins completely – there was no in-between. And besides, does it not say in the Scriptures that he who visits not the sins of the father on the son is blessed in the Almighty's eyes?'

The King grunted noncommittally. 'Never mind fathers, now you're sounding like your aunt,' he said over his shoulder.

They both chuckled – ever since she had been saved from perdition by Horskram, Lady Walsa had taken to praying and reading the *Book of Holy Scripture* every day. Princess Hjala was fond of jesting that if she were a man her aunt would have joined the Argolian Order long since.

'No good will come of it all the same,' continued the King grimly as he finished off his wine. 'This war will be as bloody as the last one – and this time I will have to be severe with the surviving ringleaders. It would be suicide to be so clement again. So if it's war Krulheim wants, he'd better make sure he wins or dies in glory on the battlefield – because his life is forfeit if he falls to the Crown alive! Thank Reus he's got no children of his own – at least I've been spared having to make that decision again.'

'And what of the other southron barons?' Hjala pursued.

The King turned to face his daughter, his grey eyes keen. 'You mean the brother of your late husband Ulfric? Lord Aelrod will not be spared either.

He and every last man of the southron noble houses – their lands, titles and lives are forfeit. Their children I shall send into exile, to live abroad as beggars – I'll not kill babes in cold blood, not even now, but I won't spare them the rod either this time around, mark my words!'

Princess Hjala had let her hands fall to her sides where they clenched into fists of suppressed anger. She hated it when her father reminded her of her dead husband, a man she had loathed at first sight. Especially now, given that his younger brother had allied himself with the new rebellion. Forestalling another uprising had been the whole point of her marriage to Lord Ulfric of Saltcaste in the first place.

'I am sorry that my nuptials were not sufficient to prevent another rebellion,' she said coldly.

Her father's voice softened as he took her gently by the shoulders. 'Hjala, Hjala – daughter dearest!' he said. 'Think not that I blame thee – why, you've suffered more than any woman deserves to! It grieves me to know that my only daughter has had to endure such sorrows – ach, truly the Almighty tests us in strange ways!'

Hjala shook her head to clear away the incipient tears. Unbidden, the bloated faces of her drowning children came floating across the vision of her mind's eye, tiny bubbles streaming from their mouths through the murky waters of her darkest imaginings.

Blinking a couple of times, she forced the thought into the back of her mind as she replied stoically: 'Never mind my grief, at least it is old. All across the realm folk low-born and high are suffering fresh tragedies. No, you are right to be ruthless, father. This time when you ride victorious across the battlefield, you must be merciless – for all our sakes! The southron threat must be extinguished once and for all.'

The page boy returned to inform His Majesty that a board had been laid in the chamber next door. Without further word on the gloomy subject of war, the two royals went to take their meal. As they did Princess Hjala wondered at their audacity, talking of being ruthless in victory. By land and sea, the rebels outnumbered them nearly twofold.

⇥ CHAPTER V ⇤

A Tryst For Old Lovers

Princess Hjala pulled her fur blanket further up towards her chin to ward against the chill of early morning; it would be some time before the spring sunshine spread its warmth across her expansive chamber. The windows were covered with thin panes of translucent bone; she disliked shutters and preferred to wake at the first touch of dawn. Oftentimes she awoke long before, for her slumber was frequently troubled and uneasy.

Happily last night that had not proved to be the case, although she had still forgone a full night's sleep. At least it was for the best of reasons, she reflected as she turned to stroke Torgun where he lay half asleep beside her. Both of them were naked beneath the blanket, another reason for her feeling cold. But then she had wanted to know him completely last night – it had been so long since she had lain with him.

Of course it had not been meant to happen at all. Their romance was three years dead, ever since her swain had announced he was joining the White Valravyn and must keep himself pure for the cause. At the time she had remonstrated wildly – Torgun was perhaps the only man she had ever truly loved, assuming she could fathom was love really was.

It was nonsensical, she had pointed out: the Order was military, not religious; devoted to king and country, not god and temple like the Bethlers of the Pilgrim Kingdoms. Plenty of ravens had wives and mistresses – they didn't get to see them often, but they kept them nonetheless. Why even his aunt, Lady Karlya, was married to a raven, none other than his own commander Tarlquist.

But her remonstrations had come to nothing. To be a knight of the Order meant to renounce all other ties, in his stubborn opinion – let others do as they will, he had been gently insistent on that point.

Besides that, his connection to a member of the royal house was too politically sensitive (though he had hardly put it like that) not to conflict with his new duties.

And so she had reconciled herself to the inevitable, and learned a bitter lesson: that whilst her paramour might love courtly romance, he loved glory on the battlefield better. For all his charming airs and graces, his outward humbleness, his gallantry and gentleness, in that respect he was a typical knight.

But during the dancing after last night's supper – a relatively meagre affair of three courses, ordained by her father in sympathy for victims of the civil war – they had shared a few movements together. And that, it seemed, had rekindled an old flame she had thought long burned out.

Afterwards all it had taken was a few goblets of strong wine and some kind words to cajole him up to her bedchamber.

It had been worth the effort. She felt an afterglow in her shapely body that even the morning chill could not completely banish. However, she was still a little shiverish, and so...

She let her long fingers trace their way across the blond hairs on his muscled torso as she reached down towards his sex. He turned over to face her, his eyes a curious mixture of guilt and desire.

Happily for her – for them both – Hjala saw to it that the latter soon won.

When it was over she lay cradled in his arms, enjoying the sensation of warm flesh touching. Turning to look at him again she found to her consternation that the troubled look had returned to his face.

'What is it now?' she asked, trying and failing to keep the sharpness from her tone.

'Nothing, my sweet princess,' he replied bashfully. 'As much as I am honoured by your favours... you know how I feel about this. Last night should not have happened.'

'Oh, no?' she replied, her face buckling as she propped herself up on a white arm and looked down at him with scorn. 'And I suppose what happened between you and that little strumpet Lady Merith after you won the tourney at Linden last summer shouldn't have happened either?'

The look on Torgun's face went from troubled to pained. Raising a broad forearm to cover his eyes he replied: 'Would you had never learned of that. Another mistake.' Pulling his arm away, he sat up in bed and sighed: 'Yes, it is true, the Lady Merith and I did have a... romance, for a few moons. But I broke it off with her last year before the coming of the first frosts, I swear to thee!'

He was looking at her so earnestly now – with those intense blue eyes she loved so much – that the princess had to laugh.

'Oh don't flagellate yourself about it, my sweet knight,' she said, sitting up further to face him and pulling the blanket up around them both.

'I seduced you last night knowing full well what had transpired between the two of you, or have you forgotten? Just don't lie with me all night and morning and then tell me how "guilty" you feel about it. Save that for your next confession – that's what the perfects are for, after all.'

'Aye, as you say my princess,' he muttered. 'You are right of course – my behaviour just now was churlish. Please accept my humble apologies.'

Again that earnest look. It inspired contempt in her even as she loved him for it. She doubted there was a sincerer knight in the realm. The kingdom's greatest warrior, and yet in her arms he was just a troubled and bashful youth again. She loved exercising that hold on him – even as she resented him for knowing how to break it. But she had him now – for a little while longer at least.

'You have my profound forgiveness,' she said lightly, running her fingers through his rich golden tresses and kissing him full on the lips. Even now she felt desire for him welling up inside her – she who so seldom concerned herself with pleasures of the flesh. Perhaps that was why it was so acute now, she thought reproachfully. But she wasn't done playing with her paramour's emotions just yet.

'Now tell me, my sweet paladin, how many tasks did she set you?'

Torgun looked at her uneasily, and feigned incomprehension.

'What do you mean, my royal princess?'

She laughed again, not entirely unkindly, before replying: 'The lovely Lady Merith – how many tasks did she set you, besides winning the tourney at Linden, before allowing you to enjoy her favours?'

'Why, but I wore her favour on the tourney field before I even won – '

'Not that kind of favour, Torgun, my prince among knights. I mean the favours of her bedchamber, as well you know.'

Wincing at her unseemly frankness, he tried to change the subject, but Princess Hjala was in a cruel mood and pressed him ruthlessly.

'Three – including the winning of the tourney,' he confessed at last in a subdued voice.

'Three!' she exclaimed, throwing her head back and laughing again. Her sandy brown locks, unbraided by her lover the night before, tumbled across her bare shoulders. 'Why, I knew it! They said that brazen hussy was dying to take you between her legs since she first arrived at court four years ago!'

'My princess!' exclaimed Torgun, genuinely shocked. 'This is no way to talk! Please be kind enough to moderate your language about – '

'A damsel who schemed to have you, and took you into her bed after the least amount of courtly resistance – all of this despite being married to a loyal vassal of the King at the time? And I wonder what *he* had to say about the matter? Hah – I don't see him demanding satisfaction in the lists any time soon!'

The hurt look in his eyes pained Hjala as much as it brought her pleasure. Why did she play these stupid games? No good ever came of them, nor ever would. Softening her voice she said: 'Very well, I will moderate my language as you desire – after all there is no need for improper behaviour, is there?'

Torgun was incapable of perceiving the irony in this last remark, but contented himself instead with saying: 'Sir Gunthor of Staling may demand satisfaction in the lists any time he pleases. I shall not scruple to strike at a man who beats his wife in jealous fits of rage, or oppresses his peasants in defiance of the King's law!'

'As to his jealousy, is that any wonder?' Hjala shot back. 'But you are right about his ill usage of his yeomanry, although my father has of late had stern words with him about that. These minor lordlings – my father grants them a holding in the Dominions, then they see fit to behave like Woldings all because they command a score of knights of their own!'

'I'm glad to hear our royal liege has done as you say,' muttered Torgun somewhat sullenly. 'And I hope Sir Gunthor will also be prevailed upon to treat his wife better in future.'

'He better had, if it only takes three tasks to seduce her,' the princess replied archly. Then, deftly changing the subject to avoid another quarrel, she added: 'Do you remember how many it took with me?'

A smile returned to his rugged face at the memory. 'Aye, my sweet princess. Twelve!'

'Twelve,' she repeated, smiling back at him warmly. 'You wanted it to be thirteen, one for each of the Hero King's knights, but I wouldn't hear of it. Bad luck, I said!'

'Aye, bad luck,' the young knight repeated, somewhat neutrally she thought. Even after the recent horrors he had faced, Torgun wasn't the most superstitious of knights. Far too busy concerning himself with worldly matters of king and country, she reflected, not without some bitterness.

'Do you remember the courtly lay you composed for me for your seventh task?' she pressed. 'Those sweet verses of love? I let you kiss me full on the lips for the first time after I heard them!'

Torgun was looking awkward again. 'I don't remember, my princess... verse was never a strong point of mine.'

'Oh don't be so bashful!' the princess exclaimed, slapping him playfully on a broad shoulder. 'That made it all the more special that you did it for me! Let me see, I can even remember a few lines: "My love for thee is as a burning brand/How I long to hold thee in my hands" – '

'Stop it, my sweet – now you are mocking me!' exclaimed Torgun, suddenly heaving himself out of bed. Only she had the power to irritate him so much, or so she hoped anyway. His tall and powerful frame loomed nakedly over her, and the princess felt her returning desire increase another notch.

'I am not,' she said, trying to keep the playfulness out of her voice. 'Come back to bed, my silly poet knight, and be consoled – it was the most joyous verse that ever I heard, even if it wasn't penned by the hand of Maegellin!'

'I never cared overmuch for that Thraxian bard anyway,' grumbled Torgun, sitting down on the edge of the bed. 'Too much mockery and bawdiness, not enough good solid virtues...'

'Ah, spoken like a true Northlending – what a credit you are to your country, sweet Torgun,' she replied, reaching out to stroke him again. She was only half joking too – a purer spirit could not be found in the halls of men, she felt sure of that.

'Aye,' he said, his face suddenly growing grim. 'I mean to prove that, if it is in my power to do so – I long for this war to reach its climax, all this hanging back and waiting for the accursed Woldings is driving me mad!'

The princess frowned sympathetically. 'Have patience, my lovely darling – the northerners will come soon enough. You'll have your chance for further glory and service to the realm.' Drawing closer to him she added in a husky voice that was now completely sincere: 'Come home safely.'

Meeting her gaze he replied evenly: 'Reus willing, I shall, and with a trail of ransomed knights and slain behind me! This treacherous rebellion must be crushed!'

He made a giant fist as he said this. He was genuinely angry – to a knight such as Torgun, treason was unthinkable.

In a lesser man his mannerisms might have seemed comical – but it was difficult to laugh at one so young who had already triumphed over hundreds of knights. A year after being dubbed he had begun courting Hjala – he'd been all of eighteen but even by then his reputation preceded him. Finally, after winning the Grand Tourney at Corne Hill held every year to celebrate Freidheim's victory over the Thraxians, he had become her lover.

That had been six months after their courtship began – he had spent an entire spring and summer tearing through tasks that would have taken most knights two years to accomplish, if at all.

Just six months to win her, body and soul – Hjala supposed that made her an easy conquest too, though Reus knew she had not intended to be. But then after years of a loveless marriage that had ended in tragedy, followed by more years of heartbreaking solitude... she had deserved some love and excitement in her broken life, surely?

She felt her thoughts going to a dark, watery place. Quickly she said: 'And what about this other business? Of the monk Horskram, and his secret mission? You know something of this, I trow.'

Now Torgun's face looked uneasy in a way she had not seen before. Perhaps she had misjudged him – was that a look of superstitious awe or even dread she perceived him checking?

'The friar Horskram is a noble and pious soul, or so I judge him to be,' he responded haltingly. 'Sir Wolmar seemed to think otherwise, but – '

'Oh to Gehenna with Wolmar!' she cried. 'He's a king's grandson, and he thinks that makes him a king himself! Nothing but trouble that one, I care not one jot what he thinks!'

'You'll have no disagreement from me on that count, my princess,' replied the young knight moodily. 'But the friar is clearly involved in some dark and evil matter. A dread thing pursued him and his novice by night, all the way from their monastery in the Highlands – '

'Yes, I'd gathered as much from what little he would say on the subject,' interjected Hjala. 'But what did *you* see? There have been rumours going around, of a vicious assault on the garrison at Staerkvit, something to do with this Northland warlock the traitor Thule has enlisted...'

'Whether it was the work of that wizard I cannot say,' replied Sir Torgun hesitantly. 'All I can say is that the devil we grappled with some ten nights ago was... just that. A denizen of the Other Side, conjured up by some dark sorcerer, sent to harry us.'

'Harry you? Or harry the monk and his travelling companions?'

'You are indeed shrewd, my princess. Not for nothing does your father include you in his closest councils! Alas, I cannot say – but yon monk Horskram certainly seems to think so. Whatever attacked us was dreadful powerful – it killed more than two dozen brave knights and men-at-arms, and when I managed to strike it a foul ichor bled from its loathsome carcass that notched my blade. No, I will not say more – this is not fit for a lady's ears, let alone a royal one.'

For once Hjala decided to let the last remark go. Truth to tell she did not particularly want to hear any more: this was the closest she had ever seen her paramour come to showing fear. That in itself was enough to inspire her with terror.

'Well, I suppose all will be revealed when my father calls his secret council,' was what she contented herself with saying.

The young knight nodded again. He was staring at the translucent window pane, as if trying to banish some dark memory with the spectacle of strengthening sunlight.

Hjala had dark memories of her own to suppress – but she had a better idea of how to go about it.

Leaning forward again she gently pushed her paramour to lie back down on the bed. Gripping him by his massive shoulders she straddled him in a most unladylike fashion.

'Lie back, my love,' she whispered tenderly. 'I have a yearning for the saddle before we go to break our fast.'

The young knight looked up at her with an expression of mingled desire and wonder. 'Yet again, my princess!? I hope I have not failed to satisfy you previously...'

She was smiling broadly at him now as she felt the heat rising up through her curvaceous figure, still enticing despite her middling years.

'No, not at all,' she breathed huskily. 'But the poets say a woman's appetite grows to full fruition only at her fortieth summer – and next year will be my fortieth summer...'

'Oh I see,' replied Torgun, his voice growing thick with pleasure. 'And what do these poets say of men in this matter?'

Leaning down to kiss the knight she let her unbound tresses envelop him in an amorous shroud.

'They say just the opposite: that a man is most potent in his prime. I think that makes us a happy match, sir knight. Come now, I think you are up to this final task of mine... Ah, *yes*, I think you are...'

⤐ CHAPTER VI ⤐

A Secret Council

'Remember, you're to speak only when spoken to – and even then it's probably for the best if you say as little as possible!'

Horskram's face looked stern in the pale morning light shining through the window of their room in the palace. As it always did when his mentor was telling him in advance to behave himself.

All the same – Adelko couldn't help but feel excited. He was to be included in the King's secret council, which was being held today. He didn't need his sixth sense to tell him his mentor was getting ready to make a clean breast of things. True, he already knew most of it, but he had a feeling Horskram would discuss other things that related to their perilous mission.

The other fragments of the Headstone for one thing. Since arriving at the capital he'd had plenty of time to reflect on that conundrum – not being in mortal danger every day helped too.

And the resumption of his studies had quickly rekindled his desire for knowledge. With barely a hundred tomes, the palace library was meagre in comparison to that of the Great Monastery's, but even so it had not taken him long to rediscover his love of learning. And booklearning was a great deal less painful than adventuring: the cuts on his side and forehead had scabbed over, but they still hurt. Any more of those and he'd start to look like Vaskrian.

As the two monks knelt for dawn prayers he found himself wondering about the squire. He had not seen him since he'd gone to join the muster outside the city walls with his new master a few days ago.

The Efrilunder was brave to the point of foolhardiness and plain foolish to boot. But he'd saved Adelko's life twice from the Northland mercenaries hired to kill them – once in the clearing by Lake Sørdegil, a second time in the Staerk Ranges.

He'd never thanked him properly for that, and for that he felt guilty. A good Palomedian should always recognise succour.

But there was more to it than being a good Palomedian. He genuinely liked Vaskrian – even if he was a bit touched, he'd grown strangely fond of him. He was angry and violent – exactly the things a good Argolian wasn't supposed to be – but he was honourable and genuine as well. He'd sworn an oath to protect them and he'd stuck by it. Young as he was, Adelko felt sure not all men could say the same.

He found the words of an old lay by Maegellin drifting back to him as they rose from their prayers: *A friendship forged on a dangerous road is as strong as castle steel.*

There would be plenty of the latter knocking around before long, the novice reflected grimly as a servant entered with their morning meal. His respite from danger would soon be at an end.

❖ ❖ ❖

After a snatched breakfast an escort of soldiers arrived to take them to the room appointed for the council. They were not soldiers of the Order, Adelko noticed. They wore green cloaks and tabards and the double unicorn insignia of the House of Ingwin: the watch had officially taken over the duties of the White Valravyn, which would even now be discussing battle tactics on the plains outside the city.

The room chosen for the council was in a corner turret of the palace. A medium-sized oblong chamber warmed by a hearth, it had a long mahogany table and chairs at its centre. The windows were narrow slits. It seemed in keeping with the secret nature of the meeting.

Soon they were all present. There were a dozen of them, including Horskram and Adelko. The King's brother Prince Freidhoff, his son Wolmar and the other knights Torgun and Tarlquist were the last to arrive, having come from the loyalist camp beyond the city walls.

Gazing furtively about him at the illustrious assembly, Adelko could scarcely believe he was there. The Princess Hjala sat next to Lord Ulnor the Seneschal, looking as severe and self-contained as ever, although once the novice fancied he caught her stealing a glance at Torgun that was far from neutral. But then these were tense times: perhaps his intuition was addled.

Lady Walsa bustled in making a great fuss. Sweeping haughtily into the chamber, she glared about her, her leathery face only breaking into the briefest of smiles when she set eyes on Horskram, whom she sat next to. Her garb was severe, even more so than Princess Hjala's, consisting of a plain black gown and gloves and unadorned wimple of white cloth. She was tall and probably not unhandsome in her youth, though she looked a good deal older than her fifty winters. Her eyes shone with a lustre that Adelko had seen in many a zealous monk. In a woman, he had to admit, it was quite frightening. But then he hadn't seen much of the fairer sex at the monastery.

The other two men were previously unknown to him. The skinny, awkward-looking man about the same age as Lady Walsa with a parrot face and tufts of curly greying hair he took to be Prior Holfaste: his grey habit was identical to Horskram's, and the chain he wore marked him out as the Abbot of Urling Monastery. Adelko suddenly wondered what had become of Sacristen, and whether he had managed to keep secret what was now about to be revealed to others. He found himself wishing the timorous old monk was here as well – most of these people were strangers to him and he felt out of his depth.

His High Holiness Lorthar, Arch Perfect of Strongholm Temple, did nothing to make him feel more comfortable. If Holfaste resembled a parrot, Lorthar looked like a hawk. Dressed in his white robes of office and red scapular studded with golden wheel motifs he looked as much like a wealthy noble as he did a priest. His taloned hands, gnarled by his seventy winters in the mortal vale, were encrusted with jewelled rings; about his bald head he wore a circlet of platinum, and the ceremonial staff he carried was of varnished black wood chased with gold elaborately fashioned to resemble scenes from the Scriptures.

The contrast between the richly attired Arch Perfect and the Argolian friars could not have been more marked; even the King looked somewhat plain next to him. His black eyes burned with a different kind of zeal to Lady Walsa's: where hers betrayed an overly earnest and hot-headed devotion, his displayed a cold zealotry that set Adelko's sixth sense jangling. He had hitherto only dealt with the more humble members of the Temple: simple mountain perfects, priory men and the odd mendicant. On the whole they had been pious and gentle souls, if somewhat ineffectual.

But his High Holiness Lorthar dressed like the worldliest of men, and the novice's sixth sense told him he was rarely gentle.

Presently, when the door had been closed and barred, the King cleared his throat and convened the council.

'You have all been gathered here today to help address a matter of grave import,' he began. 'I need not tell you that we are already troubled by Thule's treasonous rebellion – however it is also said the world contains many threats to peace and prosperity, far older and deadlier than the wars of men. Having conversed at length with the Argolian adept Horskram, who sits here among us, I have come to believe that the beginnings of such a threat have arisen, here and now, in this our realm.'

The King paused a few moments to let his words sink in. All about the table curious pairs of eyes belonging to some of the most accomplished and powerful people in the kingdom were fixed on Adelko's stoical mentor.

The King continued: 'I believe it is meet that I now permit Horskram to speak, and tell all of you his ill tidings. Some of you here will have heard part of the tale already, but none of you I think, save perhaps for his novice here, know the full story. Master Horskram, if you would now care to proceed...'

✤ ✤ ✤

Horskram told the story of their adventures again, only this time he told it in full. When he mentioned the Headstone fragment and described its theft from Ulfang, a furious look buckled Lorthar's features, whilst one of horror crossed Holfaste's. Lady Walsa made the sign and muttered a prayer. More of the assembled worthies followed suit when the old monk reached the part about Tintagael, and his tale of their audience with the faerie kings had some of them gaping. The story of the final encounter with the demon did nothing to calm his audience, confirmed as it was by many a nod of the head from the raven knights present. Only when he recounted how they had slain the Northland brigands afterwards was a note of general defiance struck.

Lorthar was the first to speak after the tale of their adventures was over.

'How could the Argolians have let this come to pass!?' he thundered. 'That fool Sacristen ought to be horsewhipped – I've said for years that the friars of St Argo were unfit guardians for such a powerful artefact!'

Drawing himself upright in a gesture of moral righteousness he made the sign of the wheel in most exaggerated fashion.

'And where else would you have had it kept?' retorted Prior Holfaste in his quavering voice. 'According to Brother Horskram the fragment was stolen by a demon with the power to smash stone and melt iron – what protection could the Temple have offered against such an entity?'

'The power of the prayers of true perfects!' replied his High Holiness sententiously. 'Your Order has ever delved too deep into eldritch arcana – why, it stood accused of black witchcraft but a generation ago!'

'We were exonerated and pardoned in full!' cried Holfaste.

'Only for lack of evidence,' muttered the Arch Perfect darkly.

'Lack of evidence!' spluttered the Abbot, rising from his seat angrily. 'You speak of evidence! Need I remind you that all the evidence pointed to our chief accusers being the culprits themselves! Why, the Arch Perfect of Montrevellyn was subsequently found to have succumbed to the temptations of Sha'amiel the Deceiver! He was burned at the stake in the main square in Rima, along with several dozen of his followers – perfects of the Temple all! Do you remember that, Lorthar?'

'Aye, I do,' replied the high priest, unmoved. 'I remember how His High Holiness Abelard and his so-called co-conspirators were condemned at the word of a man who had just recently stood trial himself for witchcraft and demonology. Oh, you Argolians turned the tables on the Temple nicely, that I'll grant you!'

Now it was Horskram's turn to rise from his seat, his face black with anger. 'This is outrageous!' he shouted at the Arch Perfect. 'Grand Master Hannequin's powers of divination had been attested to on scores of occasions ere that dreadful episode men call the Purge! The divination was carried out with all due process – I myself was a part of it. The truth is, Lorthar, that the True Temple's perfecthood had long become seduced by the temptations of the Fallen One. For generations you have envied us our knowledge and piety, for our example shames you daily – we spend our lives in prayer and studying, learning the ways of men and angels, aye and demons too, that we may better abjure them for the sake of mortalkind! Whilst you and your ilk lavish yourselves with money squeezed from the poor faithful, and live in fine houses in the cities. The Temple is a disgrace to the Creed, and it has been for an age! When Sha'amiel possessed Abelard he was pushing at an open door!'

Holfaste had retreated into himself during Horskram's tirade, which was perhaps going a step too far. Lorthar had turned purple with rage.

'How dare you!' he said in a strangled whisper. 'You dare to criticise the Mother Temple, of which your Order is but a limb! Such contumely! Such blasphemy! This is typical of the Argolians, and how arrogant you have become! Would that we had burned *you* in the square, and not the other way around!'

'Guard your tongue when addressing a true servant of Reus' will!' cried Lady Walsa in a voice as leathery as her skin. 'Horskram has done more to advance the Palomedian cause in his lifetime than you and your priestly ilk have done in a century! I don't recall the perfects coming to my aid when I lay possessed by devilspawn – it was an Argolian friar who saved me! And afterwards I learned that it had been noised about among the Temple that I was being justly punished by the Almighty for leading a wanton life!'

The Arch Perfect tried to interject but she would not let him. Adelko understood her fearsome reputation. 'Oh, aye, I do not dispute that,' she went on, 'and ever since I have strived to change my ways, so that my soul is ne'er weakened again by venality and indulgence. But from whose example did I learn this? From Brother Horskram's! What example do you set, Lorthar, with your rich furs, and your jewels, and your vain pomp? Look at you – you dress like an overweening merchant! Is it any wonder the Argolians look upon you and your like with such contempt?'

'I will not be upbraided by a woman,' replied Lorthar icily.

'I'm a woman of royal blood, and I'll upbraid you as much as I see fit,' replied Lady Walsa in a voice thick with scorn. 'Never mind this Sacristen – I should have *you* horsewhipped, you fraudulent popinjay!'

'Enough!' roared the King, rising to his feet in turn. 'I did not convene this council so we could have a religious debate! Lorthar, you will henceforth refrain from using this unfortunate occasion as an excuse for indulging your prejudices against the Argolian Order – rant against it all you will under your own roof, but not under mine! And cousin Walsa – you will kindly refrain from taking the bait and pouring fuel on the fire!'

Turning to the Argolians he said in a gentler voice: 'Holfaste and Horskram, please be seated and rest assured – no one was more against the travesty that was the Purge than I was, and fie on those Pangonians for ever allowing such a ridiculous trial to take place on their soil! I swear that such a thing will never happen on mine whilst I rule. Now, does anybody have any useful questions or observations?'

'I... I do,' said Adelko in a small voice. Horskram turned to look at him and scowled. 'I thought I told you that you were here strictly as an observer,' he hissed.

'Yes well, as to that Brother Horskram,' the King interjected. 'Given that thus far you have spoken only to argue, I hold it time that someone else spoke up. I would hear what the youth has to say. Speak on, novice, your King commands it.'

'Well,' continued Adelko, blushing furiously. 'It's just that, we've heard all about the fragment that was stolen, and where it came from, but I'd like to know a bit more about the others. That is to say... their whereabouts and how they came to be there.'

'And what use would that be?' asked Sir Wolmar haughtily. 'There were four fragments. One was in our country and has been stolen. What need is there to know of the others? I find myself agreeing with his High Holiness – these Argolians thirst for too much knowledge, methinks.'

'Yes, you would say that,' sneered Sir Tarlquist. 'You've mistrusted the friars since first we laid eyes on them.'

'Aye, and has that mistrust proved ill founded?' Wolmar shot back. 'They brought a demon on our garrison at Staerkvit, or have you forgotten that?'

'Perhaps you also blame our yeomanry for bringing Thule's robber knights down on their backs,' said Sir Torgun mildly. 'Nay,

I think the young monk's question is a wise one – we should know the full context of the problem we are dealing with.'

'I agree with Sir Torgun,' said Princess Hjala, smiling coolly at the knight. 'Let us hear more of this Headstone and its history.'

'Aye, let us have more of it then,' said the King decisively. 'Horskram, if you will.'

The adept nodded, pointedly ignoring Lorthar's burning stare.

'Of the other three fragments, one was kept on the Island Realms as I have already said. As far as I am aware it is still there now, guarded closely by the descendants of Caedmon the Far-Sighted. It was he who first called together the Westerling clans and druidic synod to deal with the Headstone fragments seven centuries ago.'

'Let it stay there!' interjected Lorthar sharply. 'Such a wicked thing belongs in a benighted far-flung land, where devils are worshipped openly by pagan sorcerers!'

'For once I agree with his High Holiness,' said Holfaste drily. 'No need to alert the distant clans of that forgotten realm, surely? And it's said they rarely welcome visitors from outside in any case.'

'As to that,' replied Horskram. 'We shall no doubt decide presently. But for now let me tell the council of the third fragment, which was taken up by an island chieftain that the *Westerling Chronicles* name Corann. It had already been resolved that one piece should be borne north, to Olav Iron-Hand of whom I have already spoken. The remainder it was decreed should be taken east and south respectively. So Corann agreed to take the third fragment across the ocean to Thraxia, whose lands had been settled for long centuries by exiled Westerling tribes after the Wars of Kith and Kin.

'Taking ship with a stout vanguard of his most trusted warriors, Corann reached Thraxia without incident. But before long, the chronicles say, he found himself embroiled in a messy war between two mainland chieftains, Cadwyn and Curulyn. The former lord promised to take the shard from him in return for his military assistance against the latter. Corann agreed to do this for the sake of his sworn mission. During the ensuing conflict, which Cadwyn won thanks to his unexpected ally's aid, many of Corann's men were killed. After the battle Cadwyn sent Corann on to his great fortress in the Forest of Roarkil, in the Thraxian province of Umbria.

'Cadwyn sent an escort of his own troops with Corann and his surviving men, but on his orders they murdered the remaining Islanders in the depths of the woods; for having learned of the rich treasures brought by Corann to use as possible leverage on his errand,

Cadwyn had resolved to kill him and take his spoil for himself. From this foul deed Cadwyn became ever known as The Treacherous, and even among fellow mainlanders he was thereafter called the False Friend. But of the wars of revenge that followed, and of his justly deserved death at the hand of Caedmon in the Battle of Cullingan Fields, other tales tell.'

'Yes, yes, I'm sure they do,' sneered Lorthar. 'Is this to be a useful story, or another chance for the Argolians to show off their knowledge?' Holfaste stared at the high priest and shook his head despairingly, but Horskram ignored him and continued.

'Repairing to Roarkil Fortress, Cadwyn now fancied himself ultimately victorious, for he had the stone, Corann's treasure, and conquest of his neighbour's lands. But before long his victory proved a pyrrhic one, as the shades of the men he had so foully murdered returned to haunt the forest and beset his castle every night. After forty days, by which time the ghosts of Corann and his soldiers had driven many of their killers including Cadwyn's son Druca to madness with their banshee wailings, the murderous chieftain could bear no more. Taking the remainder of his retinue with him, he fled Roarkil forever, abandoning it to the spirits of the men he had slain. With it he left the fragment of the Headstone, on the counsel of his mistress, Adretica the Prophetess, a sorceress of some repute whose witcheries had helped him divine Corann's fortune in the first place.

'And there it lay for another two centuries, for none dared to approach Roarkil anymore. None that is, until a party of adventurers, drawn by rumours of the treasures left behind by Cadwyn in his haste, dared to enter its precinct and plunder it. Though more than one of them was left broken in body and mind by this effort, the survivors managed to bear away the fragment of the Headstone, little knowing what artefact they had obtained, for by this time the tale of Søren had passed into legend.'

'You mention Roarkil Forest again,' interrupted Lorthar while Horskram paused for breath. 'How very interesting that your failed attempt to rid the world of this Andragorix whom you suspect of being behind your demonic pursuer took place in the very same haunted tower... Did you really try to kill him, I wonder? Or are you in fact in league with him?'

The perfect was staring at Horskram now with an expression that Adelko supposed was meant to be cunning. To him it looked positively malignant. The King intervened before Horskram could respond.

'Your High Holiness, I believe I have made myself clear on this matter already! I would respectfully ask that you desist from casting base aspersions on the learned friar's character and piety, or by the Almighty that we both serve, I'll have you ejected from this council!'

That seemed to pacify the Arch Perfect, though he looked from the King to Horskram with eyes that smouldered.

'Thank you, Your Majesty,' said Horskram humbly, before continuing.

'What happened immediately after is not firmly established and can be only vaguely gleaned, from second-hand testimonies and ill-verified accounts, but it was generally believed that the curse which brought so much misery upon Olav Iron-Hand and his descendants visited itself on the plunderers of the third fragment. Before long the surviving adventurers were driven to fractious dissent, and having borne the stone across the Malarok Passes of the Hyrkrainians and into the southern lowlands of Northalde, they soon fell to quarrelling over what to do with it. Venturing into the depths of the Argael Forest, it would appear that the hapless freebooters finally succumbed to madness and slew each other. The fragment must have lain, forgotten by all, for generations afterwards, until it was discovered by a travelling merchant called Manfried of Wernost.'

Horskram went on to recount how the fragment was taken from among the skeletal remains of the freebooters by Manfried and sold to Alaric the Prescient, a black magician of ill repute whose dastardly practices finally drove his more godly neighbours to overthrow him.

'The fragment was found by Alaric's slayer, Lord Ludvic Stone-Cursed, who took it back with him to his seat at Graukolos, where it has been kept ever since,' the monk finished.

'And we cannot be sure it is still safe there,' added Holfaste. 'For the Wheel of St Albared no longer protects it. That means it could be stolen just as the fragment in our keeping was – if the holy prayers of our Order were not enough to prevent a blasphemous devil from stealing it, I don't see how a castle of knights will do any good!'

'No indeed,' replied Horskram. 'That is why we must go to Graukolos as soon as this war is over and warn – '

'Let me save you the journey,' interrupted the King. 'For the fragment at Graukolos has already been stolen.'

The council turned as one to look at their liege. 'Your Majesty, how do you know this?' asked Horskram, aghast.

The King sighed and frowned deeply. 'The day before you arrived at the palace, I received a messenger from the Eorl of Dulsinor in Vorstlund, telling me so.'

'But, Your Majesty, why did you not tell me as soon as you knew my business?' Horskram demanded, quite forgetting his place.

'Let me remind you, master monk, that as King it is *my* business to tell *my* subjects what I want them to hear when I want them to hear it,' replied Freidheim scowling. 'But to answer your question,

I didn't want you gallivanting off on your own before this council was held, which I knew there was a chance of you doing once you learned another fragment had been taken.'

Horskram was unplacated. 'But this is a loss of vital time, Your Majesty! This cannot be mere coincidence – now we know for sure that somebody is trying to reunite the Headstone! Hannequin must be warned, we must send word to the Islanders too - '

'If the Islanders are as vigilant and enthralled by the powers of the Other Side as they say, they will be well prepared enough,' replied the King dismissively. 'And in case you haven't noticed, the kingdom's at war, by both land and sea. You won't be able to travel any further until it's resolved, so there's no use in your hurrying off. Your mission is bound up with the fortunes of this war, whether you like it or not. In any case, I believe you told me only a few days ago that your quest will be severely compromised without the help that you detoured to Strongholm to seek in the first place – there was no chance of your getting that without this council, so I thought it might as well wait until now.'

Horskram sat back, mollified if not entirely pleased. 'And what details did this messenger give – can you tell me that much, Your Majesty?'

'Very few, I'm afraid. All he seemed to know was that it had been spirited away during a feast to celebrate the Eorl's daughter's nuptials. Half the castle was drunk when the fragment was stolen by the sounds of it, which is typical of Vorstlending folk. Some supernatural agent, talk of burrowing under a crypt where they'd kept the cursed thing all those years. Something tells me his liege didn't want to part with too many... specifics. Given everything I've just heard here, I'm beginning to see why.'

Horskram scowled and shook his head in frustration.

'What of the fourth and final fragment?' asked Princess Hjala. 'I would like to hear more about that as well – where is it being kept? Presumably we will have to alert its keepers too.'

'We would if we knew where or who they are,' replied Holfaste. 'Alas, the location of the fourth fragment has been a mystery ever since it was taken from the Island Realms by the boy Cael some seven centuries ago.'

'Cael? Who is he?' asked the princess.

'Few have heard of him,' said Horskram, resuming the story. 'The *Westerling Chronicles* tell how after the All Meet of Islanders had decided what to do with the first three fragments they fell into a quandary over what to do with the fourth and final piece. West was their home, while the north and east would take their agents swiftly into familiar countries – but in sailing south one could as soon reach the Other Side as another earthly land. The assembled worthies pondered long upon the matter, the chronicles say, until the stars began to sparkle in the night skies and a chill wind swept the high place they had chosen for their meeting.'

This time Lorthar restrained himself to a roll of the eyes. Though he disliked the vindictive perfect, Adelko had to wonder whether now really was the time for Horskram's storytelling theatrics.

'Presently a youth spoke up,' continued the adept, oblivious. 'His name was Cael, and he was not a high-born chieftain or a great warrior, but a humble shipwright's son who had taken holy orders a few years before, and been assigned to one of the druids present, whom the chronicles name Maponus.

'And the chronicles tell us he offered to take the fourth piece and bear it to the Sassanian lands of the Far South. "For I have read much of those lands when my master was not present," he said, "and the Library of Kell near Skulla's eastern shores holds many a scroll and tome detailing the lands of the Known World." Hearing this Caedmon is said to have asked Cael why he should speak out of turn so.'

Horskram couldn't resist a sidelong glance at Adelko as he said this. The meaning wasn't lost on him, and he felt himself blushing again as his mentor continued his tale.

'"I humbly apologise if I have offended, my lord," the youth is said to have replied. "My name is Cael, and I'm naught of a great warrior nor a leader of men but I do know something of the Sassanian lands from my studies, and thanks to my father I also know how to sail a boat as well as any here, if I may be so bold. These stones, you say, must be scattered to the Four Winds, and kept as far apart as can be, for the good of the world. Well, I can think of naught further to the south than the realms of Sassania, where it is written that the deserts stretch for endless leagues and the people bow down before One God and admit no other. Let me take the fourth fragment, and with the good grace of the Moon Goddess I'll bear it to some far and distant place where none will ever find it."

'So impressed were the assembled worthies by Cael's impassioned outburst that no one spoke for a short time. But at first the chieftains were reluctant to let the youth go, for he had only seen seventeen summers.

'"Tis too few for such a challenge," Caedmon is said to have told him. "You would be waylaid as soon as your boat hit land, assuming you survived such a perilous sea journey, for the leagues lie long and the waves count rolls without number until one reaches the lands of the hot South. But even then, what of the customs there do you know? Do you even speak their language?"

'At that, the legend has it, Cael proceeded to amaze his elders by reciting various dialogues in the Old Sassanic tongue. After that the chieftains, druids and high priestesses needed no further convincing, and Cael was despatched to bear the fourth fragment to the Far South and find whatever resting place for it as he might. None of the mariners or warriors who went with him ever returned, and for generations it was thought the boat had floundered beneath the waves, taking the fragment with it to the bottom of the ocean.'

'Would that not have been the best method of disposal?' asked Visigard. 'Not just for the fourth fragment, but for all four of them? The ocean deeps seem fairly remote from the touch of men, after all.'

Horskram shook his head. 'Many a wise man has suggested that,' he answered. 'But the waters of the world are not without their own denizens, and who is to say what submarine wickedness the Headstone might have wreaked if it had fallen into the hands of the Seakindred or the Tritons that keep their watery kingdoms beneath the waves? And as we have recently been reminded, there are warlocks who know only too well how to command the sea.'

Visigard sat back frowning, the self-congratulatory expression erased from his whiskered face. Horskram went on with his account.

'In any case, slender but significant tales that emerged from the Sassanian lands in subsequent centuries suggest that Cael did indeed reach his destination. These are desert stories, whispered fearfully by the elders of nomadic tribes as the wind ravages their tents at night. They speak of wayfarers lost in the parching heat, who espy an oasis on the horizon. Stumbling joyfully into its bowers they see that they are not alone, for by the sparkling pool sits a hunched and emaciated figure, who shivers uncontrollably despite the blazing heat.

'Approaching gingerly they forget their raging thirst, as a naked fear dries their throats more rapidly than any sun could. For the skeletal figure before them is barely human, more ghost than man; his skin hangs off his gnarled bones in strips as he stares at his newfound companions with eyes that hang loosely in their sockets, speaking silently of centuries of hardship and suffering.

'Clutched tightly to his chest is what appears to be a lump of stone the size of a man's torso, bearing strange markings. Through near fleshless lips he mouths words in a cracked and heavily accented voice, words that float across time and space to the ears of the transfixed listener. And as the fireside tales have it, those words say: "Will you please take my burden from me? I have borne it so long, you see, and it is so cold and heavy. I long to part with it, and yet I find I cannot give it freely..."'

⁜ ⁜ ⁜

Horskram sat back, his story done. Several of the council members exchanged fearful glances. Lorthar made the sign again. 'A foul and cursed thing,' he muttered. 'Would that such an evil had not fallen into our times.'

'It has been with us since the world was young,' said Horskram. 'But at least from Cael's story we can take one small crumb of comfort – the fourth fragment is lost to humanity, for the time being at least.'

'But a sorcerer powerful enough to conjure up demons and perhaps communicate with henchmen across great distances will not be confounded forever, I fear,' suggested Holfaste.

'No indeed,' acknowledged Horskram. 'That is why the sooner we tell the Grand Master of this, the better. I don't say that Hannequin is omniscient, but he will have a better idea of what to do about this than anyone I can think of.'

'Might I ask,' said Lorthar coldly, addressing the King, 'if the Grand Master of the Argolians is so all-wise and powerful, why Your Majesty has bothered to summon me here? It seems that respect for the True Temple is at a low ebb in this room – hardly surprising in a nation that increasingly seems to put king before god!'

'The True Temple has thrived well enough under my rule,' replied Freidheim coldly. 'Just don't expect me and my heirs to dance to its tune – your temples and your priories, aye and your monasteries too, stand on my soil! But to answer your question in a manner that I trust will satisfy your pride, you are here because this mission needs your help. Without it, it may not succeed. Horskram, now I believe is the time for your petition.'

If he was nervous, the adept showed no sign of it as he looked across the table at Lorthar and said: 'Your High Holiness, as you have already heard, we have been doggedly pursued by hellspawn ever since we discovered the theft. Perhaps I am wrong to insist that alerting our headquarters is a priority – as I have already said, Hannequin is not omniscient. But through the ages I think that our Order has proven its ability to fight the powers of darkness, and its mightiest and wisest members are in Rima. The Island Realms need to be warned that somebody is trying to reunite the Headstone. Graukolos must be visited, its master and his servants questioned, the scene of the crime there examined closely for clues. The final fragment remains a mystery but we must also decide what to do about it – whether it is wiser to try to find it ourselves before our unknown warlock does, or hope that the druids prove better guardians of the third piece and that the fourth is never found.

'These are decisions that must be taken by all the relevant parties – I have little doubt that once informed Hannequin will inform the Supreme Perfect in Rima anyway, but now that you know I will understand if you choose to notify him yourself. I leave that in your hands, and in any case until this rebellion is crushed they will be tied just as ours are. But know that I mean to continue with my journey after this war is over – our King has granted me permission to do so. I intend to travel to Rima via Graukolos as planned.'

The Arch Perfect shrugged. 'So what of it, monk? I cannot stop you, but why should your travelling plans be of any concern to me?'

'As you may have fathomed from my story, whoever is behind the theft at the monastery knows that we know, and has wanted us dead since then,' replied Horskram. 'Lorthar, think on it – why are there no devils knocking down our walls by night? Why has the thing that pursued us so relentlessly since Ulfang not maligned us since we arrived within the girdle of the Strang Ranges?'

'Perhaps this sorcerer has realised that you meant to forswear your secrecy – indeed it has proved so,' answered Lorthar. 'Now your secret is known by some of the most powerful people in the realm – there is no point in killing you any more.'

'Aye, some of what you say is true enough,' Horskram had to allow. 'But I cannot take that chance – a black magician trying to reunite the Headstone would still have good reason for eliminating a meddlesome monk who insists on alerting the most powerful members of his Order. If he kills us, he may only delay the inevitable now that all here know of the theft, but every day's delay buys him or her more time to find the other pieces he seeks! Lorthar, I think you know what it is I am asking you. You must give me a drop of the Redeemer's blood.'

The Arch Perfect laughed. It was not a pretty sound, harsh and cynical and full of malice it seemed to Adelko.

'Ah,' he said, still chuckling. 'I think you grey friars have spent over much time at the lectern and not enough preaching the word of the Redeemer! What nonsensical poet's lays have you been reading, Horskram – even an Argolian should know better than to believe in such myths! I must confess I had wondered what this "sanctuary" yon faerie spirits spoke of during your ungodly audience was supposed to be referring to! But tell me, are you really such a blasphemous fool as to pay any heed to the rhyming words of the false fays of Tintagael?'

'Nevertheless it has long been rumoured that the blood of Palom is in your keeping,' countered Horskram levelly. 'It is said it was first brought here by the Seventh Acolyte Alysius – why, the most sacrosanct part of Strongholm Temple is named after him.'

The Arch Perfect had resumed his sniggering. 'Really, Horskram, you genuinely surprise me! I have long suspected the grey friars of iniquitous doings, but I had never thought them gullible enough to be taken in by such fireside tales!'

He seemed genuinely amused, but Adelko sensed there was something beneath the scornful mockery, a palpable unease. The priest was hiding something.

Holfaste and Horskram must also have been served by their sixth sense, for both monks now pressed their religious rival.

'And yet if it be myth, how indeed does one explain the dearth of possessions, witchcraft and other diabolical happenings within the Strang Ranges?' asked Holfaste pointedly. 'As Prior of the local chapter I can assure you my tenure has not been a particularly eventful one – the only cases we have ever been called upon to investigate lay beyond the ranges.'

'And with good reason,' chimed Horskram. 'That is because the power of the Redeemer protects this corner of the King's Dominions – it is a blessing from Reus that His Prophet should be with us in the flesh. A blessing you and your forebears have jealously guarded for centuries, fearing that your rivals in Rima might try to wrest it from you.'

'This is pure nonsense!' cried the Arch Perfect. 'Invidious lies, designed to stir up hatred against the Mother Temple! Your Majesty, I call upon you to arrest these men for defamation!'

'We are not trying to defame the Temple,' said Horskram. 'We are merely trying to fathom the truth. I have long suspected that the legend is true, that the far-flung city of the north shrouded in mist that the tales of St Alric speak of is none other than Strongholm. The lack of supernatural incursions in the area throughout the ages would certainly bear this out – for only a greater demon of some power would be able to stand the proximity of the Redeemer's flesh and blood without suffering terrible agonies.'

'Nonetheless, the tale is a myth, and nothing more,' said Lorthar, looking distinctly uneasy now. 'There is no such relic in St Alysius' Bethel – it is the power of the prayers of its perfecthood alone that keeps the devilspawn at bay.'

'I can't say I've ever noticed that being the case on my travels,' sneered Horskram. 'And I have journeyed far and wide across the countries of the Known World.'

'Lorthar,' said the King. 'I will not pretend I have not heard this rumour either – for it has long been an open secret. As a ruler of men I understand only too well the need to keep one's precious things hidden, for the connivance of one's rivals is a thing justly to be feared. But need I remind you that this is a secret council – not one word of what is spoken here shall be breathed to the outside world. If you confirm the legend to be true,

I swear to thee by all the saints I shall put to death any who reveal it to anyone outside this room, be they kith or kin of mine. Does this satisfy you?'

The Arch Perfect looked stubbornly down at the table.

'Oh for heaven's sake, Lorthar,' spat Lady Walsa, 'it's been a well-known fact for generations that a relic of our saviour is kept within the Temple at Strongholm. We all know you have it, but won't reveal it because you're afraid the Supreme Perfect will want it for himself in Rima.' She fixed him with a penetrating stare. 'Come come, man, we may not agree on everything, but we're all good Northlendings – do you really think we'd do something that would jeopardise our Temple here for the benefit of those dreadful Pangonians?'

'Lady Walsa has the right of it,' added Holfaste. 'Think on what she has said, your High Holiness, there is a ring of truth to it.'

'Indeed,' put in Horskram. 'You will know full well after what I and my ilk suffered at their hands that I am no friend to the Pangonian perfecthood either.'

The Arch Perfect stared at the mahogany table for what seemed a long time. Then he spoke.

'I do not say that what you have said is true, but let us suppose for the sake of argument that it is. You want the Strongholm Temple to do what it has not done since St Alric came begging for a drop of Palom's blood, that his liege Vasirius might be cured of the White Blood Witch's curse. What it did for a saint you would have it do for you, a monk of an Order that is no friend of ours.'

'*Sir* Alric was but a knight when he came into this land on his sacred mission,' Horskram reminded him. 'And as to the lack of friendship between the monks of St Argo and the Temple perfects, whose fault is that? We did not level faulty accusations of witchcraft, aye though we suffered for such at the hands of the Temple!'

'In any case it is not only the Argolians you would resent giving a portion of Strongholm's most precious relic to,' put in Holfaste. 'You fear that if you give it to Horskram it risks falling into the hands of your brethren at the Supreme Temple in Rima.'

'And with good reason,' snarled Lorthar. 'Considering the Temple at Rima was found to contain a nest of idolators and devil-worshippers in its very midst!'

'At the very trial you decried but a moment ago as us turning the tables on the Temple!' cried Horskram in exasperation. 'Where will your circular reasoning end, Lorthar?'

'There is nothing circular about it,' replied the Arch Perfect. 'I did not deny the actual existence of a diabolical cult within the Mother Temple –

I merely suggested it was very convenient that the Argolians managed to deflect the accusations mounted against them by uncovering devil worshippers within the Pangonian Temple!'

'We disproved the accusations before we rooted out the demonologists in the Temple who had denounced us in the first place!' said Holfaste, growing angry again. 'But you know this well enough, Lorthar – now you are twisting facts to suit your own ends.'

'You will refer to me as your High Holiness, Prior,' said Lorthar venomously. 'And I am twisting nothing, for the Almighty shines the light of truth in the eyes of His most faithful subjects. The truth is that the Temple at Rima has fallen into corrupt ways, just as the Argolian Order has – only the pure perfecthood of Northalde can be entrusted with so precious a relic as the blood of the Redeemer himself.'

Prior Holfaste shook his head exasperatedly. Lady Walsa sneered contemptuously. 'The pure perfecthood of Northalde, don't make me laugh – the only thing that's pure about you is that platinum circlet you think it's your duty to flaunt in Reus' name. And the only light shining in your eyes is that from the gems dangling off your fingers. A blinding light it is too!'

'I must say very well put, my lady,' said Horskram softly, just as Wolmar rose from his seat and shouted: 'How dare you speak to the Arch Perfect like this, cousin Walsa! He is the most sacred personage among us, and that makes him Reus' deputy in this realm, along with mine uncle the King! You should all be listening to him, not mocking him!'

'Your son is a true knight, Prince Freidhoff,' said the Arch Perfect, nodding approvingly. The High Commander merely sat stoically as he had done throughout the meeting, and kept his counsel.

But Lady Walsa was not done yet. 'I'm your first cousin, once removed, Sir Wolmar,' she replied acidly. 'So that'll be *Lady* Walsa to you. As for your newfound piety, I've yet to be convinced – I think this is another one of your hot-headed endeavours to cause trouble for its own sake. The day you stop bedding tavern wenches and getting them with children you refuse to acknowledge, that's the day I'll believe in your Palomedian faith! Really, Freidhoff, you ought to discipline your son better – you're no better than your brother. In fact the pair of you are hopeless. Too sanguine by far, if you ask me...'

Lady Walsa launched into one of her infamous diatribes, taking both men to task for ungodly, reckless behaviour on all manner of fronts, while Wolmar choked on rage. The royal brothers did little more than exchange weary looks and shake their heads. When she was done the King got up again.

'Well, thank you cousin, for that instructive moral sermon – I am sure that your great rival in piety Lorthar here could have done little better,' he said. 'Now if we could please get back to matters in hand... Your High Holiness, assuming the legend of St Alysius is true, will you not at least consider granting Horskram's request? These are dark times, if half of what we've just heard is to be believed.'

'Assuming said legend is true, which I still do not own, the learned friar managed to get this far without the Redeemer's blood,' answered the perfect stubbornly. 'Why should he not be able to complete his journey without it?'

'Your High Holiness, as I believe I already suggested when recounting the story of my journey,' resumed Horskram patiently, 'whoever conjured up the devil to pursue us was probably already sorely taxed by having to control the first demon that stole the fragment. But with two fragments now spirited away, he or she may well be able to focus all his or her energies on conjuring up a single entity, one that we have no chance of fighting unaided. Adelko and I barely managed to repulse the lesser thing sent after us as it is!'

'But you said the theft took place weeks ago,' persisted the Arch Perfect. 'Why surely this unknown sorcerer, this Andragorix or whoever, would have had ample time to spirit the fragment away and then concentrate his or her energies on despatching you long before you reached the sanctuary of Strongholm?'

'A worthy point, your High Holiness,' said Holfaste. 'But you forget that the second fragment was also stolen during that time – another demon that needed binding, presumably as powerful as the first. And also, from what we've gleaned during witch trials over the years, it can take a black magician weeks to recover from the ordeal of binding the more potent spirits of the Other Side. Horskram is right – it is only a matter of time before our mystery warlock recovers his full powers. My learned colleague has risked much already on our behalf – to abandon him to devilspawn and further jeopardise our mission would be the height of ingratitude and sheer folly!'

'And just who is this mystery warlock, I should like to know?' said Princess Hjala suddenly. 'You are all so busy arguing about the reliquary and apportioning blame for the theft that you are overlooking one of the most important issues facing us – learning who is behind it and where they are. Torgun, Tarlquist and Wolmar have already spoken at other councils of the interference of a warlock in our battle against Thule and his rebels – could this Sea Wizard be involved? It seems to me as though the present uprising and Horskram's mission might well be linked!'

'You are indeed as shrewd as your father says, Your Highness,' said Horskram, inclining his head towards the Princess. 'Thus far I have two chief suspects in this foul business – one of them is Andragorix, the other is this Sea Wizard we have been hearing so much of lately.'

At the King's behest the knights recounted their story of the watery apparitions at the siege of Salmor.

'You mentioned how the brigands you slew on the road from Staerkvit seemed to have been in thrall to a wizard commanding similar powers...' said Holfaste.

'We do not know that for sure,' rejoined Horskram. 'But there do appear to be some similarities, yes: the wizard who commissioned and enthralled the Northland mercenaries sent to kill us hailed from the Frozen Principalities, according to the one we managed to question briefly. And it is noised abroad that this Sea Wizard is a renegade priest from the Northlands, where Sjórkunan is still worshipped as a god and his priesthood routinely practise magic.'

'But what of Andragorix?' queried Prior Holfaste. 'He hasn't been heard of for many a moon. The last we heard, he was somewhere in Vorstlund.'

'That would place him ideally for the theft at Graukolos,' mused Horskram. 'But no – I have no concrete evidence that he has resumed his diabolical scheming in earnest. Certainly his lust for power is a matter of record – had not Belinos and I sought him out he would no doubt by now be meddling in the affairs of Thraxia with his gramarye and trying to subjugate that realm to his will.'

'Wait,' Adelko piped up, breaking his mentor's injunction for a second time. 'Somebody *is* meddling in Thraxia though – not him, but another witch. The Thraxian knight Sir Braxus told Vaskrian and me when we met him the other day... Abrexta the Prescient they called her.'

'They called the Vorstlending mage Alaric that, before the second fragment corrupted his mind,' said Horskram thoughtfully. 'Adelko, are you sure this is true?'

'It is true,' said the King. 'A few days ago I finally found time to grant Sir Braxus of Gaellen the audience he craved. King Cadwy has been enthralled by a witch, and visits ruinous policies on his realm while mountain clans take advantage of his ensorcellment and run amok. He wanted my help to temporarily depose his liege and overthrow this Abrexta and her followers.'

'How very interesting,' said Horskram. 'So now we may add a third suspect to our list... Three witches, one of them a noted black magician of depraved character, the other two meddling in the worldly affairs of men. The more I see of this, the less I like it. It seems we must now add Thraxia to our list of countries to visit – though it lies on the way to the Island Realms in any case.'

'If this now concerns his kingdom too, perhaps we should invite the Thraxian knight to this meeting?' suggested Tarlquist.

The King frowned as he mulled this over. 'Perhaps he should be made a party to this, but not yet – I would rather not go divulging what we know to foreigners until we are more certain as to who is behind what.'

Horskram voiced his assent to this, but Lorthar scowled and muttered: 'Last time I looked, Grand Master Hannequin and the Supreme Perfect of Rima were foreigners.'

Ignoring him, the King rose and said: 'We have taken long counsel here today, and heard many unsettling tales. Now the time has come to decide what to do. Master Horskram, I have already given you leave to journey on when this war is done and seek your leader for whatever wisdom he can offer. But now I think it becomes clear that your cause and mine dovetail – for it seems at least possible that this Sea Wizard is involved in your affairs as much as he is in mine. So I would say to thee – when the time comes ride out with us, and if we can capture this warlock alive he shall be given up to you for questioning before we put his head in a noose. You have my word as your King on that.'

Horskram nodded. 'My thanks, Your Majesty. If it be Reus' will that he falls to us alive, I shall be grateful for the opportunity to question him.'

The King turned to the Arch Perfect. 'Lorthar, you have heard the story in full, or as much of it as we know. Thus far you have steadfastly refused to countenance giving up a single drop of our saviour's blood or even acknowledge its existence. Know that as your King, I do wish with all my heart that you relent in this.'

The perfect drew himself up proudly and, casting a venomous glance at the three Argolians, turned to the King and said: 'It is written in the Scriptures: "Render unto kings of men their lands to rule; but their souls my apostles shall command, yea, and all their disciples hereafter." As the noble knight Sir Wolmar so rightly reminds you all, here in Northalde I am that disciple. And though I hold from you all temporal lands as is right, in this matter, which concerns the Redeemer's blood and thus the souls of us all, I cannot and will not be compelled.'

Finishing his bombastic speech the Arch Perfect stared brazenly at the King with a smugly sanctimonious expression.

The King looked vexed for a few moments, then his expression cleared. 'Your High Holiness, you are indeed right,' he sighed. 'In this matter I cannot compel you, for as you say your will must be free in this matter.'

Horskram seemed about to protest, but the King went on without a pause. 'That is why I must now do something that pains me, and which for all the world I would have averted. *Guards!*'

Sweeping over to the door, the King unbolted it to allow four men of the Royal Guards to bustle in. Pointing at the gaping Arch Perfect he thundered:

'Arrest this man! Take him down to the dungeons directly, and permit him to speak with no man or woman on his way there. His High Holiness Lorthar stands accused of high treason, for defying the will of his King. He will languish in gaol until such time as this war is done and he may stand trial. Until then he will receive no visitors, except when his gaoler visits him twice a day to feed him.'

The stunned perfect managed a single strangled word.

'*What?*'

'Oh I may not be able to compel you in matters of the cloth, Lorthar, but that doesn't mean I can't attaint you when you break the laws of my land,' said Freidheim darkly. 'Defying your King is an act of treason – is that not written in the statutes? Your very own Scriptures say so: "Render unto kings of men their lands to rule." Well, your precious Temple – and everything in it – sits on my lands.'

Turning to Lord Ulnor he said: 'You will send word to Lorthar's deputy that pending his superior's trial he is acting Arch Perfect. You will also explain my request, and what has just befallen his predecessor for refusing it – I trust he will prove a wiser man in this matter. He will also be strongly advised to dispense with Temple politicking and make prompt confession as to the contents of his precinct when his King commands it.'

'It shall be done at once, Your Majesty,' said Ulnor, before sweeping out of the chamber on his cane.

'Well what are you waiting for?' growled the King at his startled guards. 'Get this traitor out of my sight – I've enough of them to deal with thanks to Thule, Reus knows.'

'You haven't heard the last of this!' Lorthar managed to scream as the guards dragged him from the room. 'His Supreme Holiness will hear of this, mark my words! You've just made an enemy you can't hope to defeat in battle – you will be sundered from the Temple for this!'

'We'll see about that,' replied the King, looking singularly unmoved. 'I don't think his Supreme Holiness will be overly pleased when he learns what you've been keeping back from him for years – think of all the pilgrimages you've denied good Palomedians! I'm sure the Supreme Perfect and I will be able to come to a happy arrangement on the matter – so no need for any sunderings! Oh, one last thing – see that this traitor is stripped of all his baubles, I'll think I'll have them requisitioned for the war effort. That will be all – now get him to the dungeons where he belongs!'

The former Arch Perfect of Strongholm wailed all the way down the stairs as the guards dragged him off.

The King slammed the door shut behind them.

'Uncle, this is sheer madness – ' began Wolmar, his eyes bulging.

'Silence!' roared the King. 'Silence or I'll have my brother expel you from the Order! I've had enough of your mouth!'

Wolmar cringed back into his seat like a beaten dog.

'Brother,' said Prince Freidhoff, breaking his silence. 'I apologise for my son's temerity, but he has a point I think – this is rash indeed.'

But the King was in no mood to brook any more dissent. Waving his huge hand he said: 'I've heard enough. I know when I'm making powerful enemies, and I've also reigned long enough to know when a more powerful enemy is hatching plans. True, we don't even know yet who we are rightly facing, but if everything I've heard today is true, then whoever they are, they mean to cover us all in darkness. If the Fay Folk fear what's brewing enough to aid mortals, I'll warrant the wars of kings will seem like a storm in a flagon if this malefactor has his or her way! That is what you have rightly been getting at all along isn't it, Horskram?'

The adept, who looked as astonished as everyone else, nodded humbly and said: 'Aye, my liege, it is.'

The King fixed him with a beady look. 'Then hear this, master adept,' he intoned. 'I've just put my royal neck on the line for the sake of you and your quest, and my aid does not come without a price. This Redeemer's blood I have secured for you – and in so giving it, I do charge you, as your rightful sovereign, to seek out this black sorcerer. And if it happen that he or she is doing evil on my soil, you will do everything in your power to overthrow them. Yea, if it costs you your life to do so! Do you solemnly swear to this?'

To Adelko's surprise his mentor knelt. 'I do so swear,' he said gravely, his eyes to the ground as he made the sign. 'All I have ever wanted is to oppose the servants of darkness and defeat them where I can. I pray that your trust in me does not prove unwarranted, and may the Redeemer light my path and guide me in all ways.'

'Very good, you may rise,' said the King peremptorily. 'Most of the rest of you have duties to attend to – well get to them, we've a war to fight! Everyone in this room is sworn to secrecy about everything they have heard here – save for you and your novice Horskram, you may divulge what you already knew as you see fit. The rest of you: it's treason and the dungeons with Lorthar if you breathe a word of this to anyone without my say-so. Is that firmly understood?'

As one the remaining councillors nodded. It was most firmly understood.

'Very good,' rejoined the King. 'Now let's to it! There's a traitorous upstart waiting to meet us in battle – and I have a feeling that's only going to be the beginning of our troubles.'

⇥ CHAPTER VII ⇤

A Muſter at Dawn

Eight thousand fighting men. After three weeks in a city of twenty thousand people, it seemed a slender hope for a kingdom.

Not that they weren't an impressive sight to Adelko. The pitched tents of the loyalist muster sprawled before him, sporting hundreds of pennants, each one bearing its own unique coat of arms. Each section of the camp was earmarked by a standard, one for each lord who had brought knights and other soldiers to the coming conflict. The section belonging to the White Valravyn was conspicuous by its absence of heraldry: a single standard bearing their age-old symbol ruffled alone in the breeze.

'That's where I've been staying,' said Vaskrian with more than a hint of pride in his voice. He was pointing at the clutch of pavilions centred on the standard bearing the double unicorn insignia of the Ruling House of Ingwin. As a vassal holding lands directly from the King, his new master was part of the contingent that styled itself the Royal Knights.

'We'll break camp in an hour, so I can't stay long,' the squire added breathlessly. 'The Royals have been picked to take the vanguard, along with the White Valravyn – that means we'll be part of the central charge when we get to Linden!'

He looked as fevered as he had ever done to Adelko, which was saying a lot. The novice guessed that even their shared adventures paled next to the prospect of his first proper war.

He didn't share his friend's enthusiasm. He'd gotten more than used to the luxury of living in a palace, albeit a martial one belonging to a hardened warrior-king: the prospect of returning to the road with a war waiting at the end of it didn't appeal.

He caught himself, feeling suddenly ashamed. Who was he to complain? He would be riding with the King's entourage, afforded relative comforts during the journey. When that was over he would watch the fighting from a safe distance with Horskram, Freidheim and his closest advisers. Well, safe unless they lost.

The camp suddenly rang with the blaring of trumpets.

'It's the order to strike camp,' said Vaskrian. 'Where's your guvnor? I should say goodbye to him – chances are we won't see much of each other during the march.'

Adelko glanced over his shoulder, back towards the city gates.

'He'll be along in a minute, I should think,' the novice replied. 'He'll be coming with the royal entourage – they're supposed to arrive in time for the King to give a speech to the army before we set off.'

'Surprised he let you out of his sight for so long,' quipped the squire. He had a point. Adelko had sent him a messenger, arranging to meet at dawn on the fields between Strongholm and the muster camp. Horskram had indeed been indulgent, complying with his novice's request. Adelko liked to think it had something to do with his contribution to the secret council last week. True, he'd broken his mentor's injunction yet again, but some good had clearly come of it. Surely even the irascible old adept could see how much his adventures had improved him. He might not be strong like Vaskrian or the knights they'd met, but he'd proved he could think clearly under pressure.

A second series of trumpet blasts sounded. These were from the turrets atop the gatehouse guarding the entrance to Strongholm.

'That'll be them now,' said Adelko. He was on the point of turning back to face his friend when his eye was drawn to the left. On the other side of the gates from where they were, another camp huddled against the grey city walls. Unlike the muster, now a bustle of activity pulling down tents and saddling horses, they were a pitiful sight. The refugees fleeing Thule's depredations had multiplied during the first week of their sojourn in the capital; the King had been forced to order them settled outside Strongholm. They numbered a good ten thousand at least – already the loyalist victims of war outnumbered those who would fight their cause.

The new-born sun was rising on a mild day, but that did little to raise his spirits. Its inchoate rays tinged the seas of the Strang Estuary an ominous red that put him in mind of Prince Thorsvald's efforts to hold off the rebel fleet. The last they had heard, the Sealord was putting up a valiant fight – but that had been three days ago and things could change quickly in a war. Especially when you were outnumbered.

Besides that, he felt homesick. He'd caught his first glimpse of the Highlanders a few days ago, when he'd been taking in the view from the palace rooftop.

He had been about to make his way back down when he'd heard it. The unmistakable sound of a highland horn. They had come riding in from the north-west, mounted on shaggy mountain ponies:

a six-hundred strong host of bearded, braided men bearing a myriad of brightly coloured banners. The sound of clan pipes mingling with the horn blast heralding their arrival had driven a phantom knife through his heart; the bitter-sweet longing for a home left far behind.

In keeping with their fiercely independent nature the clans had set up their own camp, a little apart from the main muster. Adelko could see them joining themselves to the middle host now, rugged warriors dressed in studded leather jerkins and carrying stout axes.

Each banner bore its own distinct pattern of interlocking shapes, woven from threads of different hues. A sash worn by every warrior mirrored the design appropriate to their clan. So very different from the knights' pennants with their pictorial devices.

Scouring the banners, Adelko had found the one he was looking for: the yellow and green diamonds of Clan MacLingen, which ruled the stretch of Highlands he'd grown up in. Perhaps old Whaelfric, his local clansman, would be among them.

'I'd best be going,' said Vaskrian regretfully. 'Too bad I can't say farewell to the old monk in person, but I have to get Sir Ulfstan ready for the march.'

'I'll give Master Horskram your best wishes,' replied Adelko, wondering how much the adept would care for those. His mentor had given little indication that he thought any better of the headstrong squire since Staerkvit. 'What's he like, your new master?' asked the novice, changing the subject.

Vaskrian wrinkled his nose. 'Not much to say, really. Don't think he's half the man my old guvnor was. You know how it is – there's bluebloods that can fight, and there's bluebloods that only think they can.'

Adelko merely nodded. He sixth sense told him that beneath his excitement his friend was concealing a profound dissatisfaction. Evidently the squire's hopes of a knighthood weren't being encouraged by his new master.

Vaskrian turned to go. Adelko bit his lip. Now was the time. 'Vaskrian...'

The squire turned to look at him again.

'What ails you?' he asked, suddenly frowning when he caught the look on Adelko's face.

Adelko flushed. How did you thank someone for saving your life? And then the answer came. It was simple. You thanked them.

'I – I don't think I ever got around to saying... you saved my neck from those Northland brigands, twice. If it wasn't for you I'd probably be dead.'

The squire grinned. The morning breeze caught his long unruly hair, making him look like the rakehell he was.

'Think nothing of it!' he smiled. 'I swore an oath to protect you both, didn't I? I may not be a knight yet, but that doesn't mean I can't act like one.'

'No, I suppose not,' faltered Adelko. 'It's just... I don't know that I'll ever be able to repay you.'

'No need,' said the squire, clapping him hard on the shoulder. Under different circumstances that might have been irritating, but as it was Adelko felt strangely touched. 'Like I said, I swore an oath – I didn't take coin to fight like those wretches we killed. If you want to repay me, just remember what I did. And tell everyone! Especially if they're a blueblood!'

They shared a laugh at that. And then Vaskrian turned, mounted his courser and was gone, galloping back towards the camp.

Adelko felt his spirits lighten a little. A friendship forged on the road indeed. He wondered if he'd see that friend again.

✠ ✠ ✠

His old guvnor would have shouted at him. Upbraided him for being late. Told him to get a move on. Sir Ulfstan did none of those things.

As Vaskrian pulled up before his master's pavilion, the knight sat back from the breakfast he had prepared for him before going to meet Adelko and sighed contentedly.

'Ah, there you are,' he said languidly. 'I wondered where you'd got to.' Looking around him at the fast dwindling tents of the encampment, he said flatly: 'I think we should be leaving now. Something about a war to fight. We're to ride in the vanguard I believe.'

Hurriedly Vaskrian dismounted and bustled over to the tent, proffering excuses as he did.

Ulfstan silenced him with a wave of the hand. 'Don't bother explaining. I don't need an explanation. You're a commoner, after all – can't be expected to be timely. Especially not an Efrilunder. Really, the things a war drives a man to. A northern toerag for a squire, I'll never live this down!'

He gave a snort of dismissive laughter. Vaskrian felt himself flush to the ears as he began pulling the tent down. Such remarks were typical of his new master. Somehow the knight's offhand manner made them even harder to bear than Rutgar's coarse jibes, or any of the other blueblood taunts he'd had to put up with back home.

That lot said things with intent – you knew they wanted to rile you. That meant they cared about what you thought, one way or another.

But Ulfstan didn't give a fallen angel's damnation about what Vaskrian thought. When he said things like that, he wasn't saying them to hurt or taunt. He was simply stating things as he saw them.

Sir Ulfstan stood and stretched his arms, yawning. He looked for all the world as if he'd just awoken from a heavy night of carousing, not to the first war in fifteen years of his kingdom's history.

There was absolutely nothing striking about his appearance. He was of average height, medium build, neither comely nor ugly. His mousy hair was receding slightly with the advance of early middle age. Everything about him screamed ordinary.

Everything except his family name that is. He could trace his noble ancestry back for generations – apparently one of his forebears had been the younger son of some forgotten lord or other. Sir Ulfstan had inherited the family estate that age-old scion had managed to carve out for himself, a good-sized plot of land some twenty miles out of Strongholm.

And of course that meant Sir Ulfstan of Alfheim was anything but ordinary.

Swallowing his bitterness Vaskrian went about his duties. The camp had thinned to virtually nothing about them: the vanguard was nearly entirely drawn up. Just waiting on lackadaisical knights and their disobedient squires.

But it was the rear that caught Vaskrian's eye. That was composed of the Efrilunders. He caught Lord Fenrig's standard shivering in the breeze. It was a customary shield motif, the field divided horizontally into two variations. The upper half was tinctured pale blue and bore a device depicting a pair of intertwining roses, one red, the other white; the lower half was a chequered design picked out in the same colours. The sight of it made him anxious and a little homesick at the same time. Next to it were those of Lord Vymar of Harrang, whose tourney he'd missed a seeming lifetime ago, and Lord Aesgir of Sjorvard, who had disembarked his troops in Strongholm harbour a tenday ago.

The Woldings were to ride in the middle section. They had arrived maddeningly late, just the day before yesterday, hauling their beefy carcasses to the fight on stout nags. They had brought trained footsoldiers and a pressed levy with them too – the latter were the sorriest-looking bunch of peasants Vaskrian had ever seen.

He shook his head as he watched them being bullied into line by the serjeants in charge of the middle army formation. Wolding conscripts. Perhaps the one benefit those ragged serfs could be said to bring was a complete indifference to death. For death would be a blessing for such miserable folk.

Returning to work, the squire packed the tent away and loaded it on to his master's sumpter. He'd taken care of most of the preparations before meeting Adelko. He was fully accoutred himself; his swaddled ribs still ached beneath his mail shirt but he was young and strong and on the mend nicely. All he needed to do was arm Sir Ulfstan and they were ready.

'I hope you've not neglected my armour,' said the knight as Vaskrian began helping him into his boiled leather undertunic and leggings. 'I want those links mirror bright, my boy – if I've to fight this wretched war then I mean to do it in style. The sooner we send those rebel traitors packing, the sooner I can get back to my life.'

This is supposed to be your life you idiot, thought Vaskrian as he fastened the straps. *The whole point of being a knight is to fight, not whore and drink and play at dice.*

Fetching his master's hauberk he helped him into it. Sir Branas had never particularly cared for polishing: as long as his armour had no chinks or dints and functioned properly he wasn't fussed. Sir Ulfstan had insisted to the contrary however, and Vaskrian had spent hours buffing up every link. That wasn't the least of the grudges he bore the haughty knight.

He missed Sir Branas more by the day. But thinking on the old veteran had his mind going to strange places. A hunched figure leered at him from the darkest corner of his consciousness, strange voices whispered to him in forgotten tongues...

Shaking his head to clear it, he pulled suddenly on one of the fastenings binding the hauberk in place.

'Not so hard!' snapped Sir Ulfstan. 'What in Reus' name do they teach you up in the provinces?'

'Sorry, sire,' muttered Vaskrian, scowling. The knight's back was to him, so at least he didn't have to dissemble completely.

Sir Ulfstan shook his head. 'An Efrilund commoner for a squire, this really is the worst,' he sighed. 'Be assured that I'll be handing you back to Lord Fenrig after the war. I shall just have to do without a squire until my other nephew comes of age this autumn.'

Another deadpan rebuke. This one didn't rile him – it made his heart sink. A pity he couldn't stab Sir Ulfstan as he had Derrick. But then what good would that do even if he could?

And his hopes had been so high. When Lord Visigard had singled him out to be squired off to a landed vassal of the King, he'd thought his future made. A prestigious position and a war on the way.

But now he knew there'd be no glory for him no matter what he did. Sir Branas had been quick to put him back in his place, but he'd given credit where he thought it due. Sir Ulfstan would never even countenance the idea of a common squire's worth in the field.

At least he'd been spared having to approach Lord Fenrig and explain what had happened. But once the war was over Ulfstan would dismiss him and the King's injunction would no longer stand – his loyalty would default back to the Jarl of Hroghar, and he'd have to make a full disclosure of events.

And how exactly would he explain poor Branas's death anyway? He could barely remember their frightful adventure in the forest. And then there was the matter of Sir Anrod and Derrick. Word would be getting around by now. Before, under the auspices of his old guvnor, he'd been self-assured: if anyone wanted to make anything of that, they'd have to seek out Sir Branas first.

But with the old knight gone it would be left to Fenrig to decide what to do with him. He might decide Vaskrian was too much trouble and release him from service.

What would he do then? He wasn't worried about Anrod or Derrick's family – they could come looking for him for all he cared. He wouldn't back down now, not even for a blueblood.

But his chances of getting another position as a squire would be minimal. Knights in other jarldoms would require a letter of introduction, even the Woldings were picky about that sort of thing.

Never mind a knighthood – his very squirehood was in jeopardy.

With a heavy heart he finished buckling on Sir Ulfstan's armour and fetched his tabard. It sported a light grey field with a red turret device blazoned on top. Even his coat of arms was dull.

Sword, shield and dagger came next and then they were done. Without another word the two of them took to the saddle and rode to join the vanguard.

They were the last ones to take their place, but that didn't seem to bother Sir Ulfstan. It didn't bother Vaskrian much either – what did it matter what people thought of him now?

✢ ✢ ✢

Adelko gazed at the bristling forest of spears, their tips glinting in the rising sun. The three army formations were bolstered by the usual host of ancillaries: wayns bearing food supplies, craftsmen, washerwomen and other necessaries for the march to war.

Next to him his mentor sat still in the saddle, his cowl drawn up as though he did not wish to be seen. A sidelong glance at the old monk's face beneath his hood told him nothing of his feelings; but his sixth sense said enough. Beside an Argolian's customary disapproval of violence he felt a sense of shame: he guessed Horskram's past as a knight was playing on his mind. Sir Horskram – it sounded all wrong. If it seemed so to Adelko, he could imagine what it felt like to the adept.

Nearby the King was saying farewell to his family and closest advisers. Princess Hjala's face looked wan and sad as she embraced her father. They were said to be unusually close for a monarch and daughter, all the more so since the Queen had died of the ague two years ago. Freidheim still mourned her deeply, though his Northlending stoicism prevented him from showing it.

Adelko had been at court long enough to learn the princess had had her own share of tragedy too. Her husband and three children had been carried off to a watery grave ten years ago, when the former baron of Saltcaste's ship was wrecked during a voyage from Port Urring to Strongholm. She had been too ill to travel with them at the time; by a cruel twist of fate she survived her malady only to be faced with the lifelong pain of loss. Her sandy-brown hair was tied back in a severe braid, and though tall and handsome like her father she wore little ornamentation.

Lady Walsa approached them, riding on a sleek black palfrey. She had insisted on praying with Horskram every sunset during their stay at the palace. If Adelko had not known better, he could almost have sworn the crinkly old dame was in love with his mentor.

Horskram inclined his head as she drew level with them, though he did not remove his hood.

'May the blessings of the Almighty go with you on your journey, Brother Horskram,' she said seriously. 'Your doings will far exceed this dreadful civil war, I trow.'

Looking somewhat abashed Horskram cleared his throat and replied: 'As to that, Your Highness, only He can say. But the Redeemer has heard our prayers, and lent us his flesh that we might strive in his name.'

Lady Walsa stared deep into the old monk's eyes. Her leathery face looked intent and serious.

'You have been chosen to carry out the Almighty's will,' she intoned. 'How else could it be that you now bear what has not been born for more than a hundred years? I shall pray for you, Brother Horskram, though I fear the prayers of a humble wretch like me will be as naught next to yours.'

Adelko blinked in surprise. Had he really just heard the fierce old matriarch refer to herself as 'a humble wretch'? Perhaps she was in love with his mentor after all.

'We are all humble in the Almighty's eyes,' was all Horskram had to say to that. 'Pray for me, Your Highness, and for all of us.'

The old monk inclined his head again. Lady Walsa gave an almost imperceptible nod of the head, then turned her steed away to rejoin the royal entourage. Horskram resumed staring at the assembled army with blank eyes, and held his peace.

Lord Ulnor was talking quietly with the King as Walsa rejoined them. The seneschal hailed from a high house of his own, being a blood relative of Walsa's demented husband the Jarl of Stromlund. Perhaps now was a good time to be mad, Adelko reflected grimly – it felt as though the whole realm had gone insane, tearing itself apart for the sake of vanity and greed.

Next to them Lord Toros, Jarl of Vandheim and elder brother to Sir Torgun, was embracing his wife, a plain-looking girl of about eighteen summers. He was of similar stature to his celebrated younger brother, with the same mane of blond hair. Somewhat less powerfully built, his face was older and wiser, though he had not seen thirty summers.

Torgun was there also, exchanging quiet words with their sister, Princess Aeselif. A beautiful damsel, she strongly resembled her brothers, but her comely face was riven with anxiety. She was married to Prince Wolfram, who even now struggled to hold Linden. Their son Prince Freidhrim, a boy of eight summers, stood at her side, clutching her pale hand with an innocence Adelko envied. He would one day inherit the throne, if he lived.

The boy might inherit sooner rather than later if things went ill at Linden. Then again, if that happened, he might inherit nothing more than a trip to the axeman's block. The word about court was that Thule was not expected to be merciful in victory.

Torgun stepped over to embrace Princess Hjala. Adelko's sixth sense flared: their two houses were linked by Aeselif's marriage to Wolfram, but there was something stronger than mere kinship by proxy between those two. He sensed a lingering bitterness too – and it wasn't coming from Sir Torgun.

His thoughts were interrupted by the sound of horses approaching. Turning he saw Sir Braxus and his six compatriots come riding up, fully armoured and ready for war.

The Thraxian knight called out a cheery greeting as he pulled up his charger before them.

'Good morning, monks, and a high morning it is!' he cried, gesturing towards the army with an extravagant sweep of the arm. 'A fine day to go riding off to war and glory, no?'

Horskram said nothing, and continued to stare at the men drawn up in the field, some waiting more patiently than others for their King to address them before signalling the march to Linden.

'What are you doing here?' asked Adelko. 'This isn't even your fight!'

Sir Braxus frowned. The knight next to him, the older one Sir Vertrix, looked for all the world as if he agreed with that statement. He shook his head and muttered something unintelligible.

'Well, it is now,' replied Sir Braxus, somewhat lamely Adelko thought. 'Your King won't listen to our petition while he has a war of his own to fight

– but I reckon he might just listen when he's sitting on the field of victory. He might listen especially to a lord's son who helped him to that victory.'

Horskram broke his silence then. A short stab of contemptuous laughter escaped the cowl.

Braxus stared at him, a returning smile freezing on his lips. 'Something amuses you, master adept?'

Horskram met his gaze. 'No, not really,' he replied flatly. 'I don't find anything about this situation amusing. Your folly however, does furnish me with a momentary light relief.'

The Thraxian knight's face darkened. Sir Vertrix looked troubled and conflicted. The other knights and their squires, who could not understand the exchange, exchanged bemused glances. It was then Adelko noticed that a squire was missing – Sir Braxus rode to war without a second. But then he supposed that was what the knights of the White Valravyn all did all the time. Perhaps he was trying to prove a point, something about a lord's son being self-sufficient.

'Folly is it?' replied Braxus unsmiling. 'So you say, but you may find that my kingdom's problems are not so different from your own... your novice here is as reticent as you are, Brother Horskram, but it's clear there's some devilry at work in your realm just as there is in mine. Why else would an Argolian be joining the march to war?'

'Why indeed?' returned Horskram laconically, turning to stare at the army again. He did not meet the knight's gaze again.

'Suit yourself,' said Braxus, shrugging his mailed shoulders. 'Adelko, it is at any rate pleasant to see you again – where is your young friend?'

Adelko nodded towards the vanguard. 'With the Royal Knights – he's been squired off to a vassal of the King.'

'Ah yes, I remember now,' said Braxus. 'Well I may not see much of him during the march – but we shall see plenty of each other, Adelko! We'll be riding with the King's entourage as guests of honour – Thraxians part of the King of Northalde's honour guard, who'd have thought it?'

Sir Vertrix's expression looked sour as the Thraxians rode off to join the king's personal contingent of knights. Adelko guessed the old veteran remembered Corne Hill well. Braxus had reminded him of something though.

'I met Vaskrian at dawn,' he told his mentor. 'He said to give you his best wishes.'

Horskram turned cold eyes on him. 'Did he now? How very thoughtful of him.'

Something in his sarcastic tone grated on the novice.

'I... I thanked him too,' he pressed. 'For saving my life. Twice.'

Horskram mulled over his words. 'He saved you from the sword, by the sword,' was all he said.

'Well... he can't be that bad then,' persisted Adelko. 'I mean, he swore an oath to protect us, and he kept to it. I know he's headstrong and foolish but – '

'He's a killer!' yelled Horskram suddenly. 'Don't you understand that? Vaskrian, yon Thraxians, every experienced man in this field, yea even our King himself – they are all killers!'

'But – '

'No buts Adelko – you are a novice of the Argolian Order, sworn to peace and only to fight in self-defence. And even then you aren't supposed to take life – and that means you don't befriend those that do! I fear your adventures have clouded your judgement – perhaps I should never have brought you along after all. Clearly your moral fortitude is vulnerable to pressure.'

Adelko felt a surge of anger then. It was a rare emotion for him – he rarely got angry about anything. But after weeks of danger he felt stretched thin. Why did his mentor have to be so relentlessly grim and unpleasant?

'But these men have no choice!' he said. 'Thule started this war – and it's only because the King let him live after the last one that he's even able to in the first place! Vaskrian killed those men because they were trying to kill us – and if he hadn't I'd be dead by now! How can you be so... so ungrateful?'

Horskram sneered. 'Ah, he muddles his way through a few misadventures and now the novice presumes to teach the master on moral equivalence! Well, go to it then, lad – befriend this fool squire if you think it best. Befriend every hardened sworder in the land if it pleases you. Just remember that if any one of them had to kill you in service, they would do it without hesitation.'

'That's not fair!' yelled Adelko. 'Vaskrian would never kill an Argolian! He only kills bad men.'

Horskram laughed bitterly. 'Ah, have I taught you nothing these past months?' he said ruefully. 'Let me tell you precisely what Vaskrian is, seeing as it seems to have passed you by. He is a glorified young thug. He hopes to earn himself a title, so he can enrich himself and kill with impunity whenever he feels like it. That is his motivation – nothing more. He doesn't care a fallen angel's damnation about you – he saved you only to enhance his own reputation.'

The old monk flung his arms up in mock adulation. 'Vaskrian – esquire of Hroghar, saver of hapless young monks! Vaskrian – killer of traitors in service to his King! Vaskrian – killer for hire, full stop. Do you understand?'

'No, I don't,' said Adelko defiantly. 'He isn't for hire – he doesn't fight for coin, he said so himself.'

'No, Adelko, he doesn't fight for coin – his ambitions are higher than that. He fights for the living he one day hopes to attain, for the plot of land he hopes to receive for services rendered. He kills for his own advancement, his own personal glory. The rest is just gold-plating on steel.'

Adelko was about to retort. Then he stopped.

Remember what I did. Tell everyone. Especially if they're a blueblood.

The squire's own words. The ones he'd laughed at that very morning.

He should have held his peace then. He should know better than to try and outfoot his mentor in a debate on moral logic. But he still felt angry. He wasn't done arguing yet.

'So what does that make you?'

The words were spoken quietly. They caught his mentor by surprise.

'What does what make me?' replied the adept icily.

'You used to be a knight once – and a crusader to boot. Fighting in a holy war our Order refuses to condone. How many men have you killed, Master Horskram?'

A pained look crossed his mentor's face. Adelko regretted his words instantly.

'I... have repented my sins,' was all he said. He turned away again, looking bleakly at the assembled knights and soldiers as the King rode up to address them on a gorgeously caparisoned Farovian destrier.

Adelko could not bring himself to stop. It was as if somebody else were speaking with his voice.

'But you've still killed men, Master Horskram,' he said softly. 'They're still dead. No matter what you've done since, or what you ever do, their blood will always be on your hands.'

He was half expecting an angry rebuke, to be told to guard his tongue and know his place. It didn't come.

'Aye, it will,' replied the adept sadly. 'And my soul shall ever be tainted with it, until the day the Angel of Death sees fit to bring me before him. That is why, for all the world, I would not have you seduced by the way of the sword, Adelko. A pure spirit is a precious thing.'

The adept laid a tanned hand on Adelko's shoulder and looked him square in the eyes. 'In time, if you survive, you will become an Argolian journeyman, perhaps even an adept. As the years pass you will realise that compromises must be made, to serve the greater good.'

'But I do realise! That's what I've been arguing just now, about Vaskrian and the others...'

'Not that kind of compromise, Adelko. Next to perjuring one's soul, to kill a man is the worst thing a Palomedian can do.'

Something occurred to Adelko just then.

'But – even Palom himself was a killer, before he forsook the sword. He spent his early years leading the revolt against the Thalamians while trying to bring the Creed to Urovia. And he is our Prophet!'

Horskram nodded. The sadness had not left his voice. 'Aye, that is true. And some among our Order say his cruel death was a punishment, meted out by the Almighty – for his own indulgence in moral equivalence.'

That brought Adelko up short. Everyone knew the Redeemer had been a warrior-prophet who eventually became a pacifist before being tortured and executed in Tyrannos. But he'd never thought about it like that before.

'You will have to make moral compromises, as we all must,' the adept continued. 'But killing should never be one of them. To consort with those that do so without hesitation, without compunction, is a grave sin.'

'I understand, really I do,' said Adelko. 'But if there was hope for Palom, and hope for you – surely there's hope for Vaskrian? At least he tries to do the right thing sometimes, even if he is a killer.'

Horskram sighed and shook his head wearily. 'Do we absolve the unrepentant murderer because he loves his wife? Or cares for his children? Think on it Adelko – that young hotblood you call friend is tearing up the highway towards perdition. And I don't see him getting off that horse very soon.'

'But... if that's true of Vaskrian, then it's true of half the people in this army. Torgun, Braxus... all of them, even the King. Their souls are all forfeit.'

The adept sighed, his face bleak beneath his hood. 'Now perhaps you appreciate why I do not share that idiot Thraxian's exuberance over this war.'

The two monks said nothing more after that, listening in silence to the King's speech.

Freidheim was a good speaker. No, he was more than that. He was a magnificent speaker. The effect of his words on the men was visible; as he exhorted them to deeds of valour in service to the loyalist cause, Adelko could see every man from landed knight to common footsoldier stand a little straighter. Even the poor Wolding peasants seemed to stir, clutching their rusted pitchforks more firmly, a glimmer of pride kindling their hopeless eyes.

The King was a magnificent speaker. His speech made Adelko feel sick and troubled.

A great cheer went up when Freidheim finished, drawing his sword with a flourish and brandishing it high over his head. The walls of Strongholm resounded with clarion calls and the army began its march to Linden. Adelko and Horskram fell in with the King's retinue, riding before the vanguard. As they made their way past a crowd of womenfolk and men too young or old to fight, their discourse on Palom took the novice's mind back to an unexpected place.

He remembered the Fays' words in Tintagael Forest.

The warrior-prophet's blood was shed, that mortal man might thrive instead.

Cryptic words, intended to steer them towards the Redeemer's blood for their own protection. They had a bitter irony to them now. To thrive on bloodshed: was that the Almighty's plan for His creation?

The faerie couplet stayed with him. Staring at the horizon he recalled another, from their penultimate verse.

A crooked path you now must tread, gloom gathers on the road ahead.

Was that just a warning specific to their mission, he now wondered, or a metaphor for any life? He pictured the Fays, ensconced in their sylvan sanctuary, laughing down through the ages at the ways of mortal men.

⊱ CHAPTER VIII ⊰

The Net Tightens

'Father, what is the meaning of this?' Adhelina's face was flushed and angry. The pair of them had not been getting on well of late as it was; this latest absurdity only heightened the tension.

'It's a precautionary measure,' growled her father, without turning from the window overlooking the middle ward. From the practice yard far below the faint sound of clanging drifted up as the knights and soldiers went about their daily regimen.

'A precautionary measure?' repeated the heiress of Dulsinor incredulously. 'An armed guard on my chamber door day and night! What are you fearing father, that a rival lover may seek me out in my boudoir?'

Her father turned to face her. A mountain of a man, his temper could inspire fear in many a knight, but not his only daughter.

'More likely that a rival baron may send an assassin to prevent this alliance with the stroke of a knife!' he thundered. 'You're supposed to be the great reader in the family – surely you recall the tale of Hardred the Melancholy?'

This unexpected remark brought Adhelina up short. She had to think a moment to remember the story. Hardred had been the Second Eorl of Dulsinor. He had inherited the Griffenwyrd from his grandfather Ranveldt Longyear more than two centuries ago, and earned his lugubrious epithet after his daughter Alois was murdered on the eve of her wedding. She had been engaged to a powerful Pangonian warlord, and the House of Markward had stood to gain from the blood alliance... until the then Eorl of Upper Thulia had had her assassinated to prevent the match from happening.

That had been the start of the blood feud between the two Griffenwyrds, which continued to this day. For many years afterwards the House of Markward had taken to putting an armed guard on female family members for a moon before their weddings, and it had gradually grown to be something of a custom.

But it had been dropped a few generations ago. The night-time guard had always struck Adhelina as rather silly given that Alois had been murdered during a hunting expedition.

'But you cannot mean to revive such a foolish custom!' she exclaimed. 'The Lady Alois was killed in the Glimmerholt – why, no assassin could hope to penetrate the walls of Graukolos!'

'Oh no?' replied the Eorl. 'Don't be too sure... the Eorl of Upper Thulia's been making threats.'

'Threats? What kind of threats?'

'Just before he left, his emissary, that lickspittle Malthus, said his liege would stop at nothing to prevent this alliance being sealed with your marriage.'

Adhelina was sorely tempted to shower praise on the Eorl of Upper Thulia, but thought better of it. 'I think you are taking a hotblood's word too literally,' was what she said.

'Then you should think again,' replied her father darkly. 'I haven't ruled this long and stayed alive by ignoring threats, veiled or otherwise. The guard stays until the wedding – they're to accompany you on all your errands, though thanks to Hettie you shouldn't need to do any of those yourself.'

Walking over to his only daughter he took her firmly yet gently by the shoulders.

'We may not have agreed on much of late,' he said, looking earnestly down into her face. 'But believe me when I say that I love you, and am doing what is best for you, in the long run. You may not see that now, but in time I hope you will.'

Adhelina nodded slowly, feigning resignation. Her thoughts were awhirl. She could not risk pushing this point too far, her father mustn't suspect anything...

'Well as long as I still have the privacy of my chambers...' she said in voice that was meant to be small.

'Of course!' said her father, smiling for once. 'After all, I'll not have common soldiers invading the sanctity of my virginal daughter's boudoir!'

Adhelina nearly flinched when he said this. She did not enjoy the subject of her virginity – the price of preserving her freedom had been to deny her body's desires. While she remained unmarried under her father's close watch there was little chance of her ever being courted by a paramour, for few would dare even try. Now after all that struggle and sacrifice she was on course to being deflowered by a man she found repulsive. The thought had only spurred her on in her plans of escape.

But now those plans looked set to be scuppered – by one hasty remark from some foolish knight, and the echo of an old family tragedy.

'Very well, father,' she said demurely. 'If that is all, I think I will return to my chambers now.'

⁘ ⁘ ⁘

Back in her main chamber Adhelina paced circles frantically whilst Hettie did her best to calm her down.

'Sit down and have some herbal tea, m'lady,' she proffered. 'Look, I've just made it!'

'Oh fie on tea, I need a stiff drink!' said Adhelina hotly.

'Well, that can be arranged,' replied her lady-in-waiting. Rising to her feet she went to speak to the two guards outside before exiting. Before long she returned with a servant in tow carrying a jug of wine and two goblets on a silver tray. Adhelina had not ceased her pacing, but with the servant gone and the door barred she was at last prevailed upon to take a seat and have a drink.

'You'll make yourself ill with all that frantic pacing,' muttered Hettie, taking a sip of the ruby-coloured vintage.

Adhelina took a great draught before setting her goblet down on her walnut table with an exasperated *thunk*. It was a lovely dry red from southern Pangonia but not too strong, and did little to soothe her troubled spirits.

'Oh Hettie, what are we to do?' she lamented, moderating her voice so the guards outside would not hear. 'This spoils all our plans... how are we to sneak away in the dead of night with sentries on the blasted door?'

Hettie stared dolefully into her cup. 'I know not, m'lady,' she replied in a subdued voice.

Sighing deeply Adhelina turned to stare across her room, clogged as always with myriad bunches of herbs hanging up to dry.

And that was when the solution to her problem occurred to her.

⁘ ⁘ ⁘

Time drew on towards the day of the wedding. The castle was a hive of activity throughout, as cooks prepared a feast of gargantuan proportions even by Vorstlending standards; the draymen and drovers of Merkstaed were kept continually busy with repeated orders for ale, wine and meat. Hundreds of knights and ladies would attend the ceremony, even the Great Hall would be stretched to fit them all in.

The heiress of Dulsinor could not look upon all these preparations without a twinge of guilt, and though she still loathed her affianced with all her soul she also could not help feeling for her father – he would be mortified by her disappearance.

In keeping with custom she would not see her betrothed before the day of their wedding – that was good, it meant if all went according to plan she would never see him again.

She and Hettie had quarrelled over the date of their escape before she had gone to town on her three clandestine errands. Hettie felt that if it must be escape then the sooner the better, so as not to allow the preparations to get too far advanced.

Adhelina saw things differently. She still hoped futilely that her father would somehow relent, or more likely that the Lanraks would try to insert some last-minute clause into the agreement that Wilhelm would find unacceptable, leading to his calling off the wedding.

That too proved a vain hope. The days stretched on pitilessly without any such occurrence. Once she tried to persuade her father to at least delay the wedding, but he only roared her out of his solar. Messengers from Stornelund confirmed what Adhelina dreaded most; the Lanraks were perfectly contented with all arrangements as they stood, and the ceremony would take place on the appointed day. The heiress of Dulsinor resigned herself to her escape plan, and together she and Hettie finalised it.

They did not lack for furs and warm clothes, although with spring drawing towards summer they probably would not need them, save at night. The money left over from Adhelina's brooch would be enough to purchase lodgings along the way to Meerborg in any case, and perhaps bribe a few innkeepers into silence.

Besides that she had plenty of finery that her father had gifted her over the years that she could sell when she got to the Free City. Her white gold ruby circlet, a collection of silver and gold bracelets, many of them studded with semi-precious stones, several other brooches and pairs of earrings and one or two pendants of similar value to the piece she had sent Hettie to pawn, a pouch full of gold and silver rings that she rarely wore, the most valuable of which was studded with emeralds. That had been another coming of age present from her father, back when their relationship had been a warm one.

Before she had disappointed him, she thought bitterly as she watched Hettie seal up the pouch.

Yes, it was a veritable king's ransom of jewellery – and up until now she had never thought she would have a use for any of it. She had never been one for ornamentation, preferring to dress simply in imitation of the Marionite monks she so admired. She would never see old Lorsch, the prior of Lothag Monastery again, she reflected sadly; the kindly old monk had taught her many things about herb lore since she was a child, patiently indulging the lord of the keep's only daughter.

She hoped she had proved an able student over the years – not least because everything now depended on her craft.

⁜ ⁜ ⁜

Her last meal beneath the walls of Graukolos was a nervous one, and she could barely swallow a bite. This would not draw any suspicion, she knew – what maiden wasn't nervous before her wedding? Sitting with her father at the high table she gazed about the Great Hall and tried to take in all its details one last time: the rich hangings depicting her ancestral coat of arms, and the scenes of hunting, warfare and tourneying that her father so enjoyed.

Gazing into the blazing firepit nearest to her she wondered if she would gain a glimpse of her future in the flames, as the mystics claimed one sometimes could. All that stared back at her was an orange flicker which dazzled her eyes as the fire scowled hotly. She did not think this a good presentiment.

She stinted on the wine and asked to be excused early. Her father, by now merrily in his cups, waved her away casually. Berthal looked over at her, with old eyes that seemed sad.

Did he have an inkling? No, he could not – he was far too ingenuous ever to suspect her of such a monstrous crime. As she smiled as fully as she could at him and rose from her seat, Adhelina felt a sense of everything falling away from her. It seemed then as if the world she had known was breaking into tiny pieces around her, whilst some unknown force propelled her up and up, into an infinity without colour or form.

My unknown future, she realised suddenly.

Gripping the back of her chair to steady herself she took a deep breath and a last look around the hall where she had eaten almost every day of her life since she was old enough to dine with the grown-ups.

From his seat near her Father Tobias looked up, his fat lips coated with grease, round black eyes peering at her.

'My lady, are you well?' he asked politely.

'I am... quite well,' she responded, hastily gathering her wits. 'This wine is a little too strong for my liking is all. I shall retire to rest now, I think.'

The sententious perfect nodded and began an impromptu sermon about the wisdom of young high-born ladies steering clear of drink and other vices. She left him in mid-speech: she would certainly not miss his hypocritical moralising.

As she left the hall she reflected that perhaps packing her small collection of books hadn't been such a good idea: clearly her imagination was inflamed by all that reading. Only now she was about to step into a real-life adventure of her own. The thought both thrilled and terrified her.

Making her way back to her chambers she nodded curtly at the two guards on the door before entering and bolting it behind her. Taking one last look at the bottom of the portal she nodded decisively: the gap between it and the floor was a good finger's breadth at least. That would serve nicely.

Walking over to the walnut table she checked the herbal concoction she had prepared in a wooden bowl and made sure the flint and tinder next to it was dry and ready. Then she looked over the supplies Hettie had packed one last time.

Her jewels were secreted in leathern pouches that she would wear next to her body, beneath the folds of her robes. Her herbs and poultices she had taken down from their hangings and packed into a bag. Another contained some food Hettie had managed to scrounge from the kitchens. It could not be too much without arousing suspicion: some bread, dried fruits and hard cheeses that would keep on the road. Not enough to get them to Meerborg, but they could purchase more on the way.

She had yet to make up her mind whether they should stay at any inns. It might be too risky – but then she could hardly pitch up at the nearest knight's manor and demand lodgings as the Eorl's runaway daughter.

Pursing her lips as she considered the matter again she made sure the maps were also tucked safely into another bag that contained a change of clothes for both of them and a few other odds and ends. Once they collected their steeds from Merkstaed they would transfer most of this to the saddle bags Hettie had also purchased.

Taking a last fretful look out of the window across the broad expanse of fields and the river below, Adhelina could see the odd cottage fire defying the darkened firmament with a bright stab of orange. Off to the south-east the myriad lights of Merkstaed clustered thickly, wordlessly calling her to the first stage of her new adventure. Adhelina suppressed a shiver as the night breeze swept in.

Turning from the window she was about to light another lantern but then thought better of it. She was tired, the last few weeks of plotting had left her enervated. Best to get some rest before Hettie returned from her final supper at the castle – she would be needing all her strength before too long.

Casting herself down on her bed Adhelina soon drifted off into sleep, despite not having her lady-in-waiting's reassuring warmth next to her.

She dreamed strange dreams.

She saw four riders making breakneck pace towards a dark forest. The forest looked thoroughly alien and unnatural, and she felt an urge to cry a warning to the riders from where she floated high above its writhing bourne. But a screaming pack of barbarians pursued them hotly, waving crude axes and swords that gleamed dully in the strange light. The hapless riders had no choice but to plunge headlong into the forest...

Then the scene changed. This time she saw a great host moving across the rolling plains of a land unknown to her. Knights in gleaming armour carried banners that rippled in the breeze; two unicorns danced about a white raven, and against the horizon towards which they moved a great castle burned...

Then she saw herself, in another forest. It was less malignant than the other one, but no less old; the boughs of gnarled oaks loomed over her menacingly, and beyond them a gibbous moon shone brightly against the black skies. Hettie was with her and they were holding hands. Next to them walked a cloaked and hooded figure with a sword at his belt. Suddenly they found themselves in a clearing. From beneath the damp eaves on all sides there loomed white-faced giants, reaching for them with two-fingered hands. Eyes and mouths gaped at them from otherwise blank, featureless faces...

❖ ❖ ❖

Adhelina woke with a start. She was covered in a cold sweat, and it took her several moments to remember where she was. Then she heard a sharp report on the door followed by a voice.

'M'lady! Are you in there? It's me, Hettie! Unbolt the door!'

Pulling herself upright Adhelina strode briskly over and unbolted it. Opening it she saw her lady-in-waiting and both guards peering at her with anxious faces.

'I fell asleep,' said Adhelina. 'Too much wine is all. Nothing to worry about.'

This mollified the guards, who resumed their posts to either side of the door. Adhelina shut and barred it again after Hettie had stepped inside.

'I had the most frightful dreams,' she said distractedly as Hettie went to check their bags herself one last time.

'I'm hardly surprised,' Hettie replied absently as she busied herself. 'My nerves are all a'jangle – I was sat next to Lady Mila, you know her, the wife of Sir Jordun of Ingolstein, and what d'you think she's on about the whole evening? "Must be excited now your mistress is getting married, Hettie – it'll soon be time to find you a husband as well! Who knows, with your mistress' influence you might even get married to a well-off vassal like I was!"'

Hettie rolled her eyes, trying to make light of the situation. 'Lord Almighty, that was the last thing I wanted to talk about on tonight of all nights!'

'Yes well, it's hardly surprising that's all anyone should want to talk to you about just before my big day,' replied Adhelina.

Her voice still sounded more distracted than sarcastic in her ears. Though the memory of her dreams was already fading it still left an unpleasant imprint at the back of her mind.

Hettie must have sensed this. Fixing her mistress with a quizzical stare she asked: 'Are you quite well, m'lady? Last-minute nerves getting to you I should imagine, no wonder you're having nightmares! There's some wine left over – shall I pour you some?'

Adhelina shook her head. 'Heavens no, that's the last thing I need right now. I'll be fine – let me make one last pot of herbal tea, to see us on our way.'

Hettie nodded dumbly, but continued to fix her mistress with the same quizzical look. Then she suddenly walked over to her and took her by the hands.

'Oh Adhelina!' she said earnestly. 'You know... if you don't want to go through with this, it isn't too late – to turn back I mean.'

Gazing down into her dearest friend's eyes Adhelina could see in a heartbeat that this was what she wanted her to say with all her heart.

With a twinge of profound sadness and pity she shook her head and said: 'It *is* too late, dearest Hettie – I made up my mind a long time ago. You know, in a funny way I feel that it was always going come to this... that somehow I've known my whole life it would. Dreams can point the way to our destinies, and some birds were never meant to be caged.'

Hettie's look changed to one of consternation. 'What are you speaking of now?' she frowned. 'Why, but you're babbling – are you sure you are well?'

Adhelina smiled and nodded. 'I am quite well, Hettie – indeed in some ways I think I may never have been quite so well, though I am all afraid too. But listen, if you don't want to come with me, you don't have to – you've already helped me, you can stay here if you like.'

Hettie's frown deepened. 'And do what? Explain to your father how I let you slip out from under my nose?'

'You could say I drugged you, why I could even - '

Hettie shook her head. 'I won't hear this, m'lady. If you're going, I'm going. Simple as that. We agreed on this a fortnight ago and I won't waste time and energy debating it.'

Adhelina hugged Hettie and kissed her tenderly on the forehead. 'Dearest Hettie, I believe the whole world wouldn't hold half its allure for me if I didn't have you by my side! How I love thee!'

'And I you, my mistress,' replied Hettie, blinking away tears. 'I wouldn't be parted from you for half the world, nor all of it either!'

Adhelina felt her nerves subside a little. It was good to know she wouldn't be facing her new unpredictable life alone. By the time they settled down to one last brew she almost felt calm.

When they were done guzzling tea, Adhelina bade Hettie fetch the thick scarves they would use as veils.

'Remember, it's very potent, so not even having the window open will avail you if you inhale a full draught,' she whispered. The crackling of the fire Hettie had made to ward off the night-time chill also served to muffle their voices – but even so whispering seemed more appropriate when discussing their escape.

'Very good, m'lady: but how will you get the guards to inhale it on the other side of the door?' Hettie whispered back.

'Easy – the gap beneath it's more than a finger wide,' explained Adhelina. 'I'll use my old bellows I need for getting inhalant poultices into vials to suck up as many of the fumes as I can and then just blow them under the door. They won't know what's hit them!'

'Will it... poison them?' asked Hettie nervously. 'The guards are only doing their duty, after all.'

Adhelina just laughed. 'No, don't be silly! Morphonus' Root is a powerful sleeping agent – it'll put you out for hours, but it won't harm you! And I've written a note explaining everything, so father will know not to punish them for falling asleep on the job.'

Hettie bit her lip. 'Assuming he doesn't just have their heads off straight away,' she said reproachfully. 'As you've always pointed out yourself, your father's a man of action not words.'

'But old Berthal can read, and so can Lotho,' replied Adhelina, unmoved. 'And there's Tobias, pompous fool that he is. If my father struggles with his letters, there are those who can help him. And I don't believe he would have loyal men summarily executed without investigating the matter first.'

Hettie sighed nervously. 'I can only pray you are right, m'lady,' she said. 'I wouldn't want their deaths on my conscience.'

'Don't worry, I'll leave the note in plain view. They won't be punished unduly.'

Privately she could only hope she was right about that – her father was going to be furious when he found her gone. But she had to do this: she felt with all her heart it was her life on the line too, in a manner of speaking at least.

After that it was a matter of hunkering down and waiting for the appointed hour. They dressed for the road and gathered their bags about them. The guards on the door would not be relieved until dawn –

that would give them plenty of time to put some distance between themselves and the castle, assuming their rendezvous with the ostler at the Wytching Hour went as planned.

Thinking on this Adhelina suddenly felt nervous again – Hettie had portrayed him as a slippery character, whose loyalty was uncertain at best. She hoped he would be loyal to the prospect of gaining further coin, and pushed the doubt from her mind.

The fire was burning low in the grate when the time came to go. It was just over an hour before midnight – all the castle occupants would be sound asleep by now. Wrapping their veils of thick cloth tightly about their faces the damsels prepared to make good their escape.

Taking up the wooden bowl Adhelina placed it gingerly on the floor by the door. Then she brought the bellows and her flint and tinder over. Hettie stood behind, sweating uncomfortably in her thick clothing, their bags at the ready beside her.

Taking up the flint and tinder Adhelina struck it and soon had a flame burning. She set light to the herbs prepared in the bowl before her. They began to burn immediately, emitting a thick, pungent smoke. Taking up the bellows quickly Adhelina teased as much of the fumes as she could into them before gingerly putting the nozzle to the gap beneath the door and squeezing.

She knew she had to move swiftly: as like as not the guards would be less than alert after standing still for several hours, but they would soon notice the strange smoke wafting around their knees.

Fortunately the root was powerful, and she had put in enough to knock out a dozen horses. Holding her breath she sucked in more of the cloying smoke, before pumping it under the door again. Twice more she repeated the exercise, still holding her breath.

Still she did not hear the guards stir.

Some of the stray wisps that she hadn't caught were starting to drift across her chamber; frantically Adhelina fought to keep her breath as she sucked up another gout of smoke and pumped it underneath the door.

Glancing over she saw Hettie, whose face was turning purple beneath her veil with the effort of holding her breath. If they had to take another breath their scarves might just protect them, but there was a chance they'd fall victim to the root too...

Then, like a blessing, the sound she had longed for came from the other side of the door.

'Hey, can you smell anything?' she heard one of the soldiers ask, followed directly by the sound of a mailed warrior slumping to the floor and the clatter of a spear being dropped. Two heartbeats later, the sound was repeated.

Motioning quickly to Hettie, Adhelina rose and unbarred the door. Flinging it open she saw both guards lying on the floor, one on top of the other, as tendrils of thick smoke curled towards the ceiling and danced hypnotic patterns in the smouldering torchlight.

Grabbing their bags both women nipped down the stairs as quickly and quietly as they could, gratefully inhaling deep lungfuls of untainted air.

Tiptoeing past servants' quarters and guest chambers the two made their way to the bottom of the tower and into the south wing of the inner ward.

The ground floor of the tower abutted directly onto the south wing's entrance chamber, and passing through the gothic archway connecting the two they emerged at its western end. Opposite them a grand crumbling staircase of cracked and pitted stone led up to the extended series of chambers reserved for her father and his servants. In the northern wall a pair of barred double doors led out into the ward's flagstoned courtyard. The doors were flanked to either side by gothic-arched windows.

Keeping well away from these, they approached the side of the staircase closest to the eastern wall. Set against this were the four statues of the erstwhile rulers of Dulsinor, their graven forms staring sightlessly out at the windows looking into the courtyard.

The statue of Ulmo was second from the left. He was portrayed as a stocky, muscle-bound warrior clad in crude mail and helmet. His braided beard came down to his midriff and his broad hands rested on the hilt of his double-headed axe.

'Keep an eye out, in case anyone comes from the courtyard!' hissed Adhelina. 'I need to find the secret catch.'

Reaching into her bag she pulled out her flint and tinder and a taper. She knelt to light it, before holding up the flaming brand to get a better look at Ulmo. She knew this was the riskiest part of their escape: a sleepless servant chancing to gaze out of a window from across the courtyard might just notice a light burning in the entrance hall where there should not have been. But it was a risk she had to take.

⁜ ⁜ ⁜

Hettie glanced about her nervously as time slipped by with a painful slowness.

'I've got it!' whispered Adhelina triumphantly, reaching around to the side of the statue where it met the ordure-stained wall behind and grasping the likeness of a dagger hilt at Ulmo's belt. There was a distinct clicking sound as the disguised lever responded.

'Here, help me pull it, old Ulmo's heavy!' said Adhelina.

With some effort they managed to open the secret door, of which Ulmo's statue was but the frontispiece. Hettie had half expected it to make a dreadfully loud screeching noise – after all, how often had the secret door been used in the six hundred years since it was built?

But amazingly, it opened on hinges that moved as soundlessly as if they had been oiled just yesterday.

'I can't believe it still works after all this time!' exclaimed Hettie.

Her mistress turned to favour her with a girlish grin. 'I told you old Goriath knew a thing or two!' she said.

Beyond the door a narrow flight of spiral stairs disappeared down into stygian blackness.

Hettie swallowed hard. 'Do we really have to do this, m'lady?' If she hadn't been whispering her voice would have been small regardless.

'Of course we do – stop asking silly questions. Don't worry, I don't mind going first.'

That did little to settle Hettie's nerves as they stepped through the doorway. On the other side of the door was a great ring of rusted iron – wide enough for two to grasp it at once. They had to shoulder their packs and squeeze together side by side at the top of the stairwell to pull the door shut behind them. Fortunately Goriath had also thoughtfully installed sconces for their tapers just inside the door.

The door closed with another smooth click. Hettie wrinkled her nose in disgust as she caught the foetid air.

'I hope Goriath remembered to design air holes – I don't fancy choking to death underground!' she said.

'Of course he did,' replied Adhelina excitably. 'Look, you can see them at regular intervals going down the shaft! You can even find them where they exit on the hill up above if you care to look for them – only a genius like Goriath could have worked out how to design such things!'

'A genius – or a black magician,' muttered Hettie disconsolately. 'Let's be getting on – the sooner we're back outside again the better I'll like it!'

Taking the tapers the two damsels began their descent. The spiral stairs descended for what seemed like an age to Hettie. Sure enough, Goriath had built small apertures at regular intervals in the shaft down which the crooked stairs now took them, but all the same she began to feel dreadfully claustrophobic. The deeper they went the warmer and danker the air became; were it not for her veil Hettie felt she would have been gagging by the time they reached the bottom, where a tunnel stretched ahead of them.

This ran level at first before inclining upwards at a steady gradient. The tunnel walls were earthen but supported by stout beams that appeared not to have been worn away by time. Once or twice she thought she caught a glimpse of some peculiar markings on them; weird alien characters that made her feel uncomfortable. Her muffled breathing sounded loud and ragged in her ears, and Hettie had to summon all her fortitude not to succumb to panic.

If her mistress felt anything similar she gave no indication of it. When they got to within thirty paces of the exit they began to feel a cool breeze; this steadily strengthened as the tunnel continued to rise. It terminated at a great round door fashioned of bronze. There was no discernible handle.

Adhelina stared at the door, her face buckled up with consternation.

'What is it?' hissed Hettie behind her.

'I completely forgot – the exit door can only be opened by a secret catch as well!'

'Well, surely you knew that! Didn't Berthal tell you?'

Adhelina shook her head dolefully. 'When we first got on to the subject he said the secret exit had two doors operated by hidden mechanisms – but he only told me where the first one was! I was so enthralled by that, I completely forgot to ask him about the second!'

'Oh, what do we do now?!' Hettie wailed, raising her voice for the first time since they had left their chamber.

'We don't panic is what,' answered Adhelina irritably.

But Adhelina wasn't really annoyed with Hettie. In truth it was herself she was angry with – how could she have been so stupid? In her desire to escape she had seen only what she wanted to, and forgotten any detail that might cause her to hesitate.

Forcing herself to remain calm she bent to examine the round bronze door. It was smooth and polished: like the oak beams that supported the tunnel it had withstood time far better than it should have done. All around its circumference could be seen more eldritch markings: probably the sorcerer's script, part of the ancient language of magick first taught to men thousands of years ago by the Unseen.

That made her extremely reluctant to touch them, but screwing up her courage she did so, gingerly poking and prodding for any signs of another secret catch or lever.

All to no avail. After a while she turned to face Hettie, her heart sinking.

'I can't find anything!' she said. She almost felt like crying. They had come so far, everything had worked out so well...

'But... if we can't get out, that means we'll have to turn back,' said Hettie in a small voice. 'The guards – how will we explain...'

Her voice trailed off as they stared at one another helplessly. Their torches were starting to burn low.

'Do we have any more tapers?' Adhelina hissed. Hettie nodded, opening her bag and rummaging around until she found a fresh pair. They lit these off the old ones as they considered the problem.

'Try to think,' Hettie urged her. 'What did Berthal say to you exactly?'

'I don't recall,' replied Adhelina. 'It was several years ago. He said something along the lines of "there are two doors at either end of the secret tunnel, both of which can only be opened by a secret catch". Then he told me about the catch on the first door, but he never mentioned anything about the second one. Oh, how could I be such a fool as to forget something like that!'

Hettie looked deep in thought now. Suddenly she looked up, a fresh light in her eyes. A light that said something had dawned on her.

'But wait...' she said hesitantly. 'That just doesn't make sense.'

'What doesn't make sense?' This time Adhelina tried to mask her irritation. She had expected something better than that.

But Hettie obviously had something on her mind. 'Did Berthal say the second door could be seen from outside?' she asked.

'Well of course not – a fine secret escape tunnel it would be if everyone could see it!' barked Adhelina, exasperated. 'No, on the other side this will be covered with sward, it'll be a seamless part of the rest of the hill. To all appearances at any rate.'

'Well... then it definitely doesn't make sense.'

'What doesn't make sense? Hettie, *you're* not making sense – please explain yourself!'

'Well, picture it if you will, m'lady – you're a lord whose castle is under siege and you've decided to flee as a last resort. Of course no one can know how to open the first door because you don't want people pursuing you, assuming they find out where the secret door is in the first place. But why put an inside lock on the second door?'

Adhelina shrugged. 'An extra precaution I suppose – in case pursuers find their way through the first door and chase you down the tunnel.'

Hettie shook her head. 'Begging your pardon m'lady, I may not have your book learning but that just doesn't ring true – what if the catch broke? If that happened on the first door you'd still have the freedom of the castle at least, but if it happened down here you'd be stuck! And you've searched the thing high and low – there's clearly no hidden catch!'

'But Berthal said – oh, Goriath was canny beyond mortal ken, he must have hidden it somewhere... perhaps in the tunnel walls.' Adhelina began casting around frantically, her sputtering taper painting frightful shadows on the unrevealing earthen walls.

'Goriath for all his powers was a man when all's said and done – and so is Berthal,' said Hettie, her voice unusually firm.

Adhelina stared at her. 'So what are you suggesting? That there's no lock on this door at all? We simply push it open just like that?'

'Well, it might be worth pointing out that we haven't even *tried* to push it open yet...'

Adhelina turned back to face the door. It looked heavy-set enough, sunk into the damp earth like the head of a giant tent peg.

Yet still, what harm was there in trying?

'All right,' said Adhelina, handing her taper to Hettie. 'Step back and give me a little more room. I'm going to try.'

Adhelina was strong for her sex, but she was expecting the door to be a stout obstacle. She gawped as it gave way after a few moments of pressure, opening on concealed hinges that behaved as though freshly oiled. The night air rushed in to greet them, and both women blinked as stars greeted them across the darkened firmament.

'I don't believe it,' breathed Adhelina. 'You were right and Berthal got it wrong! I don't know what to say!'

'Berthal doesn't know everything,' replied Hettie archly as they stepped out. 'He forgets a lot of things, according to the castle knights I've spoken to... He's a good and faithful servant to your father, but he's seen more than seventy winters! You just don't remember things so well at that age.'

'No, I don't suppose you do!' replied Adhelina, beaming. 'But come, let's be off! First let's close this door...'

The door had brought them out at the southern tip of the hill on which the castle stood, just as Adhelina's map had said it would. When it was shut it was as though it had never been there.

'Well, let's hope the last part of our escape plan is as successful,' said Adhelina, holding her taper aloft. 'Come on, it's this way to Merkstaed!'

⁜ ⁜ ⁜

The streets of the town were dark when they reached it, all its occupants having said their prayers and gone to bed. A drunk lurched out at them from an alley as they were making their way across the deserted town square, but he was too far in his cups to do more than harass them with incoherent remarks.

All the same, Adhelina was anxious to not to linger in Merkstaed. Footpads had been known to prowl its streets at night, although the town watch would most likely keep that from happening. But of course, in their present circumstances, running into a bunch of guardsmen could prove just as catastrophic.

They reached the *Flying Fish* without further incident. The stabling yard was dark but Hettie had memorised where the ostler's sleeping quarters were. In any case she didn't have to venture in to wake him, for he stepped out to greet them looking haggard and tired.

'Well there you are,' he muttered irritably. 'I was wondering whether you were going to turn up! Missing a well earned night's kip for you!'

'Your services are being paid for in full,' Hettie reminded him, putting on her haughty voice again. Adhelina could not help smiling behind her veil. Though her lady-in-waiting was a noblewoman, she was on the very lowest rung of her class and seldom put on airs and graces.

'Aye, speaking of which...' The ostler extended a grubby hand for the rest of his pay. His eyes gleamed in the moonlight. Adhelina disliked him immediately.

'Let us have our horses first – then I will pay you the remainder,' replied Hettie.

'Oh aye,' he smirked, 'of course, my lady – or should I say my *ladies*...'

Adhelina felt a surge of anxiety as the ostler fixed her with a gimlet stare, before turning abruptly to fetch their horses from the stable.

No, surely he could not have guessed...

Adhelina had little time to voice her fears to Hettie, for the ostler soon returned with their horses. They appeared to have been kept well. Leading them out into the yard he stepped up to Hettie and extended his palm again.

'Another five silver marks, that was the price we agreed,' he said.

'Here,' said Hettie, pressing the coins into his hand. He glanced at them and smiled a gap-toothed smile before putting the jingling coins casually in his pocket.

Adhelina was about to step over to a horse and mount when she heard an altogether different sort of jingling behind her. Whirling around she saw two soldiers of the watch, dressed in rude mail. Their swords were drawn, their unhealthy-looking faces cruel and greedy beneath their pot helms.

'Ah, that'll be my friends from the watch,' said the ostler breezily, before addressing the new arrivals: 'I was wondering when you would turn up as well! Good job you're all as bad at timekeeping as each other, or that might have scuppered my plans.'

'You said they was high-born ladies, Reefe,' said one of the watchmen, addressing the ostler as they stepped into the yard. 'And high-born ladies always keep folks waiting. Well now, my fine dames, Reefe here tells me you've been wanting to leave town in the dead of night. Strange that you should wait a fortnight to do that – sounds to me like you've had your hands tied.'

'My companion has had to wait for me,' Adhelina said quickly, using the cover story she and Hettie had rehearsed in case the ostler should ask any awkward questions. 'I am not minded to disclose the reasons for my delay to common guardsmen. Now if you'll stand aside - '

The watchman who had spoken favoured her with a gap-toothed grin of his own. In the mingled light of the flaring tapers and wan moonlight they looked a foul pair of rogues. Every watch had its rotten apples.

'I don't think so,' he sneered. 'Any woman who goes about at night veiled and hooded like a common footpad don't deserve to be treated as no noblewoman, if y'ask me. Besides that, Reefe here tells me you're a merchant's lass - that might make you rich, but yer still a commoner.' He inched forwards.

Hettie rounded on the ostler. 'What is the meaning of this, you churl?' she demanded, genuinely angry. 'We paid for your silence!'

The ostler appeared unruffled. 'Indeed you did, my lady,' he replied in his mocking voice. 'And I reckon them as can afford to pay ten silver marks for a man's silence and service have a lot more than that stashed away on their persons!'

'I'll see you hang for this, you rogue!' Hettie spat.

'Begging your pardon,' interjected the watchman, as he and his silent companion advanced towards them. 'But it seems to me as if it's *you* who's on the wrong side o' the law - we'll find out what crime you're running from, *after* we take the rest o' your coin.'

Without warning Adhelina flung her taper at the watchman's face. He lurched out of the way, but it gave her the moment she needed to dash towards the horses. Following suit, Hettie lunged at the ostler with her own torch. He gave a yelp of pain as she caught him a singeing blow across the eyebrow, forcing him to let go of the horses' reins.

That was all the advantage she gained. Bounding over, the silent watchman seized her by her cloak and flung her roughly to the ground. The other closed in on Adhelina as she tried desperately to mount one of the horses, and grasping her by the arm he pressed his sword to her throat.

'I wouldn't be trying any of that, your ladyship,' he leered at her.

'Ho there, men of the watch, what is this now - surely not arresting respectable ladies in the middle of the night?'

The voice was strange, high-pitched yet rough, and thickly accented.

The five protagonists turned to look at the newcomer. Dressed in a brown cloak and hood and brigandine and vambraces of studded leather, he cut a short, nimble figure as he strolled lightly from the inn towards them. A sword was girt at his side and a poignard sheathed at his boot. His face could not be seen beneath his hood.

'Get back inside yonder inn,' growled the watchman, still holding Adhelina firmly. 'This is watch business, and none of yours, mercenary!'

'As to that,' replied the stranger, taking another step towards them. 'I still don't see what business the watch has arresting two defenceless women at this time of night.'

'Good folk have no business being abroad at the Wytching Hour, veiled and cloaked, that's why!' snarled the watchman, turning the blade of his sword towards the cowled freesword. 'Now get you gone, before I arrest you too.'

'Perhaps you should,' replied the foreigner breezily, taking another step. 'After all here I am, also abroad at the hour of darkness, my face concealed.' He spread his arms invitingly.

'Right, if that's how you want to play it,' snarled the watchman. 'Reefe! Stop crying over a woman's blow and grab hold of her! Derk, you can have the honour of gutting this foreign pig if he resists arrest!'

The watchman named Derk grinned evilly at this and advanced towards the hooded stranger. Reefe grabbed hold of Hettie and pulled her up from the ground, pinning her arms behind her.

In an instant the stranger's sword was out of its sheath, its gently curving blade displaying a razor edge that was anything but gentle.

Not a sword, Adhelina thought momentarily, *a falchion – a rare weapon in these parts.*

Without taking his eyes off the slowly advancing watchman the outlander crouched in readiness for him but addressed Adhelina: 'You there, with the other watchman – why are you being arrested?'

'No reason other than to rob us,' Adhelina shot back, hope of rescue rising in her as her quick mind assessed the situation. 'This lickspittle ostler has obviously taken them into his confidence. We need to get out of the country – if you help us I can promise you a rich reward, far greater than any mere coin we carry.'

The foreign freesword parried the watchman's first crude stroke, nimbly stepping to one side and launching a lightning riposte. The startled guardsman only saved himself by lurching clumsily backwards. That bought them more time to talk.

'Very well, what guarantees can you give me of this reward?' said the mercenary, without taking his hooded eyes off his assailant.

'None,' replied Adhelina firmly, 'but I can pay you a handsome sum now if you'll deal with these guards without killing them or waking up half the town.'

'Damn your eyes, shut up!' snarled the guard holding Adhelina, pressing his blade against her neck again.

But the brief exchange seemed to have made up the foreign fighter's mind. Stepping in lightly he goaded Derk into attacking again, a clumsy lunge that he evaded easily before stepping within the hapless watchman's guard. Grasping his sword arm firmly at the elbow, the hooded foreigner brought the pommel of his falchion round into the side of his head just below the helm with a resounding *crack*. Adhelina could not help wincing as he fell to the ground like a sack of turnips.

Cursing, the other watchman let her go and dashed towards the mercenary. Crouching low he waited for him to close the distance between them... and in a whirlwind of motion he had spun around behind the watchman with breathtaking speed, striking him senseless with another pommel-blow to the back of the head.

With scarcely a pause for breath he turned and advanced on the ostler, who was holding Hettie before him.

'I'll yell for the rest of the watch,' he said hesitantly, clutching her tightly.

'All right,' said the freesword. 'No need for that. After all we can always rob the ladies and share the spoil ourselves. Not convinced? Here, look, I'll put my sword down...'

Kneeling slowly he placed the falchion on the ground. Only one of the two tapers remained alight; its expiring flames guttered at the feet of the ostler. Adhelina moved slowly into the fading circle of light.

'Know when you are beaten,' she said in a quiet voice. 'Release my companion and let us leave peacefully. You still have your reward money.'

The ostler turned towards her, his face full of fear. As he did so he instinctively brought Hettie around with him, exposing his flank to the mysterious mercenary.

The latter did not need a second invitation. Picking up a nearby rock he flung it with unerring accuracy at the ostler's head. Letting go of Hettie he took two tottering steps sideways before slumping to the ground senseless.

'Three foes vanquished quickly and quietly without bringing charge of murder on us,' said the foreigner coolly, picking up his falchion and sheathing it. 'I think I will claim my payment now.'

He approached Adhelina, extending a gloved hand.

'I... I don't handle money,' she said uncertainly.

'Here,' said Hettie, stepping forward. 'Here's two gold regums for your trouble. We don't have enough to give you any more.'

'But we can give you a rich reward if you get us to Meerborg unscathed,' added Adhelina quickly.

The mercenary seemed to eye them both suspiciously in the dying light of the taper, although the depth of his hood made it hard to tell.

'How do I know you are telling the truth?' he demanded gruffly. 'I could just rob you here at sword-point.'

'You could,' replied Adhelina boldly. 'But then you would lose a greater reward. See us to Meerborg safely – I have goods and chattels there, and can make it well worth your while. Rob us now and you stand to gain little else – my servant is the only one of us who carries any coin. If you think the rest of her purse's contents are worth passing up such an opportunity for, go ahead and rob us.'

Both damsels held their breath for the second time that night as the strange foreigner weighed their words.

Then he said: 'Very well – I accept your offer. But I want five regums now. The rest of the reward we can talk over later.'

Hettie glanced at her mistress, who nodded. The taper had almost gone out, leaving them under the light of moon and stars. Hettie pressed the coins into the stranger's hand.

'We'd better get moving,' he said in his strange high voice. 'I made as little noise as I could, and yon inn is full of drunken freeswords and merchants, but all the same it is best not to take chances, yes? Here, help me get these three oafs into the stable – they can sleep where my horse has been staying!'

They did this hurriedly. As the outlander led his own horse – a swift courser of foreign breed – out into the yard, Hettie found time to whisper to her mistress.

'M'lady, is this wise? We don't know this foreigner from the First Son! What's to stop him double-crossing us on the road and robbing us?'

As they stepped back into the yard Adhelina shot back a worried glance at Hettie. 'I know – but what choice do we really have now?'

They said no more to each other as their uncertain new guardian paused to light a torch before taking to the saddle. The two damsels followed suit, the three of them passing out of the yard and making their way at a brisk trot towards the outskirts of town. Then, spurring their horses into a swift gallop, they plunged into the night-shrouded countryside.

⚔ CHAPTER IX ⚔

Battle Is Joined

From the inner wall battlements Bernal, castellan of Linden Castle, stared at the bleak spectacle bequeathed him by the fortunes of war.

All about him was a tumult of cries, the ring of steel on steel and the crash of exploding rock. At the southern end of the outer wall, the gates heaved and trembled as the attackers renewed their onslaught, undeterred by the heavy rocks being dropped through the machicolations overlooking it. From the east, belfries mounted on warships in the river pulverised the outer battlements with trebuchet and catapult, as the escalades below attempted once again to mount them. Arrows and quarrels zinged back and forth through the soot-smeared air as archers and crossbowmen searched for targets and found them.

There was burning on both sides. Firebombs catapulted from the trebuchets mounted on the castle's outer turrets had set several of the big cogs aflame; in retaliation they had shot fire of their own high over the ramparts, setting the outer ward stables alight. That had sparked a general panic before the roaring flames were quenched into smoky silence by the best efforts of the garrison; most of the horses were now under control, although the enemy had taken advantage of the distraction to redouble their efforts to breach Linden's first line of defences.

Bernal knew it was only a matter of time, and short time at that, before they succeeded. Corpses of slain soldiers clogged the mud on his side of the wall, but there were many more piled up on the unforgiving slopes of the rocky hill without: the beleaguered defenders had extracted a grisly toll for entrance to the outer ward.

Turning to face him, Prince Wolfram hefted his sword and grinned. His eyes burned with a zealous love of battle. 'The time has come!' he cried above the din. 'The gates will soon be breached and we cannot expect the riverside wall to hold much longer. Marshall all the troops – we're riding out to meet the rebels!'

Bernal, a stout man in early middle age, dressed in full battle armour like his prince, frowned. 'Your Royal Highness, the first wall and outer ward are all but lost! We should conserve our strength and do our best to defend the second – it is our last line of defence!'

'Nay,' snarled Wolfram, his handsome features contorting with frightful passion. 'I shall not have it said I cowered behind both of Linden's walls and waited for the enemy to defeat us! Marshall all the men I say – we shall anticipate them in the outer ward below!'

'But sire, your father must be nigh with his army,' protested Bernal. 'We cannot risk the castle being taken before he arrives!'

'It shall not be taken!' yelled Wolfram, already brushing past the castellan towards the stairs leading back down towards the inner ward. 'By Reus, we'll send these rebel traitors scurrying back over yonder walls they've worked so hard to breach!'

Struggling to keep up and protesting all the way, Bernal followed his youthful prince as he strode through the courtyard barking orders at every knight and man-at-arms he laid eyes on.

Compared to the besieging army they were a meagre sight: no more than four hundred fighting men altogether, besides the harried crossbowmen on the walls whose number had dwindled daily since the siege began.

But Bernal knew they would follow Wolfram in his madcap charge anyway. His prince had that rare gift: the power to inspire men with the same courage that burned in him night and day. His father had been the same – but where Freidheim was also a skilled tactician his eldest son was reckless and bold. As far as Wolfram was concerned, the Almighty was on his side: raw courage and skill at arms would take care of the rest.

Mounting his Farovian destrier, the heir to the throne he was fighting to preserve mustered knights and soldiers around him and ordered the gate leading to the outer ward opened.

Shaking his head Bernal strode over to remonstrate one last time. Though he respected his liege's prowess, his overconfidence was going to get them all needlessly killed. Better to hunker down and protract the siege – surely the King's army would get here soon. If they could just hold out a little longer...

✥ ✥ ✥

When the invaders finally succeeded in breaking down the outer ward gates and came roaring into the courtyard, they found two hundred mounted knights waiting for them.

At first it seemed as though Wolfram's foolhardy tactics would pay off: the rebels had clearly expected the garrison to remain cowering behind the inner walls. The prince and his knights cut a swathe through the unsuspecting footsoldiers, slaying on the left hand and the right until the earth was thick with an iron blanket of armoured corpses.

But by now the attackers on the walls had finally succeeded in gaining the purchase they had fought so hard to obtain, and in their wake came more archers. As their comrades lost no time in slaying the remainder of loyalist crossbowmen on the battlements, the rebel bowmen began picking off knights, using bodkin heads designed to pierce armour.

As more enemy soldiers began to pour in through the breached gates and down from the walls the melee thickened, and with the mounted knights presenting an easy target above the heads of the common footsoldiers they began lose to ground, pushed ever back toward the inner gates...

From his vantage point on the inner wall Bernal saw all of this. He had eventually prevailed upon Wolfram to spare him the men-at-arms, so that they might at least hold the inner ward for a while if the doughty prince should fail.

But as he saw men dismounted, their horses slain beneath them by their desperate attackers, his hopes that it would not come to that began to fade. Even now he could see the first company of rebel knights in the distance, preparing to ride up the road towards the broken gates and enter the fray; the archers positioned on the palisades were holding their fire, trusting to their better-placed comrades on the walls to do their murderous work without inflicting casualties on their own side. On the river the siege-mounted catapults were also holding off so as not to spoil this effort.

We are lost, he thought resignedly. Prince Wolfram would pay for his vain courage with his life or liberty, and most likely two hundred good knights would go down with him, slain or maimed or held prisoner for ransom. With great reluctance the old castellan prepared to give the order to lower the twin portcullises guarding the inner ward.

And then things went from bad to worse. A great cry went up from the courtyard down below.

'Prince Wolfram is injured! His Royal Highness has been shot!'

With frantic eyes the castellan scoured the ugly human tapestry of iron and blood below him for signs of his liege, his heart quickening. And then he saw him: just below his battle standard the prince lurched in the saddle like a rag doll abandoned by its puppeteer. Protruding from the eye slit of his helm was a feathered shaft.

Dashing along the parapet the castellan yelled at a battle herald: 'Sound the retreat!'

The herald did as he was told and Bernal prayed the men below would have presence of mind enough to remember protocol in the thick of battle:

with the prince dead or incapacitated the castellan resumed command of the castle and its garrison.

As the herald repeated the summons to withdraw twice and thrice the castellan lumbered down the thick stone steps to the courtyard.

'Erith!' he barked at the nearest serjeant. 'Keep the gates open to receive our sortie – get the rest of the crossbowmen to put up covering fire and have the foot ready to repulse any rebels that try to slip in!'

Turning to another serjeant he added: 'Tokar, be ready to close both gates at my signal! Have men ready at the murder-holes! Saving the prince is a priority – you're only to close the gates on my orders! The rest of you – close ranks in the courtyard and be prepared to fight any rebels that break through!'

Drawing his sword the castellan felt some of his old fighting spirit return to him.

'By Reus, if this is to be our last stand we'll make it a good one!'

The courtyard was a flurry of activity as men scrambled to obey his orders. The entrance to the inner ward was a long wide passage with the portcullises at either end. The innermost one was reinforced with a stout door of iron-shod oak. The castellan ordered another company of men to stand ready to shut it at his command.

Addressing another serjeant on the battlements above him he cried: 'Lorbo! Keep me informed, dammit! Tell me what is passing without!'

Lorbo, a flustered young man who had been promoted early, stammered back a response: 'Prince Wolfram's knights are trying to get him free, sire – they're fighting fiercely... the enemy soldiers are trying to get to them...'

Bernal tried to make out what was being described to him, but all he could see through the gatehouse's far exit was a mass of men fighting. A sortie of rebel soldiers, suddenly breaking free of the general melee and espying the open gates, made a dash towards them.

Bernal gave the order to fire. Crossbow bolts zinged and the men fell dead and dying. Now knights belonging to the garrison began to pour in, obscuring his view.

'Lorbo, what's happening up there?' barked the castellan. 'Is the prince secure?'

The only answer he got from the hapless serjeant was a strangled cry as a shaft pierced his neck. The old castellan swore loudly as his corpse fell to the courtyard, along with those of the herald and several other men still deployed on the ramparts.

'Dammit, the enemy archers on the outer walls must have switched their fire to target ours! Crossbowmen – get up on the battlements and give them a return volley, on the double!'

It was a forlorn hope. By now the outer battlements would be thick with enemy archers, more than a match for the rump of crossbowmen who now hurried to obey his orders.

'Knights regroup!' he yelled at the mounted warriors fleeing back into the courtyard. 'Get ready to receive the enemy! Soldiers on the gates stand by to close on my orders!'

Bernal was motioning to his squire to bring his warhorse over as he barked orders; handing the lad his sword he mounted up in one swift but painful motion. He was getting too old for this. Taking the blade again he nudged his charger over to join the knights. More continued to pour through, riding down enemy soldiers as they did, though several of them were picked off by archers before they could reach safety.

As the tide of retreating loyalists began to thicken Bernal felt his heart lighten somewhat. *Thank Reus,* he thought, *they're obeying the herald's summons.* Perhaps they could salvage the situation after all. But where was the prince?

And then he saw. Riding through the gates they came, hell for leather, half a dozen knights including the standard bearer. Two of them supported their liege in the saddle whilst a bleeding squire led his horse by the reins.

'Get the prince to a room and have Sandon see to him immediately!' yelled Bernal without taking his eyes off the gates.

In truth he doubted the castle chirurgeon could do much more than ease his prince's passing now, but with the castle about to fall he had more pressing matters to concern him.

A few dozen other loyalist knights and squires came hurtling in... and then there was a rush of enemy soldiers, making a mad dash in their wake.

'Close the gates!' he screamed, his voice hoarse with shouting above the mad din of battle. 'Close the gates I say!'

With a twin screech the portcullises came crashing down. Several enemy soldiers were pinned by the innermost one; their dying screams were matched by those of their comrades behind as they fell victim to the burning pitch dropped through the murder holes. These faded as the soldiers within the courtyard pushed the oak door to with a mighty heave, ramming a thick bar in place to hold it.

'Uthor!' yelled Bernal, addressing the serjeant in charge of the remaining crossbowmen on the walls. 'How are you speeding up there?'

From where he was kneeling behind the battlements Uthor shouted back: 'Their archers outnumber us at least five to one, but they've no cover on the inner part of the walls. We're giving as good as we get - '

An arrow glanced off his helm as he said this, causing him to crouch lower as he addressed his commander in chief. 'But they're bringing up men with kite shields to protect them! They don't have much room to

manoeuvre up there but they're making the best of it they can – we'll do
our best to discourage them.'

'Good, see that you do,' yelled the castellan. 'We've a few hours
before sunset. When night comes I want a watch posted on all sides
of the walls – let's get a few of our own kites up there too! Where's
Sir Orfius, did he survive the sortie?'

'I'm here, sire.' His second-in-command came riding up. His surcoat
was torn and stained with blood, but he appeared to have escaped injury.

'Orfius, take a headcount – I want to know exactly how many we
are left. Judging by what I see, this reckless business has cost us dear.'

'It has cost the enemy dear too, sire, rest assured,' replied Orfius.

Bernal sighed inwardly. Few good knights would speak ill
of Wolfram's impetuous gallantry, though it had nearly ended in
disaster. But for all his misgivings, Bernal was not about to dissent –
not when the heir to the throne lay dying, as was probably the case.

'Good – at least it wasn't all for naught then,' he said brusquely.
'I'll see the Prince now.'

※ ※ ※

They had taken him to a room in the north-west tower, furthest away
from the fighting. It was crowded with Wolfram's anxious knights.
The Prince was still covered in full armour – the arrow that had
pierced the eye slit of his helm was precariously lodged, making the
chirurgeon Sandon's job all the more difficult. Gently nudging the
knights aside the castellan gazed on the fallen royal with sad eyes.

'Is the wound mortal?' he asked the chirurgeon in a hushed voice.

Sandon, a slight man dressed in the blood-red robes of his
calling, passed a hand through his thinning black hair and replied
nervously: 'He yet lives, my lord, though without removing the helm
it is difficult to assess the extent of the damage.'

'Well remove it,' said Bernal simply.

Sandon licked his lips nervously. 'I cannot do that without
removing the arrow – but if I do so without being able to examine
the wound first, it might worsen it.'

'Well, what choice do we have, man?' answered Bernal curtly. Bending
to inspect the shaft more closely he added: 'This looks like a bodkin arrow
to me – a broadhead most like would not have been able to pierce his eye
slit. You should be able to remove it without worsening the injury.'

'I have your leave to act then, my lord?'

'Yes, yes, dammit – you have my leave and authority. Get the damned
arrow out of him and take his helm off. Then... just do what you can.'

The surgeon nodded slowly. In the flickering lantern light of the shuttered room the castellan could see how afraid the commoner was.

Placing a hand on his thin shoulder he said firmly but gently: 'Sandon, you have ever served Linden well – if any man can save our prince now it is you. Do your utmost to save our future king – I swear an oath before all these good knights I shall not hold you responsible if he dies. Just do what you can.'

Exhaling tremulously the chirurgeon nodded and said: 'I shall need my tools, my assistant and a bowl of warm water.'

'They shall be yours directly,' answered the castellan, before turning to address the Prince's knights. 'I think it were better if Sandon had more space to go about his work – the rest of you get down to the courtyard and join the headcount.'

'But, sire, we are the Prince's own knights – we should be here with him!' one of them protested. Wolfram's men were mostly hot-headed youngbloods just like himself.

'I'll send for Father Ubo, our resident perfect,' replied Bernal. 'He can pray for our prince, that should be sufficient. Now, while you are in my castle you will do as I say – get back down to the courtyard, for all we know there may be more fighting to do before dark.'

Given the protracted nature of siege warfare Bernal knew this was unlikely, but he made his point. With grim and surly faces the battle-weary knights shuffled out of the chamber and left Sandon to do his work.

The process was long and painful, but Bernal watched it all as Ubo prayed silently next to him throughout. When the surgeon extracted the arrow the prince let out a great groan. Blood flowed freely from the unseen injury, staining his tabard and the bed sheets beneath it. Gingerly removing his helmet with the help of his assistant, an apprentice of thirteen summers, Sandon made a sorrowful exclamation.

For their handsome prince would never be handsome again. The bodkin had penetrated the eye slit with enough force to put out his left eye: where before had twinkled a keen blue iris now a red gouge gaped hideously.

Fortunately for the prince, the arrow had struck at such an angle that it had not entered his brain, but rather had torn through the eye and carved a great furrow across the bridge of his nose, from where the white of bone could be seen glinting in the lantern light.

Bernal shut his eyes and muttered a silent prayer of his own as Sandon went about his work, first giving the Prince an opiate to dull the pain. After he had washed the wound, cleaning out the gaping eye socket as best he could and applying a poultice to aid healing, he dressed it with clean bandages.

The castle was fortunate in its chirurgeon. Sandon had trained in Rima, where the standards of medicine were somewhat better than in the north, and studied for a while with a chapter of Marionite monks in the foothills of the Hyrkrainians. That made him a better man of his profession than many; if his skills could not make Prince Wolfram whole again, they might yet save his life.

When at last it was done Sandon turned to face his commander, his lined face grave but even. 'I have done what I can for him,' he said. 'Reus willing, he will heal and survive his hurt, grievous though it is.'

Bernal let out a trembling sigh of relief. 'Well done, Sandon, well done. If the Prince lives I shall reward thee well for this – as no doubt will the King, when he gets here.'

Sandon's face betrayed no emotion as he replied: 'You are over kind, my lord. Now if it please you I would suggest that we leave him to rest – though Ubo can stay to pray for him a while. Just let him do so silently.'

'I shall pray as I see fit,' said the fat perfect with a frown. 'For know that it is the power of prayer that will save our prince, not the artifice of mortal men.'

Sandon said nothing, merely nodding deferentially.

'Stay and pray for him a while by all means,' said the castellan with a frown of his own. 'But when the sun sets I want you with the other wounded – they too shall need the power of prayer though in the meantime I should think they'll be more than happy to receive Sandon's ministrations.'

Bernal pointedly met the perfect's misgiving look with a glare. The priest bowed perfunctorily and returned to his prayer book. The castellan ushered Sandon and his assistant out of the room, scowling as he closed the door gently behind him.

Truth be told, he'd never had much use for perfects – they were all words and no action.

✛ ✛ ✛

Back outside in the courtyard Bernal broke the news, as good as it could be under the circumstances, to the garrison, which let out a great cheer when they learned their future king might survive.

Turning to his second, he received grimmer news. Of two hundred bold knights just seventy-three had returned – the rest had either been slain, injured or captured. A few others had made it back but were seriously wounded – more work for Sandon. The inner walls had been firmly garrisoned with heavily armoured foot, and in the fading light the enemy could be seen massing its ranks in the outer ward.

'How many do they have out there?' growled Bernal as frightened servants began to light torches about the courtyard.

'From what we can glean they've filled the precinct with archers and heavily armoured foot – several hundred of both,' said Sir Orfius.

'What of their horse? I saw a company of knights preparing to make the ascent not long after they broke the outer gates.'

Orfius shook his head. 'No knights, sire, just archers and footmen. They've plenty of those on the outer walls too.'

Bernal frowned. 'What about beyond the outer walls? What are their movements?'

'It's getting too dark to see clearly, sire, but they do not appear to be moving towards Linden in any great numbers.'

Bernal raised an eyebrow. 'Really? That is passing strange, unless – '

His incipient thought was confirmed suddenly by an exultant cry from a sentry on the north-east turret of the inner ward. 'My lord! It's the King's army! The King's army has arrived! We're saved!'

⁜ ⁜ ⁜

From the vanguard Vaskrian felt a twinge as he looked on the white walls of Linden for a second time. Perched atop a rocky hill overlooking the Ørling tributary of the Vyborg and its once-fertile fields, it was a beautiful castle; he remembered it well from the previous summer. Back then it had just been a spectacular backdrop for the pageantry and heroics of the tourney. Now it was revealed in its true purpose: a bastion designed to stand up to the challenge of siege warfare.

Smoke rose from its white-walled battlements: the greatest castle in Northalde besides Staerkvit had been burning. The ugly scorch marks scarring the fields said more than one hamlet had shared in that fate. Vaskrian wondered briefly what had happened to the occupants, then pushed the grim thought away. Now wasn't the time. He'd see to it personally they were avenged, anyway.

As they drew nearer they could make out the palisaded rebel encampment; men swarmed up the eastern walls like ants as cogs bearing siege engines bombarded them without respite.

Vaskrian steeled his nerves as the realisation dawned on him fully at last. This was the real thing – no more tournament melees, no more brawling, no more duels of honour, dangerous as those could be. This was *war*. The thought filled him with excitement tinged – maybe just a little – with fear. Once more he checked his master's weapons, and his own.

⁜ ⁜ ⁜

By the time they were within parleying distance it was clear that the outer walls of the castle had been breached. Across the river the din of battle could be heard distantly.

Adelko and his mentor were encamped on a grassy knoll with Freidheim and his closest advisers.

The knoll overlooked the camp and Adelko could see cooks, armourers, bladesmiths, chirurgeons and washerwomen going about their business in the firelight. No common prostitutes would be found amidst the gaggle of camp followers though: the King had expressly forbade the harlots of Strongholm to join the march to ply their usual trade, saying he would not have the battle for his throne used as an excuse for rampant whoring.

'Well, we'd better send parleys out – naught but a formality but still decorum should be observed I suppose,' growled the King. He was in an ill mood, having been prevailed upon not to fight personally after a heated argument with his advisers. Though a mighty warrior in his day who had aged well, he was sorely out of practice. He had not even competed in a tourney for more than a decade.

'At least I get a ringside seat,' he grumbled. 'Can't join in the slaughter because my trusted advisers would fall to pieces without me if I perished in the field, but still I can have fun watching it, eh?'

The knights and lords about him exchanged uneasy glances and wisely held their peace.

Presently a sortie of messengers led by a herald returned and informed them of Krulheim's position: he had taken the outer ward of Linden, which was now sorely invested, and demanded that the loyalist army surrender the throne if they knew what was good for them.

'Tell him no such terms will be agreed,' sighed the King wearily. 'We'll meet him in pitched battle on the fields before Linden at dawn tomorrow, according to standard conventions of formation – assuming a traitor who consorts with pagan wizards is still capable of conventional behaviour.'

The messengers nodded and galloped off again. The wind picked up as they waited on the knoll. Adelko folded his hands in the sleeves of his habit. He felt tense and anxious. His mentor's sombre presence next to him did nothing to ease his bleak mood.

Before long the herald returned with Thule's final answer. 'Thule agrees to the terms of battle,' he said, his face unsmiling beneath his helm. 'We engage the rebels at first light.'

✥ ✥ ✥

The morning brought with it a cold, clear day. At the King's orders his army drew up its ranks into three hosts: the vanguard of knights took the centre, with the Highlanders stiffening the left and right flanks of footsoldiers. The yeoman levies were also divided between these two, and behind all three hosts the archers were arranged, ready at command to shower their enemies with a lethal rain of shafts.

His heart thumping, Vaskrian gazed across the fields. Several hundred yards away, Thule had drawn up his own forces in a similar arrangement. His knights occupied the centre, with armoured footsoldiers flanking them to the left and right. These were bolstered by a great horde of peasant levies; true to earlier reports they were better equipped than usual. The Northland berserkers had also joined up with them: to either side a motley slew of battle-hungry barbarians could be seen chewing their broad shields. Above them a rude standard proclaimed the Frozen Thane Hardrada's sigil: a silver warrior-mermaid dressed for war on a sky-blue background. Behind these Thule's own archers would be drawn up, ready to answer like for like with a rain of ruin of their own.

'They are almost double our number on either flank,' said Sir Ulfstan as Vaskrian handed him his spear. 'We must smash their centre and rally to help our comrades on foot.'

Vaskrian nodded absently. As if he hadn't known that.

'And don't get carried away,' added the knight, lowering his visor. 'There's been talk of telling squires to attack anyone they can because we're outnumbered. I don't want it heard that mine overstepped the mark – you're to attack commoners only, understand? War or not you're to remember your place.'

Prince Freidhoff had issued an order instructing squires to strike down any foe they could, commoner or noble. Now Ulfstan was going against that order – even though it had come from the commander of the army in the field, a man who answered only to the King.

The blueblood fool's blinkered prejudice would have irked Vaskrian at any other time. But now he was barely listening – his mind was roaring with a berserker fury of its own. With the field of battle spread before him, all the despondency he had felt on the march to war had dropped away.

So he wouldn't get any credit from his master. So the odds were against them. So what? It didn't matter any more. The only thing that mattered was that they were going to fight. For real, on a scale he'd never experienced before.

He'd waited his whole life for this moment: it was time to show the bluebloods how well a common serjeant's son could fight. Even if they didn't sing his praises for it, they'd know. *He'd* know.

He drew the old man's blade and looked it over. Was there a slight greenish tinge to it in the cold sunlight? That brought back the hint of darker memories; he could feel them pushing at the growing tide of his battle rage. But the sword felt good in his hand, very good. That feeling pushed the murky thoughts to the back of his mind.

He knew he'd been to dark places. That didn't matter either. Today was a blood day. And blood would wash the past away.

✤ ✤ ✤

From his place in the vanguard, Sir Tarlquist gripped his lance and prepared to lower at the High Commander's order.

Beside him sat Sir Torgun. He looked just the same as he would have done riding to a tournament melee – calm and self-assured. If he felt afraid at the prospect of his first real war, he gave no sign. Nearest to them in the vanguard were the High Commander, his son Wolmar, the deputy chief Toric of Runstadt, Sir Aronn, Sir Redrun, and the chequered twins Doric and Cirod. Some of the best knights in the land, ready to carve up some rebel hide.

The plan of attack had been agreed at war council the previous night. The vanguard was to meet Thule's, and smash it as quickly as it could. This was the loyalist faction's only real hope: Krulheim's foot vastly outnumbered theirs, and without swift aid from their victorious horse they would most likely be routed.

If that happened all was lost – there would be nothing to do but fall back beyond the Vyborg, leaving Linden unsaved, and prepare for an inevitable siege of the capital. They had made plans for one alternative strategy should this seem likely to happen, but it was very risky.

Thinking on this Tarlquist felt his gut tighten. It was not fear for his own skin that troubled him – he had put such concerns aside when he joined the Order years ago – but fear of what would befall the kingdom if Krulheim won.

Doubtless the rebel upstart would exact bloody vengeance on all the noble families who had opposed him, and his father in the last war. And when that was done, what kind of king would the pretender prove to be? Freidheim had earned his reputation as a just ruler: in peacetime he had worked hard to try and rule for the benefit of all his people, difficult as that was. Tarlquist knew that made him a rarity among kings.

He didn't fancy the chances of a vengeful traitor proving anywhere near as benevolent. Krulheim might offer some concessions to his own; southerners who'd served the lords on his side. But he doubted that the King's Law would survive in its present form. The Order of the White

Valravyn would be broken up – commoners and lordlings alike would be left to fend for themselves and fight each other for scraps across a lawless realm.

It was loyalty to his rightful liege that impelled him to war above all. But behind that, Tarlquist knew, there was the wellbeing of an entire kingdom at stake.

A rebel victory that put Thule on the Pine Throne would be nothing short of disaster.

The thought that he might never see his wife Karlya again also troubled him. He barely saw her enough as it was: his duty was to the Order and he only got to spend time with her once a month, on conjugal visits to Staerkvit.

Thinking on that made him feel sad. He hadn't loved her all that much when he first married her, but love had grown gradually over the years. Reus knew how, given the little time they'd had together. Absence made the heart grow fonder, he supposed. Their marriage had been a childless one: there was a time when he had been sad about that too but now, on the eve of deadly conflict, it almost seemed like a blessing in disguise.

In any case, his real family were the knights around him. He'd known that for years. The truth was, he was probably closer to his wife's nephew Torgun – he certainly saw more of the promising young knight than he did of his wife. But perhaps that was for the best. Men and women would come and go, but the Order would endure. If Thule didn't win, that was.

Banishing his gloomy thoughts, Tarlquist steeled himself for a heroic effort on behalf of king and country.

�֍ �֍ ✖

The sun rose slowly, illuminating a field pregnant with the tense stillness that comes before battle. Long it lingered, the silence broken only by the hungry cawing of crows as they circled in anticipation of the coming feast, and the prayers of perfects on both sides.

And then it came: the clarion call to war.

With a great roar the vanguard of the King's Army kicked its horses into stride as lances were lowered into nooks. This was met by an answering roar from Thule's knights, who couched and charged, thundering across the green sward to meet their enemies.

Watching this, Adelko felt a curious sense of relief. He had half expected the Sea Wizard to suddenly rear his ugly head, casting some foul spell that would doom their chances. But of that much-reported warlock and his sorcerous ways there was no sign. Beside the young monk, his mentor stood stock still and stared across the field, his face a stony mask beneath his cowl.

✠ ✠ ✠

Sir Torgun's lance shattered in his hand as the two hosts met with a splintering crunch. His foe hurtled from the saddle and was dead before he hit the ground, Torgun's broken spear transfixed through his heart. In an instant his sword was out of its scabbard. Laying about him, he downed another knight with a mighty swipe, shearing through a chink in his armour and sending him low, a fountain of red spurting from his neck.

Another knight lunged at him – Torgun took the sword on his shield before bringing his own blade down in an arc onto his head. His opponent was wearing a great helm, but the force of his blow was strong enough to crumple it. The knight shuddered and lurched back in the saddle, his sword slipping from nerveless fingers. Torgun switched to a thrust, the point of his blade piercing through surcoat and hauberk with a pitiless force and entering the man's entrails. As the man sloughed off his horse dying, Torgun was already wheeling his charger around in search of another opponent.

Gore from his second foe was dripping down his nose guard, but he didn't let it distract him and stayed focused on the mayhem unfolding around him. A frightened squire flashed before his gaze – but he ignored this unworthy adversary and instead spurred his horse towards another knight, a great big burly man wielding a morning star to devastating effect. He had just downed a raven, his face exploding in a shower of blood and bone as he fell from his horse.

Torgun drove hard at him. The burly knight took his first blow on his shield, which bore a portcullis as a coat of arms. He renewed his onslaught, cutting left and right in rapid succession. But the knight moved quickly for his size, ducking one blow and blocking the other with his shield. Then, twisting in the saddle, he brought his morning star round in a great loop. This passed above Torgun's shield, striking him in the side of the helm with a force that set his ears ringing and jostled his teeth in his mouth.

But the hardy knight had suffered more than one knock like that in his time. Roaring a great war-cry he spurred his horse at his foe again. This time the burly knight's own steed responded, snapping fiercely at Torgun's. The sudden reaction threw the knight off balance for just a moment, presenting his flank to Torgun's line of attack.

A moment was all he needed. Suddenly lunging low he caught the knight beneath his hauberk, thrusting deep into his thigh and beyond into his horse's flank. Horse and rider screamed as one, and the fierce black charger reared and threw its master to the ground to lie bleeding and groaning in the churned mud.

'Torgun, behind you!'

The shouted warning from Tarlquist came not a moment too soon. Torgun turned just enough to interpose his shield between his head and a descending axe. Just then Tarlquist spurred forwards and thrust his blood-slick blade into the rebel knight's side. He screamed and lurched off his horse into the mud and blood.

'Well met, Sir Tarlquist!' cried Torgun above the noise. 'Let's find more rebels to slay!'

'Aye, let's do that, Sir Torgun!' answered Tarlquist with a wolfish grin.

The joy of battle was on them, subsuming all fear. Together they pressed further into the melee, searching for new foes to wet their blades.

⁜ ⁜ ⁜

Vaskrian's first experience of war consumed him in shroud of steel. No sooner were the two hosts joined than he found himself separated from Sir Ulfstan. He had been riding in his master's wake but lost sight of him as soon as the armies met.

Riding his courser into the fray he passed a myriad of knights clashing noisily before coming up against his first opponent: a battle-scarred squire of some twenty summers, clad in a shabby brigandine and wielding a shield like his own and a cruelly spiked mace. The older squire gave a hateful sneer as he lashed out at Vaskrian. He parried with his shield before trying a sword thrust to his midriff, but the rebel squire was too quick and twisted in the saddle to avoid the strike.

The attack left Vaskrian momentarily off-guard. His opponent took advantage of this to strike again. With an agonising crunch his mace bit into Vaskrian's left shoulder. And his ribs had been healing up so nicely. Biting his lip hard to avoid crying out he felt blood run into his mouth but recovered in time to counter attack, aiming a thrust at the squire's unprotected face. The squire blocked with his own shield, before counter counter-attacking.

Vaskrian was pressed back before a flurry of blows, and forced to parry any overhead strikes with his sword, for he now could not lift his shield above his injured shoulder. He saw his life flash before his eyes... but then his overconfident foe made one fatal mistake, bringing his mace around in a sidewise swipe at Vaskrian's head. With a speed born of instinct he ducked the blow. The wild attack left his foe momentarily unguarded – taking his sword in both hands he slashed from left to right across his face. The squire screamed and dropped his weapon, clutching at the wound as blood streamed through his fingers. Without hesitation Vaskrian finished him off, thrusting his sword deep into his bowels.

His battle lust went up another notch. The aching in his shoulder diminished. Spurring his horse through the riot of blood and steel he cut down another squire, a timid-looking noble of barely sixteen winters. He felt no pity, only the joy of battle. Hadn't his master said something about not attacking bluebloods? Ridiculous notion.

Speaking of which, where was Ulfstan? The melee had thinned slightly – it appeared that the rebel knights were giving ground. All around was a surge of violence as mounted warriors clashed at close quarters with sword and axe and mace.

A war cry alerted him to another attack – this one from the ground as a dismounted knight charged at him with a sword. Clearly he had been badly wounded – his light helm revealed a face streaked with flowing blood, and his shield arm was bent at an awkward angle, presumably broken in his fall. His injuries must have robbed him of all self-possession, for a squire would be considered an unworthy opponent to aggress by most self-respecting knights.

Vaskrian had little time to consider this as he parried the knight's first blow. The second came quickly, but by the time Vaskrian returned the attack it was clear that his opponent was fading fast. Hacking down at him frenziedly Vaskrian's initial blows were turned by the knight's mail – but his final cut found a weak spot and sheared through his collar bone in a spurt of blood.

The knight slumped to his knees and looked up at his killer with an expression of profound pain and bewilderment.

'A... squire,' was all he managed to say, before keeling over.

Vaskrian felt something hit him hard on the top of his helm. His ears rang and his vision swam. He felt himself falling slowly backwards into a black pool of night. Then he felt nothing.

✢ ✢ ✢

Adelko watched the battle unfold anxiously. The King and a rump of his knights did likewise. Most of them were unknown to Adelko – Ulnor had been left at Strongholm, to supervise the last defence of the city if it should become necessary, whilst every fighting man of status had been deployed in the field. Beside him his mentor remained as impassive as ever, looking upon the spectacle with grim eyes.

The knights on either side had been first into the fray – Adelko knew that much of the day depended on the success of their vanguard, but with several thousand knights and squires fighting each other it was hard to discern who had the advantage. Thinking of his friend

Vaskrian in the thick of it, he mouthed a prayer for him. He still didn't entirely agree with what his mentor had said on the eve of the march, although the spectacle of war was sickening enough.

The flanks were next to meet. As these advanced towards each other both sides gave the order for their archers to fire.

That was the worst part of the battle for Adelko, who watched with his heart in his mouth as men fell by the dozen before the pitiless hail of shafts. The advancing footsoldiers left a carpet of corpses in their wake as they charged to meet the foe, who sustained similar casualties. The screams of the dying and wounded footsoldiers drowned out the distant din of mounted knights clashing, and the young monk's stomach heaved as he saw some of the men trying to crawl back towards the camp, their bodies feathered with arrows. Even at this distance he could see that some of them wore the colours of his own Highland people.

As the foot battle was joined it soon became apparent that they were dreadfully outnumbered. Before long all semblance of formation on either side was lost, and serried ranks gave way to a seething mass of men and horse, as mounted warriors did battle with footmen and vice versa.

The distant cries and screams and ring of steel on steel continued interminably as the sun climbed slowly towards its zenith.

And then a series of clarion calls came. Far and wide they rang out across the corpse-strewn field.

'What does that mean?' asked Adelko.

Horskram's face remained icy as he said: 'It means a general retreat. Our strength is overmatched and we must withdraw the field.'

'Withdraw...? But that means they'll come for us here – what about the King?'

Horskram turned to look at Freidheim, whose face was as inscrutable as his.

'I'm sure His Majesty is more than aware of the situation,' was all he said.

✥ ✥ ✥

Krulheim heard the clarions and rejoiced. He had led his own knights into the fray as befitted a true king, and slain more than his fair share. Even so, they had been hard pressed by the White Valravyn that morning, and had it been simply down to their horse the battle would probably have gone ill for them. But once the main body of his army had joined battle, the tide had quickly turned, for not even those myrmidons could hope to prevail over such weight of numbers.

Or so it had turned out, anyway.

The knights commanded by loyalist jarls could be seen riding hell for leather towards the east, leaving the White Valravyn and the Royal Knights to fight a brave rearguard action to protect their fleeing footsoldiers.

Krulheim was on the verge of ordering a new attack, when things went out of his hands. The Northland berserkers, filled with bloodlust and greed for loot, broke formation and charged pell-mell after the fleeing footsoldiers, highlanders and levies towards the King's camp. Many of the southron levies, their blood up, followed suit. The loyalist knights who had not fled the field, inspired by the dwindling numbers on the enemy side, renewed their attack against the rebel knights, the more disciplined regular footsoldiers and those yeomen whose commanders had had presence enough to keep them from breaking ranks.

Krulheim spat into the bloodied earth at his charger's feet. He turned to Sir Jord. He too had done his share of killing: his tabard was covered in the blood of loyalist knights and footsoldiers.

'You see what comes of this alliance, Jord!' snarled Krulheim. 'I never should have made a pact with such Northland brigands!'

Jord glanced sidelong at him, but kept his counsel.

'Pah!' the pretender snorted. 'What does it matter anyway? Half their horse flee the field, and their footsoldiers are all but finished. The day is ours, I say!'

This time Jord did not so much as look at his liege. Instead he watched the tumultuous battlefield, his lined face set grim.

✣ ✣ ✣

Adelko watched with his heart in his mouth as thousands of berserkers and peasant levies screamed after their retreating footsoldiers. Off to his left those knights commanded by the Efrilunders and other jarls loyal to the King were fleeing the field.

'But they're abandoning us!' he cried. 'They're running away!'

'It would appear so,' said Horskram grimly. His face remained expressionless. The faces of the King and his personal bodyguard of knights were taut and tense. Helplessly Adelko watched as the horde of fleeing footsoldiers hurtled back across the field towards them.

Suddenly the King turned and motioned to a herald next to him, who raised a horn to his lips and blew three short sharp blasts. The fleeing knights, who had been dwindling on the horizon, suddenly wheeled around and began riding back towards the fray.

Their target was unmistakeable.

Simultaneously the footsoldiers who had been fleeing abruptly turned and stood their ground. Their pursuers outnumbered them hugely, and for a few minutes there was fierce fighting. It was close enough for Adelko to fancy he could smell the blood being spilt now, as the enemy cut a dreadful swathe through the hard-pressed loyalists.

But they managed to hold on just long enough for the returning knights to smash the berserkers and common footsoldiers in the flank, riding them down and slaying on the left hand and the right. The Northlanders turned and fought viciously, transported by berserker courage, but the peasant levies panicked and quickly broke into a rout.

Even the Northlanders were no match for the combined forces of their mounted opponents and the King's hardy men-at-arms, and soon their bodies were piling up atop the others already littering the bloody sward.

✢ ✢ ✢

Embroiled once more in combat at close quarters, Thule had no idea of what was occurring in the wider field. Not that he cared. With a great blow of his war axe he cut down another raven. He felt a great rush of exultation – Ragnar's ministrations had left him feeling fearless, and rightly so. He had cut down two more knights by the time he came face to face with the High Commander of the White Valravyn.

'How very fitting,' he snarled from a mouth made feral by bloodshed. 'The King sends his little brother to do his dirty work for him.'

'As to that, Krulheim,' replied Freidhoff, lowering his visor, 'there will be nothing dirty about ridding the realm of a traitor such as thee.'

They joined battle. No one about them on either side interfered. They fought long and hard, trading fierce strokes, and soon both knights' shields were in splintered tatters. Then Freidhoff made a skilful feint at Krulheim's head – he raised his iron-shod axe haft to parry but the High Commander changed the direction of his attack at the last moment, thrusting his sword deep through a chink in his armour just beneath the shoulder.

And Krulheim laughed.

Freidhoff's eyes widened behind his visor as he wrenched his blade free of the wound – not a drop of blood stained his sword. Clutching his battleaxe in two hands Krulheim aimed a swipe at Freidhoff. He raised his shield instinctively to ward off the blow, remembering too late that it was in tatters. The sharp blade sheared through the remnants of the shield and the mail beneath, biting deep into flesh and bone. With a great cry Freidhoff brought his sword down onto Krulheim's shoulder. It was a powerful cut, enough to break through his mail, but again he merely laughed.

Blood was spurting from Freidhoff's maimed arm, which hung limply at his side, kept in one piece only by a few threads of flesh and mangled sinew.

Raising the war axe over his shoulder again the self-style Prince of Thule aimed another cut at his head. The High Commander tried to parry... but he was faint from shock and loss of blood and his reactions were slow.

Krulheim's axe smashed heavily into his helm, crumpling the visor inwards with enough force to break his nose. With a gasp he slipped from his horse to lie prone in the churned mud. With a malignant sneer Krulheim prepared to dismount from his horse and administer the *coup de grace*, but at that moment Sir Wolmar was on him in a frenzy, raining furious blows on him.

Such was the shock of his attack that Krulheim found himself swiftly disarmed, although none of Wolmar's other blows did him any harm. But then why would they?

Laughing madly he drew his sword and returned the young knight's onslaught in kind.

Things would have gone ill for Wolmar had not Torgun intervened, spurring his charger at Krulheim and forcing him back with another salvo of attacks. Just then another surge of rebel soldiers, by now a hotchpotch of regular foot and pressed conscripts, pushed forwards to menace the loyalist knights with long spears. Krulheim, Torgun and Wolmar all became separated from one another as a sortie of Saltcaste's knights joined their part of the battle.

Of the fallen High Commander there was no sign. No matter – he was sure he had incapacitated the Order's precious leader at the very least. Let the high-and-mighty ravens think that over, if they survived the day.

✣ ✣ ✣

With the berserkers slaughtered and more than half of Thule's peasant levies in rout, the King's victorious forces lost no time in riding back up the field to rejoin their comrades.

By now it was past noon. Adelko had felt his emotions go from the depths of despair to the height of joy in that time, as what had happened finally dawned on him.

'It was a feint!' he exclaimed. 'They never really meant to flee the field at all! It was just a ruse to draw out Thule's men!'

'Welcome to the wily ways of warfare,' was all his mentor said.

For his part the King was now grinning broadly, as were most of his attendant knights.

'Well, Horskram,' he proclaimed loudly. 'What think you of my tactics? I may be too old to fight a war, but I'm still not too old to plan one! I knew those Northland barbarians and that jumped-up rabble could be counted on to take the bait!'

'Your Majesty is indeed wise in the ways of war,' answered Horskram levelly. 'Though may I be so bold as to say it was a dangerous manoeuvre that could easily have gone awry, with disastrous consequences.'

The King glared at the old monk. 'War is ever decided on dangerous manoeuvres, master monk,' he replied testily.

✢ ✢ ✢

From where he was in the vanguard with the Royal Knights, Sir Braxus could see nothing but men and horses about him. It had been a hard morning's fighting, and his limbs ached.

At least that was his only complaint. Regan had not been so lucky – he'd taken a nasty spear injury to the thigh, his squire Conric had had to drag him out of the battle for treatment. And Braxus' own steed had been taken out from under him, forcing him to continue the fight on foot.

As a man-at-arms charged at him wielding a spear he found himself briefly wondering whether volunteering for someone else's war had been such a good idea after all – there was little glory to be had in killing commoners.

As he nimbly dodged the soldier's first spear thrust before stepping in to open his throat with an arcing slice of his sword, he consoled himself with the thought that he had at least managed to slay three brave knights before being unhorsed. That would give him something to sing about in his next song.

✢ ✢ ✢

Vaskrian's eyes fluttered open. Everything was the same as he remembered – the noise of war and armoured men all about him, screaming as their weapons clashed or found flesh. He was lying in the mud, a soldier's corpse on top of him. With an effort he pushed the dead man's body off him and struggled to sit upright.

His head was pounding and his left shoulder throbbed painfully. His ribs were aching too. His target shield was still strapped to his arm. Of the helm that had saved his life there was no sign – he could only suppose it had rolled off his head when he fell from his horse senseless. His side also ached, from the fall he supposed. Thank Reus he hadn't fallen on to his broken ribs – they hurt enough as it was.

Lurching painfully to his feet he reached out to stop himself falling back to the ground... and found his hand clutching his father's sword where it lay in the mud beside him. Grasping it he staggered to his feet again and steadied himself. The blade was still bright despite the day's use. As the smell of war brought him back to his senses he loped off in search of more foes to fight.

✣ ✣ ✣

Braxus engaged his next opponent. He was a tough-looking sinewy serjeant who fought well for a commoner, but the agile Thraxian soon had him off guard, and before he could recover he took three fingers off his sword hand. As he knelt clutching his mangled hand in agony Braxus finished him off with a quick thrust.

His next attacker launched at him without warning – another dismounted knight. The two fought for some time, trading blows, before Braxus saw a gap in his defence and lunged at his midriff. His foot slipped in the mud just as he did, and he suddenly found himself lying prone on the ground.

Hadn't he been in this position quite recently?

His opponent loomed above him, his shield sporting a silver falcon haloed with stars. At the last moment Braxus rolled aside, dodging the blow aimed at his head, and lurched to his feet. His armour slowed him down, and he barely had time to raise his own shield to ward off a follow-up attack. That put him on the back foot again, but this time he was able to circle around his assailant, and he soon recovered the initiative.

From then on it was no contest. He was swifter and smarter than his opponent. Wrongfooting him with a skilful feint he passed his sword through a chink in his armour. The knight sank to his knees, raking at his hauberk, frantically trying to close his gauntleted hands around the wound that now spilled his lifeblood into the already reddened earth.

Braxus had no time to rejoice in his victory, for just then a knight rode past him, catching him a passing blow with a mace that caught him in the back and knocked him face down into the mud.

He lay winded for a while, before recovering enough to roll on to his back... and then he saw two ugly yeomen standing over him, their hand axes raised to strike. Prone again – and no chance of recovery this time, with two foes menacing him.

He was just thinking what an ignominious death this would be when suddenly a bloodied squire dressed in a mail byrnie and wielding a sword and shield charged into view. With one cut he sliced through the first peasant's brigandine: he fell to his knees screaming as his entrails poured onto the ground right next to the Thraxian's head.

The second yeoman turned to face his new attacker – but sitting upright and pulling his dirk from his boot Braxus thrust it deep into his calf. It was always a handy place to keep a dagger. With a cry the yeoman buckled, and before he hit the ground the chestnut-haired squire struck his head from his shoulders.

'Why if it isn't Vaskrian, esquire of Hroghar!' exclaimed Braxus as the squire helped him to his feet, wincing all the while. He looked to be in a lot of pain and blood was trickling down the side of his head, but the hardy youth seemed equal to it.

'You are well met indeed!' cried Braxus, going to slap him on the back before thinking better of it. 'Where is your knightly master?'

'I don't know!' replied Vaskrian, shouting to be heard above the clamour. 'I lost him at the start of the battle!'

'Well I've lost my squire, so that makes us a fine pair!' replied the Thraxian, sheathing his dirk and picking up his sword. 'Stay close by me, Vaskrian, and we'll fight to live another day yet!'

⁙ ⁙ ⁙

It was fully an hour past noon when Thule's forces sounded a general retreat. Adelko felt a profound sense of relief wash over him. That had been close – far too close for comfort. He hoped Vaskrian and all the other fighters he knew were still alive. The King and his knights were exchanging hearty congratulations. Horskram remained as stoical and impassive as ever.

The loyalist knights who were still mounted lost no time in mowing down those fleeing on foot, before sweeping through the enemy camp and ransacking it. Most of its occupants, witnessing the turning tide of war, had long fled; likewise the cogs bearing the siege engines and catapults were moving swiftly upriver, away from the castle they had come to take.

Though he knew little of boats, Adelko thought they moved with an unnatural speed. Glancing over at his mentor, he saw him frown; evidently he was thinking much the same thing.

Further evidence of the Sea Wizard's meddling soon became apparent, for where there had been clear blue skies of a sudden there came lowering clouds from north and south, quickly followed by a torrential downpour that discouraged all thoughts of further pursuit.

Despite the blood and rain the King's forces returned to the camp in high spirits: the cost of victory was yet to be counted, but the battle for Linden Castle had been won.

As he peered out from under a hastily erected awning at the victorious warriors returning across a field obscured by hundreds of rain-drenched corpses, Adelko found it hard to share their elation. Even now common soldiers were busily despatching the enemy dying and wounded – save for those of noble blood, who would be treated by chirurgeons and held prisoner pending ransom, as the chivalrous code dictated.

Of their own wounded, common and noble alike, many were beyond saving. One glance at the bloody field was enough to tell the young monk that the price of war had been heavy on both sides.

Clarion calls were being exchanged by the garrison at Linden and the King's Army, the investing sortie having fled the outer ward. At the cost of many lives, the last bastion of the King's Dominions had been saved, the rebel invaders repulsed.

Oblivious, the crows descended greedily to their feast.

⇒ CHAPTER X ⇐

A Brief Respite

King Freidheim looked at his son with sorrowful eyes. His face looked peaceful enough in his drugged sleep, and Sandor's bandages concealed the worst of his wound, but even so it was a grievous sight for any loving father. And for all his faults, Freidheim was a loving father.

Without taking his eyes off his heir the King asked tersely: 'Will he live?'

'His Royal Highness is out of immediate danger,' replied Sandor, the castle chirurgeon, in the nervous voice of a messenger afraid to give bad news. 'Right now the gravest peril he faces is the risk of infection. If that does not happen, there is no reason why he should not recover. He is young and strong - '

'And if the wound becomes infected?'

The chirurgeon lowered his eyes to the rushes. 'Then death will be a mercy.'

The King merely nodded. 'Then do whatever you must. My son's life is in your hands – let no fear of royal authority bind them. Just... do what you can.'

Without another word the King swept out of the chamber with Bernal in tow. He suppressed his feelings of grief. Grief was a luxury an embattled king could not afford.

The rain had abated shortly before sunset, and the skies above the castle courtyard were dark but clear. Soldiers were busy clearing up corpses in the torchlight.

'I shall be taking all the knights who survived the siege of Linden with me for the next battle,' said Freidheim brusquely. 'The rest of the garrison is yours – I'll leave you to clear up this mess as best you can.'

'As you will, Your Majesty,' replied Bernal deferentially. 'Including those prisoners of war we rescued from the invaders, you should have well over a hundred able-bodied knights to add to your own.'

'Good, we shall need them,' said the King.

He knew only too well how right he was. The rest of the day had been spent counting the dead on both sides, treating wounded loyalists and despatching injured rebels or taking them prisoner.

He had not yet given orders what to do with Thule's captured knights. Although custom dictated that their families be allowed to ransom them when the war was over, it was being noised about the camp that a treasonous war was another matter. In times gone by the King might have overlooked this and cleaved to the laws of chivalry regardless, but given the present state of affairs he felt increasingly disinclined to be merciful.

Now, with his son and heir lying injured and disfigured, what he would do next was anybody's guess. Anybody's guess but his.

✢ ✢ ✢

Returning to the camp the King marched into his tent and found his war council assembled.

'My son's life hangs in the balance, but Reus willing he shall be spared – albeit less one eye and those handsome looks of his,' was all he said on the subject of Wolfram.

He waved aside the chorus of horrified gasps. 'Enough. I do not wish to dwell on my own private tragedy, public a matter as that is. Let's to business – what of our casualties, and the enemy's?'

Lord Toros, Jarl of Vandheim, was first to speak up. Torgun's older brother, not as handy in the field but a wiser man, as befitted a firstborn heir to lands. Two finer sons the House of Hamlyn could not have asked for. But then Hamlyn had ever been staunch and loyal to the Pine Throne.

'We pursued the fleeing enemy as far as we could before the rains made it impossible to continue further,' the Jarl began. 'We cut down plenty before that happened however. According to our tallies, we slew more than two hundred of their bowmen and a like amount of trained foot. His peasant levies also suffered – we estimate we killed around five hundred before the rains saved them.'

Lord Fenrig, Jarl of Hroghar, a bald thick-set man with a bushy brown beard and moustache, was next to speak.

'Added to the tally of those killed on the battlefield and during the siege of Linden, we estimate Thule's losses to amount to no less than fifteen hundred men-at-arms and two thousand conscripts,' he said gruffly.

'I see,' replied the King unsmiling. 'And what of their knights?'

It was Lord Aesgir's turn to speak. Twirling his flamboyant corn-yellow mustachios he slapped his girth with a gauntleted hand and cleared his throat dramatically. The scions of Sjórvard had ever been an irrepressible bunch. But then their ancestral home lay by the sea that all true-blooded Northlendings yearned for. A Northlending's ancestry was in the sea.

'The tally is unchanged since you went to see your son, Your Majesty,' said Lord Aesgir brightly. 'Thule has lost six hundred knights, of which a third are alive in our keeping for ransom. About half of those are seriously injured. Also, two hundred squires, of which fifty have been captured for ransom. The others are dead or dying. We have also captured Lord Johan, one of the key conspirators, and two other principal barons in the rebel faction have fallen – Lord Aelrod of Saltcaste was slain in the closing minutes of battle by Sir Torgun, and a lesser baron, Lord Crumly of High Crannock, lies dying of his wounds even as we speak.'

'This is very good,' said the King with satisfaction. 'Lord Johan will be hanged as a traitor tomorrow. I do hereby attaint him and all his fellow conspirator barons, and strip them and their families of all lands and titles. Something I should have done years ago.'

A general murmur of approval went around the crowded tent. It appeared as though the King had at last learned when to be merciful and when not. The thought of his erstwhile clemency being perceived as weakness left a bitter taste in Freidheim's mouth. No matter how one tried, ruling a realm always led to bloody deeds eventually. That was the ugly reality of kingship.

'We should also not expect all of Thule's levies to return to him,' put in Lord Visigard. 'Of the four thousand that we did not kill, it is likely that many will choose to desert and turn outlaw rather than rejoin a failing rebellion.'

'And the Northland berserkers serving Hardrada?' pressed Freidheim. 'Did any survive the slaughter?'

'Few,' replied Visigard. 'For their way is to fight to the bitter death. However we did manage to take some two hundred alive.'

'They shall all be put to the sword come morning,' declared the King. 'Northlanders shall not be suffered to wreak ruin and devastation on our land. That should send a message to the Ice Thanes.'

The Thraxian knight Sir Braxus had proved most illuminating on that subject. So the Northland princes were stirring up trouble again – sending their sea-carls abroad to make slaughter on the mainland. There would be a reckoning for that – and a right bloody one too. Half of him hoped he would not be alive to have to do it. The other half that still housed his old warrior spirit hoped otherwise.

Most of the assembled nobles were nodding their approval. No doubt they thought it good that their King was not getting carried away with any of his foolish merciful notions today.

Swallowing his bitterness and taking a deep breath Freidheim asked: 'And what of our own losses? Come, let's have it.'

'All told, not so bad as might have been expected, thanks to the success of our strategy,' replied Visigard. 'We lost three hundred brave knights, including a hundred of the Order. A hundred squires were killed or injured, and most if not all of the Wolding levies are gone – we have thirteen hundred peasant foot left. We lost five hundred men-at-arms.'

'What of the Highlanders?'

A short rotund warrior, dressed in colourful robes with interlocking patterns over a mail byrnie, stepped forward. Lord Whaelin, who had been chosen among the dozen clan leaders to act as a spokesman for all. With his outlandish appearance and bushy red beard and hair, he was looked down on by most of the lowland nobles in the tent. But if he noticed or cared he gave little indication of it. The King privately had to admire him for that.

'Six hundred clansmen rode down from the north t'elp ye, Yer Majesty,' said Lord Whaelin. 'And perhaps half that number remain able and ready t'fight s'more if need be.'

The King nodded evenly. 'My thanks, Lord Whaelin. Now what is the overall tally? Do we now outnumber the enemy?'

Lord Toros spoke up again. 'With the rebel levies being unquantifiable that is difficult to assess,' he said cautiously. 'But it seems likely that we do.'

'Good. Tomorrow we'll get news from our scouts as to where they are headed. Most likely they will have fallen back to one of the castles they took earlier.'

'Salmor is the most likely of those,' suggested Visigard. 'Though that means forsaking much of the ground they have gained, it is the most defensible castle in their possession next to Thule itself.'

'We cannot be sure they will choose a defensive option at all,' warned Lord Vymar of Harrang, a tall pale man with close-cropped hair and a hawkish face. 'They may choose to meet us in the open field again.'

'They may, if they've still the stomach for it,' replied the King. 'But Thule knows full well that if he can hold Salmor he still gets much of what he wants – oh he won't plant his dirty backside on my throne, but he could still shore up his treasonous secession for years if he consolidates his defences. Mark my words, kingdoms have been broken up over less!'

They were interrupted by the sudden entry of Sir Toric. His ugly face was pale and anguished.

'Toric, you're late,' the King began, but his voice trailed off as he saw Toric blinking back tears.

'What is it?' he demanded sternly. Then the realisation suddenly dawned on him. He felt an invisible hand grip his guts. 'My brother...'

'... is dead,' the bull-necked deputy commander finished for him. 'We found his corpse in the field just now.'

Freidheim felt a sick heaving in the pit of his stomach as the tent erupted.

'How?' he asked through tightened lips after waving a hand for silence.

'Torgun and Wolmar both say they saw the High Commander engage Krulheim,' blurted Toric. 'Things seemed to be going against the Pretender, but when Prince Freidhoff dealt him a blow that should have been mortal, he just laughed! The last they saw of him, he'd been grievously injured and toppled from his horse...'

'Yes, yes, we know that already!' cried the King in exasperation, fighting back tears of his own. How many more personal tragedies must he endure today? How much more must his people endure before this madness was quashed?

He motioned for the raven to continue.

'When we found him,' Toric continued dolefully, 'he'd been butchered... by what looked to be axes...' His voice trailed off and he hung his head.

Freidheim felt the invisible hand tighten. Inhaling deeply he measured his words.

'You are telling me that my royal brother, the head of the most prestigious Order in the realm, was despatched by a traitor fighting under some kind of sorcerous protection, and then left to be finished off by common soldiers?'

His voice was ice cold in his own ears. It sounded almost as though someone else were speaking.

'It would appear so,' said Sir Toric without looking up.

'I see.' The King stood still, saying nothing. The tent was pregnant with silence. Then he spoke.

'Lord Toric, you are now High Commander of the Order of the White Valravyn – serve me well, as my brother did. He shall be buried with full honours tomorrow. Lord Aesgir, how many enemy knights did you say are in our keeping for ransom?'

'Some two hundred, Your Majesty.' The yellow-haired jarl didn't look so cheerful now.

'Then that's two hundred ransoms we'll be doing without,' said the King. 'They shall all be hanged as traitors on the morrow, along with Johan. I do hereby attaint every single noble family that holds lands from the erstwhile barons that have risen up against me. When this war is over their holdings shall be given to men of my choosing. The King's Dominions shall henceforth stretch from the Rymold to the Argael.'

Several of the assembled lords appeared to think this an excellent policy, and nodded approvingly, but the Wolding barons looked deeply suspicious, and even the faces of the Efrilund lords were unsettled. One of the latter, Fenrig, had the courage to voice what they were thinking.

'I hope Your Majesty will not next be considering extending them north of the Rymold,' he said cautiously.

'Reus dammit, man!' shouted the King, losing his temper. 'I've just lost my brother and nearly lost my first son, and hundreds of other good men besides! These lords and knights rose against me in rebellion! REBELLION! How many homesteads have they pillaged and burned these last six weeks? How many peasants have they violated and slaughtered? And how do you know I wasn't planning to install an Efrilunder in one of the southern provinces in any case?'

The three lords looked visibly mollified.

'Ah, that reassures you does it?' said Freidheim, trying and failing to keep the bitterness out of his voice. 'Well, then be reassured – if I have to make your younger sons southern lords to keep you happy, I'll do so! Now if that's all the bad news for one day, I'd like to retire – we've another long march ahead of us tomorrow. I want to finish this accursed business as soon as I can.'

He was about to leave when Visigard spoke again.

'What of the squires held captive, Your Majesty – shall we ransom them, or...?'

The King paused to consider this. 'How many are worth anything?'

'Some thirty are from noble families. The rest are common men who were promoted to lifelong knightly servitude. They won't fetch anything – we can dispose of them perhaps.'

The King shook his head. 'Nay, I've nothing against an ordinary man following orders and trying to make his way in the world,' he said wearily. 'The twenty commoners will be held prisoner and released after the war. As for the other thirty, they can hang tomorrow with the rest of their noble kin – I've learned the hard way what happens when you spare a lordling's life out of pity.'

Without another word Freidheim stalked from the tent. He didn't know which was worse – watching men die in the heat of battle, or coldly ordering their execution. He did know one thing though – he was sick of war. He had seen enough killing to last a lifetime. But then that probably had something to do with the fact that it had.

✧ ✧ ✧

Making his way through the camp Adelko went in search of his Highland kin. A yearning to make contact with his own people had grown steadily in him during the march to war. Now war had been joined he wanted to set eyes on them all the more – before any more of them died.

Was that homesickness? He supposed so, but the tumultuous events of the day had robbed him of any ability to assess his feelings. He was making his way past a campfire in the Stromlending contingent when he spotted Horskram sitting with a knight. His surprise tapered off as he remembered that his mentor hailed from the lands around Lake Strom.

Just then the knight happened to glance over at him. Waving a mailed arm he called him over cheerfully.

'And you must be Adelko!' he exclaimed as the novice approached. 'My uncle was just telling me all about you!'

Walking deeper into the circle of light Adelko drew level with the pair of them and bowed low.

'Adelko of Narvik, novice of Ulfang, at your service,' he said deferentially.

The knight laughed at this, a merry twinkle in his eyes. 'Well, uncle, you've certainly taught the boy more manners than you ever had!'

The two were clearly related. The knight bore a strong resemblance to his mentor: he had the same aquiline features and hooked nose. His black beard was streaked with incipient grey – he looked to be about forty winters. He was of similar build and stature to Horskram.

'This is my nephew, Sir Manfry of Vilno, vassal to the Jarl of Stromlund,' said Horskram. 'And I would appreciate it, Manfry, if you would be more civil to your elders, even a poor monk such as I am.'

'Why nonsense!' cried Manfry, motioning for Adelko to sit and join them. 'You weren't always a poor friar – in your day you couched a lance as well as the next man, my father included! Adelko, did you know that your master once reached the jousting final at Linden?'

Adelko was by now not entirely surprised to learn this, although he still could not picture his mentor as a mail-clad knight.

'No...' he faltered. 'I mean, begging your pardon Master Horskram, but I've seen him fight with a quarterstaff and he's very good at it...'

'Quarterstaves?' exclaimed Sir Manfry with an air of mock incredulity. 'Why nonsense! Brother Horskram here – or *Sir* Horskram as they used to call him back then – was once accounted one of the best swords in the jarldom! Now remind me uncle, who was it you lost to in that final at Linden?'

Adelko was half expecting to hear a rebuke from his curmudgeonly master, but to his surprise the old monk's face took on a slightly dreamy look as he said with a half smile: 'Sir Freye of Orlin – the best knight I ever couched a lance against, bar none. At least the runner-up prize was generous at Linden – I gave it all to the Temple of course.'

'Always the pious one – even back then!' chuckled Manfry. Though they looked similar, in demeanour they could not have been more different – Manfry was jollier than a court jester.

'If I'd known better, I'd have given it to the Order of St Argo,' replied Horskram reproachfully, his face darkening again. 'But I was young in years, and still had much to learn.'

He fell to his characteristic brooding again, staring glumly into the fire. But Manfry was having none of it.

'Oh nonsense! Why, you've made up for it tenfold since with your service to the Order! Come come, uncle, I understand how you feel about bloodshed these days, but there's no denying we've just won a remarkable victory against a bunch of treasonous rebels – who some say have thrown their lot in with a black magician! That alone should be good cause enough to rest your soul! Upon my troth, this is a time to celebrate, not commiserate! I'll call for horns of ale – Adelko, you're having one too.'

'Begging your pardon, sire, but I was hoping to seek kin of my own, well in a manner of speaking – do you know where the Highlanders are encamped?'

Sir Manfry fixed him with a quizzical look. 'Why, are the clansmen your kin?'

'No,' faltered Adelko. 'I'm of much more humble stock – my father is a blacksmith in Narvik, a highland village. But I just wanted... well, to see some of my own people. It's been so long since I did.'

'He spends years dreaming of leaving his homeland behind, and when he finally does, he gets homesick,' muttered Horskram with a wry shake of the head.

'Oh stuff and nonsense, uncle!' said Sir Manfry dismissively. 'You of all people should be wise enough to know that the heart's desires twist and turn like an old road – keep heading in the same direction as you were Adelko, and you should find them presently! Their camp's just beyond ours – doughty men those Highlanders, for foreigners anyway! But when you are done visiting your kin, you must come back and drink a horn with us.'

'That I shall do gladly,' replied Adelko happily, before bounding off.

It was not long before he reached the Highlanders' campsite. Like all the other contingents, they had brought along an entourage of craftsmen, cooks and the like to support the warriors' needs, although theirs was noticeably smaller than those of the lowland knights – clansmen prided themselves on self-sufficiency.

The camp was crowned with the same banners he had seen from atop the King's palace, each one a riot of clan colours. Adelko soon found his own – the interlocking yellow and green diamonds of the MacLingens who ruled his part of the Highlands.

Two battle-stained clansmen greeted him as he approached the campfire. They were both clad in mail hauberks, swaddled with the woollen saches sporting their colours. Each one leaned on a double-headed war-axe. Their crimson beards were braided after the manner of the Highland warrior caste.

'And what service may we do a man of the cloth?' asked one, gruffly but not unkindly.

Adelko was about to reply when a familiar voice called out his name. Turning he saw a tall, muscular man dressed in artisan's garb walking towards him.

'Adelko!' he repeated. 'Bless my eyes, but can it be you?'

It took Adelko several moments to register who he was looking at. The artisan was a stout fellow of about twenty summers – his forearms and apron were covered with soot, and his face was blackened too. But this close it was unmistakeable.

'Arik!' cried Adelko. 'Arik, can it really be you?'

'Adelko!' cried Arik again, taking his youngest brother in a mighty embrace. 'It really *is* you! Almighty be praised! I could not have hoped to see you here, of all places!'

'He works in mysterious ways,' said Adelko, choking back tears.

Quickly the two took a place by the fire and Arik called for horns of ale. Adelko pressed him eagerly for news of home.

'Father is still hale,' he said, quaffing from a frothing horn. 'Though a little slower about the forge these days. Malrok will take over the family business when the time comes.'

That surprised Adelko. Usually the eldest did this, leaving the younger sons to seek a trade elsewhere as best they could. Arik shook his head when he pointed this out.

'Nay, it's a household life for me Adelko!' he said cheerfully. 'I was taken in by old Whaelfric two summers ago – I'm an armourer these days. No more horseshoes for me – Malrok is welcome to them!'

'What about Silma?' asked Adelko, suddenly remembering his elder brother's betrothed. 'Did you...'

A mixed expression crossed Arik's soot-smeared face.

'Aye, we married – shortly after you left with Master Horskram to join the Order,' he replied. 'We have two children – we had a third but she was stillborn.' Though the sadness in his face was obvious as he said this, Adelko could sense it had other sources.

'What is it, Arik?' he pressed gently. 'You can tell me.' It felt peculiar to be addressing his older brother as a fellow adult for the first time.

A pained look crossed Arik's face. 'Ah...' he faltered, waving his horn as if searching for the right words. 'Adelko, you're a monk of the Order now, and will never have to face such problems. Silma... well she is still as beautiful to me as the day I first courted her but... married life is different. It changes a person, I tell you. She isn't happy about my being here.'

'Where is she now?' asked Adelko.

'She's back at Whaelfric's homestead, where we have modest lodgings. Reus knows I've set her up better than my father or anyone else in Narvik could have hoped to – but dammit Adelko, that woman is never happy! I don't know what more a man can do to satisfy his wife...'

Seeing the look of anguish on his elder brother's face Adelko felt a stab of pity. Perhaps a celibate life wasn't such a bad one after all – the adepts at the monastery taught that gratifying earthly desires always brought one to misery in the end.

'Ah, but let us not dwell on such things!' said Arik suddenly, banishing his black mood. 'We've won a great battle today, though it's cost us dear – hopefully in a few days' time we'll win another one!'

Adelko felt his high spirits dampen. 'Will it be fought so soon?' he asked hesitantly.

'Oh I should think so,' replied his brother, taking another slug of ale. 'That's what the clansmen are saying anyway – there's no time to lose and we must press our advantage.'

Adelko nodded and pressed his brother for more news of home. War was the last thing he wanted to talk about now.

'Well now,' said Arik, thankfully warming to the subject, 'Malrok is courting too – a young lass by the name of Magda who lives in Rykken. I hope he has better luck in his choice of wife than I did!'

Adelko did his best to suppress a shudder as memory of the exorcism there came back to him – the very encounter that had set them off on their frightful quest. He'd thought about it more than once since Horskram had recounted it again, at the secret council in Strongholm three weeks ago. Something about Belaach's words didn't add up, but he couldn't put his finger on it. But then a demon's words were intended to trick and confound – he should pay little heed to them.

Arik was too caught up in his stories to notice his younger brother's troubled expression. 'And speaking of marriage, you'll never guess what,' he said, the smile returning to his honest face. 'Albhra married Ludo!'

'What?' exclaimed Adelko, his ugly thoughts vanishing in a trice. 'Ludo the fiddler married Albhra the harridan? I don't believe it!'

'Oh, come on!' guffawed Arik. 'Those two were bound to do it eventually – Reus knows a man and a woman can't argue that much without having strong feelings for each other! Perhaps I should bear that in mind when I think of Silma!'

'What about my old friends? What of Ulam?'

Arik frowned. 'He turned out to be a bad sort. Caught thieving from the granary last winter. Malgar would have had him shunned for it, only Radna was moved to pity for the lad. Last I heard, he keeps foul company, drinking his father's house dry and doing not a stroke of work. He'll be banished for real before long.'

Adelko frowned back. Ulam had always been a mischief-maker, the ringleader in any village prank among the boys. But then he himself had been no angel in his youth. He wondered if he might have turned out the same way had it not been for Horskram's intervention. He pushed the thought away and inquired further after Narvik's three headmen.

'Well, old Balor passed three winters ago,' replied Arik, making the sign. 'But at least thanks to your master his passing was a godly one. Dreadful business that was – how is the old monk, by the way? Still hale I hope.'

'Still hale and very much here,' replied Adelko. 'I've been seconded to him for the best part of the last year.'

Arik raised his eyebrows. He was clearly impressed. 'Bless me, young Adelko, but you do move up fast in the world! And I thought I was doing well! Even us Highlanders know Master Horskram's name precedes him throughout the lowlands! But tell me of yourself – how do the pair of you come to be here? I thought you Argolians are supposed to be off fighting werewolves and demons when you're not shut up in the monastery praying and studying.'

Adelko related as much of his story as he felt he could without jeopardising their mission or frightening his brother too much. Though Arik had matured into a sturdy young man, his was an ordinary soul and his mind would only be able to stand so much.

The two of them had got through another horn of ale by the time Adelko was done.

'Well that is a tale and no mistake,' said Arik at last, his face looking anxious in the firelight. 'Adelko, I'm just a simple armourer, and this war is about the most adventurous thing I've yet seen – but it sounds to me as if Master Horskram has taken you to some dangerous places! I do hope he'll take care to see you safe on the rest of your journey.'

Despite the cheering ale Adelko felt as anxious as his brother looked. He knew full well by now that for all his acumen Horskram was far from immortal or infallible. In the business they had undertaken he could guarantee no one's safety, not even his own.

Forcing a smile he replied: 'Horskram is both wise and powerful, and I learn new things from him every day. If anyone can see us through, he will.'

Arik nodded absently, seemingly contented with this response. Then looking again at his younger brother he grinned over his empty horn.

'But by all the archangels, Adelko, it's good to see you!'

'It's good to see you too!' said Adelko, his joy returning to banish his dark thoughts.

They embraced again and called for another round of ale – the victorious camp was in high spirits and the quartermasters were being generous.

The two talked long into the night, of Narvik and their old life together, of shared memories, and of the other villagers including Aunt Madrice. Adelko was pleased to hear she was still in good health and shrewd as ever.

'She thinks of you always and says a prayer for you every night,' said Arik earnestly. 'You know, when this war is done and your private quest is finished, you should go back home and visit. Everyone would love to see you – and they'd be right proud of you too.'

A wistful sadness came over Adelko then. He had no idea when that would be, or if he would even live to do it.

When at last the curfew was called he rose, somewhat groggily after a fourth horn of ale, to bid his brother farewell and return to his tent. They arranged to meet again at the final victory feast, Almighty willing.

His mentor was fast asleep when he entered the tent they shared. Curling up on his pallet Adelko drifted off a few seconds later. He dreamed vivid happy dreams that night, of a joyous homecoming and long-lost family and friends rediscovered. The wan morning that awakened him was far from welcome.

⊰ CHAPTER XI ⊱

The Blade and the Noose

'Left, up, down, right, right, left, down, up, up, up, right, left!' Braxus called out the commands; the ring of steel on steel followed a split second later as Vaskrian responded to his commands.

They had been at it for a good fifteen minutes when the Thraxian called a halt.

'Good, very good,' he told the flushed squire. 'You defend well, and your footwork isn't bad at all – but it could be better. If you take service with me, I'll teach you some Thraxian moves in that area that should help you. In all honesty, you Northlendings have ever been better riders and swordsmen than us on the whole – but you don't move as well. I think we can be of benefit to one another, Vaskrian.'

The foreign knight was smiling encouragingly, but even so Vaskrian wasn't sure.

Could he really be seen to take service with a foreigner?

Braxus must have read his expression, for he suddenly frowned and said: 'Come, what ails thee lad? Is this proposition not agreeable to you?'

'It is, sire,' replied Vaskrian with uncharacteristic caution. 'It's just that... I still haven't told Lord Fenrig about Sir Branas, and now with Sir Ulfstan dead too...'

'... you are once more a squire without a knight to serve,' Sir Braxus finished for him. 'Just as I am a knight without a squire, for as I've told you poor Paidlin will never walk again without a crutch. Plus you saved my life on yonder battlefield – I owe you a boon, lad, and I mean to repay my debt in full.'

The handsome knight fixed him with keen green eyes. Vaskrian felt there was no hiding the complete truth from his shrewd prospective new master.

'All right, what you say is true enough, sire,' he blurted. 'It's just that, well, begging your knightly pardon, but you are a Thraxian. I'd always thought I'd finish my squirehood in service to a fellow countryman.'

To his surprise Braxus laughed.

'So that's what really troubles you!' he chuckled. 'Well, I could ask to have you flogged for such impertinence – but don't worry, I won't! As for your concerns about king and country, be at ease – it's not unheard of for knights to take foreign squires on. All that is required is the usual – a leave of pardon granted by your liege lord.'

Vaskrian bit his lip. 'Yes, that's the other thing I suppose – I'm not sure if Fenrig will...'

Grasping the squire by the shoulders Braxus looked him square in the eye. 'Listen to me, Vaskrian,' he said seriously. 'I may not stand on ceremony very often, but I am still a lord's son in my own right. One day I shall be a lord of men and command my own armies in the field. When that day comes, if you have served me as well as I think you will, I may be moved to grant you what you most desire.'

Vaskrian stared back at him, beautiful hope kindling his spirit. 'You mean...'

'I can't make men knights now, as you well know,' said Sir Braxus. 'But when I inherit my father's lands and title, I will be able to. And frankly I see no reason why common birth should preclude a doughty fighter with promise from being elevated to knighthood. I told you already, we Thraxians are not so stiff, so formal, as you Northlendings. We recognise merit when we see it.'

Vaskrian nodded, making up his mind quickly. Neither Branas nor Ulfstan had given him so much as a hint that he would ever have such reward for his hard work. And neither of those men had been heir to a jarldom – or whatever the Thraxian equivalent was.

Taking a knee in the mud, he laid his sword at the Thraxian's feet and said: 'Then I am yours to command, sir knight – take me where you will.'

Braxus laughed again. 'Get up! You Northlendings, so earnest all the time – no wonder you never produce any decent poets! First we must tie up a few loose ends with your soon-to-be erstwhile liege lord. Then we'll have oath-swearings aplenty, mark my words! Just leave me to do the talking...'

✛ ✛ ✛

Lord Fenrig's camp was a bustle of flesh and steel and leather. It was a cloudy morning but even so the men were in high spirits despite their hangovers. There would be ample opportunity to work off the revels of the previous night – word had been given that the King's Army would strike camp and march at noon, after the executions. Scouts had come in with early reports suggesting that Thule was falling back towards Salmor as expected.

Fenrig was conferring with his marshal in the midst of the tents being dismantled when they approached him. About them knights and soldiers were putting on their armour and preparing to leave.

'Sir Braxus of Gaellen, knight of Thraxia and heir to the Ward of High Dréuth, at your service!' he declared with a florid bow.

Lord Fenrig raised a bushy eyebrow at this, his marshal favouring the knight with a flat stare. Clearly they were both unimpressed.

Unabashed, Braxus continued: 'I am come to present to you a squire of your land, formerly in service to Sir Branas of Veerholt.'

Fenrig frowned at this. 'Formerly, you say? That doesn't bode well – yon squire is known to me. I elevated him above his station in return for a favour his father did me.'

That seemed an underwhelming way to describe having your life saved from a Wolding axe, but Vaskrian knew better than to make the point. Bluebloods – they hated to acknowledge their debts. Especially when that debt meant you owed everything to a mere commoner.

'As for Sir Branas, what of him?' demanded the Jarl sternly. 'He went missing some weeks ago – set out for a tourney at Harrang but never got there. Hasn't been seen since.'

'Yes, well I'm afraid you won't be seeing him again,' replied the Thraxian candidly. 'He perished in the wilderness.'

'I see,' replied Fenrig. 'How?'

'He perished in the wilderness,' repeated Braxus. 'In the forest you Northlendings call Tintagael, to be precise.'

Both men gaped. They looked impressed now.

'Tintagael?' exclaimed the marshal, a lean man of sixty winters with a shock of white hair. 'What madness possessed him to venture there?'

'It would appear,' continued Braxus as though he were telling a tale of ordinary events, 'from the account that young Vaskrian here has given me, that during the course of his journey to this Harrang you speak of, Sir Branas fell in with two friars of the Argolian Order.'

The two nobles exchanged uncertain glances.

'The monks appear to have gotten themselves into a spot of bother and were being chased by brigands for some unknown reason,' said Braxus. 'The old knight, valiant worthy that he was, swore an oath to protect them on their journey to Strongholm. During said journey they were pursued by said brigands, who greatly overmatched them. Branas – and it must be said his no less valiant squire here – were for facing them nonetheless, but the cowardly monks chose instead to seek uncertain refuge in Tintagael.'

Vaskrian was about to say something when he felt Braxus' foot kick his own sharply. He bit his tongue.

'During their sojourn there,' continued the knight, 'they were bewitched by the faerie folk, so that the poor lad cannot remember what passed.

But suffice to say, when they awoke from their ensorcelled nightmare the three of them were free of the forest – but of Sir Branas there was no trace.'

The two knights made the sign, their faces pale. Braxus returned the pious gesture with all the sincerity of a disgruntled peasant tugging his forelock at a sozzled and inept lord of the manor.

'Yon squire would have sought you out to tell you this awful tale – which I could barely extract from him, such a horrible ordeal as it clearly was – but upon arriving at Strongholm he was immediately seconded to one of the King's knights, Sir Ulfstan of Alfheim. That worthy, I am sad to report, was killed in the first charge at yesterday's battle. As such the youth is without a knightly master once again.'

'And how does this concern you?' asked Lord Fenrig coldly.

'I lost my own squire to Northland reavers during the journey to your fair country, and am too far from home to requisition another of my kinsfolk. As such, I would fain take Vaskrian of Hroghar into my service, by your leave… and with all due courtesy.'

The Northlending noblemen frowned at each other as they considered the request. Fixing Vaskrian with steely eyes, Lord Fenrig said: 'Thus far it is the foreigner who has spoken for you. Do you solemnly swear that he is telling the truth as you told it to him?'

'I do,' said Vaskrian bashfully.

'And do you solemnly swear that you have told him the truth?'

'I do,' the squire repeated.

Drawing himself up and puffing out his burly chest Fenrig turned to look at Braxus again.

'And you can vouch that you will provide for this young man, and keep him as a squire ought to be kept?'

Vaskrian winced inwardly. The question was pointed: it certainly would not have been asked of any Northlending heir to a lord.

'I can so vouch, my lord,' replied the Thraxian, taking the slight on the chin. 'In fact I shall keep him as well as any future lord of men can.'

Fenrig considered for a few more moments. Then he said: 'Very well, in that case I do formally release Vaskrian, esquire of Hroghar, from my service. From henceforth you shall be Vaskrian, esquire of High Dréuth, for as long as this worthy knight sees fit to keep you in his service. I trust you shall not forsake the noble ways of your countrymen in foreign company.'

'No my lord!' gushed Vaskrian, bowing low. 'I swear to thee I shall not.' He was too elated by his sudden change in fortunes to notice the second slight aimed at his new master.

'Rise,' said Fenrig peremptorily. 'I shall not trouble to ask what a Thraxian is doing fighting in the King's Army – I can only suppose that in these desperate times His Majesty has need of all the help he can get.'

Braxus looked as if he was about to answer this third slight when a familiar voice called out: 'Vaskrian! Churl of Hroghar!'

The voice was thick with anger and contempt. Though he had come far since he last heard it, it was unmistakeable.

Sir Rutgar was clad in full armour, carrying his helm under his arm as he strode over towards them. His head was swathed in a bloody bandage, but otherwise he appeared to be in rude health. Or rude at least.

'Well, well – fancy seeing you here,' he sneered as he drew level with Vaskrian. 'Still scrubbing pots for the real fighters, I hope?'

Vaskrian stood rigid, his face flushed scarlet. His moment of joy had been turned to ashes by the sudden reappearance of his arch rival. He wished with all his heart he could break Rutgar's smug face open, or cut his throat as he had done Derrick's.

Braxus eyed the newcomer coldly as he continued to pour scorn on his squire. When he was done the Thraxian spoke calmly. 'I do not believe we have met before...'

'Sir Rutgar,' replied the other knight haughtily. 'And who are you? A dirty foreigner by the looks – and sounds – of it.'

'Rutgar!' barked Fenrig. 'Guard your tongue! Chastising a low-born squire is one thing, but this is a lord's heir you now speak to – foreigner or no.'

Typical noble, Vaskrian reflected ruefully: Fenrig didn't permit his vassals the same liberties he was happy to take himself.

'Forgive me, my lord,' said Rutgar, favouring Braxus with a curt bow. 'I did not realise who you were.'

'*Sir* Braxus will do,' replied the Thraxian coldly. 'Where I come from we don't use lordly titles until we're actually lords ourselves. But I accept your apology for the insult offered to my person. Now I will accept likewise for the insult offered to my squire.'

Rutgar looked confusedly from Lord Fenrig to the unsmiling Thraxian and back again.

'It is as the Thraxian says it is,' confirmed Fenrig. 'I have just now released Vaskrian from my service. He serves Sir Braxus of Gaellen now.'

Rutgar stared at Vaskrian and Braxus. 'You surely don't expect me to apologise for insulting this common churl?' he spluttered.

'No,' replied Braxus evenly. 'I expect you to apologise *to* this common churl.'

'Steady now,' warned Lord Fenrig. 'This man is a knight in my service – he is of noble blood and will do no such thing.'

'Very well,' Braxus allowed. 'In that case I will be content with an apology made to myself on my squire's behalf.'

Rutgar turned red with rage. 'Fie on that! I'll not apologise! You have your answer, sir!'

'Then here is mine,' replied Braxus, still unsmiling. 'For the insult you have thus offered me, I have no choice but to seek satisfaction. When this war is done – if we are both still alive and able – I will seek that satisfaction in sight of man and deity. Think on your harsh and hasty words, sir knight, and ask about the camp for word of my deeds in the field. You shall find them worthy of consideration – I hope you are as skilled with lance and sword as you are with that sharp tongue of yours.'

The Thraxian motioned for Vaskrian to follow him, bidding a courteous farewell to the Jarl and his marshal. Rutgar simply stood and stared, a stupid expression printed across his stupid face.

'Well, that was a satisfactory piece of business,' breezed the knight as they walked back to their part of the camp. 'I knew that when Hroghar heard of your misadventures in Tintagael he would be loath to keep you on – that forest is dreadfully feared in these lands and he probably thinks you're cursed.'

But the horrors of Tintagael were the last thing on Vaskrian's mind.

'What about Rutgar? Do you really mean to fight him?'

'Well seeing as you are forbidden by chivalrous law from doing so, I hardly see any alternative,' replied Braxus casually. 'So, can you tell me anything about this Rutgar? Does he fight as well as he talks?'

'Why no!' said Vaskrian, grinning. And he told his new master of their mock fight the previous summer.

'Oh ho, now I see why he bears you such a grudge!' laughed Braxus. 'And of course now he is a knight and you are not, he too is bound by custom not to seek redress! What a merry bind! In truth, such a consideration should be beneath him now, but clearly his pride rankles him.'

'I wish I *could* fight him again,' muttered Vaskrian disconsolately, thinking of the unfair drubbing he'd gotten at Hroghar. That was weeks ago now, but the recollection still pained him far more than the bruises he'd received.

'You'll get plenty of worthier opponents before your life is done,' Braxus assured him, 'so rest easy! I'll take care of this Rutgar – assuming the next battle doesn't.'

That of course was a strong possibility. The coming conflict might take care of many of them.

✤ ✤ ✤

'Why are we here, Master Horskram?'

Adelko felt sick. Last night's joyous reunion with his brother was already a distant memory, cruelly pushed aside by the horrible spectacle he was now forced to witness. And he'd thought watching a battle was bad enough.

Horskram's face was unrelenting beneath his cowl. 'For your edification,' he replied flatly. 'This is what comes of war. Perhaps if you see it with your own eyes you will understand better what I was trying to tell you at Strongholm just before we marched.'

The executions had begun at dawn. Johan and two hundred knights were to meet the noose on the fields, in sight of the devastation they had helped to wreak. It was the last thing they would see with mortal eyes.

Most of the loyalists who had turned up to watch thought this a fitting punishment, although Adelko had heard one or two knights mutter that it was ill fitting a nobleman should be hanged, whilst a foreigner met a warrior's death – the surviving reavers and the seacarls commanding them were to be beheaded.

'The King insists that they are not technically traitors,' Horskram had explained. 'And so he will give them their due, barbarians or no. But then our King is an honourable man.'

Adelko felt his gorge rise as the next clutch of prisoners was shoved towards the row of gallows. They were hanging them a dozen at a time. The fresh corpses were piled in a mound beside the rest of the enemy dead. When the executions were done this would be set alight in accordance with custom. The loyalist dead would be given a proper burial by the surviving townsfolk of Linden.

Adelko winced as he caught the face of the second condemned noble from the right. Presumably a squire, he couldn't have been much older than he was. His arm was in a bloodied sling; his dirt-streaked face looked petrified in the wan light. Even at this range it was obvious he was weeping.

'Some of them... they're so young,' said Adelko hoarsely. He felt like crying himself.

'As were many of Thule's innocent victims,' answered Horskram. 'Blood must answer for blood – this is the King's justice. The last time he deviated from that tradition, he set in place the chain of events that led to this very uprising. Hard choices, and sacrifices regardless of which one you make – this is the way of the sword, Adelko. Mark it well.'

The twelve captives had their heads placed in nooses. The perfects said prayers for their souls, although Adelko had heard more than one spectator voice doubt as to whether the Almighty would allow traitors into His halls.

More than half the assembled spectators were commoners. Ordinary men and women: soldiers, victuallers, smiths and folk from Lindentown.

All here to see the blood-soaked fields play host to yet more killings. And they seemed to be enjoying it. The King had forbidden drinking among his army ahead of the midday march, but the drunken townsfolk were making a proper celebration of it. As they had done when they lynched collaborators among their own the previous evening, after Thule's forces fled Lindentown.

Freidheim himself presided over the executions. He sat in a makeshift chair on the same knoll from where they had watched the battle unfold. In his hand was a featureless black rod carved of ebony – the royal staff of execution. He held it aloft, his face implacable and unsmiling. Then he lowered it firmly.

The herald watching him from beside the gallows called out the command. 'Release!'

Adelko heard the squire scream. Was it 'no don't' or 'mother' he cried before the hangman's rope broke his neck? He would never know.

At least the next batch were all seasoned campaigners. Twelve of Thule's knights, disarmed and clad only in hose and undertunics, were shoved towards the makeshift podium. Most of them were injured, and one or two had lost limbs. Not that they would be missing them for much longer.

The soldiers conducting the executions were about to place the nooses when one of the condemned knights cried out.

'This is an outrage!' the nobleman yelled. He was a young man in his early twenties. He looked well-made and handsome: he wouldn't have seemed out of place among the knights Adelko had met on his adventures.

'What kind of King executes men of noble blood, hanging them as common criminals?' spluttered the knight as a burly serjeant forced a noose around his neck. 'My family can pay my ransom – all captured fighters of noble blood should be ransomed! This goes against the Code of Chivalry!'

The assembled crowd started booing and jeering the knight, but Lord Visigard turned to look at the King.

'He raises a fair point, Your Majesty,' said the old raven. 'This is in breach of all protocol. Are you sure you wish to proceed?'

The King turned to stare at the whiskered knight. Visigard swallowed hard. 'Forgive me, Your Majesty,' he stuttered. 'I spoke out of turn.'

Turning back to the gallows, the King shook his head. 'Nay Visigard, you spoke like an honourable knight. Unfortunately a King cannot always afford to behave as such – I've learned that the hard way.'

Raising the rod he brought it down with a swish.

'Release!' cried the herald.

Twelve more men danced on the gallows.

The executions went on. The crowd thickened as more people came to witness the spectacle. They were here to see the main event –

Freidheim had decreed that Lord Johan and the other captured barons and marshals would be the last Northlendings to be hanged.

As soldiers marched the barrel-chested jarl to his death, the crowd started baying. At least this execution wouldn't be so hard to watch – from what Adelko had heard the Jarl of Orack deserved to die as much as any man.

Johan took the podium along with the last of the captive rebels. There were only seven left – besides Johan there were two minor barons, Lord Porvald of Geldangg and Lord Valgaut of Horsen. The rest were marshals who had served the rebel lords, commanding their troops.

Johan's corpulent face cracked a sneer as the rope went around his neck. If he was scared he showed no sign of it – there would be no weeping from this one.

Nor would there be any contrition, as they soon learned. As a courtesy to their former high status, Freidheim permitted the seven condemned nobles a final word before they met their deaths.

'You have been found guilty of treason,' boomed the King, his stentorian voice silencing the raging crowd. 'You have conspired to murder the people of this realm under the spurious pretext of an unlawful war – have you anything to say before sentence is passed?'

Johan grinned. 'I have done what any man of noble blood would have in my position,' he bellowed. 'For years my people were subjugated, made to pay reparations for a just war against an oppressor! The Kingdom of Thule has a right to exist – a right that has been usurped for generations by the House of Ingwin, and the House of Caarl before that! I am no traitor, nor any man here – we stayed loyal to our true king, Krulheim of Thule!'

A defiant chorus of 'ayes' went up as the six other condemned men voiced their approval as one. They were quickly drowned out by the crowd screaming for their blood.

'Hang 'em high!' yelled one.

'Show them what happens when they kill for a false king!' cried another.

'Murderers all – make 'em swing!'

'Bastards dishonoured my daughter and slaughtered my sons...'

Lord Visigard was staring anxiously at the King. His face betrayed no emotion as he lifted the rod.

Down it came.

'Release!'

Seven more men danced. Johan's bloated corpse swung wildly on the gibbet. For one second Adelko thought the creaking thing might break, but it stayed firm.

A great cheer went up from the crowd.

The King turned to Visigard and nodded. The Royal Marshal gave the signal and soldiers began pulling the corpses off the gibbets, to add to the fly-encrusted mound nearby.

When that was done they started to dismantle the gallows. The crowd began to thin. The Northlending executions were over.

The Northlanders were up next.

'Doubtless the execution of foreign mercenaries will prove a less alluring spectacle for the good folk of Linden,' said Horskram grimly. 'Curious how treasonous killers seem to excite the passions more than merely opportunistic ones.'

Adelko had nothing to say to that. At least this was a fitting place for his mentor's gallows humour.

The beheadings were done twenty at a time. Sickened as he was, Adelko had enough presence of mind to register surprise when he learned these executions would be performed by knights.

'There isn't time to get a trained headsman to perform two hundred executions properly,' explained Horskram. 'So its death by the sword for our foreign friends. Only knights have the training to use greatswords – the next best thing to an axe for decapitation.'

Turning to one side Adelko vomited up his breakfast.

'Don't trouble yourself over much,' Horskram deadpanned. 'I think yon reavers will be honoured to die at the hands of fellow warriors.'

And it was true. To a man, the Northlanders met their deaths stoically, their heads held high before they were lopped from their shoulders. Some cried out before dying – but Adelko knew enough Norric to recognise a pagan prayer when he heard one.

'They are praying to Tyrnor,' said Horskram, making the sign and shaking his head disapprovingly. 'Whom they venerate as a god of war. They are beseeching him to recognise their deaths as dying in battle, so they can be admitted to the Halls of Eternal Fighting and Feasting in Gods-home.'

'Tyrnor... but that's the Norric name for Azazel, the archdemon embodying violence!' exclaimed Adelko, also making the sign. Azazel wasn't one of the Seven Princes of Perfidy, but he was a greater devil all the same, belonging to the First Tier. To worship such as a god was gross blasphemy, if not outright demonolatry.

His mentor turned to fix him with a steely look. 'They are pagan idolators, Adelko – what do you expect from such benighted souls?'

Adelko shook his head as he watched the hand-picked swordsmen behead the barbarian reavers. The bloody executions were bad enough – but these men were also condemning their very souls to everlasting torment. The sheer folly of it horrified him more than anything else he had seen today.

He had more prosaic reasons to be concerned by the Norric prayer, however.

'What's that last part they keep saying?' he ventured. 'Something about "our brothers will avenge us with pine and steel"?'

'It means just what it says – Hardrada will not forget this. He will build more ships and recruit more men. A new strife is stirring in the world – old treaties are being forgotten, peace breached. This I fear will be but the first foray from the Frozen Wastes.'

Adelko thought for a minute as soldiers seconding the knights gathered up corpses and heads and dragged them over to a second growing pile of flesh. 'But... this Hardrada lost two thousand men,' he said presently. 'How many more can he have?'

'Admittedly not many for now,' replied Horskram. 'He must have staked a lot on backing the winning side – I wouldn't be surprised if our mysterious friend the Sea Wizard had a hand in putting him up to such a huge gamble. But I'll warrant that he isn't the only Ice Thane contemplating a return to war and plunder. The other Northland princes will be stirring too before long.'

Adelko felt a chill descend over him as they dragged the last of the reavers' corpses off the field. So this was only the beginning. He thought of Braxus and Thraxia's troubles with its highland clans. His mentor was right – war was brewing across realms. And the sorcerous alliance they were working so hard to uncover might just be behind it all.

As the twin piles of corpses went up in flames he fished in his habit for a rag and placed it to his mouth and nose. Watching greasy smoke rise from the grisly bonfire of roasting flesh, he wondered if such things might not soon become commonplace.

For all his mentor's misgivings and efforts to the contrary, it looked for all the world as though the sword would have its day.

✛ ✛ ✛

By noon the clarions were sounding. As Freidheim's army, now dwindled to just over six thousand men, filed slowly past the stinking hecatomb of burning and rotting corpses, Adelko pressed the rag more tightly to his face.

He was thoroughly relieved when they moved out of sight and smell of it into green fields. Yet even these told a woeful tale, written across the land in burned villages and hanged corpses – victims of Johan's depredations. A few survivors ran towards the army and begged them for food to replace their scorched crops, but none was forthcoming.

As the sound of their hopeless pleas mingled with the cawing of greedy crows, Adelko found himself wishing he could stop up his ears as well.

⇥ CHAPTER XII ⇤

A Forced Detour

They rode hard through the night. At dawn the three of them veered off the main road to snatch a few hours' sleep against the side of a hillock. With nothing but their thick cloaks for a blanket and mattress, it was miserable sleep, but Hettie supposed they would have to get used to such hardship for a while.

They woke to find the outland mercenary roasting a piglet for a belated breakfast. A curiously fashioned bow and quiver of arrows were placed at his side, along with his falchion. His hood was still drawn over his head, despite the mild spring weather.

'You both slept longer than I would have liked,' he said in his strange high accent. 'I've made us something to eat. Better get it down you quick – I'd like to put more distance between us and Merkstaed. I've no doubt those fool watchmen will be making their report.'

Rubbing the sleep from her eyes Adhelina raised herself and stumbled over to the fire. She wasn't inclined to disagree – they had more reasons than their strange bodyguard could know for putting distance between themselves and the town her father owned.

As they bent to their coarse meal Adhelina glanced inquisitively at the foreign stranger.

'Where are you from?' she asked between perfunctory mouthfuls of unseasoned meat. 'I've met a fair few foreigners in my time but I don't recognise your accent.'

The hooded mercenary gave a short laugh that sounded more like a sneer. 'Nor should you. I hail from a far-off land, where things are more different than you could possibly imagine. Finish your food. We should leave soon.'

Adhelina did not demur. She had one last question though. 'You speak our language well. How long have you been in Vorstlund?'

'Less than a year,' replied the freesword in his sing-song voice. 'But I learn foreign tongues quickly. I spent many years in service in the Imperial lands to the east – their language shares similarities with yours, I think. So to learn Vorstlending, it was not so difficult.'

Adhelina nodded, doing her best to smile and be affable. 'I learn languages quickly too,' she said. 'I agree with you about the similarities between the Imperial tongue and our own.'

But the freesword said nothing further, and finished his breakfast in silence.

⁘ ⁘ ⁘

They rode hard for the rest of the day, passing the odd travelling merchant and drover. Close to nightfall they passed an inn, and though Hettie implored her mistress to stop she refused.

Their nameless protector agreed that it was too risky, and so once more they sought refuge in the wilderness, bedding down in a copse of birch trees in some hills overlooking the highway. Their meal was a meagre one – strips of meat from the morning's kill supplemented by some of the food Hettie had purloined from the castle kitchens, washed down with mouthfuls of water taken from a nearby stream.

The weather was fairly clement, but even so the night-time brought a chill. Their laconic guardian built a small fire to warm them. During their day's journey he had said little. He never removed his hood, making him seem all the more sinister.

Hettie didn't trust him one shred, and made sure her mistress knew this several times. Adhelina consoled herself with the thought that at least he had not tried to rob them that morning while they were asleep.

Even so, as she watched the freesword sat crossed-legged before the fire, slowly and methodically sharpening his falchion to a razor edge, she felt a shiver run down her spine.

Just who was this mysterious character – could he really be trusted to get them to Meerborg safely? And even if he could, what then?

That she could sell some of her jewellery and reward him richly for his services, she did not doubt. But the truth was that she carried all her worldly fortune on her – he had only to suspect she was lying, and he could reach out and take everything...

She had seen him fight at Merkstaed using non-lethal force, effortlessly incapacitating three able-bodied men – two of them fighting types, albeit of the lowest kind. The hardened outlander could make light work of them both if he wished.

Thinking these uncomfortable thoughts, Adhelina caught him gazing at her intently. Drawing her cloak more tightly around her, she retired to sleep in the crook of a tree.

✧ ✧ ✧

The next morning Hettie rose and went to make her water on the edge of the copse. From there she could see the highway, and the flowing waters of the Graufluss beyond it in the pale light. She had just finished and was about to rise when she caught her breath and froze.

Riding along the highway at a quick pace was a small group of knights. They were lightly armoured and mounted on swift coursers – as she peered down at them she caught the flash of weak sunlight on the surcoat of the foremost.

It was too far to be sure, but the colours looked familiar... their wearer had long flame-coloured hair that streamed behind him in a steady breeze...

She caught her breath. *Balthor.*

The men rode past her, oblivious to her presence above the road, rounded a bend, and were lost to sight. Getting up she scrambled back towards the camp, breathing hard.

She found Adhelina there alone, checking their bags and making ready to leave. The fire had been stamped out. Of the outlander there was no sign.

'Adhelina!' she gasped.

Her mistress turned to her, suddenly anxious as she caught the look on Hettie's face.

'Hettie? What's the matter?' she ventured.

'I was at toilet on the edge of the copse,' breathed Hettie frantically. 'And... I think I saw Sir Balthor, riding with a company of knights! It was hard to be certain at that distance, but I'm fairly sure it was him!'

Her mistress frowned, her face buckling up in consternation.

'But... how can they have overtaken us?' she mused aloud. 'We had at least six hours' head start on them... unless... Oh no, they must have changed horses yesterday and ridden through the night to catch up with us!'

Hettie's heart sank as her mistress confirmed her own fearful notion: as a knight of the land Balthor would be able to requisition fresh steeds at will from any inn, castle or homestead he passed.

'How many did you see?' demanded Adhelina.

'Besides him there were three others,' replied Hettie.

'Four fresh horses would be easily obtainable by a knight of Balthor's esteem riding on urgent business of my father,' said Adhelina dolefully. 'Oh Hettie, what fools we've been! I should have reckoned on this – our pursuers have an advantage that we don't!'

'Yes, along with a knight's stamina,' added Hettie disconsolately. 'I'm not sure I'd be up to riding day and night without sleep, even if our poor horses were!'

At that moment they were distracted by the sound of the outlander returning.

'Where have you been?' asked Hettie unreasonably. Her nerves were clearly showing.

'I went to answer nature's call, just the same as you,' he replied affably from beneath his hood. 'Are the ladies ready to depart? We have another good day's riding before us, but after that I think we should reach Meerborg – '

'We aren't going to Meerborg,' said Adhelina abruptly. 'That is to say... we can't, not by the main road. We need to strike off, that way – ' She pointed vaguely north. 'Into the wilderness. We must stay off the road, for the next few days at least.'

If they could have seen his face the mercenary would no doubt have looked surprised. He paused for a few moments, before saying: 'I see. Something you have seen on the road, I think, discourages you from using it.'

The two damsels glanced at each other, then turned back and nodded as one.

'We must find another route to Meerborg,' repeated Adhelina firmly. 'One less direct. You shall be paid for your extra efforts of course.'

The mercenary paused again. 'You will at least tell me what it is you have seen that frightens you so,' he said. 'For I cannot protect you without knowing what dangers pursue us.'

Adhelina frowned, then said: 'We are indeed pursued – my lady in waiting saw armed men on the road just now.'

'I see,' said the freesword neutrally. 'And how can you be sure that this has anything to do with what happened in Merkstaed? Or is it more to do with the reasons why you needed swift horses in the first place?'

In the wan light of dawn they could not see his eyes, but Hettie felt sure they would have had a cunning glint to them if they were visible.

'Perhaps a little of both,' replied Adhelina, doing her best to look expressionless. 'But if you've to have any chance of getting us safely to Meerborg and claiming your reward, you had better do as we say immediately.'

✣ ✣ ✣

The way was not easy. This part of Dulsinor was mostly hilly and strangled by dense undergrowth, and there were no roads to follow. Several times they had to dismount and lead their horses through precarious ways. It was past noon when they were forced to abandon the idea of striking directly north before veering east to reach the Free City.

'We cannot do it this way,' said the outlander firmly after they had stopped at a stream to water their horses and eat a little. 'We must turn back for the road or seek another direction altogether.'

Adhelina pulled out her map and consulted it.

'Look,' she said presently, pointing at it, 'we can strike east – that should get us out of these dreadful hills! Then we can join up with the east-west road here that leads from the Argael Forest to the Free City and approach it from the west.'

The cowled mercenary peered over Adhelina's shoulder to study the map. For an instant Hettie was tempted to reach out and pull the hood back – his continual air of mystery was maddening. Recalling the fight at Merkstaed she thought better of it.

'Yes, I think we could do this,' he replied at length. 'It should take us no more than a day to get out of the hills if we head north-west, then we can skirt their edges and journey north-east to catch the eastern road to Meerborg.'

A merry zigzag, Hettie thought disconsolately. But she kept her opinion to herself.

✣ ✣ ✣

The journey out of the hill-lands took them longer than expected, for they had to make several detours and became lost more than once. It was approaching dusk on the day after they had looked at the map when they decided to make camp again for the night. At least there was little chance of Balthor and his men finding them in the middle of this blasted wilderness, Adhelina reflected.

Twilight was filtering through the branches of a few ragged trees in the dell they had chosen when the sound of cracking twigs alerted them to fresh danger. Looking up the three wayfarers saw four raggedly dressed men descending the hills towards them. They carried rude axes and rusty swords. It was clear by the looks on their faces that they did not mean well.

'Greetings strangers,' said the outlander in an unruffled voice, rising slowly from the fire he had been busy preparing. 'May we be of any assistance?' His hand moved lightly to the hilt of his sword.

The biggest of the men, a greasy unkempt fellow of middling height and more than middling girth, sneered, revealing teeth that were blackened and rotted.

'Strangers?' he replied in a voice that was surprisingly soft. 'I don't think we're the strangers...! You're on our territory, y'see, and there's a fine to pay... those ladies look ever so pretty, and ever so *rich*...'

The four men edged closer, moving down into the dell, sickly grins on their dirt-streaked faces.

'Why of course,' replied the outlander affably. 'If you'll just let me get you something...'

He reached down towards his bag. At that moment the four outlaws charged with a single yell. In the flash of an eye the outlander came up fast, drawing his dirk from his boot and sending it cartwheeling through the air to impale the lead brigand through the throat. The other three closed on him.

Stepping back he drew his falchion with blinding speed, parrying the first clumsy stroke and slaying another outlaw with a lightning riposte, trailing an arc of blood through the gloaming as he opened his jugular.

The remaining two pressed him hard, but the foreigner moved with astonishing swiftness, dancing and whirling around and between them. When he cut down another brigand in a shower of red the last turned and began to run back up the dell. Without hesitation the mercenary reached for his bow, and nocking a shaft he loosed. The last outlaw fell with a scream, the arrow lodged in his back.

He wasn't quite dead. Adhelina winced at the sight of him trying to claw his way up out of the dell, groaning pitifully all the while. Calmly walking over to the dead leader and pulling the dirk from his throat, the outlander scrambled up the hill and grasped the final brigand's head by his mop of lank hair.

The outlaw made a last desperate attempt to save himself, reaching around frantically and clutching at the mercenary's hood. Without respite the outlander pushed his knee into the brigand's injured back, forcing him down before cutting his throat from ear to ear.

As the last outlaw choked to death on his own blood, their saviour hopped lightly back down into the middle of the dell, where the two damsels were staring aghast. The whole fight had taken less than a minute.

Perhaps the thrill of battle had temporarily robbed the freesword of caution, for he had apparently forgotten about his hood, pulled back by the desperate strength of a dying man. The twilight showed a face that was ugly and rude, crowned by short tufts of hair cropped irregularly, with keen eyes and tanned skin. A face that was unmistakeably female.

'But... you're a *woman*!' gasped Hettie, completely forgetting the slaughter she had just witnessed.

'It would certainly appear so,' replied the outlander with a wry smile, sitting down to clean her weapons.

Adhelina was staring at her benefactress incredulously. 'But, no woman can fight like that! It doesn't make sense!'

'Where I come from, only the women fight,' said the swordswoman dismissively as she began to clean her dirk. 'And I can assure you they fight a lot better than yon brigands did.'

Adhelina gasped as her copious reading provided her with the answer to another riddle.

'You belong to the fabled tribe of Harijans that dwell across the Great Inland Sea!' she exclaimed. 'Where women fight and rule as men do!'

'No, not as men do,' corrected the woman warrior, spitting contemptuously as she finished cleaning her blade. 'We fight and rule *better* than men do. Men are good for only a few things,' she added with a wolfish grin that Hettie found disturbing. 'We keep some of them as thralls, to serve us as menials and provide us with children – and satisfaction to those of us who are too weak to live without such pleasures of the flesh. When we are done with them we cut their throats, just as I did with yonder brigand.'

'How barbaric and awful!' exclaimed Adhelina in disgust.

'Oh really?' replied the Harijan, fixing her with keen black eyes. 'And is it not the same but in reverse in these lands? The Imperial folk are a little better than your people in this regard, but since I am in this country I have been sickened by what I see. You women should *fight* – then perhaps your menfolk would have a reckoning on their hands!'

'But how can we fight when men have all the power?' demanded Adhelina angrily. 'Why, all my life I've been cossetted, aye even though I am a woman noble born! It took all our ingenuity just to escape the castle I'd grown up in - '

Adhelina stopped dead as she realised what she had just said.

The Harijan was watching her keenly now. 'Yes, go on – do not stop. I think it is time you told me more of yourself. After all, today you have learned more of me.'

Adhelina blushed and looked at Hettie uncertainly. She'd get no help there – her oldest friend was dumbstruck. Struggling to control her rising rage, the runaway heiress of Dulsinor cursed herself inwardly.

She stood like that for a while, clenching and unclenching her hands, forcing herself to calm down. The Harijan sheathed her dirk and picked up her bloody falchion to clean. She glanced up at the damsels expectantly as she ran a crimson cloth up and down the curved blade.

Taking a deep breath Adhelina sat down on another rock near the Harijan. Hettie followed suit.

'If I tell you my name, and that of my companion, may we at least know yours?' she asked, trying to sound charming.

A smile creased the Harijan's ugly brown face. Her skin was like the boiled leather she wore for armour. 'Of course. It is Anupe. At your service.' She returned to cleaning her falchion.

Adhelina told her their story whilst Hettie busied herself making the fire, keeping a watchful eye on Anupe all the time. She held back the details of her wealth.

When she had finished, Anupe sat back, stretched out her wiry arms, and whistled.

'Well! That is a fine tale to hear in this country, and no mistake! Perhaps I was wrong to dismiss the courage of the women of the Vorstlendings, for it is clear that you have taken a risk in making a bid for your precious freedom! And so you plan to take ship from Meerborg for the Empire and set yourself up there – but I hope these riches you speak of are enough, less my reward of course. Life in the imperial cities is expensive, I can assure you!'

'Yes well, as to your reward doubt it not,' said Adhelina guiltily. 'But as for my own fortunes, I have skills I can rely on should my coin dwindle.'

'Oh really?' inquired Anupe. 'And what skills would a pampered noblewoman of the so-called Free Kingdoms have to offer a civilised folk such as the Imperials, I wonder?'

'I am an accomplished healer,' replied Adhelina proudly. 'And my book-learning surpasses most of my countrymen.'

'As to the latter, that will help you little in the Imperial lands,' replied the Harijan. 'For all well-born folk there are taught the strange symbols of knowledge. But as a healer, if you are as good as you say you are, you might find a living of sorts... and from the story of your escape it seems you have knowledge of other herbs?'

Adhelina flushed, feeling guilty again.

'Well, yes, I know how to prepare all sorts of poultices and concoctions – not all of them benign to tell the truth.'

'Benign?'

'For the good.'

'Ah, you speak of poisons! Then in that case rest assured you shall have work aplenty in the Empire! Your future is secure, if only you can get there!'

Adhelina swallowed nervously. She did not care much for Anupe's gallows humour, especially given it seemed to carry a grain of truth. But a more pressing matter was on her mind. Screwing up her courage she voiced it.

'So... knowing what you know and who pursues us – you'll still help us?'

Anupe took a deep breath as she mulled this over. The stars were appearing in the clear night sky. Adhelina tried to focus on those and the warmth of the fire she had lit, ignoring the corpses around them. She had seen enough dead men in her father's last war not to be traumatised, though the prospect of bedding down for the night with the dead was unpleasant.

'That depends,' said Anupe, answering her question at last. 'If you are concerned that your story makes me afraid to help, don't worry! For Anupe is never afraid of men! In fact, if anything it makes me wish to help you even more – the pair of you are the closest to brave women I have yet met in this accursed country! But there still remains the matter of my reward, for I too wish to go to the Empire.'

That surprised Adhelina. 'Really? Then why did you leave it in the first place?'

Anupe sighed. 'My tale is a long one, much longer than yours, and it is getting too late to tell it all. Enough for now to say that I have spent years wandering far from my homeland, which I did not leave willingly. I spent some of those years in service with the Imperial Legions, which sometimes take in Harijan recruits such as myself. But certain complications arose... and I thought it best to leave the Empire for a while.'

She scowled, spitting into the fire as if for emphasis. Adhelina tried not to show how appalled she was by the Harijan's lack of civilised manners. Oblivious to her aristocratic sensibilities, Anupe continued: 'So I took ship to Meerborg nearly a year ago. I had hoped to find work as a freesword in this land, but here they dislike women who fight even more than the Imperials do! This is why I have been obliged to wear a hood – quite ridiculous! Yet the only way I can get any work is by hiding my true sex – I, a proud member of the Harijan race, lowered to this!'

Her eyes flared angrily. She had seen the Harijan knock three men senseless and kill four more in the space of a few days, but this was the first time Adhelina had seen her genuinely angry.

'No,' she continued. 'I have had enough of this place. I want to buy passage on a merchant ship back to the Twin Cities, the great trading ports of the northern imperial lands. I will take my chances in the Empire again. Who knows? Perhaps I will even make the long journey home, though I doubt my people will accept me now.'

'Why?' asked Adhelina. There was a sadness in Anupe's voice now. In spite of the immense difference between them Adhelina felt a growing empathy for the embattled Harijan.

'Because,' sighed Anupe, 'my people believe that once a Harijan has been taken into captivity, she is tainted by the customs of men. We are a fiercely independent folk, and we guard that independence jealously.'

'I see.' Adhelina felt as though she understood, but wasn't sure she really did.

'But at least back in the Empire I have some chance of a life,' Anupe continued. 'So... that brings us back to the question of my reward. The more money I have to take with me, the better my chances are.'

'You will have your reward, as I have said, once we get to Meerborg.'

'Mmm, yes, so you have said. But one thing concerns me – this money of yours, is it not your father's in truth? And I presume even now his knights –

this Balthor you spoke of – will be at Meerborg. Will he not force whatever merchant you have entrusted your valuables to there to hand them over?'

Adhelina had to think fast. 'The valuables I speak of were secreted away a fortnight ago,' she dissembled nervously. 'I managed to have Hettie here bribe a passing merchant into taking them with him back to Meerborg, to keep them there under lock and key. The merchant does not know my true identity – he is under strict instructions not to release them to anyone but Hettie, who gave him a false name. He will of course know her, and only her, by sight. So you see there is absolutely no connection between my name and the valuables in question.'

✤ ✤ ✤

Hettie gulped nervously as her mistress spun her elegant web of lies. She really didn't like being embroiled in them, especially not without being told first. Anupe frowned as she considered their story.

As she waited nervously for the Harijan to reply, Hettie could not help thinking that the lie probably would have been a good idea in reality – travelling incognito with all her mistress's worldly goods on her person now seemed like the height of foolishness. But then if everyone thought as well on the spot as they did in hindsight there'd be no need for wise men or seers, she supposed.

'Very well,' said Anupe at last. 'I am content on this point, and I am trusting your word that my reward will be a good one – for if not, know that your father's men will seem like nothing next to my anger!'

She put a calloused brown hand meaningfully on the hilt of her falchion. Hettie was about to protest but Adhelina waved her back.

'Rest assured your reward when we get to Meerborg will be more than ample,' she said firmly.

'Very good,' said Anupe nodding. 'That just leaves one final problem. How we get into Meerborg.'

The two damsels looked at her nonplussed. 'But, we've already taken care of that,' said Adhelina. 'We take the east road and – '

Anupe laughed and shook her head. 'Are you so blind to what is in front of you?' she asked. 'You have just said yourselves that this Balthor and his men will be riding into Meerborg even now. Oh, he may not be able to find your hidden treasure, but he can certainly pay a visit to the merchant houses and tell them to be on the lookout for a runaway bride and her servant! The merchant houses rule Meerborg – that might not affect your treasure if you have concealed your identities as well as you say, but it will make it difficult for you to get into the city...'

Adhelina and Hettie exchanged pained looks. They had tried so hard to be cunning in planning their escape, but it was rapidly becoming clear that they were out of their depth.

'But, surely if we ride hard the next few days, we can reach the city and slip in?' offered Hettie, doing her best to sound optimistic.

Adhelina shook her head. 'No, no, Anupe's right – it's too risky,' she said. 'All the guards will be alerted by the time we reach Meerborg. They'll probably be expecting us to enter by the south gate, but they'll just as likely notify the guards on the other gates too. Dammit! What do we do now?'

'It is indeed a problem to consider,' replied the Harijan laconically.

They sat in sullen silence for a while. The night cold drew in. The fire continued to crackle. The dead men stayed dead.

Then Adhelina looked up, her eyes sparkling in the firelight.

'There's one way they won't think to check,' she said firmly. 'And even if they did they probably wouldn't be able to do it effectively.'

'We are – how do you say? – all ears,' said Anupe.

'We take ship *to* Meerborg,' Adhelina replied. 'It's the last thing they'll expect! We arrive there via the docks, transact our business as quickly as we can, and then take another ship bound for the Empire! Think on it – Meerborg's harbour is said to be busy night and day, it would be so much easier for us to slip in unnoticed!'

Anupe nodded slowly, considering this. 'Yes, yes,' she said presently. 'I have seen the docks there many times – what you say is true enough. But from where do we sail to Meerborg?'

Adhelina scrabbled around in her bag for her map, drawing it out and holding it to the light.

'There's a fishing village up here,' she began, pointing to a place marked about twenty miles up the coast from the Free City.

Anupe shook her head. 'No, that will never do,' she said. 'A fishing village would not have the boats to take us, never mind our horses. And their small vessels would not be fit for such a voyage in any case.'

'Then what?' Adhelina bit her lip as she scoured the map, following the north-westerly coastline of the country she was trying to flee.

'We need to widen our detour,' she said finally. 'The nearest port that services Meerborg lies across the border, in Northalde – we need to get to Port Urring, and double back by sea from there.'

Anupe raised a raven eyebrow. 'You want to go to Northalde? You do know there is a war going on there, don't you? The last I heard, trade between Meerborg and Strongholm had all but ceased.'

'Strongholm and Meerborg yes,' pressed Adhelina. 'But not necessarily Urring – it's located in the south, where the secessionist rebels are based, if I remember rightly. At least we have some chance – and if the Northlendings are too busy fighting a war against each other, then all the less chance that they'll take any notice of a runaway noblewoman from Vorstlund.'

Anupe laughed again, though this time there was less of a sneer to her laughter. 'Hah, you may not fight like a warrior, but you certainly think like one, Adhelina of Dulsinor!' she chuckled. 'Well then, that is settled – Meerborg by way of Urring! So it seems I am destined to see one more "free" kingdom before I return to the Empire! I trust that my reward will be increased to allow for the extra time spent protecting you.'

Adhelina sighed. 'The reward will be everything you could want it to be,' she answered. 'You have my word and my life on it.'

Hettie listened to this exchange in silence. And she didn't like what she heard.

'My lady?' she said in a small voice.

'Yes, what is it?' asked her mistress, somewhat impatiently.

'Won't we have to travel through the Argael to get to Northalde?'

Adhelina stared at her impatiently. 'Yes, what of it?'

'It's just that... my family used to say it was haunted – they say it's inhabited by Wadwos, and that a woods witch lives there...'

'Well, we'll just have to take our chances with the Wadwos and the witches, Hettie,' replied Adhelina testily, stuffing the map back into her bag. 'As long we stick to the main road through the forest, we should be fine.'

As they turned in for the night, Hettie couldn't help thinking that this was just what they had initially intended for their journey to Meerborg. But so far, sticking to the main road had proved more than difficult.

Wrapping herself tightly in her cloak, she tried not to think about the journey ahead, or the four dead men in the dell who had gone to sleep forever.

⊷ CHAPTER XIII ⊷

Bloodshed And Sorcery

'This had better work.' Krulheim's face was anxious as he surveyed his troop formations from the battlements of Salmor, the first castle he had taken in his rebellious campaign.

Standing tall next to him, a full head above his own, the sorcerous priest he called ally scowled.

'Have my ministrations failed you yet?' he asked curtly. 'Did my moat magic not dismay the enemy the last time they sought to relieve this castle? Did I not bid the waves carry our ships more swiftly? Did my shielding charm not protect you on the field of battle? Did the rains not come to aid your escape when all seemed lost?'

His good eye glinted like hoarfrost as he asked the questions pointedly and methodically. It was the last one that rankled most, even more than the penultimate question.

'It was a retreat, not an escape,' replied Thule irritably. 'How was I to know Freidheim would employ such devilish tactics? Pulling out his men only to have them return to the field – he fights like a heathen Sassanian, not a true knight!'

'True knights don't use magic charms to protect them from injuries in the field,' Ragnar reminded him with an icy smile.

Krulheim turned on him at that, his eyes blazing. 'Aye, that much I know! 'Twas you who insisted!' he cried. 'If it were not for your accursed magic runes daubed on my body, I'd have claimed Prince Freidhoff's life fairly!'

'If it were not for the magic runes daubed on your body, it would be a bloodstained corpse by now,' snapped the Sea Wizard. 'Everyone saw the High Commander best you fairly – it is only thanks to my runecasting that you live!'

The Young Pretender turned away, stung by the truth of the words. Putting his head in his hands he leaned against the crenelation and groaned. His every chivalrous instinct had screamed out against submitting to the Sea Wizard's diabolical ministrations, yet he had been so persuasive...

in this as he was in everything. In fact the would-be King of Thule found it daily harder to refuse him anything.

'Why? Why?' he sighed desperately, looking helplessly at the grim skies up above. 'I should not have consented to this – our defeat at Linden is the Almighty's punishment for turning to your sorcerous tricks instead of fighting fairly like real men!'

'The Almighty only helps those who help themselves,' replied the Northland priest implacably. 'And did you not help yourself? My charm made your flesh as invulnerable to a blade as the ocean waters – just as I said it would. And now you have rid yourself of a powerful enemy as a result of it – is this not helping yourself?'

The pagan priest's logic was relentless, but all the same Krulheim knew in the depths of his soul that he had erred. Perhaps fatally.

'Leave me,' he said abruptly. 'Send for Jord, I would have words with him.'

'As you wish, Your Royal Highness,' replied the priest with a nonchalant air before leaving. He still deferred to Thule, but the hapless prince increasingly felt that his blasphemous ally was ruled by no one.

Presently Sir Jord arrived to join him on the battlements.

'You called for me, Your Highness?' he asked. His face looked more careworn and lined than usual. He had not sustained any injuries during the battle for Linden, but he looked grave.

'Yes,' replied Thule impatiently. 'I wanted to know how the battle formations were going.'

Jord raised an eyebrow at this obvious question. 'They are just as you see before you,' he answered with an expansive sweep of his arm. 'We have a thousand levies and three hundred men-at-arms drawn up before the castle moat and gates. Another thousand conscripts are up in the hills to our right, with seven hundred archers for company. We've another two hundred ensconced in the hills to the left – just enough to keep their scouts or any advance sorties at bay. We don't want them creeping up on us from that direction as they did last time. The palisade straddling the gap between the hills and the castle is nearly complete – we'll put another seven hundred bowmen behind that. I've kept back the last two hundred for the castle walls, along with the original two-hundred strong garrison of men-at-arms you left here.'

Thule nodded grimly. 'And the knights?' he asked.

Jord hesitated before answering. 'They shall be deployed as you saw fit to deploy them,' he said neutrally.

'You mean as Ragnar saw fit to deploy them,' answered the prince reproachfully.

The battle-weary marshal appeared to be about to answer this, then stopped himself. A few moments of silence slid by. Then, abruptly, Jord reached out and put a calloused hand on his liege's arm.

'Your Highness, it is not too late to change your mind,' he said with sudden urgency. 'I beg of you, do not do this. For too long we have been in thrall to this foreign devil-worshipper – the Almighty is punishing us for it!'

Thule shut his eyes tightly, his face anguished. 'It is... too late,' he said resignedly. 'We have come too far to turn back now. This is my last gambit, Jord – I must and will hold Salmor. It is our only chance of making good our secession.'

'Then let us hold it as befits true knights!' rejoined Jord earnestly. 'Let us ride now to meet them in the field!'

Thule shook his head sorrowfully. 'I chanced all on a lightning strike, and chance has failed me. Our scouts confirm that they now have twice the number of knights and trained foot as we do. We exceed them only in archers and conscript levies – and half the latter have deserted us, the craven peasants!'

'We exceeded them when we rode against them at Linden,' his marshal reminded him. 'And they managed to defeat us! Come, let us turn the tables on them! They won't be expecting us to ride out again – let us discuss a real battle plan, you and I!'

But Thule only shook his head again. 'Nay, Jord, it is too late for such changes of heart. Our scouts tell us the enemy are nigh two days' march from us – soon they will be upon us. We must trust once more to the Sea Wizard's machinations and hope they are enough to see us through.'

Jord said nothing. He looked downcast and sullen, like a man who has given up a last fleeting hope of success.

'Then if that will be all, I'd better return to my duties,' was all he said.

Krulheim was about to let him go when suddenly he turned and said: 'One last thing. Tell the seneschal on your way out to have the servants prepare me a bath.'

Jord looked at him askance. Bathing on the eve of war was hardly commonplace – some even held that doing so cleansed a man of the natural oils that gave him his vitality.

'Aye, my prince, I will do so, if that is what you wish,' he said in bafflement.

'I do so wish it,' muttered Thule, returning to stare across the fields and hills of the land he had so briefly conquered. 'If this enterprise is to fail then I will meet Azrael valiantly, as befits a true knight.'

✤ ✤ ✤

Dusk was drawing in when the King's Army reached the vicinity of Salmor. It was too dark to see the castle clearly: its high turrets and battlements sketched black lines against the dwindling skies, surrounded by the rough humps of the hill-land ranges to either side. Nestled between these, flat colourless fields beckoned sinisterly.

Adelko was saddle-sore: they were nearly two weeks out of the capital, and the novice had thoroughly missed the comfort of his bed in the palace. At least now he was beginning to forget what that felt like – he was well and truly back to a hard life of adventuring.

Next to him Vaskrian fidgeted in his own saddle. Adelko knew him well enough by now to fathom that his hardy friend's discomfort was anything but physical. Now he was a squire to Sir Braxus he rode with them in the King's contingent – but that kept him apart from the main body of the army. And Vaskrian did so love to be in the thick of things.

The squire frowned as he watched the army set up camp, deploy scouts and post sentries. He'd lost his helm in the Battle of Linden, and acquired a fresh bandage instead, which he'd removed on the last day of the march. Either he healed quickly, or he prided his appearance above his health. Probably the latter – Adelko had heard knights were full of such bravado.

Braxus gave the order for Vaskrian to see to their tent and horses. Vaskrian nodded and dismounted. The Thraxian repeated the command in his own tongue for the benefit of his compatriots. There were only four of them left, besides Braxus. Sir Regan had been left at Linden to recover from his injuries. His squire had stayed behind to tend him. That left Sir Bryant and Sir Vertrix and their own squires. They seemed to have escaped the fight largely unscathed – except for Bryant's squire, who had earned himself a gash running the length of his cheek. Another inch and he would have lost an eye. The cut had been crudely stitched up – if he felt any pain the lad was putting a brave face on it.

A liveried squire to the House of Ingwin hustled over to see to the monks' needs as he had done throughout the march. He was some young lordling from the House of Vandheim; of an age with Vaskrian, he could not have been more different otherwise. Looking at the pudgy youth, whose physique was scarcely better than his own, Adelko supposed that not all the scions of Sir Torgun's house could be heroes.

As an esquire assigned personally to the King, at least he'd get to stay out of trouble – for now.

✣ ✣ ✣

When the pavilions had been set up the army settled down to bivouac. Ale and wine were strictly rationed – enough to dull the nerves and get a good night's sleep before fighting, but no more. The evening meal was a subdued one, but lack of drink wasn't the only reason for that.

The journey south had been enough to dampen even the brightest of spirits.

They had found both Rookhammer and Blakelock burned-out shells, part of the scorched-earth tactics the enemy had adopted in retreat. Worse, the garrison at Blakelock been put to the sword, sharing the earlier fate of their brethren at Rookhammer. Hewn and rotting corpses disgraced the precincts of both castles, another grisly feast for the crows and the flies and the worms. Of Thule's own troops there had been no sign.

'A ruthless tactic, but a sensible one,' Braxus had sighed as they rode past, leaving the corpses in their wake. 'Thule knows he'll need every advantage he can get, now his own numbers are dwindling.'

'It's unchivalrous!' Vaskrian had raged, unable to hold his temper. 'Those men had surrendered, at the original siege of the castle!'

'Then perhaps they should not have surrendered,' replied Braxus, unsmiling. 'War does not always have a place for chivalry – think on all those men your King hanged at Linden. And it's chivalrous notions on his part that led to this uprising in the first place.'

Vaskrian had said no more at that, and ridden on in sullen silence. Adelko had glanced sidelong at his mentor, half-expecting him to chime in, but he'd held his peace. And yet something in the way he had looked at the Thraxian then had suggested a new-found respect for the young knight.

But it wasn't the slaughtered garrisons that troubled Adelko most, bad as that was. During the week-long march from Linden they passed scores of burned villages, mass gallows like the one just beyond Lindentown screaming a silent testimony to the ugly privations of war. A once bountiful land had been reduced to a living hell on earth. Adelko found himself making the sign repeatedly.

Here and there the odd cluster of white-robed Marionite monks could be seen doing their best to tend the sick and wounded. But perhaps worse than the bite of blade, the awful desperation of starvation was setting in, for the attackers had pillaged all the ready food they needed before slaughtering livestock and burning fields of crops. As the unyielding spectacle of desolation unfolded around him, Adelko fancied that the Fallen One's city of burning brass could not have furnished worse.

'In fact this is just what Abaddon lusts to see when he peers from his dark kingdom into the mortal vale,' said Horskram when Adelko gave voice to that thought. 'For though he had a hand in the world's making, he would rather see it ruined and laid waste than suffer us to live in it unruled by his will.'

'But why doesn't the Almighty *do* something?' Adelko had wailed. 'It's His creation that's being ruined!'

'His creation, that He gave to us, to do with freely as we will,' Horskram reminded him. 'If we choose to wreak havoc on His gift, He cannot intervene – He has only done so once in all of human history, as you will recall. And even that was not without great cost and human suffering.'

'But... why could He not have made us *better*?' the novice persisted. 'Why give us all this bounty and make us so flawed?'

'Our flaws come from the hand of the Fallen One,' Horskram sighed. 'Perhaps it is true as some sects claim that the Almighty is not truly omniscient, not so far as his archangels are concerned anyway. For it is written that in the Dawn Of Time He trusted Abaddon, the wisest of all archangels, and could not foresee the poison he would inject into His creation by making mortalkind so clever and so... individual.'

Horskram paused, as if not entirely satisfied by the last word. Then he continued: 'Others hold that Abaddon did not even realise it himself at first, but rather thought he was augmenting mortalkind – whereas in truth he served nothing more than his own vanity and pride. These cankered traits grew in him, as this theory has it, until they had thoroughly corrupted him, and before long his lust for power turned to frustration and anger. The rest, as they say, is history.'

Adelko had pondered that long on the rest of the march. But all he did was turn circles in his head, which came to hurt from too much thinking. The tradition his mentor spoke of held that Abaddon had corrupted man by making him capable of higher thought. But if that meant more lethal weapons, cunning intrigues, skilled deceptions, did it not also mean greater poets, better healers, wiser sages?

All he could conclude in the end was that the world – indeed both worlds – made little sense.

✥ ✥ ✥

Presently they were all seated in the King's pavilion to take the evening meal. True to form, Freidheim insisted that on the eve of war his board be no more lavish than the rest of the army's – but the muster had provided well, and there was food aplenty.

Adelko was too nervous to eat much in any case. He wished he could see Arik one last time before tomorrow's battle. He had tried to seek out his brother again during the march from Linden but Horskram had forbidden him: Arik would be far too busy for reminiscing. Adelko supposed the old monk was right, but resented him all the same for stopping him.

When the meal was done the tent was cleared in preparation for a war council. It was hoped that it would be the last; that tomorrow's battle would be decisive. Despite the general mood of optimism throughout the camp, fuelled by desire for revenge for the atrocities committed by Thule's men, Adelko felt anxious and subdued.

As he lay down to sleep he found his mind drifting back to Tintagael again. The strange faerie-forms loomed before him in his mind's eye, reaching towards him with distended fingers.

He heard their eerie voices in his head, pronouncing the same cryptic words they had uttered in their sylvan palace:

What perils did you hope to flee, to seek the silence of the trees?

So many perils. It seemed madness looking back on it now: they had come through all of that and lived, their minds still intact. The noise of knights and soldiers drifted across the camp. Adelko had retired early – it was an hour before curfew. He shifted uncomfortably on his pallet.

Oh mortal wise beyond your time, gifted with reckoning sublime!

The Fays' false flattery of his mentor – or was it false? Horskram had gotten them this far in one piece after all, and the faerie kings seemed willing enough to help them...

A crooked path you now must tread, gloom gathers on the road ahead...

Not his favourite part of the faerie stanzas, not since those words had returned as if to mock him after his discourse with Horskram on the morality of befriending a swordsman...

He shifted again on his pallet and opened his eyes. Why was he thinking about this now? He wondered if this were some last trick of the Fays, a way to afflict his sanity even though he had left Tintagael far behind. And yet they *had* helped them – their words about the warrior-prophet's blood and bloody strife barring the way south had been both apt and useful... possibly even to the point of saving their lives.

Sighing exasperatedly he focused his mind, repeating the Psalm of Spirit's Comforting in his head to achieve a meditative state. From there he hoped to drift into true sleep, unhindered by the memory of the Fay's unsettling couplets.

It must have worked, for soon the words diminished and he felt his mind empty and slip toward blissful darkness. But even as it did, the last words spoken by the spectral kings echoed at the penumbra of his fading consciousness:

Sanctuary-subterfuge-sanctuary-subterfuge-sanctuary-subterfuge...

✣ ✣ ✣

The morning dawned clear and cloudless. Adelko had half expected another sorcerous elemental trick, to see the sun obscured by thick clouds or heavy rains, but the clement skies and dry earth presented no obstacles. After a hasty breakfast the army began drawing up into formation while outriders scouted ahead for signs of Thule's forces.

This time the King and his advisers had opted to divide their archers, putting six hundred on each flank. Behind these marched the trained men-at-arms and the remnants of the highland foot, divided evenly into two flanking companies five hundred strong.

Foremost on either side went the remainder of the yeoman levies, some six hundred apiece: the cruel realities of war dictated that these should be sacrificed and used for arrow fodder if need be, to give the trained footsoldiers a better chance to survive the approach.

When he learned this Adelko felt his heart contract. The poorest soldiers in the army – men of humble birth like himself – would be used as fodder. Perhaps Horskram had a point after all: could anyone hope for redemption while they remained party to the ugly trade of fighting? He tried not to dwell on it – he felt miserable enough as it was with the prospect of another bloody battle before him.

At the centre rode the knights, divided into four companies, each four hundred strong. The black-and-white banner of the White Valravyn waved in the steady breeze above the first of these, the royal unicorn coat of arms flapped briskly above another. The remaining two companies sported the varied coats of arms of the barons that commanded them.

Adelko and Horskram rode before the knights with the King's contingent. As the distant grey walls of Salmor gradually sharpened into visibility the scouts came back with their first report.

'The archers in the hills to the left numbered at least five hundred, Your Majesty,' said the lead scout, falling into a canter between the King and Lord Visigard. 'They're stiffened with a large contingent of levies. As far as we can tell, the hills to the right are much less well defended – we reckon they've got two hundred bowmen up there.'

'What about the Salwood?' asked the King, without taking his eyes off the castle.

The outrider shook his head. 'We couldn't get close enough without being picked off by their archers to tell, sire.'

Adelko followed the scout's line of sight. Away to the south the dark eaves of the Salwood beckoned, still and silent as the grave. Adelko felt his sixth sense tingling.

The enemy had constructed a hasty palisade directly to the left of the castle, behind which were stationed many more archers. Drawn up before the castle moat was a motley array of trained and conscript foot, numbering fifteen hundred at the most. Of Thule's knights there was no sign.

At the King's command the army halted just out of bowshot range. Freidheim and his personal contingent broke off to the right and crested a nearby hill for a better view of the coming battle. As his squires began pitching the royal pavilion Adelko looked south again. He could see the rebel archers clearly now, clustered on the hills about them that lined the flat approach to the castle.

Surveying the field the King frowned. 'His left flank's barely defended,' he muttered to Lord Visigard. 'Unless he's hiding men in the Salwood – there's been no sign of his knights.'

'He can't be hiding them in there,' replied Visigard. 'The trees are too dense and the wood's too small for seven hundred mounted knights. Unless our reckonings are wrong, he appears to have all the rest of his army deployed.'

Adelko felt his sixth sense go up a notch. Yet again his mind went back to the faerie woods of Tintagael. Flicking the thought away he tried to concentrate on the situation before him.

'Send scouts out back the way we came,' ordered the King. 'I can't see how we've missed hundreds of mounted knights, but it's possible Thule might be planning some sort of surprise rear attack. Have them check the land close to the main road as well.'

A herald nodded and hurried off to relay the command. Turning back to face the scene before him the King frowned again and took counsel.

'We should waste no time,' insisted Sir Toric, the new High Commander of the White Valravyn. 'If he is planning a surprise attack then the sooner we join battle the better.'

'All the same we should not be too hasty,' countered Visigard. 'I'd suggest we pull back one company of knights to guard our rear, until the scouts return.'

Reluctantly the King decided to act on this advice. Adelko could almost sense the baffled irritation from the Efrilunders and Woldings as they complied with the order – with an enemy right in front of them what need was there for fencing with shadows? He could feel a palpable unease spreading through the wider army as the company of knights turned and broke formation, cantering towards the rear of the army to face south. Glancing at Horskram he found his mentor to be his same old inscrutable self.

After another brief conference it was decided to act on Toric's advice as well. At the King's command the heralds gave the order for both flanks to begin advancing towards the hills on either side. The steady beat of a drum matched their measured tread.

When the loyalist archers drew within range they stopped to nock and draw at their leaders' command. At that moment the levies charged up the hills with a great yell, the regular soldiers and highland foot following closely in their wake.

His heart once again in his mouth, Adelko watched the gruesome spectacle of battle unfold anew.

The casualties on their right side weren't so bad. Thule had fewer bowmen on the hills there, and these were soon overwhelmed by the answering fire of the loyalists. When the conscripts reached the remainder they made light work of them, massacring them so that there was little sport left for the Highlanders and heavily armoured men-at-arms charging in their wake. By the time it was over perhaps two hundred loyalist yeomen lay dead or dying on the slopes.

On the left side things fared much worse. The first hail of arrows fired by loyalist archers found meagre pickings, for they were at maximum range and the wind did not help. The rebel archers aimed their first volley at the charging levies, mowing down dozens of screaming men. The thousand-strong levy serving Thule had meanwhile charged down the hills to meet their oncoming attackers, and soon the two hosts were joined together in a bitter bloodletting, as peasants hacked and stabbed each other to death with axes, scythes and spears.

Though he was too far away to see it in much detail, Adelko felt queasy. He didn't think watching wholesale butchery was ever something he would get used to. At any rate, he prayed he never would.

The rebel archers had now switched to targeting their loyalist counterparts, to avoid hitting their own side in the melee. For a while the fight continued thus doubly, with archers picking each other off and the two hosts fighting hand to hand. But the loyalist flank, stiffened with armoured foot and Highlanders skilled at fighting on uneven ground, gradually began to gain the upper hand.

When the victorious right flank cut across the sward to join up with their fellow loyalists, the tide finally turned decisively in their favour. The remaining rebel levies broke into a rout, leaving their surviving bowmen to unleash a last deadly volley at close range against their attackers before being butchered to a man.

Watching before the royal pavilion, the King did not appear to share his generals' exuberance. The motley rebel company drawn up before the castle had not budged throughout the engagement.

'I like this not,' he muttered. 'We may have Thule on the back foot, but this seems all too easy.'

✤ ✤ ✤

When the two flanks had rejoined the knights at the centre a quick estimate of casualties was taken. Perhaps half the yeomen on the left had perished, along with a third of its regulars including the Highlanders. From the rear company of knights there was no report of any enemy on the horizon; scouts had returned during the hill skirmish to report similar non-findings.

Adelko's sixth sense flared as the King prepared to order two companies of knights, the Valravyn and the Royals, to charge the remainder of Thule's forces.

The faerie kings returned to plague his thoughts. He could see them sat before him, their gossamer forms shimmering as they spoke voiceless words of warning: *Forces of darkness are abroad, not all shall take an open road...*

The two companies of knights began jostling into position, their steeds stamping and snorting in anticipation of the coming charge.

Wounds 'neath woods are harder healed...

At the King's command the herald gave the order for the knights to couch lances. Behind them squires prepared to ride in their masters' wake. Everyone he had met on his adventures would be in that charge – Vaskrian, Braxus, Torgun, Tarlquist, Doric and Cirod...

And then the last stanza uttered by the faeries came back to him, loud and clear in his mind:

So keep your wits about you all,
Many are the Fallen One's thralls,
And though trees may offer refuge,
Yet others conceal subterfuge...

The knights lowered their spears and prepared to charge. The remaining enemy footsoldiers prepared to receive them. Adelko found his gaze moving beyond them to where the trees of the Salwood stood stock still. Brooding and menacing they looked; not a leaf or branch stirred.

And though trees may offer refuge, yet others conceal subterfuge...

And suddenly he knew. 'Your Majesty!' he cried suddenly, turning to address the King. 'Don't give the order to charge! It's the trees! Thule's knights *are the trees!*'

Horskram blinked, staring at his novice in bafflement. The King, who had been on the point of ordering his herald to blow the signalling note, turned and stared at Adelko.

'What nonsense are you speaking, lad?' he thundered. 'A novice should know better than to interfere in a war!'

But Adelko had never felt more sure of himself. 'No, don't you see? The knights *are* the trees!' he yelled again.

'Adelko!' cried Horskram, recovering his wits. 'Be silent! This is no time for your antics!'

'Thule's knights cannot possibly be hiding in the trees,' said Visigard sternly. 'Did you not hear what I said before?'

'No, not *in* the trees,' insisted Adelko, shaking his head. 'They *are* the trees – those aren't real trees you're seeing! The Sea Wizard must have disguised Thule's knights using his magic!'

'Stuff and nonsense,' roared the King. 'Horskram, you will remove your novice from my presence at once. Herald – '

'But look!' cried Adelko as his mentor seized him roughly by the arm. 'The trees can't be real – there's been a steady breeze all morning but their leaves aren't moving!'

Horskram turned instantly to look at the forest. It was true. Though the bracing wind continued to ruffle their habits and the surcoats of the knights, the line of trees stood still as stone.

'Wait,' said Horskram, letting go of Adelko's arm. 'He's right – look at yonder trees, they aren't moving.'

Visigard rolled his eyes and looked at his King, who was staring at the Salwood with thoughtful eyes. Down on the field the knights' horses were stirring impatiently, their armour and spurs jingling as their battle standards flapped in the breeze.

The King measured his words carefully. 'Are you trying to tell me, Master Horskram, that yonder trees are *knights?*'

'I'm saying that my novice is right about them not moving in the wind – and if everything we've heard about this Sea Wizard is true, he has the power to meld elemental magic with illusion. Think on the earlier battle here.'

'So what do you suggest?' snapped the King irritably, motioning for the herald to hold off.

'If you give the order to charge and Adelko is right, you will leave your flank exposed to a ferocious charge – he will serve you the same turn as you did him,' said Horskram. 'If he breaks your formation with most of his remaining horse and foot intact, he puts himself back almost on a level footing with your remainder. And though the Efrilunders be stout men of arms, I would not stake the outcome of a battle on the oafish Woldings you'll have left besides.'

'He has the right of it, sire,' put in Sir Toric. 'As strange as it seems, if that is a company of knights seven hundred strong, they are poised to regain the initiative – that's a chance we can't take.'

'So what do you suggest we do?' demanded Visigard, his eyes bulging. 'Order our men to charge at a clump of trees?'

'If you give them such an order you will be calling the Sea Wizard's bluff,' said Horskram. 'If Adelko is right, they will have no choice but to return the charge, or else be swept away. As soon as Thule's knights move – if it is them – the glamour disguising them should be broken.'

'And if your novice is wrong, he'll have our best men charging at trees!' cried Visigard, his whiskered face flushing.

'The decision is yours, Your Majesty,' said Horskram flatly.

The King said nothing, looking thoughtfully from the woods to the rebel footsoldiers and back again.

⁜ ⁜ ⁜

'What's keeping them?' muttered Tarlquist. 'They've had us sitting here ready to charge for more than five minutes.'

'I don't know,' replied Torgun. His face was unusually pensive beneath his helm. That didn't do much for Tarlquist's jangling nerves – he'd had a bad feeling about today since he rose to bathe his face and hands.

'Well I hope they get a move on,' said Aronn, his ruddy face a deeper red than usual. 'If we wait here all day Thule's knights are bound to show up eventually. We should dispose of his remaining foot while we have the chance!'

'Perhaps it's the missing knights that concern high command right now,' suggested Torgun.

'Aye, perhaps,' returned Tarlquist sullenly. Even so, this delay didn't make sense – for once he was inclined to agree with hot-headed Aronn. A swift charge would see the remaining rebel foot crushed and dispersed. Just what was high command playing at?

He glanced nervously at the moat enclosing Salmor. No sign of ghostly knights this time – but that didn't mean their conjurer wasn't still at large.

Taking a deep breath he steeled himself. Mustn't show fear in front of the men – a brave man felt fear and mastered it. He repeated that to himself several times, words his father had told him years ago, when he was but a green page.

Together with Sir Wolmar, who since his father's death had said little to anybody, and the twin knights, who said little to anybody at the best of times, Tarlquist waited restlessly with the rest of the vanguard for the order to charge.

Then an order came. But not the one they had expected.

'What?' Wolmar exclaimed, breaking his self-imposed silence.

'We're to about face along with the Royals and make for the woods,' confirmed Sir Redrun. Promoted to Deputy High Commander in place of Toric, he had just relayed high command's order to Sir Tarlquist. 'The Efrilunders and Woldings are to charge the foot.'

'Have they gone completely mad?' gaped Aronn. 'There are no soldiers in that wood – and it's too cramped to hide knights. We'll be smashed to pieces charging it!'

'Nevertheless, orders are orders,' replied Redrun firmly. 'We're to couch and charge the Salwood as if it were a living enemy.'

A great tumult was growing across the wider company as news of the controversial order spread. Up and down the lines commanders and their deputies had to shout down a general dissent and reissue the command directly.

'I don't pretend that there is aught but rank foolishness in this,' said Sir Tarlquist reluctantly, addressing his men. 'But the order comes direct from the King himself, and we are sworn to obey him in everything.'

That settled the matter. Even sullen Wolmar saw no choice but to acquiesce. Amid great confusion the entire company of the White Valravyn pulled around and changed formation, preparing for what seemed like a direct assault on nothing more threatening than leaves and branches. Next to them the Royal Knights could be seen doing likewise.

When the clarion call came both companies spurred their horses forwards. No battle roar came from either; not a single throat uttered so much as a cry. Eight hundred heavily armoured knights thundered wordlessly towards the Salwood.

Clutching spear and shield as he digged his spurs tightly into his horse's flanks, Tarlquist watched the forest loom nearer by the second. Off to the side he could hear the Woldings and Efrilunders striking up a war cry as they charged the waiting army of footsoldiers.

Carried by their swift Farovian destriers, the knights of the White Valravyn would smash themselves to pieces against the unyielding boughs of the dense wood. Sir Tarlquist was just saying his prayers and thinking what an ignominious and absurd death he rode to when something strange happened.

The line of trees before him shimmered. Once, twice, then all of a sudden melting away... and where before had beckoned static green and brown there now appeared a surging tide of colour, as Thule's seven hundred knights charged to meet them.

As they closed to do battle, a great cheer went up through the ranks of the White Valravyn. Sir Tarlquist joined his voice to it, bellowing a war cry that sounded more relieved than fierce to his ears.

✢ ✢ ✢

In the clashing thick of battle, Wolmar lay about him with an unquenchable fury. Left and right he hewed, striking down knights. A dreadful rage augmented the strength of his limbs. Once he ran a hapless squire through, gutting him mercilessly on the point of his sword. 'Father, help me!' were the youth's last words as he slid off the saddle, his entrails flying in his wake.

Wolmar found time to spare a sneer for his fallen opponent. Crying for his father instead of dying like a man in the field – pathetic. Even if he'd been a loyalist, such a weakling only deserved to die.

Wolmar was thinking of his father too – but not like that. Driving his dappled Farovian through the melee the princeling hoped his prayers would be answered.

They were. Before long he saw it – a stylised black shield divided by a single white triangular line, with a rose, a dagger and a gauntlet picked out in red at the three corners. Thule's standard, beckoning him on to sweet revenge.

A dismounted knight lunged at him from the ground as he rode towards it, but Wolmar disarmed him with a sidewise swipe of his sword, taking off several of the man's fingers in the process.

'Thule! Traitor and killer of my father – turn and face me!' he roared as he galloped towards him.

The pretender to a throne that was lost obliged him. Thule had fought with a fierce fury of his own that afternoon; his tabard was drenched and stained with the crimson tide of war.

'And who would you be, raven knight?' he called mockingly, his voice tinny beneath his helm as he raised his dripping blade. 'Come! Come and die on my sword, like the rest of your brothers!'

With a war-cry that was more a scream of naked anger Wolmar launched himself at Krulheim. The two fought savagely, all thoughts of finer swordplay forgotten as they hacked at one another frenziedly. Then of a sudden Wolmar switched to a thrust; reacting quickly Krulheim turned the blow and attempted a riposte at his unprotected throat.

Dodging the counter-attack Wolmar spurred his horse in closer, bringing his shield around and smashing it into his adversary's face. Thule's helm protected him from injury, but the sheer force of the unexpected blow was enough to drive him back in the saddle. Pressing his advantage, Wolmar delivered a thundering overhead strike with his sword that caught Krulheim square in the chest. Again his armour saved him from serious injury, but the impact sent him crashing from his charger.

Wolmar was about to press his advantage when Krulheim's dismounted squire, a stout lad of about eighteen summers, stabbed his horse's flank with a spear. The point was driven hard enough to puncture the barding, and as his mount reared in agony Wolmar was forced to lurch clumsily off the saddle to avoid being thrown.

Before he could fully recover the desperate squire attacked him, lunging at him with his spear. Falling to one knee Wolmar threw his shield up just in time. Getting to his feet he cleaved the squire's head in twain at an oblique angle, the lop-sided top flying upwards in a spurt of blood and brains.

Wolmar turned to face Krulheim, who had recovered from his fall and now awaited him in a half crouch.

Wolmar extended the point of his bloodied sword towards his foe and snarled beneath his dinted helm. No words – an animal noise of pure hatred escaped feral lips.

And then they were joined again, driving one another back and forth and circling hungrily for an opening. Gradually both men's battle rage subsided into a coolly lethal focus, as each sought to end the other's life. Here and there one attacked, the other parried or dodged and countered, but neither could gain the upper hand.

And then suddenly Wolmar's sword was buried inches deep in Krulheim's calf just below the knee. A cunning feint to the stomach had served him well, and Krulheim had taken the bait.

Pulling his blade free and taking a step back Wolmar half expected Krulheim to laugh unscathed in his face, but with a groan the pretender sank to his good knee as blood flowed freely over his mail from the cut in his leg.

'Come then!' spat the erstwhile lord of Thule. 'Come finish it, if you dare!'

Wolmar did dare. Springing forwards he brought his blade down towards the side of his opponent's head in a lightning stroke. Krulheim raised his own blade to defend himself... but his sword shattered beneath Wolmar's furious blow, which rang loudly off his helm. Abandoning the remnant of his sword Krulheim reached for a dagger at his belt – but Wolmar kicked it from his hand as he drew it. In a last desperate gambit Krulheim tried a shield-swipe of his own. Anticipating this, Wolmar dodged it.

The failed blow with a clumsy weapon toppled Krulheim, and as he lay on his side Wolmar sat down on him hard, pinning both his arms under the weight of his own armoured body. Shrugging off his shield he began to unlace Thule's helm, whilst holding his sword aloft. Krulheim struggled, trying desperately to throw his attacker off, but Wolmar steadied himself and would not be thrown.

Pulling off the great helm he tossed it aside contemptuously, revealing Krulheim's mailed head. A trickle of blood ran down his face: his sword-shattering blow must have done some damage.

Not nearly enough.

Clutching the coif Wolmar yanked it back in a single swift motion. Krulheim's long brown locks spilled out. They were surprisingly clean for a man who had just spent seven weeks on campaign, but the son of Freidhoff did not concern himself with that.

Standing up, his feet straddling Krulheim's prone body, he raised his sword high in the air, point downwards, and prepared to deal the death blow. He half expected Thule to make some last desperate attempt to trip him, and was prepared in case he did, but the Pretender did not move. Gazing straight above him into the heavens, he mouthed a few words: 'Oh Reus Almighty, forgive me my sins.'

Wolmar sneered at that. 'Now you shall eat my sword,' he said coldly, before thrusting it down through Krulheim's mouth, pinning his head to the ground. His body shuddered and jerked, once, twice, thrice, as the vengeful knight drove the blade further down, down, deep into the dark earth...

And then Krulheim moved no more.

Slumping across Thule's corpse, Sir Wolmar wept for his father.

✢ ✢ ✢

Tarlquist limped across the battlefield, biting on agony. He knew he must have broken his thigh when he was sent hurtling from the saddle at the first charge. At least he had broken his spear on his opponent's breast: that would be one less knight fetching a ransom.

He had dropped his shield, picking up a broken spear shaft to use as a crutch. Clutching his sword in his free hand he cast about for foes – he would not lie wounded or plead for mercy whilst his comrades were fighting and dying around him.

Soon he found what he was looking for – another dismounted knight. This one appeared to be injured too. His helm had been knocked off his head, which boasted an ugly gash that streamed blood.

Yelling war-cries, the two wounded warriors assailed each other. Unable to move properly, Tarlquist had no option but to stand his ground and rely solely on the strength of his right arm. Reus knew how he managed that, but he did: his opponent, half blinded by his own blood, lunged unsteadily at him, allowing Tarlquist to parry and riposte with a deadly thrust to the throat.

As his foe expired in a gurgling heap another knight who had just been knocked off his horse crashed into him, knocking him to the ground. Tarlquist felt an agonising stab of pain shoot up his thigh, and for a while he lay prone. Then, raising himself to a sitting position he found the knight, one of the King's, lying next to him. He was bleeding profusely from where a sword or spear had pierced his mailed chest. Leaning over him Tarlquist tried to mouth a few words of comfort to ease his passing.

'Hold me, I'm cold,' was all he said, before his hazel eyes frosted over in death.

With a groan Tarlquist struggled to get back on his feet. It was a painful and by now exhausting effort, but again he somehow managed it. Limping along through the mud he fell again as a panicked riderless horse veered towards him. He made a desperate grasp for its spurs but clutched thin air. He was just steeling himself to get to his feet again when he heard a great cry go up around him.

'They're shooting at us from the castle! They're killing their own as well!'

Several knights around him toppled from their horses as a stinging volley of deadly shafts fell among them – both Thule's men and loyalists were among the victims.

With a curse Tarlquist heaved himself upright again, leaning heavily on his makeshift crutch as he loped along. There must be someone else to fight, somewhere...

His breathing was coming in ragged gasps and he stood a moment to clear his vision. It was then that he felt something hard and thin hit him in the back.

With a stuttered cry he pitched forwards into the mud. His back exploded in pain: this wasn't like the broken leg, it was sharper, more acute and searching. Coughing face down he saw a great gobbet of blood come spewing into the turf beneath him. He could taste it in his mouth. It was only then that he noticed he wasn't wearing his helm any more.

Stubbornly he grasped hold of the spear shaft with both hands, using it to lever himself up from the ground and standing on his one good leg. The pain in his back had grown more intense; he could feel it spreading across to his chest as he coughed up another gout of blood.

'Ah me,' he said to no one in particular, raising his eyes to the bright skies. 'And so this is an end of it. Reus love me, but it could have been a more noble weapon...'

The Almighty must have heard his half prayer. A few moments later, a knight wielding a mace came galloping towards him. A mad look was in his eyes, the frenzied expression of someone who knows he is doomed to die and welcomes death.

Leaning down in the saddle as he hurtled past Tarlquist, he swung the mace in a great arc towards his head. The spiked ball of iron grew suddenly large as it rushed to meet his face –

✧ ✧ ✧

Most of the warriors crowding the King's tent were covered in blood, the mail links of their armour turned a rusted red colour. Adelko could smell the cloying stink of it. Surreptitiously he reached for his cloth and tried not to gag.

'Jord's in charge now,' said Lord Toric. 'Him, and that hedge wizard of theirs. We'll see if they can be prevailed upon to see sense.'

'I wouldn't count on it,' offered Braxus lightly. 'Seeing as you've made a point of killing every man of noble blood on their side that you've captured, they'll know what's waiting for them if they surrender.'

Several of the bloodstained Northlendings standing near him looked darkly at him. The Thraxian had fought once more in the vanguard, sustaining only a flesh wound to the right shoulder and slaying several more knights. Adelko felt that had it not been for this service the bull-necked High Commander might have taken his words unkindly.

As it was he said: 'They still have the Jarl of Salmor and many other good knights prisoner. And Reus willing they won't have heard about the executions at Linden yet. We should be able to bargain with them.'

The King frowned. He clearly did not like to be reminded that his ruthless act of retribution might have put the lives of Lord Salmor and all his retinue in danger.

'There'll be no more bloodshed if I can help it,' he growled. 'Except that warlock – I want his pagan head on a spike.'

'We should proceed with caution where this Sea Wizard is concerned,' said Horskram. 'We do not yet know the full extent of his powers.'

'Aye,' growled the King, glancing at the adept sidelong. 'And that is precisely why you are invited to a post-war council, master monk. You and your novice have already proved shrewd enough at unpicking his sorcerous schemes – I would not have him rob us of a just victory with his unnatural chicanery.'

Freidheim's foremost knights and nobles were all gathered in the King's tent whilst the army rested in the field. All agreed that the first thing to do was sue for a parley – with the war all but over there was no sense in losing more loyal men to Jord's last clutch of archers on the walls. The corpses of the slain on both sides remained unidentified – all except the Pretender himself. That had been settled decisively when Sir Wolmar had brought his head back to camp and tossed it on the table in the middle of the tent.

A great cheer had gone up then, with knights and nobles crowding round to embrace Wolmar and clap him on the back. Even Torgun joined his voice to this praise, although Aronn hung back and scowled, a disconsolate look on his ruddy face. Adelko shared his sentiments – war hero or not, Wolmar was still an unpleasant character who would have seen him tortured beneath Staerkvit for no good reason.

It was true enough as Horskram said that all knights were killers – but some killers were clearly more malicious than others.

After he had exposed Thule's magicked knights, victory in the Battle of Salmor had been just a matter of time. As the White Valravyn and the Royals engaged the last of Thule's horse the other loyalist knights had smashed the last of the Pretender's foot. There were still his archers behind the palisade to be reckoned with, but having occupied the hills overlooking it the King's bowmen began picking them off. In the meantime the surviving Highlanders, being canny footsoldiers, had managed to skirt the foothills and outflank the rebel archers, bypassing the wooden stockades and ditches of the palisade. When this happened they lost morale and scattered: after that it was an easy matter for the King's footsoldiers to pick them off as they tried to flee through the hills.

In a last desperate attempt to inflict casualties ahead of a possible siege of the castle, Jord had ordered the archers on the walls to fire at will on friend and foe alike. But even this had not been not enough to turn the tide, for the Wolding knights and the Efrilunders, making light work of the remnants of Thule's foot, soon joined their efforts to bringing down the remainder of his knights. Few of the latter survived to be executed. Lord Magnus, the last of the rebel barons, perished with his knights, the former being feathered by shafts fired at Jord's command.

The slaughter done, the King's Army had withdrawn beyond range of the castle bowmen to take counsel.

Now it was simply a matter of deciding who to send to the parley with Jord. They were busy discussing this when a messenger burst into the tent.

'Your Majesty, they're waving the flag of surrender!' he blurted, taking a knee.

The assembled worthies exchanged suspicious glances at this. Jord was known to be a staunch knight, even if he was a traitor. Surrendering before discussing terms while he still held the castle seemed unlikely.

Exiting the tent to a man they soon saw the truth of the messenger's words. From atop the castle ramparts a broad white cloth could be seen waving.

'Surely not without a parley first!' exclaimed Lord Toros, raising an eyebrow. Though the war was lost, Jord could with just a few hundred men and ample provision hold a stout castle like Salmor for weeks, perhaps even months.

'It may be a trick,' said Visigard. 'To lure us into range and pick us off again.'

Lord Aesgir shook his head. 'I doubt it. Jord is no fool, this madcap business aside. He knows his future survival depends on us one way or another – he won't survive a siege forever. Surrendering immediately is odd, however.'

'Well we won't learn the truth of it by standing here debating uselessly,' rumbled the King. 'Horskram – you shall go with the contingent of parley, in case our friend the Sea Wizard tries anything. This could be one of his ploys, methinks.'

Horskram nodded his assent. 'You're coming with me, Adelko,' he said, turning to his novice. 'Seeing as you've already proved to be so observant where pagan sorcery is concerned, you might prove useful again.'

Adelko swallowed and said nothing. He didn't fancy war would improve as a spectacle within bowshot range.

They soon had the answer to their puzzle. As they moved forward cautiously they could see something else besides the white flag mounting the battlements. Two heads atop spikes. As they drew closer they saw the archers leaning on their bows. Before them stood a mail-clad warrior – no knight, but a grizzled serjeant.

'The battle for Salmor has been won by the King,' declared the herald in charge of the contingent. 'We are here to accept your surrender. Where is your commander?'

'That'd be me, sire,' replied the serjeant, his greasy hair blowing in the wind. 'We've put paid to the marshal here' – he indicated the nearest severed head – 'and his bastard grandson. There's no more high-born folk left in the castle, save the ones on your side. The rest of us is just common soldiers, wot was obeying orders. We don't want no trouble, we just want to go home to our families.'

The herald blinked. 'You executed Jord and his grandson? That was ill done – the lad could have been no more than fourteen summers.'

'We don't want no more trouble,' repeated the frightened serjeant. 'Jord was for fighting on, y'see – said he'd sooner go down with a sword in his hand than surrender to the King. Would've made us all fight with 'im – his grandson too. Said everything he'd done, he'd done it for him.'

'I see,' answered the herald. 'And what are your terms of surrender?'

'We want the King's pledge that all common soldiers wot served Thule will be free to go. We'll disarm of course – we just want to go home.'

'And that is the extent of your terms?' inquired the herald.

'That's right, sire,' replied the serjeant.

The herald seemed about to accept this and go but Horskram whispered something to him. Turning back to the serjeant he asked: 'And where is the Northland priest men call the Sea Wizard?'

'Gone,' replied the serjeant. 'We tried to get 'im too, but when we smashed down the doors to his chamber there was nothing – just his odds and sods, a load of queer-looking things that none of the men rightly wanted to touch. We searched the whole castle for him – he's vanished, ain't no one seen sight nor sound of him since he barred himself in his room when the battle turned against us.'

The sortie retired to relay its findings to the King. The terms were agreed – in spite of much protestation from many of the knights including Wolmar, who said it was a travesty to let the killing of two nobles by common soldiers go unpunished.

Freidheim shouted them all down. 'A common soldier or archer kills a noble knight on the field of battle, no one bats an eyelid,' he growled. 'And I'd only have had to hang the pair of them as traitors anyway. No, these men have saved me another ugly job. I've a good mind to recruit them – we'll be needing every sword we can get to hold the new lands of the King's Dominions.'

✣ ✣ ✣

Adelko and Horskram sat down to a bowl of beef stew long after dusk. The garrison had given up the castle and consented to be disarmed, Salmor and his knights freed from the dungeons. As night drew in a wave of euphoria spread through the loyalist army camp; casks of wine and ale were breached and meat was roasted over fires.

The monks had spent the rest of the day joining the perfects giving the Last Rites to the hundreds of dead and dying. Sir Tarlquist was among them. His corpse had been found, an arrow protruding from his back and the front of his skull smashed open, leaving a bloody ruin where his face had been. He was only recognisable by a signet ring he wore.

Thinking on this Adelko mouthed a second prayer for the dead knight as he stared sadly into the fire. At Horskram's behest they had taken leave of the King's contingent to eat and drink among the Royal Knights, joining his nephew. Sir Manfry was still the height of cheerfulness despite having broken his shield arm in the battle.

'Still able to wield a flagon, what!' he said gaily, his eyes glowing feverishly in his moustachioed face.

Adelko tried to smile back, but found it difficult. He felt exhausted. Saying prayers all day was draining work. But then, he hadn't been doing any fighting: what right had he to feel tired? A wave of guilt washed over him to complement his melancholy mood.

'Now, young Adelko,' continued Manfry, oblivious, 'before seeking out your darling brother again, I must insist you make good on your unkept promise and drink a stoop with us first!'

All about them the camp was a riot of celebration tinged with sorrow. There was no time like war to remind men of the precious value of life. The sorting of the dead and treating of the wounded would go on long after the victory feast, which would be held at Salmor in a couple of days. And as for the lands that Thule in his prideful ambition had seen fit to lay waste, such hurts would be healed in no short time. How many hundreds or thousands had died or had their lives ruined by one short war?

Pushing away his miserable thoughts Adelko agreed to stay for a stoop of ale. He longed to visit Arik again now Horskram had given him permission, but it was hard to refuse the jovial Manfry. Besides, this time they would have the whole night to drink away the gloom of war together.

Or so he thought, until Horskram addressed him halfway through his first flagon. The ale was strong, and he could feel his spirits beginning to rise again.

'I hope you aren't planning on getting uproariously drunk with your brother tonight, Adelko,' he said, fixing the novice with piercing eyes.

'Oh leave him be, uncle!' laughed Manfry. 'If everything I've heard today is true, he's as much a hero in this war as any knight! Why, if it wasn't for his seeing through that sea mage chap's frightful delusions, we mightn't be sitting here celebrating at all!'

Adelko started at that thought. He had been so busy it genuinely hadn't occurred to him that his small part in the battle may have been pivotal.

But his mentor replied seriously: 'Yes, and that's exactly why I want young Adelko bright-eyed first thing tomorrow – we still haven't got to the bottom of the Sea Wizard and his said frightful delusions. The King promised me leave to question him should he be captured. That hasn't come to pass – but the least I can do is inspect the warlock's chambers at Salmor. I've had a word with the King in private and he's sent strict instructions to Lord Kelmor that they are not to be touched until we've had a look for ourselves.'

The adept turned to scrutinise the novice again. 'And seeing as you have proved yourself to be so acute, young Adelko, I shall be taking you with me when I go there at dawn.'

Adelko's heart sank again. So much for a badly needed night of revels – but then he supposed he hadn't become a monk for such things.

Quaffing the rest of his stoop, he bade Manfry a fond farewell and promised Horskram he would be back at a reasonable hour. Then he went in search of his brother. They'd get a few ales in before bedtime at least.

As he passed groups of knights and soldiers singing and drinking by firelight, Adelko reflected wryly that an Argolian's work was never done.

⟜ CHAPTER XIV ⟝

A Villain Unmasked

Dismissing the weary guardsman Lord Kelmor opened the door and ushered both monks inside a spacious chamber. It overlooked the southern grounds of the castle estate; dawn light streamed through a window where the shutters had been left wide open.

The room was spartanly furnished, but tables and chairs were hardly what drew the eye to its contents. Rude shelves to one side were crammed with strange books covered in peculiar markings, many of them bound in an odd-looking sea-green hide.

They immediately put Adelko in mind of the books he had seen at the Abbot's inner sanctum weeks ago. Ancient scrolls of vellum and parchment peered from between the tomes; he could see similar markings on their worn surfaces. Not even the old Sassanic texts he had looked at in Ulfang matched their alien foreignness.

The secret language of magic. The one Horskram had told him of back in the cave on the fringes of the Brenning Wold. The arcane tongue taught to the Varyans by the Unseen, in the long-ago days when archangels had walked on earth and visited mortalkind. He presumed this was its written form – words of an ancient power that they were fighting to suppress, before it overwhelmed them.

A table was crammed with odd paraphernalia: vials and phials containing liquids and powders of different colours. A pestle and mortar lay in the midst of the clutter. In it was a thick paste, again of a sea-green hue. Curious instruments there were too, tweezers and sharp knives and other metal tools Adelko didn't recognise that resembled tiny square-headed spoons.

Set on a wooden plinth in the middle of the chamber was a wide shallow basin crafted of silver. Its ancient rim had been wrought to resemble creatures of the sea. Dolphins and seakindred and tritons were embossed on its polished surface, and other more nameless creatures of the unfathomed deeps: horrid-looking alien things, with tentacles and suckers and malignant eyes fashioned to reflect a queer intelligence. They reminded Adelko of the demon at Staerkvit, when it had finally revealed itself in all its unnatural loathsomeness. Shuddering, he made the sign.

As they drew closer they saw that the basin was filled to just below the brim with clear water. On a smaller table besides stood a silver ewer containing more.

'The Sea Wizard's scrying tool,' breathed Horskram softly. 'He will have used this to spy on his foes, perhaps to communicate with other adepts of the art of far-seeing.'

'Ye Almighty,' breathed Salmorlund, also making the sign. 'That my own holding was used for such dastardly practices! This shames me as much as losing the castle itself.'

'Be of some cheer, my lord,' replied Horskram. 'Your castle is yours again, and I shall put a blessing on this chamber once we have examined the paraphernalia and destroyed it. But first we must inspect.'

This the two monks did under Horskram's careful supervision, the Jarl hanging back nervously. Much of the equipment was of unknown purpose to Adelko, whose career as a witch-hunter had barely begun in earnest.

'It is clear that our warlock was accomplished in Thaumaturgy, Scrying and Enchantment,' the adept said presently, citing the Seven Schools of Magick. 'The first and last would explain his powers over the elements and his mastery of illusion. And we now can say for almost certain that he was behind the original band of brigands sent to kill us on our journey from Ulfang.'

Their search had uncovered more of the strange blue-jewelled necklaces they had found on the Northlanders; even now they glowed softly at the edges with a resentful green light.

'However,' added Horskram, 'without being able to operate his scrying pool we cannot determine if he was in collusion with other warlocks.' The old monk rubbed a hand over his beard, looking pensive. Adelko stared at the room and its bizarrely blasphemous contents, also at a loss for a solution.

After some moments Lord Kelmor spoke up. 'Master monk, I hesitate to offer this counsel, for I would not rightly be party to any sin, but... I think I may know of someone who might be able to help.'

Horskram, still deep in thought, looked at the Jarl of Salmor absently. 'Hmm, and who might that be?'

Salmorlund licked his lips nervously. He bore little signs of his captivity – Thule had treated him well along with the other noble prisoners, doubtless hoping to augment his coffers with a tidy ransom after the war. The occupants of Blakelock and Rookhammer had not been so lucky – Thule's ruthlessness had apparently escalated with his ill-fated campaign.

'Not long before the war broke out, my men apprehended an old crone,' the Jarl continued. 'She hails from the foothills of the mountains – she had been accused by her fellow villagers of being a witch. Of course, we had no way of being certain of that until an Argolian could be fetched, but the peasants were convinced of it and would have lynched her had my soldiers not intervened.

'It was resolved to bring her back to Salmor and keep her in the dungeons until one of your Order could be summoned to interrogate her. Then of course Thule launched his campaign and such trifling concerns were pushed far from my mind.'

'Accusations of witchcraft, founded or no, are never trifling concerns,' replied Horskram testily, but Adelko could sense elation in his tone as well. 'Where is this crone now?' he asked. 'Can you bring her to me?'

'Aye, that I can, master monk,' replied Lord Kelmor.

'Then do so,' replied Horskram. 'Is she chained?'

'I believe she is, in links of cold iron.'

'Good. Keep her thus for the nonce – we don't want her trying to charm her way out of difficulty if she is a genuine witch.'

Presently the crone was brought before them. She was a filthy sight. Her bleached hair was matted with the dirt of the dungeons, her ragged homespun stained and blotched. When two guards dragged her into the room she looked up at the monks and smiled. Adelko could count her teeth on the fingers of a mangled hand. She was tiny – at least a head shorter than average, and her back was crooked and hunched.

Adelko was put briefly in mind of the awful Hag in Tintagael; suppressing a shiver at the memory he banished the thought.

'What is your name?' Horskram asked her coldly.

'Ulla, begging my lord's pardon,' replied the crone, still grinning.

'I am no lord,' replied Horskram. 'But a monk of the Order of St Argo. I have brought many a witch to justice in my time.'

The crone appeared unperturbed, merely smiling again and raising her shackled hands in a gesture of supplication.

'Oh, very good!' she cackled. 'Very good! I am at your service!'

'That remains to be seen,' answered Horskram levelly. 'You stand accused by the folk of Wethering of witchcraft,' he continued, Salmor having apprised him of the details of her case while she was being fetched. 'What have you to say to these accusations?'

The crone shook her head furiously. 'No, my lord monk! No! It isn't true! They're lying, every one of them!'

But Adelko had registered the keen eye with which she took in the room's contents. He was already beginning to form his own judgment of her guilt or innocence.

Taking out his circifix Horskram brandished it and muttered a prayer. The crone did not flinch, but plainly looked uncomfortable. Such a reaction usually meant the likelihood of a Right-Handed practitioner: most black magicians of Left-Hand Path would have registered instant loathing at the sight of the holy rood – only the most powerful would be strong enough to resist displaying instant revulsion.

Horskram questioned her closely for the better part of an hour, with Adelko observing, just as they had done at Lönkopang the previous year when they apprehended the witch there.

Now as then the principle was the same: the trick was not simply to catch out a suspect witch with clever questioning, to get them to say something that would incriminate themselves. That method had been tried by the mainstream perfects for centuries, often with disastrous results, and many an innocent had been hanged or burned at the stake as a result of their clumsy gropings after the truth.

But an Argolian's sixth sense was attuned from an early age, honed and refined through years of meditation, prayer and fasting. The object of their interrogations was to provoke an emotional response from the subject; by doing so they would be able to uncover a suspect's psychic spoor. Because the latter tended to be much stronger in a practising witch, this would quickly enable a skilled Argolian to spot one.

As the interrogation drew to a close it was fast becoming apparent that the villagers of Wethering had had good reason to accuse the crone. Though she deftly evaded all of Horskram's questions, saying nothing that directly incriminated her, her psyche told a myriad of tales.

Every time Horskram mentioned one of the Seven Schools of Magick the novice could sense her pulse quicken. The two schools she responded to most strongly were Alchemy and Scrying. When he thrust the *Holy Book of Psalms and Scriptures* at Ulla and called on her to renounce her worship of the Unseen as pagan gods and embrace them instead as archangels at the Almighty's right hand, she acquiesced with a gap-toothed leer.

But her resentment and insincerity were palpable; the novice could feel the tension rising in her like the growing heat from a kindling fire as she said the words. Her skeletal hand quivered as it rested on the leather cover of the sacred tome – her spiritual anguish was just as perceptible to his attuned sixth sense.

'We have our witch,' intoned Horskram finally. 'Ulla – you have been found guilty of practising Right-Handed Magick. Though this is a lesser crime than following the darker Left-Hand Path, I am still obliged to have you branded as a witch. These chains you now wear shall remain on you for life, and all shall know you for what you are by the mark. Do you have anything to say before the sentence is carried out?'

'No, please, lord monk!' begged the witch, crawling on her knees towards him, her manacled hands raised in a pathetic gesture of supplication. 'Don't brand me, I beg of you! I was only spying on my neighbours... and I might have made a potion or two – to make the younger lads fall in love with me.'

Horskram stared down at her in disgust. 'Foul and lecherous crone,' he said coldly. 'You made blasphemous pacts with the spirits of the Other Side so you might cater to your depraved lusts, and gain advantage over your honest neighbours by spying on them! You used your ill-gotten powers to turn man against wife, while you preyed on their children for your own abominable satisfaction! Let the sentence be carried out henceforth, and consider yourself fortunate not to be hanged! You are banished from returning to Wethering, on pain of death!'

The crone wailed as the soldiers stepped forwards and hauled her up from the ground. Even now Adelko couldn't help but feel some pity for her – he had rarely seen his master so cold, not even at the previous witch trial they had conducted together.

The men were dragging her off when Horskram cried: 'But wait! Hold her here a little longer.'

A gleam of hope returned to the witch's eyes as Horskram asked: 'Now your status as a witch is in no doubt, do you recognise much of what you see in this room?'

The gleam intensified. 'Some of it... my lord monk. Yes, yes, lots of nice, interesting things in here, oh yes... I'd heard tell there was a mighty mage staying here, oh yes, so I'd heard, mmm...!'

Horskram's voice was still cold as he asked her: 'Yonder scrying pool – do you think you can use it?'

The witch cocked her filthy head to one side. 'Well, I might... would need to look at the words, though, mm, yes, the words...'

Salmor's expression turned from one of disgust to bafflement as he glanced over at Horskram.

'She means the proper incantation. It will be written down in one of yonder tomes, inscribed in the sorcerer's script.' Ignoring the nonplussed look on the Jarl's face he turned to face the crone again and proclaimed: 'We seek the sorcerer who was using this paraphernalia. That, and we needs must learn if he had any accomplices of his calling. If we free you of your shackles, do you think you can operate his scrying pool?'

'Well, yes... I suppose I could,' replied the crone. 'Ulla can be nice yes, nice and helpful. What help will Ulla get for her services?'

'I can reverse the sentence, if you pledge to do as asked and don't try to magick us when we free you from your chains,' replied Horskram.

A look of joy suffused the old crone's crumpled features. 'Oh, you'd let Ulla go! Free?'

Salmorlund was staring at Horskram aghast, but the monk raised his hand to indicate silence. 'You will still be forbidden from returning to Wethering – but you'll be set free, yes. Doubtless the Jarl will want to banish you from his lands, but so long as you leave them, you will be free to go wherever else you will – *if* you help us.'

'Oh yes, yes!' breathed the crone. 'Ulla will help! Ulla swears to help and not try any tricks – just get these chains off!'

At Horskram's bidding the Jarl reluctantly had his men strike them off. The crone rubbed her spindly wrists with a reedy sigh of satisfaction. The two monks kept a close watch on her, ready in case she tried to enthral them.

'She does not appear to be overly versed in the ways of the enchantress,' said the adept, 'relying instead on her potions to seduce her victims. All the same, we should be careful. Ulla! Know this – two stout soldiers will be here at all times, ready to strike off your head if I sense you are trying to ensorcell us in any way. Be warned – I am now strongly attuned to your psyche. Try anything untoward, and I shall be the first to know of it.'

But Ulla was scarcely listening to him, and was already rifling greedily through the Sea Wizard's library.

It did not take her long to find the one she was looking for.

'Oh yes, yes!' she hissed. 'A great and mighty wizard this one, lots of books, lots of spells... he knew an awful lot, this one!'

'Just find the one we need,' said Horskram sternly. 'I need that scrying pool activated, and we don't have all day.'

While the crone was busy poring over manuscripts, Horskram offered up a prayer, imploring the Redeemer and Almighty to forgive them the sin they had to condone to do His work.

When he was finished Ulla was ready. Horskram took her aside and whispered some final instructions in her ear.

'Everyone else stand back behind yon witch,' he said, turning to address the rest of them. 'Salmor, have your men ready with their blades drawn just in case.'

Salmor gave the order and they all withdrew a few paces behind Ulla. Adelko could feel his sixth sense tingling, myriad needles probing at his psyche. As much as he felt anxious, part of him was excited too: after everything they had been through, now at last they might learn

who else was behind the attacks on them. Not to mention an insane plot
to harness a power that would bring about hell on earth.

With the tome open on the table beside her the witch touched the
surface of the pool and began to recite the incantation. The words were
foul to the ear; they sounded harsh and unnatural on human lips.

Adelko found himself wondering how the Unseen, the very
Archangels themselves, could have taught something so foul to the
Almighty's foremost creation. But then perhaps the language of magick
had not seemed so foul in the long-gone days of the Platinum Age.

The crone's face was a mask of concentration as she mouthed the
words, over and over, touching the pool gently with each incomprehensible
line. From where he was Adelko could not see into the pool, but he could
discern a strange light begin to emanate from it. The sunlight streaming in
through the open window seemed to grow darker, and the novice fancied
he could hear sounds that had no origin in his vicinity.

And then the surface of the pool began to cast a shimmering light
across the room; it ran up the walls like quicksilver before turning a deep
sea-green colour. It changed again to a bloody crimson, before deepening
into black and blotting out the sunlight altogether. He watched in darkness
before colour and light returned to the room; he fancied he saw the
vague semblance of a human face stretched macabrely across the walls.

Then a voice filled the chamber. Clear and cold it was, almost
without emotion.

'Who are you? Where is Ragnar?'

The distended lips of the reflected face moved in ghostly time with
the icy words. Adelko shivered, his body breaking out into a cold sweat.

'He-he is busy with the war, he has l-left me to commune on
his behalf,' stammered the crone. She was trying to remember all of
Horskram's instructions, but what she saw in the pool clearly terrified her.

The voice came again. This time it was underscored with contempt.

'What? Has that Northland hedge wizard dared to take an
apprentice without my leave? He might have picked a prettier one.
Where is he? How does the war speed? Has he succeeded in putting
that fool Krulheim on the Pine Throne yet?'

'The-the war rages on, my lord,' stammered the crone. 'The th-
throne is not yet won.'

'Yes, I'd fathomed as much from his lack of communication, you
wretch!' There was bitter hatred in the voice now, an unreasoning hatred
of all things living it seemed to Adelko. 'When Ragnar returns, tell him
to contact me directly – I didn't take him into my service so he could
send his lackeys to tell me the obvious! What else have you to say?'

Trembling, the witch licked her sore-coated lips and said: 'Ragnar t-told me to ask you if the fragments are safe.'

A moment's silence. Then a sibilant hiss came from the pool. There was a deadly susurration to it, more menacing by far than any of its previous tones.

'*What did you say?*'

'R-Ragnar asks where the fragments are being kept. H-he says he knows you have them.'

'Who told him of this? Oh, but wait... I see! So the meddlesome monk has been captured! Excellent! Where is he? Is he still alive? I would have him brought to me if so – but why does Ragnar send the likes of you to discuss such important matters?! Begone, you cur – send for your master immediately, do you hear me? At once! If he has to transform himself into a raven and fly all the way back to Salmor – I want to see him now!'

'He-he is not present, my lord,' was all the crone could stammer.

'Where is the monk?' yelled the voice from the pool, cracked and harsh with mounting fury. 'Where is he?'

At this point Horskram stepped forwards, gently moving the witch to one side and squaring up to face the pool.

'Here he is,' said the adept softly. 'I cannot say you are well met, Andragorix.'

Laughter filled the room. It was clearly from a human throat, but the sound set Adelko's teeth on edge. He thought it every bit as evil as the hideous shriek of the thing that had pursued them between Ulfang and Strongholm. Only it was undeniably human – and somehow that made it even worse.

'So, you have overcome my Northland hedge wizard!' the voice exclaimed mockingly. 'I might have known! Horskram of Vilno, master monk of the Order – you just won't die, will you?'

'Your devilish servant did its best to try,' the adept replied levelly. 'But the Redeemer watches over his own.'

'Ah, my demonic servitor gave you a merry chase, eh?' chuckled the voice of Andragorix. 'But you won't be able to cower at Strongholm forever – even now you are beyond range of that which protected you. Oh, I know my old legends as well as you do, Horskram! It is only a matter of time before I recover my strength – you'll never reach that fool Hannequin alive, mark my words!'

'There are others who can tell him of your crimes if we fail,' replied Horskram, unperturbed. 'But in any case, I do not think you will be sending any more of your servitors to trouble us.'

The adept reached deep into the folds of his habit and withdrew something on a slender iron chain. Hanging from it was a tiny crystal phial.

As he held it up above the pool, its unearthly light caught the red dot of a single drop of blood.

The revolted screech that escaped from the pool had everyone in the room but Horskram flinching.

'No, no! Not that! Put it away! Get that out of my sight, oh mother no...'

Horskram's lip curled in disgust. 'Don't call on your witch mother's trapped spirit to help you now – look upon the blood of the Redeemer, poltroon, and despair!'

Andragorix must have recovered himself, for he quickly retorted: 'Ha! Do you think I am a devil, and can be turned by such talismans of your false faith? There are plenty of ways to kill you that a relic won't protect you from!'

'Granted,' replied Horskram. 'But to do that you'll have to face us yourself. Where are the fragments, Andragorix?'

The voice from the pool sneered. 'Safe and sound, quite beyond your feeble grasp! Awaiting their brothers to rejoin them!'

'Andragorix, know this – wherever you are, I am coming for you,' said Horskram in a voice that was flat and emotionless. 'And when I find you, this time I shall not be merciful. You are quite mad, and must be stopped at all costs.'

Another hoot of maniacal laughter shot from the shimmering pool. 'Oh hear, mother, now he threatens us! Tell me, how is Sir Belinos? Did he smell good after I cooked his flesh? I hope you didn't have too much trouble burying his remains.'

The voice was cruelly mocking now. But Horskram remained ungoaded. 'Belinos is in the Heavenly Halls, where his soul rightly belongs,' he replied calmly, making the sign. 'I'm sure he was pleased to take your hand with him.'

'Oh that?' replied Andragorix. 'Never mind – I made myself a new one! Those idiot druids were good for teaching me some things – do you like my silver hand, Horskram? I'll use it to tear out your spleen before long!'

'I would fain give you the opportunity to try,' answered the adept. 'Just tell me where you are – and I'll come and face you. You and your servants against me and whatever companions will join me. Let's settle this business between us once and for all!'

The voice laughed again. 'Oh ho, I always forget you used to be a knight! Spoken like one, truly – the duel of honour, eh? Ah no, I think not, Brother Horskram – you'll have to work a bit harder than that to find me! Until then, be assured I'll be keeping a close eye on you – now I know better than to rely on an idiot pagan priest to watch you while I attend to more important matters. And rest assured, I've plenty of other servants I can send to test you, ones that won't flinch at the sight of a prophet's blood!'

The pool suddenly went dark. A moment of stygian blackness, and then daylight was streaming through the window again, and all was as it had been before. Horskram stepped back from the pool, making the sign and intoning a quick prayer.

'We have learned all there is to learn,' he said presently. 'Let us clear the room and have all the paraphernalia destroyed. Then I will put a blessing on the room and it can be used once more for cleaner purposes.'

The crone, who had been cowering in a corner, now shuffled up to Horskram. 'Now you'll let me go, lord monk?' she inquired, looking at him with beady, hopeful eyes.

Horskram turned to eye her coldly. Then he looked over at Kelmor and said: 'My lord, have your men seize this witch immediately.'

The crone wailed piteously as Salmorlund gave the order.

'Gag her and bind her at once, before she tries any chicanery!' cried Horskram.

This was quickly done, Adelko looking on aghast. Ulla was a lecherous and greedy old crone, a hedge witch of low character. But she'd never really harmed anyone – and she'd just helped them identify one of the most dangerous black magicians in the Free Kingdoms. Surely this was no way to repay her?

Squaring up to her, Horskram declared: 'Ulla, the mark of the witch shall be branded on your forehead directly, so that all may know you in future. With Salmorlund's consent I do also banish you from all his lands including Wethering, on pain of death if you return.'

'I do so consent,' intoned the Jarl.

'Very well,' rejoined Horskram. 'Then you have a tenday to quit the Jarldom of Salmorlund. If you are found within its environs after that, you shall be put to death.'

Adelko finally found his voice as the soldiers dragged the gagging crone off to the dungeons with Salmor following behind. 'But Master Horskram, you promised you'd set her free!' he cried.

'She is a pagan witch!' snarled the adept, rounding on him. 'No promises can hold when dealing with such.'

'But, you lied...!'

'Yes, Adelko, I lied,' replied his master in a surly voice. 'You may have noticed on our travels that I've done so several times, when need has dictated. Sometimes the greater good must be served with a lesser evil, as I've already told you. At least yon witch shall keep her life. Next to the sins of half the men you have kept company with these past weeks, I think this a small one, don't you?'

'But it still isn't right,' Adelko protested. 'That witch helped us to identify Andragorix, and you just tossed her aside after using her! It doesn't seem... well, fair.'

'Oh for Heaven's sake, Adelko!' snapped Horskram. 'Now is hardly the time for such trifling moral scruples! You've just witnessed a war! Think on everything you've seen this past fortnight, everything your King has had to do, far greater evils than I have just done, in order to save the kingdom and return it to peace. And now a branded hedge witch troubles your conscience? Don't make me laugh.'

Adelko felt another rare burst of anger surge through him. His mentor's cynicism appalled him.

'So what gives you the right to sit in judgment – after everything you've done?' he yelled. 'That old crone might be a witch and a thief and a... lecher, but I bet she never killed anyone! "Let he who is without sin hammer the first nail" – that's what Palom himself said!'

Adelko fixed his mentor with a look that was both triumphant and angry. Surely he had him now – the words the Redeemer had spoken when he abolished executions in his army were common knowledge among students of Scripture.

Horskram returned his gaze and held it. Then he laughed. 'Ah, you have learned much, Adelko – as high as my praise of you has been, yet still I have underestimated you. Let he who is without sin hammer the first nail indeed! And are you without sin, that judges me so harshly?'

'I... no. I'm not. No mortal is – every good Palomedian knows that. But I don't lie. And I don't have any blood on my hands either.'

A queer light entered the adept's hard blue eyes. 'Do you not? And what of the Battle of Salmor? Does the swordsmith not play a part in the deaths dealt by the sword?'

'I don't know what you're talking about, Master Horskram. I'm no maker of weapons – I'm just a novice in the Order.'

'Ah, just a novice in the Order,' replied Horskram with mocking acquiescence. 'A novice who played a crucial part in winning a battle, if I remember rightly.'

Horskram fell silent and stared at him pointedly. Adelko didn't like where this was going. He felt awash with a muddle of emotions. It was suddenly difficult to think straight.

'How many brave knights of Thule's perished because you were canny enough to see through the Sea Wizard's disguise and turn the tables on them?' pressed Horskram. 'Your second sight dealt Thule's men a sounder blow than a hundred blades of Strongholm steel could have done.'

Adelko was about to interject but Horskram forestalled him.

'Oh I know – treasonous knights died so loyal ones might live,' he continued. 'But can you say for sure that all of Thule's men were bad? Or that all the King's men are good? Think on Wolmar, as cruel and vain a knight as any that lived – quite possibly your perception saved his life too! Good and evil, noble and base – the lines between such are not so clear as we would like to believe, Adelko.'

Without another word, Horskram turned and stalked from the chamber.

Adelko stood alone in the room for a while, struggling to collect thoughts that were now troubled and confused. A timorous servant came to bar the door pending the chamber's clearing and reconsecration. Gathering his wits, Adelko left.

A window in the corridor outside faced north. Blankly he looked out of it while the servant hurriedly barred the door behind him. Gazing on the hewn and punctured corpses of the slain piled up on the hills and fields around Salmor, he felt a surge of guilt.

And he realised then that his mentor was right – neither good nor bad, but just simply right.

He thought of the hundreds of knights the King had hanged, of the hundreds more dead and butchered yeomen they had ridden past. In his mind's eye he saw the hopeless eyes of the peasant women at court on his first day at Strongholm, victims of the angry lust of frenzied soldiers.

What, indeed, was one more lie and a branded hedge witch on top of all of that? He was involved in high events now, and every decision had high consequences.

I would not have you seduced by the way of the sword, Adelko. A pure spirit is a precious thing.

His mentor's words, on the eve of the march to war. He realised then what Horskram had been trying to tell him. But it was too late for such warnings now. Maybe he hadn't killed anyone directly, but he had intervened in the work of killers, and that changed everything.

The side he had picked might well have been the right one – but even that would not excuse him from judgment, in the end.

Adelko hung his head, and a sorrow came over him. All his life he had thirsted for adventure. Now it had found him with a vengeance, and there could be no turning back. His innocence was gone forever.

⊰ CHAPTER XV ⊱

A Farewell Feast

King Freidheim turned from the window as Horskram finished relaying the events of the morning. They were alone in a chamber in a turret of the castle, from where he had been observing the preparations for the victory feast.

Salmor had been a hubbub of activity all day, as servants scurried to and fro. All the knights and lords would be crammed into the great hall, to celebrate the crushed rebellion with their King and his loyal barons. Outside, in fields directly south of the castle, trestle tables were being set up for the commoners who had taken part in the war, for summer was near and the nights were increasingly warm.

Freidheim prided himself on being able to concentrate on more than one thing at a time, but his scrutiny of the preparations had soon waned as the monk's latest story unfolded.

'Reus Almighty!' breathed Freidheim, walking over to sit in a chair and motioning for Horskram to do likewise. 'So you mean to tell me this Andragorix was behind Thule's bloody uprising all along! Reus be damned!'

He knew he shouldn't blaspheme, especially not before an Argolian. But the way he saw it, he was King and could blaspheme any time he damn well pleased.

'Not directly, as I have just endeavoured to explain,' rejoined Horskram, tactfully overlooking his transgression. 'But presumably he was able to seduce the ambitious Northland priest to his will, who in turn was set to pouring poison in Thule's ear. Thus will the servants of the Fallen One ever work, playing pawn over pawn.'

'And this Ragnar, what of him?'

'It seems likely that he transformed himself into a raven or other swift bird as soon as he saw all was lost,' replied Horskram. 'Andragorix himself intimated he had that power. Plus one of the windows to his chamber was open.'

The King pursed his lips as he considered this. The mysterious monk's story still did not quite add up.

'But one thing, Horskram,' he pressed. 'One thing puzzles me. If this Andragorix had scrying powers as you say he did, how then were you able to use that old crone to hoodwink him into thinking the war wasn't lost? Wouldn't he have divined as much using his black arts already?'

'I was wondering if that gambit would pay off,' replied Horskram. 'But in his closing words he said he'd had "other matters" to attend to. He also let slip that his strength was not at optimum – from what we know of sorcerers, they can become psychically fatigued by their efforts, just as a warrior in the field can grow tired after one sword-stroke or forced march too many.'

'I'm sure my men could tell you plenty about that just now!' rejoined the King with a booming laugh. His recent victory had left him feeling more contented than usual. Wars were unpleasant, but by Reus it still felt good to win one.

'Just so,' continued Horskram. 'It also became clear during our discourse that Andragorix had been relying on the Sea Wizard to keep tabs on Adelko and me during our journey – it was he who commissioned the Northland brigands to pursue us, having probably flown to Port Cravern to hire them at his master's command. But even this conclusion doesn't solve the mystery of just what has been occupying him – I have my suspicions in that area however.'

'And those are?'

'Assuming Andragorix is responsible for the thefts of both fragments, he would need his powers free to command the agents he used to steal them. And then there is the matter of the other two fragments – he will no doubt be laying plans to steal the third from the Island Realms, and be searching for the fourth in the Sassanian Sultanates. Even a wizard of his stature must grow weary after such efforts, so it makes sense that he was relying on Ragnar to spy on us in the meantime. I think it likely that, once we reached divine sanctuary at Strongholm, he gave up on the chase for a while and turned to focus his energies on those other tasks, leaving Ragnar to keep him informed of the war and our movements.'

Freidheim still wasn't satisfied.

'But why this war, Horskram?' he demanded. 'Why bring ruin on my kingdom – it has little to do with his mad quest for these fragments as far as I can see!'

Horskram's face was set grim as he answered. 'Whoever seeks to reunite the Headstone seeks to have power over many kingdoms not one. There are rulers who would gladly throw their lot in with such a person, if they saw their own benefit in it. But there are other rulers, perhaps rarer, who would seek to oppose such a worldwide tyranny, and do everything in their power to stop it. You are such a prince, Your Majesty. For that reason, it made perfect sense to try and supplant you while the Headstone remains incomplete – and replace you with a more pliant ruler.'

The King, though flattered, was not wholly convinced. 'But why not simply wait until the Headstone is reunited, if it's so damnably powerful? Why bother with all that intrigue?'

'The fourth fragment remains unaccounted for,' Horskram reminded him. 'Andragorix may never find it. Even then it is said that only a mighty sorcerer could ever hope to wield its power – Morwena clearly sought to, seven centuries ago. But whether any latter-day warlock can ever hope to do such a thing remains uncertain at best.'

'Then this Andragorix is mad!' exclaimed the King.

'Oh, yes, quite,' Horskram confirmed. 'But not so mad as to realise that if world domination is what he desires, a good way to start is by bringing the kingdom of his birth under his control. I say this to you, Your Majesty – Andragorix may not yet be powerful or knowledgeable enough to use the Headstone, or even canny enough to reunite it, but his powers have clearly grown since I fought him in Roarkil. I sensed that much today. What has fuelled those powers, I cannot yet say. But the fact that he is ambitious enough to seek to take over a realm from afar shows how confident he is in them. And it's obvious his plans are far more elaborate than we can yet fathom. I fear we have answered a few questions, merely to be presented with others.'

The monk sighed and leaned back in his chair, staring out of a window at the darkening skies. The sun would be setting soon.

'And you were unable to determine Andragorix's whereabouts during your interrogation?' asked the King.

'It was hardly an interrogation, more a sparring of words,' sighed Horskram. 'And no, he gave little enough away.'

The King frowned. 'So why not send to Urling Monastery, have Prior Holfaste sanction a... what d'ye call it?'

'A divination?' supplied Horskram. 'That would have been my preference initially – back at Ulfang, when all this mess began. Sacristen would not hear of it, and I cursed his abject secrecy at the time. But since then... I'm more inclined to agree with the abbot. Andragorix may have revealed himself, but there is still too much about this situation that we do not know. I still feel that the fewer people we tell, the better.

Even if that means forgoing a divination. To hold one at Urling, Holfaste would have to tell all his adepts Andragorix was at large. That would inevitably lead to questions as to how we know and what he is up to.'

'So what?' asked Freidheim bluntly. 'Everyone who was at the council knows – and it won't be long before I can get a messenger to your precious Hannequin. When the rebel fleet hears of our victory on land they will doubtless flee or surrender to Thorsvald. That means the Wyvern should soon be open to us again. As you said yourself at the council, once your Grand Master knows he'll inform the Pangonian King and the Supreme Perfect. Why all the need for secrecy?'

The adept tapped his lips thoughtfully and gazed distractedly out of the window. Dammit but the man's recondite musings were irritating – if not downright suspicious.

'The Temple will learn of the theft before long,' the King pressed. 'And don't count on me to have that pompous idiot Lorthar executed, though I may yet. But if I do, rest assured it won't be to save your Order from being embarrassed!'

'There is a good deal more to it than being embarrassed, Your Majesty,' returned Horskram, far too sharply for his King's liking. 'But it's more than just Temple politics that stays my hand...' His face grew anxious. 'Every time I think of any more people being privy to this affair my sixth sense jangles.'

Freidheim stared at him. 'Your what?'

Horskram sighed. 'Tis a psychic attunement that Argolians cultivate from an early age. It makes us sensitive to witchcraft and can also heighten our intuition in certain matters... I am sorry, sire, I wish I could be more concrete on the matter, but to one not gifted with the sense it is difficult to explain... with all due respect.'

The King shifted uncomfortably and huffed irritably. Argolians and their blasted mysticism. Sixth sense, divinations – in their own way, they were almost as bad as the sorcerers they claimed to oppose. Perhaps it was with good reason that Lorthar and his ilk distrusted them so. He thought of the erstwhile Arch Perfect, languishing in the dungeons beneath Strongholm. He damn well hoped he had chosen the right side in this preternatural struggle.

'Besides,' continued Horskram, 'I am no longer convinced a divination at Urling would do us much good.'

The King glared at Horskram suspiciously.

'And why is that?' he growled.

'Andragorix will almost certainly have placed a blanketing spell on his new lair,' replied Horskram. 'Before, I would have been confident that an Argolian chapter would be able to channel enough of the Redeemer's elan to break through such a defence. But after the power I sensed in him today...' The monk shook his head. 'Urling monastery is smaller than Ulfang, its adepthood less potent – and largely untested thanks to the sanctity of the Redeemer's blood. And even Ulfang, I now think, would be hard pressed to divine past Andragorix's witcheries. In fact the only chapter I can think of that might muster enough spiritual essence to do such a thing - '

'Is the Grand Monastery in Rima,' the King finished for him resignedly.

'Precisely, Your Majesty,' rejoined Horskram with a deferential nod that Freidheim found infuriating. 'So if I'm to find him before I go there, I must think of some other way to do it.'

'Well you better had,' replied Freidheim sternly. 'Hopefully I need not remind you that you have sworn your King an oath to seek out Andragorix and destroy him.'

'And that I shall,' Horskram reassured him. 'As soon as I know his whereabouts. The last I heard he was in Vorstlund, but that was many moons ago. He could be anywhere in the Free Kingdoms by now, perhaps beyond.'

The King shook his head, feeling thoroughly exasperated. 'Well this is a merry dance and no mistake!' he exclaimed.

'There is nothing merry about it,' replied Horskram glumly.

❖ ❖ ❖

Adelko sipped his stoop of ale and tried to lose himself in the music, as servants moved about the castle courtyard lighting torches. Braxus was in fine form on the harp, and his compatriots were in good voice; the troubadours had gathered quite a crowd in the run-up to the feast, and the ward was teeming with carousing knights and soldiers. Mail and shield had been discarded in favour of doublet and hose, giving the Thraxian lordling a chance to show off his finest clothes: slashed russet-red silk with black velvet undercloth, and an elegant cocked cap of matching colours. He broke off his playing to take a sweetmeat from a tray – and flirt with the serving wench bearing it.

Vaskrian was as happy as Adelko had ever seen him – clearly he had done well out of the fortunes of war, his purse jingled with silver marks to prove it. He'd managed to avoid further injury in the last battle, and killed a few more rebels. Or so he had told Adelko, several times.

The novice didn't care to hear it – he was heartily sick of war. His mentor's hard words that morning had left him nursing a guilty conscience that even the potent combination of Northlending ale and Thraxian song could not entirely dispel.

'Will you be eating in the hall tonight?' the squire asked him, his face flushed with success – and the copious amounts of beer he had already downed.

Adelko shook his head and forced a smile. 'I could have – Master Horskram has a place at the table of honour, and the King said I could have the same, for spotting Thule's knights.'

The squire suddenly looked crestfallen. 'You turned down a place at the King's table? Why in the Known World did you do that?'

'I want to sit with my brother Arik – out there in the good green fields,' replied Adelko, motioning vaguely beyond the castle precinct with his half-empty horn. 'It's where I belong – I'm no hero, Vaskrian, just a novice of the Order.'

Vaskrian frowned and shrugged his shoulders. 'Suit yourself,' he replied nonchalantly. 'I'm eating in the hall – I'll have to carve for Sir Braxus first of course, but they say the spread will be staggering – even for us squires!'

'I should think so,' replied Adelko, taking another swig. Kelmor's lands had been spared Johan's scorched earth tactics – presumably Thule had felt confident of holding that much land indefinitely at least. The ale was fruity and frothy on his tongue; brought up from Lord Kelmor's cellars, it was as good as anything Sholto brewed back at Ulfang. 'Salmorlund's had the kitchen staff working day and night – I've heard he's even pressed some of the men-at-arms that served Thule into service.'

'I'm sure they'll be happy with that,' replied the squire with rare sarcasm. 'Well, they're lucky to be keeping their heads – hope they don't poison the food, though!'

Adelko winced at the ugly thought. After all they had been through and survived, being poisoned at a celebration feast sounded like an ignominious – and painful – death.

Just then Braxus started up again. Adelko recognised the song immediately – it was the Northlending bard Halreth's *Lay of Sleeping Steel*. A well-known tune in those parts, written to celebrate the final defeat of the Northland reavers a hundred years ago. That had ended in the signing of the Treaty of Ryøskil, and King Aelfric III, son and heir to the Hero King Thorsvald, had commissioned Halreth to write a song celebrating the end of the long war with the Ice Thanes.

'Ah, one of my favourites,' slurred Vaskrian as he grabbed another horn off a passing wench. 'You can't beat old Halreth for a good tune.'

'I know he's playing local stuff to please the crowd, but I can't see why Braxus is playing *Sleeping Steel* – the peace it celebrates has just been broken in our time,' replied Adelko glumly. 'Then again, I don't suppose he was going to play Vakka's *Lay of Blood's Rest.*'

That particular ditty had been penned by the contemporary of Halreth some ten years before – to celebrate a crushing defeat of the Thraxians by the Hero King. It had been revived after Freidheim did likewise at the Battle of Corne Hill, the year before Adelko was born.

'They don't have much luck against us, your new master's people, do they?' mused the novice, following his sombre train of thought. 'I wonder, how did Braxus and his countrymen feel when we passed Corne Hill on the march to Salmor? They didn't look too pleased – especially not when half the army started cheering it as a good omen.'

The ale was starting to go to his head. Given his mood it wasn't likely to be a good kind of drunk.

Vaskrian screwed up his face. 'What's got into you?' he demanded, frowning now. 'You've been in an ill humour all afternoon! I don't understand – we *won*, Adelko. And you played a big part in that. This is a time to celebrate, not sour your ale with one miserable remark after another! And as for Sir Braxus, you leave him out of this – Thraxian or no, he fought in our war on our side. Or have you already forgotten that?'

Adelko sighed, downing the rest of his drink. There was no use trying to explain his feelings to the hot-headed squire – but there was no need to poison his humour either.

'I'm sorry, Vaskrian,' he sighed. 'I'm just tired, that's all. This morning was... draining.'

Vaskrian fixed him with a stare. 'Look, I don't need your sixth sight or whatever you bloody call it to see that it was more than just draining. You've hardly told me anything about it! Reus' sake, I'm your friend, Adelko – you should be able to talk to me about this kind of stuff.'

Adelko nodded perfunctorily, staring absently about the courtyard. Several of the knights and soldiers had begun to dance with the serving wenches, who seemed happy enough to be distracted from their duties. A general mood of euphoria was permeating the ward, one he couldn't share.

'We've identified who was trying to have us killed,' replied Adelko, lowering his voice despite the noisy laughter and music. 'It wasn't only Ragnar... there's another warlock behind it all. He's called Andragorix – you may remember Horskram mentioned him at Staerkvit, when the High Commander interrogated us.'

Prince Freidhoff. Another noble corpse made by the war. Hard to believe the stern old patrician was rotting in the ground. Reus willing, his soul was on its way to a better place. Once he would have taken that for granted: but after everything Horskram had said he wasn't so sure anymore.

'So is he the one behind that theft you're all so concerned about?' The squire sounded positively nonchalant. But then he hadn't been at the secret council – the gravity of the fragment thefts would be largely lost on him, unlettered as he was. Adelko could not have envied his ignorance more.

'It looks that way,' he said, as Vaskrian turned to grab him another horn from a passing wench. Taking the fresh stoop gratefully, Adelko sighed: 'So he'll be our next assignment.'

Vaskrian grinned. 'Really Adelko, you need to cheer up. After helping to put down an armed rebellion, what's one more wizard? Why at this rate, you'll be a chief monk in no time!'

Adelko had to smile at that. 'We don't have chief monks you idiot – they're called abbots, remember?'

'Whatever you say. Hey, did you see that wench just now? She was definitely looking, know what I mean? Reckon we'll have some fun tonight, eh?'

Adelko flushed. 'You know I can't... I mean I'm sworn...' He looked at the ground, his face burning.

Vaskrian smiled again, not unkindly. Then he leaned forward, a conspiratorial look on his face. 'But surely, on account of you being a war hero and all, just this once your master might, y'know, let you...'

'No!' replied Adelko, genuinely shocked. 'That wouldn't be proper at all! Argolians are forbidden – '

'Oh fie on that!' laughed the squire. 'Why, I'll bet your old mentor had a few wenches in his time, back when he was a knight. Oh, I've heard about his wild youth – he looks at me like I'm a man gone wood half the time, but I reckon there was more of Vaskrian of Hroghar in Horskram of Vilno than he cares to admit.'

After everything he'd learned about his mentor, Adelko could almost entertain the possibility. Almost.

'Hmm... they say he was a very pious knight, though,' said the novice, mulling it over as he took another sip of ale. However inappropriate the squire's bawdy conversation was, it was certainly good to get his mind

off his gloomy thoughts. 'I really don't see him being quite the knight...
you plan on being.'

'Oh I don't know, Adelko,' replied Vaskrian, grinning devilishly.
'I can definitely see him riding a few nags in his time... Maybe he
read them scripture while he was doing it! Commit the sin and, what
d'yer call it, absolve the sin at the same time...'

'Vaskrian!' Adelko was even redder than he had been just a
minute ago. 'Of all the blasphemous things you could say...!'

The squire was miming along with his filthy words now, moving
his hips back and forwards and pretending to read from a book.
Behind him Adelko could see Regan and Bryant looking at him
curiously and exchanging bemused glances.

And then he started laughing. Maybe it was the ale. Maybe it really
was that funny. Or maybe a youth of fourteen summers with his whole life ahead
of him could only stay sad for so long. Whatever it was, that laughter was
the best he'd enjoyed since he and Yalba and Arik and Hargus had shared
a gourd of cider, the same spilled gourd that had changed his life forever.

They both laughed for a seeming age, bent over double, ale spilling
messily from their cups. The sound mingled with Braxus' clear high alto
as he took the music up another notch; it mingled with the revelry and
joy that swirled in the courtyard about them, the stomping of feet and
raucous babble of voices as noble and commoner alike forgot decorum
and lost themselves in the purest joy of all, the joy of being alive.

They were halfway through their next drink, clapping each other
merrily on the shoulders and laughing loudly when Adelko screwed
up the courage to ask his friend the question he'd been afraid to.

'What will you do next? After the feast I mean?'

Vaskrian shrugged. 'Don't know – it's not up to me, is it? Braxus
is my guvnor now – where he goes, I go.'

Adelko nodded sadly. He knew what that meant.

'Well...' he faltered. 'I never thought I'd hear myself saying this
to a man of the sword but... I'm going to miss you.'

Vaskrian gazed at him, a slightly wistful look entering his
dark eyes. Then he laughed again. 'Don't get maudlin on me again,
Adelko! We haven't parted company yet! And there's a whole night's
celebrating to get through – I shall need you along! I'm sure we'll
meet up for a few more after the eating's done!'

'Aye,' Adelko nodded. 'I'd like that. I'd like you to meet my brother too.'

'There we go then,' replied Vaskrian, putting a wiry arm around
the monk and clinking horns with him. 'No need for sad farewells
just yet! We'll cross that bridge when we come to it!'

Just then they were startled by a commotion. A group of ravens came tearing into the courtyard at a gallop. As they dismounted Adelko recognised Sir Torgun. His face was grave as he handed the reins to an ostler and stalked towards the keep, closely followed by his knights.

'What do you think that's all about?' asked Adelko, feeling suddenly anxious. The music had stopped abruptly. Sir Braxus had left off playing some time ago to get a few ales in and start wenching, but by then the castle troubadours had arrived. Their sudden silence filled the courtyard, now awash with muttering.

'Dunno,' said the squire. 'Torgun's been promoted to Commander, to replace poor ol' Tarlquist as head of his company. I think he was sent riding south with a larger detachment to secure Thule's holding.'

'Do you think they're holding out?' asked Adelko nervously.

'I doubt it,' replied Vaskrian. 'From what I hear Thule emptied his lands of able-bodied men to fight his war. Only a fool would try to hold Thule Castle against all the King's men. He did look concerned though.'

From somewhere in the courtyard a piper started up again, closely followed by drums and harp. The castle quickly returned to its twilight revel. Adelko looked at Vaskrian and shrugged. No point worrying about it now – if the past weeks were anything to go by, he'd learn of any fresh trouble soon enough.

✥ ✥ ✥

The King was just about to dismiss Horskram and retire to prepare for the feast when there came a knock at the door.

Reus' teeth, was a king's work was ever done?

'Enter!' he bellowed.

A guard poked his armoured head around the door. 'Sir Torgun of Vandheim is without, sire,' he said. 'He craves an audience with you directly. Says it's urgent.'

The King rolled his eyes. 'Heavens! Those rug rats had better not be holding out at Thule Castle or I'll have it razed! All right, let him in. Horskram, you may as well stay – I've come to value your counsel, even your novice is wise beyond his tender years.'

Horskram acquiesced with another one of his deferential nods. The King had bid him stay for a cup of wine. He'd hoped to wheedle more out of the wily adept as to his plans, but he had dissembled evasively. Damned secretive Argolians – still, they had just helped him win the war.

Torgun strode in, taking a knee.

'Get up, Torgun, and have out with it,' said the King, in no mood for formalities.

'Thule Castle is secure, Your Majesty,' said Torgun, rising swiftly.

'Good. Then why the long face?'

'During our reconnaissance of Thule's lands we heard disturbing stories,' said Torgun, licking his lips. 'Most of the levies who fled the field at Linden appear to have returned to the lands of their birth, only they have turned outlaw. They're causing trouble and turning on their own folk.'

'That is no great surprise,' replied the King. 'We'll rest up and celebrate our victory in the field, and then we'll deal with any remnants. Seeing as I intend to annex the southron fiefs to my dominions, I've been expecting to meet resistance anyway. We'll have more than just a few rag-tag outlaws to deal with too – there'll be younger sons and brothers of disinherited knights looking to stake their claim. When the feasting's done I'm going to begin parcelling out the baronies that belonged to the rebels, we'll create new lords and knights - '

'Begging your royal pardon,' Torgun interrupted. 'But this isn't the only news I bring.'

The King frowned. 'Well, what else could there be? Don't tell me the Sea Wizard has resurfaced!'

'Not as far as we know,' said Torgun. 'But we've heard strange stories – coming out of the Argael Forest.'

The King exchanged glances with Horskram. 'The Argael? But that's right on the border of my kingdom. What has that to do with anything?'

'We met a lone mercenary not far from the south highway,' said Torgun. 'A freesword returning from Vorstlund. He was grievously wounded and being tended to at a manor belonging to one of Thule's dead knights.'

'Dead disinherited knights,' the King corrected. 'Go on.'

'He said he'd been in a party of bodyguards, travelling through the forest with a group of merchants on their way to trade with the southrons.'

'Not caring a fig that those same southrons were wreaking havoc up north I'll be bound,' exclaimed Freidheim. 'Pah, a pox on those up-jumped market hawkers, they're all the same!'

'I share your opinions of the merchant class,' interjected Horskram. 'But perhaps we should let Sir Torgun finish his story.'

'Yes, yes,' said the King with an impatient wave of the hand. 'Sir Torgun, pray continue.'

'His party was attacked. He was the only survivor, and barely at that.' Torgun paused. 'He claims the attackers were beast-folk of the woods.'

'Wadwos?' asked Horskram, looking suddenly very interested.

'Just so,' confirmed Torgun. 'He says they were clumsy, but hugely strong – white-faced brutes with strange hands and stranger faces, loathsome to look upon. They set upon them at dusk when they were busy making camp. They were a large group, at least a dozen strong, well armed. From the way the freesword told it, they sounded well organised too. I thought you should know, Your Majesty, as it happened on the Northlending side of the forest.'

The King and the adept exchanged glances again.

'But that doesn't make any sense,' said Horskram. 'From what I know of Wadwos, hugely strong and malicious though they are, they seldom cooperate. They mostly live alone, and are as like to turn on one another as they are to prey on ordinary mortals.'

Sir Torgun nodded gravely. 'I once slew a Wadwo myself, master monk, and my experience of them is likewise.'

'So what does this mean?' sighed the King. 'Have I defeated an army of rebel traitors only to be faced with a slavering pack of beastmen in my back yard?'

'There is more, Your Majesty,' said Torgun. 'During their journey – before they were attacked – the merchants and their bodyguards encountered frightened groups of woodfolk abandoning their homes. They say a dreadful curse has descended on the forest – they also spoke of another warlock who walks abroad at night, chanting fell sorceries beneath the trees.'

'Ragnar?' asked the King.

'Nay,' replied Torgun, shaking his head. 'Another elementalist by the sounds of it – they call her the Earth Witch.'

'I've heard of her,' mused the King. 'Legend has it she keeps the deepest part of the Argael as her private realm, and suffers none to tread there. But few if any have ever had contact with her – to tell the truth I never really believed it.'

'No, I think the legend is true,' said Horskram thoughtfully. 'She is a Right-Handed practitioner of fearsome repute, a pagan priestess who worships the Moon Goddess and can bend nature to her will. Some say she hails from the Island Realms, where she learned her craft of the druids before being banished as punishment for a failed attempt to wrest power from her rivals. Others say that she was born in the Argael, and that her mother was a Terrus – an earth spirit.'

Torgun gaped. 'A spirit and a mortal bearing offspring in coitus! Is such a thing possible?'

'It has been known,' replied Horskram laconically, briefly making the sign. 'But nobody knows her true origins for sure. Unlike most warlocks she seldom stirs from her lair and never troubles those that leave her alone. That's why we Argolians have never had cause to seek her out.'

'Well, if the freesword is to be believed, something has her stirred up,' said Torgun. 'The wood-dwellers he spoke of said she's been seen beyond the heart of the forest where she usually dwells.'

'Could she be behind the Wadwos?' ventured the King. Once again he was getting the sinking feeling that matters had taken a turn that went well beyond his experience. Perhaps he should consider employing an Argolian as a court adviser in future. Secretive or not, they were undeniably useful.

Horskram shook his head. 'I don't think so. Wadwos are an abomination – the descendants of failed attempts by the Elder Wizards to create a race of super-soldiers thousands of years ago. It's unlikely a Right-Handed warlock would have any dealings with beastmen – such wizards are more wont to harness the Elementi, what you would call nature spirits, to their will. It would take a Left-Handed sorcerer of considerable power to enthral such creatures... I don't think I need to spell out who it might be.'

Torgun looked confused.

'He means Andragorix,' said the King, before telling him of the morning's events.

Torgun made the sign. 'So Andragorix was behind the war and now he's amassing a loathsome army of his own! Dastard!'

'Well we don't know the latter part for sure but it would appear so,' said Horskram. 'And that might explain what is depleting his psychic strength – ensorcelling an army of Wadwos would require considerable sorceries. One would have to be a past master in the School of Enchantment, and prepared to expend a good deal of energy...' A thin smile crossed the monk's face. 'In any case, at least now we have a better idea of where he could be. Indeed, this is an excellent development.'

'How so?' asked the King.

'Why it's quite elementary, Your Majesty,' replied Horskram, sounding almost affable now. 'If Andragorix is behind the beastmen, he'll be somewhere in the vicinity of the forest – not even he could hope to ensorcell a pack of Wadwos from afar. So he was toying with me this morning – I might have guessed.'

Both Torgun and the King looked at Horskram quizzically.

'He must have known I would learn about the beastmen before long,' explained the adept. 'He isn't going to make it easy by spelling it out for me, because that would ruin his game, you see. But I think he wants to be found – he's itching for a confrontation.'

'That doesn't make sense,' replied Freidheim. 'Last time you encountered him, he lost a hand and nearly his life. Why should he seek to meet you again?'

'You forget what kind of man this is,' answered Horskram gravely. 'In fact even to call him such is perhaps wide of the mark – after a near lifetime of servitude to the Fallen One he is more a living demon than a man.'

Torgun and Freidheim exchanged uneasy glances. 'I fear this requires more explanation, though the subject is in serious danger of ruining my appetite!' said the King, glancing ruefully out of the window at the deepening dusk.

'Andragorix is a fetishist in the classical sense,' said Horskram. 'He is a living embodiment of the Seven Princes of Perfidy, to whom he has given himself up, body and soul. Lust, envy, greed... such dark drives consume him night and day. But to these we may also add vanity and pride, wrath and cruelty – and therein lies his weakness. His pride and anger will demand that he have an opportunity to be revenged by inflicting pain and torment on me. And in his vanity he will gloat at the idea of showing the world that he finally bested me. He may have mocked me for seeking a duel of honour, but he himself craves a duel – a duel of vengeance in a place of his choosing.'

'What will you do?' asked Sir Torgun. 'If what you say is true then it sounds as if you plan on walking into a very death trap.'

'And I have sworn an oath to His Majesty that I will do everything in my power to destroy Andragorix,' returned Horskram, glancing sidelong at the King, 'rendering such concerns immaterial.'

He turned to meet the King's gaze fully. 'Moreover, I believe Your Majesty has been viewing me with considerable scepticism this past hour – and with all due respect I would fain put your mind at rest. I may be secretive when the need arises, but be assured my liege, I am without doubt the lesser of evils presented before you.'

The King allowed himself a wry smile at that. 'I see this sixth sense of yours serves you well, Brother Horskram – perhaps I was wrong to look askance at an Argolian.'

Horskram shook his head. 'Nay, Your Majesty, you would not be much of a king if you took everything at face value like a trusting fool,' he said with characteristic candour. 'In any case it looks nigh certain

Andragorix is behind the theft of the fragments and has them in his keeping. I shall seek him in the Argael – dangerous as that will be, it's too good a lead to pass up.'

'But how will you find him?' queried Torgun. 'The Argael is vast – you can hardly go scouring it branch and tree, all the more so if there's a horde of Wadwos at large!'

'Thank you, sir knight, I'm well aware of the conundrum,' replied Horskram tartly. 'This matter bears some consideration…'

'Well, you can consider it over another cup of wine in the hall – I've a victory feast to preside over and I need to get dressed,' said the King, starting to rise.

'… although I think the obvious course of action presents itself clearly enough,' continued the monk, as though no one had spoken.

The King frowned. 'Well, out with it!' he growled, sitting down again heavily.

'Wait! Should you speak so candidly?' exclaimed Torgun suddenly. 'What if Andragorix hears us, even now?'

Horskram smiled wanly. 'He cannot hear us. He can only see us – to attain far-hearing he must have another scrying tool connected to his own.'

Torgun blinked, looking none the wiser.

'The surviving mercenary spoke of rumours that the Earth Witch has stirred from her lair,' continued Horskram, running a hand over his beard thoughtfully. 'From what little we know, that is certainly not like her – she is so reclusive her real name is unknown. For years she has kept her lair protected with her sorceries, suffering none to encroach. Divided and leaderless, the beastmen of the woods would pose little threat to the spirit guardians bound to her will…'

'… but united under another wizard, they might,' breathed the King as realisation dawned on him. 'Reus almighty! He's fighting her for mastery of the forest!'

'No wonder she's so stirred up,' replied Horskram, nodding. 'Andragorix isn't content with overthrowing kings – he also seeks to supplant rival sorcerers. While his pawns have been busy trying to undermine realms, he is trying to annex those parts of the world where not even kings hold sway. That is quite in keeping with his twisted ambition, as not all warlocks would choose to ally themselves with him, especially not those of the Right-Hand path, who often hold themselves to be "good" or white witches.'

The monk's curling lip showed what he thought of that last notion.

'And what does this mean to us?' asked Torgun, looking perplexed.

'It means my enemy's enemy is my friend,' replied Horskram, suddenly looking as if he had tasted vinegar. 'Andragorix is probably too well shielded by now for a divination to avail us much without the power of Rima behind it – but a rival witch, who is in daily contest with him, and thus attuned to his psychic spoor...' Suddenly raising his eyes to the heavens, the old monk made the sign again. 'May Reus forgive me the sin I am about to commit,' he intoned.

'Surely you don't mean what I think you do?' asked the King dubiously. 'You've already made one alliance with a witch today – how many more do you plan on making to keep your oath?'

'As few as possible,' replied Horskram grimly. 'But faced with the circumstances, I don't see a better alternative. At least we have some idea where this Earth Witch is – I shall seek her out and persuade her to help me find Andragorix.'

⁙ ⁙ ⁙

Adelko awoke with a thumping headache. Turning over on his bed he saw his mentor was up, staring out of the window across the castle grounds. Groaning he turned over on his back, trying to ignore his churning guts.

The victors had celebrated in style. The castle walls had rung with the sounds of music and merriment, the brazier-lit fields echoing them as the common folk showed they could drink and feast like their lordly masters given half a chance.

Adelko had got uproariously drunk, celebrating with his brother Arik and the rest of the Highlanders till dawn. Vaskrian had descended from the castle to join them shortly after the Wytching Hour, disappearing with a comely wench on his arm just before sunrise.

Sir Braxus had found time to join the commoners too, for they had a love of the lyrical music of his countrymen that surpassed the stoical appreciation of the haughty Northlending nobles. The Highlanders especially loved to hear him, and many even knew the words to his songs thanks to their Westerling ancestry. Adelko foggily remembered linking arms with Arik and Whaelfric as they had sung along to Maegellin's *Lay of High Firth* and other classics.

Braxus had also disappeared just before dawn, with two comely wenches, one for each arm.

Adelko didn't remember much about what happened after that. How had he got back to his chamber? He didn't even know where it was – they had only moved there from the camp a few hours before the feast.

Reus Almighty but it hurt to think.

His painful reverie was interrupted by Horskram proffering him a cup of water. At least it looked fresh.

'Drink this and get up,' he said curtly. 'We must speak with the King.'

'What, right now?' protested Adelko. 'What time is it?'

'Time to be getting up and doing as you are told,' answered Horskram sternly. Sunlight was streaming through the window. The cock must have crowed some hours ago. Wincing, the young monk hauled himself upright and quaffed the water, trying to focus on that and not the room spinning around him.

The castle was quiet as a pair of soldiers escorted them to the wing of the castle given over to the King's use. Most of the lords and knights guesting at Salmor would spend the day recovering before returning to the serious business of war's aftermath, remaining there in anticipation of reward for their efforts.

'The King will have plenty enough to occupy himself before the day is out,' said Horskram. 'For as the loremaster Arodotus says, administering the peace is as much hard work as winning the war.'

Adelko nodded perfunctorily. His head throbbed with every step; right now the last thing he needed was one of his mentor's impromptu lessons.

As they approached the King's chamber they saw Braxus being ushered out by a page. His looked vexed and angry.

'Good day, Sir Braxus,' said Horskram politely.

'What's so good about it I should like to know!' snarled Braxus, before unceremoniously emptying the contents of his troubled mind. 'I rode to war for your King, risking my life. My old squire was crippled on the journey here, and the rest of us are nursing injuries besides. And all for naught! Freidheim has refused my suit, fobbing me off with half-hearted assurances that he'll reconsider my case once his own affairs are in order. And when will that day emerge, I wonder? Oh, but how am I to face my father with this sorry news?'

His face was more distraught than angry now, another of his turbulent mood swings. Vaskrian had mentioned his new master could be somewhat mercurial.

'Be of some cheer,' replied Horskram levelly. 'You have won honour and renown on the field of battle, and I think gained a handy new squire in young Vaskrian. The Almighty oft bestows blessings where least looked for, as the prophet sayeth.'

'Don't bandy Scripture with me, Horskram,' snapped the knight testily. 'Blessings won't help raise an army against an ensorcelled King who is ruining his realm! Abrexta will probably have him signing away the whole kingdom by the time I return – empty handed!'

That seemed to give Horskram pause for thought.

'Will you wait without while I see the King before I leave?' he asked suddenly.

Braxus fixed him with a quizzical look. 'Certainly, if you wish it. But why?'

'I am sure yon novice would fain bid his friend farewell before you both leave for Thraxia,' replied Horskram easily. 'And I may need to have words with you as well. It just reoccurred to me now that our causes may be linked.'

The Thraxian stared at him nonplussed before shrugging his shoulders. He looked like a man recovering from a late night himself – although from what Adelko had seen it wasn't ale or wine he'd indulged in to excess.

'Whatever you will,' he sighed. 'But mind you don't take too long! Now my suit has been refused I've no wish to linger here!'

The two monks were ushered into the King's chamber. Sir Torgun was present, along with Lord Visigard.

'Ah, Horskram,' said the King. 'Come in and sit down. Adelko, a seat for you as well. I'll have you treated as an honoured guest after your contribution to the war! You are henceforth welcome at my court at any time.'

'Thank you, Your Majesty,' replied Adelko, his young face flushing. He still felt uneasy about his part in the Battle of Salmor, but all the same it felt good to be praised by your King. Technically such thinking smacked of vanity and pride, but then again they were all stained with sin anyway... He would pray for redemption when he next got the chance, for now it was nice to be appreciated.

'Is everything in order for your journey?' asked the King, addressing Horskram.

The adept nodded. 'Your page informed me this morning. The supplies from the kitchens are more than welcome, as is the ready coin you have furnished us with.'

'Think nothing of it,' replied Freidheim affably. 'Anything to help you fulfil your vow. May it smooth your path, if it can be smoothed. But bread and coin are not the only things I will give you. Your way is dangerous, far too dangerous for a pair of monks to travel alone, methinks. I'm sending Sir Torgun here with you, along with Sir Aronn and the Chequered Twins. I can't spare any more I'm afraid, but they'll accompany you until you have rooted out Andragorix, or determined beyond doubt that he is not in my kingdom. None of the knights going with you but Torgun here know of the true nature of your mission. I hope this pleases you.'

Horskram nodded deferentially. 'Very much so, Your Majesty. If beastmen are our next enemy, then I fear we shall need every trusty sword we can get. And I trust Sir Aronn is suitably recovered from last night to join us.'

Even serious Torgun, clad as ever in his mail and surcoat, had to smile at that. 'It is nothing a white raven cannot survive,' he replied. 'Though his wounded pride may take a little time to recover.'

'What happened?' asked Adelko. He felt a momentary twinge of regret at having missed the feasting in the Great Hall.

The King laughed. 'He drank far too much Pangonian red is what happened! Got so damn drunk his face looked like a bloody beetroot. He had to be excused after vomiting over the dessert – all that fine work, ruined! Kelmor's poor cook will never recover, I'm sure. Fashions a huge multi-coloured jelly to look like Salmor Castle, and one of my best knights is sick in it!

'At least he was only sick in one turret, sire, as Horskram's nephew Sir Manfry pointed out at the time,' said Visigard, cracking a smile. 'The rest of it was quite edible.'

They all started laughing at that. Even Horskram could not resist a smile.

'All right, that's enough merriment,' said the King, though he was still chuckling. 'So, Horskram, your honour guard, in various stages of recovery, duly assigned.'

Torgun stepped forward and bowed stiffly.

'It will be an honour to serve you in your quest,' he said formally.

'It'll be an honour to have you,' replied Horskram courteously. 'I hear tell you are the best knight in the realm.'

'I know nothing of that, master monk,' replied Sir Torgun modestly.

'Stuff and nonsense!' roared the King. 'Horskram speaks the truth – I wouldn't be sending you otherwise. No, I had considered keeping you back, to help with the pacification of the south – but you were made for greater things, Torgun, than harrying outlaws and rebel remnants. Your destiny lies elsewhere, I trow.'

'Your Majesty,' said Torgun, clicking his spurs. Though the modest knight gave little away, Adelko could sense how pleased he was.

'If it should be your will to protect yon monks further along the road, even after Andragorix is dealt with, you have my blessing,' the King added. 'Just make sure the rest of the men get back in one piece – if that's feasible – when you're done with him.'

'I shall, Your Majesty,' replied Torgun seriously.

'Very good, that settles that then,' said the King. 'It only remains for me to wish you all good speed on your journey – oh, and I've despatched a messenger to take ship from Port Urring to Meerborg, with a message for the Grand Master of your Order in Rima.'

There was a silence. Torgun looked at the ground uneasily.

Horskram raised an eyebrow. 'May I ask who, Your Majesty?'

'I've sent Wolmar,' replied the King. 'He already knows the secret of your mission, and besides that I needed to get him out of the kingdom, before he wreaks some havoc of his own. The other ravens had to stop him riding off drunk to butcher some southland peasants halfway through the feast.'

'He still grieves deeply for his father, poor man – can't stomach the fact that it was common soldiers who dealt the death blow,' explained Visigard.

'Vengeful spirit that one – best channelled elsewhere,' added the King. 'Hopefully Grand Master Hannequin will bless some sense into him.'

Horskram was not amused by the King's humour. 'With all due respect, Your Majesty – ' he began.

' – you would like to take it upon yourself to congratulate me on my cleverness in this appointment. Thank you! But no need for it – there's an end to the matter. He left this morning.'

'I see,' replied Horskram, giving it up as lost. 'There is one other final thing I wanted to ask of you.'

The King looked at him suspiciously. 'What is it?'

'On our way in, we passed Sir Braxus – '

The King snorted. 'Oh yes, him. Don't concern yourself with that foreigner. Fool Thraxian thinks that by warning me the Northland thanes have broken the Treaty of Ryøskil and lending me half a dozen swords he'd convince me to send an army back with him over the mountains! Doesn't he realise I've a third of a kingdom to pacify?'

'Yes, his expectations were foolish,' agreed Horskram. 'I said so all along. However, it does appear that his problems are linked to ours. A sorceress wheedles her way into a king's bed and ensorcells him... her ambitions sound much akin to Andragorix's.'

'Yes, well I hadn't given much thought to that,' the King admitted bluntly. 'Been too busy. Well what of it? I can't send an army with him, you know that.'

'No, but perhaps he could be persuaded to join our mission...' ventured Horskram.

'Why? Andragorix is our concern, not his.'

'He may well be everyone's concern if he has his way,' replied Horskram gravely. 'And most likely we'll have to pass through Thraxia at some point, to warn the Islanders beyond that the fragment in their keeping is under threat.'

'Hmm, that's a roundabout way to get back home,' mused the King, shaking his head. 'I still don't see why he'd do it. Why do you want him so badly anyway? Are some of the best knights in our land not enough for you?'

'Far from it, Your Majesty,' Horskram assured him. 'But as I said, we'll need every trusty sword we can get. Sir Braxus may have character flaws, but he's proved his mettle in the field. And my experience of the Thraxians – with all due respect Sir Torgun – is that they are less afraid of the dark arts than we Northlendings on the whole. Sir Belinos of Runcymede was a Thraxian, and he served me well against Andragorix – even in his death throes he dealt him a crippling blow. My sixth sense tells me that Braxus may prove unusually useful, beyond mere skill at arms.'

The King frowned. 'Well, if you say so. All right, so you've worked with Thraxians before, and you find them useful men to have along in witch hunts. Fair enough – but you'll have to go and talk to him yourself, it's naught to do with me.'

Horskram paused momentarily. Then he said: 'Your Majesty knows full well that he isn't likely to listen to me without leverage. You could... provide that leverage.'

'How?' Both Visigard and the King looked at the old monk askance.

'You could call him back in here and promise him you'll seriously reconsider his petition if he agrees to help us find Andragorix and slay him.'

'Why of all the cheek...!' gasped the King. 'You dare! Fie! Argolians, give them a horse and they want the whole stable! No! Absolutely not!'

'Think on it, Your Majesty,' persisted Horskram. 'If everything we've been piecing together is forming the picture we think it is, you may soon be riding to war in Thraxia, or elsewhere, before long anyway. And you mentioned yourself just now that the Northlanders appear to have returned to their old piratical ways after generations of relative peace. How long before another berserker army lands on the mainland? Something big is afoot, that much is clear. Andragorix, the Sea Wizard, this Abrexta the Prescient... they're all linked somehow. Some devilish cunning work is being done – an alliance of warlocks that means ordinary men no good. You say you don't want to ride to war against Thraxia – but it may be that Thraxia rides to war against you before long if Abrexta is part of Andragorix's conspiracy.'

The King paused and thought long and hard on that. Torgun stood stock still and said nothing. Visigard held his silence, but shook his head and looked at the ground. Adelko's spirits perked up – Vaskrian might be coming with them after all.

At last the King spoke. 'If I call this Thraxian knight back in, it means telling him everything... we can hardly keep him in the dark and make an effective proposition.'

'Everything,' agreed Horskram.

Braxus was admitted back into the King's chamber wearing a surprised look on his face. This increased to a look of wonder as the

King told him the whole story. Then he made his proposition. At that Braxus frowned, rubbing his neatly trimmed beard.

'That's a lot of tale-telling to take in at once,' he said laconically.

'Well, you're the amateur bard,' replied the King testily. 'So take it in and decide! I want your answer before you leave this room.'

Braxus took a deep breath and considered some more. 'And what guarantees do I have that you will keep your word?' he asked presently.

The King's face darkened. 'You have my word as King of this land,' he growled. 'I won't stand by and watch the realms of men put under a wizard's thrall one by one. If it means another bloody war to stop it happening, then so be it! But first you must help the Argolian friars. Andragorix must be stopped – after that we can make plans to deal with this Abrexta. Your realm will have to muddle on in the meantime, I'm afraid – I have been persuaded by Brother Horskram that it is in my interests to help you, but my own realm's concerns are still a priority. And it looks as if Andragorix is a likely ringleader in this conspiracy.'

Braxus nodded again. 'I'd have stopped short of calling Abrexta a Left-Handed witch,' he mused. 'A Right-Handed bitch would have been more my description. But in light of what you say... aye, she could very well be in league with other warlocks. Thraxia is no stranger to sorcerers but we haven't had one as ambitious or dangerous as this in many a year...'

He paused again to consider. The King drummed his fingers impatiently on the desk before him.

'All right, Your Majesty – done! I'll go,' said Braxus presently. 'But I'll need to send my countrymen back to give the news to my father, and he'll need to know the full story behind why I'm not returning with them – else it's my head when I do get back!'

'Just tell him to be discreet with the knowledge,' said Horskram, looking distinctly uneasy. 'And your men too.'

'Don't worry!' replied the knight with a charming smile. 'I'll write it down myself – no danger of my knights learning anything, none of them can read.'

'What about Vaskrian?' Adelko blurted out. 'Will he be coming too?'

'Well I hardly see how a knight can ride without a squire – begging your pardon, Sir Torgun, but not all of us cherish the life of a poor bachelor – so yes, of course he'll be coming,' replied the Thraxian, still smiling.

Adelko beamed like a village idiot until he caught Horskram glaring at him disapprovingly.

'There is just one other matter I needs must settle before I join your party however,' ventured Braxus.

The King frowned. 'What?'

'A duel of honour... during the war I had words with a knight in Lord Fenrig of Hroghar's service, one Sir Rutgar. He offered churlish insults to my squire and refused to apologise for the slight this offered me. I would fain have satisfaction before I leave.'

The King raised an eyebrow. 'Sir Rutgar, you say? In the Jarl of Hroghar's company?' He glanced at Lord Visigard. 'Haven't I heard that name recently?'

Lord Visigard frowned. 'Indeed, Your Majesty – he was on this morning's tally of wounded.' The whiskered old patrician looked distinctly disapproving.

'Wounded, you say?' pressed Braxus. 'Too seriously injured to fight soon?' Despite having complained of his injuries the Thraxian looked positively disappointed.

'Yes, wounded,' continued Visigard. 'Though I daresay that is not why you will wish to forego your duel with him. Frankly, such a man is beneath your consideration, Sir Braxus.'

'Oh, and how is that?'

'His name was brought before me this morning, by Lord Fenrig himself – he has instructed that the knight in question be expressly removed from receiving his share of the spoils of war. The dues of cowardice, as stipulated by the Code of Chivalry.'

Braxus could hardly repress a grin as he said: 'Oh really, pray tell... I am sure my young squire would fain hear of this as much as I would.'

Lord Visigard looked abashed as he shuffled his feet. 'Please be sure that such behaviour is far from typical of we gallant Northlendings,' he said seriously. 'He fell from his horse and broke his arm and leg while fleeing the field in a cowardly panic. He is now convalescing in the camp, his name a disgrace and his reputation in tatters.'

Torgun shook his head, his cheeks colouring. 'The man is a disgrace to his liege lord and a living stain on this country's honour,' he said.

'Ah indeed,' said Braxus, trying not to grin more broadly. ''Tis a pity. I had so looked forward to chastising him in the lists but... as you say, quite beneath my concern now. In light of that I consider the matter closed – seeking redress from such a churl would hardly be fitting.'

Torgun and Visigard exchanged looks. Braxus tried not to laugh. Freidheim made a dismissive gesture.

'Well, that settles everything,' he said. 'Now if you'll excuse me, I've a broken kingdom to mend.'

⁘ ⁘ ⁘

The sun rose on the courtyard, slowly illuminating the grey stones of the castle keep. Adelko basked in its nascent warmth, a welcome antidote to the chilly dawn air. There were eight of them drawn up in the middle of the courtyard, mounted and ready to leave.

Vaskrian, his long untidy hair ruffling in the breeze, looked at him and grinned. Adelko could not help grinning back despite the fresh dangers that lay ahead. He'd had two days to recover from his debauch, and he felt fairly fresh himself.

It was like something out of the old tales he had read at the monastery: a motley band of adventurers about to ride off into the wilderness on a mad and dangerous quest.

Sir Braxus sat on a fine-looking roan charger, dressed in mail and fully armed. If half of what Vaskrian had told him was true, he suspected the laden sumpter that whickered between master and squire was burdened as much with court clothing and musical instruments as spare weapons and travelling kit.

The four knights of the White Valravyn who would be their honour guard were clad exactly as they had been when Adelko first met them on the road to Strongholm. Their dappled Farovian destriers snorted impatiently; the novice caught Braxus glancing at these with an envious glint in his eye.

Next to him Horskram sat unmoving in the saddle. Ever the same, he looked as if he might have been carved of granite, painted grey and fleshy brown to resemble a well-travelled monk of the Order.

The two of them had spoken little since the feast. Horskram had briefed him curtly on the next stage of their mission but hadn't said much else to him besides. Adelko did not need his sixth sense to tell him that relations between mentor and novice were not at their best. It must have been apparent – Horskram's nephew Sir Manfry had done his best to reassure him when they'd said their goodbyes yesterday. Old Horskram, bark worse than bite, nothing to worry about, a good fellow really deep down...

But even the jovial knight's usual cheer hadn't been enough to put his mind at rest. Where they were going, he sensed, even good men might fall to blows with one another – literally or otherwise.

He banished the thought from his mind. It was the 1st of Rodmonath: the start of summer and an auspicious day to begin their new mission. Now wasn't the time for gloomy thoughts. He would find a way to make peace with his estranged mentor – after everything they had been through, surely that wouldn't prove impossible.

The guards on the gate raised the portcullis and they nudged their horses into a canter. No one was there to see them off – that way fewer questions would be asked about their departure. They crossed the moat and turned up the east road towards the highway that would take them over the River Thule and all the way to the Argael Forest.

As they joined it and turned south, Adelko mulled over the next episode of his real-life adventure. They went to seek an uncertain ally, against an enemy whose whereabouts were still undetermined. Both were warlocks – the very kind of people his Order had sworn to oppose.

Set a thief to catch a thief, the young monk reflected philosophically.

All the same, it did seem a strange turn of events – but then what hadn't been strange about the past two months?

He thought of his brother, to whom he had bid a tearful farewell the previous night. He had been unable even then to tell him the true nature of their dangerous business. That made him sad, but it sustained him too: he supposed that people like him had to keep horrible secrets, so people like his brother wouldn't have to.

As the company rode down the rutted highway he clung to the thought, which brought him a strange yet lonely comfort. The road stretched ahead, pulling him through quiet fields and hedgerows towards his destiny.

• • •

GLOSSARY OF NAMES

Here follows an overview of some of the more common names relating to legends, geography, history, religion, magic and supernatural entities that feature in this book. It is not intended to be exhaustive but may be used as a reference to guide the reader.

Abaddon Foremost among demonkind; led the revolt against **Reus** and the loyal angels and **archangels** during the Battle for Heaven and Earth at the Dawn of Time. Was condemned to languish in the Kingdom of **Gehenna** on the **Other Side**, but has been influential in the affairs of mortalkind ever since. Corrupted **Ma'amun**, foremost among the **Elder Wizards** of **Varya**, by teaching him the **Left Hand Path** of sorcery. Also known as the Fallen One, the Dark Angel, the Author of Evil, and the King of Gehenna in **Urovia**; known as Sha'itan, Loth and the Cloven Hoofed God in other cultures.

Acolytes Palomedes' seven closest advisers and disciples who afterwards were instrumental in spreading the **Creed** – a religion based on his teachings and life examples – throughout **Urovia**. Generally heralded as bringing spiritual salvation to benighted peoples, though dissenters argue that their teachings were flawed interpretations of the **Redeemer**'s beliefs and practices.

Ancient Thalamy Also known as the Thalamian Empire, a **Golden Age** hegemony that straddled the Sundering Sea and incorporated the modern kingdoms of Thalamy, **Pangonia**, Mercadia, the southern reaches of the **Urovian New Empire** and northern **Sassania**, lasting for several centuries until its destruction by Wulfric of Gothia.

Antaeus Legendary mariner and adventurer belonging to the **Golden Age**, said by some to have been the son of the **archangel** Aqualcus, worshipped as a god in pagan times before the coming of the Faith and the **Creed**. Hailed from **Ancient Thalamy** in the Era of Warring City-States before the empire was consolidated. His exploits against **Gygants**, Ifriti, Seakindred, **Wyrms**, **Wadwos**, warlocks and other supernatural foes are celebrated in song and poetry throughout **Urovia**.

Anti-angels Demonkind or evil spirits; angels who sided with **Abaddon** in the Battle for Heaven and Earth at the Dawn of Time.

Archangels   Most powerful of the angels who stayed loyal to **Reus**; foremost among them are the **Seven Seraphim**.

Archdemons   Most powerful of demonkind along with **Abaddon** himself; foremost among them are the seven **Princes of Perfidy**.

Argael   A large stretch of primaeval forest straddling the border between **Northalde** and **Vorstlund**. Long the haunt of **Wadwos**, it was formerly much bigger until the rise of the **Free Kingdoms** saw much of it pared back. Its centremost part is rumoured to be the enchanted lair of the Earth Witch, a right-hand sorceress of fearsome repute.

Argolian Order   Founded by St Argo five hundred years ago, this learned order of monks and friars is tasked with fighting evil spirits and hunting down witches and warlocks throughout the **Free Kingdoms** and **Pilgrim Kingdoms**. It is also celebrated for its learning.

Ashokainan   A legendary left-hand wizard who reputedly lived for hundreds of years until **Søren** slew him seven centuries ago. One of the most powerful warlocks to walk the Known World since the demise of the Priest-Kings of **Varya**.

Avatar   A collective name intended to summarise a complex terminology that covers all supernatural entities regarded as a manifestation of **Reus Almighty** (i.e. a direct extension of His being). This includes **archangels**, angels and their demonic opposites; the word is also commonly used to describe such entities sent to earth in mortal form to guide mankind for good or ill. The term can also be used to describe a saint who is rewarded for a virtuous life by being exalted to the ranks of the **Unseen** upon death. Most religious scholars across the Faith and **Creed** agree that the **Two Prophets** fall into the former category of avatar (i.e. that they were angels or archangels sent to earth to help mortalkind), though some cleave to the second interpretation (that they were mortals rewarded in the Afterlife for their service to mankind).

Azrael   The Angel of Death, tasked by **Reus** with judging the souls of the dead, determining whether they go to **Gehenna** or the **Heavenly Halls**. Known by many different names across cultures throughout history, including Orcus, Osirian, Mortis, Mahatsu and Imraan.

Battle of Aumric Fields   Decisive battle in the Wars of the Southern Secession fought fifteen years ago in **Northalde**. Brought the southron rebel uprising to an end, when King Freidheim II slew its leader Jarl Kanga.

Battle of Corne Hill   Decisive battle of the northerly **Border Wars** that saw **Thraxia** and its Vorstlending mercenary allies crushed by the **Northlendings** half a century ago; this cemented the young King

Freidheim II's reputation as the greatest ruler of **Northalde** since the Hero King Thorsvald, and paved the way for an era of peace and prosperity in the kingdom.

Border Wars   Series of internecine conflicts between **Pangonia**, **Thraxia** and **Northalde** that lasted for a couple of centuries. The wars between the latter two kingdoms culminated in the **Battle of Corne Hill**.

Breaking of the World   Cataclysm visited on the Known World by **Reus** and the **Archangels** five thousand years ago as punishment for **Ma'amun**'s attempt to open the gates of **Gehenna** at the behest of his master **Abaddon**. Resulted in the destruction of the **Varyan** civilisation and substantially altered the geography of the **Urovian** and **Sassanian** continents. Ushered in the **First Age of Darkness**, during which nearly all the vast learning of the Varyan Empire was lost.

Brenning Wold   Stretch of gently rolling hill-lands lying between the **Highlands** and **Efrilund** in the Kingdom of **Northalde**. Ruled over by half a dozen petty barons (known collectively as the Wolding Barons). Fiercely independent, these pay only lip service to the King, whom they appease by paying taxes whilst scorning to apply his laws, each one ruling his petty fiefdom as a despot.

Cael   A learned youth from the **Island Realms** tasked with taking the fourth fragment of the **Headstone of Ma'amun** to **Sassania** after it was broken by **Søren**. Disappeared with the fragment centuries ago, though since rumoured to have become one of the undead, wandering the deserts of the hot southlands.

Creed   Monotheistic religion founded by the **acolytes** of **Palomedes**, one of the **Two Prophets**, who opposed the tyranny of the **Thalamian Empire**. It falls into two mainstream churches: the Orthodox Temple in the **Urovian New Empire** and the **True Temple** in Western **Urovia** and the **Pilgrim Kingdoms**.

Dulsinor   Lands in northern **Vorstlund** ruled by the House of Markward, current incumbent Eorl Wilhelm Stonefist. The Eorldom is one of nine principal states that compose the Vorstlending realm.

Efrilund   Stretch of the kingdom of **Northalde** comprising lands lying between the **King's Dominions** in the south and the **Wold** and **Highlands** to the north. Ruled over by three jarls: Lord Vymar of Harrang, Lord Fenrig of Hroghar, and Lord Asgeir of Sjórvard. These are loyal provinces and though not directly ruled by the King generally apply most of his laws.

Elder Wizards   Ancient race of warlocks who ruled over the Known World from their island homeland of **Varya** for a thousand years until the **Breaking of the World**. Foremost among them was **Ma'amun**, who became corrupted by **Abaddon** after he learned the **Left-Hand Path** of black magic at his feet. Also known as the Priest-Kings of Varya and the Magi.

Elementi   Race of spirits belonging to the **Other Side** corresponding to the four elements: Terrus (earth), Aethi (air), Saraphi (fire) and Lymphi (water).

Faith   Principal and monotheistic religion of **Sassania** based on the teachings of the Prophet Sha'abat, who preceded the coming of **Palomedes** by several generations. Unlike Palomedes, Sha'abat was never a warrior and always counselled peaceful resolution of conflict wherever possible. However, this has not prevented adherents of the Faith from making war in his name.

Fay Folk   Race of malicious spirits who cross over from the **Other Side** to dwell in earthly haunts such as forests and mountains. Though not strictly demonkind they are generally feared and shunned by mortals, upon whom they often prey for sport. Also known as pixies, elves, sprites, will 'o' wisps, vylivigs and the Faerie Kindred.

First Age of Darkness   A thousand-year period of backwardness and strife directly succeeding the **Breaking of the World**; few civilisations if any flourished during this bleak era.

First Clarion   Marked the Dawn of Time and the creation of the Universe by **Reus Almighty**, who set his angels to work creating the galaxies, solar systems and planets thereafter. Scholars dispute over what timeframe this occurred, with estimates varying between a few hundred years to aeons in mortal reckoning.

Free Kingdoms   Collective name given to the six principal realms of Western Urovia: **Northalde, Thraxia, Pangonia, Vorstlund**, Mercadia and Thalamy. The epithet 'free' comes from the fact that slavery was abolished throughout these realms with the coming of the **Creed** – although serfdom and other types of feudal bondage still persist.

Frozen Principalities   Name given to a string of petty kingdoms belonging to the Northlanders, barbarian tribes who still worship angels and demons as gods and cling to their age-old customs. Also known as the Frozen Wastes, these lands are ruled over by the Ice Thegns and their seacarls and housecarls – fierce warriors who pledge fealty to their liegelords.

Gaellentir   Stretch of lands in northern **Thraxia** ruled over by Clan Fitzrow, the present head of house being Lord Braun of Gaellen. The Ward of Gaellentir has been hard pressed by highland rebels for some time, who threaten its very existence.

Gaunt   A malignant ghost that dwells half in the **Other Side** and half in the mortal vale. Seeks to drag unsuspecting mortals into its own ghastly half-world through terror and trickery.

Gehenna   The island prison on the **Other Side** to which **Abaddon** and his demonic followers were banished by **Reus** after the Battle for Heaven and Earth was lost. At its heart lies the City of Burning Brass, divided into Five Tiers – the first and highest of these is reserved for **Abaddon** himself, the **Seven Princes of Perfidy** and other archdemons.

Golden Age   New era of civilisation that flourished after the end of the **First Age of Darkness** some four thousand years ago and lasted for three millennia. During this time the civilisations of Sendhé and Ancient Thalamy flourished; much lore was relearned or rediscovered, though the glory of mortalkind never attained that achieved during the apogee of the preceding **Platinum Age**.

Great World Serpent   The first of **Reus Almighty**'s sentient creations along with Aurgelmir the Titan. Fathered the race of Wyrms with Hydrae the Many Headed (whom **Søren** slew on his Seventh and final Deed). According to legend, the Great World Serpent's body was used to create the world when Reus crushed him and Aurgelmir together to stop them destroying the Universe with their constant fighting. The same legend states that the World Serpent lies coiled at the centre of the earth, surrounded by the flesh of Aurgelmir; should he ever be woken from his slumber the Known World will fall apart and be destroyed. As such, the Great World Serpent is also referred to as He Who Must Not Be Disturbed, particularly among the Northlanders of the **Frozen Principalities**.

Gygant   A race of giants, believed to be **Reus'** first attempts to fashion mortalkind from the rock and clay of the earth (itself created from Aurgelmir the Titan, who is thus also known as the Father of Giants). Many times larger than their human descendants, though extremely violent and stupid, Gygants terrorised early human settlements until the **Elder Wizards** slew most of them and enslaved the rest. Today there are only believed to be a handful left alive, mostly in remote mountain retreats far away from mortalkind.

Hag   An evil spirit that kills its victims by entering their dreams and frightening them to death, feeding off their life-force. A very rare apparition, it is not known whether it is kindred to demonkind or belongs to an altogether different race of spirit.

Hamlyn   One of the oldest and richest noble houses in **Northalde**, which rules a strip of fine coastal land that constitutes an enclave within the **King's Dominions**. As well as deriving much of its wealth from the trading privileges this grants, the House of Hamlyn also benefits from an abundance of silver mines on its lands.

Headstone of Ma'amun Tablet of incalculable power wrought by Ma'amun five thousand years ago; inscribed with hieroglyphic writing said to represent additions he made to the Sorcerer's Script under the tutelage of **Abaddon.** It is said to contain the power to break the hold placed on the Fallen One by **Reus** and summon him and his followers back to the mortal vale. It is not clear whether Ma'amun sought to control Abaddon or serve him, and as such whether the Headstone will enable its user to bind him to his or her will.

Heavenly Halls The Kingdom of **Reus**, where the **Seven Seraphim** sit at his side and the rest of the **archangels** and angels dwell. The most splendid of the island realms of the **Other Side**, where the souls of those judged fit by **Azrael** are sent to reside until the Hour of All's Ending and Judgment Day.

Highlands Informal name given to craggy stretch of lands lying north of the **Brenning Wold** and east of the Hyrkrainian Mountains that divide **Northalde** from **Thraxia**; its inhabitants are mixed Northlending and native stock, the latter being descended from the same clans who fled the **Island Realms** and settled **Thraxia** two millennia ago.

Ingwin Ruling royal house of the Kingdom of **Northalde**; current incumbent is Freidheim II. Coat of arms is two rearing white unicorns facing each other on a purple background.

Island Realms Series of islands, the two principal ones being Kaluryn and Skulla, ruled over by the Marcher Lords and Druids, lying in the Great Western Ocean. The most westerly known civilisation, the Island Realms cling steadfastly to their ancient beliefs, having been visited by Kaia the Moon Goddess during the **First Age of Darkness** and taught the **Right Hand Path** of magick lost to man when the **Varyan** Empire was destroyed at the **Breaking of the World**. Also known as the Western Isles, Druidsbourne, and the Islands of World's Ending.

King's Dominions Stretch of rich lands between **Efrilund** to the north and the Southern Provinces ruled directly by the **Northlending** King. Here royal law is strongest; consequently this is the wealthiest and most stable part of **Northalde**.

Left Hand Path Black magic, derived from the teachings of **Abaddon** to **Ma'amun** more than five thousand years ago. Comprises Necromancy and Demonology, the two **Schools of Magick** most closely aligned to the Left Hand Path. However, some sorcerers who practise left-hand magic claim it is not necessarily wholly evil of itself, for instance those who use it to ask the dead for advice.

Ma'amun   Most powerful of the **Elder Wizards**, became corrupted by **Abaddon**, who taught him the **Left Hand Path** and encouraged him to extend his powers. Ma'amun was slain along with all the other Magi at the **Breaking of the World**, when the **Unseen** punished him for perverting the Gift of Magick and daring to challenge the Laws of Reus. His shade is believed to be trapped in **Gehenna**, where he languishes in the City of Burning Brass ruled by his erstwhile teacher along with all the other souls of the damned.

Maegellin   Thraxian bard who lived three centuries ago; widely held to be the greatest poet and songsmith of the **Silver Age**, surpassing even the classical poets of the **Golden Age**. Most noted works include *The Tales of Antaeus the Mariner* and *The Seven Deeds of Søren*.

Morwena   Beloved of **Søren**; a sorceress of fearsome repute who hailed from the **Island Realms**. Ensorcelled the great hero and sent him on his Seven Deeds, which were ultimately purposed to recover the **Headstone of Ma'amun** from the Forbidden City on the Island of **Varya**. Slain by Søren after she spurned him on completion of his Final Deed, in which he brought the Headstone from Varya to the Island Realms.

Northalde   One of the **Free Kingdoms**, settled by Northland reavers from the **Frozen Principalities** seven hundred years ago. Has undergone something of a revival under the reign of Freidheim II since its power diminished from its zenith more than a century ago under the reign of the Hero King Thorsvald. Comprises the lands north of the Argael and west of the Hyrkrainian mountains that divide the north-west peninsular of Western **Urovia** between it and the kingdom of **Thraxia**. **Northlendings** are famed for their skill in warfare, horsemanship, shipwrighting, weaponsmithing and castle-building.

Northlending   Inhabitant of the Kingdom of **Northalde** in north-western **Urovia**; not to be confused with Northlander, an inhabitant of the **Frozen Principalities**.

Other Side   Collective name given to all the dwelling places of spirits, **elementi**, **fays**, demons, angels and **Reus Almighty** Himself. Said to be an endless sea of vapour punctuated by islands, including the **Heavenly Halls**, **Gehenna**, and Azhoanarn where **Azrael** dwells. All supernatural beings hail from the Other Side, and this is consequently where warlocks of all bents derive their powers using the Language of Magick and the Sorcerer's Script.

Palomedes   Second of the **Two Prophets**; inspired the **Creed**, the major religion of **Urovia**. Born to a soldier in Ushalayim about a thousand years ago in what is now the **Pilgrim Kingdoms**. Initially intended to follow his father into the Thalamian Legions but began hearing the Voice of **Reus** shortly after coming of age at fourteen. Resolved to use his martial skills to lead a revolution against the tyrannical Thalamian Empire and acquired a great following, but later forsook the sword and led his supporters in a campaign of passive resistance. Was finally apprehended by the Thalamians after being betrayed by his former lieutenant Antiochus the Red-Handed, taken to Tyrannos and broken on the **Wheel** at the Emperor's command. Also known by his abbreviated name, Palom, and his most common epithet, the **Redeemer**.

Pangonia   Most powerful of the **Free Kingdoms**, though its influence has waned somewhat since its apogee under the Chivalrous King Vasirius, who ruled some two centuries ago. Its capital Rima is also the headquarters of the **True Temple** and the **Argolian Order**. Currently ruled by King Carolus III of the House of Ambelin, a scheming, ambitious monarch known also as the 'wily' and the 'greedy' for heavy taxes imposed on his barons.

Pilgrim Kingdoms   Collective name given to northern **Sassanian** territories carved out by **Urovian** crusaders a century ago, consisting of the Kingdom of Ushalayim, named after its principal city, where **Palomedes** the **Redeemer** was born, the Kingdom of Keraka and the Kingdom of Ranishmend.

Pilgrim Wars   Series of crusades – holy wars against the heathen **Sassanians** sanctioned by the **True Temple** – begun more than a hundred years ago that recaptured the holy city of Ushalayim where **Palomedes** the **Redeemer** was born. Many factions besides the victorious crusading dynasties have profited from the Pilgrim Wars, most notably the merchant houses of Mercadia, most southerly of the **Free Kingdoms**. However, the Pilgrim Wars have not been endorsed by all Palomedians: the Orthodox Temple has openly voiced its disapproval, whilst the **Argolian Order** has refused to condemn or condone them. And few knights from the northerly Free Kingdoms of **Thraxia** and **Northalde** have taken the **Wheel**, with most crusaders originating from Mercadia, **Vorstlund**, **Pangonia** and Thalamy.

Platinum Age   A thousand-year epoch during which the **Elder Wizards** ruled all of the Known World from the Island of **Varya**; during this time mankind, though in bondage to the Priest-Kings, reputedly lived in a state of ease, comfort and luxury unparalleled in mortal history. According to some scholars the average lifespan exceeded a century and even the lowest of birth were well educated and literate. This era came to an abrupt end some five millennia ago when the **Unseen** punished **Ma'amun** for daring to challenge their authority by destroying Varya and much of the Known World, laying waste to the great civilisation it had built.

Princes of Perfidy Collective name given to the seven most powerful **archdemons** who serve **Abaddon**: Sha'amiel (**avatar** of greed and bigotry); Azathol (vanity and hubris); Zolthoth (wrath); Ta'ussaswazelim (cruelty); Chreosoaneuryon (gluttony); Satyrus (lust and sexual depravity); and Invidia (envy). The Seven Princes are themselves dark emanations of the **Seven Seraphim** and thus have their celestial opposites among the **archangels**, whose virtues they seek to corrupt and subvert.

Purge Calamitous event a generation ago that saw the **Argolian Order** falsely accused and tried for witchcraft by clerics of the mainstream **True Temple** in Rima. Many Argolians were tortured and made false confessions which they later retracted. The Order eventually succeeded in refuting the charges and even turned the tables on their accusers – a divination led by Hannequin, Grand Master of the Order, revealed many of their accusers to have been themselves acting under the influence of the **archdemon** Sha'amiel. The guilty perfects were burned alive in the main square at Rima. However, in another twist, since then the Temple has been held to be itself 'purged' of all wrongdoing, its traitors having been brought to justice, whilst much suspicion continues to fall on the Argolians, whose psychic and spiritual abilities are held by many to be akin to sorcery itself.

Redeemer Common epithet by which **Palomedes** is referred to among believers of the **Creed**.

Rent Between Worlds The name given to the gap between the mortal vale and the **Other Side** that wizards of all kinds use to draw upon the supernatural powers essential to sorcery, using the Language of Magick and the Sorcerer's Script. This gap was greatly widened during the **Platinum Age** when the **Elder Wizards** ruled the Known World, and is said to be responsible for all manifestations in the mortal vale, be it **elementi**, demonkind, **fays**, **gaunts** or other supernatural entities. The Rent widens in accordance with how much sorcery is being used; hence if a warlock is particularly active in one area, the Rent there will be widened, increasing the likelihood of possessions, hauntings and other apparitions.

Reus Almighty God; responsible for the creation of the Universe and everything in it, including the Known World, the **Other Side**, **archangels**, angels, spirits, **elementi**, mortalkind and the animal kingdom. Sages differ on whether His power is truly infinite or simply incalculable according to the reckonings of mortalkind. The

Almighty was unknown to pre-Faith mortals, who worshipped the **archangels** and **archdemons** as gods in their own right during the **Platinum** and **Golden Ages**.

Right Hand Path   More benign white magic originally taught to the **Varyans** by the **Archangels** to help them fashion their civilisation during the **Platinum Age**. Some thinkers, the **Argolians** among them, hold that all magic is a mistake, and that even the Right-Hand Path can be used to do evil in the wrong hands. Others such as the pagan followers of Kaia The Moon Goddess – who retaught aspects of white magic to the folk of the **Island Realms** during the **First Age of Darkness** – disagree on this point.

Saltcaste   One of the richest of the **Southern Provinces** of **Northalde**, along with **Thule**; its lands abut on the Wyvern Sea, giving it access to much trade. Joined the rebellion against the King during the War of the Southern Secession a generation ago; current ruler is Lord Aelrød.

Sassania   Lands of the hot south lying beyond the Sundering Sea that comprise the Four Sultanates, the **Pilgrim Kingdoms** and various other petty principalities. Principal religion is the Faith, founded by the First Prophet Sha'abat several generations before the coming of **Palomedes**.

Second Age of Darkness   Another period of decline marked in Western **Urovia** by the destruction of the Thalamian Empire after Tyrannos was sacked by Wulfric of Gothia more than nine hundred years ago. It is generally agreed to have ended with the consolidation of barbarian petty kingdoms into the six **Free Kingdoms** more than three centuries ago, ushering in the advent of the present **Silver Age**. Note that other cultures differ in their reckoning of the Second Age of Darkness; for instance the **Urovian New Empire** dates its ending with the completion of the Hundred Years Conquest slightly earlier, while the **Sassanians** date its beginning from the demise of the last Rightly Guided Sultan, two generations after Wulfric sacked Tyrannos.

Seven Schools of Magick   The core disciplines of sorcery practised by warlocks and witches of varying bent and aptitude throughout the Known World. These are: Thaumaturgy, Transformation, Enchantment, Scrying, Alchemy, Necromancy and Demonology. The first five are broadly classified under the more benign **Right Hand Path**; the last two belong to the darker **Left Hand Path**.

Seven Seraphim   Foremost among the **Archangels**, those that sit at the right hand of **Reus Almighty**. They are: Logos (**avatar** of prosperity and tolerance); Siona (grace and dignity); Virtus (courage); Stygnos (stoicism and fortitude); Euphrosakritos (merriment); Luviah (love); and Aeriti (aspiration). The Seraphim are opposed by their dark emanations the **Princes of Perfidy**, who represent twisted or corrupted forms of the virtues they embody.

Silver Age The present age; regarded by most Western **Urovians** as beginning with the consolidation of the **Free Kingdoms** some 350 years ago. Distinct from the previous **Golden Age** in that it is an era in which **Reus Almighty** has made Himself known to mortalkind – yet civilisation in Western Urovia is acknowledged by the learned to lag far behind that of the preceding epoch.

Sixth Sense Special talent particular to the **Argolian Order**, honed by years of prayer and meditation. Its abilities are somewhat vague and thus difficult to define, but broadly speaking they allow a monk of the order to detect the following, with varying degrees of accuracy: when a person is lying or concealing something; when danger (particularly supernatural danger) is near; past pain or sorrow that continues to plague a victim; the presence of a warlock or witch and the type of magick being used; and a demon's psychic spoor.

Søren Legendary hero who hailed from the **Frozen Principalities** and came over with the First Reavers who began conquering and settling what is now **Northalde** seven centuries ago. Reputed to have been fathered on a mortal maiden by the archangel Sjórkunan, Lord of Oceans, whom the Northlanders worship as a god. Is most famed for his adventures thereafter, when seeking the westerly **Island Realms** in his magic ship Jürmengaard he stumbled upon the sorceress **Morwena**'s lair in the ruins of one of the **Watchtowers of the Magi**. She ensorcelled him into performing his Seven Deeds, the last of which saw the **Headstone of Ma'amun** recovered from the Forbidden City of **Varya**. Søren subsequently slew Morwena and broke the Headstone into four pieces, before taking his ship and sailing out across the Great Western Ocean, never to be seen again by mortal eyes. Has gone by various epithets during and after his lifetime, including the Doomed, Irongrip, Wavetamer and Wyrmslayer.

Southern Provinces Collection of half a dozen small but prosperous baronies or jarldoms that comprise the lands of **Northalde** lying south of the **King's Dominions**. The southron lords have a long-standing grievance with King Freidheim for war reparations imposed on them after being defeated during the **Battle of Aumric Fields**.

Stornelund One of the richest of the nine baronies that compose the realm of **Vorstlund**, neighboured by **Dulsinor** to the west and Ostveld to the south. Ruled over by the House of Lanrak; the current Herzog is Lord Hengist – a vain, inept and bibulous man unworthy of the title.

True Temple   The church of the **Creed** that holds sway in Western **Urovia**, with the Supreme Perfect headquartered in Rima, the capital of **Pangonia**. Its name differentiates it from the Orthodox Temple, which administers the Creed in the **Urovian New Empire** east of the Great White Mountains. The True Temple was created by a schism, known as the Sundering of the Temple, six hundred years ago.

Thraxia   One of the **Free Kingdoms** of Western **Urovia**, composing the lands west of the Hyrkrainian Mountains that divide it from **Northalde**. Originally settled by clans fleeing the **Island Realms** after the Wars of Kith and Kin two thousand years ago. The last of the kingdoms to embrace the **Creed**, Thraxia has somewhat more tolerance for right hand magic than the other western kingdoms, although the **Left Hand Path** is punished severely. Thraxians are famed far and wide for the excellence of their poetry and music, and their greatest bard **Maegellin** is celebrated throughout the Free Kingdoms and beyond. Their skill at hunting and their fine mead are also noteworthy.

Thule   The most prosperous of the jarldoms of the **Southern Provinces** of **Northalde**, along with **Saltcaste** to the south. It was the Jarl of Thule, Kanga, who led the southron uprising against the King in the War of the Southern Secession. Had severe taxes imposed on it after losing the war in the **Battle of Aumric Fields**.

Tintagael   Name given to a haunted forest in the westernmost fiefs of the **King's Dominions** and the ancient **Watchtower of the Magi** on its outskirts. Long the earthly sojourn of the **Fay Folk**, who exploited the **Rent Between Worlds** caused by the sorcery emanating from the Watchtower to cross over from the **Other Side**. Nowadays few wayfarers dare venture inside it, and of those who do fewer still emerge.

Two Prophets   Collective name given to the **avatars**, Sha'abat and **Palomedes**, whose teachings inspired the Faith and **Creed** respectively and brought the knowledge of **Reus Almighty** to mortalkind. Due to religious conflict, particularly the **Pilgrim Wars**, adherents of both religions respectively call the prophets 'true' and 'false' – though some loremasters acknowledge both. Note that the term 'false prophet' is also used to describe those possessed or impersonated by **archdemons** in order to lead mortalkind astray.

Ulfang   Name given to the largest **Argolian** monastery in **Northalde**, situated in the **Highlands**. The Great Monastery, as it is colloquially known, was founded on the ruins of a pagan shrine used by Northland priests who came over with the reavers that founded Northalde.

Un-angels   Collective name given given to 'neutral' entities that are considered neither angels nor demons. Foremost among them are **Azrael**, judge of souls; Kaia, worshipped as a nature goddess throughout pagan communities in the **Island Realms**; and Nurë, the archangel of fire, prayed to by smiths of all kinds. The **Fay Folk** are also considered by many loremasters to be lesser un-angels, being far from good but not truly evil.

Unseen   Collective noun given to all inhabitants of the **Other Side** after the **Breaking of the World**, when angels and other supernatural entities ceased to walk openly among mortalkind. Throughout the **Golden Age** they are said to have reappeared occasionally, though with diminishing frequency, and by the advent of the **Silver Age** such manifestations had become virtually unknown. Note that demonkind will manifest in the form of possessions and in response to summonings by a demonologist meddling with the Other Side using the **Left Hand Path**.

Urovia   Name given to all the lands lying north of the Sundering Sea and the Great Inland Sea, as far the Steppes of Koth that lie beyond the Mercenary Kingdoms to the east of the **Urovian New Empire**. Nowadays Urovian culture is usually associated with the **Creed**; but note that the Three Emirates lying directly south of the Mercenary Kingdoms and Koth are considered **Sassanian** by virtue of their religion and culture.

Urovian New Empire   The most powerful and technologically advanced country of the **Silver Age**, a land empire comprising seven former kingdoms that were consolidated four centuries ago by the House of Usharok during the Hundred Years' Conquest. Protected by a string of fortresses in the Great White Mountains to the west and the Great Wall to the east, the Empire guards its secrets jealously and trades selectively with its neighbours. It is said to have preserved or relearned much of the lore of **Ancient Thalamy**, and former outlying provinces of that fallen empire are now part of the New Empire. Its capital, Illyrium, is said to be the greatest **Urovian** city since Ancient Tyrannos, and is the seat of the Imperator, the Ruling Senate, and the Orthodox Temple.

Varya   Name given to the civilisation and the island city that spawned it more than six thousand years ago in the midst of the Great Inland Sea. Inspired by the **Archangels**, who regularly visited them and taught them the Language of Magick among many other arts and crafts, the Varyans founded an empire that covered the Known World, from the **Island Realms** in the West to the Steppes of Koth in the East. They were ruled over by the Synod of **Elder Wizards**, said to number some five dozen warlocks of power unsurpassed before or since. This empire lasted about a thousand years until it was destroyed by the **Unseen** at the **Breaking of the World**, by which time it had fallen into demonolatry, decadence and corruption thanks to **Ma'amun**, foremost among the Elder Wizards, who was seduced by **Abaddon** during his astral wanderings through the **Other Side**. Varya is also frequently referred to in texts as Seneca, the name given to it in Decorlangue, the language of **Ancient Thalamy**.

Vorstlund   Formerly a kingdom until the Partition Crisis some two centuries ago, Vorstlund is now a loose federation of nine baronies, although it is still classed as being one of the **Free Kingdoms**. Vorstlendings are known for their gluttony and generosity, but can also be quick to anger and are doughty fighters.

Wadwo   The result of disastrous experiments by the **Elder Wizards** to create a race of superhuman soldiers, Wadwos are generally solitary, near-mindless creatures of humanoid but grossly distorted aspect who dwell in remote forests and mountain lairs. Also known as ogres, woses and beastmen, they are possessed of huge strength but are clumsy and ill-disciplined.

Watchtowers of the Magi   A series of huge towers built by the **Elder Wizards** to watch over their vast domains across the Known World. Many were destroyed during the **Breaking of the World**, but some survived partially intact, including the Watchtowers of **Tintagael** in **Northalde**, the Valley of the Barrow Kings in the **Island Realms**, and Mount Brazen in the Great White Mountains dividing the **Free Kingdoms** from the **Urovian New Empire**.

Wheel   Chief symbol of the **Creed**, derived from the execution of its prophet **Palomedes** on a torture wheel in Tyrannos a thousand years ago. The sign of the Wheel is made by first touching the forehead and then splaying the fingers of the hand across one's chest, in representation of the spokes the **Redeemer**'s limbs were broken on.

White Valravyn   Chivalrous order founded by the Hero King Thorsvald of **Northalde** a hundred years ago, in memory of the warrior saint Ulred; charged with upholding Royal Law throughout the **King's Dominions** and bringing justice to all during peacetime, defending the realm in times of war, and the King's personal security. Revived during the reign of Freidheim II after falling out of favour during the rule of King Aelfric III. The Order's prestige means it draws the greatest and most ambitious knights of the realm to its ranks. Its present High Commander is Prince Freidhoff, younger brother to the King. It is headquartered at Staerkvit, one of Northalde's greatest castles, which lies on lands in the Dominions that the Order rules directly on royal grant.

Wyrm   Also known as dragons and wyverns; the ancient offspring of the **Great World Serpent** and Hydrae the Many-Headed. Now an extinct species, after the last of the great venom-spitting reptiles was slain by the Pangonian knight Sir Azelin of Valacia some years ago.